THE EMPEROR

THE EMPEROR

THE TELNARIAN HISTORIES
VOLUME V

John Norman

OPEN ROAD

INTEGRATED MEDIA

NEW YORK

978-1-5040-5817-9

Distributed in 2019 by Open Road Distribution
180 Maiden Lane
New York, NY 10038
www.openroadmedia.com

INITIAL NOTES, IN THE WAY OF A PREFACE

The orthodoxy is clear.

It is comforting to know the orthodoxy. That makes it easier to dissemble, to pretend, and lie.

I am regarded as harmless. At least I suppose so. I hope so. That is my protection. An eccentric scholar, puttering in libraries, carefully turning the brittle, yellow pages of old manuscripts, copies of copies of copies, and yet already ancient in their own right, is not to be feared.

And yet spies are about.

They are not so hard to recognize.

What is it they fear, the learned ones, the holy ones, that spies must be about?

It is now said that the empire never existed.

That is the orthodoxy, the new orthodoxy.

One must learn it. One must pretend to believe it. Or, at least, it would be wise to do so. Few wish to be found missing.

One wonders where they are, or if they are.

There are always alternative explanations, of course, one supposes, for anything, and certainly for ruins, medals, and coins, for artifacts and carved stones, for unusual words in a language, seemingly of alien origin, for unusual place names, for surprising names of days and months, and holidays. And what of certain practices, sayings, and melodies?

It is hard to change all those things.

There are always explanations.

But the peasants remain fond of old melodies.

I, too, like them. They are seemingly very old.

I am puzzled about time and space.

Time, I am told, has been tamed by clocks and space by the three-knot cord and the marked wheel.

But I am still puzzled how time could begin or space end. How long was it before time began? Why did it begin then and not at another time? If it stops, how long will it be stopped? Would it start again? Is there something before the start of space, or something beyond its end, and if so, what? Is space in a space, and that space in another space, and so on? Is the straight line the clue to space and time? I do not think so. Perhaps time and space are circles and do not need beginnings or ends. But from whence the circle, then, and from whence its source, and from whence the source of that source, and so on? These questions do not seem satisfactorily answered by the clock and the three-knot cord, even the marked wheel.

Far off, better than twenty sleeps by cart, is the city, our great and populous center of culture and learning. The city, as is well-known, is the cup in which is found the wine of civilization. In it are many wise men. That is not surprising, of course, given the population of the city, which numbers more than two thousand inhabitants. Once, in the benighted and wicked times, before the sanctified petrification of the orthodoxy, following several votes in some four councils, I am told it was not unknown for scholars to entertain the hypothesis that the Telnarian Empire once existed, though, of course, long ago and far-away. I, personally, do not think it was far away, not if it encompassed worlds, and countless systems. Too, I have seen the traces of walls and roads. Indeed, such things are within walking distance of the village. Once its ships, I suspect, crossed our skies. I wonder what it would be, to see such a ship, now, one whose ports of call would be the satellites of stars. Several times, in the past year, I have given lodging to travelers. Those who ask me, in passing, of Telnaria, and the empire, so casually, over a cup of wine, I reprove with politeness, but firmness, reiterating the orthodoxy, as I assume they are spies. Scholars are, after all, suspect, as are any inquiring minds. When all is known, there is no need for inquiry. It could but lead one astray.

What is most fascinating to me, of course, is difficult to put into words, perhaps because words, in their origins and utilities, for the most part, deal with familiar things in familiar ways. They have their localities and neighborhoods. Things precede words, and when one comes upon a certain thing, a new thing, really new, or a new thought, really new, it may not yet have its word. No word has yet noticed it.

I shall begin, tentatively, timidly, hoping for much, expecting little.

The world is ours, designed for our comfort and happiness. The kindly orthodoxy assures us of this. The newly discovered, inverted bowl of the sky, now graced with its lamp of the day and its lamps of the night, supplied for our convenience, protects and shelters us. The sea gives us fish and the land its fruits. Further, we are at the center of the universe, visible proof of our importance. Can one not see the universe, all about one? How tiny, how small, how fragile, how alone, how vulnerable we would feel, if these things were not so! What if our sturdy platform were to spin, and what if our house were hurled into the sky, harnessed to a ball of fire? What if our world were a little world and our sun a little sun, a world and a sun amongst countless worlds and suns, a world and sun scarcely numbered amongst the countless grains on the beaches of space? Are you diminished? Are you afraid?

But what is loneliness, and horror and fear, to one, to another is a thing welcome, a prospect, an excitement, an invitation, a provocation, the opening of a door, a challenge, a liberation. One leaves the room, and puts one's foot upon the porch of tomorrow. In a world perhaps vast would there not be much to do, many places to go, many ways to be? Might not that first step be the first step of a species into forever?

We have our world, small and orderly. It is a pleasant, comfortable world, particularly if one does as one is told, and thinks what one is told to think. We are told it is the one world, the only world. But if there is one world, why might there not be others? Indeed, would it not be more likely, all things considered, that there would be no world at all? But there is clearly at least one world. It would be strange, would it not, were there only one thing of a kind, one flower, one stone, one beast. But worlds, of course, are not flowers, stones, or beasts. A world is in a place, say, this place. But where is this place? Is it in another place? Perhaps there are places we do not understand as places. Could our places be the only places? What if there are many places, other places, unaware of one another, perhaps sometimes closer to one another than they understand, places which might be their own threads in some large tapestry, perhaps one tapestry amongst others. Are the strands interwoven? Do they sometimes cross and touch one another? And what of the twistings of time, so strange, time, so patient, so unconcerned with beginnings and ends?

What is "now," and what is "then"?

Could it be that "then" is sometimes "now"?

Could we ourselves be the ancients, and know nothing of it?
Suppose the wheel of time turns.

Would that not make today yesterday, and yesterday tomorrow?

I would dismiss such fancies, were it not for something that happened long ago. I was young. I still wore the youth's brimless cap and the youth's striped jacket. It was a dark, cold day. It was windy, and raining. I was returning home. I paused amongst the ruins. In such a time, and on such day, none would be likely to see me. I did not wish to be again punished. The men avoided the ruins, except for occasionally carrying off stone. I wandered about, curious. I would not be noticed, not today. I turned, at last, wet and shivering, but enough contented, to leave, but suddenly cried out in fear, and stood half blinded by a burst of sunlight. I raised my arm wildly, as though to fend a blow. I tried to see in the brightness. I stepped back, frightened, and my sleeve, ever so briefly, brushed a tall, stately, golden column. Then again it was dark and rainy, and I stood alone, in the soaked moss and grass, in the wind and cold, amongst crumbled stone and fallen, broken columns.

I have never forgotten that moment.

I had seen Telnaria.

The rumors, fleet through the guarded passes, where dimensions touch dimensions, coursed even the most obscure geodesics, the most remote paths between stars, to the most distant outposts of the *limitanei*. Thousands of species on thousands of worlds attended to disputed whispers, whispers of an empire, one crumbling, one stable and eternal, one dying, one living, one fallen, one risen, one older than suns, one newer than spring.

The roads between worlds can be long, certainly where the passes are not used, or are closed. It is well known that the light one sees, streaming from a star, may have taken millennia to reach the observing eye, the ready eye which notes it, seeing it this night, anew, afresh. Indeed, the star may have perished long before the announcement of its birth is received. So, too, in parts of the empire, the latest news may be fresh, and scanned with anxious intent, but the events of which it speaks may be ancient.

But let us return to our account, an account of the dark and troubled times.

We see an empire beleaguered and diminished. A million years, perhaps millions, have expended or reduced resources once thought limitless. Reality consists of polarities and contrasts. Ships exist which can voyage amongst stars. Sometimes they are noted, as roaring streaks of light, by the vacant, lifted eyes of simple men, tilling fields with pointed sticks. Power is nursed and hoarded. It is still possible to explode the core of a planet, but, on many worlds, imperial troops, occasionally contacted, if at all, are armed with little more than bows and blades. The empire is vast. Some worlds fade from imperial view, forgotten, worlds whose records are missing, mislaid, removed or destroyed. Some worlds repudiate the empire, boldly declaring their independence, and the empire may not notice, or feel it worthwhile to expend resources in their recovery. There are worlds which do not know they are claimed. Other worlds, exposed and vulnerable, are well taxed, in coin or *munera*, forced labor, imposed by agents, licensed tax farmers. Populations may be relocated, transported to sites convenient to vast projects, the irrigation of deserts, the working of quarries and mines, the manning of heavy manufactories, thought inappropriate to, if not inimical to, more salubrious worlds. Inhospitable worlds are rendered congenial by canals and seed. Men plant flowers they will never see bloom, carry stone to build cities they will never enjoy. Riches reign, adjacent to destitution. Palaces soar, ringed by hovels; temples loom, scorning juxtaposed squalor. Urbanized proletariats are restless, idle, and dangerous. They must be amused and fed. The tiniest of incidents may be seized upon, in eagerness, affording an excuse for destruction, looting, and arson. How stimulating is carnage, under the cloak of anonymity! Consider, too, the contrast between preferred worlds, to which resources are drained, and less-prized worlds, remote and neglected, exploited, or once-exploited, many now denuded of arable soil, minerals, and game. Where authority is lax, bandits thrive. Strong men defend themselves, and mete out justice, compatible with their interests. Enclaves flourish. Private armies abound. Crowns are forged. Rogues become monarchs. Technology is coveted. A pistol can create a king. A cartridge can purchase a woman.

And beyond perimeters, baleful eyes, gleaming and envious, regard an empire and its wealth, both conceived as spoils. There, beyond the perimeters, lurking, ever more bold, prowl the hungry wolves of space, hundreds of barbarian nations, some armed with ships and weaponry equal to the empire's own, supplied by recalcitrant, ambitious worlds. Rude folk, violent and angry, like storms, gathering strength, see in palaces little more than torches with which to illuminate the night, and little more in temples than hangars for their machines and stables for their horses.

What follows may be easier to understand, much easier, I think, if one keeps clearly in mind the weight of an institutional inertia, accumulated over thousands of years, vested in an enormous civil service, distributed throughout thousands of imperial worlds, and the doings, sometimes dark and alarming, which may occur in a small locality, for example, in the aisles of a senate or the chambers of a court. Over centuries and generations, despite the comings and goings of emperors, the empire has endured, almost as if by habit. Clerks have kept their records, officials have discharged their duties, soldiers have manned their posts. Indeed, even as the hand of the empire might be extended or withdrawn, be present or absent, whether in the shadow of silver standards or beneath the rudely inscribed, snapping pennon of a bandit king, merchants have bought and sold, herdsmen have tended their flocks, fishermen have cast their nets, peasants have sown their fields and reaped their crops. For thousands of years, in the lives of millions, in thousands of rational species, it made little difference who graced the high throne in Telnar, seat of the imperial palace. Did Telnar even exist? Perhaps you knew one whose grandfather had once been there. And what was an Emperor, but a far-off name? In the lives of the great majority of the far-flung populations of the empire, far removed from the corridors of power, from those of ambition and intrigue, little depended on the success or failure of an assassin's knife or a draught of poisoned wine; little depended on the success or failure of one plot or coup, or another. Even dynastic squabbles, as in the time of the four emperors, fierce, hard-fought, and ruthless as they might have been, seldom afflicted more than a dozen worlds. Now, however, in the times of which I shall speak, all this was to change.

THE EMPEROR

CHAPTER ONE

"By Orak, father of the gods, and Umba, his consort, it is mad-ness," cried lean Iaachus, Arbiter of Protocol, turning on his heel, violently, his sable cloak swirling, mirrored in the broad, polished tiles before the dais, on which was now mounted but a single throne, the high throne. Another throne, the throne of the empress mother, once behind and to the right of the high throne, from which she might whisper into the ear of the boy emperor, had been removed. Gone, too, from the wide, lower step to the left, were the princess thrones, hitherto reserved for golden-haired, arrogant Viviana and her younger sister, quiet, dark-haired Alacida. The high throne, now the single throne, massive and large-armed, was not now, in virtue of an unforeseen accident of birth, occupied by a half-slumped, fragile, wretched shape, coiled inward upon itself, sometimes trembling, a shape dull-eyed and slow-speaking, timid Aesilesius, now a youth of some seven-teen or eighteen years, but seemingly, in mind, no more than five or six, coached in responses, terrified of insects, saliva at his jaw, sometimes giggling, clutching some toy.

"The empire is madness," said Julian, "the *vi-cat* is madness, all is madness, life is madness." The speaker was, if casually re-garded, a modestly ranked officer, a lieutenant, in the imperial navy; yet, as a scion of the Aureliani, a family high amongst the imperial *honestori*, he was entitled, in his dress uniform, to the three purple cords. He was a patriot of the empire, according to his lights. Too, he was a cousin of Aesilesius. He was feared by some, including Iaachus, the Arbiter of Protocol, as a pretender to the throne. Most importantly, in our present context, he was a participant in the recent coup.

"One does what one can," said Tuvo Ausonius, former civil servant on Miton, by all lights an unlikely party to have found itself implicated in recent, surprising events.

"What of the empress mother?" inquired Julian.

"She rages, confined to her quarters," said Tuvo Aúsonius.

The empress mother, as she had planned, had returned promptly after the nuptials, proceeding through the cheering streets in her own carriage, that she might welcome in person the arrival of the wedding party at the palace.

She had been immediately taken into custody.

"Interesting," said Julian, "how the most powerful woman in Telnaria becomes helpless, behind a locked door."

"The power of women," said Iaachus, "is only the power of men who will do their bidding."

"Such a bidding," said Julian, "may be declined."

"And so worlds might change," said Iaachus.

"And thousands of new slave markets might be formed," said Julian.

"In collars," said Iaachus, "women are in no doubt as to their sex, their meaning, and purpose."

"I shudder," said Tuvo Ausonius. "I was a same."

Certain worlds of the empire, such as Terennia and Miton, were "same worlds," worlds in which it is pretended, in the light of certain prescribed ends, largely political, that the sexes are identical. As in many other cultural experiments, or inventions, of one sort or another, one must put truth aside and do one's best to ignore human nature. An example of the lengths to which one might go on the "same worlds," one might mention the "curtain and frame," a type of garmenture designed to conceal the delights of the female body, which delights, of course, however deplorably, regrettably, or embarrassingly, would continue, one supposes, even beneath the obscuring armor of the curtain-and-frame ensemble, to exist.

"Your Sesella," said Julian, "was not a same."

"No," said Tuvo, "she was a free woman, a stewardess, in the employ of *Wings Between Worlds*."

"She looked well at your feet, stripped, in her collar," said Julian.

"It seems she wishes to be there," said Tuvo.

"But it does not now matter, one way or the other," said Julian. "The collar is on her, the rose is burned into her thigh. She will stay there. She is helpless. She is where she belongs."

"If you wish, dear Tuvo," said Iaachus, "you might restore her to the dignity and honor of freedom."

"She does not wish to be so restored," said Tuvo.

"But if she did?" inquired Iaachus.

"I would keep her where she is, or sell her," said Tuvo.

"The whip might be helpful," said Julian.

"Doubtless," said Tuvo.

"Could you use the whip on her?" asked Julian.

"Of course," said Tuvo. "She is a slave."

"Excellent," said Iaachus.

"It seems," said Julian, "our dear Ausonius is no longer a same."

"He has become a man," said Iaachus.

"How could one be other," asked Julian, "once having tasted the mastery?"

"I no longer hear the crowds outside," said Iaachus.

"When I left the empress mother," said Tuvo Ausonius, "she was shaking, beside herself with fury."

"She is cruel and vicious, but old, and frail," said Iaachus. "I fear for her. I shall have her sedated."

"Do you think your consideration will win you a pardon?" asked Julian.

"No," said the Arbiter of Protocol.

"Perhaps an easier death?" said Julian.

"You do not know the empress mother," said Iaachus.

"We have gone far, too far," said Julian. "There is no turning back."

"Clearly," said Iaachus.

"Rurik should report shortly," said Julian.

The Rurik instanced was Rurik, fierce, bearded Rurik, the Tenth Consul of Larial VII, of the Larial Farnichi. He maintained a small, private army in an enclave close to Telnar, somewhat northeast of the city. The two anomalies here, the presence on Telnaria of so august a personage as the Tenth Consul of Larial VII, surprisingly neither received nor acknowledged publicly, and the existence of troops independent of the imperial military so close to the capital might be accounted for in virtue of certain recent events. Two mighty merchant families, the Larial Calasalii and the Larial Farnichi, both maintaining private armies, had opposed one another for generations, on several worlds, struggling to control trade routes, competing for markets and raw materials, attempting to form monopolies, waylaying caravans, seizing shipments, confiscating ferries and shuttles, burning trade posts, and such. This trade war, one of the worst in the galaxy, could not indefinitely escape the notice of the empire which, beleaguered by appeals and complaints, must needs eventually stir, or, at least, seem to stir. Imperial proposals as to the partition of districts, markets, and territories having failed, and commands pertaining to the cessation of hostilities having been ignored, the empire, itself limited in its resources, lapsed into a watchful, benign inertness. Restricted by the logistics of war, by the scarcities of materiel, and threatened by invasions from without and insurrections from within, the empire was unwilling to invest ships, men, and materiel to cope with two private forces, those of the Larial Calasalii and the Larial Farnichi, both formidable in their own right. It was at this point that representatives of the Larial Farnichi, well aware of the severe costs of the trade war, and the harm it must inevitably impose on rational mercantile interests, approached the empire, not as a stubborn adversary, but as a congenial, prospective ally. In short, the empire, unwilling to do battle singly with two desperate, dangerous armies, took the side of the Larial Farnichi, with the result that the combined, overwhelming forces of the empire and the Larial Farnichi brought the trade war to a rapid close, much to the detriment of the Larial Calasalii. It was rumored that a considerable amount of gold, variously and judiciously distributed, may have done much to lubricate the gears which, turning, produced this change of policy. In any event, the empire ceased to be a neutral mediator and engaged itself as a committed partisan. The forces of the Larial Calasalii, soon defeated and surrendered, were disbanded, and their goods and properties, their buildings, ships, and such, were seized as spoils of war, shortly thereafter being divided between the Larial Farnichi and the empire. Some weeks later, by means of a secret vote of the senate, the Larial Calasalii was outlawed. Its surviving members were seized and impounded. This took place in a series of coordinated, early-morning raids. The men were consigned, on the whole, to labor gangs. The women were enslaved, and made available to the Larial Farnichi. They kept those they wished, whom they might find of some interest, and the others were remanded to hundreds of markets on a variety of worlds. This disposition of the females of the enemy is common in both civilized and barbarian worlds. Conquerors enjoy owning the women of the enemy, as other forms of booty. Women, as is well known, make excellent slave beasts. It was also rumored that more had been involved in the aforementioned series of incidents than the exchange of large quantities of gold. Supposedly secret arrangements had been emplaced. How, otherwise, could it be explained that the Tenth Consul of Larial VII, Rurik, of the Larial Farnichi, his presence never officially acknowledged, should maintain a villa and enclave, one quartering troops, so near the capital?

At that moment, a servitor appeared in the threshold of the throne room, at the end of the long, scarlet carpet leading toward the dais.

"Lords!" he called, lifting his hand.

But a large, brusque figure thrust him aside and strode toward the dais. He moved quickly and with assurance. He still bore a side arm, the guards not daring to deprive him of the article in question.

The carpet was fifty *maxipaces* in length, supposedly commemorative of the first fifty worlds of the Telnarian Empire.

The figure advanced toward the dais.

The two leaves of the door to the throne room, large, black, polished, and intricately carved, were tied back with golden cords, and flanked by high, scarlet curtains. Behind these curtains were also two leaves, not of wood, but of thick steel, supposedly capable of withstanding the blast of a Telnarian rifle at close range.

The large figure halted, at the foot of the dais, before the throne.

"The square has been cleared," he announced.

"As far as the entrance to Palace Street?" inquired Iaachus.

"Farther," said Rurik, Tenth Consul of Larial VII.

"I would know more," said Julian, he of the Aureliani.

"Matters proceed apace," said Rurik.

"The princesses?" inquired Iaachus.

"They withdrew, in consternation," said Rurik. It might be mentioned, as the reader has doubtless already suspected, that the Tenth Consul of Larial VII was a party to the coup to which attention was earlier drawn. Indeed, it is not unlikely that it was in anticipation of some such employment that he and his men had been brought to Telnar. The reader may recall that certain unverified conjectures had been entertained to the effect that more than gold, perhaps private arrangements or understandings, might have been involved in the empire's recent intervention in a certain trade war.

Having been assured by Rurik that matters were proceeding apace, this seems an opportune moment to attend to such matters, supposedly proceeding apace, and, perhaps more importantly, the context within which they were taking place, the context in terms of which they appear intelligible and plausible, if not warranted and excusable.

I trust the reader will forgive this interlude, which seems inevitable.

The jewel of power is a gem much coveted.

That is not difficult to understand.

What treasure can compare with the treasure of power; even gold is of little moment, except for the power it can buy.

Let us briefly think on this matter.

Consider the Telnarian Empire, with its thousands of worlds, and abundances of rational species. It is vast, complex, and unwieldy; it is strong and weak, loved and hated, rich and poor, luxurious and impoverished. On some worlds, the sight of the silver standards inspires terror. On other worlds, innocent species inspect claiming stones whose significance they do not understand. The enemies of the empire are not merely barbarians without and the discontented within, not merely the scarcity of resources and the inefficiency of ponderous bureaucracies, but the unmanageable immensities of space and time themselves, militating against effective governance. Yet, despite such considerations, the institution of the empire, spanning galaxies, maintained largely by the routines of an almost autonomous civil service, endures. In all this vastness, it seems that the tiny dot of Telnaria would be scarcely noticed. Nonetheless, it was on just such a dot, on just such a speck, millennia ago, that the silver standards were first raised. It is in her name that ships were launched and worlds claimed. It is to her emperors, coming and going, prosperous and ill-fated, that allegiance is pledged. And it is to her coffers, ultimately, that the scanned and selected wealth of galaxies will find its way. All is traced back to Telnaria; is she not the origin, might, and meaning; the symbol and fact, the sword and staff, the hope and law, the terror and comfort, the threat and consolation, the burden and safeguard, the protector and despoiler, the empire itself?

Her capital is Telnar.

And now, on the royal dais, platform of imperial power, there reposes a single throne.

Men would kill to seize it; who would dare to claim it?

The jewel of power is a gem much coveted, surely; but, too, it is a gem dangerous to possess.

The most obvious danger to the empire, if not the greatest, are the barbarian nations. Prominent amongst these are the peoples referred to in the imperial records as the Aatii. Their leader is Abrogastes, called the Far-Grasper.

Over recent generations, due to a variety of causes, the empire has found itself in ever greater jeopardy. Citizenship on many worlds within the empire was once a muchly sought guerdon, an important and valued prize to be earned by years of service, most often in the military, commonly by undertaking the hazardous duties of the *limitanei*, troops maintaining frontier outposts. Later, as emperors sought popularity, it was awarded universally, throughout the empire, in mere virtue of birth. Accordingly, being free, it was taken for granted, and ignored. Where all are citizens, citizenship is no longer precious. Manual labor came to be looked down upon, as not fit for free men. Too, as resources grew more scarce, arable lands being eroded and mines exhausted, seas being overfished and forests emptied of game, millions, *humiliori*, flocked to thousands of cities, to be entertained and fed, constituting demanding, dangerous, inflammable crowds. The social and cognitive elite of the empire, the *honestori*, once cognizant of their station, and accustomed to accepting its presumed duties, administrative and military, the mirror of their privileges, now well-fixed and comfortable, sometimes rich, turned to other matters, not merely horses and dogs, gardens and villas, carriages and yachts, porcelains and statuary, pastries and wines, dice and cards, and such, but business, often the buying and selling of tenements and the lending of money, occupations formerly thought more appropriate for the *humiliori*. In any event, in view of a combination of circumstances, some of which we have alluded to, the empire grew ever more at risk. Those unwilling to accept the sacrifices of defending the empire mocked patriotism. Cowardice presented itself as a hitherto unrecognized form of courage. Many resolved not to note the darkening of skies, and the impending storms, rising at the borders. Had the empire not always been? Was it not eternal? Surely it would survive, as always in the past. Others, if needed, would undertake the watches, guard the gate, man the walls, and, if needed, stand in the breech. One other factor posing a dreadful threat to the empire might be noted, even in this cursory summary, particularly as it will have some bearing on events shortly to transpire. This factor, for want of a better word, might be referred to as political, or, perhaps indifferently, as religious.

Now, while populations remained oblivious of, or only dimly aware of, the dangers in which the empire stood, this was not universally the case. Some in the empire, and some who were powerful and highly placed, were only too acutely aware of the peril. One of these we have met, Julian of the Aureliani. He had reasoned that if the empire is to survive it must be defended, and if it was not to be defended by its own, it must be defended by others. In the light of this recognition, he was prepared to embark on a controversial and dangerous path, the recruitment of barbarians to deal with barbarians. How better to guard sheep from wolves but by wolves, other wolves, wolves who did not fear wolves, wolves as fierce and terrible as those who looked upon vulnerable docile flocks with hunger and greed? Clearly the risks entailed in so bold a stratagem were considerable. What if the guards themselves should fall upon the flocks? What if wolves should enleague themselves with wolves, forming an irresistible pack, ravaging and feeding, festive with blood, doing slaughter with impunity?

One of the classic strengths of the empire was its capacity to capitalize on, or even abet or generate, hostilities amongst barbarian peoples, that they might concern themselves with seeking one another's blood, that they might weaken one another, even exhaust themselves in tribal combat, leaving remnants and tatters which an armed, watchful empire need not fear.

Two such nations were the Alemanni, spoken of in imperial records as the Aatii, and the Vandals, or Vandalii. Both of these nations, in many ways, were much alike; both, for example, were originally forest peoples. Indeed, a trace of this origin lingers in the very name of the Vandals, or Vandalii, in which it is not difficult to see a reference to the "Van," an archaic word for a forested area. The Vandals, then, might be understood as the "folk of the Vanland," the forest land, or forest country. Indeed, the enmity between the Alemanni and the Vandals, of centuries standing, may have begun in territorial competition. The Alemanni, consisting of eleven tribes, the largest and most dangerous being the Drisriaks, constituted the greatest single threat to the empire. Naturally then it had occurred to Julian to recruit, arm, and train, if possible, Vandals to confront and withstand the Aatii, or Alemanni. The Vandal nation consists of five tribes, the Otungs, Darisi, Haakons, Basungs, and Wolfungs, the largest being the Otungs and the smallest the Wolfungs. A particular individual, of obscure origin, an arena killer and bodyguard, as we have recounted elsewhere, had come to the chieftainship of the Wolfungs. This individual, recruited by Julian, and having received a commission, a captainship, in the imperial auxiliaries, ventured to Tangara, though it was the Killing Time, to enlist Otungs, in the process of which, in bloody selections, honored by so fierce a people, he became the king of the Otungs.

Some weeks ago, the aforementioned Abrogastes, cunning Abrogastes, the Far-Grasper, king of the Drisriaks, having suborned certain officers charged with the defense of Telnar, had raided the city and abducted the boy emperor's sisters, Viviana and Alacida, with the end in view of marrying them, forcibly or otherwise, to two of his sons, Ingeld and Hrothgar, thus establishing, in time, prospective heirs to the throne.

Entering into these dark, intricate, troubled matters, is the ambition of the exarch of Telnar, Sidonicus. One may rule through the sword; but one may also rule through the mind. In the past several years, a new religion, in a number of variations, all claiming to be based on the teachings of a gentle, anarchistic Ogg, or salamanderine, Floon, from the swamp world of Zirus, has been spreading throughout the empire. Sidonicus and those like him, unlike the devout rank and file, clerical and lay, pacifistic and otherworldly, concerned with the welfare of their *koos*, hoping one day to sit at the table of the god, *Karch*, taken now to be the only god, are only too well aware of, and keenly interested in, the enormities of power latent in the manipulation and control of belief.

Sidonicus intends to rule the empire, one way or another, either by means of the empire itself or by means of its enemies. If the empire will declare his particular version of the Floonian faith the official religion of the empire and outlaw, persecute, and destroy all other versions and religions, he will supply the empire with millions upon millions of new soldiers, Floonians, no longer repudiating service to the empire, but now willing, and even eager, to die for it. The Floonian faithful, after all, will believe whatever emanates from the high temples, whatever is blessed by, and proclaimed by, the exarchs, on whom *Karch* has putatively bestowed an inability to err. Let there be new understandings, more profound interpretations. Distinctions need only be drawn, new texts need only be discovered, or invented, and so on. Unfolding revelation is supple. Too, whereas it would be iniquitous to defend an empire willing to tolerate false gods, it would be a sacred duty to defend an empire ruled by *Karch* himself, his wishes and intentions made clear by his ministrants.

But, as might be supposed, not only would many in the empire be reluctant to abandon familiar gods and the traditional imperial policy of religious tolerance, which had kept peace amongst thousands of religions for thousands of years, but many, too, would not be eager to be forced to accept, or pretend to accept, what to them seemed a mass of eccentric beliefs from a tiny, distant, despised world, ranging from the implausible to the unintelligible and inconsistent.

Sidonicus, of course, versed as he was in the politics of power, realized that those who held power would not be likely to relinquish it willingly. Therefore, he must seek out those who want power.

He obtained, by means of a renegade Otung, Urta, from a *festung* on Tangara, the *festung* of Sim Giadini, the legendary Vandal's medallion and chain, the holder of which unites and commands the Vandal Nation. This artifact he had delivered to Ingeld, an ambitious son of Abrogastes. By means of it, Ingeld, who could already marshal considerable Alemanni support, could also command, due to the power of the artifact or talisman, Vandals. United, the Alemanni and Vandals, as Sidonicus reasoned, could crush and destroy the empire, or, better, seize it and its wealth. The price, of course, would be the conversion of the barbarian peoples. If Sidonicus could not convert the empire, he could convert the conquerors of the empire, who might then, in turn, by the sword if necessary, see to the conversion of the empire.

This plan was foiled by Julian, who, having seen the medallion and chain, had hundreds, if not more, of duplicates made and scattered throughout the worlds, this putting in doubt the authenticity of any single medallion and chain.

Afterwards, as recounted elsewhere, the authentic medallion and chain was recovered from the holding of Ingeld on Tenguthax-ichai, this negating its intended exploitation, the enleaguement of Alemanni and Vandals in a fearsome coalition under Alemanni command. And later, the recovered artifact, identified by its former, long-time custodian, Brother Benjamin, himself, like Floon, a salamanderine, served to unite the Vandals.

This brings us to the present, and the immediate events which precipitated the aforementioned coup. The raid of Abrogastes will be recalled, that issuing in the abduction of the boy emperor's sisters, Viviana and Alacida.

Citizens of the empire, in their complacency and arrogance, while fearing barbarians as fierce and mighty, as bold and ruthless, as might be ravening beasts, commonly look down upon them as rude, simple, artless folk. Citizens, nursed in, and protected by, the precincts of civilization, are seldom adequately apprised of the dark selections, natural, social, and cultural, whose knives have shaped and carved out barbarian peoples. Barbarian peoples do not lack culture; it is only that their culture is different. These selections favor not only raw aptitudes and attitudes, as those of the empire might suppose, but intelligence and thought, planning and foresight. Many a woman of the empire, for example, enslaved by a barbarian, has discovered that the severe, uncompromising beast who now owns her, and so thoroughly masters her, is likely to be wiser and shrewder, far more intelligent and less easy to fool, than the males to whom her former freedom had accustomed her. There is no doubt that Abrogastes, for example, was bold, and fierce, but he, no more than the *vi-cat*, would not attack prey he had not scouted. He who would attack is well advised to study his enemy. One assumes the enemy is intelligent; one attempts to be more intelligent.

Consider now the following.

A weakly held throne is a throne in jeopardy.

Many may be the paths to a throne, and these paths are not mutually exclusive. But beware the fruit which would seem too easily picked. Paths may be narrow, steep, and treacherous. The path to victory may lead to defeat. It could be no accident that the empire has endured for thousands of years. There are many paths. Choose your path with care. Poisons and daggers, insurrections and civil wars, may lead to thrones; but alliances and adoptions, births and deaths, too, may lead to thrones. Some paths may be less dangerous than others, less costly to tread. A path of peace and law is not obviously inferior to one of ships, men, and blood. It is highly likely that Abrogastes had apprised himself of the empire's rules of succession. Indeed, it is likely that he was more familiar with them than many a courtier or herald.

There is no doubt that Atalana, the empress mother, was the most powerful woman in the empire, as she, though subject to the varying influences of others, ruled, in effect, through her son, the boy emperor, Aesilesius. On the other hand, it was not she, but Aesilesius, who was emperor. The throne, in Telnarian tradition, and in the *pandect* of Telnar, is to be occupied by a male, the oldest son of the reigning emperor being the first heir to the throne, followed, in turn, by the younger sons. Then would come male grandchildren, and so on. Next in line would be brothers and nephews of the reigning emperor, followed by male first cousins, second cousins, and such. Indeed, Julian himself was a second cousin of the emperor, and, thus, was in the line of succession, however remotely. Needless to say, in the history of the empire, tradition and law tend to be most prominent, and most righteously stressed, by the party it might favor. Certainly such things have been overlooked, or abrogated, on numerous occasions. Laws, innocent of the sword's backing, can be conveniently suspended, ignored, revoked, or changed. Indeed, on several occasions, an emperor has seen to the crowning of an empress, whose authority and power is then, during his lifetime, second only to his own. The simple fact of possession counts for much. Scions of a number of families, over millennia, had seized the throne, commonly in consequence of civil wars, and instituted new lines of succession. Law does not always command the sword; it may as often be the sword's servant. How often it is that passion fosters perception, that desire generates belief; that will precedes reason, that justification follows deed!

The boy, Aesilesius, seems an unlikely occupant of the throne. Might he not be easily disposed of, or swept aside?

Let the union of Viviana with Ingeld, or that of Alacida with Hrothgar, now produce one or more sons. Such issue, then, being nephews of the childless emperor, would be in line for the throne.

There are, as was noted, many paths to a throne.

There was, however, one grievous, unanticipated flaw in the cunning plan of Abrogastes, a flaw which he, even in his profound understanding of intrigue and steel, had not foreseen, the possibility of its preemption by others, a treacherous son and an individual whose form of power was at that time foreign to his understanding, treasonous Ingeld and ambitious Sidonicus, the exarch of Telnar.

Sidonicus, on the grounds that the invisible, alleged to exist, was more important than the visible, the *koos* superior to the body, and such, claimed the superiority of the temple to the palace, the superiority of faith, his particular version of the controversial, and often obscure, teachings of Floon, to law, the state, and such. As the mind controls the body so, too, the temple should control the palace. For example, he will claim that no emperor can be legitimately enthroned without being crowned by the exarch of Telnar. What incredible power thus redounds to the exarch! Further, the empire is to foster a particular faith, and obey the will of the god *Karch*, taken now to be the one and only god, the will of *Karch* being conveyed by the ministrants of *Karch*, in particular, the exarch of Telnar. As there was one emperor, so, too, there would be one exarch of Telnar, and as the *koos* was superior to the body, so, too, the exarch would be superior to the emperor. Domination was the ambition of Sidonicus, domination through the mind, through superstition and lies, through belief and invention, through terror and guilt. It was not merely that his faith was to become the one and only recipient of offerings, exchanging its imaginary benefits for tangible assets, a spectacular triumph of economic fraud, but, ideally, it was to creep into, and infect, all thought, all phases of life.

"So the princesses withdrew?" said Iaachus.

"In consternation," repeated Rurik.

"What of the noble grooms, Ingeld and Hrothgar?" pressed Iaachus.

"Ingeld is dark and deep," said Rurik. "He will act."

"And Hrothgar?" asked Iaachus.

"Affairs of state mean little to him," said Julian, "one way or another. He takes the wind as it blows, the rain as it falls. He thinks of little but *bror* and falcons, horses and slaves."

"He is a lusty fellow," said Rurik. "He was on the brink, I fear, when interrupted, of making himself known to the fair Alacida."

"In the carriage itself?" asked Tuvo Ausonius.

"Yes," said Rurik. "Are you surprised?"

"Alacida is a princess, not a slave," said Tuvo, aghast.

"The city is secure?" said Julian.

"Major streets, the senate house, the palace," said Rurik.

In accord with the plan of the coup, assembly had been prohibited, martial law proclaimed, and a curfew imposed.

"The city guard?" asked Iaachus.

"It offered no resistance, as anticipated," said Rurik. "It is few in number and poorly armed."

The forces enacting the coup were threefold, and numbered in the hundreds. The first party, and the smallest, consisted of several officers, and contingents of their men, recruited from the imperial navy, loyal to Julian. Second, there were the men of Rurik, who had been garrisoned in an enclave near Telnar, a small private army of sorts, drawn from the large private forces of the Larial Farnichi, the great merchant family, whose original house had been founded on Larial VII. Lastly, the largest of the three groups, were Otungs, hair-cropped and beard-shaven, in the uniforms of imperial auxiliaries.

"The announcement was made of a new order, of right, propriety, and justice, that the empire is restored, that law is upheld," said Iaachus.

"Of course," said Rurik.

"We may be unable to hold the city indefinitely," said Julian.

"The city itself will have much to say about that," said Tuvo Ausonius.

"Games will be held," said Iaachus, "bread distributed."

"Still I am apprehensive," said Tuvo Ausonius. "For days the city prepared for the nuptials of the princesses with the two sons of Abrogastes. Little else was spoken of. Perfumes anointed columns and thresholds. Alleys were washed, facades painted. Banners and ribbons bedecked the streets. Flowers were imported, even from Inez IV. Musicians played, and choirs sang. Guests arrived, from a hundred worlds. Gifts flowed in, as well, even from barbarian worlds. Then, in a most impressive ceremony, in the high temple itself, lasting hours, the nuptials were performed, by the noble exarch, Sidonicus himself."

"I did not see it," said Iaachus. "Doubtless it was impressive."

"It is dangerous to deprive people of their holidays, their festivals," said Tuvo.

"But," said Iaachus, Arbiter of Protocol, "we have not done so. They have had their holiday."

"What has transpired here, in Telnar, cannot long be kept secret," said Tuvo Ausonius.

"Nor need it be," said Iaachus. "What occurs in one room in a palace may not be of much concern in another room. What occurs in one city may not be of much interest in another. Many times the throne has changed its occupant and the empire, persisting, has scarcely noted it. A rock drops into the water; do not expect the ocean to tremble."

"What of the emperor?" asked Tuvo Ausonius.

"You mean, of course, what of the former occupant of the throne," said Julian, "he, the boy, young Aesilesius?"

"As you wish," said Tuvo Ausonius, uncertainly.

"He is content," said Julian. "He has a toy."

"The doors of the senate have been closed," said Rurik.

"They will remain closed, until we have need of the senate," said Iaachus.

"I trust the curfew will be enforced," said Julian.

"There will be Otungs in the streets," said Rurik.

"It was necessary to act," said Julian. "The empress mother was taking instruction from the exarch of Telnar himself. She is old and frail, easily flattered, easily confused, easily subject to influence. The exarch's power waxes. Soon she might be smudged with the sacred oil from one or another of the holy pools of Zirus. Would she not then become but another tool of sleek, pompous, clever Sidonicus? And Ingeld and Hrothgar loom, spouses of the princesses Viviana and Alacida. In time new heirs are spawned. How ascendant then become the Alemanni, their agents, their blood then within the palace itself! Soon the emperor is killed, thrust aside, forced to abdicate. It was necessary to act. It was necessary to protect the throne."

"I trust," said Iaachus, glancing at the throne and its occupant, "that the throne is protected."

"There is something I do not understand," said Julian. "The plan of Abrogastes was shrewd and daring, abducting the princesses and somehow, presumably on Tenguthaxichai, influencing them to accept the suits of Ingeld and Hrothgar, who knows what means were employed, but what has all this to do with the exarch of Telnar, and recourse to his solemnization of such unions? Does this not seem to concede unusual power, or prestige, to the exarch? It is difficult to see the hand of Abrogastes in this."

"I do not think the hand of Abrogastes is in the matter, at all," said Iaachus. "I see Sidonicus and Ingeld here. Surely it was some agent of Sidonicus who transmitted the stolen medallion and chain to Ingeld."

"Where is Abrogastes?" asked Julian.

"He was not listed amongst the honored guests invited to the nuptials," said Tuvo Ausonius.

"Is that not strange?" asked Julian.

"Perhaps he returned to a barbarian world," said Rurik, "perhaps Tenguthaxichai."

"Why?" asked Julian.

"Perhaps his work was done," said Rurik. "Perhaps he feared assassination in Telnar."

"I wonder where he may be," said Julian.

"We do not know," said Rurik.

"Men such as Abrogastes do not simply disappear," said Iaachus.

"I wonder," said Julian.

"The next move, if it be made——," said Iaachus.

"It will be," said Julian.

"——will not be ours," said Iaachus.

"Whose?" asked Tuvo Ausonius.

"That of Ingeld," said Rurik.

"Or that of Sidonicus," said Iaachus.

"How so?" asked Rurik. "Sidonicus is a man of peace. Ministrants of *Karch* do not even bear arms. Too, there are the very teachings of Floon, an inoffensive, loving Ogg, presumably insane, praising snakes and insects, wandering about, blessing flowers, trees, and rocks."

"One need not bear arms if others will bear them for you," said Iaachus. "Indeed, is that not the shrewdest, safest way to bear arms, letting others take your risks and face your dangers, letting others loose your arrows and fire your pistols, while you remain to the side, wrapped in holiness, perhaps even publicly deploring the violence you have been at pains to instigate?"

"How is it possible?" asked Rurik.

"Seeds planted, words spoken, agents dispatched, hints released, like bats, sermons preached, prayers uttered," said Iaachus, "and riots are raised, and men bearing torches rush into the streets."

"But the teachings of Floon?" protested Rurik.

"What have they to do with Floonianism?" asked Iaachus.

"In mobs there is power," said Julian.

"And anonymity and license," said Tuvo Ausonius.

"The dogs of war, snarling and howling, lurk within many hearts," said Iaachus. "They beg only to be released."

"We must wait," said Rurik.

"I fear so," said Julian.

"Might we not seize Ingeld and Hrothgar?" asked Tuvo Ausonius.

"That would precipitate open war," said Iaachus.

"Then Sidonicus?" said Rurik.

"The empire would be in flames," said Iaachus.

"Then we wait," said Rurik.

"But surely," said Iaachus, "we may wait pleasantly."

"'Pleasantly'?" asked Julian.

"Wine is at hand," said Iaachus.

The tolling of a distant bell was heard, its peals taken up by others about the city.

"The curfew," said Rurik.

"A decanter awaits, of ruby *kana*," said Iaachus, "and a light collation, as well. Do not fear to drink or eat with the Arbiter of Protocol. He shall partake first."

"And perhaps earlier, of an antidote," said Julian.

"That is possible," said Iaachus.

"You are implicated in these matters, as well as we," said Julian.

"What better foundation for trust could there be?" smiled Iaachus.

"True," said Julian.

"Muchly so," said bearded Rurik.

Iaachus, Arbiter of Protocol, then turned about, smiling, and clapped his hands, sharply.

A door opened, to the side, and a lovely gray-eyed, brown-haired slave entered, bare-armed and barefoot, closely collared, in a long gown, belted with a belly chain, from which dangled two small cuffs, suitable for her slender wrists. This arrangement not only belts the slave's gown in, snugly, accentuating her figure, but allows the slave's hands, if one wishes, to be fastened before her body, or behind her back. Too, such an accouterment symbolizes, as well, that she who wears it is a slave. She bore a tray on which reposed a decanter of *kana*, and five small glasses. She placed the tray on a nearby table, slightly to the side. She then, without speaking, returned to the room to the side, and, shortly thereafter, returned, bearing another tray, which she placed similarly, on which was arranged finger bowls and napkins, and a variety of crisp breads, fruits, and cheeses.

"Only one slave serves?" inquired Rurik.

"Let us trust," said Iaachus, "that one slave is not too many."

"I see," said Rurik.

"Who knows of what might be spoken in this room, this evening," said Iaachus.

Rurik watched the slave, carefully filling the tiny glasses.

"Do you like my slave?" asked Iaachus.

"Yours, not a palace slave?" asked Rurik.

"Yes, mine," said Iaachus.

"I recall now," said Rurik.

"It is sometimes difficult to note slaves," said Iaachus. "Well trained, they are unobtrusive."

"She has served us before," said Rurik.

"Yes," said the Arbiter of Protocol.

"Very nice," said Rurik.

"Perhaps seventy-five *darins*," speculated Julian.

The slave kept her head down.

"I call her 'Elena'," said Iaachus. "She was once a lady-in-waiting to the empress mother."

"Incredible," said Rurik.

"I gather she was displeasing," said Julian.

"A slight smile, at an ill-chosen time," said Iaachus.

"I see," said Julian.

"I saw no point in having her bound and cast into a *carnarium*, outside the city," said Iaachus, "so I decided to keep her. Perhaps you can suspect why."

"Yes," said Rurik.

"It is an excellent *kana*," said Tuvo Ausonius.

"I trust," said Julian, "it contains no subtle, tasteless additive."

"Some poisons," said Iaachus, "actually improve the taste of a *kana*."

"Not a *kana* as fine as this," said Rurik.

"No," said Iaachus.

"Slave," said Julian.

"Master?" she said, addressed, frightened.

"Do you think you would bring seventy-five *darins* on the block?" he asked.

"No, Master," she said, "not nearly so much."

"Would you like to be sold, Elena?" asked Iaachus.

"No, Master!" she said, hastily. She turned white. She was obviously frightened, terribly frightened. "Do not sell me, Master!" she whispered, terribly distraught, beggingly.

"But it could be done, easily, could it not?" he said.

"Yes, Master," she said. "I am a slave."

"You understand that, clearly, do you not?" he asked.

"Yes, Master," she whispered. "I am a slave."

Rurik laughed.

"Master?" asked the slave, frightened.

"Do you like being a slave?" he asked.

"Do not make me speak," she begged. Free women may lie. Slaves may not.

"Speak," he said, sternly.

"Yes, Master," she said.

"Do you love being a slave?" he demanded.

"Yes, Master," she said.

"Worthless, meaningless slave," he said.

"Yes, Master," she said.

One gathers it is not unusual for slaves to be scorned. They are, after all, only slaves.

"Do you love your master?" demanded Rurik.

"Yes, yes, yes, Master," she wept, and fell to her knees by the table, her head down covering her face with her hands. And then, she lifted her head to the Arbiter of Protocol, her master, her eyes bright with tears, tears streaming down her cheeks. "Please do not whip me, Master," she said. "Please do not sell me!"

"Resume serving," said Iaachus.

"Yes, Master," she said, gratefully, rising.

"It is interesting," said Julian, "how love often comes with the collar."

"It is not so hard to understand," said Rurik. "It is hard to be a man's slave, and not, in time, become his, in all ways."

"Being a man's slave is the deepest part of a woman," said Julian. "It is what they want, in their deepest heart. How else can they fulfill the deepest part of their nature?"

"The whip is a useful instrument in reminding a woman of her bondage," said Iaachus. "Under the whip, she knows she is a slave."

"The Larial Farnichi," said Rurik to Iaachus, "owe the empire much."

"I would know nothing of that," said Iaachus, warily.

"Of course," said Rurik.

Rurik reached for one of the crisp breads.

"Slave," said Rurik.

"Master?" said the gray-eyed slave.

He broke off a bit of cheese and placed it on the bread.

"What do you know," he asked, "of the Larial Calasalii?"

The slave looked at Iaachus, quickly, frightened.

"You have been addressed, my dear," said Iaachus.

"Only what all know, Master," she responded. "It was scattered and reduced, outlawed and impounded, its men impressed, its women enslaved."

"Your gown is attractive," said Rurik.

"A slave is pleased, if Master is pleased," she said.

"I brought a blond slave to the palace recently," he said.

"That is known to me, Master," she said.

"You saw her earlier, at another repast," he said.

"Yes, Master," she said.

Rurik finished the bit of bread and cheese to which he had helped himself. He then availed himself of a finger bowl and a napkin.

"How is she clothed?" he asked.

Surely he knew. Was he not her master?

"Tunicked," she said, "briefly, in little more than a rag. She must be a muchly despised slave."

"A slave tunic is perhaps too much for her," he said.

"Masters determine whether or not we will be clothed, and, if clothed, how," she said.

"She was of the Larial Calasalii," said Rurik.

"Once the noble Lady Publennia, of that noble family," said Elena.

"Disinherited, disowned, put aside, stricken from their records," said Rurik, "a cast-aside wastrel, vain and petty."

Elena lowered her head.

"You spoke her former name, that name she so sullied," he said. "Did you know her?"

"Our Elena met her briefly," said Iaachus, "aiding her in the restoration of her garmenture, following an interview of state. It had to do with a mission of some delicacy, undertaken on behalf of the empire." Iaachus risked a glance to the side, to the dais on which reposed the throne, the single throne, to which we have earlier alluded. He then returned his attention to Rurik. "I fear the Lady Publennia was impatient, and somewhat cruel to our dear Elena," he said.

"May I speak, Master?" asked Elena.

"Certainly," said Iaachus.

"Such things are within the entitlements of the free woman," she said.

"You were not so, in your freedom," said Iaachus.

"I bear her no animus," she said, "nor may I do so, as I am a slave."

"Where is she now?" asked Rurik, Tenth Consul of the Larial Farnichi.

"On her chain, in the kitchen," she said.

"You are nicely gowned," said Rurik.

"Master?" asked Elena, puzzled.

"Is she ankle-chained or neck-chained?" asked Rurik.

"Neck-chained, Master," said Elena, "and, I fear, the chain is fastened quite closely to the floor ring."

"I ordered it so," said Rurik. "Have her freed of her chain, and have her crawl here, in her rag, head down, to my knee."

"Surely, no, Master," protested Elena.

"She is no more than a worthless slave, and a former slut of the hated Larial Calasalii," he said.

"She was a free woman," said Elena, "a scion of the highest *honestori*, a patrician, even of the senatorial class."

"Women are worthless when free," said Rurik. "They have value only in a collar."

"Yes, Master," said Elena.

She then, frightened, turned about and hurried from the room, leaving by the portal through which she had begun the serving.

"The *kana* is excellent," said Rurik to Iaachus.

"I am pleased that you are pleased," said Iaachus.

Shortly thereafter a blonde, blue-eyed slave, head down, on all fours, entered the room, and crawled to Rurik's place, where she put her head down to the floor, at his side.

"This slut was once of the Larial Calasalii," said Rurik. "You see her now appropriately, at the feet of her master."

"The women of the defeated," said Iaachus, "belong by right to the victors."

"You may beg to kiss the feet of your master," said Rurik to the slave.

"I beg to kiss the feet of my master," said the slave.

"Do so," said Rurik.

"Behold, lovely Elena," said Rurik, "the former Lady Publennia, of the Larial Calasalii, a slave."

"Please be kind to her, Master," said Elena.

Rurik laughed. "Be kind," he laughed, "to a slave?"

The blonde slave, trembling, continued her ministrations.

"She looks well there, at a master's feet," said Julian.

"They all do," said Iaachus.

Rurik reached down, put his hands on the slave's collar, one on each side, and pulled her head up, so that she, now kneeling, must face him, looking into the eyes of her master.

"You are collared, slave," he said.

"Yes, Master," she said.

"The collar looks well on your neck," he said.

"Thank you, Master," she said.

"Can you remove it?"

"No, Master," she said.

Slave collars are not made to be removed by those whose throats they grace.

"It belongs there," he said.

"I fear so, Master," she said.

He looked at her, with the look of one who is a natural master of women.

"Yes, Master," she said, "it belongs there. It belongs on my neck. My neck is suitably encircled with the badge of servitude."

"Why?" he asked.

"Because I am a woman, Master," she said.

"You see, dear Elena," said Iaachus, "you need no longer fear her. Her neck, like yours, is now in a collar."

"Yes, Master," said Elena.

"The women of the Larial Calasalii are spoils of war," he said.

"Is not every woman, in a sense, Master, the spoils of war?" asked Elena.

"To whom will they belong, who will possess them?" said Iaachus.

"Yes Master," said Elena. "Unowned, unpossessed, we are meaningless, lost, and forlorn. In defeat we find our victory, in submission our redemption, in the collar, owned and mastered, our freedom."

"I rise," said Iaachus, "to lift a glass of *kana*."

Julian, Rurik, and Tuvo Ausonius, too, rose.

"It may be our last glass of *kana*," said Julian.

All eyes turned toward the throne.

Another presence had long loomed in the room, large, and brooding.

Those individuals with whom we have been particularly concerned, Iaachus, Julian, Rurik, and Tuvo Ausonius, had scarcely glanced at this presence, in this evincing a neglect which was conspicuous in its inattention. Not regarded, it was regarded. Unacknowledged, it was devastatingly acknowledged. It was like a sound one pretended not to hear. How then could it be more fearsomely intrusive? Might one not hesitate before looking over a precipice, or into a crater? One might keep one's eyes averted from a corridor, apprehensive of what might tread therein, approaching. If one shared a room with a watchful golden beast, of whose nature one was unsure, one might well avoid eye contact. Might not the crater burst with fire; might not what is expected, even invited, prove, in its reality, unwelcome; might not the beast spring?

"I will drink now," said Otto, chieftain of the Wolfungs, king of the Otungs.

Hitherto he had gestured Elena away, when she had approached with *kana*. She had not dared to meet the eyes of that shape, that anomalous thing then before her, reposed upon that high-backed, wide-armed chair, of which there could be but one in the thousands of worlds, a shape massive, and yet alert, feral, and supple, incongruous in such a place, unexpected in such an ensconcement.

Surely such a thing belonged not here, in a palace, but in a forest, or arena. Would it not be more fittingly placed in a saddle, raiding villages on Tangara, or waiting at the foot of a corsair's boarding ladder, on the inland sea of Menon IV?

Otto, comporting with the regulations of the imperial auxiliaries, was clean shaven. His hair was close-cropped. No longer did long, blond, braided hair dangle behind him. Within the imperial mantle, loose about his shoulders, he wore his uniform, that of a captain of the auxiliaries. Some people see no further than such things. Do they think that a barbarian must wear skins and carry an ax? Do they not know that the difference between *civilitas* and *barbaritas* is not a matter of accent or garmenture? Do they not know it lies deeper? Do they not know it lies in the heart?

Otto had been lost in thought, for, in the doings of worlds, there is much to consider, and much occurs which cannot be considered, as it is waiting, patient and unknown.

Elena swiftly lifted one of the small glasses, preparing to hurry to the dais, and climb the steps to the throne.

"Hold," said Julian. "He would *drink*." He indicated the decanter.

"Yes, Master," said Elena, taking the vessel in two hands.

She hurried to the dais, and climbed the steps to the foot of the throne, before which she knelt, head down, and, with two hands, lifted the vessel to the figure on the throne, who accepted it and, with a gesture, as a slave may be dismissed, dismissed her. She hurried back to Iaachus.

Iaachus, Julian, Rurik, and Tuvo Ausonius stood, glasses in hand, facing the throne. Until a few hours ago the men in this chamber had been muchly fellows, bonded in an enterprise of import, warily congenial, informal with one another. But now one sat upon a throne.

"Friend Rurik," called Otto, adjusting the imperial mantle, "I think I know your slave. Present her."

The blonde slave cried out with misery, but was pulled to the feet by her hair, and thrust by Rurik toward the throne, his left hand in her hair, tightly, her head held back, and his right hand holding her small right wrist up, high, behind her. She whimpered. She was on her tip toes. Before the throne he released her hair and wrist, but held her upright, by the arms, from behind.

"The slave," he said.

"She was a woman of the empire," said the figure on the throne. "I, as I understand it, am a barbarian. Thus, present her as a woman of the empire is properly presented to a barbarian."

"Assuredly," said Rurik.

The slave cried out as her tiny garment was torn from her.

She sank to her knees before the throne, looking up at a free man. She did not attempt to cover herself with her hands. Such an indiscretion can bring the whip. A slave's body, as that of any other animal, is public. Her body is not hers to do with as she pleases, but the master's, to do with as he pleases.

"We have met before," said Otto, "on Tangara, only then you had a small dagger, its blade thought to be coated with poison."

The slave put her head down, not speaking.

"I would have you speak your principal, clearly, in this room," said Otto. "Who employed you? Who put you to the dark work of the assassin, which work, suspected, was foiled?"

"I dare not speak, Master," she said.

"Surely you know, or suspect, my dear Ottonius," said Iaachus, from the side, the glass still in hand. "It was I, and it was I, too, who engineered the flawed attempt on Vellmer, on the villa of Julian. I acted, as always, for the health of the empire, as I perceive it. I sought to frustrate our friend Julian's designs upon the throne, depriving him of the means whereby he would seek that end, the recruitment of barbarians."

"I have no designs upon the throne," said Julian, "and the recruitment of barbarians, I fear, is essential to the preservation of the empire."

"I see little to choose from," said Iaachus, "between Alemanni and Otungs."

"But you have chosen," said Julian.

"Yes," said Iaachus, "should the princesses Viviana and Alacida produce sons, those sons will, as nephews to a childless emperor, stand next in the line of succession."

"But," said Rurik, "they would find the throne otherwise occupied."

"If we can hold Telnar, and Telnaria," said Julian.

"Now," said Iaachus, "all matters public, each proclaimed and clear, I await my fate."

"You are, of course, safe," said Otto. "You are needed, in a thousand ways."

"Such," said Iaachus, "was my surmise."

"What of Aesilesius?" asked Rurik.

"What of him?" asked Iaachus, warily.

"I have looked in upon him from time to time, he amongst his toys," said Otto. "I am thinking of looking in upon him once more."

"There is nothing to be gained," said Iaachus, apprehensively, "from a timid, retarded boy, twisted and misshapen, lost amongst toys, who can scarcely speak, who cannot control his own saliva, who can barely write his name, or, having written it, understand what he has written."

"Perhaps you are thinking of looking in upon him—one last time?" said Rurik.

Otto was silent.

"I beg of you, noble Ottonius," said Iaachus, "do not kill him, he or the empress mother."

"Yet, alive," said Rurik, "they leave room for hope, hope for a dynastic restoration. They might prove rallying points for a rising resistance."

"Let them live," said Iaachus. "An old woman and a retarded boy are unlikely rallying points. And if you should kill them, a far more plausible rallying point looms."

"Who?" asked Rurik.

"Julian, Julian, of the Aureliani," said Iaachus.

"I seek no throne," said Julian, angrily.

All looked to the throne.

"They will live," said Otto. "I am not one to kill old women and boys. My sword does not seek such blood."

"How is it then," asked Rurik, "that you would look in upon Aesilesius?"

"Perhaps," said Otto, "in a dark, terrible world, one of blood, intrigue, and steel, it is pleasant to look in upon a child, pleased with its toys."

Rurik swept his boot against the thigh of the kneeling blonde slave. "Return to the kitchen," he said, "and have yourself chained again, your neck even closer to the floor ring. I shall decide later whether or not to whip you."

"Please do not whip me, Master," she said. "The whip hurts so! It hurts so!"

"But under it," he said, "you well know yourself a slave, do you not?"

"What woman would not, Master?" she wept.

"To the kitchen," he said.

"Yes, Master," she said, seizing up the shreds of her tiny tunic, and fleeing from the room.

Rurik then returned to the table.

"I propose a toast," said Iaachus, "to Ottonius, Ottonius the First, Emperor of Telnaria!"

Iaachus, Julian, Rurik, and Tuvo Ausonius lifted their small glasses.

All noted that he upon the throne had not raised the decanter, it small in that large, bronzed hand.

"To the empire!" said Julian, lifting his glass higher.

"Our empire," added Rurik, Tenth Consul of Larial VII.

The figure upon the throne, mayhap some seven feet in height, and mighty in breadth, then rose to its feet.

"—*The* empire," it said.

Otto put back his head and drained the decanter, emptying it as though it might have been a horn of *bror*.

The others, too, then drank.

The decanter was then flung down, and it shattered into fragments. The others, too, then cast down their glasses.

"Things must now begin again," said Iaachus. "All is new."

CHAPTER TWO

"The palace was closed to us!" cried Ingeld. "Were we not to be welcomed by the empress mother? Was the emperor not to be clad in his regalia, and put upon his throne, to welcome us? We were turned back, back! Fools who cheered us approaching the palace, cheered us as heartily on our return to the temple!"

"I trust you returned in stately fashion, waving, returning the salutations of the crowd," said ponderous Sidonicus, exarch of Telnar.

"Scarcely," said Ingeld. "Plans were obviously awry. We returned in haste, drivers lashing the horses."

"I have had word put out," said Sidonicus, "that your return to the temple had been planned, to acknowledge the final superiority of the temple to the palace."

"Burn your temples!" snarled Ingeld. "See if they can resist the torch and sword! What good are they, save as a tool to be used by the palace, a prop to power?"

"We may discuss such matters later," said Sidonicus. "In the meantime I am sure each of us will continue to find profit in the friendship of the other."

"Treachery!" said Ingeld.

"Not on my part, I assure you," said Sidonicus.

"Would we were on Tenguthaxichai," said Ingeld. "It would be the Horse Death for you!"

"Who turned you back?" asked Sidonicus.

"Officers of the imperial navy," said Ingeld.

"Where was the city guard?" asked Sidonicus.

"Withdrawn, apparently dismissed," said Ingeld.

"Naval officers?" said Sidonicus.

"By their uniforms," said Ingeld.

"You submitted?" said Sidonicus.

"They were armed," said Ingeld. "One cartridge would burn the horses and carriage."

"I see the hand of Julian, of the Aureliani, in this," said Sidonicus.

"What is going on?" demanded Ingeld.

"I have more than a hundred spies in the streets," said Sidonicus. "We shall soon know."

CHAPTER THREE

"What are the bells for?" asked Lady Gia Alexia, she of the Telnar Darsai, waiting across the street from the home of the rhetor and attorney, Titus Gelinus.

The air was thundering with the joyful peal of perhaps a thousand bells, their sound rising to the clouds, shaking the sky, falling like bright, shimmering rain on the capital.

"It is freedom and joy, Lady," said a guardsman, "signaling the accession of Ottonius, the First, Emperor of Telnaria. Men flock gladly into the streets, assembly now welcome. The curfew is lifted. In the square before the palace, the scented fountains again flow. Food is distributed. Avail yourself of free tickets for the games, the theaters, and races. And the portals of the senate will again open, tomorrow, that august body, guarantor of the majesty of the empire, guardian of law, convening for the first time in weeks."

"A monster is on the throne," said the Lady Gia Alexia. "Little is known of him. Who is he? Some assert that he may even be a barbarian. What of the emperor, of the empress mother? Where are they? Why do they not appear in public? Unruly crowds are easily distracted and bribed. The senate is worthless, waiting only to receive its instructions."

But the angry ruminations of the Lady Gia Alexia, however virulently expressed, fell on no ears but her own, for the guardsman had turned away.

It may be recalled that we have met the Lady Gia Alexia earlier, for it was she, a once-scorned acquaintance of the Lady Publennia, of the Larial Calasalii, who, on a street in Telnar, following the raid of Abrogastes, that raid which had resulted in the abduction of the princesses Viviana and Alacida, had discovered and claimed for her own a loose slave, one blonde-haired and blue-eyed. She had treated this slave rather badly, we fear, though one is scarcely concerned with such things in the case of a slave. To be sure, it is generally recognized that, as the slave is a domestic animal, she, as any other domestic animal, is likely to prove a much better, and more valuable, domestic animal if attention is given to her welfare, seeing that she is well fed and such. This prudential solicitude in no way, of course, compromises the fact that she is to be kept, at all times, under perfect discipline. That goes without saying. She is a slave. In any event, the Lady Gia Alexia soon sold her slave to a merchant, Tenrik, Tenrik of Tenrik's Woman Market, insisting however, as a condition of the sale, that the small placard hung about her neck, on its cords, advertising her, as such things do a slave, should make clear that she had been of the Larial Calasalii. She had then brought the slave to the attention of a scion of the Larial Farnichi, Rurik, Tenth Consul of Larial VII, who was well pleased to acquire a Calasalii prize, even one now collared. In this way the Lady Gia Alexia received not only twenty-five *darins* from Tenrik, for her slave, but a gold *darin* for her aid in locating a Calasalii woman, and one of interest, for a scion of the Larial Farnichi. And it was thus that the former Lady Publennia, of the Larial Calasalii, came into the collar of her current master, Rurik, Tenth Consul of Larial VII.

The location of the Lady Gia Alexia, where she was, in the Lycon district, waiting across the street from the home of the rhetor and attorney, Titus Gelinus, should not be attributed to accident. It was not a simple matter of casual happenstance, but, rather, of intent. The noble Gelinus, young, handsome, wealthy, and vigorous, and much accomplished for his age, was well known in Telnar, at least in certain circles. His figure, voice, and gestures were familiar to those who frequented the law courts, not only as disputants or participants, who often feared him, but as thrill seekers who looked for entertainment, the curious, idle, and bored, amongst whom we might number Lady Gia Alexia. Perhaps a word is in order at this point, pertaining to the legal culture in Telnar at the time in question. The characteristic which I shall enumerate is, of course, not unique to Telnar, at the time in question, or at other times, for that matter. It pertains, or its flavor pertains, much more broadly. To begin with, we must distinguish between formal sciences, such as geometry, and board games, such as Miton draughts, and the law. In the case of geometry, the criteria for a proof are understood, and a proposed proof is either a proof or not. One can tell. Similarly, in the draughts of Miton, the criteria for winning, losing, and drawing are understood, and a given game is either won or not won, or drawn. One can tell. In law, on the other hand, persuasion is paramount. Who can convince who of what? It would be rather as though, in geometry, it was not really important whether a proof was a proof, or not, but rather whether or not one could convince someone that something was a proof, whether it was or not. And, in the case of draughts, it would not really be important whether or not the game was won, lost, or drawn, but, rather, whether one could convince someone that it had been, say, lost or drawn. Also, in geometry and draughts, the meanings of terms are clear. In law, "interpretation" is often important, which allows one to change rules and reassign meanings in such a way as to favor one or another outcome.

This characteristic, the paramountcy of persuasion, was particularly prominent in Telnar at the time in question. Rhetoricians, and teachers of rhetoric, flourished. Indeed, as private individuals in Telnaria often pleaded their own cases, the skills and goods provided by the rhetorician, often at considerable expense, were avidly sought. It is clear, then, that the skill to make the worse case appear the better, and even the worst case appear the best, is one of great value, particularly to one who has the worse or worst case.

One other characteristic might be mentioned, which seems worth noting, though officially it fails to reach the threshold of existence. This has to do with, first, the influence or pressure of the audience, so to speak, at a given trial, and, second, more broadly, the influence or pressure of the environing social milieu. Crowds have their favorites, and want certain results. It is impossible that a judge or jury not be aware of such things, and the possible repercussions, physical, economic, and social, which might follow unpopular decisions. Since one is not dealing with geometry or draughts, prudential elasticities are likely to characterize legal rulings and decisions. For example, in Telnar, courts resemble theaters and trials resemble sporting events. The court has its audience, and the trial its spectators, crowds, in effect, which are not reluctant to make their views, and their likes and dislikes, known. Attorneys play to the crowd, for its views are often persuasive, as well as to judges or juries. Indeed, large segments of the crowd may consist of one claque or another. Some individuals hang about the courts, hoping to be recruited for one claque or another. The usual fee is a quarter *darin*. Sometimes these op-

posing claques come to blows. In passing, it might be noted that
Titus Gelinus, as least as far as was known, had never resorted to
the device of hiring a claque. His view in this matter was not so
much that such a practice was unworthy, or such, as that, in his
case, it was not needed. In any event, as certain actors, dancers,
riders, gladiators, and such may have their followings, so, too, in
Telnar, certain successful lawyers had their followings. And not
the least of these would be the brilliant, flamboyant, and dramatic
Titus Gelinus. When he was to appear in court, the tiers would be
filled. And one sure to be ensconced somewhere in those crowded
tiers would be the Lady Gia Alexia. The mere appearance of Titus
Gelinus in the court room would bring applause. Then, when
he inverted the sand glass, to measure his time for speaking, the
crowd would lean forward, intent, that not a word be missed. It
was alleged that he had never lost a case, except, of course, to suborned juries, some of which he actually won over, or prejudiced,
hostile judges, jealous of his popularity and skills. He commanded
the highest fees in Telnar for his services. Needless to say, such
a young, handsome, wealthy, successful advocate would not be
long unnoted by many of the free women of Telnar. And certainly
one of the most determined and resolute of these many admirers
would be the Lady Gia Alexia. Indeed, the blonde-haired, blue-
eyed slave, once of the Larial Calasalii, now the rightless property
of Rurik, Tenth Consul of Larial VII, had, when the slave of the
Lady Gia Alexia, carried various notes to Titus Gelinus on her behalf, apparently petitioning for an assignation. These efforts of the
Lady Gia Alexia, mediated by the slave's erranding, had, however,
been unsuccessful. Indeed, a number of times the Lady Gia Alexia
had expressed her frustration and disappointment to her slave,
that by means of the switch.

The Lady Gia Alexia suddenly gasped for breath, shaken, and
then, deliberately, breathed in, deeply, forcibly. She must appear
her elegant, casual, serene self. Her presence here was but a coincidence. She hoped not to swoon. Her heart raced. She felt anoma-
lously warm. She feared that her reaction might be unfitting for
a free woman. Surely it was! How very conscious she was then of
her body. No longer was it unfelt, inert, ignored, and unnoticed,
as though it might be elsewhere or absent. How frightful for her,
that it was reactive, despite the care with which it was sheathed,
wrapped, and swathed. Fully clothed, she felt exposed. A frightful thought gripped her. If she could feel such feelings within the

layers of defenses contrived on her behalf by her society, what might be her weakness, and helplessness, if she were denied such bastions of protection, if all that stood between her and the wind, the air, and sunlight, and the lustful gaze of men was naught but a thin, tiny scrap of cheap cloth? And what if she had a collar on her neck, and knew what it proclaimed, what she was, and what she was for?

Across that street, in the fashionable Lycon district that morning, the door to the residence of Titus Gelinus had just opened.

She caught a glimpse of the tall, robed figure in the portal, turned, perhaps addressing some last remark or instruction to a secretary or servant.

She hurried across the street, that she might encounter him, inadvertently, as each pursued their independent way. It might even be possible, if all went well, to seize a moment to chat, if one could make oneself heard for the bells. After all, the weather was pleasant and much of late had transpired in Telnar.

Her veil might loosen, she feared, which could happen, such things occasionally did, but surely this calamity would be amenable to an embarrassed, expeditious repair. But it should have slipped far enough, and for long enough, for an alert observer to be startled at the beauty it normally served to conceal.

One thing pleased her, in particular.

This morning no petitioners, no cloud of clients, hung about the portal, waiting to accompany Gelinus to the courts.

This had to do, of course, with the holiday, that of the imperial accession, in recognition of which all official business, that of the courts included, was suspended.

Might this not provide an opportunity to meet with him alone?

Surely she hoped so.

She had not known, of course, that he would definitely take leave of his residence today. But it did seem a plausible day for him to be about, the courts not in session, to attend to postponed errands, to visit friends, or such. She hoped he would not visit the brothels or the woman markets. This was not, of course, the first day that the Lady Gia Alexia had found herself in the vicinity of the house of Gelinus. Her presence in the vicinity had been frequently noted.

Something crossed her mind, only to be quickly dismissed, a thought as meaningless as the flight of a small bird, passing overhead, somewhat to the side, that the senate would meet tomorrow, after a hiatus of several weeks. The guardsman, she recalled, had said something about the reconvening of the senate.

Yes, it was he, Titus Gelinus! And he was approaching!

She stumbled a little, but righted herself, promptly. It would not do to be clumsy. She trusted her legs would not fail her.

She proceeded toward him, seeming not to notice him.

But he had glimpsed her and he had stopped, and was looking about. Was he thinking of turning back, of going to the other side of the street?

But then he resumed his gait, perhaps annoyed, certainly resolved.

How well he walked, his robes about him.

Was it not impressive, like an argosy or galleon under sail?

Why should he seem angry?

"Oh!" said the Lady Gia Alexia, looking up, startled. Surely she had not meant to block his way. "I am so clumsy," she said. "Forgive me, noble sir."

"The fault is mine," he said. "I should have been more careful. I beg your pardon, noble lady."

It seemed he was intent upon pursuing his way.

"Why," she said, amazed, looking up at him, not abandoning her location, "are you not the rhetor, the advocate, Titus Gelinus?"

"I am he," he admitted.

"I once saw you, in court," she said. "I had a friend who was a litigant. For her sake I thought I should attend. Normally I would not do such a thing."

"Certainly not," said Gelinus. "The tiers are no place for a lady such as you, the matter made clear by your habiliments, the quality and taste of your ensemble. The tiers can be rowdy. Too, attendance being open, that to ensure public scrutiny, it is impossible to deny access to any stratum of the public."

"How true," she acknowledged, wistfully. It is true that there is much in the world which cannot easily be changed, or avoided.

"If you would pardon me—," he said, and seemed ready to press past her.

"You were brilliant," she said. "You won the case, of course."

"One is sometimes fortunate," he said.

"It is hard to speak for the bells," she said.

"True," he said.

"Much depends, of course," she said, "on the judge, the jury, and such."

"It is often thought so," he said, "particularly by those who are unfamiliar with the matter."

"I am the Lady Gia Alexia," she said, "of the Telnar Darsai."

"I thought you might be," he said.

"Oh?" she said.

"Does your business not often bring you to the Lycon district?" he asked.

"Occasionally," she said.

"I have, over the past several months, received a number of notes, on ribboned, scented paper, from a woman identifying herself as the Lady Gia Alexia, of the Telnar Darsai," he said.

"It was I," she said.

"I receive many such notes," he said.

"Oh?" she said.

"From women, pleading for a meeting, doubtless having in mind a clandestine assignation," he said.

"How dreadful!" she said.

"It is amusing, in its way," he said.

"I have solicited such a meeting, more than once," she said, "but, I assure you, for no such purpose."

"I am pleased to hear it," he said, but did not seem all that pleased.

"I wished only to consult with you on certain obscure points of law," she said, "points which I found of interest."

"You are interested in the law?" he asked.

"Very much so," she said.

"What obscure points?" he asked.

"Points which I found obscure," she said.

"I see," he said. "If you will now excuse me, I must be on my way."

"Might we not have lunch together, to discuss the law?" she said.

"I have an appointment," he said.

"Might I not accompany you?" she asked. "We could walk together."

"I think not," he said.

"Who is she?" asked the Lady Gia Alexia.

"I undertake a matter of business," he said, annoyed, "at the house of the senate."

"The senate does not meet until tomorrow," she said.

"Precisely," he said.

"You are to meet with the moderator of the senate, with certain members?" she asked.

"I bid you, noble lady, farewell," he said, politely but firmly.

"A moment," she said, "the breeze. I must adjust my veil." Her small hands went to the vicinity of her right ear, to lift and tighten the veil, readjusting the clasp, but her fingers bungled the operation, and the veil, instead of being quickly and safely resecured, as was her intent, dropped about her shoulders, much to her dismay.

"Ah!" he said.

"Look away, kind sir," she begged.

With this understandable request he immediately, thoughtfully, complied.

"Forgive me, sir," she said. "I shall detain you no longer."

"Perhaps" he said, "you might write to me again sometime, to discuss points of law."

"Perhaps," she said. "We must wait and see."

He then bowed, and continued on his way.

The Lady Gia Alexia, who knew herself to be very beautiful, was much pleased. Indeed, some had speculated, privately, of course, that she might even be beautiful enough to stand stripped on a slave shelf, chained and collared, with a sales placard hung about her neck. Beautiful women sell best, of course. What man does not want one or more beautiful slaves?

"I have kindled a fire," she thought. "It is now up to me to see if I shall stoke it, or feed it, or refuse it, depriving it of fuel, leaving behind only agony and ashes. Certainly I shall manage it, regulate it, and make use of it as I will. Fire is useful, very useful."

Looking after Titus Gelinus, she wondered what might be his business with the senate. Certainly he was not a senator.

Could it be, she wondered, that the senate might now be in session, that a secret meeting was in progress?

The peal of the bells was meanwhile continuing, celebrating the accession of a new emperor, Ottonius, the First.

CHAPTER FOUR

"We shall soon be returned to the palace!" said blond-haired Viviana.

"It is all arranged," said Sidonicus, his weighty, thoughtful, swollen, purple-clad figure, content, now grievously sessile, settled comfortably in the flattened cushions of the broad, towering chair of the exarch, a chair designed to resemble, or rival, the imperial throne. His eyes seemed half shut, given the fatness of his cheeks, and his short, pudgy fingers played with the golden replica of a burning rack, slung on its chain about his neck. It was on such a device, long ago, that the prophet, Floon, an Ogg, had been incinerated, only to appear later, it seems, unharmed, in a thousand forms on a thousand worlds. It is easier to take seriously the words of a prophet when it wears the genetic cloak of one's own species.

"You are confident in the matter?" asked thin, uneasy, crafty-eyed Ingeld, from behind the latticework of the golden screen which separated him and his brother, Hrothgar, from Sidonicus, and the princesses, Viviana and Alacida. Such screens, openly latticed, had separated Ingeld and Viviana, and Hrothgar and Alacida, during the lengthy ceremony in the temple. Now, from the interior of the room, given the lighting, supplied by means of candles, one could note Ingeld and Hrothgar as little more than shadowy figures on the other side of the screen and, presumably, to Ingeld and Hrothgar, the figures in the room, Sidonicus, Viviana, and Alacida, despite the lighting, would not have appeared much better. Similar screens, widely latticed that they might be easily seen through, had separated the brides and grooms during the ceremony. The symbolism seems to be that that which separates men from women is golden. In most Floonianism, which was characterized by dozens of sects, with different theologies and practices, sex was regarded rather along the lines of being, if not a necessary evil, at least a dangerous temptation which might lure one away from the life of the *koos*, which was invisible and for which no evidence existed. It remained an inexplicable mystery why *Karch* had not arranged a more sober and less interesting way of reproducing a species. It did not seem to occur to most Floonians that *Karch*, if it existed, might have known what it was doing. Floon himself did not seem to express himself on this matter. Rather it was inferred by others, usually generations later, what he might have said if he had chosen to say something. Floon's failure to express himself on the matter was most likely not the result of his having reservations about sex, or disapproving of it, say, for its possibility of distracting one from, or interfering with, the pursuit of the life of the *koos*, as the result of his not having any interest in the matter, as he seems to have been a salamander-ine neuter, like many others of his species.

On the other hand, perhaps the question was, what does biology have to do with the *koos*? Indeed, if there is no such thing as a *koos*, one might wonder what anything might have to do with it. Reasonably clearly, if there is no such thing as a *koos*, biology cannot threaten it, nor, indeed, could anything else threaten it. As it does not exist, it is quite safe. Why then, assuming, as a possibility, there is no such thing as a *koos*, as there does not seem to be, why should someone invent it? What would it be good for? As it turns out, it could be good for many things.

Let us think about the matter.

First of all, the *koos* is different from the body and, as defined, is superior to the body. You are not really what you seem to be, but something else. You are essentially a *koos*. Indeed, it is not clear why you would even need a body. It seems unnecessary. The body, at any rate, is the house of the *koos*, its temporary residence. Moreover, the body can make things difficult for the *koos*. It is also not clear why *Karch* would have arranged things in this fashion, but that is a mystery, beyond human understanding, as is often the case. On the other hand, if the *koos* is a human invention, things fall into place nicely.

Let us think further about the matter.

Human beings have needs, for example, to breathe, eat foods, drink fluids, and so on. Suppose it were now practical to condition human beings in such a way as to be ashamed of breathing, eating, drinking, and such, and to regard such things as regrettable, demeaning, weak, unworthy, degrading, and so on, as being, say, second best to, or inferior to, not breathing, starving, thirst-

ing, and so on. How grateful they would then be, to be allowed, at certain times, and under certain conditions, to be permitted to breathe, eat, or drink. The device is psychologically simple. Create guilt, incredibly enough in connection with something natural, inevitable, and wonderful, indeed, something biologically central to human existence, and then make a living from this crime. This trick, rather clearly, will not work where breathing, eating, and drinking are concerned. People would die. In the case of sex, on the other hand, things are much more promising. Where sex is concerned, one is likely, in most cases, to be no more than sick and miserable, though, to be sure, lives can be shortened and minds lost. Sex provides a splendid field for guilt manipulators, many of whom have succumbed to the same disease they, often, in their innocence, would foist on others. In most of the religions in the Telnarian Empire, on the other hand, sex is accepted gratefully, even with rejoicing, most often as a gift of the gods.

The guilt industry, on the other hand, proceeds as follows.

Disparage a natural part of life, a basic human need, the expression of which is inevitable, and, indeed, biologically central to human life. Produce suspicion and fear. Manufacture shame. Create guilt. Then one rations sex, parceling it out, refusing it, withholding it, permitting it, and so on.

One controls the mind.

One reaps the profit.

One administers poison and then sells the antidote.

"How long am I to remain behind this screen?" shouted Hrothgar, not pleased.

"Be patient," said Ingeld.

Alacida shuddered.

"Not long, my son," said Sidonicus, in a kindly, tolerant fashion.

The ministrants of Floon often spoke so. In this way, they implicitly placed their interlocutor in a position of inferiority, or subordination, as might be a child to a wise and knowing parent, which higher role they implicitly arrogated to themselves.

"I am not your son," said Hrothgar. "I am the son of Abrogastes, king of the Drisriaks, first tribe of the Alemanni."

"It is a way of speaking," purred the exarch.

"If you do not touch women, as you claim," said Hrothgar, "how could you have a son?"

"He could adopt one," said Viviana, annoyed.

"Alas," said Sidonicus, "I may not even do that."

"Or have one willed to you," said Viviana.

"Impossible," said Sidonicus.

"How then could you have a son?" asked Viviana, puzzled.

"It is a manner of speaking," said Sidonicus.

"I thought," said Ingeld, who had inquired into certain doctrinal matters, "parenthood was ascribed, or the expression justified, in virtue of a ministrant's smudging with oil imported from one of the sacred pools of Zirus."

"Quite true," said Sidonicus, "but I think that origin is a bit far-fetched. For example, it would scarcely justify a ministrant's using the expression 'son' of those whom he had not smudged."

"I see," said Ingeld.

"To be sure," said Sidonicus, "matters might change."

"Unfolding revelation?" said Ingeld.

"Precisely," said Sidonicus.

It should be noted here that Ingeld and Hrothgar had not the least reservations pertaining to sex, no more than to breathing, eating, drinking, and such, nor, for that matter, neither had Viviana and Alacida. It would not have occurred to them. Indeed, such reservations would pertain to few in the empire, save those who had been instructed in the tenets of Floonianism. Floon himself had been deprived of that advantage. Should he have exercised the poor judgment of reappearing in the empire, not only might he not recognize the religion founded in his name, but he would be at risk for heresy, and, most likely, at least in certain quarters, be subjected for a second time to the horrors of the burning rack.

"You do these things through the mind," said Ingeld.

"Of course," said Sidonicus.

"You would seek to control even thoughts?" said Ingeld.

"Particularly thoughts," said Sidonicus, "as they are wayward, unpredictable, and uncontrollable."

"And natural feelings, natural urges?" said Ingeld.

"Of course," said Sidonicus.

"You tell them they must not think of a blue *torodont*, and, then, naturally, they cannot help but think of a blue *torodont*?" asked Ingeld.

"Do not make my work difficult," said Sidonicus.

"You would make them feel ashamed of natural feelings, natural urges?" asked Viviana.

"Let us speak of more pressing matters," said Sidonicus.

"That is the trick," said Ingeld. "You make them believe they have done wrong, for this thought or that deed, fill them with apprehension, guilt, and shame, make them miserable and frightened, and then you offer to remove the wrong, for which kindness they are tearfully grateful, the charge for the removal of the wrong, the rescue, the forgiveness, and such, being coin, supporting the ministrants, maintaining the temples, and so on."

"Orak would not behave so abominably," said Viviana.

"Orak is a false god," said Sidonicus.

"How do you know?" asked Viviana.

"I see this as very clever," said Ingeld, "where one can get away with it, a shrewd business, an interesting way to earn a living, a fascinating way to gain prestige, to become important, to garner power, and such, but what I do not understand is how anyone could take it seriously."

"That is a great problem," said Sidonicus, "particularly at first, as the holy truths of faith are likely to seem farcical gibberish to the unenlightened mind."

"True," said Viviana.

"It is a problem," said Sidonicus.

"How does one obtain an enlightened mind?" asked Viviana.

"By accepting the holy truths of faith," said Sidonicus.

"Supporting the ministrants and the temples," said Ingeld, "is little enough, I suppose, to pay for having an infinitely valuable *koos*, which makes one inestimably important, and a chance to sit forever at the table of *Karch*."

"What if," asked Viviana, "they die and, having died, are dead?"

"Then," said Ingeld, "they will never learn they were wrong. They will suffer not the least disappointment."

"They will have sacrificed their entire life, their one life, for a lie," said Viviana.

"Many men," said Ingeld, "sacrifice their life for one lie or another."

"True," said Sidonicus. "What does it matter?"

"I suppose some lies are better than other lies," said Viviana.

"Certainly," said Ingeld, "some are more profitably exploited than others."

"Many men," said Sidonicus, "wish to believe in something, and it is easiest to believe in what one wants to believe."

"And you, and others, will give them something they would like to believe," said Ingeld.

"It is a kindness," said Sidonicus.

"One fools oneself?" said Viviana.

"One is kind to oneself," said Sidonicus.

"It is still difficult for me to understand how you manage to perpetrate your fraud," said Ingeld.

"The true faith," said Sidonicus, reprovingly. "You do touch upon a sensitive point, namely, the offense to reason, plausibility, likelihood, evidence, and such. Ideally, one begins with children, ignorant, trusting little brutes, who will believe whatever they are told."

"In capturing the child," said Ingeld, "you capture the man."

"That is the hope," said Sidonicus.

"They are victims, defenseless victims," said Viviana.

"Dear daughter," said Sidonicus, "one prefers 'fortunate beneficiaries'."

"Am I truly spoused?" inquired Hrothgar, from behind the golden screen.

"Of course," said Sidonicus.

"According to the rites of the exarch," said Ingeld.

"I am not truly spoused," said Hrothgar.

A small squeak of surprise emanated from Alacida.

"How is that?" asked Sidonicus.

"I have given no horses, no dogs, no cattle, no pigs for her," said Hrothgar, "not even one pig."

"Such things are not necessary," said Sidonicus.

"One pays even for a slave," said Hrothgar, "unless one takes her by force."

An apprehensive sound escaped Alacida.

"I assure you," said Sidonicus, "you are spoused."

"According to the rites of the exarch," said Ingeld, "no matter how absurd, pointless, empty, fraudulent, or silly they may be."

"Please," protested Sidonicus.

"How long then," said Hrothgar, growling behind the screen, as though it might be the bars of a cage, "until I seize the royal slut and tear away her robes?"

"I am sure we are both eager, brother," said Ingeld, "but be patient. This is the game of the exarch."

Hrothgar then, who was not noted for his patience, with his tasseled horse boot, kicked away the golden screen, violently, and it flew across the room with a rattle of metal, several of its flat, narrow pieces scattered about.

Sidonicus rose from the exarch's throne, aghast, while Viviana leaped back, and Alacida screamed.

"So much for your golden screen!" said Hrothgar, glaring at the startled exarch.

Ingeld interposed himself between Hrothgar and the exarch.

"Patience, brother," counseled Ingeld. "This is the exarch's game. Another may be played at another time."

Hrothgar leaned forward, menacingly. Ingeld was a slighter man than Hrothgar, who was an *arn* bear of a man, but Ingeld held his ground. For all his temper, and size, Hrothgar commonly yielded to Ingeld, granting Ingeld's depth and shrewdness. Too, Ingeld was the older brother, which, amongst the Alemanni, conscious of order and hierarchy, was important. The first son of Abrogastes was Ortog, who had left the Drisriaks, to found his own tribe, the Ortungen. This secessionist movement was defeated by Abrogastes, and its remnants scattered. Most believed that Ortog had been killed by Abrogastes on Tenguthaxichai. Ingeld was the second son of Abrogastes. Hrothgar seems to have been either the third or fourth son of Abrogastes. The records are not clear on the matter. Similarly, it seems likely that Abrogastes, as was not uncommon with barbarians, particularly chieftains, kings, and high men, had more than one wife and a number of sons and daughters. The only offspring of Abrogastes on which we have explicit information, however, are Ortog, Ingeld, Hrothgar, and a daughter, Gerune, who had joined her bother Ortog, in his attempted secession.

"How long!" demanded Hrothgar, scowling fiercely over Ingeld's shoulder at the understandably uneasy exarch.

"Alacida has fainted," said Viviana, holding her sister in her arms.

"Not long, my son, I mean, forgive me, noble Hrothgar," said Sidonicus. "Not long, indeed. These glorious marriages may be soon consummated, in the palace itself. That is the place to do such things, for the sake of propriety, and appearance. Indeed, we may even dispense, by my personal exarchical dispensation, with the ten days allotted for the dismantling of the golden screens."

"Be patient, brother," cautioned Ingeld, facing his brother, his hands on his brother's arms.

This advice drew only an angry, feral noise from Hrothgar, but he did not thrust his brother aside.

As Hrothgar did not understand the reference to the golden screens, and various readers, as well, might find it obscure, a brief note would seem to be in order.

The reference to the dismantling of the golden screen has to do with marital stipulations or prescriptions enjoined in a number of Floonian sects. The reader may recall that it was deemed golden to keep men and women apart. The marriage ceremony itself had taken place with brides and grooms separated by such screens. Such a screen, too, as has been noted, was emplaced in the exarch's chamber to keep Viviana and Alacida separated from Ingeld and Hrothgar. The latticework of such screens, too, as has been noted, is such that the brides and grooms are well aware of one another's presence, and proximity, and can even, in a sense, see one another. In this way, they are acutely, painfully, aware of one another's presence. Then, in their own domicile, over a period of ten days, the screen is dismantled, bit by bit, to the accompaniment of prayers and condign services. Then, at the end of ten days, the screen removed, the couple, however regrettably, but necessarily, if offspring are to be produced, may consummate the marriage. It is recommended, of course, that this shameful, but necessary, act, be performed in the dark, under covers, as briefly as possible, and with as little pleasure as possible, as pleasure is inimical to the life of the *koos*. Needless to say, it is difficult to resist temptation, which *Karch*, for some reason, had made it difficult to resist, and, one supposes, it is occasionally yielded to, this lapse to be followed by regret, shame, guilt, and such, for which the ministrants of Floon are prepared to supply a remedy. And so it goes, on and on. The ministrants of Floon, of course, at least in theory, and doubtless often in practice, are celibate. It should also be added that normal Floonians, of limited means, are unlikely to have golden screens, at least screens of genuine gold. In their case, screens of baser metals, painted with gold paint, are used. These, suitably blessed, are obtained from ministrants, following the receipt of an appropriate donation.

When burly Hrothgar, muttering and scowling, turned away from Ingeld, and strode angrily to the side, fists clenched, Sidonicus deemed it safe to settle again, affably, into the exarchical throne. Floon himself, wandering about in the swamps of Zirus, overflowing with the joys and beauties of life, celebrating the hardness of rocks, the flight of insects, the stealth of reptilian constrictors, and such, had apparently lived and died in abject poverty, which he seemed not to have noticed. This oversight, however, had imposed no obligation on those who waxed rich in his name to follow his example. In name they shared his poverty; in fact, they did quite well.

"How soon shall we be returned to the palace?" asked blond-haired Viviana.

"Soon," said Sidonicus. "It is all arranged."

"It has to do with the senate?" asked Ingeld.

"It is meeting now, secretly," said Sidonicus. "Tomorrow, when it convenes, it will challenge the accession of the barbarian, Ottonius. It will assert the ancient senatorial right, long in abeyance, of ratifying or failing to ratify an imperial accession. It will not recognize the usurper, Ottonius. It will denounce the usurpation and demand the restoration of Aesilesius."

"Or some other candidate," said Ingeld.

"Possibly," said Sidonicus, "but that need not be feared."

"Aesilesius, as it is explained to me," said Ingeld, "is a retarded boy, enamored of toys, terrified of insects."

"He will do very nicely," said Sidonicus.

"Perhaps you mean the empress mother will do very nicely?" said Ingeld.

"Perhaps," said Sidonicus. "In any event, the empress mother is taking instruction with me. She will soon be ready to be smudged with holy oil, imported from one of the sacred pools of Zirus."

"What if the senate ratifies the accession of the Otung?" said Ingeld.

"It will not," said Sidonicus. "The senate hastens to reclaim its ancient prerogative."

"It, too, is eager for power," said Ingeld.

"Of course," said Sidonicus. "The wine of power is a heady wine. And gold follows power."

"Beware you do not hatch a new monster, one with five hundred and one heads," said Ingeld.

"A word of the emperor may recess, or dissolve, the senate," said Sidonicus. "And five hundred and one heads may be lopped off as easily as one."

"What if," asked Ingeld, "the Otung and his party decline to accept the predetermined verdict, the decision, the ruling, of the senate?"

"They must," said Sidonicus. "If they do not, the city will rise, Telnar will burn, civil war will ensue."

"Would that my father were here, and not on Tenguthaxichai," said Hrothgar. "He would laugh with steel. He loves war."

Sidonicus and Ingeld exchanged glances.

"It seems," said Ingeld to the exarch, "you have planned well."

"Tomorrow evening," said Sidonicus, "you will all be returned to the palace."

"Good," said Hrothgar, eying Alacida, who had not yet recovered consciousness.

CHAPTER FIVE

"He speaks well," said Julian, of the Aureliani, to Rurik, Tenth Consul of Larial VII, both occupying curule chairs of honor.

"Were it not to mean my head," said Rurik, "I might be persuaded."

"One must struggle, surely," said Julian, "not to succumb to such eloquence."

"He is not a senator, I take it," said Rurik.

"No," said Julian, "he is a rhetor, a fellow from the courts."

"A professional speaker?"

"I believe so," said Julian.

"He is quite good," said Rurik.

"That is why he is here," said Julian.

"Still it is difficult to stay awake, after the first two hours," said Rurik.

"Do not nap," said Julian. "It would be disrespectful."

"I did not realize there were so many precedents, and so many legal opinions to be recognized, if not deferred to."

"It is hard to keep track," said Julian. "I stopped trying somewhere after the two hundredth citation."

"Do you suppose he really believes that the matter will be decided in virtue of such considerations?" asked Rurik.

"He may," said Julian. "It is a naivety of jurists."

"The senate thinks the matter is already decided," said Rurik.

"They must nonetheless go through certain motions, observe certain procedures, pretend to deliberate, and then vote," said Julian.

"As was decided yesterday," said Rurik.

"Yes," said Julian.

"I like the senate building," said Rurik. "From the outside it is stately, with its broad steps, its friezes, the deep porch and columns."

"It is one of the most impressive buildings in Telnar," said Julian. "Its message is clear. Behold patience, might, wisdom, and the majesty of the law. Buildings have their say, as well as men."

"I have never been inside before," said Rurik.

He looked to the steeply rising semicircle of marble tiers, on which some five hundred senators, each in his senatorial robe, white trimmed with purple, were ranged, some intent, or seemingly so, some reading, or writing, perhaps notes or letters, some looking about, some chatting, and some, we fear, asleep.

At a lower level, to the right, as one looked toward the tiers, there were two tables, one below the other. At the lower table sat Clearchus Pyrides, senator from Inez IV, who, as moderator of the senate, attended to order, procedure, and the recognition of speakers. Behind him and above him, at the higher table, was Timon Safarius Rhodius, of the Telnar Rhodii, *primarius* of the senate. His was the most powerful voice in the senate. Subject to some constraints, such as the right of a senator to appeal to the entire body, he controlled the agenda, might rule on the legitimacy of motions, could impose limits on debate, and had the final say on procedural questions. His "no," or veto, could be overridden only by three fifths of the senate. Also, at present, he was evincing visible signs of exasperation.

"It is an impressive chamber," said Julian.

"Very much so," said Rurik.

The chamber was spacious, domed, and well lit, by encircling, vaulted windows. It apparently followed the instructions, or plans, of the previous four, or more, senate buildings. Telnarians tend to be fond of tradition. Some of its predecessors, despite repairs, alterations, and such, had been replaced, having fallen into dilapidation, or desuetude. Others had, from time to time, perished in fires, some spreading through the city, some consequent on civil wars. Twice, earlier senate buildings had been the victims of rioting, or sabotage. Once the senate had met in open fields, outside the city. Beyond the last fifteen hundred years or so the records are silent. The origins of the senate, as an institution, were lost in antiquity. It presumably emerged, or at least the supposition seems likely, from something like an assembly of elders or a village council. Testifying to the ancientness of the institution, it was thought to antedate even the enthronement of emperors. Its power varied a great deal over its history, waxing and waning, sometimes constituting an executive organ of the state, particularly during interregnums, sometimes serving as an advisory or consultative body, sometimes constituting little more than a claque, celebrating imperial decisions, sometimes serving as little more than an ornamental relic of tradition, whose approbation or disapprobation was neither sought nor noted. To be fair, it was entrusted with a number of routine matters, such as the appointment and reappointment of certain officials, most significantly provincial governors, these often nominated by the emperor, all such actions, of course, being subject to imperial approval.

"I trust, noble speaker," called Timon Safarius Rhodius, of the Telnar Rhodii, *primarius* of the senate, down to the floor, to the speaker's rostrum, "the senate is now well convinced of the appropriateness of the proposed action, and is prepared to cast its shards, of approval or disapproval."

The tiers seemed to welcome this observation.

"Noble *primarius*," said the speaker, "my case is nearly complete, and it requires very little before it soars to its triumphant, irresistible conclusion. My case, justifying the intended action, and, in passing, clarifying and upholding the rights and power of this august body, utterer of the final and supreme word in Telnaria, entered into the records, will be consulted, quoted, and esteemed for millennia."

Vigorous applause greeted this, but it lapsed almost immediately, as the tiers, awakening, realized the speaker had not, despite this seeming peroration, actually finished speaking.

"Very well," said the *primarius*, wearily, "continue."

"Such a stunning period," said Julian, "would better serve in a synoptic summation."

"I am hungry," said Rurik.

Slaves were not allowed in the senate chamber, as in many public buildings. Similarly, they were not allowed in temples. Had slaves been present, they might have been dispatched on errands, such as returning with one tidbit or another, with something to allay hunger or thirst. Slaves were not allowed in the courts either, except as witnesses, their testimony commonly being taken under torture.

"Patience," said Julian. "Our dear Timon, the *primarius*, I think, has just about had enough."

As the speaker continued to add citations, and ever more devastating arguments to buttress his case, in particular the supremacy of the senate in all questions of Telnarian governance, an opportunity presents itself to remark on the nature of the senate itself, in particular on its constituents. The reader is already familiar, from numerous references in these histories, with the distinction between the *humiliori* and the *honestori*. He may also recall that one has occasionally spoken of the "high or highest *honestori*." Now, amongst the highest *honestori* are the patricians, and amongst those are those of the "senatorial class." It is from members, male members, of the senatorial class that the senate is mainly formed. Whereas an emperor may appoint senators, as he will, from any class, the senate, almost always, selects its own members, and those, naturally enough, from the "senatorial class." Many of the senate seats are, in effect, if not in law, heredi-tary, descending from father to son. Others are kept much within families. Certain individuals of the high *honestori*, the patrician class, who are wealthy, popular, or influential, may be nominated by the senate for membership in the senatorial class, following which nomination they are often selected for the senate. Their family then belongs to the senatorial class. It might be mentioned that the distinction between the *humiliori* and the *honestori* is a social, or class, distinction. It has no necessary connection with wealth or power. For example, several of the largest fortunes in the empire were to be found amongst the *humiliori*.

"I deem it time," said Timon Safarius Rhodius, he of the Telnar Rhodii, *primarius* of the senate, rising to his feet, "that the shards be cast."

"Yes," urged several members of the senate.

"Noble *primarius*," protested the speaker, "I am nearly fin-ished."

"We of the senate," said the *primarius*, "if I have the sense of the body, are ready to cast our shards."

"Yes," agreed several members.

"No!" cried the speaker.

"Be at ease, noble speaker," said the *primarius*, "you have al-ready succeeded in convincing us."

"Yes," cried a number of senators.

"*Primarius*!" protested the speaker.

"The outcome was resolved yesterday evening," said Rurik.

"The expected outcome," said Julian.

"May I, on behalf of the entire senate," said Timon, "thank the noble speaker for his research, his juristic scholarship, his legal pro-bity, and his formidable reasoning, and, too, for the eloquence with which he has overwhelmed and dismissed any possible objections, or cavils. I will now call for the casting of the shards, and I fully expect that every shard will favor the action now before us."

"Every shard!" called out several of the senators.

"*Primarius!*" cried the speaker.

Timon then began the applause, and, amidst the applause, and many grateful shouts, these expressing the body's gratitude to the speaker, the speaker, though it was difficult to tell for the noise, apparently continued to speak, angrily, and, a bit later, from a particularly dramatic gesture, and expression, apparently finished his case. He then stood there, his case seemingly submitted, and humbly inclined his head.

This brought an even larger expression of gratitude from the body.

He then looked up, his handsome features far less than fully pleased.

At a gesture from the *primarius*, the chamber was restored to order, a seemly decorum then prevailing.

The speaker had gathered up his notes, thrust them into a satchel, and was proceeding, swiftly, angrily, to the chamber exit.

"Have no fear, noble Gelinus," called the *primarius*, after the retreating figure. "All will be entered into the records. The clerks will see to it, every syllable, every syllable."

But Titus Gelinus, rhetor and attorney, had left the chamber.

"The moderator of the senate," said the *primarius*, "may now initiate the casting of the shards."

At this point, Clearchus Pyrides opened a large book, in which were inscribed the names of the senators.

Although the expression 'casting of shards', or such, had been utilized, and often, it might be noted that, at this time in the history of the senate, actual shards were not cast, deposited, say, in a white bowl or a black bowl. That had not been done for better than a thousand years. In this period, shards were cast, so to speak, by a voice vote, each senator responding to his name as the moderator called the senate roll. Change may be denied, disguised, or minimized, and the semblance of tradition maintained, in many ways. One way is to give old names to new things.

"I rise to a point of order," said Julian, of the Aureliani.

"That has precedence," acknowledged Timon.

"I do not recall," said Julian, "that the senate has received imperial permission to sit, and, lacking this permission, as is well known, business cannot be legally transacted, nothing legal or binding may be enacted, and so on. Accordingly, this session is illegal, and any action taken, or to be taken, is null and void."

There were many cries of protest, and some sounds of fear, from the senate.

"Do you speak for the emperor?" inquired Timon.

"Yes," said Julian.

"Aesilesius?" said Timon.

"Ottonius, the First," said Julian.

"Ottonius is not emperor," said Timon. "He is a usurper."

"Usurpers become emperors," said Julian.

"He is not emperor," said Timon.

"He who sits upon the throne, holds the sword, and commands men and ships is emperor," said Julian.

"He is a barbarian," said Timon.

"He is a citizen of the empire," said Julian, "born and raised on the provincial world of Tangara, in the *festung* village of Sim Giadini."

"He cannot be emperor until his accession is ratified, and we are met here today to consider that question, whether or not his accession will be ratified," said Timon.

"And doubtless that question is hotly contested," said Julian.

"Possibly," said Timon. "We shall see by the casting of shards."

"The bells announcing the accession pealed," said Julian.

"Perhaps prematurely," said Timon. "We shall see."

"You take the noble Aesilesius to be emperor," said Julian.

"Yes," said Timon.

"He, then," asked Julian, "authorized this sitting of the senate?"

"The senate does not need an imperial authorization to sit," said Timon.

"That, I take it, is a point at issue," said Julian.

"The senate," said Timon, "is the supreme agent of governance in Telnaria. It is sovereign, superior even to the throne."

"I gather that that is another point at issue," said Julian.

"Surely you heard the arguments of the noble rhetor and attorney, Titus Gelinus," said Timon.

"Indeed," said Julian.

"They are weighty," said Timon.

"Not as weighty," said Julian, touching the holster at his hip, "as a single pistol."

"We are senators of Telnaria," said Timon. "We do not fear force. We do not succumb to intimidation. I shall order you ejected from this hallowed chamber."

"Chamber of *filchen,*" said Rurik, under his breath, "chamber of self-satisfied, entrenched hypocrites, cowards, and sycophants."

"Noble senators," said Julian, lifting his head, turning to better face the steep semicircle of tiers, housing the five hundred and one senators, some of whom were exhibiting visible signs of agitation, "I bring you cordial greetings from your emperor, Ottonius, the First. He expresses profound respect for your noble body, its undying concern for the welfare of the empire, and its history and traditions. He is cognizant of its invaluable work in the past and present, and hopes that it will enjoy a future no less important and glorious."

There was a half-hearted ripple of applause from the tiers.

"Furthermore," said Julian, "though this is an irregular, indeed, an illegal, sitting of the senate, it not having been authorized by the emperor, I have been instructed by the emperor to waive the requirement of authorization, which I now do."

"I do not understand," said Timon, the *primarius*, uncertainly.

"This meeting of the senate," said Julian, "is now authorized; it is now legal."

"The emperor is a fool," said someone in the tiers.

"We do not need such an authorization," said Timon.

"In any event," said Julian, "you now have it."

"A fool, indeed," said someone else in the tiers.

"Moderator," said the *primarius*, "proceed. Let the shards be cast."

"The question on the floor, I take it," said Julian, "though it may have been occasionally lost in the forensic richness of the former speaker's eloquence, had to do with the ratification of the accession of Ottonius, the First."

"That is correct, noble representative of the would-be usurper, Ottonius," said the *primarius*.

"How do you think the vote will go?" asked Julian.

"The shards have not yet been cast," said Timon.

This announcement was greeted with some laughter from the tiers.

"But I would anticipate," said Timon, "that five hundred and one shards will be cast against ratification, which, ratification denied, precludes any claim to legitimacy. In this way, usurpation is confronted, order is restored, and a pretender is removed from power."

This remark brought applause, and enthusiastic, even boister-ous, exclamations of approval from the tiers.

"It is unfortunate," said Julian, "that you lack men and ships, an army and navy."

"We have the backing of the empire!" said Timon.

"I was unaware you had taken a poll," said Julian.

"We stand for the empire," said Timon.

"Another point at issue," said Julian.

"Proceed," said Timon to Clearchus Pyrides, the moderator of the senate.

"Surely," said Julian to the *primarius*, "you do not think the emperor has authorized this sitting of the senate for the purpose of putting an end to his reign."

"Let the shards be cast!" demanded a senator in the fourth tier, rising to his feet.

At that point, a servitor of the senate, uniformed, distraught, rushed into the chamber, halted, and pointed back, wildly, to the exit. "The senate is surrounded!" he cried.

"A thousand Otungs," said Julian.

At the same time, a dozen men in the livery of the Farnichi entered the chamber, armed. Two others followed, and placed a large box on the table of the moderator.

"What is the meaning of this!" cried Timon.

"Open the box," said Julian.

Clearchus Pyrides, the moderator of the senate, thrust back the lid of the box, and then stepped back, white-faced.

"For those of you in the higher tiers, who might find it diffi-cult to see," said Julian, "the box contains five hundred and one daggers, each small, short-bladed, and razor sharp, of the finest steel, adapted for the opening of veins. On each ivory hilt, from the tusk of the *torodont*, incised in purple, symbolic of the sena-tor's white robe with purple trimming, is the name of a senator. There is, accordingly, such a dagger for each of you. You are, I take it, familiar with the meaning of such articles. They pro-vide a means whereby one may serve the empire. There are many ways in which the empire may be served. This is one. When such a dagger is delivered to a public official, or prominent per-son, he has the option of putting it to use, or not. It is up to him. He has the option of willingly putting it to use and honorably willing his goods to the state or declining to make use of it, and being seized for death by torture, followed by having his goods confiscated by the state, and his family sold into slavery. The choice is his."

"Surely you jest," said Timon.

"One dagger has your name upon it," said Julian. "Shall it be delivered?"

"I think," said Timon, "it will not be necessary to cast the shards. Let us move, rather, that the accession of our beloved emperor, Ottonius, the First, is herewith ratified, by acclaim."

"Not at all," said Julian, sternly. "We will have no precedent established here, that the ratification of the senate is in any way relevant to an imperial accession. It is not."

"I do not understand, esteemed scion of the Aureliani," said Timon. "What are we to do?"

"You may," said Julian, "withdraw the question of ratification, and substitute a new motion, one of rejoicing, a motion warmly and enthusiastically celebrating the accession of the emperor."

"The question of ratification," said Timon, "is withdrawn. Let it be noted, further, that the senate warmly and enthusiastically celebrates the accession of our new emperor, our beloved Ottonius, the First."

"Perhaps, too, three days of holiday might be urged," said Julian.

"It is the hope of the senate," said Timon, "that the emperor will agree to our request of three days of holiday."

"I am sure he will be agreeable," said Julian.

"Well," said Rurik, rising. "The business is done. Let us go. I am hungry."

CHAPTER SIX

"You are a fool!" cried Ingeld! "A fool!"

"Beware," said Sidonicus, "how you address the exarch of Telnar!"

"What can you do?" inquired Ingeld. "Denounce me? Remove me from the brotherhood of Floon?"

"Beware!" said Sidonicus.

"What is it to me, to be denounced by a pompous, obese, unctuous, purple-robed fraud?" snarled Ingeld. "Who cares if you denounce me? Where is your army, your navy, your ships? Are your words backed with weapons? If not, they are no more than the tooting of horns, a shaking of air, and the pounding of drums, all noise, and empty inside. And how can you remove me from a brotherhood which I despise, and to which I do not belong, and would not belong!"

"The time will come," said Sidonicus, "when even emperors will tremble at the words of the exarch of Telnar! A pronouncement of the exarch will void the oaths of subjects, free them from pledged loyalties, dissolve all bonds of allegiance, nullify all obligations and duties. Subjects will fear to obey, lest they anger *Karch*. Commands, issued, will not be obeyed. Armies, ordered to march, will not move. Who would dare to put his *koos* at risk, serving a benighted sovereign, one denied the approbation of *Karch*? Unobeyed, an emperor is only another man, a weak, frightened man, alone and helpless. Confusion will ensue. Paralysis will obtain. The state will totter."

"Live in terms of such an egregious nightmare," said Ingeld, scornfully. "It is absurd.

"You are clever, Drisriak," said Sidonicus, "but you do not know the mind and its power. You have a brain, but you would find it of little use, if your hands and arms, and your legs and feet, did not obey it."

"Please, noble spouse," said Viviana to Ingeld, "be at peace with the exarch. He is our ally."

"If you were a collared slave," said Ingeld, "I would put you under the whip for daring to speak without permission!"

"I am not a slave," said Viviana. "I am a princess of the royal blood, and I am germane to your ambitions, and perhaps mine."

"In collars, dear sister," said dark-haired Alacida, "we would be quite useless."

"It is only in a collar," said Hrothgar, "that a woman is useful."

"Noble spouse!" protested Alacida.

"A woman does not know what it is to be a woman," said Hrothgar, "until she, in chains, has crawled to a man's feet."

Alacida, her eyes wide, shuddering, shrank back from Hrothgar, alarmed by unfamiliar sensations.

He would no longer permit screens, gold or otherwise, between himself and Alacida, but, at the insistence of the exarch, an insistence abetted by Ingeld, he and his brother stood apart from the two princesses.

"I understand the plan," said Hrothgar. "It was the plan of my father, Abrogastes, the nuptials, and such, to ally our blood with that of royal Telnaria, and produce sons, and, this done, to sweep aside the boy emperor, and rule."

"Yes, dear Hrothgar," said Sidonicus. "And, for my part in this, my version of Floonianism is to be denominated the official religion of the empire, and the empire will see to it, with all its might, that all other religions, including all other versions of Floonianism, will be outlawed, crushed, and extirpated."

"There will then be only one temple, so to speak," said Viviana, "and only one bowl for coins?"

"As it happens," said Sidonicus, "that is a mere consequence. The important thing is that there is only one true faith, mine, which is fitting, as there is only one true god, mine, *Karch*."

"When did *Karch* become the only god?" asked Viviana.

"He has always been the only god," said Sidonicus. "It is merely that this was not always clearly recognized."

"There are many Floonian sects," said Ingeld, "differing amongst themselves, which base their beliefs on a large number of Floonian texts."

"False texts," said Sidonicus. "We will have a council and separate the many false texts from the true texts, thus establishing a definitive list of true texts."

"Which favor your version Floonianism?" said Viviana.

"As they are the true texts, certainly," said Sidonicus.

"My father," said Hrothgar, "devised this business of nuptial alliances, to have a key to the empire, a key of law and blood, but he did not intend to install a religion, not even one of the religions found amongst the Alemanni, let alone that of a particular Floonian sect."

"Let us not discuss the matter, brother," said Ingeld.

"Where is dreadful Abrogastes?" asked Viviana.

"He is on Tenguthaxichai," said Hrothgar.

"Your plans, noble exarch, those of which you were so sure," said Ingeld to Sidonicus, "failed, abominably."

"Much went awry," said Sidonicus, fingering the small replica of a gold burning rack on its chain about his neck. "We did not anticipate the coup, the seizure of the throne by the barbarian, Otto, a miserable Otung. In that I see, too, the hand of Julian, villain of the Aureliani. I was making excellent progress with the empress mother, instructing her in the holy truths of Floonianism. I could have ruled through her, by means of her influence on the young Aesilesius. She was almost ready to be smudged with the consecrated oil from the one of the sacred pools of Zirus, one in which Floon himself might once have waded. Now I lack access to her. She has either been done away with, or sequestered. Indeed, as far as I know, young Aesilesius may have been done away with."

"The bells pealed," said Viviana. "The people accepted the accession. They are fed, and entertained. What more concerns them? They cheer mindlessly and hasten to the imperial pantries, and the theaters, games, and circus."

"We could have turned it all back," said Sidonicus.

"Oh, yes," said Ingeld, "the reliable, glorious senate, guardian of the empire, champion of liberty, another one of your brilliant plans."

"It was all arranged," said Sidonicus. "I do not understand what happened. Our plans were drawn with such care. Timon Safarius Rhodius, the *primarius* of the senate, our natural ally, was enlisted. The senate, unquestioning, even enthusiastic, was in total agreement. In a secret meeting the vote was organized, set to take place yesterday. We had even arranged, for the sake of appearance and seeming deliberation, for a local jurist to supply the legal and forensic finery expected on such occasions. There were to be five hundred and one votes against ratification, which would delegitimize the coup, bring the empire to the point of civil war, and force the usurper from the throne, to stand trial, a shackled prisoner, in the courts, which the senate controls."

"Instead," said Ingeld, "the senate unanimously celebrated the accession, and called for three days of holiday."

"I do not understand what happened," said Sidonicus.

"The senators seem reluctant to make clear what occurred in the senate chamber," said Ingeld.

"Sooner or later," said Sidonicus, "it will all come out."

"They dare not reverse themselves," said Viviana. "They would face disgrace if they did so, or admitted that they had yielded to some form of intimidation."

"Perhaps they were bribed," said Hrothgar.

"Doubtless they were," said Viviana. "I suspect they were offered a bribe which was most persuasive."

"What bribe?" asked Hrothgar.

"Their lives," said Viviana.

"You boast power," said Ingeld to Sidonicus. "Use it! Summon fury. Call for an uprising, fill the streets with angry crowds, vocal and unruly, demanding right and justice."

"Opinions differ as to right and justice," said Viviana. "What have a thousand conflicting claims and views in common but the words? Are they not vessels into which anything may be poured?"

"Enflame men," said Ingeld to Sidonicus, ignoring the princess, Viviana. "Hand them torches, point at that which you wish burned."

"And how is he to bring war into the streets?" asked Viviana. "The city is content, well fed and entertained. Shall they abandon the free theaters, refuse the games, ignore the races? And the bells have pealed. The senate itself celebrates the accession, holiday reigns!"

"Call then to your darker cohorts," said Ingeld to Sidonicus, "your discontented and rabid, the violent and simple, ever eager for an excuse to steal and destroy. They ask only the cloak of anonymity. License them with a prayer. They live for blood and spoil. Get them, the nameless and unknown, into the streets, looting and burning."

"And they would be slaughtered," said Sidonicus. "We are not now dealing with civilized guardsmen, subject to political constraints, fearing to strike a blow, knowing they might be punished for doing their duty. Otungs are about, barbarians. They do not stand aside; they act. My darker cohorts, as you call them, would not long be my cohorts, if they knew themselves in jeopardy. They enjoy their carnivals, surely, but only insofar as they may be enjoyed in safety. Too, I do not wish to risk them. I may need them sometime."

"Then," said Ingeld, angrily, "it seems you are without resources."

"Not at all," said Sidonicus. "There is a time to act, and a time to bide one's time."

"I do not understand," said Ingeld.

"Some," said Sidonicus, "have access to the palace, for example, guards, servants, and slaves, and, of course, certain high officers and certain high officials, even the moderator of the senate, and the *primarius* of the senate."

"So?" asked Ingeld.

"Both the grandfather and the father of the emperor died of poison," said Sidonicus.

CHAPTER SEVEN

"We know nothing of the empire," said Flora. That was her slave name and, being a slave, she had no other. Slaves have no names in their own right, which is to be expected, as they lack rights. As other animals they are named by their masters. Flora had once been an arrogant and beautiful officer of a court on Terennia, which had sentenced a peasant from Tangara, named Dog, to the arena. She had later fallen into the hands of the same peasant, who later rose to the chieftainship of the Wolfungs, on Varna, the smallest tribe of the Vandalii. In his arms, on Varna, helpless and spasmodic, in a naming tag, she was subjected to lessons which she had no choice but to learn, that she was a woman, and a slave. Later, no longer hers, but his, she lived for his glance, and his least touch.

"Were we not on Vellmer," said Renata, another slave, touching her collar, "but on Inez IV, or even Tangara, we might hear something." Renata had been a free woman on a summer world, on which was found one of the summer palaces of the emperor. The name of that summer world does not appear in the records. On that world, overwhelmed with understanding and need, she had exercised the right of a free woman, that of petitioning bondage. Her petition was accepted and she was enslaved. No longer then were the options of the free at her disposal. She was then a slave, and utterly incapable of altering her condition. The man before whom she had knelt and petitioned bondage was he who had been known as Dog, and was then Otto, or, as now, at least in the common parlance of the empire, Ottonius.

"Vellmer is not isolated," said another slave, ruefully, a slender, dark-haired slave, whose collar identified her as 'Sesella,' another slave name, and her owner as a Tuvo Ausonius. "It is we who are isolated, as slaves. It is not that Vellmer is without news. It is we who are without news."

The particular location of this conversation was in one of the villas of Julian of the Aureliani. It was from this very villa that, long ago, Otto had departed, at the behest of Julian, for Tangara, to recruit barbarians, Otungs, for the auxiliary forces of the empire.

"I have listened in my serving," said Gerune, "but I learned nothing."

"It is strange," said Flora. "Commonly masters speak freely before slaves."

"Yes," said Renata. "It is as though we were not present."

"They do not think of us as present," said Flora.

"We might as well be furniture," said Gerune, "mere objects of convenience, meaningless domestic beasts, hovering about, attentive to summoning."

"Of course," said Sesella, "we are nothing, we are slaves."

"How is it then," asked Flora, "that men will kill for us, that they will risk their lives to get us in their ropes, that wars are fought to bring us into collars?"

"Men enjoy owning us," said Renata.

"It is fitting," said Sesella. "We are property. We are the property sex."

"How outraged I would pretend to be, when I was free," said Flora, "to hear such things, but, how, too, I secretly longed for a master, and the chains of a slave."

"Our fulfillment is love, service, and the collar," said Renata.

"It is what we are for," said Sesella.

Flora suddenly sobbed.

"What is wrong?" asked Sesella.

"I am lonely, I am needful," said Flora. "I want my master."

"We all want our masters," said Sesella.

"Have we been forgotten?" said Renata. "Are they done with us? Are we to be sold?"

"I would be pleased," said Flora, "even to feel his whip, to know that he has not forgotten me, that I mean at least enough to him, as a lowly slave, to be whipped."

"The cruelest punishment," said Sesella, "is to be ignored."

"Better a thousand times the whip," said Renata.

"We want to be free in our collars to love and serve our masters, with our whole being, and heart," said Flora.

"Yet we hear nothing!" said Renata.

"Nothing!" said Flora.

"Still," said Gerune, "is that not strange, that we hear nothing, even of the empire, even of the worlds, that no political crumbs fall from the table, that no word slips from a goblet's rim? Do armies no longer march, nor ships fly?"

"I carried wine to grooms," said Sesella, "and they stopped speaking."

"When much occurs," said Renata, "either there is much news, or no news."

"If anyone should hear," said Flora, "it is you, Gerune. You are the slave of Master Julian himself, master of this fine villa, he so notable on Vellmer, of the high patricians, cousin to the emperor, one involved intimately, I am sure, in the affairs of the empire."

Gerune was of barbarian origin. She was originally a member of the Drisriaks, the largest and foremost tribe of the Alemanni nation. Indeed, she was a daughter of Abrogastes himself, the Far-Grasper, king of the Drisriaks. She had joined her brother, Ortog, in his secession from the Drisriaks, to form his own tribe, the Ortungen. Ortog and many of the Ortungs, or Ortungen, were surprised on Tenguthaxichai by Abrogastes, an attack which muchly reduced and scattered the Ortungs. It was generally believed that Abrogastes had slain Ortog on Tenguthaxichai. Gerune had been captured in the same raid. On Tenguthaxichai, spared, she became the slave of a tender of pigs, a prisoner of Otto, chieftain of the Wolfungs. That prisoner had been Julian, he of the Aureliani.

"Yet I have heard nothing," said Gerune, thrusting back her long hair, in its two braids, done in the Alemanni fashion.

"Why would news be kept from us?" asked Flora.

"Hoe the vegetables," said Sesella. "The garden master approaches."

CHAPTER EIGHT

"How is it, noble lady," said Titus Gelinus, "that you have not permitted me, until now, to call upon you?"

"I have been occupied," said the Lady Gia Alexia, in her silken house robe, lying back, half-reclined, her figure gracefully turned, on the couch.

"But now?" asked Gelinus.

"I respond at last to your notes," she said. "I have the afternoon free."

"You torture me," he said angrily.

"Not at all," she said. "I am unaware of your suffering, or its possible cause."

"Do you not know what you have done to me?" he said.

"I have no idea what you might mean," she said.

"You are as cunning as a *vi-cat*," he said, "and as cruel."

"I do not know what you mean," she said.

"You receive me, recumbent," he said, "in a house robe."

"In my own home," she said, "I see no need for formality."

"Yet, though indoors," he said, "you greet me—veiled!"

"Would it not be unseemly to entertain a stranger otherwise?" she inquired.

"Are we such strangers?" he asked.

"How we be otherwise?" she asked.

"In the Lycon district, outside my house, on an unforgettable morning," he said, "your veil was disengaged."

"An inadvertence," she said.

"I saw your beauty!" he said.

"Noble sir," she said, "do not shame me."

"A stroke of lightning," he said, "a sunrise, from clouds the sun, a glimpse, a flash, of beauty."

"What woe for a woman," she said, "that her beauty might wreak so mighty an effect."

"In particular," he said, "when she is so innocent and unwilling."

"When the straw burns," she said, "is the torch to be blamed?"

"I have sent rich gifts, received, but unacknowledged. I have sent gold, accepted, but unnoted. I offered you rooms in my house."

"It is difficult to overlook the offensiveness of such an insult," she said.

"You want more, of course."

"It is so hard to understand you," she said.

"I cannot concentrate," he said. "I am distracted. My work founders."

"What has that to do with me?" she said.

"*Vi-cat*," he said.

"You are no longer the wonder and glory of the courts," she said. "Your address to the senate, in the matter of the ratification, must have been dismal."

"I do not understand," he said. "It was brilliant, well-researched, prodigiously documented, argued with cogency, administered with force. There should have been a unanimous vote against ratification!"

"Instead," she said, "the motion to deny ratification was withdrawn, the accession of the barbarian was celebrated, and days of holiday were urged."

"I do not understand," he said.

"Perhaps," she said, "your case was less persuasive than you supposed."

"It makes no sense to me," he said. "The moderator of the senate, on behalf of the *primarius* himself, invited me to speak against ratification and on behalf of the senate, arguing for its primacy in Telnarian governance. As I understood it, the senate was predisposed to favor such a case. This did not call for the skills of a Titus Gelinus; a stumbling dolt could have won such a case."

"And yet you did not," observed the Lady Gia Alexia.

"I have fallen," said Titus Gelinus. "All crumbles. I lose clients. Litigants do not petition for my services. Men laugh. My enemies rejoice."

"A far more serious blow is dealt to your fortunes," said the Lady Gia Alexia.

"What is that?" he asked.

"Judges and juries will no longer favor you," she said. "They are afraid."

"Why?" he asked.

"It is feared," she said, "that you lack the favor of the emperor."

"I am still wealthy," he said.

"For now," she said.

"May I call upon you again?" he asked.

"Feel free to do so," she said, "when men once more acclaim you and seek your services, when crowds fight again for space on the benches, hoping to hear you, when you again stand high in Telnar, when you are once more the wonder and glory of the courts."

CHAPTER NINE

"I weary of signing documents," said Otto.

"It takes little effort to put your sign, the sword, on each," said Iaachus.

The hot wax would then be put in place, and imprinted with the imperial seal, with its embedded tassel or ribbon. The small imperial seal was commonly used, but on documents of greater importance the large seal was used. It was formed of three components which, when fitted together and locked, formed a single device. Each component was in the keeping of a separate person, each a trustee of the imperial seal. In this way no single person could affix the seal. Since the accession of Otto to the throne, the three individuals designated to be trustees of the seal were Julian, Iaachus, and Tuvo Ausonius. Smaller communications, instructions to officials, summonses to the imperial presence, authorizations, commendations, personal letters, and such, were commonly sealed by means of a signet ring. The use of signet rings was quite common at this point in the history of the empire and few individuals of importance, whether connected with the state or not, lacked such a ring.

"I like," said Otto, "to have the contents of documents made known to me."

"Much is routine and repetitious," said Iaachus.

"Even so," said Otto.

"Of course," said Iaachus.

The documents were commonly read aloud to Otto, or summarized in detail, for his consideration.

Otto, as many in the empire, was illiterate. As a peasant of the *festung* village of Sim Giadini, he had never learned to read. That skill was not thought necessary for the peasantry. What had it to do with the seasons, with land, soil, seed, sunlight, and rain? Indeed, literacy was not highly prized by many in the empire, particularly in the barbarian nations. Many warriors, for example, held it in contempt, as a skill more fitting for clerks, rune readers, and spell casters than wielders of weapons. Often kings could not read. They could, of course, as men of means, hire readers, as one might hire cooks and valets. Astute leaders, sometimes brilliant and learned men, often feigned illiteracy, or indifferent literary skills, in order to retain the respect, devotion, and loyalty of rude, simple men.

"Dear Iaachus," said Julian, "surely it is more important to read men and deeds than words."

"I have no objection," said Iaachus, "to those who can read both."

"How hold the borders?" asked Otto.

"Minor incursions, small raids, threatening gestures, little outside of the ordinary," said Julian.

"That is not so strange," said Iaachus. "The Aatii have for generations posed the greatest threat to the empire, and now it seems that Abrogastes, the Aatii Drisriak, is essaying a subtler assault on the empire, one of legal invasion, of alliances, of blood and nuptials. Such things risk no ships, no armies."

"In this way, too," said Tuvo Ausonius, "he defers the risks of encountering imperially trained, imperially armed Otungs, blood enemies, now interposed between himself and the empire."

"The coup was necessary," said Julian, "to protect the throne from the designs of Abrogastes."

"But not, perhaps, from those of Julian, of the Aureliani," said Iaachus.

"Abrogastes is clever," said Otto, "whether at a conference table or on the bridge of a Lion Ship. Many trails lead to a mountain of gold. If one trail proves impractical, he will seek another."

"On a dozen worlds," said Tuvo Ausonius, "Lion Ships are poised."

"Should he not have attacked, following the coup?" asked Iaachus.

"I think he is patient, like the adder," said Julian, "watchful, like the *vi-cat*."

"But," said Tuvo, "it has been weeks since the coup."

"True," mused Julian.

"Where is Abrogastes?" asked Otto.

"It is said," said Tuvo Ausonius, "on Tenguthaxichai."

"Dangerous is an enemy one cannot see," said Otto.

"Or one you do not suspect," said Iaachus, regarding Julian.

"True," said Julian, regarding Iaachus.

"It was not my plan to enlist barbarians," said Iaachus.

"It was necessary," said Julian.

"In any event," said Iaachus, "worlds orbit their suns, men buy and sell, the bureaucracy functions, and what has occurred in Telnar seems scarcely noticed elsewhere."

"It is nearly time," said Iaachus, "to receive reports, to greet envoys, to meet with petitioners."

"As I understand it," said Julian to Iaachus, "you are permitting Sidonicus, the exarch, access to the palace and he continues to instruct the empress mother in his peculiar beliefs."

"With the consent of Ottonius, of course," said Iaachus. "In this way the exarch is assured that the empress mother still lives. This quells rumors that she, and the boy, Aesilesius, have been murdered in the palace."

"You understand of course," said Julian, "that he hopes to rule the empire through her, by means of her influence on the retarded boy, Aesilesius, whom he hopes to restore to the throne."

"Certainly," said Iaachus.

"And if he chose to spread rumors of her murder," said Julian, "she need merely be produced, publicly, in carefully arranged appearances."

"What if he, himself, should arrange her murder, by some slow acting poison, then ascribing her demise to Ottonius, the emperor?" asked Tuvo Ausonius.

"Precautions are taken," said Iaachus. "No foodstuffs, no pastries, fruit, candies, wines, or such. Too, he wants her alive, to serve as a tool for his own ambitions."

"I am afraid of his influence on the empress mother," said Julian. "She is vain, and susceptible to flattery. We have listened, unnoticed. Sidonicus even reassures her of her attractiveness."

"Surely that is astonishing, for a Floonian ministant, with their views of such matters," said Tuvo.

"She was once a beautiful woman," said Iaachus.

"She is now a vain, shrewish, withered, painted hag," said Julian.

"Be kind," said Iaachus. "Let her cling to her memories."

"Do not permit her to come under the influence of Sidonicus," said Julian.

"It is important that she does," said Iaachus. "It is part of my plan."

"Sidonicus may be more dangerous to the empire than Abrogastes," said Julian.

"That is why my plan must succeed," said Iaachus.

CHAPTER TEN

Orontius Rhodius, of the Telnar Rhodii, Envoy of the Senate to the Palace, cousin of the senate's *primarius*, Timon Safarius Rhodius, of the Telnar Rhodii, his credentials proffered and accepted by Iaachus, the palace's Arbiter of Protocol, inclined his head politely to Ottonius, the First, and backed away from the steps below the throne. He then turned and withdrew.

"I trust that is the last of them," said Otto, "that the audience is done."

"Being an emperor," said Iaachus, "does require stamina."

"I know war, the hunt, the saddle," said Otto, "not words."

"You did quite well," said Iaachus, "in your blunt way."

"I am of the peasantry," said Otto. "I know no other way."

"You may do for an emperor, my friend," said Iaachus, "but I think you fall short as a diplomat."

"Abrogastes," said Otto, "might manage both."

"Quite possibly," said Iaachus. "I do not know him."

"And how does a diplomat speak?" asked Otto.

"In such a way that his speech is not clear, in such a way that it might mean one thing to one fellow, and something else to another. In this way, the diplomat commits himself to little or nothing, and preserves his options. His assurances and promises sparkle but are so general that it is not clear what, if anything, has been assured or promised; his threats are menacing but vague. Do they portend a frown, or a war of annihilation? He moves in such a way that others are not certain of his move, even if he has moved."

"It is not the Otung way," said Otto."

"I cannot speak, of course," said Iaachus, "for barbarians."

"There were many petitioners," said Otto.

"Too many," said Iaachus. "One might carry a concealed dagger."

"Let them be searched," said Otto.

"They are," said Iaachus, "but not all blades are easily detectible, a thumbnail, the edge of a button, the side of a buckle, painted with a deadly, transparent poison, one which requires only a scratch to kill."

"I suspect," said Otto, "you may be familiar with such substances."

"No more than many another," said Iaachus.

"I gather," said Otto, "you disapproved of some of my decisions in the matter of the petitioners."

"You will improve in such matters with more experience," said Iaachus.

"I judged as seemed good to me," said Otto.

"That was obvious," said Iaachus. "But you should judge as seems good to the empire. You are difficult to advise. Image is all; politics must rule. You refused to allow me to hire and coach petitioners, as is commonly done, that a show may be performed, one redounding to the charity, glory, and honor of the empire. You even ignored my most blatant signals of affirmation or negation. Do you think these things have to do with individual cases, with fairness, fittingness, right, justice, propriety, or such? All must be viewed with respect to consequences. One petitioner, seemingly penurious, is to be lavishly gifted, and another not. This demonstrates not only the generosity of the emperor but his astuteness, as the average person could see not the least difference between the two cases. And the rich or well-to-do, despite the merit of their claims, are, at least publicly, to be refused, reduced, and chastened. Thus one pleases the multitude and conceals the relationship between the throne and wealth."

"It is a game, a play?" said Otto.

"A game the empire must best win," said Iaachus, "a play it is well advised to see performed."

Otto and Iaachus were then alone in the throne room, save for the guards at the entrance and exits.

"I will give no audience tomorrow," said Otto.

"As you will," said Iaachus.

"Nor the following day," said Otto.

"Nor for the foreseeable future?" asked Iaachus.

"We shall see," said Otto.

"I am deep," said Iaachus, "but I sometimes think you are deeper."

"I am a plain, simple man," said Otto.

"I am not sure of that," said Iaachus.

"How is that?" asked Otto.

"The matter of the palace library," he said.

"I was curious," said Otto.

"You cannot read," said Iaachus.

"Others can," said Otto.

Otto then rose from the throne, cast back the regal robes, and descended the steps of the dais.

He turned to the Arbiter of Protocol. "I seek your advice," he said.

"Your majesty?" said the Arbiter.

"Come with me," said Otto. He then, followed by the Arbiter, made his way to a table at the side of the room, near one of the rear exits. On this table there was a medium-sized box, a fourteen- to eighteen-inch cube.

Otto removed the lid and laid it aside. He then lifted from the box a soft, yellow object, which he placed on the table.

"What is it?" asked Iaachus.

"A gift for Aesilesius," said Otto.

"What is it?" pressed Iaachus.

"Surely it is obvious," said Otto. "It is a stuffed animal, a small stuffed animal, a toy *torodont*."

"What is it—really?" asked Iaachus, frightened.

"That, I trust," said Otto.

"You wanted my advice?" said Iaachus.

"Yes," said Otto, "do you think he will like it?"

"It is truly a toy, and not a killing device?" asked Iaachus.

"I trust so," said Otto. "Look, you turn this key, and it moves."

Otto then demonstrated this feature of the object. "There is a spring inside," he said.

"It will not explode?" said Iaachus.

"I certainly hope not," said Otto. "Do you think he will like it?"

"Any boy of five would find it a delight," said Iaachus. "Aesilesius might have to be taught how to turn the key."

"I can teach him that," said Otto.

"The tusks are of cloth," said Iaachus.

"Yes," said Otto, "he will not be able to hurt himself on them."

"*Torodont*s are not yellow," said Iaachus, "but brown, gray, and sometimes black."

"But yellow is such a pretty color," said Otto. "I do not think he will mind."

"He will love it," said Iaachus.

"Good," said Otto.

"You do not intend to kill him, while he plays with it?" said Iaachus.

"I do not understand," said Otto.

"Many would see to it that possible claimants to the throne are eliminated," said Iaachus. "Some, upon accession, have killed their brothers. Many would regard it as politically astute to put away young Aesilesius, as naive and harmless as he is, and, indeed, the empress mother, as well. They might constitute rallying points for resistance. Consider potential difficulties with the senate, or ambitious generals on provincial worlds, eager to move on Telnar."

"'Put away'?" said Otto.

"It might be done easily, privately, in the palace, suffocating by a pillow, strangulation by a bowstring," said Iaachus, "or publicly, arranging the charade of a trial, finding them guilty of treason, or such, followed by an execution."

"A judicious, legalized murder?" said Otto.

"Precedents exist," said Iaachus.

"What do you advise?" asked Otto.

"Restraint," said Iaachus.

"There is strange talk in the palace," said Otto. "—the matter of the empress mother's custards."

"Absurd talk," said Iaachus.

"What do you make of it?" asked Otto.

"It is false," said Iaachus.

"No," said Otto. "It is true."

"Custards, the empress mother's favorite dessert, mysteriously appearing in her quarters?"

"Yes," said Otto, "which happenings, as you have doubtless heard, the empress mother, doors being locked, and such, humbly and gratefully accepts as miracles, blessings attending her progress in Floonian studies."

"Absurd," said Iaachus.

"What do you make of it?" asked Otto.

"Such things are smuggled to her by Sidonicus," said Iaachus.

"No," said Otto. "We have made sure of that."

"I trust," said Iaachus, "it is not you who are responsible, amusing yourself in some macabre way, building eagerness and trust in an old woman, who will one day partake of the last custard, thick with poison."

"No," said Otto.

"If you wished her death, you could bring it about easily, with as little as a gesture, an expression."

"So what, then, do you make of it all, dear Arbiter?" asked Otto.

"The matter is perfectly clear," said Iaachus. "The empress mother has bribed her guards."

"And what of "miracles"?" asked Otto.

"The empress mother lies, to protect the guards, and assure the continuance of the custards."

"The guards claim ignorance," said Otto.

"They lie, to avoid a reprimand, to escape discipline," said Iaachus.

"The guards are Ulrich, Vandar, Citherix, and others, Otungs, with me since Tangara, since the Killing Time in the Hall of the King Naming. I would place my life in their hands."

"They, or at least one of them," said Iaachus, "have been suborned."

Otto picked up the stuffed toy, the small yellow *torodont*. "Do you really think that Aesilesius will like this?" asked Otto.

"Yes," said Iaachus.

Otto then replaced the toy in the box.

"What do you think of the matter of the custards?" said Iaachus.

"I think," said Otto, "it confirms something I have long suspected."

"This has something to do with your inquiries in the palace library?" said Iaachus.

"Possibly," said Otto.

"You will have the gift delivered to Aesilesius?" said Iaachus.

"I will deliver it myself," said Otto. "And I am thinking of giving him another gift, as well."

"The gift of death?" asked Iaachus, uneasily.

"Speculate," said Otto.

"You unnerve me," said Iaachus. "I do not understand you. I do not know what you mean."

"I profit from your lessons," said Otto.

"I do not understand," said Iaachus.

"I am making progress, am I not?" asked Otto.

"In what?" asked Iaachus.

"In diplomacy," said Otto.

CHAPTER ELEVEN

"I advised against this," said Julian. "It is dangerous."

"It is good to get out of the palace," said Otto.

"The hour is late," said Julian. "We should have guards, lanterns."

"That would attract attention," said Otto.

"Few know you, save by name and title," said Julian. "But I might be recognized."

"Cloaked, and hooded, that is unlikely," said Otto.

"We may have been observed, leaving the palace," said Julian.

"It is unlikely," said Otto.

"I do not care for these sorties, either by day or night," said Julian. "You do not even inform the Arbiter or the Tenth Consul."

"The fewer who know the better," said Otto.

"Do you not fear assassination?" asked Julian.

"I am aware of the danger," said Otto. "Who, if he should occupy a throne, is not?"

"You put our plans at risk," said Julian.

"I will not have the palace be a prison," said Otto.

"At least," said Julian, "this evening you have chosen a gentler, more refined district for this ill-advised, nocturnal wandering."

"One wanders with intent," said Otto.

"In such dangerous darkness?" said Julian.

"I do not wish it noted that a certain threshold has been crossed," said Otto.

"Then you have a particular destination in mind," said Julian. "This is not the casual interrogation of encountered citizens, the sitting about in restaurants or taverns, unnoticed, listening to conversations, sounding out the state of the city?"

"No," said Otto.

"High men use spies for that sort of thing," said Julian.

"I have spies out," said Otto.

"Yet you yourself venture forth," said Julian.

"And thus," said Otto, "may better assess the reports of spies."

"You could send another," said Julian.

"I am my own best spy," said Otto.

"You jeopardize our projects," said Julian.

"It is long since I have ridden on Vellmer, or hunted in the forests of Varna," said Otto.

"I thought so," said Julian. "More is involved here than intelligence and statecraft."

"The *arn* bear must leave his cave, the *vi-cat* its lair," said Otto.

"Consider the hour," said Julian. "Even here, in the Lycon district, we might be set upon."

"I have not laughed with steel since a dark night on the north shore of the Turning Serpent," said Otto.

"I fear you would welcome such an encounter," said Julian.

"There are too many in Telnar," said Otto, "who kill and rob by night."

"It is a large city," said Julian.

"Even so," said Otto.

"Did Sidonicus know of these wanderings," said Julian, "we could be overwhelmed by a frenzy of assassins."

"But he is a ministrant," said Otto, "a ministrant of Floon, and such would be contrary to the teachings of Floon."

"What has Floonianism to do with Floon?" asked Julian. "Floon, if he ever existed, and is not an invention of miscreants intent on exploiting fear, loneliness, discontent, jealousy, envy, and rage, is ignored, forgotten, and betrayed. He who controls the dagger need not touch it with his own hand."

"We are here," said Otto, stopping before a sturdy portal, and lifting the heavy, hinged knocker from its metal plate to the side.

"The house of Titus Gelinus," said Julian.

Otto then smote the heavy metal knocker against the metal plate, again and again, decisively, even violently.

"Open," he said, loudly, authoritatively, "open in the name of the emperor!"

CHAPTER TWELVE

"Stand them there, in the sun, where I may better see them," said the house master, reclined in his chair, in the shade, under the porch roof.

He sipped his drink, looked at the four slaves, placed his drink on the small table to his left, and then turned to the stranger sitting next to him.

The stranger handed him a paper, which the house master, in turn, handed to the keeper, who looked at the paper, and then nodded, affirmatively.

The stranger, who wore the sash of a civil servant, of the third level, then rose to his feet and took back the paper from the keeper, which paper he placed in his satchel. He then went to the short line of slaves, and walked about them. They stood, heads bowed. Slaves, they dared not meet the eyes of the free man without permission.

"They are tanned," he said.

"Garden slaves," said the house master.

"Are they wholly tanned?" asked the civil servant.

"Remove your tunics," said the keeper.

"You see," said the house master.

"Excellent," said the civil servant.

"Our keeper is skilled," said the house master, and the keeper looked away, surely gratified, perhaps embarrassed. "One protects them from being burned, but works them naked, as well. The tanning stocks do the rest."

"A uniform shade sells better," said the civil servant.

"Of course," said the house master.

"They seem uneasy, agitated," said the civil servant.

"They are uncertain as to the meaning of their presenting," said the house master.

The civil servant then went to each girl, and thrust up her chin, examining her features. None of the slaves met his eyes. When he released her chin, the slave again lowered her head.

"We will replace the house collars with shipping collars," said the civil servant. "What is wrong?" he asked one of the slaves.

"Nothing, Master," she said. "Forgive me, Master."

"Have they been given names?" asked the civil servant.

"Yes," said the house master. "We prefer them to have names. It makes it easier to refer to them and command them."

"Of course," said the civil servant, "as with any animal."

"We call that one 'Flora'," said the keeper.

"So what is wrong, Flora?" asked the civil servant.

"Nothing, Master," she said. "Forgive me, Master."

"You are a very pretty beast, Flora," said the civil servant.

"Thank you, Master," she said.

"You might bring as much as forty *darins*," he said.

"Thank you, Master," she said.

Slave girls are vain creatures, and often much concerned with the price they will bring. Even free women, it is said, perhaps standing naked before their mirrors, in the privacy of their own chambers, might wonder about such things. The slave girl, of course, publicly exhibited and vended, need not leave such matters to idle conjecture.

"That one," said the keeper, "is Renata; the slender, dark-haired one is Sesella, and the blonde is Gerune."

"Gerune looks barbarian," said the civil servant.

"She doubtless was," said the keeper.

"Are you a barbarian?" asked the civil servant.

"I was once Drisriak," she said, "and then of the Ortungen."

"It must be quite an honor for you, a mere barbarian," said the civil servant, "now to belong to gentlemen."

"A slave is a slave," she said. "It does not matter to whom she belongs."

"It is rumored," said the house master, "that even women of the empire sometimes fall into the hands of barbarians."

"Is it true?" the civil servant asked Gerune.

"Yes, Master," she said, "and they are well-owned. They whimper, and beg, and roll and crawl, and lick and kiss, and, supine, leap uncontrollably, obediently and pleadingly, to the least touch of their masters."

"Shall I beat her?" asked the keeper.

"No," said the civil servant.

"They cannot help themselves," said Gerune, "no more than I, we are slaves, only slaves."

"I see," said the civil servant.

"Slavery is the natural destiny, and fulfillment, of the female," said Gerune. "She is whole only in a man's collar."

"Perhaps I should call this to the attention of some free women I know," said the civil servant.

"Better to strip them, put them to their knees, and collar them," said Gerune.

"I take it," said the house master, "all is in order."

"Yes," said the civil servant.

"What do you think of them?" asked the house master.

"Superb," said the civil servant. "They are part of a consignment of six. We have already picked up the others, one from Tangara, one from Varna."

"Kneel," said the keeper, "in line, your right side to the porch, your wrists behind your back."

"May I speak, Master?" asked Renata, on her knees, her hands behind her, of the civil servant.

"If you wish," he said.

"We have heard little on Vellmer," she said. "How goes the empire?"

"Some things change," he said, "some things remain the same."

"Thank you, Master," said Renata, tears in her eyes.

"May I speak, Master?" asked Flora.

"If you wish," he said, at the same time turning about and signaling to two men to the side, two who had accompanied him to the house, who carried some collars, chains, and some light, linked bracelets, suitable for confining the wrists of female slaves. In the distance, near the villa gate, there was a small slave wagon, it drawn by two horses.

"You spoke of shipping collars," said Flora.

"Yes," he said. "You are all going on a little trip."

"We do not understand," said Flora. "We have, or have had, Masters. Are they done with us? Do they no longer want us? Have they sold us? Are we to be sold? Are we to be sold on Vellmer? Are we to be sold elsewhere? Where are we to be taken? What is to be done with us?"

"You will find out," he said.

"Master!" begged Flora.

"You are slaves," he said.

"Yes, yes, we are slaves!" wept Flora. "We will find out! We are slaves! It will be done with us as masters please."

"Be silent," he said.

"Yes, Master," she said.

Shortly thereafter the hands of the slaves were braceleted behind their backs, light shipping collars were locked on their necks, and the house collars were removed. In this way, there was not an instant in which a slave's neck was not in one collar or another. They were then fastened together by a neck chain, ordered to their feet, and directed, single file, toward the waiting slave wagon, near the villa gate.

At the slave wagon, the ramp at the rear was lowered, and they were assisted into the wagon. A link toward the center of the chain was padlocked into a ring forward in the wagon bed. In this way, two girls were on each side of the wagon, and no slave could leave the wagon. The ramp was then raised, and bolted shut. They could see one another, as some light filtered through the cracks and slats of the wagon sides.

The keeper gathered up the tunics, watched for a time, until the wagon exited the villa grounds, and then withdrew.

The house master and the civil servant returned to their drinks.

CHAPTER THIRTEEN

"We are here," had said Otto, stopping before a sturdy portal, and lifting the heavy, hinged knocker from its metal plate to the side.

"The house of Titus Gelinus," had observed Julian.

Otto then smote the heavy metal knocker against the metal plate, again and again, decisively, even violently.

"Open," he had said, loudly, authoritatively, "open in the name of the emperor!"

After a short time, some two or three minutes, the door opened, revealing a worn, disconsolate, haggard Titus Gelinus. "I have been expecting you," he said. "You need not deliver me the dagger. I will use my own knife. I prefer it. I have already prepared the vessel, set by the couch. Indeed, had you been an hour later, your visit would have been unnecessary."

"Titus Gelinus?" said Julian.

"Surely you know me," he said.

"Titus Gelinus?" said Julian, uncertainly.

"Yes," said Gelinus. "Forgive my vanity. I thought myself well-known. I flatter myself that I was once well-known."

"You are Titus Gelinus?" asked Julian.

"Yes," said Gelinus. "I understand now. I so certify the matter. You want the admission, the certification, for legal purposes, before delivering the imperial dagger."

"I did not recognize you," said Julian. "Forgive me. I was not sure. Perhaps it is the light, the shadows. You seem much changed."

"I have eaten little of late," he said. "I have not slept well. I am unsteady, and distracted. My work fails. I am absent from the courts. Men shun me. I am despised and mocked."

Julian thrust back the hood on his cloak. "Do you know me?" he asked.

"Julian, Julian, scion of the Aureliani?" said Gelinus.

"Yes," said Julian. "Doubtless you remember me from the recent sitting of the senate."

"I find this hard to believe, you here," said Gelinus. "How can it be you? How is it that one of your stature, one of the Aureliani, is involved in these dark calls, fit only for lackeys, that one such as you would consent to undertake so menial and cruel a delivery, the dreaded dagger of supposed mercy, rightfulness, and honor? And I see, from the giant at your side, that all precautions have been taken, that, should I falter or bungle, or dally, I will be assisted, or the desired result, in one way or another, will be obtained."

"And why," asked Julian, "do you expect the dagger?"

"In the senate," he said, "I spoke against the emperor."

"And you spoke well, as I understand it," said Otto.

"We do not bring the dagger," said Julian.

"I see," said Gelinus. "I am so hated, that I am to perish in a less noble, less honorable manner. I am to be demeaned and humiliated even in death. Doubtless your friend, the giant, will arrange a noose, fit for a coward, that I may be discovered hanging in a closet, dangling like a *varda* in a poultry dealer's stall."

Julian turned to Otto. "I may speak your identity?" he asked.

"Surely" said Otto.

"Noble Gelinus," said Julian, "May I present to you your emperor, Ottonius, the First."

"Here," said Titus Gelinus, startled, his eyes wide, "here, abroad, so alone, in the night? Come inside, quickly!"

Julian and Otto were ushered within, and Titus Gelinus closed the door and bolted it, securely, with two beams.

"There is little light here," said Julian.

"Lamps require oil," said Gelinus, "and oil costs money. I lived foolishly, at the edge of my means, and then the means vanished."

"Light more lamps," said Otto.

"You have not come to bring the dagger?" asked Gelinus.

"No," said Julian, "nor lamp oil."

"Forgive me," said Gelinus, and hastened about, lighting four lamps, to better illuminate the atrium.

"Your basin needs cleaning," said Julian. He was referring to the long, rectangular basin in the center of the room. It was muchly bereft of water, and contained some debris.

"I no longer have slaves," said Titus Gelinus. "Indeed, I do not know how much longer I can keep the house, nor, indeed, if I can sell it. Many seem reluctant to bid upon it. I think they would fear to own it."

"Why is that?" asked Otto.

"Because it is mine," said Titus Gelinus.

In a few moments Julian and Otto had been introduced into a stately reception chamber adjoining the atrium, in which chamber, once lamps were lit, they were seated on two of four large, intricately carved, high-backed chairs, these arranged about a large, lacquered, thick-topped, circular table, similarly carved.

"There were six chairs," said Titus Gelinus. "I managed to sell two through a dealer. Could I bring you some wine? I have a little left, but it is not of high quality."

"I have not come here to drink," said Otto.

"Of course," said Gelinus. "There is no taster."

"You would do," said Julian.

"Of course," said Gelinus.

"It is my understanding," said Otto, "that your fortunes have declined."

"Muchly so," said Gelinus. "I have been ruined. Men will no longer retain me. Some I thought friends now avoid me. I am held in contempt. My reputation vanishes. It is fog and smoke. My finances collapse. It is cinders and ashes. Banks will not advance me a *darin*. Men fear to deal with me, even to be seen with me. Amusingly, no longer am I even besieged with notes from free women, begging for trysts, hoping for assignations."

"And to what do you owe these ill fortunes?" inquired Otto.

"In the last sitting of the senate," he said, "I spoke against the emperor."

"Perhaps," said Otto, "you spoke in favor of the emperor, your eloquence swaying a committed, hostile senate to reconsider, to alter its position, to yield to your view."

"I do not understand," said Titus Gelinus.

"Did the senate not acclaim the accession and even urge days of holiday?" asked Otto.

"Yes?" said Titus Gelinus.

"I think," said Julian, "I see the road of the emperor, the route he follows. Given what the senate did, who in the senate would dare to question your role in their decision?"

"But," said Gelinus, "I am out of favor with the emperor."

"I am the emperor," said Otto.

"And you are here, at night," marveled Gelinus.

"Some business," said Otto, "is not best handled in the palace, in the throne room."

"I attend," said Gelinus, wonderingly.

"How," asked Otto, "would you like it to be made clear that you stand high in the favor of the emperor, indeed, that you were never out of favor?"

"I would be restored," said Gelinus, "I would be healthy, I would be esteemed and sought."

"You would be higher than ever before," said Julian.

"There is an envoy from the senate to the palace, Orontius, of the Telnar Rhodii," said Otto. "I think it appropriate then that there should be an envoy from the palace to the senate."

Titus Gelinus regarded the seated emperor, just across the table from him, with amazement.

"You could, of course," said Otto, "independently continue your normal legal practice, representing clients, consulting, accepting and refusing cases, and such."

"A general understanding that you stand high in the favor of the emperor, even to being the palace's envoy to the senate," said Julian, "would not be likely to harm your legal practice. It might even be of interest to judges, of some concern to juries, and such."

"You would offer me such a post?" said Gelinus, disbelievingly.

"It is in my mind," said Otto.

"Why me?" asked Gelinus.

"That I am here to learn," said Otto.

"I do not understand," said Gelinus.

"The boy, Aesilesius, and the empress mother live," said Otto.

"I am pleased to hear it," said Gelinus.

"I do not wish to kill them in the palace," said Otto.

"I trust not," said Gelinus.

"It would be awkward, injudicious, even embarrassing," said Otto.

"Doubtless," said Gelinus.

"Too," said Otto, "such a private action, however convenient and practical, would deny us a public action which might have enormous political value, one which might reduce possible resistance and serve to assure the stability of our regime."

"I do not think I understand," said Gelinus.

"I think you do," said Julian.

"One charges Aesilesius and the empress mother with treason, a capital offense, even amongst barbarian tribes," said Otto.

"I see," said Titus Gelinus. "One then arranges a sham trial, complete with incriminating letters, compromising notes, and traitorous documents, all cleverly forged, and then abets the farce with overwhelming, if meretricious, testimony, following which one obtains the desired verdict, and then proceeds to carry out the inevitable, preordained sentence."

"Following which," said Julian, "the current regime is seen as legitimate, vindicated, and justified."

"Can you initiate, and carry through, such a proceeding?" asked Otto.

"Of course," said Titus Gelinus.

"Proceed," said Otto.

"No," said Titus Gelinus.

"'No'?" inquired Otto.

"No," said Titus Gelinus, "better the dagger, the knife, the cutting of veins, the thrusting of the blade into my own heart."

"You spoke of your knife," said Otto. "Fetch it."

Titus Gelinus, moving stiffly, unsteadily, as though made of wood, went to a chest, set on a small table at the side of the room, and brought forth a knife, presumably the one he had mentioned earlier. He then returned to the table, the knife in hand.

"So," said Titus Gelinus, "you have brought the knife, after all."

"Beware," whispered Julian to Otto.

"Am I to plunge it into my own heart?" asked Titus Gelinus.

"Would you do so?" asked Otto.

"I would have no choice," said Titus Gelinus.

"Do you wish to die?" asked Otto.

"No," said Titus Gelinus.

"Perhaps," said Otto, parting the garments covering his chest, "you would prefer to plunge it into mine?"

"No!" said Julian, leaping to his feet, but Otto, with a motion of his arm, thrust Julian back.

"I am not an assassin, I am not a murderer," said Titus Gelinus, and dropped the knife to the surface of the table.

"Am I to understand," said Otto, "that you refuse to undertake the project I have described, the prosecution of Aesilesius and Atalana, the empress mother?"

"Yes," said Titus Gelinus.

"What now," asked Otto, "do you think your life is worth?"

"Now that you have confided your plan to me, now that I have learned of it, and have declined to be of service, nothing," said Titus Gelinus.

"You will not undertake the proceeding?" asked Otto.

"No," said Titus Gelinus.

"Your decision is absolute and final?" asked Otto.

"Yes," said Titus Gelinus.

"Splendid," said Otto. "I have discovered what I wished to know." He then lifted the knife from the table and returned it, handle first, to Titus Gelinus. "You will not be needing this," he said.

"I do not understand," said Titus Gelinus.

"What would you have done if he had struck at you?" asked Julian.

"Broken his arm, and then his neck," said Otto.

"What is going on?" asked Titus Gelinus.

"You asked earlier," said Otto, "why you, of others, would be chosen for a post such as that of the palace's envoy to the senate, and I told you that I was here to learn that. I have now learned it."

"I do not understand," said Titus Gelinus.

"You would die before you would compromise your honor," said Otto. "It is the Otung way, the Drisriak way, the way of the Vandalii, the way of the Alemanni."

"And once the way of the empire," said Julian.

"And may once be its way again," said Otto.

"What am I to do?" asked Titus Gelinus.

"No one is to know of this meeting," said Otto. "In the morning, you are to come to the palace. You will then be invested with suitable credentials, designating you the emperor's envoy to the senate."

"What if the senate will not accept such credentials?" asked Titus Gelinus.

"Then," said Otto, "the senate will not meet."

"But I spoke against you," said Titus Gelinus.

"How is that possible," smiled Otto, "given the senate's action?"

"But I did speak against you," said Titus Gelinus.

"Emperors, as well as chieftains, captains, and kings," said Otto, "have need of men who do not fear to speak against them."

Otto and Julian then, accompanied by Titus Gelinus, left the reception chamber and made their way through the atrium to the door. Titus Gelinus removed the two beams with which he had barred the door.

"Be careful in the streets," said Titus Gelinus.

Otto laughed.

"I shall be careful for us both," said Julian. "The emperor is in a good mood. It will be more dangerous in the streets than some might realize."

"Until morning, envoy," said Otto.

"Until morning, your majesty," said Titus Gelinus.

Otto turned about, in the doorway.

"Your majesty?" asked Titus Gelinus.

"I restore your fortunes," said Otto. "I am pleased. I would do more. Is there anything else I might do for you?"

"Well," said Titus Gelinus, "—there is a woman."

CHAPTER FOURTEEN

The tall, sturdy, bearded figure struggled in his ropes, violently, before the throne.

"Shall we throw him to his knees?" inquired a guardsman, one of four who accompanied the roped figure.

"Let him stand," said Otto.

"You!" said the roped figure, looking up.

"I have long sought you," said Otto. Then he said to the guardsmen. "Unbind him."

"He is dangerous, your majesty," protested the guardsman.

"I am more dangerous," said Otto. "Now leave us."

"Your majesty?" said the guardsman.

"Now," said Otto.

The two men were then left alone in the throne room.

"Am I not to be slain?" asked the figure.

Otto descended from the throne, and stood before the prisoner. The man was large, but Otto was better than a head taller.

"You are Drisriak, are you not?" asked Otto.

"Ortung," said the figure.

"Good," said Otto. "I had hoped it would still be so."

"I remember you from Tenguthaxichai," it said.

"Most think you died there, at the hand of your father, Abrogastes," said Otto.

"I thought he meant to kill me, but failed, missing his intended stroke by an inch," said the figure. "It was only later I realized he had spared me."

"But had succeeded in giving the impression of meting out a deserved punishment to a dissident son, a secessionist from the Drisriaks."

"I recovered, gathered some followers. I am sure there must be others about."

"I thought you would still be in the delta of the Turning Serpent," said Otto, "not far from your four, concealed Lion Ships."

"You know of them?" said the figure.

"They are safe," said Otto. "I sent agents to contact you. I had hoped to invite you to the palace."

"I would decline such an invitation," he said, "as I would an invitation to dine with a hungry *vi-cat*."

"But you were nowhere to be found," said Otto. "Then you were apprehended at the Telnar river wharves, questioned, and set upon as an Alemanni spy."

"Two guardsmen I flung into the river," he said, "three I smote unconscious, and then all went black."

"Perhaps then you can understand the advisability of the ropes," said Otto.

"How did you know it was I?" he asked.

"I did not know," said Otto, "but I thought it likely from the description. Too, when my people could not locate you in the delta, and the river ships were moored, and the Lion Ships slept in their sheds, I thought you might venture to Telnar."

The figure crossed his arms on his chest and faced Otto, regarding him boldly.

"Good," said Otto, "you have the look of a king."

"I am a king," said the figure, "king of the Ortungen, son of mighty Abrogastes, the Far-Grasper, king of the Drisriaks, high tribe of the Alemanni."

"A rebel king, a break-away king," said Otto.

"What do you intend to do with me?" asked Ortog.

"We could fight," said Otto.

"I know your skills," said Ortog. "It would be an easy way to commit murder."

"I am not a murderer," said Otto.

"You kill easily," said Ortog.

"The two things are not the same," said Otto.

"My fate?" asked Ortog.

"Do not belittle your skills," said Otto.

"My fate?" repeated Ortog.

"You have, as I understand it," said Otto, "engaged in the craft of a river pirate."

"I needed gold," said Ortog, "to gather and arm my followers, that the banner of the Ortungs be once more unfurled."

"You have captured and enslaved, and sold, women of the empire," said Otto.

"Of course," said Ortog, "women are property, spoils, and loot, and they all belong in the collar. Their greatest happiness is to be owned, to find themselves helpless, subject to the whip, on a man's chain."

"True," said Otto.

"My fate?" asked Ortog.

"You stand boldly," said Otto. "Do you not fear your fate?"

"No," said Ortog.

"Yet," said Otto, "there are mines to be worked, galleys to be rowed, quarries from which stone is to be removed."

"Where is Abrogastes?" asked Ortog.

"It is said," said Otto, "he is on Tenguthaxichai."

"He is not on Tenguthaxichai," said Ortog.

"I suspected not," said Otto.

"I think he is in Telnar," said Ortog.

"I think you are right," said Otto.

"That is why I came to Telnar," said Ortog.

"Of course," said Otto. "And why do you think I wished to contact you, and bring you to the palace?"

"We are allies?" asked Ortog.

"For the time," said Otto.

"Abrogastes is your enemy," said Ortog.

"Is he not yours, as well?" asked Otto.

"Yes," said Ortog, "but he is also my father."

CHAPTER FIFTEEN

The Lady Gia Alexia, trembling, seated before her mirror, dabbed the perfumed swab ever so gently to the sides of her throat. One must be subtle, one must be refined. She then, satisfied with what her mirror revealed to her, lifted her veil, diaphanous enough to suggest what it feigned to conceal, opaque enough to deny the final satisfaction it seemed to offer, and fastened it in place, its silken yellow against the light blue hood, with two silver pins. She then rose up, and stepped back, admiring the silken yellow sheathing which, cunningly drawn about her, flattered a figure whose striking contours, those of thighs, hips, waist, and bosom, were in little need of flattery. A large, but light silken cloak, blue in color, like the hood, was about her shoulders, secured with a golden clasp. The silken cloak, with its dimensions, could be cast back, casually, or, as one wished, might be adjusted, opened or closed, swept a bit to the side or back, in such a way as to permit or deny access to the ensemble within, and the delights it did so much to suggest, and so little to obscure. Cloaks, like fans, can be used to tease, taunt, and flirt. The values of clothing, like those of speech, manners, and gestures, far transcends the boundaries of utilitarian considerations. A cloak, for example, may speak as nimbly and fluently as a fan. Bundled about one, held tightly and modestly, one can hide, head down, apparently timidly, shyly, within it; thrown back, and spread, it can frame one with an at-tractive, portable vista should the background afford nothing better, such as a garden, a meadow, an aspect of columns, a vine-covered wall, or such; much depends, of course, on the man one might wish to intrigue. A beach may do for one fellow, and a library might do as well, or better, for another. It is well known that an identical object may appear quite differently against a dif-ferent background or in a different context. One sees with more than the eye. Is it not easy to see what one wishes to see, hear what one wishes to hear, and believe what one wishes to believe?

In any event, imagination may enhance vision, and speculation compete with fact. Truth may not need to hide, but it frequently does.

The Lady Gia Alexia, as might be supposed, was much startled and muchly taken aback by the seemingly inexplicable transformation in the fortunes of the rhetor and advocate, Titus Gelinus. From a squalid nadir of exclusion and shame, from a plummeting fall into disgrace and destitution, he had, it seemed, overnight, sprung to a pinnacle of acclaim and success. It was his eloquence, it seemed, which had convinced a wavering senate to celebrate the accession of Ottonius, the First, thus stabilizing a new, possibly dubious, possibly precarious regime. Indeed, his work had been so overwhelmingly persuasive that the enraptured senate had even urged three days of holiday, to which request the emperor had graciously assented.

Needless to say, the startled Lady Gia Alexia, muchly distraught, fearing she had misstepped grievously, had immediately set about repairing any possible damages which might have somehow jeopardized her relationship with the rhetor. She must express her concern that he might have misunderstood or misinterpreted her behavior. Surely he could not have done so. What a mistake that would have been! How tragic that would have been! She hoped she had not given him any cause to doubt her admiration, interest, friendship, and devotion, or, to speak sensitively, the overwhelming physical attraction she felt for him, which she, as a free woman, had, in prescribed propriety, struggled so to conceal. How keenly she had lamented his misfortunes. Had she not felt them as she would her own, were they so grievous? She could explain all. Might he not permit her to explain her former feigned indifference to his difficulties? Could he not understand that it was all a pretense, no more than a foolish free woman's test to determine the sincerity of a swain's fervor, a facade he was to sweep aside, a wall he was to climb, a veil he was to remove, a subterfuge through which he was to see? She wished to clarify all that might be misunderstood or obscure. He was not to doubt her unwavering devotion. She must be given an opportunity to see him, to speak with him. Do not let her be tormented, fearing she may have been misunderstood. How terrible that would be! She must see him; she must speak with him. All could be made clear.

It had been several days, better than a month, since Telnar had been shocked to learn of the restitution of the fortunes of Titus

Gelinus. Not only had he been rescued from a particularly dreadful cloud of obloquy, the result, it seemed, of outrageous misinformation, but had been elevated to an envoyship, one so important as that of palace envoy to the senate. Clearly he stood high in the favor of the emperor. Former friends now renewed their calls and invitations. Clients who had recently eschewed his company now again lingered at his door. Banks again welcomed his business and merchants once more solicited his custom. Too, commensurate with his restored popularity, he was again muchly sought in the courts, countless litigants competing for his services. Judges even rearranged their schedules that they might hear his cases. Too, it seems that many free women now recollected his charms, and his house was once more the recipient of numerous delicate missives attesting their interest.

Among the latter missives were surely those of the Lady Gia Alexia.

She had written several notes which, if received, were unanswered. Soon her efforts had become desperate and persistent. The notes had become ever more frequent and urgent. She found this seeming neglect alarming. She was aware, of course, as an intelligent woman, of the signs of male infatuation. Surely they are not difficult to discern. Had not Titus Gelinus exhibited them helplessly, even pathetically? In the Lycon district, she had laid her snare, baited it well, and snapped it shut, deliciously, triumphantly. The large, handsome beast, and his position, wealth, and prospects, she was sure, were then hers. Much might have proceeded expeditiously from that point on had it not been for the seeming downfall of Titus Gelinus, following the sitting of the senate. She castigated herself for her lack of patience. If only she had anticipated his return to favor! Had she pretended loyalty to him in his adversity, and had he been simple enough to accept it as genuine, how advantageous would be her position at present! But, alas, she had not only dissociated herself from him, long refusing to answer his notes and declining to accept his calls, but had finally, for her pleasure, and as a sop to her disappointed vanity, allowed him into her presence, to make clear to him what he had lost, and her contempt for him, and, beyond this, unfortunately, she had been gratified to torment him, by a provocative garment and a seductive attitude, these contradicted by veiling, thus managing at one stroke to both arouse and frustrate him, to stimulate him and make simul-

taneously clear to him the inaccessibility of the fruits she chose
to suggest. It was now obvious to her that her behavior had
been tragically inept, quite possibly rendering the resumption
of her earlier designs impractical. Yet, she was certain that the
former interest and attention of the rhetor had been more than
authentic. He had suffered, torn by desire and need. She was
sure of that. Thus, she had retained the hope that his passion
might be renewed. Might not ashes, stirred, reveal obstinate,
still-glowing coals? And might not former flames, given the ap-
plication of a suitable tinder, rage again?

Thus, when her last note, after all this time, had been answered, her apprehensions had been set much at rest. She had not
been forgotten. She was no longer being ignored. Reconciliation
was possible. Relieved and elated, she had clutched that brief, polite note, inviting her to call, as she might have clutched the key
to a chest of treasure which, in a sense, she took it to be. She had
little doubt that she could explain away any misapprehensions he
might entertain having to do with her previous words or actions.
She required only the opportunity to do so. His desire for her, still
afire she was now sure, would lead him to accept any construction
of the past she might choose to foist upon him. Indeed she could
manage matters in such a way, she was sure, that he would regard
himself as having been at fault, and she as having been the innocent victim of his misunderstanding. He wanted her. She was sure
of that. She would have him, then, on any terms she might wish.
It is easy to believe what one wishes to believe; desire can pave
the road to a multitude of destinations.

The Lady Gia Alexia stood back, regarding herself in the mirror, the blue hood and cloak, the yellow veil and the cunning
sheathing. "Excellent," she thought, "sensuous, yet refined, seductive, yet tasteful. One shows little, and suggests much. Beware, noble Gelinus. I am formidable. You will soon be mine." She
would have preferred, of course, that the rhetor had called upon
her, but, currently, that would be unseemly. He was a man of position and wealth, even the palace's envoy to the senate, and she
was only of the Darsai, of Telnar, a recognized family, but not of
the highest *honestori*. But who knew how high in the social strata
of Telnar a lovely, clever girl might ascend?

It was her plan, in any event, to waste no time, but, rather, to
hire a cart and driver, and have herself conveyed promptly, discreetly, to the residence of the rhetor.

As she turned about, and prepared to leave the apartment, a knock, polite but firm, was heard from the door.

"Who is there?" she inquired, annoyed, for her mind was on important things. "Servitors," she was told, "come to convey the Lady Gia Alexia, of the Darsai, of Telnar, to the house of Titus Gelinus."

"Excellent," she thought. "He cannot come himself, but he sends for me! He is eager, accommodating."

"You have a cart?" she inquired, through the door.

"Surely," was the response.

She undid the door, and confronted two individuals, in the livery of the palace. This, in itself, was impressive to her, and an indication of the new importance of Titus Gelinus, that he might have access to the palace staff. He could now draw on such resources, as he held an imperial post, that of envoy to the senate.

"Please enter, sirs," she said.

The two servitors entered the apartment, and stood to the side.

"How thoughtful of the noble Titus Gelinus," she said, "to send a cart for me."

This overture, apparently idle and conversational, received no response, and so the Lady Gia Alexia thought it best to proceed. "I suppose you are often applied to these errands," she said, "that you frequently supply the noble Gelinus with such services." Who, curious, suspicious, and jealous, would not be interested in such things?

"No, Lady," said one of the men, he presumably senior of the two.

"'No'?" she said.

"No, Lady," he said. "The charge we undertake here is not only unusual, but, to the best of my knowledge, unprecedented."

This response much pleased the Lady Gia Alexia.

Indeed, she was thrilled.

"I am alone, I am unique, I am special?" she asked.

"It seems so, Lady," he responded.

"These are men," thought the Lady Gia Alexia. "They are servitors, lackeys of a sort, but men. I shall enjoy this. I shall test my powers. I shall watch." "A moment, sirs," she said. She then turned, and withdrew to the mirror, where she surveyed herself, appraisingly. She adjusted her hood and veil, dallied with the clasp of the cloak, looked down, pressing her small feet deeper into the matching yellow slippers, turned a bit, lifting the yellow sheathing, to inspect a well-turned ankle, and then, carefully, drew down, turned, and tightened the yellow sheathing. She also, as was her intent, used this opportunity to inform herself, in the mirror, of the first reactions of the servitors, while they would not be likely to consider themselves observed. To her annoyance and disappointment, however, it seemed her display had been mostly for naught, as their attention, for the most part, had seemed to be directed elsewhere. "Lackeys," she thought. "Bumpkins, boors, dolts!"

"I am ready," she said, turning away from the mirror, facing back, toward the center of the room.

"We must make one stop," said the foremost of the two servitors, "before we convey you to the house of Titus Gelinus."

"Very well," she said.

"You are the Lady Gia Alexia, of the Darsai, of Telnar, are you not?" asked the foremost of the two servitors.

"Certainly," said the Lady Gia Alexia. "Let us leave, at once."

"You must do one thing first," he said.

"What?" said the Lady Gia Alexia.

"Remove your clothing," he said, "instantly, completely."

CHAPTER SIXTEEN

"May I introduce Ortog, king of the Ortungen," said Otto.

Iaachus, Arbiter of Protocol; Julian of the Aureliani; Rurik, Tenth Consul of Larial VII; and Tuvo Ausonius, once a civil servant on Miton, rose to their feet.

"I thought the Ortungen were no more," said Rurik.

"Here is their king," said Otto.

"Should he not be in chains?" asked Iaachus, uneasily.

"I think not," said Otto.

"But he is Aatii, our foe," said Iaachus.

"Alemanni," said Ortog.

"Would you care to chain him?" asked Otto.

"No," said Iaachus, quickly.

This meeting did not appear on the agenda of the emperor. Some meetings, it seems, escape the notice of official schedules.

"Ortog," said Otto, "is apprised of the actions of his father, Abrogastes, often called the Far-Grasper, in particular, the surprise raid on Telnar, which raid succeeded in the abduction of the princesses, Viviana and Alacida, and his plan to use the princesses, wedded to two of his sons, Ingeld and Hrothgar, in such a way as to eventually intrude Alemanni blood into the imperial line of succession."

"The plan," said Rurik, "is daring and brilliant."

"It is the plan of Abrogastes," said Otto.

"What I do not understand," said Ortog, "is how such a raid succeeded."

"Treachery," said Otto. "The raid was not opposed. Telnar's defensive batteries, capable of burning fleets out of the sky, remained silent. The high command of the batteries was suborned, that command consisting of three men, Phidias, once the captain of the freighter, *Narcona*, and two of his former officers, Corelius and Lysis. These three traitors accompanied Abrogastes and his royal prisoners, the princesses, to Tenguthaxichai."

"The nuptials of the princesses and the two sons of Abrogastes, as you probably know," said Rurik to Ortog, "were celebrated in Telnar, in a ceremony presided over by the exarch of Telnar, a man named Sidonicus."

"Abrogastes, contrary to expectation," said Julian, "was not present at the ceremony."

"It was supposed," said Otto, "he remained on Tenguthaxichai."

"He is not on Tenguthaxichai," said Ortog.

"Where then is he?" asked Tuvo Ausonius.

"Ortog and I," said Otto, "suspect he is in Telnar."

"Presumably he would have accompanied Ingeld, Hrothgar, and the princesses to Telnar," said Ortog, "if only to see that all went well."

"But he seems," said Otto, "to have disappeared."

"King Ortog," said Iaachus, "as you know your father, and have a sense of his thinking, what variety of nuptials would your father have favored?"

"It would be of no interest to my father," said Ortog. "The payment of a bride price would do, provided it was public, recognized, and took place in Telnar, the capital of the empire."

"He had no particular preference," asked Iaachus, "no favored sect, faith, or service?"

"My father," said Ortog, "believes in what he can see, feel, and hear. He scoffs at the thousands of faiths, each competing to be more absurd than the other. He sees no more reason to believe in invisible gods than invisible *torodonts* or *garn* pigs."

"Then," said Iaachus, "I believe I can explain the disappearance of your father."

"Speak!" demanded Ortog.

"You have heard," asked Iaachus, "of the medallion and chain?"

"Of course," said Ortog, "it is important to the Vandalii."

"Sidonicus, exarch of Telnar," said Iaachus, "conspired to bring it into the possession of Ingeld, the Drisriak, that he might command not only the Aatii but, by means of the artifact or talisman, the Vandalii, as well, and thus overwhelm the empire."

"How was my father involved in this?" asked Ortog.

"He was not," said Iaachus.

"Ingeld then far exceeded his place," said Ortog.

"What limits does ambition know?" asked Iaachus.

"And what price asked the exarch for this perfidy?" asked Ortog.

"Presumably the conversion of the conquered empire to his particular faith," said Iaachus. "Sidonicus would bargain similarly with the empire. If the empire were to make his faith the official faith of the empire, enforce it on all citizens, and persecute and extirpate all other faiths, thus gathering all religious wealth to his own temples, he would rearrange dogma in such a way that millions of currently pacifistic Floonians, normally eschewing military service and withholding allegiance to the empire, refusing even the simplest of civic duties, would then spring to arms, prepared to die for a state, now holy, which they had hitherto repudiated."

"What has this to do with the disappearance of my father?" asked Ortog.

"Would your father uproot and destroy thousands of religions, would he enforce one absurdity on an empire already familiar with thousands, would he deny the right of free belief and freedom of heart and conscience to millions, would he convert, change his life, give up his own mind and will, divert wealth to superstition, bow down to parasites, share power with charlatans, celebrate hypocrites who send others forth to do their torturing and killing, while they remain behind, housed in pompous, sanctified safety?"

"Never," said Ortog. "I understand the sword, the spear, the pistol, the rifle, but I do not understand the things you speak of."

"It is a new kind of war," said Otto.

"I fear," said Iaachus, "your father is dead."

"Ingeld and Hrothgar would never permit it," said Ortog.

"They may not know of it," said Iaachus.

"I suspect," said Otto, "Abrogastes is alive. He would presumably be of more value to captors as a prisoner, a possible hostage, something with which one might bargain, than dead."

"My father," said Ortog, "must be freed or avenged."

"*Barbaritas*," said Otto.

"*Barbaritas*," said Ortog.

"We do not even know where he is," said Julian.

"But how could my father be seized?" asked Ortog. "He is shrewd, wary, suspicious, dangerous."

"Betrayal," said Otto, "betrayal by those he trusted."

"Ingeld?" said Julian.

"Possibly," said Otto.

"Hrothgar?" asked Julian.

"No," said Ortog. "Hrothgar is simple, jovial, and lusty. He cares for drink, dogs, horses, falcons, and slaves, not gold, not power."

"Ingeld then?" said Julian.

"Possibly," said Otto.

"But," said Iaachus, "the presence and actions of Ingeld and Hrothgar are well known."

"Then, more likely, others, less conspicuous, would act," said Julian.

"Others," said Otto, "who might have accompanied Abrogastes from Tenguthaxichai, and might act before his presence became public."

"You speak as though you have someone in mind," said Julian.

"A servant who betrays one master," said Otto, "may well betray another."

"Those who betrayed the batteries, making possible the raid of Abrogastes?" said Julian.

"Yes," said Otto, "Phidias, Corelius, and Lysis."

"Those who fled Tangara, thinking you slain, leaving the assassin slave to her fate?" said Julian.

"Yes," said Otto.

"A third betrayal then," said Tuvo Ausonius.

"Do you think they are in Telnar?" asked Rurik.

"Yes," said Otto, "but, doubtless, inconspicuously, unobtrusively."

"You would hope, through them," said Rurik, "to be led to Abrogastes."

"It would be my hope," said Otto.

"There must be many in Telnar who could recognize them," said Julian.

"If it were known they were sought," said Otto, "I suspect they would be whisked away, or found in some alley, their throats cut."

"Then they must be sought inconspicuously, unobtrusively," said Julian.

"Precisely," said Otto.

"But who could do so?" asked Rurik.

"One who knows them well, one who has had dealings with them, one who could not fail to recognize them," said Otto.

"Who?" asked Ortog.

"Rurik, friend," said Otto, "have you not a slave, a Filene or Cornhair, a former Calasalii woman?"

"I have," said Rurik, Tenth Consul of Larial VII.

CHAPTER SEVENTEEN

"Stop struggling," said the driver, turning back, looking back, into the canvased cart.

"Let her struggle," said his fellow, sitting beside him on the wagon bench. "What does it matter?"

"Rope burns," said the driver, returning his attention to the reins and horses.

"Is she that stupid?" said his fellow.

"Many are, at first," said the driver. "They do not yet realize the rose is in their thigh, the collar on their neck."

"They soon learn," said his companion.

"You have seen her," said the driver.

"So?" said his companion.

"Who would want her?" asked the driver.

"She is not bad," said his companion.

"Fifteen *darins*, twenty?" asked the driver.

"Perhaps," said his companion.

On the rude, heavy, unvarnished planks of the wagon bed, behind the men, a small figure, muchly agitated, rolled and turned, struggling, trying absurdly to free itself, its body swathed with ropes, from ankles to shoulders. Whereas the ropage was plentiful and thick, it did little, as it was tight, to leave in doubt the nature of the contours it so snugly encircled, namely, that the figure they bound was that of a woman, and quite possibly one of interest, one of the sort for which men might pay, the sort they are accustomed to buy. The figure, though it was not easy to tell from the ropes, was naked, absolutely so, save, of course, for some strips of cloth, some of which were over her eyes and some of which, some back between her teeth, and some over her mouth as well, made it difficult for her to articulate her distress, should she have been concerned to make it known. She could utter tiny noises. One last item was a light, close-fitting metal collar. It was locked on her neck.

"Turn here," said the driver's companion. "This is the Lycon district."

The driver and his companion were dressed nondescriptively. Few could have told them from common cartsmen. No longer were they in the livery of the palace. Even the cart, though canvased, to be sure, was plain, nondescript. It was not strikingly painted, that it might call attention to itself, and, surely, it bore no company emblem nor flew any company pennon. It was indistinguishable from hundreds of others, private wagons, rental wagons, cheap wagons, engaged in small-load haulings within the city and its environs.

"There," said the driver's fellow, or companion, "the house."

"Yes," said the driver.

The cart was drawn to the side, and the driver set the brake.

The small roped figure supine on the planking was lifted from the cart in the arms of the driver's fellow, and the driver strode to the door of the house, lifted the heavy metal knocker and struck it twice, politely, against its metal plate.

The door was answered by a young, strong, handsome fellow in a house tunic who invited the driver and his fellow within, and indicated that their delivery should be placed on the tiles of the atrium between the atrium basin and the door. As in many such houses, there was a chest in the atrium, placed within the atrium, to the right of the door as one would enter. The lid of this chest was chest-high, as most men might stand. Some objects were on this lid, amongst them two goblets, each filled with a draft of wine. The fellow in the house, after chatting briefly with the driver and his fellow, and receiving some papers from the driver, which he put aside, served the driver and his fellow with the wine. While these pleasantries were taking place, the small figure lay supine, neglected, on the tiles. It moved somewhat, but it no longer struggled violently; perhaps it now well realized the meaninglessness of such efforts, realized that it was utterly helpless, that it was well tied, indeed, even as a slave might be tied; perhaps, too, it was uncomfortable, the smooth, sensitive, silken skin, now raw and sore, fearing to do further contest with its thick, tight, rough, pitiless constraints. Even she knew that slaves, if bound, and not chained, shackled, or braceleted, were commonly bound with ribbons, silken cordage, thongs, or narrow, flat leather straps, that there would be no reduction in their market value. On the other hand, now that it had been delivered, perhaps it merely realized that it was well advised to be patient, to wait, and see what might ensue.

After a few minutes, the fellow in the house tunic, the goblets emptied, took some chaining from the lid of the chest and cast it to the floor beside the small figure, where the driver and his companion, preparing to take their leave, were bending down to remove its impediments, the many loops of rope with which it had been so closely encircled. "Shackle her," he said, "and stand her."

This was done and the small figure, still blindfolded and gagged, now shackled hand and foot, stood before the men, loops of rope like cast-aside vines to the side. The fellow in the house tunic walked about her.

"Is she satisfactory?" asked the driver.

"We must wait and see," said the fellow in the house tunic.

"If she is not satisfactory," said the driver, gathering up, and looping, rope, "she may be thrown to the dogs. She cost nothing."

"In that sense, my dear," said the fellow in the house tunic to the shackled figure, "costing nothing, you are worthless."

Angry, muffled sounds greeted this assessment.

"She might be worth a *darin* or two," said the driver, "on some mud world, as a work slut."

The small figure, raging in frustration, violently shook the chains linking her wrists.

"It can be arranged," said the driver.

The small figure was still. It trembled.

"We shall see how she works out," said the fellow in the house tunic.

The driver had now gathered up and looped the rope. He left the loops wide enough to be looped over and about his body.

"Shall I remove the blindfold?" asked the driver's companion.

"Certainly," said the handsome fellow.

The rolls of obscuring cloth were unwrapped from the figure's head, and her eyes, after blinking and darting about, blazed with fury.

She was held in place, firmly, by the upper left arm, by the driver's fellow, lest she be tempted to rush forth, trying to attack, as she could, the young man in the house tunic.

"The mouth binding?" inquired the driver, the several loops of rope now looped over his body, from the right shoulder to the left hip.

"Yes," said the young man.

In a moment the several bands of cloth, those covering her mouth, and those drawn back between her teeth, were removed.

"I knew your voice," she screamed. "You, Titus Gelinus! Wretch! Abductor! What is the meaning of this! Release me, instantly!"

Titus Gelinus moved to her, took her by the hair, and, holding her head in place, slapped her once quite sharply.

"Have you requested permission to speak?" he asked.

She may have then considered another outburst but, seeing the palm of his hand poised, she restrained what might have proved to be a most unfortunate impulse.

She looked at him for a long, troubled, moment. Then she said, "May I speak?"

"Certainly," he said.

"You monster!" she screamed. "Surely this is some mad joke in the poorest of taste! Take away these chains! Reprimand these bumpkins! Chastise them, severely! Beware the perpetuation of follies such as this! Relieve me of these chains! I am a free woman! Get this collar off my neck! Do you think I am a slave? Bring me clothing! Let me go. Release me, instantly! Now! Now!"

"She is very loud," said the driver.

"Perhaps she thinks she is a free woman," said his fellow.

"I am a free woman!" screamed the occupant of the shackles, stamping her small foot on the tiles, which shook the chain on her ankles.

They were closely pinioned, separated by no more than five or six links. So pinioned a slave is quite helpless. She must move with care, lest she fall.

"You are to speak henceforth, my dear," said Titus Gelinus, "softly, with respect, with deference, clearly, and with excellent diction. Women such as you are not permitted to be slovenly about such things."

"Such as I?" she said.

"Yes," he said. "Female slaves."

"I am not a slave!" she said.

"In that conjecture, you are mistaken," he said.

"With your permission, noble envoy?" said the driver, the foremost of the seeming cartsmen. "We have duties in the palace."

"By all means," said Titus Gelinus. "Be thanked for your prompt and efficient service."

The driver and his companion then exited the house of Titus Gelinus.

"Are they truly of the palace?" asked the occupant of the shackles.

"Yes," said Titus Gelinus.

"I do not understand," she said.

"You need to understand little more, my dear," said the rhetor, "than that there is now a brand incised in your thigh and a collar on your neck."

"How dare you have me brought here?" she demanded.

"I thought you might wish to come," he said.

"I did," she said. "I was eager, but not to be conveyed hither as a roped captive."

"A roped slave," he said. "Recall the stop on the way here."

"You did not truly fool me," she said, "despite the blindfold. As soon as you spoke, I recognized your voice."

"You will become quite familiar with my voice," he said, "and you will learn to respond to it with alacrity."

"Take off these chains," she said.

"The point of the blindfold, and the gag, in your case," he said, "was primarily instructional, namely, that you begin to familiarize yourself with a slave's helplessness, being unable to see or speak."

"This joke has gone far enough," she said.

"Are you standing in the presence of a free man?" he asked.

"I shall call guardsmen!" she said.

"Do so," said he. "They would return you to me, promptly, for punishment."

"Beg my forgiveness!" she said. "I might forgive you. And sweeten your pleading with gold, a plenitude of gold!"

"But," said he, "as a slave you can own nothing. You do not even own your own collar."

"I cannot be enslaved," she said. "I am a free woman."

"You are enslaved," he said. "And most slaves were once free women."

"How could I be enslaved?" she asked.

"Quite easily," he said.

"With what justification?" she asked.

"With no justification," he said. "Let me put your mind at rest. The matter is entirely arbitrary. One could, of course, if one wished, invent a number of pretexts, but this was not done, not in your case. For example, one might claim you were enslaved for the good of the empire, or, alternatively, that it is morally appropriate that cheap, dishonest, mercenary, scheming women such as you be enslaved, that you might become good for something, at last, or, again, that you be enslaved as a debtress, and given to me for having satisfied your debts which, incidentally, I did, but none of these pretexts were resorted to. As I said, the matter was quite arbitrary. In your case, I merely thought that you should be a slave and, if so, why should you not be my slave."

"I shall appeal to the emperor," she said.

"It might be difficult to make it through the guards," he said. "Too, the emperor seldom grants audiences to slaves. If you wish, however, I could present you to the emperor."

She looked at him, wildly.

"It was he," said Titus Gelinus, "who selected you for slavery."

"He does not even know me," she said.

"But I do," said Titus Gelinus, "and the emperor, happily, was pleased to look kindly on my suggestion."

"You beast," she said.

"Actually," said he "it is you who are now the beast. I am a free man."

"How could the emperor do such a thing?" she asked.

"Quite easily," he said. "He is emperor."

"But—" she said.

"The emperor is a barbarian, an Otung, I believe," said Titus Gelinus, "and, as a barbarian, tends to view the reduction of free women to slavery not only with approval, but zest."

"Please, kind and noble Gelinus," she said, "remove my chains, free me, clothe me, and let us once more return to the delicacy of *civilitas*, for I am sure you know the warmth of my feelings for you, and, I suspect, I know those of you for me."

"Do you wish to know what your collar reads?" asked Titus Gelinus.

"No," she said.

"I shall tell you," he said. "It reads 'I am Pig. I am owned by Titus Gelinus, of Telnar'."

"'Pig'?" she said.

"It is an endearing name," he said. "Many peasant girls in the empire are named 'Pig'."

"I am not of the peasantry," she said.

"True," he said, "as a slave, you are a thousand times below the peasantry."

"Let us talk," she said.

"You are still standing," he said.

"Yes," she said defiantly, lifting her head.

At this point, Titus Gelinus turned and went to the chest at the side of the room and removed from it another object, which he uncurled and then snapped, sharply.

A gasp of anguish and alarm escaped Pig, though nothing had touched her.

She did, however, under his stern gaze, slip down to her knees.

"Good," he said. "That is better. You are now where you belong, on your knees, before a free man."

"I can explain everything, thoughtful, kind, understanding, noble Gelinus," she said, kneeling before him, in her chains. "In the time of your tribulation, I was dismayed. I grieved for you and suffered as you suffered. You cannot guess the keenness of my sorrow. When your many notes came I, overcome with love, and need, could not bring myself to answer them. I dared not, foolish I, lest I betray the depth of my feelings for you, which I feared were unbecoming to a free woman. Convention constricts. Society is cruel. Inertness is praised. Coldness is to be pretended, no matter how fiercely blazes the furnace of the heart. We are to conceal our feelings lest we be taken for amorous beasts, rushing about, rutting at will. How we must guard ourselves, despite ourselves, and our true feelings, lest we, noble free women, be taken as wanton! So I feared, foolishly, to answer your notes, that I not betray myself as a free woman, and thus earn your rightful scorn. And then I resolved, unable longer to resist seeing you, to answer one of your dear notes, and invite you to my domicile. But then, oh, terrible, unhappy day, I resolved to see if your love was as strong as mine, so I pretended coldness, indifference, and scorn, to see if you would, nonetheless, persist in your attentions. I set forth a wall only that it might be shattered, I posed an obstacle meant solely to be overcome, all this a tragically misconceived stratagem to test your fervor. Forgive me, dear Gelinus, for my foolishness! But should you, too, not be chastised for not seeing through so transparent an artifice? Is all this not as much, or more, your fault as mine? Should you not beg my forgiveness as much as I beg yours?"

"No," he said.

"'No'?" she said.

"I shall explain your duties, my pretty slave," he said.

"'Slave'!" she cried.

"Yes," he said, "slave, that and no more. You are as much a slave as any woman captured, the prize of a raid, the loot of a war, chained to a post, with a placard on your neck, as much as a slut from the breeding farms, brought to Telnar in the crowded, hose-washed bins of a common slave ship."

"How dare you speak so to me?" she cried.

"A master speaks to a slave as he wishes," he said, "and the slave hopes to please."

"I have no master!" she cried, from her knees.

"He is Titus Gelinus, of Telnar," he said, "and beware, lest you be punished as a lying slave. Only free women may lie and you are not a free woman."

"But I love you!" she cried.

He snapped the whip, and she, startled and frightened, cried out in misery.

"Kneel up," he said, "more straightly. Good. Now lift your arms, and put your wrist chain behind the back of your neck."

She did so.

"Good," he said. "Your breasts lift nicely. They are attractive. I like good lines in a pet animal."

"Please!" she protested.

"Now," he said, "put your head down, to the tiles."

"These are slave positions!" she wept.

Again the whip snapped and she, alarmed, put her head down to the tiles.

"I have long wanted to have you so before me," he said.

"You degrade a free woman," she wept.

"You are no longer free," he said. "You are now an object, an article of goods, merchandise, a beast, an animal, to be done with as an owner might please. You can be bought and sold, gifted, traded, exchanged. You are goods, a slave!"

"Please, no, noble Gelinus!" she said.

"Do you dare soil the name of a free man," he asked, "by putting it on the lips of a slave? Surely you know how a slave addresses a free man or a free woman."

"Mercy," she begged.

"Kneel up," he said. "Now take your hands from behind the back of your neck, put them before you, at your nicely rounded little belly. Good. Now attend me closely, Pig, and I will explain our relationship. Most simply, you are a slave, and I am your master. Obedience is to be instantaneous, and unquestioning. You exist for the service and pleasure of your master. It is what you are for. You must understand, in your deepest heart, in every particle of your small, luscious body, that you are a slave, and only a slave. You are to think, speak, and act as a slave. When you look in the mirror you are to see a slave; when you kneel, you are to know that it is a slave who kneels; when you speak, you are to know that it is a slave who speaks. You are to feel as a slave and hope as a slave. Most simply, you are a slave."

"Be kind," she begged.

"You are to strive to be pleasing at all times, in all ways," he said. "I hope you will be successful. The more pleasing a slave is the less likely it is that she will be beaten. On the other hand, as a former free woman, you are well aware that a slave may be beaten at any time for any reason, or for no reason. I might, for example, lash you once in a while if only to remind you that you are a slave. We do not wish our girls to forget that. In the beginning, in the house, you will be naked and chained. Later, I expect to remove the chains but keep you naked. In time, if I am satisfied with your service, I might let you have a tunic. I might even, should I be so moved, eventually give you a better name, a more attractive name for a female slave, for slaves are commonly lovely. But I promise nothing, pretty Pig."

"Release me," she said. "I demand it!"

He regarded her.

"I beg it!" she said.

"How well women look," he said, "as you are, as they should be, on their knees, naked, and chained."

"Release me, noble sir," she begged.

"You are now as you should be, slut," he said, "—a slave."

"No, no!" she wept.

"I am thinking of you primarily, at least presently, as a work slave," he said. "For example, I will want you, soon, on your hands and knees, with a brush and water, to scrub the tiles of the atrium, and clean the atrium basin for, as you can see, over the past weeks, it has accumulated a good deal of leaves and other sorts of debris."

"I," she said, "the Lady Gia Alexia, she of the Telnar Darsai?"

"Beware, Pig," he said.

"I am free," she said.

"The house is large and there will be a good deal of work for you," he said. "The house was neglected during my time of difficulties, and, after the repair of my fortunes, these past weeks, I continued this neglect, deliberately. I had you in mind, as you

are now. Thus, I saved the work for you. And we must not forget shopping, cooking, polishing, cleaning, laundering, and such,
the full panoply of duties expected of a slave in a clean, well-run
house. Also, of course, if I entertain free women, you will be expected to serve humbly and dutifully, as befits a slave. Doubtless, some of these free women will remember you, from when
you were free. I do not think they will object to seeing you in a
collar. Indeed, I suspect they will enjoy it. I gather you were not
popular. Do not fear, however, for in your serving of free women,
I will see to it that you are clothed, that the sensibilities of the free
women not be offended. I have in mind a modest tunic which will
extend to the calves of your rather attractive legs. It will be clear,
of course, that it is your only garment. You will also, as would be
expected, serve barefoot."

"I will never be so humiliated," she said.

"You will have no choice," he said. "You will be a slave."

"I will never serve so," she said.

"It may be difficult at first," he said, "but later you will think
nothing of it. Indeed, you will feel it fitting and perfectly appropriate, as you are a slave. Indeed, you will later look forward to it,
and enjoy it, as it provides you with an additional way in which
to prove pleasing to your master. Too, after the free women leave,
it is you who will remain in the house, with your master, in your
collar."

"I will never serve so," she said.

"You are mistaken, of course," he said.

"No!" she said.

"Perhaps," he said, "if you feel the lash, you will better understand that you are now a slave."

"You would never dare to whip me," she said.

"Never dare to whip a slave, one who has not been fully pleasing?" he said.

"I am not a slave," she said.

"I should also mention," he said, "though it scarcely requires
to be mentioned, that, amongst your other duties, those of a female slave, is the providing of your master with inordinate sexual
pleasure, at any time, in any place, in any way he may desire. You
may, too, of course, as a slave, beg for such pleasure on your own
behalf, but whether or not the master chooses to accede to your
request is completely up to him."

"For one is a slave," she said, bitterly.

"Precisely," he said. "He is master; she is slave. The coyness of the free woman is not permitted to her. The games of the free woman are not permitted to her, the dangling of prospects to wrangle gifts, entertainments, and suppers, the teasings and tauntings, the postponements, ambiguities, hintings, and calculations, the baiting of traps, the cunning distribution and withholding of favors, the playing off of one man against another, the provocation of jealousy, the delight in stimulating rivalries from which one may profit, the bargaining with one's smiles, presence, and body, to buy position and power. What mercenary, what merchant, can compare with the free woman?"

She shook the chains on her small wrists with frustration.

"Behold, contrariwise," said he, "this cunning, lovely, fascinating, seductive, desirable, tempting beast put in a collar where she belongs. What a delicious possession, yes, possession, she then is. Now her coyness is over. Now her games are done. No longer is she permitted hesitations, inhibitions, qualifications, or such. She is his. He takes from her what he wants, when he wants it, where he wants it, and as he wants it. When he commands her to be silent, she is silent; when he command her to kneel, she kneels; when he commands her to perform, she performs."

She looked up at him, from her knees, in her chains.

"And her obedience," he said, "as earlier noted, is to be instantaneous, and unquestioning."

She jerked helplessly at the metal which pinioned her wrists.

"The female slave, you see," he said, "is quite different from the free woman. As an object, an animal, she is completely at the disposal of the master. Thus, she is quite different from a free woman."

"Very much so," she said.

He looked at her.

"What?" she said.

"Get on your belly," he said, "hands extended well before you."

She assumed this position. He did, after all, have the whip still in hand. Girls, particularly unclothed, are wary of the whip. It might be used.

"Be fully aware of your position," he said, "and the feeling of the tiles."

She was silent, seemingly uneasy.

"What do you feel like?" he asked.

"I feel strange sensations," she said.

"Those of a bellied slave," he said.

"Surely not," she said.

"I would expect so," he said, "as that is what you are."

"May I lift my hands in supplication?" she asked.

"If you wish," he said.

"Free me," she said, lifting her head to him, and her hands, as she could.

"No," he said.

"Why not?" she begged.

"You are now where you belong," he said, "at your master's feet."

"I am a free woman!" she cried.

"Tell it to the empire," he said, "to the rose burned into your fair thigh, to the close-fitting collar locked on your lovely throat."

"I am free!" she wept.

"I warned you about lying," he said. "You are no longer a free woman. Lying is no longer permitted to you."

"I am free, free!" she cried. "I am a free woman! I am free! Free!"

"You are clearly a slave in need of discipline," he said.

"No!" she cried.

She heard the whistle of the whip and, an instant later, the snap of the leather across her back, and, disbelievingly, her back afire, almost unable to comprehend the pain, she screamed with misery. Any resolutions she might have entertained hitherto pertaining to bravery under the whip, prior to its stroke, vanished instantly, even with the first stroke. Never again did she desire to feel such a stroke. How could it be endured again? She would do anything, anything, to avoid it stern admonition. Never had she suspected what it might be to feel herself under the lash of a master. "No!" she begged. But then she felt another stroke on her naked, slave's body, and she rolled about, weeping, trying to fend blows with her hands, trying to rise to her feet, against the chains, tripping, falling backwards, then again, twisting, went to her belly, scratching at the tiles, and then there was another stroke, and another and another, and she cried out, weeping, "Please Master, no, no! Please do not strike your slave further! She begs mercy! She will obey! She will try to please you, her master!"

"To my feet," he said.

She crawled to his feet and put her head down, sobbing, over them.

"Speak," he said.

"I am a slave," she said. "I will strive to be pleasing to my master."

"Perhaps you would now like to show your love, respect, and devotion for your master," he said.

"Yes, Master," she said.

"You may do so," he said.

She pressed her lips to his sandals, and kissed them, again and again, sobbing.

"And perhaps, too," he said, "you would like to express your joy and gratitude, that a man has seen fit to put you in a collar."

"Yes, Master," she said. "Thank you, Master."

She then continued to minister, delicately, humbly, with lips and tongue, to his feet and ankles. After a time, he drew her up, to her knees, and she held his knees and looked up at him, tears in her eyes. She knew that she, before him, and on her knees, was looking into the eyes of her master. She then pressed her cheek to the side of his leg. "I am a slave, your slave, Master," she whispered. He then pulled her to her feet, lifted her arms, and looped her wrist chain behind his own neck, thus holding her in place. "I cannot help myself, Master," she said. "I am filled with strange feelings. I have never felt them before. They overwhelm me. I am their captive. Are these the feelings of a slave, of an owned woman, so hot, so suffusive, my whole body, so helpless, so needful? You have conquered me, you own me, I am yours. Use me, as a common slave is used, as pitilessly and ruthlessly, as you will. I have nothing to say, and want nothing to say. I am a slave."

He then held her in his arms, and pressed his lips to hers, and she could scarcely move, for the grasp that held her so, and then, as she whimpered in need, he removed her wrists from the back of his neck, and thrust her back, on her back, to the tiles.

He then stood and looked down upon her.

She lay before him, looking up at him, supine, shackled.

"I have dreamed of you so, many times, pretty slave," he said.

"Yes, Master," she said.

He then bent down and removed the shackle from her right ankle.

He then again stood.

With his foot he brushed her right ankle suddenly, rudely, to the side.

She gasped, startled.

He then stood over her, between her legs.

"Master," she breathed.

"Do you understand something of your collar now?" he asked.

"Yes, Master," she said.

"Put your wrist chain behind the back of your neck," he said.

The slave complied.

"You look well at a man's feet," he said, "particularly now that his vision is unobstructed."

"A slave is grateful, if she pleases her Master," she said.

"You may now, if you wish, place your hands before your body," he said.

"Thank you, Master," she said, and hastened to do so.

She then looked up at him, at her Master.

"You seem to be a ready slave," he said, "ready for use."

She turned her head to the side.

"Are you ready for use?" he asked.

"Yes," she said, "I am ready for use."

"But it matters not," he said.

"No, Master," she said, "for I am a slave."

"Perhaps I shall now abandon you," he said.

"Do not, Master!" she said.

"Do you beg use?" he asked.

"Yes, Master," she said.

"Now be silent," he said.

"Yes, Master," she said.

But, later, she cried out, again and again, gasping and weeping, moaning and shrieking, writhing and thrashing, with the gratitude and joy of a helplessly ravished slave.

He then, toward morning, replaced the shackle on her right ankle.

"You will now sleep for a bit," he said, "here on the tiles."

"I do not know if I can sleep, Master," she said.

"I advise it," he said, "for soon you must awaken, and there will be much work for you to do."

"Yes, Master," she whispered.

He then, with a length of chain, fastened her ankle to a nearby ring, one at the foot of the atrium pool, and withdrew.

She lay in the darkness, on the tiles, on the chain, trying to grasp the transformation which had taken place in her life. "Such sensations," she thought. "Such feelings! I did not know such things could exist!" She shook her chains, a tiny bit. "I am a slave," she thought.

CHAPTER EIGHTEEN

"Please forgive the lateness of the hour, dear Timon," said Sidonicus, exarch of Telnar, to his guest, Timon Safarius Rhodius, of the Telnar Rhodii, *primarius* of the senate, "but I thought it well to be discreet. I trust that you, and our dear friend, Orontius, your esteemed envoy to the palace, came to our humble quarters, here in the rectory, as suggested, well shielded in closed, nondescript palanquins?"

"We did," said Safarius.

"Separately, by circuitous routes, alert to possible surveillance?" said Sidonicus.

"Yes," said Orontius, leaning forward on the plush couch.

"The streets were muchly deserted?" speculated Sidonicus.

"We had guards," Safarius reassured the exarch.

"Perhaps," said Sidonicus, toying with the golden replica of a burning rack on its gold chain slung about his neck, over the swollen purple robes, "you are curious as to the reason for my requesting the honor of your presence here, at so unseemly and lonely an hour."

"We are confident," said Timon Safarius Rhodius, "it concerns the well-being of the city and empire, and is thoroughly compatible with the sweet and gentle teachings of your holy prophet, the beloved Ogg, Floon."

"Clearly," said Sidonicus, "these are dark and terrible times."

"And most regrettably," said Safarius, "many are unaware of the fact, but, naively and contentedly, prosperously and happily, pursue their own affairs, as though all was well."

"The state does little to interfere with life," said Orontius, "and the people do as they please."

"And think they are thriving," said Safarius.

"There is a barbarian on the throne," said Sidonicus, "the senate is ignored, and the state has not, as is its duty, imposed the one true religion on the empire, but, rather, allows false religions and heresies to go unchecked."

"It is the error of tolerance and the crime of inaction," said Safarius.

"Of what value is the sword of the state if it does not shed the blood of the iniquitous?" said Sidonicus.

"Perhaps your god, *Karch*, who is reportedly omnipotent and omniscient, if interested, might remedy matters," said Safarius.

"Then you need do nothing," said Orontius.

"Yet I have called this meeting," said Sidonicus.

"*Karch* has overlooked the matter?" asked Safarius.

"Surely men may do the work of *Karch*, and should," said Sidonicus.

"And the exarch of Telnar may be depended on to know the work, and will, of *Karch*," said Safarius.

"Infallibility has its privileges, as well as its burdens," said Sidonicus.

"I am not a scholar in the simplicities, ambiguities, and obscurities, of Floonianism," said Safarius, "but I do not recall Floon having said anything about infallibility."

"It is implicit in the fact that, as there is one true god and one true religion," said Sidonicus, "there must be one true authority to clarify doctrine and belief."

"I know little about religions, of which there are a great many," said Orontius, "but, politically, that is a sensible, and desirable, arrangement, one army, one supreme general, and so on."

"Many assumptions are involved, of course," said Timon Safarius Rhodius, the senate's *primarius*, "for example, that one or more gods exist, that they are certain sorts of gods, have particular attributes, that they have any interest whatsoever in men, that they have a religion, that they are interested in its propagation, that they are unable or unwilling, for some reason, to establish beliefs by themselves, that a particular religion is not only the right one but only one of its many variations is the right variation, and that someone, such as the exarch, who, fortunately, happens to be of that particular variation, will be preserved from error, should be listened to, and so on."

"Precisely," said Sidonicus.

"You have not, of course," said Safarius, "invited us here this evening to convert us to your particular views."

"True," said Sidonicus. "I am aware that skepticism, denial, uncertainty, and confusion exist, that to some minds the clear truths of faith are less obvious than to others."

"Possibly," said Safarius, "because the clear truths of thousands of faiths, faiths often resolutely and fervently held, contradict one another."

"As you have suspected," said Sidonicus, "we are not gathered here to discuss the subtleties of holy things, but matters more mundane."

"Proceed," said Safarius.

"The senate," said Sidonicus, "celebrated the accession of Otto, the Usurper, even urged some days of holiday."

"We deemed it preferable to our extermination," said Safarius.

"But," said Sidonicus, "we can profit from your very embarrassment and defeat."

"How so?" asked Safarius.

"The sitting proclaimed concord between the palace and the senate," said Sidonicus. "It made the senate appear to be an ardent supporter of the current regime. Surely, politically, the palace will be interested in maintaining that appearance."

"I begin to see," said Safarius, *primarius* of the senate.

"Continue," said Orontius, envoy to the palace.

"The Usurper," said Sidonicus, "is not easily accessible. It would not be easy to serve him the dram of poison, to bring him within the compass of the assassin's dagger. He hides within the palace, cowering, not daring to show himself in public, lest the outraged citizenry rise up and tear him to pieces."

"To the best of my knowledge," said Orontius, "he does not venture outside the palace, perhaps for fear of assassination, but I would dismiss your spies, as it seems they are telling you what you wish to hear, not what passes in the taverns, streets, and markets of Telnar. The citizenry, for the most part, give little, if any, thought to either the palace or senate. Indeed, benightedly perhaps, for the most part, they prefer to live their own lives and be left alone, particularly by the state."

"What if," said Sidonicus, softly, "the senate were to invite the emperor to attend a sitting, perhaps even to preside over a sitting?"

"Or," said Safarius, "to be the recipient of certain distinctions and honors?"

"He could not refuse so gracious and generous a request," said Sidonicus, "not without jeopardizing the supposed harmony betwixt himself and the senate. He attends. He is then out of the palace, exposed and vulnerable. Some patriots, disguised in senatorial robes, enter the chamber. A dozen knives strike. The patriots rush from the chamber, brandishing bloody knives and proclaiming liberation. Has this act not been performed in a dozen places at a dozen times? The patriots are then whisked away by suddenly appearing hoverers. The senate itself, of course, is dismayed and horrified, and innocent."

"You will supply the patriots?" said Orontius.

"Of course," said Sidonicus.

"We," said Safarius, "will attend to the other arrangements."

"Excellent," said Sidonicus.

"How," asked Orontius, "do you reconcile such a deed, so clever and treacherous, with the teachings of Floon?"

"We do not, nor need we do so," said Sidonicus, "as the temple, like the senate, knows nothing of such matters."

"The temple is as shocked, and appalled, as the senate," said Safarius.

"Of course," said Sidonicus.

CHAPTER NINETEEN

"Can you see, beyond the lamps?" asked Elena.

"Not well," said Cornhair.

Elena peered out, across the large, round, half-darkened, low-ceilinged room, with its many tables, served by floor slaves. Perhaps a third of the tables were occupied. There was a rustle of conversation, the gentle susurration of small noises commonly associated with the partakings of small collations, and such.

"Why are the lamps placed as they are?" asked Pig, squinting her eyes.

"That we be illuminated, you fool," said Cornhair.

"I cannot close the tunic," said Pig, her remark accompanied by a small sound of chain. Her hands were fastened high over her head.

"Wriggle a little," suggested Cornhair.

The three slaves, and the other slaves, as well, all fastened to the same overhead display bar, had been placed in inspection tunics. Such tunics, falling nicely and loosely, attractively, about the body of the slave, from her shoulders to her knees, lack a frontal closure. Accordingly they may be easily parted, as is intended by their design, to provide an unobstructed view of the garment's occupant.

"I wish I could lower my arms," said Elena.

"You need not have come," said Cornhair.

"Your master was unwilling that you be involved in this," said Pig.

"You petitioned him earnestly," said Cornhair.

"It was important to me," said Elena. "I did not want to be left out, to be an exception, to be privileged. I wanted to serve, as others."

"Perhaps now you have thought the better of it," said Cornhair.

"No," said Elena, "but my arms are sore."

"I trust you shaved your armpits," said Cornhair, irritably.

"Of course," said Elena, "as we all do. Men like smooth slaves, silken, caressable slaves."

"Why did your master object?" asked Cornhair. "There is little danger here. Guards, incognito, are about; we are watched."

"He was reluctant to see me so displayed," said Elena.

"What does it matter?" asked Cornhair. "You are a slave."

"He wants to keep me to himself," said Elena.

"My Master," said Cornhair, "has no such reservations."

"That is because you were a Calasalii bitch," said Pig.

"And you were a low-class slut with social pretensions," said Cornhair.

"The Telnar Darsai," said Pig, "are not lower-class. They are *honestori*."

"The pretentious lesser *honestori*," said Cornhair. "They do not begin to compare with the Larial Calasalii."

"I am sorry," said Pig, "I treated you badly when I owned you."

"You were cruel, stupid, vindictive, and vengeful," said Cornhair.

"I did not realize I would one day be put in a collar," said Pig.

"Nor," said Cornhair, "that my master, Rurik, would inform your master, Titus Gelinus, of the nature of our former relationship, and then that Titus Gelinus would bind you, hand and foot, throw you naked to my feet, and furnish me with a switch."

"You well had your vengeance," said Pig.

"You abused me for weeks," said Cornhair.

"Please do not beat me further," said Pig. "The switch hurts, terribly."

"I am well aware of that," said Cornhair. "Do not think I do not remember your switch. I remember it quite well."

"Forgive me," said Pig.

"We shall see," said Cornhair.

"Do not squabble," said Elena. "The masters might not be pleased. You are now both slaves, only slaves. Be careful that you are not both lashed."

"I do not like this," said Pig, "standing here, under the lamps, so clad." She twisted her body a little, to try to bring the dangling, parted edges of the inspection tunic more closely about her body. "They will take us for brothel slaves."

"Let us hope so," said Cornhair. "That is our disguise."

"Do you see those whom you hope to recognize?" Elena asked Cornhair, in a guarded whisper.

Two men had entered the reception area together.

"No," said Cornhair.

It had been the speculation of Otto, and others, as it may be recalled, that Abrogastes, of the Drisriaks, was a captive in Telnar, quite possibly betrayed into the hands of enemies by three men, Phidias, once the captain of the freighter, *Narcona*, and two of his former officers, Corelius, and Lysis. This trio had been involved in the attempt to assassinate Otto on Tangara, and had, treasonously, silenced the defensive batteries of Telnar, enabling the daring raid of Abrogastes which had succeeded in abducting the princesses, Viviana and Alacida. It was the hope of Otto, Iaachus, Arbiter of Protocol, Julian, of the Aureliani, Rurik, the Tenth Consul of Larial VII, and their fellow, Tuvo Ausonius, that Phidias, Corelius, and Lysis, or at least one of them, might be in Telnar, and, if detected, might be utilized to discover the location of Abrogastes. Otto, and his colleagues, hoped to liberate Abrogastes, that he might frustrate the designs of Sidonicus and Ingeld, his second son. Ortog, the first son of Abrogastes, recently arrived in Telnar, enleaguing himself with Otto, and the others, was concerned, more simply, with the welfare of his father. The search for Abrogastes was, for political reasons, having largely to do with the power of Sidonicus in the empire, a secret search. It was hoped that the slave, Cornhair, who had been a co-conspirator with the treacherous trio in their attempt to assassinate Otto on Tangara, might recognize and identify one or more of them, following which it might be feasible, sooner or later, to locate and rescue Abrogastes. Needless to say, determining the location of Phidias, Corelius, or Lysis, who might be disguised, somewhere in the hundreds of districts in vast, rambling Telnar was a daunting task, one giving little promise of being brought to a successful conclusion. There was one clue, and it was on the grounds of this clue that Otto had decided to act. Phidias, Corelius, and Lysis, assuming that Cornhair had successfully employed the poisoned dagger on Tangara, had abandoned her to the mercies of Otungs and imperial soldiers. Naturally, they had assumed her dead, presumably following her capture and torture. On the other hand, following a series of events elsewhere recounted, she had, in a time of great unrest in the city, been put up for sale in an outlet of *The House of Worlds*, located on Varl Street in Telnar. She had been purchased by an unknown buyer who, by means of agents, planned to have her cast into one of Telnar's vast, reeking *carnari-*

ums, refuse pits located outside the city walls. The buyer was presumably one of the treacherous trio, or someone associated with them. As Cornhair had been a party to the plot to assassinate Otto, she might recognize and implicate them. It would then seem a matter of practical expediency to arrange for her elimination. Fortunately for the slave, however, shortly before she could be cast into the *carnarium*, the raiding fleet of Abrogastes, undeterred by defensive batteries, stormed out of the sky, doing landfall in the muchly deserted area of the *carnariums*. After the second of her would-be murderers was killed, the first having been earlier slain by his fellow, he unwilling to share gold, Cornhair was seized by raiders and carried to the palace, where Abrogastes, resistance in the city quelled, was soon to hold temporary court. When again he took ship he had had the princesses, Viviana and Alacida, with him, as his prisoners. It was shortly after that that Cornhair had fallen into the clutches of the Lady Gia Alexia, of the Telnar Darsai, a former, remote, scorned acquaintance. Otto had based his supposed clue on two factors. First, few but one of the treacherous trio, or someone associated with them, fearing much for their own lives, would consider disposing of a comely slave, presumably an object of value, in a *carnarium*. Second, it seemed of interest that, given the many markets in the city, and given the rioting and disruption in the city, that Cornhair had been discovered in this particular market. It was not a famous market, patronized by hundreds of regular customers, come from all points in the city. Its customers might then be supposed to be local, or likely to be local. Too, given the disruption in the city, presumably few at that time would wish to travel far from their own lodgings. This suggested the possibility that at least one of the treacherous trio might reside in the vicinity of the House-of-World's outlet on Varl. Beyond this, the House-of-Worlds, besides their market on Varl, also maintained a well-known restaurant and brothel, also on Varl Street, "The Pleasure Palace," one of more than a dozen such establishments, variously owned, in Telnar, which bore the same name. And thus it was, that the three slaves were placed as they were, on the display bar. The first of the three men, Phidias, Corelius, or Lysis, if recognized and identified by Cornhair, would be followed, discreetly, by Elena, freed of the bar; the second would be followed by Pig; and the third, if recognized, would be followed by Cornhair. Presumably a man who might be alert to being followed by a man would be less suspicious of a slave. To be sure, each of the slaves, would be followed, at a distance, by one or more armed servitors.

"A man approaches," whispered Pig.

"Do not fear," said Elena, "we all have yellow "hold tags" on our collars."

The "hold tag" on a girl's collar, with its number, indicates that the girl is reserved, and may not be removed from the display bar except by the fellow who has reserved her, who, of course, holds a correspondent tag, with its number.

"Oh!" said Pig, shrinking back, pulling at the chains over her head, fastening her to the display bar, as the sides of her inspection were parted, and lifted aside.

"Please, Master," she whispered, "I am reserved for another."

The sides of the garment were parted, more widely.

She turned her head to the side.

"For another," she said.

The fellow released her garment, and turned away.

"He was not one of the three?" asked Elena of Cornhair.

"No," said Cornhair.

"The three may have left the city," said Elena, "days ago."

"One does not know," said Cornhair.

"They may have separated," said Elena. "They may not be resident in this district. They may not patronize this establishment."

"True," said Cornhair.

One of the girls to the right of Cornhair, caressed, began to gasp and whimper. "I will take this one," said the fellow, and an attendant freed the girl from the display bar. The fellow then conducted her across the floor and through the curtained portals leading from the dining area to the corridor of alcoves.

"My tunic was parted," said Pig to Cornhair. "Yours was not."

"So?" said Cornhair.

"So I am more beautiful than you," said Pig.

"Another patron," said Elena.

Cornhair, angry, turned away from Pig, trying to look past the lamps, into the half-darkened dining area.

"No," she said, shaking her head.

"I am," said Pig.

"You were not even sold," said Cornhair. "You cost your master nothing. You had to be given away."

"I was the gift of an emperor," said Pig.

"The emperor had never even seen you," said Cornhair.

"I am still more beautiful than you," said Pig.

"No," said Cornhair, "you are not."

"Ai!" cried Cornhair, suddenly, dismayed, frightened, drawing back, with a rattle of chains.

The man lifted the yellow tag wired to her collar, the holding tag, and then turned about, and made his way back, quickly, through the tables.

"What is wrong?" asked Elena.

"It is he, Phidias, who was captain of the *Narcona*," said Cornhair.

"I saw him from afar, stop, regard you," said Elena. "He seemed startled. Then he approached."

"He was incredulous. He wished to be certain," whispered Cornhair. "He thought me perished, no longer of danger to him."

Cornhair had now grasped her left wrist with her right hand.

"Do not be afraid," said Elena. "There are emperor's men about, servitors of the palace, disguised as guardsmen, as patrons, as attendants."

"Was it he?" asked Pig. "Are you sure? Should there not be three men?"

"Where three are searched for," said Elena, "you are likely to find only one or two, and then another. They would enter separately."

"It was Phidias," said Cornhair.

"He knows neither myself nor Pig," said Elena. "When he leaves, one or the other of us will be freed to follow him."

"Would that I had recognized him, and not him me," moaned Cornhair.

"You have given the signal," said Elena. "Servitors are now alerted."

"He is with two others, near the door," said Pig.

"It is they," whispered Cornhair.

"The light is poor," said Elena.

"It is they," said Cornhair. "I recognize them. I know them well."

She then, again and again, after brief intervals, grasped and released her left wrist with her right hand, now three times after each interval.

"All three," said Elena, "wonderful."

"Servitors approach," said Pig.

Two apparent patrons, one and then another, each with a yellow numbered tag, released Elena and Pig from their chains and conducted them to different tables, where they had them kneel at the side, while they ordered a drink or snack, prior, presumably, to conducting their choices to the corridor of alcoves.

"Master," whispered Cornhair, for Rurik, clad as a patron, in a smith's smock, was before her.

"Were you recognized?" asked Rurik.

"Yes, Master," she said. "He said nothing, he gave no sign, but I am sure he recognized me."

"Then," said Rurik, "you must not follow him. It would be too dangerous. We will make other arrangements."

"Master fears for the life of his slave," said Cornhair.

"No," said Rurik, "it would be too dangerous for our endeavor. The entire point of our surveillance would be lost. After he had turned and killed you, he might escape."

"I see," said Cornhair.

"Slaves are cheap," he said.

"I understand," said Cornhair. "Forgive me, Master."

As two patrons were now in the vicinity, having paused, presumably to review the goods fastened to the display bar, Rurik parted Cornhair's tunic, widely, and surveyed her, appraisingly.

Cornhair, though a slave, and well apprised of the fact that she was not permitted modesty, was not overly pleased with this act on the part of Rurik, her master. It is one thing to be the bared and eager love brute of a master, begging for the assuagement of a slave's needs, and another to be thoughtlessly, blatantly, meaninglessly, publicly, routinely, contemptuously exhibited. For example, most slaves fear the keen shame of public nudity, at least outside of markets, display cages, and such, which renders even a tiny, muchly revealing slave tunic a coveted treasure. Indeed, many slaves love their tunics, and how they look in them. They know how exciting and lovely they look in a tunic, and how attractive to men. Let free women envy them their collars and tunics, which so enhance a woman's beauty. It is quite another thing, however, to be naked in the streets. This gives their masters an additional useful article to include in their arsenal of disciplinary devices. Most slaves will strive zealously to be pleasing, when the perceived alternative is to be sent into the streets naked, under the eyes of fully clothed, scorning free women.

"Is this one not worth owning?" Rurik asked the nearby patrons.

"Yes," said one.

"Nice," said the other.

"You see that I am tagged, Master," said Cornhair. "Am I not then reserved for another?"

One of the nearby patrons laughed, and the other smiled. "An outspoken slave," said the one who had laughed. "Such slaves can be improved," said he who had smiled, "by a visit from the switch." They then continued on their way.

"Do you think I do not know the meaning of the yellow tag?" asked Rurik.

"Was it not appropriate that I play my role?" asked Cornhair.

"Doubtless you think you are clever," said Rurik.

"I am very intelligent," said Cornhair.

"The more intelligent a woman is," said Rurik, "the lovelier she looks on her knees."

"I would kneel," said Cornhair, "but it is difficult to do so, given the way my master has seen fit to have me chained."

"Calasalii bitch," he said.

"Oh?" she said.

"That is where all Calasalii bitches belong," said Rurik, "at the feet of their Farnichi masters."

"But I was disowned," she said.

"No matter," he said.

"All slaves belong at the feet of their masters," said Cornhair.

Rurik then looked about, as though casually.

"You designated three," he said. "Two are at that table, far off, to the right of the entrance, as one would enter the dining area. I do not see the one you first identified."

"That was Phidias, the captain of the *Narcona*," said Cornhair.

"It is likely he is still in the building," said Rurik. "The entrances and exits are watched. When the two at the table leave, they will be followed by Elena or Pig, or both. Phidias is to be followed by a servitor, which, under the circumstances, cannot be helped. Hopefully at least one of them will lead us to Abrogastes, or his captors."

"I am sure I was recognized by Phidias," said Cornhair, "but I am similarly sure that he takes my presence here as anomalous, a coincidence, a matter of chance, however annoying or troubling. I do not think he suspects anything untoward is involved."

"I think you are right," said Rurik. "There is no sign of agitation. The two at the table seem at ease. No one moves to the exit. There is no indication of an attempt to escape, or even leave."

"Then all goes well," said Cornhair.

"Seemingly," said Rurik. He then turned away.

"Master," whispered Cornhair quickly, after him, "am I to be left here?"

"Of course," said Rurik, "the yellow tag has not been removed. Must we not play our roles?"

"I see," said Cornhair.

"And while you wait," said Rurik, "contemplate your cleverness."

"Master!" protested Cornhair.

Rurik then parted the sides of the inspection tunic, again widely, and let them fall, to the sides.

"Good," he said, approvingly.

Cornhair was silent.

"Stay where you are," said Rurik.

"I will consider doing so," said Cornhair, shaking her chains. Then she bit her lip, for she did not wish to be beaten.

But Rurik, grinning, had left.

"How helpless are slaves," thought Cornhair. "How much we are at the mercy of the free!"

Time passed, perhaps the third of an hour, or so. There seemed little that was different. Men continued to come and go, to converse, to drink and sup, and sometimes to remove slaves from the display bar, to conduct them to the corridor of alcoves, or take them to the tables, presumably later to conduct them to the alcoves. Corelius and Lysis remained at their table, to the right of the entrance as one would enter. Cornhair wondered if their choice of location had in mind the possible convenience of a discreet departure. Elena and Pig, she thought, might have to move quickly across the floor to the exit. But, presumably, Corelius and Lysis, unsuspecting, and unaware of surveillance, and thus unhurried, would not be difficult to follow. She hoped that the continued presence of Elena and Pig, kneeling at their forward table, beside presumed patrons, would not be noticed, that it would not serve to provoke curiosity, or suspicion.

"Oh," said Cornhair, softly to herself, for Corelius and Lysis were no longer at the table. Elena and Pig, accompanied by servitors, were moving toward the exit. A minute or two later, several apparent guardsmen, attendants, and patrons had filed out of the dining area. Some customers observed this evacuation, puzzled. Then things returned to normal in the dining area.

"My arms are sore," thought Cornhair. "My master is a beast. He leaves me here, chained, helpless. Perhaps I should not have been clever. Have I not yet learned that it is I who am in the collar, and he who holds the whip?"

Later, two slaves were inspected, and removed from the display bar, to be conducted toward the curtained portal leading to the corridor of alcoves. Cornhair was grateful for the yellow tag wired to her collar.

"Oh!" she said, startled, and in pain.

The point of a dagger, blade upward, was pressed into her belly.

"Be silent," said Phidias. "One thrust and movement of this blade will open your belly, hip to hip. I am desperate. I am going to have you unchained. You are to give no indication that anything is amiss. My hand will remain on the hilt of the knife, it concealed within the folds of my robes. Do not cry out. If you try to run, or escape, the knife will move, swiftly, and you will get no more than a step or two away, before you trip and fall, caught in the tangle of your own intestines. Too, I will kill the attendant. I trust you understand."

"The yellow tag," said Cornhair. "I am tagged. I cannot be removed from the bar except by one who holds the corresponding tag, with its number."

"Attendant," called Phidias, politely.

"Master?" said the attendant, summoned.

"This one," said Phidias, indicating Cornhair.

"An excellent choice," said the attendant. "It is rare that one this good is not removed earlier from the bar."

Phidias handed a small yellow tag with its number to the attendant, who put it in the wallet slung at his waist. The attendant then removed the tag from Cornhair's collar, and, reaching up, freed her of the cuffs and chains which had fastened her at the bar. He then arranged them aesthetically, dangling, at the bar, ready for a new occupant, if one should be desired. There was now, given the hour, and the number of alcoved slaves, several sets of such unoccupied chains dangling from the bar.

The attendant then withdrew.

"How is it," asked Cornhair, numbly, "that you had the tag?" She knew, of course, that it was not to have been placed with the tags available to the public, no more than the tags which had been worn by Elena and Pig.

"Its holder," said Phidias, "was persuaded to part with it."

"I see," said Cornhair.

"Let us see if we cannot find an empty alcove," said Phidias, taking Cornhair's arm in his left hand.

"Few will be available now," said Cornhair.

"Then the alley will do," said Phidias.

"Surely an alcove would be better," said Cornhair, hardly hearing herself speak.

"Of course," said Phidias.

"The body would not be discovered until morning," she said.

"You have a slave's body," said Phidias. "I thought that even from as long ago as the *Narcona*. You were a slave then, without your knowledge. We allowed you to keep your delusion of freedom, of course, fearing that you might have found the realization of your bondage troubling, which realization might then have interfered with the assassination which, as we later learned, you bungled."

Phidias brushed aside the curtain leading to the corridor of alcoves. "I trust we shall find an empty alcove," he said.

"The knife was discovered, the poison washed from the blade," said Cornhair, conducted into the ill-lit corridor.

"Unfortunately," said Phidias.

"You deserted me," said Cornhair, "even when you thought the assassination successfully accomplished."

"You were no longer needed," said Phidias, "and you knew too much."

"And was a slave," said Cornhair.

"Unbeknownst to yourself, amusingly," said Phidias.

"So I have a slave's body?" asked Cornhair.

"Obviously," said Phidias. "And you can imagine my feelings, looking upon it, on the *Narcona* and on Tangara, and yet refraining from putting it to appropriate slave use, that our projected task not be compromised."

"You must have suffered," said Cornhair.

"Men suffer much from women," said Phidias, "until the women are put in collars."

"You exercised courageous forbearance," said Cornhair.

"A forbearance," said Phidias, "which is no longer necessary."

"Now that I am a recognized slave," said Cornhair, "an indisputable slave, marked and collared."

"Precisely," said Phidias. "Most of the alcoves are closed."

"Doubtless for the night," said Cornhair. "Your grip is tight on my arm. You are hurting me."

"There must be at least one open alcove," he said. "It is not that late."

"There is always the alley," said Cornhair.

"I want more from you than a disembowelment in an alley," said Phidias.

"I gathered so," said Cornhair.

"How did you escape the *carnarium*?" asked Phidias.

"Your agents were killed," said Cornhair. "One was slain in a falling out over gold. The other was killed in the raid of Lord Abrogastes, the Drisriak."

"Behold," said Phidias, pleased. "Here is an open alcove. It may be the only one."

"They forgot to close it," said Cornhair.

"No," said Phidias. "It is left open for the next customer. If we occupy it, another will be opened."

"You have been here before," said Cornhair.

"Many times," said Phidias.

"I can scream," said Cornhair.

"Before you can open your mouth, your head would be cut half off," said Phidias. "Would you not like to live a little longer?"

"Yes," whispered Cornhair.

"'Yes'?" asked Phidias.

"Yes, Master," said Cornhair.

"I shall enjoy you, as a slave is enjoyed," said Phidias.

"Yes, Master," said Cornhair.

"I thought that on the *Narcona*, and on Tangara," said Phidias, "you might be something of a free woman, a tight purse, holding back, clinging to privileges and falsehoods, fearful of surrender, frightened of the whole yielding, jealous of your status and reserve, denying the eager beast within you, begging to be owned and mastered, hoping to be taken in hand, hoping to be subdued and ravished, terrified to recognize the slave in your belly."

"I am now in a collar, Master," said Cornhair, "and I know it is on my neck."

"And what of free women?" asked Phidias.

"I do not think," said Cornhair, "they know what it is to be in a collar."

"But might they not suspect?" asked Phidias.

"I think so," said Cornhair.

"And perhaps that is why they hate slaves so," said Phidias.

"Perhaps, Master," said Cornhair.

"I suspect," said Phidias, "that you have now, over your past months of bondage, been aroused, as a slave."

"I am now different," said Cornhair.

"And doubtless ruined for freedom," said Phidias.

"Yes, Master," said Cornhair.

"You are now slave needful," said Phidias.

"Yes, Master," said Cornhair, tensely.

"I sheathe my knife," said Phidias, "But I could crush your throat, instantly."

"I understand, Master," said Cornhair.

"We will tie your hands behind your back," said Phidias.

"Master ties a slave tightly," said Cornhair.

"Enter the alcove," said Phidias.

"Yes, Master," said Cornhair.

Cornhair bent down, and entered the alcove. Phidias followed her, and then closed and latched the door. It was completely dark.

Cornhair was thrust back, to one side, against the wall, to the left, as one entered the alcove. She slid down, and lay on her left side, bound, her knees drawn up.

"If you are satisfactory," said Phidias, from the darkness, "I may take some time with you."

Cornhair sobbed and pulled futilely at the thongs which lashed her wrists together, behind her back.

"The lamp is here, in its niche," said Phidias. "We will soon have some light."

Shortly thereafter there was the snap of a striking stone, a bright sputter of sparks, and then, a moment later, a tiny flame, by means of which the lamp was lit. Cornhair closed her eyes against the light, which seemed cruel, tenuous though it might have been. She heard Phidias snap shut the cap on the striking stone.

"There," said Phidias, with satisfaction, standing, facing Cornhair.

Cornhair, opening her eyes, cried out, suddenly, frightened, and, wide-eyed, twisting about, scrambled up to a sitting position, and then thrust herself back against the wall, her knees raised.

"Do not be afraid," said Phidias. "I do not have much time, but there is no great hurry."

Cornhair, wide-eyed, sitting up, thrust herself back, even more forcibly, against the wall.

"Of course you are afraid," said Phidias. "But you are too intelligent to cry out, or think that you can escape."

Cornhair, her back against the wall, her head up, her knees up, sat perfectly still. She did not speak. She could not speak. She did not move. She could not move.

"What is wrong with you?" asked Phidias, impatiently.

"She was once Calasalii," said the figure, knife drawn, standing behind Phidias. "Is that not enough?"

Phidias dared not turn.

"One should never enter an unfamiliar, darkened chamber without light," said the figure behind Phidias.

"Who are you?" asked Phidias, not turning.

"Particularly with your knife in its sheath," said the figure.

"What do you want?" asked Phidias.

"I come on behalf of Sulpicius," said the figure.

"I know no Sulpicius," said Phidias.

"It was he from whom you obtained a numbered tag," said the figure, at the same time putting an arm about Phidias' throat from behind. Phidias' hand darted to the hilt of his knife, but the arm about his throat, bent him backward, suddenly, violently, and Phidias cried out softly, his hand falling away from the hilt of his knife. A moment later the figure thrust the body of Phidias from the blade of the long, two-edged knife, reddened to the hilt.

"Master!" cried Cornhair, going to her knees, and pressing her head down to the carpeted floor of the alcove.

Rurik, Tenth Consul of Larial VII, of the Farnichi, wiped his blade on the robes of Phidias, and then returned the knife to its sheath.

"He would have dared touch you, without my permission," said Rurik.

"He was going to kill me," said Cornhair, daring to look up.

With a slight gesture, palm up, Rurik indicated to the slave that she might kneel up, straightly, before him.

"Of course," said Rurik. "You could identify him as a traitor, in the matter of the silent batteries and the raid of Abrogastes."

"Earlier," said Cornhair, "my presence belied his asseverations that he who is now the emperor was slain on Tangara. He purchased me and gave me to agents, to be disposed of in a *carnarium*. There was a falling out, one was killed by the other, the survivor was slain by the raiders."

"I heard," said Rurik.

"I might have been cast into a *carnarium*," said Cornhair.

"That would have been a waste of slave," said Rurik, "even one who was once Calasalii."

"Perhaps Master would have regretted the loss of a slave," said Cornhair.

"Surely," he said, "as of any animal of some value, however minimal."

"I am bound," said Cornhair, squirming a little, plaintively.

"True," said Rurik, surveying her, in the soft light of the lamp.

"I might have been slain at the display bar," said Cornhair.

"I thought you would be safe at the display bar," said Rurik. "You could not be removed from the bar without the appropriate tag, and great peril would attend killing you there, so openly, in the light. Your tag, and those of Elena and Pig, were held in security. I did not anticipate the theft of a tag."

"You thought me safe at the display bar?" said Cornhair, pleased.

"Yes," said Rurik.

"Perhaps Master is fond of a slave," said Cornhair.

"Do you wish to be cuffed?" he asked.

"No, Master," said Cornhair.

"I do regard you as worth at least a few *darins*," he said.

"Master saved my life," said Cornhair.

"The house of the Farnichi is a merchant house," he said. "Goods are goods. A *darin* is a *darin*."

"How strange and wondrous it was," she said, "and how fortunate for a slave, that Master lay in wait, in the darkness, in the alcove," said Cornhair.

"Not strange and wondrous," said Rurik. "As soon as we discovered the body of Sulpicius, and that the tag was missing, we knew Phidias would wish to remove you from the display bar, and then, as might prove possible, do away with you. He would not risk trying to remove you through the front portal, so he would utilize the corridor of alcoves, either taking you to an alcove, where the body would not be immediately found, or, less likely, risk killing you in the alley, and then attempt to escape. Clearly the alcove would seem more likely. Therefore, I waited."

"A slave is pleased," she said, "that you selected the right alcove."

"It was not difficult," he said, "nor as fortunate as it might seem. All the other alcoves were cleared, and closed, in the name of the emperor."

"What if I had been taken to the alley?" she asked.

"Men were waiting," said Rurik. "Too, if the alcove were passed, I would have followed, immediately."

"Then I was not in the danger I feared," said Cornhair.

"You were in great danger," he said, "as soon as you were released from the display bar and entered into the corridor of alcoves."

"Clearly Master was concerned," said Cornhair. "Master feared for the welfare of his slave."

"Beware," he said.

"Had Master permitted me to be slain," she said, "a servitor might have followed Master Phidias, and perhaps been led to Lord Abrogastes."

"Sulpicius was killed," said Rurik.

"But might have been later avenged," said Cornhair.

"Have you ever been lashed?" he asked.

"Forgive me, Master," she said.

"It is unfortunate that Phidias recognized you," said Rurik, "rather than being himself discreetly recognized."

"Yes, Master," said Cornhair.

"He was thusly alerted," said Rurik.

"Yes, Master," said Cornhair.

"Yet all is not lost," said Rurik. "There are two others. Either will do."

"Elena and Pig will follow them," said Cornhair.

"When it became clear to them that Phidias was determined to remove a slave from the display bar, they took their leave," said Rurik. "I think they would soon be in flight. We did not anticipate, nor I think did they, the move of Phidias. In flight, neither Elena nor Pig could match their pace. If they attempted to do so, for a time, two running slaves behind them would surely alert them to their danger."

"Then the emperor's plan has failed," said Cornhair.

"With respect to being easily, conveniently, led to Abrogates, yes," said Rurik, "but I think the servitors who were accompanying Elena and Pig will be more than capable of bringing the other two, even fleeing, into custody. Torture, a familiar device of statecraft, may then be employed, to its usual excellent effect."

"I would not care to be them," said Cornhair.

"Nor will they much care to be them, either, under the circumstances," said Rurik.

Cornhair shuddered.

"Pain may easily be avoided," said Rurik. "They need only speak, promptly, accurately, and volubly."

Rurik then hauled the body of Phidias from the alcove. A bit later, he returned.

"Master?" said Cornhair.

"I put our friend," he said, "in the alley."

"The body will be discovered," said Cornhair.

"Yes," said Rurik. "The blood is fresh."

"I do not understand," said Cornhair.

"Wild dogs roam the alleys of Telnar," said Rurik.

"I am still bound," said Cornhair.

The inspection tunic had slipped down her arms, and partly behind her.

"You look well," said Rurik, "kneeling, your hands tied behind your back."

"Should we not take our leave?" asked Cornhair.

"Presently," said Rurik.

"I am still bound," said Cornhair.

"We will return to the Farnichi enclave," said Rurik.

"Master regards his slave," said Cornhair.

A woman on her knees before a man is well aware of his scrutiny.

"Phidias had more in mind, I gather," said Rurik, "than simply killing you in an alcove."

"That, too, was my impression," said Cornhair. "Perhaps Master will now unbind a slave?"

"That would be a waste of thongs and a waste of alcove," said Rurik.

"What am I to do?" said Cornhair.

"Do you wish to be used on the carpeting of the alcove?" asked Rurik.

"I will be used whenever and however Master wishes," said Cornhair. "I am not a free woman. I am a slave."

"You see the cushions about," said Rurik. "On your knees, go to them, bend down, bite into them, softly and gently, and, holding them in your teeth, one after the other, drag them here, and arrange them, before me."

After a time, in the lamplight, Cornhair had arranged the cushions before Rurik, to his satisfaction.

"You did well, slave," said Rurik. "You may now kiss my feet, to show your gratitude, for having been permitted to serve your master."

"Yes, Master," said Cornhair.

"Now lie on the cushions, on your belly," he said.

"Yes, Master," said Cornhair.

Rurik then crouched beside her, and lifted the inspection tunic up, behind her neck, over her collar.

"I am helpless," said Cornhair.

"Of course," said Rurik.

Strange feelings suffused Cornhair. "I am grateful to be a slave," she thought, "to be permitted to be a slave. I want nothing else. I want to be such that I can be bought and sold, that I am owned as goods, that I must obey, that I am subject to the whip. How lonely and miserable I was, until I was owned, until I was collared."

CHAPTER TWENTY

"Think further, your majesty," expostulated Titus Gelinus, the palace's envoy to the senate.

"Heed the envoy's request, dear Otto," urged Julian of the Aureliani. "There is no love for you in the darkness of the senate."

"What think you, friend Tuvo?" asked Otto.

"For what my opinion may be worth, though it may well be worthless," said Tuvo Ausonius, "I share the fears of the noble envoy, Titus Gelinus, and he of the Aureliani."

Shortly before, Orontius, envoy of the senate to the palace, had smiled and backed away, respectfully, graciously, from the throne, turned, and taken his way to the great portal, by means of which he had withdrawn from the lofty, muchly draped throne room.

"You sense danger, noble Gelinus?" asked Otto.

"Very much so, your majesty," said Titus Gelinus. "I know of nothing specific, no plot, no plan, but the proposal is fraught with menace."

"Do you think I fear the senate?" asked Otto. "Has it an army, a navy, a thousand guardsmen at its personal call?"

"One does not need an army, a navy, a thousand guardsmen," said Julian. "One needs only a single dagger, a single arrow, perhaps poisoned, loosed from between two men in senatorial robes, parting to permit its passage."

"Am I not in danger within the palace itself," asked Otto, "from a suborned servitor, a malcontent in livery, a credentialed intruder?"

"Such risks are understood, and accepted," said Julian. "They accompany the throne, like its shadow, but it is one thing to accept inescapable peril, and quite another to seek it out."

"How is it that such an invitation would be offered?" asked Otto.

"I fear," said Titus Gelinus, "to lure you from the palace."

"I see the hand of Sidonicus in this," said Julian.

"The exarch?" said Otto.

"This professed token of concord has to me a strange taste," said Julian. "It suggests to me the honey of the exarch's cunning."

"What has this to do with his strange beliefs?" asked Otto.

"Beliefs are the means, not the end," said Julian. "The end is power. The exarch wants power and the senate wants power, and both see you as an obstacle to their ambitions. It is natural then that they should make common cause, reserving for the future their own deadly enmity, their own struggles for power."

"Do not accept the senate's invitation, your majesty," said Titus Gelinus. "The honors it offers, the distinctions it seems eager to lavish upon you, may bait a trap."

"Almost assuredly," said Julian.

"Perhaps the offer is genuine," said Otto. "That is possible. Can we risk that it is not so? There may be forces in the senate itself, eager for a better relationship between the palace and the senate."

"Beware," said Julian.

"Should I not welcome its support?" asked Otto. "Is it not better to rule with all in amity, however superficial that pose may be, than in open suspicion and division? Would the senate not be insulted, if I refused to accept its seemingly honest, well-intentioned invitation?"

"Let it be insulted," said Julian.

"You are Otung," said Titus Gelinus. "You occupy a throne which is foreign to you, one to which you are a stranger. There is the empire you see, and the empire you do not see. The empire you see is vast and glorious; the empire you do not see is covetous and self-seeking, subtle with intrigue, rife with danger."

"The senate," said Julian, "is an ambitious, corrupt, scheming, self-perpetuating cabal, formed from the oldest and richest families of the high *honestori*. It seeks power, not law, wealth, not justice. An emperor hoping for the welfare of the empire is not its ally, but its enemy."

"You are an alien to the senate, a threat to its ambitions," said Titus Gelinus. "Do not accept its invitation."

"I cannot refuse," said Otto. "Politics prescribes acceptance, even commands it. A refusal would be taken by many as an affront to the senate, deemed by many a venerable, honorable institution. Who would be so boorish or foolish as to decline a seeming overture of peace? Indeed, such a refusal would be understood by many as a repudiation of the senate. It could be taken as a simple brandishing of power, a contumelious gesture, the shameless act of an unmitigated tyranny."

"Let it be so understood," said Julian.

"I might be thought a coward," said Otto.

"Ah!" said Julian. "Now it is the barbarian, the Otung, who speaks."

"Perhaps," said Otto.

"Be wise," said Julian. "Do not permit yourself to be manipulated by the views of others. It is not the way of an emperor."

"Such views, as well," said Titus Gelinus, "might be only pretended, to draw you from the lair of the palace, like a proud, angry lion, to the nets and spears of hunters."

"I have never seen a sitting of the senate," said Otto. "I think I shall do so."

"Do not," said Titus Gelinus.

"I have given my word to Orontius," said Otto, "envoy of the senate to the palace."

"Deny that you have done so," said Julian. "Who would know?"

"I would know," said Otto.

"Do not go," said Titus Gelinus.

"Remain in the palace," said Julian.

"I beg you, your majesty," said Tuvo Ausonius. "Heed the words of your friends."

"At least consult with the Arbiter of Protocol," said Julian. "He will oppose the measure. He will recognize the danger. A cordial veil often conceals an inhospitable blade. Consult him. He is wily, and skilled in the machinations of statecraft."

"I have done so," said Otto. "He advises me to attend."

"Impossible," said Titus Gelinus.

"It cannot be," said Tuvo Ausonius.

"Do not trust him," said Julian.

"Ten days from now, at noon," said Otto, "the senate meets."

CHAPTER TWENTY-ONE

"You have taken action?" asked Ortog, pacing before the broad, lacquered desk of Iaachus, the Arbiter of Protocol, like a restless *vi-cat*.

"Action has been taken," said Iaachus.

"I would see Otto, king of the Otungen," said Ortog.

"It is late," said Iaachus. "The emperor is not to be disturbed."

"He would see Ortog, king of the Ortungen," said Ortog.

"Many in the empire," said Iaachus, "confuse the Otungen, a Vandal tribe, with the Ortungen, an ill-fated tribe, I gather, once associated with the Aatii."

"The Alemanni," said Ortog. "I would speak with Otto, king of the Otungen."

"Ottonius, the First," said Iaachus, "is not to be disturbed at this hour. Strict orders are in effect."

"Is he in the palace?" asked Ortog.

"Where else would he be?" asked Iaachus.

"In the streets, about, prowling, reconnoitering, inquiring, seeking information, a danger to thieves and killers."

"Unthinkable," said Iaachus.

"Is he in the palace?" demanded Ortog.

"Surely," said Iaachus.

"Do you know that—for certain?" asked Ortog.

"No," said Iaachus.

"I thought not," said Ortog.

"Why would you think he might not be?" asked Iaachus.

"He is Otung," said Ortog. "Would you keep an Otung within four walls, even gilded walls? Do you think you could do so? The Vandalii and the Alemanni, like the lion, the *vi-cat*, and the *arn* bear, are beasts of the open air, drinkers at cold pure streams, soft-treaders of leaf-carpeted passages amongst tall trees."

"It is well for you to be discreet in your visits to the palace," said Iaachus. "Keeping to a late hour is wise."

"I hoped to see Otto, king of the Otungen, privately," said Ortog.

"A guardsman, even an Otung, might slay you on sight," said Iaachus.

"I cut my hair, I shave my beard, I clothe myself in Telnarian fashion," said Ortog.

"Even so," said Iaachus, "there is something of the forest about you, in the light stealth of your step, in the quick, restless movement of your eyes."

"A *vi-cat* might lurk in the brush," said Ortog.

"We have *vi-cats* in Telnar, too," said Iaachus, "only they go on two feet, wait in doorways, and carry daggers as fangs."

"You said action had been taken?" said Ortog.

"It has been," said Iaachus.

"Does the emperor confide in you?" asked Ortog.

"He keeps few secrets from me," said Iaachus.

"And you from him?" asked Ortog.

"You are concerned for your father," said Iaachus.

"Abrogastes, king of the Drisriaks, of the Alemanni," said Ortog.

"He who attempted to slay you?" asked Iaachus.

"Who chose not to do so," said Ortog.

"He did war upon your secessionist tribe, the Ortungen," said Iaachus, "defeating it, dissolving it."

"It is reduced, but in corners and secret places, it survives," said Ortog.

"He cast it from the Aatii," said Iaachus.

"He cannot cast it from the Alemanni," said Ortog. "The Ortungen have Alemanni blood. One cannot cast out blood."

"You wish to kill him, for his sternness, his lack of understanding, for vengeance?" said Iaachus.

"No," said Ortog. "In his place I would have acted as he did."

"I do not understand," said Iaachus.

"Your emperor would understand," said Ortog.

"You respect the emperor?" said Iaachus.

"Yes," said Ortog.

"I thought the Vandalii and the Aatii, or Alemanni, if you wish, are enemies," said Iaachus.

"Blood enemies," said Ortog, "enemies to the death, but good enemies, great enemies, treasured enemies, worthy enemies, the best of enemies."

"I do not understand," said Iaachus.

"You have no tribe," said Ortog.

"I will tell you what I know of the action taken," said Iaachus. "The emperor, anticipating your concern, has authorized certain individuals, such as myself, to do so. Your location was not known, nor what actions you might yourself be undertaking in this matter, and it was not known if, when, or how you might contact us. Now, late tonight, you have made your presence known, and I have received you."

"Speak," said Ortog.

"Please take a seat," said Iaachus.

"You are nervous?" said Ortog.

"Who would not be," said Iaachus, "in the presence of a lion?"

Ortog seated himself, grasping the arms of the chair, across the wide, lacquered table from the Arbiter. He looked about himself, and seemed ready to spring to his feet.

"You are safe," said Iaachus.

"Who knows what waits behind draperies, what might spring from floors?" said Ortog. "Who knows, in a house of this sort, a Telnarian palace, if walls might not open, disgorging shieldsmen?"

"We are quite alone, your majesty," said Iaachus.

"Speak," said Ortog.

"When Abrogastes, the Drisriak, called the Far-Grasper, your father, disappeared," said Iaachus, "it was speculated that he was betrayed into the hands of enemies by three men, Phidias, a freighter captain, and two of his subordinates, a Corelius and a Lysis, men who had enabled the raid by means of which he had carried off the princesses, Viviana and Alacida. We suspect, but do not know, that Abrogastes is now a prisoner of Sidonicus, the exarch of Telnar, that because of the dangers he posed to the ambitions and policies of the exarch. It is also speculated that he may still be alive, as, presumably, he would be of more value alive than dead, as, say, a hostage, a possible object of negotiation, a leader who, suitably persuaded, might have considerable influence amongst the Aatii, and such."

"If he were killed," said Ortog, "a thousand ships would fly, a hundred imperial worlds would burn."

"His location is unknown," said Iaachus. "The emperor hoped to locate him by means of one or more of the traitors, possibly still in Telnar. The only clue, if one may dignify it so, had to do with the attempted murder of a slave, one dangerous to their interests, one purchased on Varl Street. Perhaps, then, Phidias, and his cohorts, might be in the Varl district. A popular, local rendezvous in the area was a restaurant and brothel associated with the slaving house from which the slave had been purchased. The slave was placed in this establishment, in the guise of a brothel slave. She succeeded in identifying the traitors."

"Excellent!" cried Ortog, leaping to his feet, his eyes blazing, striking the table with a massive fist.

"Phidias was killed," said Iaachus. "Corelius and Lysis, possibly uneasy, possibly alarmed by the absence of their fellow conspirator, fled, but were soon taken into custody."

"Good!" said Ortog. "Let fire, the pincers and irons, the blades and tongs, the steel splinters, the scalding fluids be applied!"

"The two were incarcerated separately, unable to communicate," said Iaachus. "Each, individually, was assured that he had been implicated by, and betrayed by, Phidias, in return for his own life."

"They rushed then, in resentment and terror, to save themselves, to cooperate, to ingratiate themselves with their captors, to reveal the location of my father," said Ortog.

"The ruse failed," said Iaachus, "perhaps in virtue of comradery, each refusing to believe that Phidias would betray them, or perhaps because they suspected Phidias was dead, as he had failed to rejoin them."

"So torture, swift and severe!" said Ortog.

"I proceed," said Iaachus. "Each, again, each again unknown to the other, was dealt with. Each was confronted with the prospect of pain. Lysis, perhaps in greater fear of speaking than of not speaking, resolved to resist. Corelius, on the other hand, at the sight of the irons and tongs, the glowing forge, shuddering, spoke quickly, clearly, and abundantly."

"Then my father is free!" exclaimed Ortog.

"Men hurried to the designated place, a small, dismal warehouse on the docks of the Turning Serpent. We found chains, signs of occupancy, a dead guard, his neck broken, but not your father. He had been removed."

"How could it be?" asked Ortog.

"Your father had doubtless been moved at least as soon as it was realized that Corelius and Lysis had been taken into custody. Indeed, the orders pertinent to his removal might have been issued as soon as it was realized they had been recognized at the Varl-Street Palace of Pleasure."

"By Kragon, god of war!" cried Ortog, clenching his fist.

"There had clearly been a struggle," said Iaachus. "A guard had been killed."

"To any hall," said Ortog, "there is always more than one trail."

"Doubtless," said Iaachus.

"Interrogate the prisoners," said Ortog. "Learn, by one means or another, who gives them fee. That will lead us to my father."

"It may be true," said Iaachus, "that there is always more than one trail to a hall, but it is no less true that many trails do not lead to any hall. It seems that Corelius and Lysis were originally approached by unidentified, masked agents, and had, throughout the whole business, the intrigue and betrayal, dealings only with such agents. In short, neither, even if they wished to do so, could lead us to their mysterious, concealed principal."

"But you suspect?" said Ortog.

"Certainly," said Iaachus. "The principal is almost assuredly Sidonicus, the exarch of Telnar."

"Or another," said Ortog.

"Another?" said Iaachus.

"Ingeld," said Ortog, "who covets the high seat of the Drisriaks."

"Perhaps both," said Iaachus.

"There is another," said Iaachus, "Hrothgar."

"Hrothgar sees only what is there to see," said Ortog. "He does not see what is not there to see."

"Corelius and Lysis have been released," said Iaachus.

"Released?" said Ortog, incredulously. "Not slain by torture?"

"No," said Iaachus.

"What madness is that?" asked Ortog.

"Corelius begged to be kept in prison," said Iaachus. "He had to be whipped into the street."

"You think, released, they will somehow lead us to my father?" asked Ortog.

"No," said Iaachus. "Your father has been moved. They will now have no better idea of his whereabouts than we."

"Why release them?" asked Ortog.

"One of them revealed the location where Abrogastes was being held. Their principal will not know which. Both will deny they did so."

"But why release them?" pressed Ortog.

"That they will be sought," said Iaachus. "And that we may then seek the seekers."

"Why would they be sought?" asked Ortog.

"To be killed, of course," said Iaachus.

CHAPTER TWENTY-TWO

"Your majesty," said Iaachus, "you recall your interest in the palace library, which I found surprising?"

"Surely," said Otto.

"I have had clerks address themselves to your inquiry, an examination of the shelves, correlated with the inventory lists."

"With what result?" asked Otto.

"Several volumes are missing, as you surmised," said Iaachus.

"I suspected it would be so," said Otto.

"The library is commonly closed, sealed," said Iaachus. "There is little call for its volumes."

"That is my understanding," said Otto.

"We do not even maintain an imperial librarian," said Iaachus.

"Why not?" asked Otto.

"There is no need to do so," said Iaachus, "as the library is unused; indeed, it is commonly sealed, its keys housed with dozens of other similarly sealed chambers, forgotten, neglected, and ignored."

"So many?" said Otto.

"Yes," said Iaachus.

"Do you not find this of interest?" asked Otto.

"The palace," said Iaachus, "is a labyrinth, old, much of it formed long ago, by different generations, with different things in mind. Scarcely a third of it is used. There is little call to inquire into obscure rooms cluttered with cabinets of relics, with crates of brittle, yellow records, with boxes of dusty, unread volumes."

"But the library itself is large, and well-furnished?" asked Otto.

"It is high-ceilinged, spacious, and impressive," said Iaachus.

"You have been there?" asked Otto.

"Twice," said Iaachus.

"You said some volumes are missing," said Otto.

"As you speculated," said Iaachus.

"By whom were they withdrawn?" asked Otto. "Surely records are kept of such things."

"There is no record of usage," said Iaachus.

"Yet volumes are missing," said Otto.

"Stolen," said Iaachus.

"Books?" asked Otto.

"Who is to account for thieves?" asked Iaachus. "Some steal jewels and gold, some steal horses and cattle, some steal women, others boots and hose, others *darins*, others, I suppose, books."

"To sell them?" said Otto.

"Presumably," said Iaachus. "Why else?"

"It would be a bold thief, would it not," asked Otto, "to practice his trade within the precincts of a palace?"

"Or a foolish one," said Iaachus.

"Perhaps," said Otto.

"What, if I may ask," said Iaachus, "aroused your curiosity in this matter?"

"Nothing," said Otto.

"The matter of a handful of books missing from shelves seems to me of little interest," said Iaachus. "It is peculiar, perhaps even annoying, but it is also trivial. Matters of state press. It is scarcely worth the attention of the emperor."

"Who has access to the library?" asked Otto.

"Among others, yourself," said Iaachus.

"Do you think I am responsible for the disappearance of the missing books?" asked Otto.

"I do not know," said Iaachus. "But, were it the case, it might explain much. Why else would you initiate so anomalous an inquiry, seemingly so uncalled for and pointless, unless you knew what would be its outcome?"

"I did not know its outcome," said Otto.

"Then, why?" asked Iaachus.

"A whim, a caprice, a suspicion I have long entertained," said Otto.

"You did not remove the books, for some reason?" asked Iaachus.

"I cannot read," said Otto.

"And, I take it," said Iaachus, "you are not secretly peddling unwanted tomes in the street, pushing a cart, crying out, begging for a quarter *darin*, or so?"

"No," smiled Otto.

"Imperial matters press," said Iaachus. "May I speak of them?"

"Of course," said Otto.

"You recall, of course," said Iaachus, "that the exarch has been given access to the palace, over the past months, to instruct the empress mother in his particular faith."

"Yes," said Otto. "You argued for such a permission."

"And for a reason," said Iaachus.

"It seems to me dangerous," said Otto.

"But a danger which, if my plan is successful, will turn the danger onto the exarch himself."

"Does the empress mother continue, from time to time, to receive mysterious custards in her quarters, which she sees as miracles, celebrating her continuing progress in Floonian studies?" asked Otto.

"Yes," said Iaachus.

"And what does Sidonicus make of this?" asked Otto.

"He spreads ambiguity about himself, like the petals of flowers," said Iaachus. "He is baffled, but he wavers between encouraging the empress mother to accept the custards as miracles, which she is sure they are, to further ensnare her in his web of belief, and cautioning her not to be disappointed, should their appearance turn out to have a more prosaic explanation. Too, interestingly, he seems terrified that the mysterious custards may actually be miraculous in nature, as that suggests that his faith might be true, rather than what he takes it to be, a well-contrived, profitable fraud. No wonder he is uneasy. Could he, in trying to lie, have unwittingly, by fearful accident, a terrifying coincidence, told the truth? How would the truth look upon its having been presented as a lie? Might not an actual god, *Karch* or another, be insulted if it found that it had been treated as a fabrication or invention? Might it not seek vengeance? Similarly, the last thing a fellow who pretends to raise ghosts wants to show up is an actual ghost."

"I gather," said Otto, "that the exarch's instruction of the empress mother is nearly complete."

"Yes," said Iaachus. "I think she is soon to be initiated into the rites of Floonianism."

"There is a ceremony involved?" asked Otto.

"Yes," said Iaachus. "It involves being smudged with a certain oil, allegedly extracted from one pool or another on Zirus."

"Interesting," said Otto.

"There is no mention of this sort of thing in the earliest texts of Floonianism," said Iaachus. "But new texts, as needed, seem to be discovered. Similarly, the earliest texts of Floonianism suggest that the "sitting at the table of *Karch*" is a lovely metaphor for love, contentment, and serenity, and has nothing to do with survival after death, going somewhere, avoiding work, enjoying mysterious banquets, and so on. Similarly, the *koos* seems to be life or consciousness itself, and, given Floon's celebration of life in general, he seemed to believe that all living things, including bushes and trees, have *koos*, or a *koos*."

"That is very different from the Floonianism of the exarch, as I understand it," said Otto.

"Quite different," said Iaachus. "What seems to be the original or primitive Floonianism is generally accounted blasphemous, even heretical, in several of the current versions of Floonianism."

"Which versions also regard one another as mistaken, blasphemous, heretical, or such?" said Otto.

"I gather it is that way," said Iaachus. "I, personally, know little about it."

"Yet, it seems," said Otto, "from your foregoing remarks, that you have made some inquiries into such matters."

"I have looked into them, a little," said Iaachus.

"Insofar as they might be relevant to the interests of the empire?" asked Otto.

"At least," said Iaachus.

"And amongst such matters," said Otto, "are doubtless certain doctrinal matters."

"In particular," said Iaachus.

"And might these have some relevance to your plan?" asked Otto.

"Possibly," said Iaachus.

"But you wish to speak to me, do you not," said Otto, "of matters dealing with the exarch?"

"Yes," said Iaachus. "The exarch wishes to have the smudging ceremony of the empress mother take place publicly, with suitable ostentation and pageantry, accompanied by harps, trumpets, and choirs of rejoicing ministrants."

"Do you think this wise?" asked Otto. "To allow the empress mother out of the palace?"

"It is in accordance with my plan," said Iaachus. "Fear neither that harm will come to her nor that she shall escape. Guards will both protect her and see to it that she is returned safely to the palace."

"You wish her to appear in public, healthy and unharmed, to dispel rumors that she has been done away with in the palace, and the body somehow disposed of, perhaps in a *carnarium*?" asked Otto.

"That is a part of my plan," said Iaachus, "but a minor part."

"What of Aesilesius?" asked Otto.

"He must remain in the palace," said Iaachus. "His appearance in public would be most unfortunate. It would come as a dreadful shock to many, a repulsive and shameful revelation, an offense and reproach to the empire. Little is known of him. Few have seen him firsthand. Much has been concealed. Consider the dismay ensuing if all Telnar were to see their former beloved emperor as what he is, a retarded child in a young man's body, his eyes unfocused, his voice squeaking and unintelligible, his frame shaking, his head lolling about, his chin streaked with spittle, his hands clutching a toy to his bosom. What if he were to see an insect, a fly about his head or a crawling beetle by his foot, and he became hysterical, rolling about, screaming in terror?"

"To be sure," said Otto, "that would detract from the ceremony of holy smudging."

"The exarch requests a meeting with you, tomorrow," said Iaachus.

"So soon?" asked Otto.

"Yes," said Iaachus. "At this meeting he will request your permission for the empress mother's public smudging ceremony. I advise that it be granted."

"I take it that it would be quite a triumph for the exarch to initiate the empress mother publicly, before all the empire, so to speak, into his particular version of Floonianism," said Otto.

"It would be an example to millions, an inestimable coup," said Iaachus, "one suggesting not only an imperial endorsement of Floonianism, but of his particular stripe of Floonianism."

"Surely this is not in the best interest of the empire, of harmony, peace, and tolerance," said Otto.

"Permit the exarch to proceed," said Iaachus, "with the permission of the throne, if not its blessing."

"Tomorrow seems very soon," said Otto.

"The exarch," said Iaachus, "wishes the ceremony to take place very soon, within the next few days."

"But surely," said Otto, "arranging such a ceremony, with all its details, would require weeks of planning."

"The ceremony is already planned," said Iaachus. "It has been planned, for weeks."

"The exarch was then confident that my permission would be obtained," said Otto.

"Yes," said Iaachus. "I assured him of that."

"I see," said Otto.

"All is in accord with my plan," said Iaachus.

"I still do not understand the haste of the exarch," said Otto.

"It is not hard to understand," said Iaachus. "He wishes to make certain that the ceremony takes place before the meeting of the senate, that over which you are to preside, or that in which you are at least to be in attendance."

"Why?" asked Otto. "What difference could it make?"

"The successful completion of the ceremony is important to the ambitions and plans of the exarch," said Iaachus, "extremely important. He is zealous that it take place, as intended, that there be no postponement or flaw."

"So?" asked Otto.

"Well," said Iaachus, "after the meeting of the senate, it is possible that the ceremony might not take place. It might be adamantly opposed; it might be strictly forbidden."

"I see," said Otto.

"After the meeting of the senate," said Iaachus, "who knows who will be on the throne?"

"I see," said Otto.

"We discussed this earlier," said Iaachus.

"I remember," said Otto.

CHAPTER TWENTY-THREE

"Have we been gathered here for this?" wept Flora.

"It pleases me," said Otto.

"No, I beg of you!" wept Flora.

"Shackle her," said Otto.

The metal clasp was put about her ankle, and snapped shut. Its chain went to the ring at the foot of the emperor's throne.

"But Renata and I were women of the empire," wept Flora.

"Women of the empire are often made slaves by those whom you call barbarians," said Otto.

"You are a barbarian!" cried Flora.

"They make excellent slaves," said Otto, "their small, silken, well-formed slave bodies, suitable for the pleasuring of masters."

"Barbarian! Barbarian!" said Flora.

"I am king of the Otungen," said Otto.

"Be merciful," begged Flora. "Have mercy on us. This is not the high seat in some rude hall, where none but fur-clad marauders are about, ignorant and lustful, singing, drunk at the tables, shouting, casting meat to their hounds, swilling their spiced *bror*. This is the imperial palace in Telnar. *Civilitas*, Master, I beg of you, *civilitas!*"

"Renata is silent," said Otto. "She curls nicely in her place. Emulate her."

"What if anyone should see?" asked Flora. "What would they think?"

"Are you concerned for your modesty?" asked Otto.

"I am not permitted modesty," said Flora.

"Do not forget it," said Otto.

Flora was chained by the right ankle, and was on the emperor's left, as he would look forward. Renata, on his other side, was chained by the left ankle.

"Remember our background, our antecedents," said Flora, plaintively.

"You served well, last night," said Otto, "at the foot of the imperial couch."

"That was different," said Flora.

"It will do those of Telnar good to see former aristocrat women of the empire, insufferable and pretentious, reduced to helpless, meaningless slaves," said Otto. "Perhaps it will give some fellows of the empire some ideas as to what such lofty creatures, given their rightful deserts, might be good for."

"*Civilitas!*" wept Flora.

"*Barbaritas,*" said Otto.

As slaves are a form of wealth, and wealth is often displayed, for one reason or another, the display of slaves is common in many cultures. To be sure, Flora was undoubtedly correct, noting, in effect, that the introduction of this practice in the imperial palace in Telnar represented something of an innovation, one of which it seems she disapproved, at least at the time. It should also be noted that Flora and Renata were not the only displayed forms of wealth placed about the throne that afternoon, nor, reckoned in *darins*, the most valuable. A number of gold coins lay across a stair, seemingly escaped from a bag of such coins, apparently left carelessly unlaced, on a higher stair. A number of silver and gold vessels were strewn about. Bolts of precious cloth were partly opened. They lay upon ornate, intricately woven rugs from Beyira II. There were several vases, red-figured and black-figured, from Naxos. A basket of pearls, white and black, lay on the third stair, to the side, from some gulf, as though it might be scarcely worth noticing, while, at the same time, placed as it was, it could scarcely help but be noticed. Various seeds, many of state-protected varieties, were in yellow envelopes, bearing the seal and ribbon of the Orchid House, on Inez IV. Illicit dealings in such seeds is a capital offense. Wines, too, rare and expensive, were in evidence, many from the cellars of the palace itself. To be sure, prominent in this plethora of treasures, seemingly casually, but actually artfully arranged, were two slaves. These were doubtless far from the most expensive items in this display of wealth, distributed about the throne, but, from the point of view of the average male, they were likely to seem of special interest. Indeed, few things are likely to be regarded as of greater interest about a throne than a lovely, stripped, chained slave, fastened to its foot. It is not merely that this is aesthetically rewarding, but it is stimulating, as well, with its aspect of biological propriety.

"Greetings, noble Rurik," said Otto, from the throne, welcoming the Tenth Consul of Larial VII, who entered the throne room from a side entrance. A leash was looped about his left wrist, which led up to the leash collar of the briefly tunicked, blue-eyed, blond-haired slave, Cornhair. Animals are often kept on leashes, and slaves, as pleasure animals, as would be expected, are no exception. As men are fond of displaying their possessions, it is not unusual to see one walking about, accompanied by a well-groomed dog or slave on its leash. Rurik unwrapped the leash from his wrist, and indicated that the slave should kneel to the side, and he then bent down and tied her hands together before her body with the leash.

"Please forgive this late notice, drawing you from the undoubted pleasures of the Farnichi enclave," said Otto, "but matters of state loom."

"Pleasures may be obtained anywhere," said Rurik, "at one's convenience."

"I wish you to be present," said Otto. "Matters of import are afoot."

"I expect, too," said Rurik, "it will not hurt for one in the livery of the Farnichi to be in evidence."

"And prominently," said Otto.

"This has to do with an audience?" said Rurik.

"Very much so," said Otto.

As they spoke, and the hour of the audience drew near, several others filed into the throne room, witnesses, officers, guardsmen, various servitors, and four clerks, to record the proceedings.

"The trustees of the imperial seal," announced a servitor.

Following on this announcement, entering through a different entrance, came Julian, of the Aureliani, Tuvo Ausonius, formerly a high civil servant on Miton, and Iaachus, the palace's Arbiter of Protocol. Tuvo Ausonius was accompanied by a dark-haired slave, Sesella, and Julian by a blue-eyed slave with long, braided, blond hair, Gerune. Julian and Tuvo then took their places, to the right of the throne. Sesella knelt beside Tuvo, and pressed her cheek against his thigh, but was brushed away. Gerune knelt behind Julian, on his left. Both slaves, Sesella and Gerune, were tunicked. Long ago, slaves in the imperial palaces, that in Telnar, as well as others, summer palaces, for example, were commonly clad in long, discreet gowns, though their arms were bared. With the accession of Ottonius, the First, however, a more familiar, and revealing, garb, one more typical of female slaves, was enjoined, save for certain occasions where it might be deemed less appropriate, as, for example, at formal state banquets.

"Friend Iaachus, dear Arbiter," said Otto, "welcome."

"Your majesty," said Iaachus, humbly.

"You are not accompanied by your lovely collar girl, the fair Elena," said Otto. "Perhaps she is being punished, for failing to obey a command instantly and perfectly?"

"No, your majesty," said Iaachus. "But I think, given the audience in prospect, it is better that she remain in my chambers, chained to my couch. I would not risk her smiling at an inopportune moment. To be sure, if she had not once done so, in the chambers of the empress mother, she might never have had my collar snapped about her throat, and that would have been a tragedy, indeed."

"There are many ways in which a woman may court the collar," said Otto. "Surely she knew the dangers of an indiscretion in the chambers of the empress mother, and yet the indiscretion occurred, seemingly inadvertently, seemingly accidentally, seemingly without thinking, but, I suspect, there was thinking, a secret, unrecognized thinking, hiding in her heart, and, of course, you were present."

"Rather than have her slain on the command of the empress mother, I requested that she be given to me as a slave," said Iaachus, "to which request the outraged empress mother, delighted, seeing in this a fitting vengeance on an errant lady-in-waiting, acceded."

"And thus," said Otto, "the girl obtains both the collar, for which she as a female yearns, and the master of her dreams."

"I would not trade her for a thousand gold pieces," said Iaachus.

"But yet you keep her under discipline," said Otto.

"Under the strictest of discipline," said Iaachus. "Under discipline she juices, thrives, and begs."

"Excellent," said Otto.

"She knows she is helpless, and a slave, that she is owned, and must obey. She wants it so. She would have it no other way. She is a slave. It is what she is, and wants to be."

"She has learned that she is a female," said Otto.

"And rejoices in her sex," said Iaachus.

"Please approach, noble Arbiter," said Otto, "and stand near the throne. I may have need of your counsel."

"Your majesty," called a servitor, at the far end of the long, red carpet leading from the state portal to the stepped dais on which the throne was mounted, "His excellency, the noble, glorious, humble Sidonicus, the exalted exarch of Telnar!"

Otto lifted his hand, that the exarch might approach.

The large figure of the exarch, with small steps, its paunch swinging, robed in exarchical purple, the small, gold replica of a burning rack slung about his neck, on its gold chain, approached, something like a third of the way down the long carpet and then halted.

Otto turned to Iaachus. "What is wrong?" asked Otto.

"He wishes to be met," whispered Iaachus, standing near the throne.

"More than half way?" asked Otto.

"It has to do with his views on the relationship of the temple and the empire," said Iaachus.

"He would have, too, the emperor descend from the throne, and welcome him?" asked Otto.

"Yes," said Iaachus.

"I see," said Otto. "And would he have me take him by the hand, and lead him forward?"

"Doubtless," said Iaachus. "Indeed, I think he is disappointed. I think he expected to have a second throne on the dais, perhaps furnished with a higher cushion, that he might, if only slightly, look down upon you."

"Down on the emperor?" asked Otto.

"It has to do," said Iaachus, "with the deemed superiority of the *koos* to the body, the temple to the state, and so on."

"Surely he does not expect me to accept his pompous fraud at face value," said Otto.

"He is powerful," said Iaachus.

"I might descend from the throne, gladly," said Otto, "to greet a herdsman or mariner, a soldier or craftsman, to meet an Otung, even to welcome a Drisriak, but not one who would betray honor and unsettle an empire for gain."

"I fear," said Iaachus, "he will be offended."

"Let us struggle to restrain our grief, that he might be discomfited," said Otto.

"We shall strive to do so," said Iaachus. "Yet the moment is sensitive."

"He requires some excuse?" said Otto.

"I think he would find it difficult to move, otherwise," said Iaachus.

"Say to him," said Otto, "that he need not hesitate in terror, to approach the throne, but has our permission to do so."

"Is this wise?" asked Iaachus.

"If," said Otto, "he must, in his view, needs have the empress mother initiated publicly into his weird, inconsistent ideology before the senate meets, which is soon, he will be cooperative, however unwillingly."

"Perhaps," said Iaachus. "Too, we must be wary of establishing precedents."

Iaachus then raised his head, and faced the exarch. "Noble, esteemed, glorious one," he called out, reassuringly, "magnificent, humble, holy one, do not hesitate. Do not tremble. Do not be afraid. You may, however unworthy you may think yourself to be, or be, do not fear to approach the throne. Do not be intimidated by its awesomeness. You may approach. The emperor, in all understanding and benignity, welcomes you."

Furious, but smiling, Sidonicus waddled toward the throne until, suddenly, at the foot of the steps, as though he had first noticed something, he cried out in horror, recoiled, turned away, and threw the broad sleeve of his fine, thick purple robe high up about his face.

Once another ministrant, Fulvius, before Ingeld, on a hall's high seat, on Tenguthaxichai, had behaved similarly.

"How is this?" he cried, turned away, as though aghast.

"Is the exarch disturbed?" asked Otto.

"I fear so," said Iaachus.

"He seems distressed," said Otto.

"I believe him to be so, or seemingly so," said Iaachus.

"Why?" asked Otto.

"The ministrants of Floon," said Iaachus, "are sworn to a most abstemious asceticism. This attracts attention. It makes them seem different, and notable. They make a virtue of this oddity. They forswear the goods of this world in favor of the goods of another world, a postulated or conjectured world, a world somewhere else."

"Where is this other world?" asked Otto.

"That seems unclear," said Iaachus.

"And how does one get to this other world?" asked Otto.

"Most often, as I understand it," said Iaachus, "by being dead."

"Remarkable," said Otto.

"To be sure," said Iaachus, "the temples of Floon abound in wealth, and the renunciation of the goods of this world does not seem inimical to acquiring them. Indeed, it seems a promising way to do just that."

"Fascinating," said Otto.

"Floonian ministrants abhor the body, spend a good deal of time attempting to subdue it, eschew sex, applaud poverty, and eat and imbibe sparsely," said Iaachus.

"The exarch does not appear to be in need of nourishment," said Otto.

"In their most common ceremony," said Iaachus, "they nibble on a crust of bread and take a sip of water."

"May I ask," said Sidonicus, "of what the noble Arbiter and the emperor speak?"

"The emperor, a scion of Tangara, a far world, knows little of the holy mysteries of Floonianism," said Iaachus. "I was trying to explain to him, insofar as I might do so, what might seem to be the motivation of your apparent distress."

"You are gracious, as well as astute," said Sidonicus, not raising his head from the shelter of his cloaked arm.

"I fear we have been insensitive," said Otto. "Please forgive us. We thought that a lavish display of imperial wealth would delight you, as you are a citizen of the empire. Might it not hearten you and reassure you of the solvency of the state? Would you, as a citizen of the empire, not rejoice in such things? But it seems not. Shall I have the gold and silver, the pearls and rugs, the wine and flower seeds removed from the dais?"

"I assure you," said Sidonicus, "I can endure, however unwillingly, to look upon gold and flower seeds."

"It must be something else then," said Iaachus.

"Yes," said Sidonicus, bravely, his arm now lowered, but his body turned away, facing to his left.

"The women, the slaves?" asked Iaachus.

"Yes," said Sidonicus.

"Why?" asked Otto, of Iaachus.

"I think it is a Floonian thing," said Iaachus.

"Strange," said Otto. "What if they were dogs?"

"Dogs, as I understand it, would be all right," said Iaachus.

"But the slaves, too, are beasts," said Otto, "lovely, exciting beasts."

"Perhaps that is the problem," said Iaachus.

"I see no problem in that," said Otto. "If there is no difficulty in the bared beauty of a horse or dog, why should there be a problem with that of a slave? The difference is merely that that of a slave is far more stimulating. She is, in the eyes of many, a far more desirable property."

"Please," begged Sidonicus, looking away, "cover the slaves."

"It is true," said Iaachus to Otto, "it is difficult to resist and subdue the body in the presence of a collared, stripped, chained slave. Biology intervenes."

"Why would one wish to resist and subdue the body?" asked Otto. "That sounds stupid, if not unhealthy."

"It is a Floonian thing," said Iaachus.

"Is it in the teachings of Floon?" asked Otto.

"Not really," said Iaachus.

"How, then, can it be a Floonian thing?" asked Otto.

"I am not an authority on such matters," said Iaachus.

"Do you fear women, your gloriousness?" asked Otto.

"Intensely," said Sidonicus. "They are dangerous, beguiling creatures, provocative and enticing. They are temptresses. They lead one astray. They lure one from the paths of righteousness. They are seductive. They are treacherous, vain, selfish, and cruel. They are more dangerous than the soft-furred *vi-cat*."

"That is why they are well put in collars," said Otto. "They are very nice, once that is done."

"Please," begged Sidonicus. "I crave your indulgence. I am a guest in the palace."

"Very well," said Otto. "We anticipated that you might have reservations, given your renunciation of wealth and your esteeming of the joys of poverty, at the display of treasure, and so we were prepared to conceal the envelopes of flower seeds, and such."

"The slaves will do," said Sidonicus.

"Very well," said Otto. "Let the slaves be covered, in the manner previously arranged."

Two servitors then approached. One carried a large, soft, golden cloth, which he draped carefully, attractively about the shoulders of Renata. The other brought forth a small swatch of coarse, rudely woven cloth, of the sort peasants use to sack vegetables. This he flung against the body of Flora, and turned away. She snatched it to herself and tried to cover her body as best she could, which was very little. She clutched it to herself. Tears burned in her eyes. She looked up, from her knees, to Otto, to her right. "Master," she whispered, in piteous, vain protest.

"You are not now in the blue robes of the court," said Otto, "nor in the charming, if shocking, gown of white *corton*. Remember Terennia, and the arena."

"Master!" she wept.

"I always thought, even during the trial, that you would look well in a collar, naked, on your knees, chained," he said. "And I was not wrong."

"Mercy, Master," she wept.

"Remember Terennia," he said, "and the arena."

"I am now your slave!" she said.

"Until I will otherwise," he said, "until I give you away, or sell you."

"I will try to be a good slave," she said. "Please keep me, Master. I beg to be kept! Please, Master!"

"I will do as I please," said Otto.

"Yes, Master," she said, her knees closely pressed together, holding the bit of cloth to her bosom.

"You may look now," said Otto to Sidonicus.

Sidonicus turned about, and looked upon the slaves, with repugnance. "How disgusting they are," he said. "It is no wonder that *Karch* has denied them a *koos*."

"Why," asked Iaachus, "if women are indeed so dangerous, so desirable, tempting, exciting, alluring, seductive, and such, would a benign, well-intentioned *Karch*, a god recommending and approving abstinence and celibacy, invent them, produce them, bring them about, or such?"

"Deep and mysterious are the ways of *Karch*," intoned the exarch.

"It is beyond reason?" inquired Iaachus.

"Yes," said Sidonicus.

"That seems clear," said Iaachus.

"Your humble gloriousness," said Otto, "I am sure you did not request this audience, which we are delighted to grant, to ponder inscrutable mysteries."

"Indeed not," said Sidonicus. "As you are doubtless aware, Atalana, the empress mother, for some months now, has been receiving instruction in Floonianism."

"A particular version of Floonianism," said Iaachus.

"Fortunately, the correct version," said Sidonicus.

"Please, proceed," said Otto.

"She wishes, and I accede to her wishes," said Sidonicus, "that she be publicly initiated into the rites of Floon, that her conversion may set an example for millions."

"It would not do to have this quietly done in the privacy of the palace?" asked Iaachus.

"It makes no difference from my point of view, of course," said the exarch.

"Good," said Otto. "Then it will be done quietly, privately, in the palace."

Sidonicus turned white. "Who, then, would know of it?" he asked.

"An announcement could be made," said Otto.

"But it might not be believed," said Sidonicus.

"What difference would that make?" asked Otto.

"None, of course," said Sidonicus, "but should the wishes of the empress mother not be recognized, and honored?"

"Of course," said Otto. "Let the smudging with the holy oil from Zirus, from some sacred pool or another, if that is what is involved, be done in any manner, at any place and time, that the empress mother wishes."

"The emperor is gracious," said Sidonicus, relieved.

"Have you heard of the mystery of the miraculous custards?" asked Iaachus.

"I have heard something of it," said Sidonicus, warily.

"The empress mother sees this as testifying to, as proving, the truth of your particular version of Floonianism," said Iaachus.

"That is my understanding," said Sidonicus.

"Perhaps you care to comment?" said Iaachus.

"*Karch* is at liberty, if he wishes, of course, to materialize miraculous custards in the quarters of the empress mother," said Sidonicus. "Indeed, it would be thoughtful for him to do so. On the other hand, surprising, currently inexplicable events have no logical relation to doctrinal truth. For example, if the custards should eventually be shown to be nonmiraculous, abhor the thought, that would not affect the verities of Floonianism. Similarly, surprising, currently inexplicable events abound. Many religions, false religions, for example, are fraught with them. Thus, surprising, currently inexplicable events cannot be taken as relevant to doctrinal truth. Thousands of competitive, mutually inconsistent religions, with their surprising, currently inexplicable events, cannot all be true."

"You seem to regard such things with trepidation," said Iaachus.

"One cannot be too careful," said Sidonicus.

"One supposes not," said Iaachus.

"It will undoubtedly take some time to prepare for a public initiation of the empress mother into the rites of Floon," said Otto. "Let us schedule it for a month following the approaching sitting of the senate. Will that be enough time?"

"Fortunately, your majesty," said Sidonicus, "anticipating that our petition might be favorably received, the preparations are already in place. The ceremony may take place two days from now, in the square before the golden temple, home of the exarchical throne."

"One day before the next meeting of the senate," said Otto.

"As it happens," said Sidonicus.

"So the city may rejoice twice, on successive days," said Iaachus.

"Yes," said Sidonicus.

"A happy time," said Otto.

"I trust so," said Sidonicus.

"I do not expect to attend the smudging ceremony," said Otto. "Politics prescribes absence."

"I understand," said Sidonicus.

"There are many religions in the empire," said Iaachus. "It would not do for the emperor to attend, lest the state appear to favor a particular religion."

"Surely it would not be inappropriate for the state to favor the one, true religion," said Sidonicus. "Indeed, it seems it would have a moral obligation to do so, and, beyond that, to enforce it upon the reluctant or recalcitrant."

"Still," said Otto, apologetically.

"I understand," said Sidonicus.

"I will attend," said Iaachus. "In that way, a representative of the palace will be present."

"Splendid," said Sidonicus. "You will have a place of honor."

"Near the empress mother, I trust," said Iaachus.

"Certainly," said Sidonicus, "and the nearer and the more prominent the better."

"And I," said Otto, "may use the time to prepare for the meeting of the senate."

"It is my understanding," said Sidonicus, "that you are to be honored."

"That, too, is my understanding," said Otto.

"My heart leaps in gladness," said Sidonicus.

"Will you not attend the meeting?" asked Otto.

"It is not well for a ministrant of Floon to dabble in secular matters," said the exarch.

"Of course," said Otto.

"We are concerned only with matters of the *koos*," said Sidonicus.

"I understand," said Otto.

"I trust you will have a pleasant and rewarding time in the senate," said Sidonicus.

"Thank you," said Otto.

CHAPTER TWENTY-FOUR

"Step carefully, great lady," said Iaachus, gently steadying the empress mother, his hand on her elbow, as she climbed the carpeted stairs to the height of the ceremonial platform, yards above the street-level pavement of the great square before the golden temple, the seat of the high ministrant, the exarch, of Telnar. Sidonicus, in his purple vestments, was already waiting on the summit of the platform, the vial of sacred chrism, allegedly from a pool on Zirus, on a silked, white pedestal to his right. His hands were folded and his eyes were cast down, a fitting attitude, given the solemnity of the occasion. He had recently risen to his feet, with some difficulty, from the plush throne behind him on the platform.

"This is nonsense," snapped the empress mother, puffing a little, as she climbed. "I would have preferred to be smudged in my study, in the palace. The whole business could have been accomplished in a minute. How long does it take to push an oily thumb on someone's forehead and mumble some unintelligible phrase in archaic Telnarian?"

"I thought you insisted on this," said Iaachus.

"I hate crowds," she said. "They oppress me. I do not care to be gaped at, particularly by idiots who post themselves in the middle of the night, to have a coign of vantage by noon the next day. Wind disarranges my gown. Dust and cinders pelt me. Bright sunlight is not good for my complexion. My beauty does not appear to my advantage in bright light. Sick people may be near, breathing out their fogs of noxious vapors. The last time I left the palace I was ill for a month. See how the fools press, crowd, and shove against one another, their simple, rapt faces craned upward. In such a crowd, assassins may lurk. How else could a mediocrity obtain fame than burn a temple or slay one greater than himself? Does the scampering *filch* who slays a lion think it then itself becomes a lion, or equal to a lion?"

"You are safe, lady," said Iaachus. "Guards are about, many in livery, and many, less conspicuously, in nondescript garb."

"It is easy to spot the fools," said the empress mother. "They are looking at the crowd, instead of me."

At this point, the empress mother and Iaachus, having attained the height of the platform, waited in place, as prescribed, while the exarch, some yards away, across the platform, hands folded, and head down, continued his ruminations.

"This arrangement, then," said Iaachus, "the music, the parades, the marches, the banners, the singing, the perfume, the large, draped platform, the location, the flowers, and choirs, the thousands of garlands, and ribbons, were not your demand?"

"No," said Atalana, the empress mother.

"The exarch, in imperial audience," said Iaachus, "assured us it was your wish."

"The exarch is a fat liar," said the empress mother.

"Your public smudging," said Iaachus, "is supposed to convince millions of others to be smudged."

"That is stupid," said Atalana. "What difference would it make? Can they not make up their own minds?"

"But you have received instruction in Floonianism, from the exarch himself," said Iaachus.

"One appreciates visitors," said the empress mother. "I have had few enough since that Otung *arn* bear, abetted by traitors, such as you, pounced on the throne. The exarch's unintelligible babble is amusing. One enjoys listening."

"But surely you are going through with this," said Iaachus.

"Of course," said the empress mother. "How else can I continue to receive miraculous custards?"

"Are you serious?" asked Iaachus.

"Sidonicus may be a pompous fool, with his pretentious gibberish," said the empress mother, "but a custard is a custard."

"I do not think I understand," said Iaachus.

"There is no arguing with custards," said the empress mother. "There must be something to the god, *Karch*, if he can produce miraculous custards."

"The kitchen could supply you with custards," said Iaachus. "You need only ask."

"Of course," said the empress mother, "but they would not be miraculous custards."

"I suppose not," granted Iaachus.

"Miraculous custards are special," said the empress mother.

"I suspect so," said Iaachus.

"I want you to know, dear Iaachus," said the empress mother, "though you are a despicable traitor, I have always been fond of you, and remain so. I suppose that is so because we are both wicked and devious."

"Oh?" said Iaachus.

"Do not pretend modesty," said the empress mother. "Also, I am grateful to you that I am still alive. Statecraft would obviously recommend my disappearance."

"The Otungen, as I understand it," said Iaachus, "do not kill women."

"I suppose they do something else with them," said the empress mother.

"Possibly," said Iaachus.

"And," said the empress mother, "I gather poor Aesilesius lives, as well."

"He is in good health," said Iaachus. "The emperor sees that he is provided with toys."

"Aesilesius is not feared," said the empress mother.

"Scarcely," said Iaachus.

"That," said Atalana, "through years of intrigue, has always been his protection."

"You ruled through him," said Iaachus.

"With your help," said the empress mother.

"I am a humble servitor," said Iaachus. "I have tried to be of assistance."

Then, from across the carpeted platform, flanked by ministrants, chief among them, Fulvius, whose raiment was only somewhat less purple than that of the exarch himself, Sidonicus looked up, piously, toward the sky, and spread his hands out, widely, as though considering something which might be paying attention to him, from amongst the clouds. At the same time, given the signal of a banner bearing the image of a burning rack, raised on the roof of the temple, a number of choirs of ministrants broke into song, one on the large platform itself, one, unseen, on the roof of the golden temple, and others here and there, in raised, fenced enclaves, about the vast, crowded square, and some, also in raised, fenced enclaves, even down the adjoining, crowded streets. At

the same time, a number of other ministrants, near Sidonicus and
Fulvius, began to swing censers about, until his portion of the
platform was enveloped in a fog of incense.

"I wish they would get on with this," said Atalana.

"You should look humble and reverent," said Iaachus.

"That is incompatible with my station," she said. "I am the
empress mother."

After a time, the choirs, at another signal, it sped from the roof
of the temple, were silent.

A hush fell over the crowd.

All eyes, at least those suitably positioned, were then on
Sidonicus.

"Oh, Mighty *Karch*," cried Sidonicus, continuing to look upward, a direction as good as any one supposes, "attend to your
humble, unworthy devotee, Sidonicus of Telnar, supreme ministrant, blessed beyond blessings, holiest of men, exarch of the
golden temple. We thank you for your mercies and blessings. We
thank you for the illuminations of the holy prophet, Floon, identical with you, though different. We thank you for your table and
the goods heaped thereon. We thank you, too, for the oil pools
of Zirus, from which comes the sacred chrism by means of which
we set apart one man from another, the clean from the unclean,
the friend from the stranger, the true from the false, the right
from the wrong, the good from the evil. We are now met here,
before the golden temple, in the presence of thousands, to in-
duct within the fold of Floon, and that of *Karch*, who are the same
and yet different, a penitent and supplicating daughter, ignoble
and ignorant, who, however unworthy, petitions admission into
the fellowship of the one true faith, the brotherhood of Floon and
Karch, who are the same and yet different."

"What is he talking about?" asked Atalana. "Who is this penitent and supplicating, ignoble and ignorant daughter?"

"I think it is supposed to be you," said Iaachus.

"I?" said the empress mother.

"I fear so," said Iaachus.

At this point, like a benign cloud of purple, the ponderous
figure of the exarch, flanked by two ministrants, swinging censers on golden chains, approached. This group was followed by
another ministrant, holding the vial of sacred oil, wrapped in a
white napkin, and he was followed by two short lines of ministrants, with folded hands.

"I do not like smelly things," said the empress mother. "Too, I trust that the smudge will be quickly wiped away, as I do not wish to be soiled any longer than is necessary."

"You should not speak so of holy incense or sacred chrism," whispered Iaachus.

"Who will tell the empress mother how to speak, or what to say?" asked Atalana.

"Not I, surely," said Iaachus.

"Greetings, noble daughter, on this blessed day," said Sidonicus.

"Greetings," said the empress mother. "I think I would like to have a word with you."

"In a moment," said Sidonicus. "Let us proceed with the ceremony."

"What is this business about an ignoble and ignorant daughter, and such?" asked the empress mother. "Who do you think you are talking about?"

"Do not concern yourself with formulaic phraseology," said Sidonicus. "Dismiss it."

"It is not important?" asked the empress mother. "It is meaningless?"

"Yes," said Sidonicus.

"Then why bother with it?" asked the empress mother.

"Please," said Sidonicus. "Let us proceed with the ceremony."

"Withdraw it," said Atalana, menacingly.

"It is withdrawn," said Sidonicus.

"Good," said the empress mother. "You may proceed."

"It is herewith certified," said Sidonicus, solemnly, "that our daughter, Atalana, having been fully instructed in the holy truths of Floonianism, accepts, and subscribes to, such holy truths, and, of her own free will, begs to be admitted into the fold of Floon and *Karch*, who are the same, and yet different."

"She is not begging," said Atalana. "The empress mother does not beg. She is willing to put up with one thing or another, if it seems appropriate. Perhaps *Karch* is somewhere, though it does not seem clear where. Too, it is hard to argue with a custard. A custard is, after all, a custard."

"'*Requests* to be admitted into the fold of Floon and *Karch*, who are the same and yet different'?" suggested Sidonicus.

"'*Agrees*'," said Atalana.

"Done," said Sidonicus, quickly holding out his hand, to the side. Instantly, the vial of oil, presumably extracted from a pool on Zirus, removed from its napkin, was placed in his hand by the ministrant who had been its custodian. Sidonicus lost no time in uncapping the vial, returning the cap, with a prayer, to the ministrant, applying the oil to his thumb, with another prayer, and handing the vial back, with another prayer, to its custodian, who then recapped it, and, with his own prayer, returned it to its napkin.

Sidonicus then lifted his oiled thumb.

"As I understand it," said Iaachus, "the empress mother has been instructed in Floonianism."

"Yes," said Sidonicus, clearly annoyed, his thumb poised.

"Fully?" asked Iaachus.

"Yes," said Sidonicus.

"I wonder if, inadvertently, one doctrine might not have been omitted," said Iaachus.

"That seems scarcely possible," said Sidonicus.

"A cardinal doctrine, not a little holy truth, but a big holy truth, indeed, a central holy truth, which might be of some interest to the empress mother?"

"Surely not," said Sidonicus.

"Surely you know the doctrine I mean," said Iaachus.

"I have no idea," said Sidonicus, turning red with rage, thumb in the air.

"That women have no *koos*," said Iaachus.

"What?" cried the empress mother.

"A minor doctrine," said Sidonicus, "scarcely worth noticing."

"I have no *koos*?" said the empress mother.

"Let us proceed with the ceremony," said Sidonicus.

"If I do not have a *koos*, you do not have a *koos* either!" said the empress mother to the exarch.

"I suspect you are right," said Iaachus.

"Why should I not have a *koos*, if you have a *koos*?" asked the empress mother.

"Most contemporary versions of Floonianism," said Iaachus, "with their praised and inculcated ascetic proclivities, do not think highly of women. They are regarded as distractions and temptations. Their existence is regarded as being inimical to the life of the *koos*. Their presence jeopardizes and endangers the *koos*. When they are about who can keep his mind on holy things?"

"Sexless women are acceptable," said Sidonicus, "though, to be sure, they have no *koos*."

"Why did you not explain this to me?" asked the empress mother.

"It slipped my mind," said Sidonicus, lowering his thumb.

"Let us proceed with the ceremony," said Fulvius, concernedly, coming to the side of Sidonicus.

"Women are seen as constituting traps, and pitfalls," said Iaachus. "They put the *koos* at risk. They scatter rocks on the road to holiness. They snare the unwary."

"Why, then, do they exist?" asked the empress mother.

"To bear males, and daughters, to give birth to males," said Iaachus.

"You seem to have inquired into theological matters," said Sidonicus to Iaachus.

"A little, here and there," said Iaachus.

"What has Floon to say of these things?" asked the empress mother.

"Contemporary Floonianism, as I understand it," said Iaachus, "has very little to do with Floon. The earliest texts suggest that Floon thought that everything alive had *koos* or a *koos*, and even some things that were not alive as we usually think of it, such as rocks and mountains."

"Such assertions must be interpreted, of course," said Sidonicus. "They must be understood correctly, as expounded by conclaves and councils."

"Holy truths do not come easily," said Iaachus. "They must be crafted with care."

"By Orak and Umba," cried the empress mother, "this is absurd, preposterous!"

"False gods!" cried Sidonicus, in horror.

"How did *Karch*, a minor god on a minor world, a minor god amongst many gods, a god little known and obscure, come to be the one and only god?" asked the empress mother.

"It was probably difficult," said Iaachus.

"What was the position of Floon on that question?" asked the empress mother.

"We do not know," said Iaachus. "Apparently he gave the matter little thought."

"I suppose it is to a religion's advantage to have its god be the one and only god," mused the empress mother.

"One would think so," said Iaachus, "politically, socially, and economically."

"Be careful that you do not tread on the shores of blasphemy," said Sidonicus.

"I tread where I please," said the empress mother. "I am the empress mother."

"Of course, great lady," said Sidonicus soothingly.

"One shore," said Iaachus, "may have many names."

"No *koos*, eh?" snapped the empress other.

"Be patient, great lady," said Sidonicus, "within weeks we could convene a new council."

"Take me home," said the empress mother.

"Guards!" called Iaachus. "Conduct the empress mother from the platform. See that she reaches the palace safely."

CHAPTER TWENTY-FIVE

"It is a bright and sunny day," said Iaachus.

"A splendid day for the senate to meet," said Otto.

"Auspicious," said Iaachus.

"Was it wise for you to accompany me to the meeting of the senate?" asked Otto.

"I thought it well to do so," said Iaachus.

"Where is our envoy to the senate, Titus Gelinus?" asked Otto.

"Inside, waiting," said Iaachus.

"Shall we enter?" asked Otto.

"Wait," said Iaachus. "We will be met, and conducted ceremonially up the steps, and within, by Clearchus Pyrides, the moderator of the senate. I see him now, descending the steps."

"Should it not be the *primarius*," asked Otto, the noble Timon Safarius Rhodius, of the Telnar Rhodii?"

"He is inside and will conduct us to our places of honor," said Iaachus. "Gelinus is already there, near our places of honor."

"And Orontius, the senate's envoy to the palace?" said Otto.

"Inside," said Iaachus, "with Gelinus."

"Your majesty, and esteemed Arbiter," said Clearchus Pyrides, "be welcomed. You do the senate honor."

"The senate does us honor," said Otto.

"One seldom sees the emperor in public," said Clearchus.

"Perhaps you should look more closely," said Otto.

"I do not understand," said the moderator, from Inez IV.

"It is nothing," said Otto.

Otto and Iaachus, well-robed, proceeding upward through a parted, respectful throng, climbed the broad, marble steps to the large, two-gated portal of the senate, following Clearchus Pyrides, moderator of the senate. Shortly thereafter, they reposed in two curule chairs, rather to the left of the portal as one would enter.

Titus Gelinus was seated nearby, and seemed agitated. He looked uneasily about. Orontius, on the other hand, the envoy of the senate to the palace, also seated nearby, seemed affable, and much at ease. He chatted in the direction of Gelinus, but to little effect, as the envoy of the palace to the senate seemed much distracted.

"How does the empress mother?" asked Otto of Iaachus.

"She is fatigued, but well," said Iaachus.

"Your plan worked splendidly," said Otto.

"It could hardly have failed," said Iaachus.

"The projected coup of Sidonicus, the initiation of the empress mother into the rites of Floon, that intended to impress millions, propagate his faith, suggest an imperial endorsement for his particular version of a particular religion, and produce an epidemic of converts," said Otto, "was a debacle."

"I posted several in the crowds and even in the nearby streets," said Iaachus, "to publicize the empress mother's dissatisfaction with the exarch, and at least one tenet of his faith."

"You are a cunning rascal," said Otto.

"The best sort of rascal," said Iaachus.

"I am grateful," said Otto. "The pretentious, subtle, bubbling poisons of Sidonicus constitute a terrible danger to the empire. They divide citizens from one another; they breed contempt, loathing, and hatred, and profit from the pain they cause and the harm they do; they sow guilt; they sicken minds; they subvert respect and peace; they tear apart the chords of harmony; they undermine law and threaten civil order."

"What evil would wear the cloak of evil?" asked Iaachus. "Evil prospers best when it wears the cloak of good."

"The exarch is not done," said Otto.

"Surely not," said Iaachus, "but the empress mother's public and patent refusal of initiation into his fellowship, particularly given the publicity leading up to the event and the prominence of its staging, dealt a grievous blow to at least one of his plans. His plot was foiled, and his ambitions thwarted. This contretemps should, if nothing less, considerably embarrass the exarch and, to some extent, reduce his prestige. Indeed, jokes are being told in the taverns."

"Doubtless a new council will be called," said Otto, "and it will be discovered that it was an indisputable article of faith, after all, all along, that women have a *koos*."

"Perhaps," said Iaachus. "It is hard to tell. The seductive and dangerous nature of women, their threat to the *koos*, and such, is stained deeply into the wool of Floonianism."

"I remember," said Otto, "that females, even female *vardas*, pigs, dogs, sheep, and such, were not allowed in the grounds of the *festung* of Sim Giadini. The brothers were horrified that such an intrusion might take place."

"The greatest political flaw of Floonianism," said Iaachus, "is its view of women."

"How is that?" asked Otto.

"Women raise and nurture the young, and form their basic views in the first crucial years, when the child is least critical and most impressionable. Later the children will not even remember how they came to be as they are, what was done to them. A religion is most vulnerable for its first generation, but if it survives the first generation, much may proceed apace. Values and views are put into the young for which, no matter how strange or improbable they may be, they will be willing to die. Fanaticisms fly at one another's throat. It is tragic. My greatest fear is that Floonianism will bring women into the fold of the *koos*, bestowing a *koos* upon them, appealing to them, courting and exalting them, making Floonianism a religion congenial to them, warm and comforting to them, making it, in effect, a religion which they think understands and treasures them. How better to secure a hold on future generations?"

"Interesting," said Otto.

"More is involved of course," said Iaachus. "Things proceed, as would be expected. Women, converted, now seek the higher life of the *koos*. They come to regard their body and its needs as troublesome impediments, to be overcome at best, or reluctantly yielded to, if one can do no better. So one is to be ashamed of one's body and its needs. Such things jeopardize and threaten the *koos*. One, too, is to be dismayed that one's beauty might stimulate male desire. How unfortunate! And how wicked are men, that they should be so stimulated! The world is mistaken. Nature is wrong. Let everyone feel guilty about everything. Let falsehood and stupidity reign. And one must strive to steel oneself against desire, so natural to a healthy body. One must regard it as regrettable, even dangerous. And so the animal is sickened and made miserable. And, should nature be acknowledged, guilt ensues, followed by sterner resolutions, and more sickness and more misery, and so it goes, over and over, and on and on."

"Surely there is profit in this for some," said Otto.

"One supposes so," said Iaachus.

"I suspect," said Otto, "given the politics involved, Sidonicus will summon a new council, which will decide to give a *koos* to women."

"Politics would surely recommend that," said Iaachus. "But I think there would be much opposition to that in much of Floonianism."

"I suspect so," said Otto. "I recall the *festung* of Sim Giadini."

"There might be divisions within councils, or even countercouncils," said
Iaachus.

"What then?" asked Otto.

"Then a new crop of orthodoxies and heresies bloom," said Iaachus, "each orthodoxy denouncing other orthodoxies as heresies, and so on, with all the predictable divisions, denunciations, and hatreds."

"And bloodshed?" said Otto.

"Presumably," said Iaachus.

"Titus Gelinus seems upset," said Otto.

"He advised strenuously against your attendance here, as I recall," said Iaachus.

"Yes," said Otto, "as did several others."

"That is my understanding," said Iaachus.

"Only you, as I recall, amongst advisers," said Otto, "were in favor of my attendance."

"I see your attendance as not only advisable, but politically imperative," said Iaachus.

"I noted, within your robes, as I brushed past you in leaving the palace," said Otto, "the handle of a dagger."

"As you move like a *vi-cat*," said Iaachus, "it was surprising to me that you were so clumsy."

"I trust that the blade, as was that of a dagger transmitted long ago to Tangara, was not coated with a thin, transparent layer of poison, such that the least scratch would, within a breath, prove lethal."

"Certainly not," said Iaachus. "I would not risk such a blade about my person. It is one thing to entrust such a blade to a dispensable assassin and quite another to carry it oneself."

"Do you notice anything unusual about the placement of our chairs?" asked Otto.

"Not really," said Iaachus.

"They are unobstructed," said Otto. "They repose near the open portal. They are to its left, as one would enter. In this way, we cannot see what might ascend the stairs, and, if it wished, swiftly cross the tiles between the portal and our position."

"It is from that direction then that the attack will come?" asked Iaachus.

"That seems likely," said Otto.

"I anticipate more than a single assassin," said Iaachus.

"There will be several," said Otto. "It would be foolish to entrust the matter to one blade."

"I wish we were clearer on matters," said Iaachus.

"We are clear enough," said Otto. "If the plot is well devised, and I assume it to be so, it has little choice but to proceed in a certain fashion."

"Not all senators are here as yet," said Iaachus, looking about.

"Put another way," said Otto, "not all places are yet filled."

"I do not think several assassins could force their way through the guards," said Iaachus.

"Perhaps they will not have to force their way," said Otto.

"The *primarius* approaches," whispered Iaachus.

"Your majesty," said Safarius, "the hour of meeting is upon us. I think it apt to begin."

"It seems several of your body are absent," said Iaachus.

"They are inadvertently delayed," said Safarius.

"Perhaps," said Iaachus, "they choose not to attend, this expressing a disinclination to support the current regime."

"Certainly not," said Safarius. "Transportation failed, hover- ers being ill-arranged, a confusion of scheduling. I have received word they will be here presently."

"Excellent," said Otto.

"Perhaps momentarily," said Safarius. He glanced to the wide portal, and then returned his attention to Otto. "As there are many honors to bestow on your majesty, and a number of speeches explaining and justifying these honors, which will take some time, I think it would be judicious to proceed, beginning with some minor business."

"By all means, do so," said Otto.

"Have you a quorum?" asked Iaachus.

"Yes, dear Arbiter," said Safarius.

"Barely," said Iaachus.

"Yes, barely," said Safarius. He then turned to Clearchus Pyrides, the moderator of the senate, seated somewhat below, at his table, and nodded.

Pyrides then lifted his small gavel, and stuck the shallow wooden plate before him, solemnly, three times. "The senate," he said, "is now in session."

CHAPTER TWENTY-SIX

"The house recognizes the noble Orontius, senator of the realm, envoy to the palace," said Pyrides.

Orontius then rose from his place.

"It is now, at long last, happily, other business done," said Orontius, "the time to engage upon the major business for which this meeting was called, that aspect of our meeting to which we have looked forward with such anticipation, our doing of honor to the friend of the poor, the defender of the needy, the dispenser of justice, the fountain of mercy, the righter of wrongs, the smoother of troubled waters, the shield and bulwark of the state, the occupant of the throne."

Polite applause greeted this announcement.

Also, unnoticed by Orontius, and, presumably, Clearchus Pyrides, there was a stirring behind them, in the tiers.

"Ho," said Orontius, looking forward, outward, toward the broad portal, "I see many of our missing senators have arrived, and are ascending the steps."

"Our back is covered, is it not?" asked Iaachus.

"Yes," said Otto, not turning about. "Changes have taken place in the tiers."

Crowded, now, in the portal, were several individuals, in the purple-trimmed robes of the senate.

"Welcome, noble colleagues," said Orontius. "You are just in time. We are just about to honor his noble majesty, our beloved Ottonius, the First."

"I trust you are ready," said Otto to Iaachus.

"I prefer the quiet of the palace," said Iaachus, slipping his right hand inside his robes.

"With your permission," said Orontius to Otto, politely, "we will proceed."

"Please do so," said Otto.

"The honor we have to bestow upon you," said Orontius, "is an unusual honor."

Otto looked up, to the level of the *primarius*, on which level Orontius had placed himself.

"Perhaps you are curious as to the nature of the honor," said Orontius.

"Perhaps," said Otto.

"It is the honor of death!" said Orontius.

There were gasps in the higher tiers, movements, a flurry of robes.

Otto rose to his feet, as did Iaachus, beside him.

"One may refuse honors," he said.

"You may not find it easy to avoid this honor," said Orontius.

"Surely," said Clearchus Pyrides, moderator of the senate, "blood is not to be spilled in this chamber!"

"Silence," said Orontius.

"This is the senate!" said Pyrides.

"Be silent!" said Orontius.

"You have called me the fountain of mercy," said Otto. "It is my observation that the merciful are seldom respected, are frequently betrayed, and seldom live long. Yet I am prepared to be merciful. If you disband and withdraw in peace, this shall be as if it had not occurred. I offer this concession in the interests of harmony, a condition which I would have obtain between the senate and the throne."

Orontius threw back his head, and laughed. Some of those crowded in the portal and, apparently, several behind them, on the broad marble stairs, laughed, as well.

"Do you truly think I fear a tardy gaggle of senators, amateurs in war, dilettantes in conspiracy?" asked Otto.

"We are not senators!" cried a burly fellow at the portal, flinging aside his senatorial robes, and brandishing a knife. "We are patriots, come to rescue the state, to extract it from the clutches of a barbarian usurper."

At the same time, those with the speaker cast aside their senatorial robes, as well, drawing and raising daggers.

"I am Otung," said Otto, "but I am also a citizen of the empire, given its foolish grant of universal citizenship, as much so as I take you to be."

"Death to the usurper!" cried a man, bravely, but he did not rush forward.

"My offer of amnesty will not be repeated," said Otto.

"Do not toy with us," laughed Orontius. "Your ruse, your pompous bluff, that of a desperate, terrified barbarian, is empty and transparent. It fails. It is propounded in vain."

"I would be clear on this," said Otto. "It is refused?"

"Do not joke with us," snarled Orontius.

"I take it that my offer is refused," said Otto.

"It is refused," said Orontius.

"As you will," said Otto.

"Behold, fellow patriots," called Orontius to the men crowded in the threshold of the senate, and even behind them, down the stairs, "the noble Iaachus, our esteemed Arbiter of Protocol, standing beside the usurper, has drawn a dagger!"

"He has, so he has!" cried one of the men at the portal. "Yes, yes," cried others.

"You are then with us!" cried Orontius, jubilantly. "We welcome you to our brotherhood of liberation. Let your blade strike the first blow! We extend to you that honor."

"I have served the empire for years," said Iaachus. "I will not betray it now. This blade is not formidable, and the arm which wields it is not strong, but it will defend to the death the empire I love."

"Strike!" cried Orontius.

"You are traitors!" said Iaachus.

"You may yet live," said Orontius. "We can use your position, support, influence, and cunning."

"No," said Iaachus.

"Strike, strike!" demanded Orontius.

"I will not strike my emperor," said Iaachus.

"Then," said Orontius, "you will die with him."

"What better place to die," said Iaachus, "than beside one's emperor, and one's friend?"

"He is a fool, to set himself amongst enemies," said Orontius.

"Perhaps," said Iaachus, "it is one way to discover one's enemies."

"I am not one," said Titus Gelinus, wrapping his cloak about his left arm and taking his place beside Otto and Iaachus.

"Welcome," said Otto.

"I am where I belong," said Titus Gelinus.

"Fools," said Orontius. He then looked scornfully away from Iaachus and Titus Gelinus, and, complacently and smugly, looked upon Otto, whom he then addressed.

"Perhaps you wonder," said Orontius, "how these patriots, more than a hundred of them, passed through the streets and, unquestioned and undetained, ascended the steps to this venerable chamber."

"I know how it is that you think they have done so," said Otto.

"Many senators are absent," said Orontius. "It was arranged so. These men then, in the garb of senators, and suitably credentialed, arrive, and are admitted to the senate chamber."

"And guards have now been dismissed?" asked Otto.

"On my authority," said Orontius.

"As they are no longer needed?" asked Otto.

"No, we do not need them," laughed Orontius, and mirth, as well, rippled amongst his cohorts.

"Do not shed blood in the senate!" begged Clearchus Pyrides, moderator of the senate.

"Do not presume to interfere, or you, too, shall die," said Orontius.

"It appears," said Otto, "the resolve of the senate is not unanimous."

"Run, flee for your lives!" cried Clearchus Pyrides.

"Beware that you do not decree your own death," warned Orontius.

"Run!" cried Pyrides.

"And where is there for him to run but to a hundred and more knives?" said Orontius.

"*Filchen!*" said Iaachus. "Traitors!"

"Run!" said Pyrides.

"I do not choose to do so," said Otto.

"We shall rush upon you," said Orontius, "and you, and those with you, will die of a thousand cuts, and we shall then hurry into the streets, displaying bloody knives, proclaiming the return of liberty."

"Shadows grow long," said Otto. "I request that you publicly name your principal."

"I decline to do so," said Orontius.

"I am sure he would approve your discretion," said Otto.

"What difference would it make now?" said Iaachus.

"None," said Orontius, "but an understanding is in place."

"Do you truly think," asked Otto, "that it was through clever deceit that your men, due to suitable robes and credentials, passed through the streets and came to this place?"

"Of course," said Orontius.

"They were permitted to do so," said Otto.

More than one of those crowded in the portal looked at one another, uneasily.

"Nonsense," said Orontius.

"And you believe the guards have been dismissed?"

"Certainly," said Orontius.

"I think you will find they have returned," said Otto.

Several of the poised assassins stirred, casting glances about, apprehensively.

"You will recall," said Otto, "the offer of amnesty was refused."

"He is trapped," said Orontius. "Be not deterred! Can you not see through such discourse, empty, futile words, babblings intended to unsettle you, to sway you from the firmness of your purpose?"

"Who will be the first to approach his emperor?" asked Otto.

"We shall attack at once, together, more than a hundred knives," said Orontius.

"Swarming, like *filchen*," said Iaachus, "tiny creatures, with the coward's courage, brave only in packs."

"There will be no defense," said Orontius.

Iaachus raised his knife. Titus Gelinus lifted his left arm, shielded in his wrapped robe.

Otto did not move. He stood quietly, regarding Orontius.

"Prepare to die!" screamed Orontius.

"Speak to your men," said Otto. "Advise them, rather, to do so."

"Attack, attack!" screamed Orontius, pointing to the three who stood by the two curule chairs.

"At them!" cried Otto, in a great, terrible voice, pointing to the crowded, mustered assassins.

At his cry, dozens of figures, shouting, uttering the mingled war cries of the Otungen, the Darisi, the Haakons, the Basungs, and the Wolfungs, the five tribes of the Vandalii, the Vandal nation, casting aside the robes of senators, clutching swords and axes, descended the tiers of the chamber.

"It is a slaughter!" said Iaachus.

"Amnesty was refused," said Otto.

"Desist, desist!" cried Clearchus Pyrides, from behind his table, his senatorial robes spattered with blood.

One of the would-be assassins, knife lifted, rushed toward Otto, but Otto, easily seizing up the heavy curule chair, with its thick, curved legs of *torodont* ivory, thrust a leg of the chair into the attacker's face, breaking through the skull, like a *varda* egg, inches back, into the attacker's head.

The knives of the assassins were poor matches for the swords and axes of their foes. Most of the assassins were cut down from behind, as they turned to run, but they were jammed in the portal of the chamber, and some were trampled, broken underfoot, necks and backs snapped, and others, rushing out, slashing about themselves against their fellows, to clear their way, reached the steps, only to be impaled on the spears of the waiting, returned guards.

"It was indeed a trap," said Titus Gelinus, his robe now loose, hanging from his left arm.

"Yes," said Otto, "mine, not theirs."

"Why did you not tell me?" asked Gelinus.

"Your agitation, your uneasiness, your fear," said Otto, "were useful. Such things assure an enemy that his plans are unknown. Had you been at ease or manifested confidence, the enemy might have suspected we had drawn plans against them."

"What of Iaachus?" asked Gelinus. "Was he informed?"

"It seemed to me," said Iaachus, "that it was necessary, for various reasons, appearance, and such, for the emperor to be on good terms, or thought to be on good terms, with the senate, and an occasion such as this fitted well into such a policy. Now any public suspicion or animosity will be directed toward the senate and not the palace. The senate will now be seen as hostile, if not literally treasonous. The emperor went more than half-way, and was rebuffed. He offered amity, even amnesty, to the senate and the senate rejected it. Today is a victory for the palace."

"Did you know of the emperor's provisions?" asked Gelinus.

"No," said Iaachus, "but I supposed there would be provisions."

"You seemed ready to die at his side," said Gelinus.

"I was alarmed," said Iaachus. "As things were going, seemingly far awry, I thought my confidence in the emperor had been misplaced, and that he, largely untutored in statecraft, had taken the senate's offer at face value, and, consequently, deplorably, was in mortal jeopardy."

"I trust your confidence was restored," said Otto.

"Fully," said Iaachus.

There were heard two screams, and two of the would-be assassins fell back amongst the tiers, tumbling back several levels.

Perhaps they had hoped to climb the stairs to one of the high windows, from which they might have cast themselves down to the street, to be sure, a fall quite likely to be fatal.

"The senate runs with blood," wept Clearchus Pyrides, moderator of the senate.

"No senator has died," said Otto. "Those present were ushered to the rear, higher on the tiers, and a great many it seems, presumably by design, were not present."

"There will be a stink, as of a slaughterhouse," said Pyrides.

"It was a slaughterhouse," said Iaachus.

"It was not a good laughing with steel," said Otto, regretfully.

"This is not the first time blood has been shed in this chamber," said Iaachus, "and I fear it will not be the last. The blades of ambition have sharp edges."

"It will take weeks to cleanse the chamber," said Pyrides.

Citherix and Vandar, Otungs, approached, thrusting a bound prisoner before them. They threw the prisoner to his knees before Otto. "This, my king," said Citherix, "is he whom you wished spared."

Orontius looked up, white-faced, from his knees.

"Unbind him," said Otto, "lift him up, straighten his robes."

Orontius then stood, unsteadily, before Otto.

"I pardon and free you," said Otto.

"I do not understand," said Orontius.

"Are my words not clear?" asked Otto.

"I alone am to be spared?" asked Orontius.

"Yes," said Otto.

"No, no!" said Orontius.

"I fear," said Otto, looking about, "there are no others to spare, even were I minded to do so."

"I do not understand," said Orontius.

"And you will continue to serve in the office of the senate's envoy to the palace, and you will receive certain well-publicized emoluments, villas, lands, and such."

"It will be thought I betrayed the plot," said Orontius.

"But we know that is not true, do we not?" asked Otto.

"They will not," said Orontius.

"Who?" asked Otto.

Terror came into the eyes of Orontius, and he turned about and bent quickly down, snatching up a fallen dagger from one of the assassins. He then threw himself violently on the dagger, its hilt braced on the tiles.

"He is dead," said Citherix, turning the body over, and rising to his feet.

"He feared to reveal his principal," said Titus Gelinus.

"Yet," said Otto, "I think there is little doubt as to who it might be."

"Have you noticed," said Iaachus, "that the noble Timon Safarius Rhodius, *primarius* of the senate, after seating us in our places of honor, seems to have left the chamber?"

"Yes," said Otto.

"Apparently he wished to dissociate himself from what was to ensue," said Iaachus, "if, perchance, things might unfold contrary to his expectation."

"Shrewd," said Gelinus.

"The office of the *primarius*," said Iaachus, "is an office not easily purchased. One does not expect it to be occupied by a dullard."

"Where one is not," said Otto, "is often as important as where one is."

"Now, the noble Orontius dead," said Gelinus, "we have no envoy from the senate to the palace."

"You will do very nicely," said Otto.

"It is impossible," said Gelinus. "I am the envoy of the palace to the senate."

"And now also the envoy of the senate to the palace," said Otto.

"That is a conflict of interest," said Gelinus.

"Not of my interest," said Otto.

"The senate is soiled," said Pyrides. "The tiles are channeled with blood. One cannot walk but on blood. The portal doors are streaked with red. The stoop is drenched. Blood, like rain, drains from step to step. Look at the bodies, heaped on one another. Consider the sopped, discarded robes. Who knew how much blood could be in a single body? The tiers, even the walls, are stained."

"You must fetch white sand, and rubbing stones, soap and water," said Otto. "Let the chamber be cleansed."

"We will begin tomorrow, men will be hired," said Pyrides.

"No," said Otto. "This work will be done by senators, those who were absent today."

"That is unthinkable," said Pyrides, aghast.

"Yet I have thought it," said Otto.

"What of the *primarius*?" asked Pyrides.

"Having been present, at least for a time, he is exempted, of course," said Otto. "Too, such char work, with brushes, on one's knees, little comports with the dignity of a *primarius*."

"How shall we dispose of the bodies?" asked Pyrides.

"Put them in carts, and deliver them to the exarch," said Otto.

"I do not understand," said Pyrides.

"He will understand," said Otto.

"He will never accept them," said Iaachus. "It would implicate him."

"Is it not incumbent upon him to accept them, in the name of Floon?" asked Otto. "Are they not to be burned or granted burial? Is this not common with a thousand religions? Too, the bodies could be despoiled, of clothing and coins, and such things be distributed to the poor."

"I think the exarch would willingly decline such good works," said Iaachus.

"Very well," said Otto. "Let the bodies be taken outside the walls."

"And cast into the *carnariums*?" asked Iaachus.

"That is the common fate for criminals, is it not?" asked Otto.

"Yes," said Iaachus.

"Then let it be done," said Otto.

"They claimed to be patriots," said Gelinus.

"That is common with criminals," said Otto.

CHAPTER TWENTY-SEVEN

"I heard what occurred in the senate four days ago," said Ortog.

"I would have preferred for the matter to have been handled more discreetly," said Otto, "but it is difficult to conceal broadcast carnage, the disposal of bodies, and such."

"Cart loads of bodies, straining mighty horses, were carried to the *carnariums*," said Ortog.

"I trust," said Otto, "the bodies were relieved of clothing and purses, and that such goods were distributed to the poor."

"Yes," said Ortog, "and many now think more kindly on the state. Indeed, there is an eagerness now in the city that more such miscreants be apprehended, that their goods might be similarly distributed."

"My friend, Titus Gelinus, our liaison with the senate," said Otto, "informs me that there was once a law to the effect that an informer, one who exposed a hitherto undetected miscreant, should the miscreant be convicted, was entitled to a share of the miscreant's confiscated wealth, as much as a half in some cases, but more commonly a tenth."

"Doubtless such an incentive inspired much zeal amongst the righteous," said Ortog.

"So much so, I am told," said Otto, "that the prisons were filled and the courts overwhelmed. Thousands of crimes were charged, mostly to well-to-do citizens, in the hope that something or other might be unearthed, and hundreds of thousands of extortions took place, given merely the threat of such a charge, to defend against which would entail considerable time and expense, not to mention the damage to one's character or reputation. On certain worlds, where Floonians, of one version or another, controlled the local governments, similar charges were made on the grounds of an alleged lack of orthodoxy or a secret espousing of heresy, charges against which, in any case, it would be difficult to defend oneself. Fortunes were occasionally made in such ways, either civilly or ecclesiastically. These arrangements also resulted in the frequent disappearance of informants, or suspected informants."

"Most gods," said Ortog, "seem little concerned with such matters."

"Would you be, if you were a god?" asked Otto.

"No," said Ortog. "Being a god would be quite enough, in itself."

"I would think so," said Otto.

"Gods are tolerant," said Ortog. "What do they care what humans think, or whether they are believed in or not? If they exist, they are presumably aware of this, and do not need reassurance. If they do not exist, the question does not come up."

"Ministrants are not always so tolerant," said Otto.

"Particularly those fellows who claim, rather arrogantly, it seems to me, and without proof, that their god is the only god," said Ortog.

"Doubtless that would make their god quite important," said Otto.

"More importantly," said Ortog, "it points all the religious gold in one direction and tries to make sure that it all ends up in one pot, their pot."

"Perhaps," said Otto.

"If one looks at things from a secular point of view," said Ortog, "many things otherwise obscure and inexplicable, controversies, claims, dogmas, creeds, orthodoxies, disputes, and such, suddenly become clear."

"Perhaps," said Otto. "But I prefer to leave such things primarily to Iaachus, my Arbiter of Protocol."

"I do not trust him," said Ortog.

"He would be pleased to hear it," said Otto. "He is a diplomat. He would be crushed if he thought he were trusted."

"I take it," said Ortog, "that the law of which you spoke, remunerating informers, and such, was abrogated."

"Yes," said Otto, "after only two years. It was incompatible with law and order, the very pretexts on which it had been brought about. It did away with trust, peace, and harmony. It divided the empire, and fostered hatred and fear. It put the empire itself in jeopardy."

"And it put those who had the power to make laws, the rich and powerful, the most in jeopardy," said Ortog.

"It seems so," said Otto.

"The relationships of gold to justice and right are intriguing," said Ortog.

"One fears they are relatives, sometimes even brothers," said Otto.

"Concerning gods, and such," said Ortog, "these things dividing men and threatening empires, how are such disputes to be resolved?"

"I do not know," said Otto. "I prefer rocks and trees, clouds and rain, even *vi-cats* and *arn* bears."

"Men are the most dangerous of animals," said Ortog, "more so than the *vi-cat* and *arn* bear."

"Too, no *vi-cat* or *arn* bear has ever killed for a meaningless idea," said Otto.

"It is easy to lie oneself into doing what one wishes," said Ortog.

"If such disputes were genuine," said Otto, "one supposes the gods would step in and decide them."

"Yet one does not hear from the gods," said Ortog.

"One supposes there is an explanation for that," said Otto.

"What could it be?" asked Ortog.

"One speculates," said Otto.

"How could such disputes be resolved?" asked Ortog.

"Apparently with hot irons and edged weapons, with confiscations, exiles, and murder fires," said Otto.

"The fellowship of such things with reason is obscure," said Ortog.

"Partisans decide what they will deem reason," said Otto.

"The attack of the self-styled patriots in the senate," said Ortog, "was surely at the instigation of the exarch of Telnar."

"One supposes so," said Otto.

"You should have burdened him with the bodies," said Ortog.

"The exarch did not wish to be involved," said Otto.

"An error," said Ortog. "He could disclaim responsibility, and then, as an act of charity, distribute the clothings and goods to the poor, presumably retaining most for the temple's coffers."

"Even so, he declined," said Otto.

"I see that as an admission of guilt," said Ortog.

"I suspect," said Otto, "he understood that an acceptance of the bodies would, on the other hand, seem an admission of guilt."

"I see his refusal as such an admission," said Ortog.

"I hope others will so see it, as well," said Otto.

"Did you know," asked Ortog, "that many of the assailants in the senate had a gold *darin* in his purse, no common gold *darin*, but a weighted *darin*?"

"Banks exchanged each, before smaller coins, a thousand of each, were distributed to the poor," said Otto.

"A gold *darin*!" said Ortog. "So much gold is seldom offered even for the most dangerous and notorious of outlaws."

"A humble Otung is flattered," said Otto.

"It seems those sworn to poverty are not without resources," said Ortog.

"Some purses are heavy, some coffers are deep," said Otto.

"I wished I had seen the missing senators, those surprisingly absent from the session, replaced by assailants, on their knees, with rubbing stones, rags, powders, and water, cleaning the senate chamber," said Ortog.

"No secret was made of this in Telnar," said Otto.

"You have many enemies," said Ortog.

"Presumably no more than before," said Otto.

"They will never forget such humiliation," said Ortog.

"Rather," said Otto, "let them rejoice."

"How so?" asked Ortog.

"I left them their lives," said Otto.

"Surely, your majesty, chieftain of the Wolfungs, king of the Otungs, holder of the medallion of the Vandalii, you have not summoned me to the palace to engage in the pleasures of incidental conversation," said Ortog.

"Indeed not, prince of the Drisriaks, king of the Ortungs, dearest amongst my enemies," said Otto.

"I await your words," said Ortog.

"You are not easy to summon," said Otto, "nor to invite."

"I shaved my beard, I cut my hair in the Telnarian fashion, I wear Telnarian garb, I speak little, I walk humbly, I affect diffidence, I change my dwelling frequently," said Ortog.

"You have been a shadow amongst shadows, a phantom in crowds, visible but not seen," said Otto. "It was for that reason that I sent men to the delta of the Turning Serpent, and seized on your behalf two slaves, called for convenience Delia and Virginia, both once apparently of Telnar, one the former Lady Delia Cotina, of the Telnar Farnacii, and the other, the former Lady Virginia Serena, of the lesser Serenii."

"I know them," said Ortog. "I obtained them, with several others, at a private villa near the Turning Serpent itself, at a secret meeting of proud, young, arrogant, rich free women who hated slaves for their attractions to men, free women who had been spurned or rejected in favor of the excitements and charms of slaves. In their hatred of slaves, they had planned revenge games, blood games in which several slaves were to be destroyed. I, contacted surreptitiously by several rich men of Telnar, who knew these women and had discovered their intent, was hired to raid the villa and foil their plan, seeing to it, if possible, that the slaves were spared. Surely there were better things to do with female slaves than expend them in diverse sports of slaughter for the entertainment of free women, for example, awarding them as shackled prizes to the victors in such sports."

"Of course," said Otto.

"I would be twice paid," said Ortog, "once by the free men amused to frustrate the intentions of the free women, and once by the free women themselves."

"By the free women?" said Otto.

"Yes," said Ortog, "become goods."

"I see," said Otto.

"They who had been intent on the amusing destruction of slaves instead found themselves stripped, chained, branded, and collared, slaves themselves."

"Excellent," said Otto.

"It was clever of you," said Ortog, "to have the criers, amongst their other announcements, in the lower, more illiterate districts, announce amongst listings of stolen goods, the theft of two slaves, Delia and Virginia."

"I knew them yours, from the delta," said Otto, "slaves reserved for you, not transported upriver for sale in Telnar."

"Slaves easy to recognize, from their collars," said Ortog.

"Yes," said Otto, "the collar identifying the owner, and bearing the slave's name."

"Few knew of those slaves," said Ortog. "Naturally, hearing both names together, surely a matter of neither chance nor accident, I was intrigued, and suspected a signal. I reported to the house specified by the crier, for those who might have information pertaining to their whereabouts."

"The house of Titus Gelinus," said Otto.

"And was informed to report to the palace."

"In the future, I trust we can arrange an easier, more reliable way to keep in touch," said Otto.

"You are Otung," said Ortog. "Surely you do not expect me to place myself frequently within the reach of your sword, or those of your men. And I preferred to avoid the palace, that I be less noticed, and my identity might remain more secure."

"I understand," said Otto. "He who comes and goes through golden portals is unlikely to do so unnoted."

"I was directed to a minor gate and was discreetly admitted," said Ortog. "Did you actually steal two slaves?"

"It was necessary," said Otto. "A false claim is easily discovered, and an undone ruse lacks profit."

"Where are the slaves?" asked Ortog.

"Safe in the palace," said Otto.

"Do they know they are here?" asked Ortog.

"No," said Otto. "They were brought here hooded, bound, gagged, in tied, leather slave sacks, in enclosed conveyances, and such."

"I see," said Ortog.

"It seems you have taught them their collars well," said Otto. "They are miserable with slave need. It is more than ten days since they have been caressed. They are now ready to crawl on their belly to any man. One merely touches them on an arm in putting their plates on the floor, and they whimper, and their eyes plead, speech, of course, forbidden them."

"They were displeasing as free women," said Ortog. "Let them now suffer in their collars."

"You may use them whenever you wish, of course," said Otto. "It is what slaves are for."

"I shall do so," said Ortog. "I am tired of striking aside street women, and am wary of taverns and brothels. A turn of speech might give me away, or an allusion I failed to grasp. Otungs are about, ancient enemies of the Alemanni, and imperial guardsmen. Stray Alemanni, unprotected, such as myself, I fear, are at risk in Telnar."

"Considering ancient enmities, that of the Vandalii and the Alemanni, and the predations of the Alemanni at the imperial borders, their intrusions into the empire, sometimes deeply, the hazards they pose to shipping, and such, you should not find that hard to understand."

"Why did you summon me, or invite me, or wish to see me?" asked Ortog.

"I have heard nothing of you for too long," said Otto.

"There is little, or nothing, of me to hear," said Ortog. "I have watched, I have listened; I have seen nothing; I have heard nothing."

"I had hoped," said Otto, "you would have discovered the secret prison of Abrogastes; and then I feared you might have done so, and had perished in the doing."

"If I am successful, you would furnish men?" asked Ortog.

"If need be, a thousand," said Otto.

"Led by Julian, of the Aureliani, or Rurik, Tenth Consul of Larial VII?" said Ortog.

"Perhaps not," said Otto. "Perhaps by another."

"Oh?" said Ortog.

"It is a long time since I have laughed with steel," said Otto.

"Sometimes," said Ortog, "a thousand can fail, where one or two men, or even a slave, can succeed."

"It is true," said Otto.

"To a hall there is always more than one trail," said Ortog.

"I have heard so," said Otto.

CHAPTER TWENTY-EIGHT

"Greetings," said Julian, of the Aureliani.

"Greetings," said Rurik, Tenth Consul of Larial VII.

"Greetings," said Tuvo Ausonius, former finance officer of Miton.

"Your majesty," said Iaachus, politely.

"Friends," said Otto, "please be seated."

The five men sat about a small conference table in a carpeted anteroom, by means of which the throne room might be reached.

"I have an item of which I would that you were apprised," said Otto. "It deals with Abrogastes."

"How goes the search?" said Iaachus.

"Poorly," said Otto.

"I am sorry to hear that," said Iaachus.

"The location of Abrogastes remains unclear," said Otto. "As you know, we suppose him to be a captive of Sidonicus, whose plans of universal conversion and ecclesiastical despotism he would oppose, and perhaps of Ingeld, a treasonous son who covets the high seat of the Drisriaks, hegemonic tribe of the Alemanni, or, as you, my friends, might have it, of the Aatii."

"Yes?" said Julian.

"Abrogastes, we further suppose," said Otto, "is likely to be in Telnar, or nearby, that in order to have his person conveniently at hand, should it be needed for political purposes."

"A valuable prisoner," said Rurik, "but one it might be danger-ous to hold."

"He would be dangerous to hold," said Otto. "He has the strength of an *arn* bear and the cunning of a *vi-cat*. And it would be a rare Drisriak ax which would not be willing to be reddened in his rescue."

"Is there no clue as to his whereabouts?" asked Iaachus.

"Our spies have been unsuccessful," said Otto. "Our surveil-lance of possible informants has yielded nothing."

"I see one hope remaining," said Iaachus. "Recall the two prisoners, Corelius and Lysis, former cohorts of the slain traitor, Phidias, cohorts we released from prison. One, Corelius, in prison, fearing torture, betrayed the hiding place of the prisoner, Abrogastes, which hiding place, unfortunately, was abandoned before we could reach it. Our enemies then know that at least one of the prisoners betrayed that secret, but they will not know whether it was one or both, and, if one, which one. We released both, assuming that an attempt on their lives would be made and we might then, if not foiling that attempt, manage to capture or follow one or more of the assailants, by means of which we might be led to Abrogastes, or to others, who might know of his whereabouts."

"This is the matter of which I wished to speak," said Otto.

"I gather, as of yet," said Iaachus, "that no attempt has been made on their lives."

"We do not know," said Otto.

"How is that?" asked Iaachus.

"They have disappeared," said Otto.

CHAPTER TWENTY-NINE

"The throne is secure," said Iaachus.

"A throne," said Otto, "is never secure."

This meeting took place in the private quarters of the emperor. Otto wore a lounging robe, and sat at a table. He indicated that the Arbiter of Protocol might sit across from him, which place the Arbiter assumed.

"Would you care for some *bror*?" asked Otto. He indicated a metal vessel dangling over a small fire, in a hearth to the side. "It is spiced, and honeyed."

"No," said Iaachus, "I value my throat and mouth."

"*Kana*, then?" inquired Otto.

"That would be welcome," said the Arbiter.

Otto rose to his feet, brought a decanter forward, removed, with a glass, from a cabinet, and served the Arbiter. He then took a metal goblet to the metal vessel over the fire and, tipping the vessel by means of a tool, inserted at the bottom of the vessel, filled the goblet, put aside the tool, and joined the Arbiter at the table. "*Bror* need not be drunk hot," he said. "Commonly, in the halls, the drinking horns are filled with *bror* at the ambient temperature."

"I was not referring to the temperature," said Iaachus.

"I see," said Otto.

"Where are your slaves?" asked Iaachus.

"I put them in their cages, naked," said Otto.

"Such things help them keep in mind that they are slaves," said Iaachus.

"I expect so," said Otto.

"And serving naked," said Iaachus.

"Clothing is a privilege," said Otto. "As a slave is an animal, she need not be clothed."

"Too," said Iaachus, "it is pleasant to be served by a naked slave."

"It is commonly done in the halls," said Otto, "particularly if the slaves are former women of the empire."

"Of course," said Iaachus. "The women of the enemy are suitable loot, as are other valuables."

"I gave them each a blanket," said Otto.

"You are generous," said Iaachus. "I suspect, given an earlier audience, granted in the throne room, that the blankets may not have been identical."

"No," said Otto. "The blanket of one, the slave, Renata, is ample, soft, and warm. She clutches it about herself gratefully, but is well aware that she is naked within it. The blanket of the other, the slave, Flora, is smaller, thinner, and of loosely woven, coarse cloth, little more than a rag."

"You treat her as a low slave," said Iaachus.

"As the lowest, and most worthless of slaves," said Otto.

"Yet she is lovely, soft, and well-bodied," said Iaachus. "Indeed, she is exceedingly well-curved."

"I like them so," said Otto.

"Surely you recognize that she is of some value," said Iaachus.

"Bared, she would market well," said Otto.

"From the recent audience, and the way in which she was used as a portion of the display," said Iaachus, "I gathered that she may be in some way special to you."

"Possibly," said Otto.

"You referred to a court, and an arena, on Terennia," said Iaachus.

"I may have," said Otto.

"That suggests a trial," said Iaachus, "and a sentencing."

"I deem it does," said Otto.

"I gather it was there that you first met," said Iaachus.

"Yes," said Otto. "She was an officer of the court, beautiful, arrogant, superior, and contemptuous, and I was a simple peasant, ignorant and untutored, recently arrived from the provincial world, Tangara."

"You were a lowly person, one without station, wealth, or connections, one easily dealt with, one despised, one without recourse, one then routinely prosecuted, summarily found guilty, and remanded to the arena," said Iaachus.

"Yes," said Otto.

"That is a form of justice which, unfortunately, is not that rare in the empire," said Iaachus.

"I fear so," said Otto.

"And she, this officer of the court, later, I gather," said Iaachus, "fell into your power."

"Yes," said Otto. "On the cruise ship, the *Alaria*, seized by the secessionist Drisriak, Ortog, son of Abrogastes, the Far-Grasper, and later on, again, on Varna, the world to which the Wolfungs had been banished, the smallest tribe of the Vandalii."

"I see now how she is special to you," said Iaachus.

"Too, on the *Alaria*," said Otto, "she betrayed her word, most treacherously, putting lives at risk."

"And now she is in your collar," said Iaachus.

"Yes," said Otto.

"Splendid," said Iaachus.

"She was a Same," said Otto.

"She is no longer a Same," said Iaachus. "I have seen her eyes, her movements, her body, its pleading readiness. She is now no more than a needful, begging slave."

"It is pleasant to have a woman so," said Otto.

"How helpless they are, so reduced," said Iaachus.

"She responds well," said Otto. "One can play upon her, as with a musical instrument, it helpless to resist the performer, bringing forth what sounds one wishes, small cries, sobs, moans, gasps, and whimpers, whimpers of pleading, gratitude, disappointment, hope, and such. Even when she is determined to resist, and tries to steel herself against feeling, she is soon, in her collar, overcome, subdued, and defeated, and, unable to help herself, leaps in my arms, unable to resist the ecstasies which I see fit to enforce upon her, if only for my amusement, those of a helpless, ravaged slave, piteously sobbing herself mine, and fearing only that I will too soon thrust her aside."

"But, too," said Iaachus, "I gather that you harvest from her at will the tumults of a master's pleasure."

"Of course," said Ott. "She knows she is helpless. She knows I take from her what I want, when I want it."

"Does she not sometimes, if only in petulance, feign frigidity, pretend to disinterest and inertness?"

"Such theatrics are soon detected," said Otto. "One touches her, kindling flame. One is patient. Soon she burns; she is then yours, a slave. Her haunches deny her tongue. Her body denies her mouth."

"A sight of the whip, even in a free woman," said Iaachus, "encourages receptivity."

"Women respond well to male domination," said Otto.

"They long for it," said Iaachus.

"It seems so," said Otto.

"The former officer of the court has undergone a considerable change in fortune," said Iaachus, "from the dignified, plush, rich robes of judicial office to a scanty tunic, if that, and a collar-encircled neck."

"It is pleasant to have her now as my slave," said Otto.

"She looks well in her collar," said Iaachus.

"I think so," said Otto.

"Women are especially beautiful in collars," said Iaachus.

"Slave collars," said Otto.

"Of course," said Iaachus.

"They are then as they should be," said Otto.

"Of course," said Iaachus.

"More *kana*?" asked Otto.

"Please," said Iaachus.

The *kana* was poured.

"It is unusual to be served by an emperor," said the Arbiter.

"Sometimes it is not wise to speak before slaves," said Otto.

"Ahh," said Iaachus. "Now I understand, as well, the lateness of the hour."

"So," said Otto, quietly, regarding Iaachus, "you think the throne is secure?"

"Passably so," said Iaachus. "Certainly more so than before. Sidonicus, the secret foe of an impartial, tolerant, secular empire, unscrupulous in policy, insane with ambition, has been dealt two serious defeats, the failure of the empress mother's conversion, a failure public, humiliating, and unmistakable, one holding the exarch up to ridicule, and the failure of more than a hundred knives in the senate to remove from the throne a most formidable enemy, an emperor."

"I am a usurper," said Otto.

"It was necessary to seize the throne," said Iaachus. "There was no viable alternative."

"Yet, still," said Otto, "I am a usurper."

"Do not be concerned," said Iaachus. "You are the emperor, Ottonius, the First. The city has accepted you. The empire is quiet. Even the senate has acclaimed you so. Too, many an emperor in the long history of the empire, and many of its greatest, most honored, and most revered emperors, have won the throne by usurpation. History is seldom polite. It respects success. Possession is paramount. Fact, sustained, confers legitimacy."

"You see the papers strewn on the table," said Otto.

"I recognize them," said Iaachus. "Do you wish them read?"

"Yes," said Otto, "again."

"They are unimportant," said Iaachus. "They are meaningless, and utterly trivial. They are relevant to nothing. I fail to see your interest in them."

"Please," said Otto.

"I do not understand," said Iaachus. "This meeting is late. None know of it. It is secret. It takes place in the emperor's private quarters. I thought surely matters of state, of delicacy and moment, were afoot. Is some radical policy to be instituted; is a terrible and cleansing raid on the city's enemies to take place at dawn; is a revolution to be forestalled, a war declared?"

"No," said Otto.

"Surely you have not invited me here tonight, in secrecy and stealth, to read to you what anyone, even a literate slave, your Renata or Flora, could read to you, at any time, and is, in any event, not worth your attention?"

"You do recognize the papers, do you not?" said Otto.

"Certainly," said Iaachus. "They are papers consequent to your earlier inquiry, lists of the volumes missing from the palace library."

"Please," said Otto. "Read to me, once more, the lists."

"As you wish," said Iaachus.

The lists were then read, again, to the emperor.

"An interesting assortment of books, do you not think?" asked Otto.

"In what way?" asked Iaachus.

"With respect to themes and subject," said Otto.

"Perhaps," said Iaachus. "There is no accounting for the tastes of thieves."

"Would it not be an unusual thief, who would prey on such books?" asked Otto.

"Perhaps," said Iaachus. "I am sure I do not know."

"It is my understanding," said Otto, "that the empress mother has continued to receive, at least from time to time, another mysterious custard."

"Apparently," said Iaachus. "And it seems that is much to her relief. Apparently she was muchly concerned, and quite apprehensive, that her reproof of the exarch, her declining of the smudg-ing, the business about the *koos*, and such, might have meant an end to such treats. Now she is sure, given the reappearance of the mysterious custards, which she understands as miraculous, that she is on good terms with the god, *Karch*, if not the exarch. Indeed, she assumes that this continuance of miracles, as she sees it, demonstrates a disagreement between the god and the exarch, a disagreement which is not in the best interests of the exarch. She even takes this as a proof that smudging has nothing to do with the gods, or, at least, *Karch*. Indeed, she hazards the eccentric speculation that the nature of a life lived, if anything, might be more important."

"How do you explain the custards?" asked Otto.

"I do not take them to be miraculous," said Iaachus.

"How would you explain them?" asked Otto.

"Trickery, bribery, deceit, something like that," said Iaachus.

"I thought we eliminated such possibilities," said Otto.

"May I speak frankly?" asked Iaachus.

"Your speech would be worthless to me, were it not frank," said Otto.

"I think," said Iaachus, "that you are behind the matter, that you are somehow, for some reason, responsible for the business."

"But I am not," said Otto.

"Truly?" asked Iaachus.

"Truly," said Otto.

"Surely you do not think that gods, if they exist, have nothing better to do than deliver free custards to grouchy old women with a taste for sweets," said Iaachus.

"Without presuming to be informed with respect to the interests and habits of gods," said Otto, "I would be very much surprised if they would occupy themselves in such a manner."

"Then you have no idea as to the explanation," said Iaachus.

"I did not say that," said Otto.

"Then you have an idea?" said Iaachus.

"Yes," said Otto.

"You know the explanation?" said Iaachus.

"I think so," said Otto.

"Does it have something to do with the missing volumes from the library?" asked Iaachus.

"Yes, in a way," said Otto.

"I trust that my emperor has his wits about him," said Iaachus.

"He thinks so," said Otto.

"I am confused and bewildered," said Iaachus. "I do not understand this meeting at all, and, least of all, can I understand why it has taken place at this hour in the private chambers of the emperor, under seeming conditions of secrecy. One would think that matters of moment, germane to the state of the empire, were involved."

"Perhaps they are," said Otto.

"I understand little of this night's business," said Iaachus.

"Before you finish your *kana*," said Otto, "I would touch on a further matter."

"Please do so," said Iaachus.

"I shall proceed," said Otto.

"I trust that this new matter is less arcane than its predecessors," said Iaachus.

"I think so," said Otto.

"I am grateful to hear that," said Iaachus.

"I am thinking of a new toy for Aesilesius," said Otto.

"That is it?" asked Iaachus.

"Yes," said Otto.

"I am sure he will be pleased," said Iaachus.

CHAPTER THIRTY

"Remove your clothing, completely, Telnarian slut!" snapped dark-haired Huta, once the high priestess of the Timbri, now the slave of Abrogastes, the Far-Grasper, on the Meeting World, Tenguthaxichai.

"Never!" cried yellow-haired Viviana, princess of Telnaria, recoiling, aghast, in her finery. "What am I doing here, here, in such a place, on this dirt, rush-strewn floor, in this wooden, high-roofed, rude hall?"

"Strip," said Huta. "Now, instantly! Lest I be displeased!"

"Who are you?" demanded Viviana.

"Huta, in whose keeping you are," said Huta.

"Despite your gown," said Viviana, "there is a collar on your neck, which, I suspect, is a slave collar, and is locked on you! I would not be surprised, either, if your left thigh was marked with the slave rose!"

"I am the slave of Abrogastes, the Far-Grasper, king of Drisriaks, hegemonic tribe of the Aatii, the Alemanni," said Huta, proudly.

"Slave!" hissed Viviana.

"The slave of a great king!" said Huta.

"A slave!" said Viviana. "I am Viviana, princess of Telnaria, sister to Aesilesius, emperor of Telnaria, sister to Alacida, princess of Telnaria, daughter to Atalana, the empress mother of Telnaria, and wedded against my will to Ingeld, prince of the Drisriaks."

"Surely you hoped to profit from that liaison," snarled Huta.

"I have seen no profit," snapped Viviana.

"Aesilesius has been put aside," said Huta. "A barbarian, an Otung, now sits upon the throne of Telnaria."

"A usurper!" cried Viviana.

"It is a done thing," said Huta.

"It is unrightful, contrary to custom and law!" said Viviana.

"It is done," laughed Huta. "The spear, as always, prevails. Custom and law, as always, yield to steel. How could it be otherwise? The accession was even accepted by, and celebrated by, the senate."

"Intimidated sycophants!" said Viviana.

"The first of your line was a usurper," said Huta.

"No!" cried Viviana.

"Do you think time, tradition, and forgetfulness, bestow legitimacy?" asked Huta. "Strength bestows legitimacy. The throne belongs to he who can hold it. Your brother was a retarded, slobbering weakling, well put aside."

"The Otung can be put aside!" said Viviana.

"That is the plan," said Huta. "You are to deliver a son to Ingeld. The barbarian then, or another, is removed. The son, though in infancy, is emperor. And Ingeld holds the regency, and becomes, in effect, the emperor."

"You forget," said Viviana, "my sister, Alacida, too, and against her will, as well, was wedded to Hrothgar, Ingeld's brother. Alacida may first bear a son."

"Do not be naive," said Huta. "Hrothgar is a jovial, simple fellow, thinking of little but his slaves and dogs, his horses and falcons. He will be easily duped."

"I do not understand," said Viviana.

"Do you truly think Ingeld would allow such a thing?" said Huta. "If Hrothgar has a son by Alacida, what do you think would be the chances of that offspring to survive the first month of its life?"

"I do not understand," said Viviana.

"Poison, illness, a tragic accident," said Huta.

"Surely not," said Viviana.

"Why are you still clothed?" asked Huta, angrily.

"I do not understand," stammered Viviana, uncertainly.

"You were instructed to remove your clothing, completely," said Huta. "Get it off, strip, wholly, instantly, now!"

"Never!" exclaimed Viviana.

Huta, in a fury, whirled about, and rushed to the high seat, seizing up a whip, it looped about an arm of the high seat, on the right side of the high seat, where it would be convenient to a right-handed individual who might occupy that coign of power.

She then, half bent over, two hands on the staff of the whip, turned to face Viviana. "It seems you must be whipped, immediately, this moment, as a slave," she said.

"No!" cried Viviana.

"Then, strip," said Huta. "Now!"

Sobbing, trembling, Viviana complied.

"Stand straight," said Huta.

Viviana raised her head and straightened her body.

Huta then straightened up, and walked about her, as might an appraising mistress, whip in hand, and then, again, faced her.

"You do not have a bad body," she said. "You might make a slave."

"Never!" said Viviana.

"I would love to see you naked on a slave block, in a mud world, being auctioned to lizard people," said Huta.

"Beware," said Viviana, "I am the bride of Ingeld, prince of the Alemanni!"

Huta laughed. "You think you are wedded?" she asked.

"Against my will," stammered Viviana.

"No horses, no gold was given," said Huta. "There was no pledge of arms, no mingling of bloods, no swearing of fathers, or kinsmen, on the spear."

"My sister and I were wedded in the great temple of Telnar, by holy Sidonicus, the exarch of Telnar himself."

"Mumbled words, meaningless noises, germane to a foolish sect, one of thousands of such sects, all equally absurd, a vapid, political charade contrived to serve the ends of power."

"I am of royal blood, of the empire," said Viviana.

"You are a Telnarian slut," said Huta, "worthy only, naked and collared, at best, to carry horns of mead to your Alemanni masters."

"Villainess!" said Viviana.

Huta raised the whip and Viviana lowered her head. Huta lowered the whip.

"Do not think that the men of the Alemanni do not prize the women of the empire," said Huta.

"Oh?" said Viviana.

"They are fond of their pretty bodies," said Huta. "Such bodies look well, stripped and collared, crawling about, begging to kiss the feet of their masters."

Viviana trembled, with rage, but did not speak.

"Some," said Huta, "sell for as much as two dogs, a horse, or even a gold *darin*."

"And the less attractive ones?" asked Viviana.

"We put them in rags and use them to tend our pigs," said Huta.

"I see," said Viviana.

"If I had my way," said Huta, "that is where you would be, save without rags."

"I see," said Viviana.

"Are you hot?" asked Huta.

"I do not understand," said Viviana.

"In the arms of Ingeld," said Huta.

"I do not understand," said Viviana.

"On the mattress, or slave mat," said Huta, impatiently.

"Please do not speak so," said Viviana, "lest I grow ill, and faint."

"Ah, yes," said Huta, "you are a free woman, of course. Forgive me. I was not thinking. Doubtless you are cold now, but, subdued, collared, and trained, perhaps with a taste of the whip, I wager your thighs will steam, and you will beg, and kick, with agreeable helplessness."

"Beware, offensive slave," said Viviana, "I shall complain to Ingeld!"

"And he would laugh, and scorn and mock you," said Huta. "It was he who put you in my keeping."

"Then," said Viviana, "I shall complain to his father, Abrogastes, king of the Drisriaks, of the Alemanni!"

Huta stepped back, and laughed. "Abrogastes," she said, "need not be feared."

"Why is that?" asked Viviana.

"You need not know," said Huta.

"You do not treat me well," said Viviana.

"And why should you be treated well?" asked Huta. "You are shallow, empty-headed, meaningless, lazy, arrogant, vain, petty, and spoiled. While men went hungry in the streets, riots stormed markets, and borders flamed, you lived for garmenture, for gossip, and display, mindful only of gowns and jewels. You were a matter of public embarrassment, even scandal. But, too, you are the sister of Aesilesius, the emperor."

"So, too, is my sister, Alacida," said Viviana.

"True," said Huta.

"Surely she is as vain and shallow as I," said Viviana.

"But you are eldest, and thus have dynastic preference," said Huta.

"How fortunate I am," said Viviana.

"I myself would prefer Alacida," said Huta. "She has changed. She is now a hundred times the woman you are."

"How is that?" asked Viviana.

"She has been in the arms of Hrothgar," said Huta. "You should see her now, how she surreptitiously touches the sleeve of his jacket, how she hangs upon his every word, how she looks upon him, as might a slave."

"Surely not!" said Viviana.

"In her heart, she is at his feet, where she belongs," said Huta.

"She loves a barbarian?" asked Viviana, scornfully.

"Hrothgar is quite taken with her," said Huta. "He is thinking of sending Aesilesius horses for her," said Huta.

"So it would be a true wedding?" asked Viviana.

"Yes," said Huta, "something meaningful, something genuine."

"I see," said Viviana, coldly.

"Ingeld loves me," said Huta.

"A slave?" said Viviana, scornfully.

"In his collar, I am his," said Huta.

"What of he who owns you, mighty Abrogastes?" said Viviana.

Huta laughed.

"I do not understand," said Viviana. "Why do you laugh?"

"Kneel, there," said Huta, "before the high seat! There, head down!"

"Never!" cried Viviana.

Huta snapped the whip, viciously, and Viviana, terrified, hurried to the wooden dais on which reposed the high seat, and knelt down before it, a bit to its left, as she knelt. She kept her head down. She saw the boards of the dais, the long, narrow cracks between them. Too, she saw, as she knelt, a heavy ring fastened in the side of the high seat. To this ring was fastened a heavy chain, terminating with a large, heavy padlock.

Viviana noted that the chain would be within easy reach of an occupant of the high seat. By means of it, the occupant could pull whatever might be fastened to that chain to him.

"Lift the chain," said Huta, "and kiss it, reverently."

Viviana lifted the chain in two hands and put her lips to it.

"Kiss it," said Huta.

Viviana put her lips quickly, angrily, to the chain and then pulled back.

"No," said Huta, her voice laden with malice, "lengthily, reverently."

"As a slave?" asked Viviana, angrily.

"Precisely," said Huta.

Viviana kissed the chain, again, sullenly, as she had been directed, but, suddenly, was startled, as unfamiliar sensations suffused her body.

Huta laughed.

Had she detected some involuntary subtlety, some small acknowledgement of a reality, in the stripped body of fair Viviana?

Viviana trembled.

Had she been betrayed by her body?

Huta set aside her whip and looped the free end of the chain about Viviana's neck, rather closely, and then, passing the lock's shackle through two links of the chain, snapped the device shut, closing the loop.

"That is how the women of the empire should be," said Huta, straightening up, and backing away, "naked, and chained."

"I am chained," whispered Viviana, wonderingly.

"Doubtless for the first time in your life," said Huta. "But do not concern yourself. For any woman who is chained, there is always a first time. And doubtless, pretty Viviana, for you, it will not be the last time. Indeed, as time goes on, you may become quite familiar with being chained."

Viviana was silent, trying to understand her feelings.

"Now," said Huta, "who is the true barbarian, I, or you, you who are naked and chained, you who are at my mercy?"

"I hate you," said Viviana.

"You are not important enough for me to hate you," said Huta, "but I do hold you in contempt, as a naked, chained, meaningless Telnarian slut."

"Vile creature!" cried Viviana.

Huta smiled, and picked up the whip.

"I am not afraid of you," wept Viviana. She grasped, with both hands, the chain that held her by the neck to the side of the high seat in the rude hall.

"This is a whip, a slave whip," said Huta, lifting the implement.

"What is that to me?" asked Viviana.

"Prepare to be whipped," said Huta.

"No!" cried Viviana.

"—as a slave," said Huta.

"No, no!" cried Viviana. "Do not! I will tell Ingeld, the prince!"

"Do you think I would dare do this, without orders?" asked Huta. "I do this on the orders of Ingeld, prince of the Drisriaks."

"No!" said Viviana.

Ingeld regards you as insufficiently responsive," said Huta.

"I loathe him!" said Viviana.

"And few orders, you cold, petty, greedy thing, would I obey with more pleasure," said Huta.

"No!" said Viviana.

"The whip will teach you to be more responsive in the arms of a man, any man," said Huta. "You will learn you are a woman under its lash!"

"No, no!" cried Viviana.

The lashing was brief, but instructive.

In those few moments Viviana, writhing and shrieking, aflame with pain, though a free woman, came to understand how it was that slaves so feared the whip, why they so struggled to escape its admonishment, why they strove so to please their masters wholly, in all ways.

"You will learn, proud princess, you are a woman," said Huta.

"Please do not hurt me more," begged Viviana.

Huta raised the whip again, menacingly.

"Mistress!" said Viviana.

"Better, royal slut," said Huta.

"Dearest, beloved Mistress!" said Viviana.

"Excellent, Telnarian pig," said Huta.

"Thank you, Mistress," said Viviana.

"You will learn to please Ingeld, will you not?" asked Huta.

"Yes, Mistress," whispered Viviana.

"Good," said Huta. "Perhaps I will bring you some gruel to-morrow, or the next day, if you beg prettily enough."

"Yes, Mistress," said Viviana. "Thank you, Mistress."

"But you will not please him too much," said Huta, "for he is mine!"

"Yes, Mistress," said Viviana. But she knew, in her heart, she would do her best to please Ingeld, and as a slave, he to whom she was wedded against her will, he whom she loathed above all men.

She, though a free woman, had felt a whip, the slave whip.

A woman who has felt it is never again the same.

CHAPTER THIRTY-ONE

Small, exquisite, red-haired Nika, briefly tunicked and collared, once the slave of the Lady Publennia of the Larial Calasalii, now Filene, or Cornhair, the property of Rurik, the Tenth Consul of Larial VII, of the Larial Farnichi, shuddered, standing outside the heavy, closed portal, reached by one of the long passageways in the imperial palace.

Her body shook.

Tears ran down her cheeks.

Nika was one of six slaves recently brought to Telnar by imperial order. She had been brought from the provincial world, Tangara. Four of the six had been brought from a holding of Julian, of the Aureliani, on Vellmer. These were Flora and Renata, slaves of the emperor, Ottonius, the First; Gerune, the slave of Julian, of the Aureliani; and Sesella, the slave of Tuvo Ausonius, once a civil servant on Miton. The sixth slave, a lithe brunette with a dancer's body, named Janina, was owned by the emperor, as well. She had been brought from the forests of Varna, from an encampment of Wolfungs, the smallest of the five tribes of the Vandalii.

"We are here," said Vandar, the Otung. "This is the portal." He had been the first, long ago, on Tangara, in the Killing Time, in the Festival of Blood, when he was a young man, to accept meat from the hero's portion, cut by a giant, blond stranger, one who had wielded a mighty sword, who had dared to bring the pelt of a white *vi-cat*, knowing its meaning, to the Hall of the King Naming. With him, in the background, stood Ulrich. He, too, had been present on that bloody night when, in the light of the long fire pit, a new king, the pelt of the *vi-cat* draped about his shoulders, had ascended the throne, the high seat, of the Otungs.

"May I speak?" asked Nika.

"Surely," said Vandar.

"Will he not show me mercy?" she whispered.

"It has been decided," said Vandar.

"The king has spoken," said Ulrich.

Ulrich, too, was an Otung. He was well aware that Otto, or Ottonius, as Telnarians preferred, was emperor. He had, in a sense, been raised upon the shields. The spear, so to speak, had prevailed. He was acclaimed by, and accepted by, the people. Had not the senate, even, celebrated his accession? Yet, an Otung, he thought of Otto less as the emperor of the vast Telnarian Empire, and more as his king, the king of the Otungs, the largest of the five tribes of the Vandalii. Similarly, the Wolfungs, many remaining on Varna, thought of him less as the emperor of Telnaria, and more as their chieftain. Such things, however obscure to outsiders, are clear to tribesmen.

Sobbing, Nika sank to her knees before the heavy door.

Vandar pounded on the door twice, and then thrust a long key into the lock, turned the key, and moved the bolt.

Ulrich seized Nika by the arms and lifted her to her feet, holding her from behind. Without his grasp, she would have fallen. She twisted her head from side to side, as though such a gesture might cast a hideous fate to the side.

Vandar thrust open the door.

Nika screamed in misery.

"Behold, noble Aesilesius," said Vandar. "The emperor, your friend, protector, and patron, Ottonius, the First, sends you a new toy. Be pleased. Amuse yourself."

Nika screamed again, and Ulrich thrust her, she stumbling, inside. Within the portal, she recovered her balance, and regarded the scene before her, aghast.

Toward one end of the chamber, there crouched a human, or nearly human, figure, something twisted and misshapen, bearing a likeness to the shape of a young man. It clutched to its bosom a stuffed animal, a yellow *torodont*.

"Forgive us, if we alarmed you, noble Aesilesius," said Vandar.

"We mean you no harm," said Ulrich. Then he said, softly, to Vandar, "Our work is done. Let us quit this place. It sickens me."

Vandar and Ulrich then withdrew. The door was closed. Nika heard the key turn again in the lock, restoring the bolt to its place.

With horror she looked upon the figure some feet away. Its eyes seemed curiously vacant. Then it seemed they saw her, and it clutched the toy, suddenly, more closely to its bosom. Saliva ran at the side of its mouth. It stood up, unsteadily, and backed away a few feet.

"I will not take your toy, Master," whispered Nika.

The figure regarded her.

Nika covered her eyes.

This weak, miserable, half-human, empty thing, she thought, once sat upon the throne of Telnaria!

When she uncovered her eyes, she saw that the creature was on the floor, on all fours, yards away, playing with the small, stuffed yellow *torodont*.

He has forgotten me, thought Nika.

She watched him play.

He made small snuffling, snorting noises, such as a small boy might suppose a *torodont* to make, and occasionally, too, uttered other sounds, presumably on behalf of the *torodont*, which bore some semblance to human speech, garbled and distorted.

Then she was frightened, for she knew nothing of such a creature. It was simple, and childlike, and innocent, and doubtless harmless, but what if it should be a petulant child, an impatient, spoiled, wayward child, a child capable of an irrational, ungoverned, irresponsible tantrum, a child who might, in a fit of anger, tear open a stuffed animal or break a toy, a child equipped with the size, force, body, and strength of a grown man?

Nika, beside herself, turned about and ran to the portal, and began, sobbing, to pound on it with her small fists.

"Help, help!" she cried. "Open the door! Have mercy! Release me! Release me, Masters! Let me go! Do not keep me here! Please, please, Masters!"

She scratched futilely, weakly, at the door, and then sank to her knees, facing the door, leaning her head against it.

"Please, please, Masters!" she wept.

She remained as she was for a time, for several minutes, but then, suddenly stiffened, frightened. A hand had been placed gently on her right shoulder.

"Do not cry," said a voice.

CHAPTER THIRTY-TWO

"Lift the lamp," said Sidonicus, exarch of Telnar.

Fulvius, ministrant of *Karch*, raised the lamp.

"Odors here are insufferable," said Sidonicus.

"It is the dampness, and the urine and excrement, that of the prisoners and the rodents," said Fulvius. "Step carefully, your excellency."

Two minions, garbed in black, hooded, were in the background, near the barred door.

"I see they are well chained," said Sidonicus, regarding the prisoners.

"Hand and foot, and neck," said Fulvius.

"Excellent," said Sidonicus.

"We put them in the garb, the gowns, of penitents," said Fulvius.

"Appropriately," said Sidonicus.

"They have much to repent," said Fulvius.

"Are they sleeping?" asked Sidonicus.

"They are faint with hunger, and sleep much," said the larger, the first, of the two minions.

"Awaken them," said Sidonicus.

The smaller of the two minions, with the jailer's staff, prodded the recumbent figures.

There was a stirring of chain, the rattle of links.

Corelius blinked against the light, dim as it was. "Dear, holy prelate!" he whispered, frightened.

"You are afraid," said Sidonicus.

"Forgive me, holy one," said Corelius. "I cannot rise, to kiss your ring."

"How is it that we are here?" asked Lysis, struggling to sit up, his eyes half closed against the light of the lamp. "I do not understand, holy one. Have we not served you well?"

"You have well served whoever pays you best," said Sidonicus.

"You conveyed the assassin, the Lady Publennia, of the Larial Calasalii, to Tangara, on behalf of Iaachus, the Arbiter of Protocol, of the palace, to slay an Otung barbarian, thence to abandon her to the mercy of his followers, but she failed. Then you served Abrogastes, the dreaded Far-Grasper, a Drisriak, of the Aatii, seeing that the defensive batteries of Telnar were silent, that he might accomplish his daring raid and seize royal Viviana and Alacida, sisters of the emperor, Aesilesius."

"He trusted you," said Fulvius.

"And we delivered him into your hands," said Corelius, "a prisoner and hostage, one of inestimable value."

"And why then are we incarcerated in this place, wherever it is?" asked Lysis.

"You know much, too much, of my involvement in certain affairs of state," said Sidonicus. "Your clumsiness put my plans at risk. You allowed yourselves, sought fugitives, from the crime of silencing the batteries, to be recognized in a brothel on Varl Street, the Pleasure Palace, and were shortly thereafter apprehended by imperial forces. We instantly moved the prisoner, Abrogastes, the Drisriak, to a new location. We anticipated that one or both of you would reveal where we had hidden him."

"I did not reveal that secret," cried Corelius.

"Nor I!" protested Lysis.

"Though I endured horrifying tortures!" said Corelius.

"One or both of you are lying," said Sidonicus. "Within the hour his former location was stormed by Otungs."

"I revealed nothing," said Corelius.

"Nor I," said Lysis. "It must have been revealed by Phidias, our leader, our captain, he of the *Narcona*."

"Yes, Phidias," said Corelius. "And where is he? Should he not be here, chained with us?"

"His body was found amidst garbage, half-eaten by dogs, in an alley behind the Pleasure Palace," said Sidonicus.

"You were released," said Fulvius.

"To be followed," said Sidonicus, "that your trail would lead to us."

"Accordingly," said Fulvius, "those who followed you were themselves followed, and dealt with, and you were brought here, to be kept safe."

"Safe?" said Corelius, apprehensively.

"Safe for us," said Fulvius.

"Which of you," asked Sidonicus, "revealed the secret hiding place of Abrogastes?"

"Not I!" exclaimed Corelius.

"Nor I!" said Lysis. "I know it was not I!"

"And I know," said Corelius, "it was not I!"

"Very well," said Sidonicus, turning to the two minions, the two somber, sable-clad, hooded figures, "kill them both."

The smaller of the two minions seized Lysis by the hair, and thrust his dagger through the gown of the penitent, into his heart. Then, wiping the blade on the gown of the penitent, he turned to Corelius.

"Wait, wait!" cried Corelius. "You have Abrogastes! His son, Ortog, Ortog of the Ortungen, is in Telnar, seeking him. Would it not be a coup to have both father and son, kings of two Aatii tribes! That is treasure deposited in the vaults of politics and power! And might not one suffice to influence the other, the father to protect the captured, threatened son, and the son to protect the captured, threatened father?"

Sidonicus put his hand on the arm of the smaller minion, staying that arm's poised, readied, stroke. "Speak," he said.

"I could be about," said Corelius. "I could allow myself, seemingly inadvertently, to be discovered by Ortog. I could then lead him, he following me, into an ambush, in which he would be apprehended. And do not reveal to me either the new hiding place of Abrogastes, or that of Ortog, if it be different. Thus, I could not betray you, even if I wished. I could not reveal what I did not know. And, if I do poorly, and you are dissatisfied, you could deal with me as you see fit."

"Unchain him," said Sidonicus, exarch of Telnar.

CHAPTER THIRTY-THREE

"What is this, dear Ottonius?" inquired Iaachus, clearly distraught, standing in the doorway of the emperor's private chambers. "What madness is it to deliver a slave to a half-mad, retarded child?"

"Aesilesius is not a child, but a youth, a young man," said Otto.

"In body a man, in mind a child," said Iaachus.

"So it would seem," said Otto.

"What a miserable fate to impose on a slave, even the least of collar-sluts," said Iaachus. "She has known the hands of men. She is a slave. Fire burns beneath her tunic. What torments and frustrations do you choose to impose upon her? And why? And what is our pathetic, unfortunate Aesilesius, however dear and beloved to us he may be, to do, or be expected to do, with a slave, he, a tragic, mindless simpleton, a twisted, drooling thing, which fears insects, which lives for toys?"

"Now he has a new toy," said Otto. "Surely you know that a slave may be a toy, a master's plaything. Do not some men purchase them for just such a purpose?"

"This must be some Otung cruelty," said Iaachus.

"You fear for the slave?" asked Otto.

"And for the youth, sweet, simple Aesilesius," said Iaachus.

"He may not be as sweet and simple as you suspect," said Otto.

"I do not understand," said Iaachus.

"He has in him the blood of emperors," said Otto.

"A failed blood," said Iaachus, "diluted, weakened, and degenerated."

"So it seems," said Otto.

"You speak mysteriously," said Iaachus.

"I have learned diplomacy from you," said Otto. The emperor then rose from the table, thrust back the rude chair he favored, and went to the side, to a shelf, from which he retrieved certain papers. "You remember these papers?" he asked.

"Surely," said Iaachus. "You have referred to them, more than once. They contain names, the names of volumes missing from the palace library, presumably stolen, perhaps long ago."

"I have had the names read to me," said Otto.

"I recall," said Iaachus. "Indeed, I once read the names to you myself."

"A peculiar collection," said Otto.

"I thought so," said Iaachus. "Different volumes, having little connection with one another, doubtless stolen by different individuals, at different times."

I understand the empress mother has received another miraculous custard or two," said Otto.

"Doubtless she stands high in the favor of the god, *Karch*, or another," said Iaachus.

"I think there is a common thread amongst these diverse, missing books," said Otto.

"I see no common thread," said Iaachus.

"There are several missing histories," said Otto, "most having to do with the Telnarian Empire. Other missing volumes have to do with statecraft and political philosophy. Others deal with techniques of administration, bureaucracy, trade, taxes, law, and coinage, even military strategy."

"I see no common thread," said Iaachus.

"Who would be well served by such studies, by such knowledge?" asked Otto.

"Some savant, some dilettante, some fraud, some madman," said Iaachus.

"Or an emperor," said Otto.

"I do not understand," said Iaachus.

"One of the volumes missing," said Otto, "an old volume, more than a century old, deals with the architecture of the palace, with additions, alterations, renovations, and such."

"So?" said Iaachus.

"So," said Otto, "I sleep with a knife under my pillow."

CHAPTER THIRTY-FOUR

"Is this not a strange place to conduct business?" asked Ortog, king of the Ortungen, a decimated, renegade tribe of the Drisriaks, the son of Abrogastes, the Far-Grasper.

"The cellar of this tavern, I have found," said Iaachus, "is a suitable venue for a discreet interview. I have used it more than once."

"I have come alone, as you suggested," said Ortog.

"Yet you have men in Telnar?" said Iaachus.

"Some, perhaps," said Ortog. "Are you not fearful that you might be recognized, outside the palace?"

"My garb is humble, I am hooded," said Iaachus.

"Have you brought me here, alone, to slay me?" asked Ortog.

"No," said Iaachus.

"You do not do your own killing?" said Ortog.

"Certainly not," said Iaachus. "The risk would be too great."

"Nonetheless," said Ortog, "you will forgive me if I do not drink with you."

"Certainly," said Iaachus.

"Does Otto, king of the Otungen, know of this meeting?" asked Ortog.

"The emperor knows of this meeting," said Iaachus. "He thought it would be too open, and too unwise, to bring you again to the palace, and he himself seldom, to my knowledge, leaves the palace, at least during the daylight hours."

"Why too open, why too unwise?" asked Ortog.

"Given certain information, recently acquired, we conjecture a plot is afoot," said Iaachus, "a plot which threatens you, and perhaps your father. It was deemed best that the palace should appear ignorant of this plot, and best that you be privately apprised of our suspicions, hence this inconspicuous rendezvous."

"What information, what plot?" asked Ortog.

"You are aware of the trio of conspirators, Phidias, Corelius, and Lysis, who disabled the Telnar batteries, allowing the raid of your father which culminated in the seizure of the princesses Viviana and Alacida, the same trio which, as it seems, was involved in the disappearance of your father. Fugitives in Telnar, they were seen in a brothel on Varl Street. Phidias was killed, and Corelius and Lysis were soon taken into custody. Corelius, fearing torture, quickly betrayed the secret place of your father's incarceration, but, before imperial forces could rescue him, he was moved. Both Corelius and Lysis were freed, that they might unwittingly lead us to their confederates, but, as you recall, both mysteriously disappeared."

"I recall," said Ortog, bitterly.

"We speculated that they were killed, or sequestered, primarily that they might not lead us to their principal."

"The exarch of Telnar," said Ortog.

"Perhaps," said Iaachus.

"Surely," said Ortog.

"We suppose him to be their principal," said Iaachus.

"Why not seize him and have him torn apart in the Horse Death?" asked Ortog.

"It is not so simple," said Iaachus. "The city would burn, worlds would flame."

"But something is now new?" said Ortog. "Something has now changed?"

"Yes," said Iaachus. "Corelius has been recognized. He had not been slain, as we had speculated. He is abroad in the city. He is making inquiries as to you, as to your whereabouts."

"He wishes to contact me," asked Ortog.

"We think not," said Iaachus. "At least not as you might think. He must realize you would be aware of his likely collusion in the disappearance of your father. Too, presumably he would not be aware of your father's new location. That information would be denied to him. Might he not have once revealed just such intelligence? Too, he would be aware that you, in barbarian fury, might break his neck or back, if you could get your hands on him."

"Why, then, would he risk encountering me?" asked Ortog.

"We conjecture," said Iaachus, "to precipitate a pursuit, a pursuit hot with reckless, single-minded fury, heedless of peril."

"A naive, barbarian pursuit," said Ortog, "as you Telnarians would see it."

"Precisely," said Iaachus.

"You think barbarians are fools," said Ortog.

"We have often underestimated the sagacity of our enemies," said Iaachus. "It is a common fault of the empire."

"So I am to be led into a trap?" said Ortog.

"We conjecture that to be their plan," said Iaachus.

"And what am I to do?" asked Ortog.

"Permit yourself to be led into a trap," said Iaachus.

CHAPTER THIRTY-FIVE

"Discard that rag, which would conceal you from me," said Ingeld.

"I am not a slave, my husband and lord," said Viviana.

"Cast it aside, and turn slowly before me," he said.

"Yes, my husband and lord," said Viviana.

"Your flanks, your shoulders, your breasts, your belly, your thighs, your calves, your ankles, are not without interest," said Ingeld.

"I am not accustomed," she said, "to be appraised, as might be a fine animal."

"Or any animal," he said.

"Yes, my husband and lord," she said.

"Surely you must, in your royal quarters, in the palace in Telnar, have viewed yourself in a full-length mirror, and wondered what you would bring, as a female, sold in the slave market."

Viviana was silent.

"Surely every female has wondered about such things," he said. "They are females."

"I have been summoned by my husband and lord," said Viviana.

"What do you think you would you bring, off the block?" asked Ingeld.

"I do not know, my husband and lord," she said.

"As a princess," said Ingeld, "thousands of *darins*, as a woman, perhaps five to seven *darins*."

Tears coursed down the fair cheeks of Viviana.

"Perhaps one day you will find out," he said, "when I am through with you—on some mud world."

"Be merciful," begged Viviana.

"You seem less haughty, less arrogant, now, than heretofore," he said.

"I am naked, before my husband and lord," she said. "I have been chained. I have been whipped."

"—as a slave?" asked Ingeld.

"Yes, my husband and lord," she said, "—as a slave."

"Excellent, noble spouse," he said. "You are doubtless now much improved."

"I trust so, my husband and lord," she said.

"Did you enjoy your gruel?" he asked.

"I am grateful to have been fed," she said.

"As a slave is grateful to be fed," he said.

"Yes, my husband and lord," she said.

"It was slave gruel," he said.

"I know," she said.

He regarded her.

"It would be easy enough to have you collared and marked," he said.

"Of what value would I then be to you?" she asked.

"Slave value," he said.

"I am not a slave," she said.

"Nor were thousands of others," he said, "seized and sold like pigs in our markets."

"My husband and lord summoned me," she said.

"You despise me," he said.

She refused to meet his eyes.

"Do you not?" he said.

"How can I despise one who may occupy the throne of Telnaria?" she asked.

"One who will occupy the throne of Telnaria," he said.

"What of your noble brother, Hrothgar?" she asked.

"He will not occupy the throne," he said, "nor does he wish to do so."

"Who knows what dawn may begin a new day?" she said.

Ingeld pointed to a position on the floor, beside the bed, toward its bottom, on the right side. "Kneel there," he said.

"'Kneel'?" she asked.

"There," he said.

"I am not a slave," she said.

"There," he said.

Viviana, of royal blood, knelt at the place indicated.

"I have grown weary of your coldness," he said, "your stiffness, your aloofness, your lack of responsiveness, your inertness, your air of superiority."

"Permit me to rise, my husband and lord," she said.

"Remain as you are," he said.

"Yes, my husband and lord," she said.

"It is hard for a woman to maintain her arrogance, her haughtiness, her dignity, her air of superiority, when she is naked, on her knees before a man."

Viviana shuddered.

"Now, noble spouse," he said, "put your two hands under the coverlets, and lift them, gently. Now put your head down to the coverlets, and kiss them, reverently. You may hope to be permitted on the surface of the couch."

Viviana trembled, keenly aware of a surprising, lovely, if unwanted, unwelcome warmth in her body.

"There are no golden screens here, Telnarian bitch," said Ingeld.

"No, my husband and lord," she said.

"Will you be pleasing?" asked Ingeld.

"I will try, my husband and lord," said Viviana. Well did she recall her whipping, when chained to the high seat in the hall. She would do much to avoid being returned to the custody of Huta.

"You are free," said Ingeld, "but you will address me now, not as husband and lord, but Master."

"Yes, Master," whispered Viviana.

"Louder!" said Ingeld, impatiently.

"Yes, Master," said Viviana.

Never in her life had she felt as she did then, never before so understood her sex, never before felt so female.

Then she cried out in misery, for Ingeld had seized her by the hair, pulled her up, and hurled her to the coverlets, spread upon the deep, soft surface of the broad couch.

She was turned about, rudely.

She looked up, wide-eyed.

Ingeld's hands thrust apart her ankles.

"Master!" she cried.

CHAPTER THIRTY-SIX

"Do not be afraid," said Aesilesius.

"Master?" whispered Nika, not turning about.

"Rise up, and stand, facing me," said Aesilesius. "I would read your collar."

"Master can read?" asked Nika, uncertainly, standing, facing he with whom she shared this unusual chamber, littered with toys.

She felt uneasy, standing so close to him, for, unbent, his frame was upright, straight and strong.

"Interesting," he said, holding the collar and lifting it, slightly. "You have been given to me."

"I am a gift of the emperor," she said.

"I am the emperor," he said.

"You speak," she said. "Your body is no longer small, twisted, contorted, and knotted."

"It is hard to hold it so," he said. "It builds up pain. When it becomes too uncomfortable, one need only whimper, and feign distraction. The audience is then soon ended."

"You are thought to be simple, and slow, feeble minded, even mad."

"And thus I have survived," he said.

"I understand none of this," she said.

"You have been named 'Nika'," he said.

"Yes, Master," she said.

"It is on your collar," he said. "Can you read?"

"No, Master," she said.

"I might teach you," he said. "But you must not reveal such a skill, for speculation would arise as to its surprising acquisition."

"I am afraid," she said.

"And well you might be," he said.

"I am now apprised of a secret which I wish had been better kept."

"It would be impractical, even an agony, would it not, to maintain such a pretense indefinitely, another in the chamber?" he said.

"Am I now to be killed?" she asked.

"It would be easy enough to do," he said. "Who would blame a retarded beast for an inadvertence, a playing too roughly with a new toy, unintentionally breaking it, not knowing his own strength, or smashing it, when frustrated, when out of temper? I have labored for years to build such a *persona*, one unpredictable, one given to moods, and fears, and outbursts."

Nika backed away. She felt the heavy door at her back.

"Your tears moved me," he said. "How dreadful for you, a young girl, vital, alive and bright, to be caged with a monstrosity."

"Master is not a monstrosity," she said. "Master is young, and handsome."

"Nineteen times, since my birth," he said, "Telnaria has orbited its primary."

"Seventeen times since mine," she said.

"You are a pretty slave, Nika," he said.

"May I kneel?" she asked.

"Why?" he asked.

"I am afraid," she said.

"Why?" he asked.

"You are a free man, I am a slave," she said.

"If you wish," he said.

Nika knelt.

"Are you more comfortable, now, on your knees?" he asked.

"Yes, Master," she said. "It is where I belong. I am a slave."

"You are uneasy, otherwise?" he asked.

"Yes, Master," she said. "Very much so, Master."

"It is interesting," he said, "having a pretty woman kneeling before one."

"And properly, Master," she said, "if she be a slave."

"I have strange feelings," he said.

"I am yours to do with as you wish," she said.

"Ah yes," he said, "I recall. You are my new toy."

"But I have feelings, Master," she said. "I cry, I laugh. I can hope, and think, and fear, and wonder, many such things."

"Who would have it otherwise?" he asked. "All that, and there is a collar on your neck, as well."

"Yes, Master. I am collared."

She put her head down.

She remained so for some time, and neither spoke.

After a time, she raised her head, and saw that he with whom she shared the chamber had withdrawn, to the back of the room, and was standing there, regarding her.

"Am I to be killed?" she asked.

"That my secret be protected?" he asked.

"Yes," she said.

"Is my secret safe with you?" he asked.

"Yes," she said, "if you wish it."

"I wonder if any would believe you," he said, "were you to speak what you know. I need only prolong the pretense. It would then be thought that you lied, to escape confinement with me. You might be killed."

"Why have you pretended so degrading and false a thing, sustaining for years such an elaborate and self-shaming hoax?" she asked. "All think you are what you present yourself to be, a witless, pathetic, vacant thing, fearful of insects, enamored of toys, a twisted, retarded child, lost in a man's body."

"I think," he said, "because I am a coward."

"I doubt you are such, Master," she said. "If you were, I think I would now be dead."

"My grandfather," he said, "was poisoned, before I was born. Being informed of that is one of my oldest memories. In me it created great fear, spawning nightmares and a child's terrors, terrors of strange foods, of strangers, of empty rooms, and dark corridors. When I was five, my father died, he, too, of poison. Traumatized, I succumbed to horrors, and lost consciousness for days. When I was recovering, I heard attendants mocking a deluded, hunchbacked retardate encountered in the streets, finding in him a butt for revolting humor. But they did not fear him. They did not take him seriously. Had he been on the throne he might not have been thought worth killing. Presumably, better, he would have been seen as a convenient puppet, by means of which others might pursue their own ends. It would be easy, if others were suitably placed, to rule through him. Alive, he might be manipulated and exploited. Dead, a dynastic schism might have been precipitated, perhaps eventuating in civil war. Thus, for better or for worse, recovering from the trauma of my father's death, and in fear for my own life, I devised the pretense of debility and incompetence. After the political murder of my father, my mother, Atalana, assumed, *de facto*, the regency, and ruled in my name. Years passed. Eventually, the regency was le-

gally terminated, but, in a sense, perforce, given my supposed
infirmities, it continued. I was frightened to ascend the throne,
and hid in a cave of my own making. Iaachus, as I understand
it, by dispensing favors here and there, in my name, to one high
family or another, kept peace in the empire. Factions were paci-
fied and carnage precluded. But surely this precarious, unstable
arrangement could not continue indefinitely. It could be only a
matter of time. A thousand things might have taken place. But
that which did, given the recruitment of barbarians to defend
the empire, was the seizure of the throne by an Otung, of the
exiled, outlawed, Vandal nation."

"You can read," she said. "How could that have come to be?"

"Easily," he said, "for tutors were engaged to teach me, and I
learned, but pretended not to learn, pretended not to keep things
in mind, pretended not to be able to remember the simplest things.
How they struggled, so patiently, so bravely, failing to understand
how successful their efforts truly were. I became skilled at reading long before they gave up, believing their task to be hopeless."

Nika sobbed.

"Why do you cry?" he asked.

"Your life is so narrow, and tragic," she said.

"I have no one but myself to blame," he said. "I was afraid as a
helpless child, small amongst looming, frightening adults, anyone
of whom, as far as I knew, might kill me. Who knew what lay behind this smile or that? I was frightened of the dark. I feared to be
with others, and I feared to be alone. I scarcely dared to sleep, or
eat, or drink. What might creep toward me in the darkness? Who
might give me poison in food, poison in drink? And I am afraid
now, still, as a man. I have refused to claim my rightful place.
My pretense as a child I have maintained into my manhood. How
could one, after years, abandon it in safety? And, shames and sorrows, I am still afraid to die. And how could I now be in greater
jeopardy? At a word from he who sits upon the throne I might
be killed. Any knock at my door might be that of an instructed,
obedient assassin."

"Poor Master," said Nika.

"So I am a fraud," he said, "and worse, a coward."

"I do not think so, Master," she said.

"I dare not abandon my pretense," he said. "It has preserved
me."

"But for so little, Master," said Nika.

"I am still alive," he said.

"Is it a life worth living?" she asked.

"In any event," he said, "matters are done now. A barbarian sits upon the throne. If he knew me as I am, whole and thoughtful, I do not doubt but what he would instantly dispose of me."

"I do not think so, Master," said Nika.

"How so?" he asked.

"I know something of him, and of others about him," she said.

"What?" he asked.

"It has to do with honor," she said.

"I have read of honor in the histories," he said. "It perished long ago."

"In the hearts of some, it lives," she said.

"In the hearts of barbarians?" he asked.

"Surely in the hearts of some," she said. "And even, surely, amongst Telnarians, in the hearts of some."

"Beware," said he, "slave."

"Forgive me, Master," she said.

"I have no honor," he said.

"Had you lacked honor," she said, "I would now be dead."

"There is a tear upon your cheek," he said. "Wipe it away."

"Yes, Master," she said.

"Use your hair," he said.

"Yes, Master," she said.

"Why do you cry?" he asked.

"For you, my Master," she said.

"I do not understand," he said.

"You are intelligent, young, strong, active, and fine," she said, "and yet you are a prisoner twice over, once in the dreadful *persona* you have contrived to create, and, again, your body, your youth and promise, incarcerated in a cell, a sealed chamber, which you may not leave, save under supervision and guard."

"Do not concern yourself with the locked chamber," he said.

"Master?" she asked.

"They think I am a prisoner in this room," he said, "but I am not."

"The door is locked," she said, "from the outside. I have seen the key."

"There are panels," he said, "passages, small hidden corridors. I may go much where I please."

She regarded him, startled.

"In the dangers of a palace," he said, "where assassins may lurk in dark thresholds, eager blades unsheathed and hungry for blood, where concealed springs may launch poisoned darts, where vipers might be uncabineted outside a portal, where the walls themselves may smoke of ambition and intrigue, of envy and malice, where intruding mobs might sweep aside surprised, inadequate defenses, wise men devised means to conceal themselves, even to move about, undetected."

"How can it be?" she said.

"Have you not heard of the miraculous custards bestowed upon the empress mother," he asked.

"I have heard of them," she whispered, wonderingly.

"The matter is simple," he said. "I surreptitiously obtain them from the kitchen and, when the empress mother is asleep, I leave them in her chamber, and withdraw, unseen, undetected."

"You can come and go as you please?" said Nika.

"Subject to precautions, of course," he said. "One must be careful. Perhaps you would like such a custard?"

"Do not risk yourself on my behalf," said Nika.

"I have stolen a knife from the kitchen," he said.

"Perhaps you should not have done so," she said.

"It was not difficult," he said.

"Have you access to the sleeping chamber of Master Ottonius?" asked Nika.

"Yes," he said. "I could kill him any night."

"Do not do so," said Nika.

"Why not?" he asked.

"He is not a bad man," she said.

"He is a barbarian," he said.

"Even so," she said.

"Do you fear for him?" he asked.

"He is large, strong, alert, wary, skilled, and dangerous. He has been trained for the arena and has fought and survived on the sand. He is a warrior. He won the throne of the Otungs, on Tangara, in a festival of blood. He is given to fits of uncontrollable rage. It is you for whom I would fear."

"For me?" he asked.

"Yes, Master," she said.

"Few have feared for me," he said.

"Perhaps more than you know," she said.

"There is no hurry," he said. "I shall bide my time. Knives are patient. He might be replaced by another, who might be worse."

"Currently," said Nika, "the empire, though fragile and tense, is stable. The imperial forces, abetted by the Vandalii, with its tribes, hold the Aatii and others at bay. Plotting and diplomacy are rampant, men scheme and plan, but mighty wars do not now rage, engulfing worlds and systems of worlds."

"I have heard of the marriages of my sisters," he said, "haughty, spoiled Viviana and gentle Alacida."

"Abrogastes, the Far-Grasper, lord of the Drisriaks, hegemonic tribe of the Aatii, has disappeared," said Nika. "Sidonicus, the exarch of Telnar, despite the example and teachings of Floon, like a fat, giant spider, grows richer, and more ambitious and powerful."

"I know so little of so much," he said.

"It is not your fault," said Nika. "You are sheltered. You are uninformed."

"What shall we do with you?" he asked.

"Master?" said Nika, uncertainly.

"I could kill you or have you killed," he said.

"Your secret would then be safe," she said.

"But I do not care to do this," he said, "though it be compatible with, even prescribed by, weighty, sober policy."

"A slave is pleased to hear of your reluctance in this matter," she said.

"More generously, if less wisely, I could whine and fret," he said, "and have you removed, as an unwanted toy. You might then be free of me."

"I do not wish to be free of you," she said.

"I do not understand," he said.

She looked away, quickly.

"Keep me," she said. "Would that not be safer? Is that not a better guarding of your secret? Keep me chained, if you wish. I am, after all, a slave. Might I not, chained if you wish, accompany you when you are taken forth from the chamber? Might I not, if unchained, be as your maid, and nurse? Might I not, if you permit it, come and go, outside, and be your eyes and ears in the palace? I might learn much, and then recount to you what I learned. Thus, by this means, you could be a thousand times better informed than you are now."

"Why do you look to the side?" he said. "Why do you not meet my eyes?"

"Forgive me, Master," she said.

"You would be my spy?" he said.

"Your bearer of news, your informant," she said.

"But," he said, "you must feign misery, and grievous sorrow over your pathetic lot."

"Of course, Master," she said.

"You seem delighted, even happy," he said.

"I am a slave, on my knees, where I belong, before a free man," she said.

He then approached her, slowly, until he stood before her, looking down at her.

"I have strange feelings," he said.

"I am a helpless slave," she said. "I am before my Master. I am wet, I am juicing, I am heated. I beg, as a helpless, rightless slave, to be caressed."

"I have never had a woman," he said.

"I am a woman, a slave," she said, "and no woman is more a woman than a slave."

"I feel strange things in my body, unaccountable, wild, sweeping, overpowering, unfamiliar things," he said, wonderingly. "What feelings are these?"

"Those of a man," she said, "with a slave at his feet."

He reached down and drew the brief tunic from her body.

"How beautiful you are," he said.

He then lifted her, and carried her to the couch, on which he placed her.

"Chain me," she said. "Chain me in place."

"Do you wish it?" he asked.

"Yes," she said.

Shortly thereafter she moved her shackled limbs.

There was a small sound, of the slightly stirred links.

"You are now quite helpless," he said.

"Now do with me what you will," she said.

CHAPTER THIRTY-SEVEN

Ingeld lay sleeping.

Viviana lay beside him, awake.

It was early. She could see a gray bit of light, a subtle illumination, at the casement. She could hear the cry of birds outside the chamber.

She wanted to touch Ingeld, but dared not do so. Might she not be beaten for hazarding so egregious an importunity?

Surely he could not feel, he so much in sleep, a tiny kiss, pressed upon his shoulder?

She dared to touch him so.

To her fear, she felt him turn toward her. He was so much larger than she! It was like a large, feral animal had turned toward her, so close, in the half-darkness. She felt weak, helpless, and small, beside him, but alive, so alive! "Please," she whispered, "again, again, Master."

"You beg it?" he asked.

"Yes, Master," she whispered. "I beg it!"

Later, Ingeld chained her, by the neck, to the foot of his couch, and returned to sleep. Viviana lay there, on the chain, on the floor, at the foot of the couch, not sleeping. She recalled Huta's warning, that she was to please Ingeld, but not too well, as he "belonged to her," as though a free man could belong to a slave! "Well, dear Huta, mere slave," thought Viviana, "we shall see about such matters. I think I can please Ingeld quite well. Who knows, he might soon rid himself of you. Perhaps I can see to that."

CHAPTER THIRTY-EIGHT

"He is strong," said one of the four men who were struggling with Ortog.

"The straps will hold him," said another.

"He recovered consciousness quickly," said another, "too quickly."

"There is much vitality in these barbarian beasts," said another.

Ortog lifted his bloodied head, and listened.

Someone seemed to be ascending steps.

Ortog had been pursuing fleeing, terrified, blond Corelius down an alley in the Varl District, but yards in his wake, when he had turned, abruptly, suddenly aware of several men who had sprung forth from two doorways behind him, one to his right, and one to his left. He had fought like an iron-burned *vi-cat* driven into an arena. One man's arm he broke, and another's neck. A kick to the side of the leg of another splintered a knee. But then a heavy object had struck him, and he fell unconscious to the stones. In a moment he was bound tightly with broad straps, and was gagged and blindfolded. He was then placed in a closed wagon which, moments ago, had turned into the alley. Corelius had not returned to aid his confederates, but, shaken and gasping, perhaps uncertain as to the outcome of the uneven struggle behind him, or of Ortog's possible eluding of, or escaping from, his attackers, had continued his flight.

Then the steps were no longer heard.

The individual who had ascended the steps was then, presumably, on the level with the others.

"Is he well-secured, well blindfolded?" asked a man's voice. Ortog did not recognize the voice.

"He is like a tethered, hooded bull, large and dangerous," said a man. "Beware, he does not plunge at you, buffeting you."

"Hold him, tightly," said the voice.

Ortog was grasped anew.

"The noble Corelius has served us well," said the voice.

"At little risk, he easily led this simple, trusting, unwary barbarian brute into the trap," said a man.

"Barbarians are stupid," said another man.

"So," said the voice, "you are the mighty Ortog, the renegade Drisriak, held, trussed, gagged, and blindfolded?"

"He was easily tricked," said a man.

"He suspected nothing," said another.

"It is as I told you," said a fellow, "barbarians are stupid."

"Remove the gag," said the voice.

This was done.

"Can you speak Telnarian?" inquired the voice.

"Enough," said Ortog, "to tell your women to strip themselves and prepare to be collared and branded as slaves."

"Strike him," said the voice.

Ortog scarcely moved, though fists struck him. He felt blood in his mouth, and under the blindfold, at the side of his face.

"There is work for such as you, large, simple beast," said the voice, "on galley benches, in quarries, and in the mines, but we have other plans for you."

"What might they be?" inquired Ortog.

"The remnants of your dissident group, the Ortungen," said the voice, "are about. With your life in our hands, we shall be assured of their tractability."

"Telnaria has little to fear from the Ortungen, since their decimation on Tenguthaxichai," said Ortog.

"True," said the voice, "but we anticipate that your enkeepment will provide us with advantages well beyond the mere pacification of some half-armed, scattered tribesmen."

"How is that?" asked Ortog.

"You are the son of Abrogastes, of the Aatii, called the Far-Grasper," said the voice.

"A son," said Ortog, "of Abrogastes, the Far-Grasper, king of the Drisriaks, hegemonic tribe of the Alemanni."

"Your father tried to kill you, on Tenguthaxichai," said the voice.

"It seems so," said Ortog.

"But the blade missed its mark."

"Not at all," said Ortog. "It entered my body at the point, and depth, intended. Its purpose was to seem mortal, while, in reality, sparing my life."

"Absurd," said the voice.

"Such a stroke would require a skilled surgeon," said a man. "It would be far beyond the skill of an uncouth, ignorant barbarian."

"Where is your father?" asked the voice.

"I suspect you know," said Ortog.

"Possibly," said the voice. "Indeed, we may arrange a family reunion."

Two men laughed, one of whom was one of the two who held Ortog.

"We will put you in separate cells," said a man, "where you can see one another, but cannot reach one another."

"Therefore," said a man, "you will be unable to kill one another."

"We may not wish to kill one another," said Ortog.

"Why else," asked a man, "would you have pursued the noble Corelius, if not to be led to Abrogastes, that you might enact your vengeance upon him, from Tenguthaxichai?"

"The noble Corelius is a coward and traitor," said Ortog.

"Beware," said a man.

"Perhaps you could put us in the same cell," said Ortog.

"The noble Corelius?" asked a man.

"Yes," said Ortog.

"If you do not hate one another, you and your father, and even, ideally, care for one another," said the voice, "that is even better for us, for each may then be used to influence the other. Through you we control the Ortungen, few as they may be, and through Abrogastes, we control the Drisriaks, and, possibly, thereby, all the tribes of the Aatii. Moreover, by threatening you, we may win concessions from Abrogastes, while, by threatening Abrogastes, we may win concessions from you."

"You are clever," said Ortog.

"The plan is that of the wise and noble Corelius," said a man.

"Who speaks?" asked Ortog.

"You need not know," said Timon Safarius Rhodius, of the Telnar Rhodii, *primarius* of the senate of Telnaria.

"Let us take him to his cell," said a man.

"Be careful on the steps," said Safarius. "There are several of them."

CHAPTER THIRTY-NINE

"You are pretty," said Atalana, the empress mother, to the kneeling slave.

"Please, gracious Mistress," said the slave, "let another attend upon your glorious son."

"Your hair," said the empress mother, "is bright red, like fire, and long."

"Please," begged the slave.

"Dear Aesilesius likes pretty things," said Atalana.

"I fear him," said the slave. "I do not know what he will do. He is a creature of tantrums and moods. He cannot control his saliva. He can barely speak. It is hard to understand him, even to know what he wants. I fear even to look upon him. His body is twisted, crooked, curled in upon itself. A fly entered his chamber yesterday and I thought he would go mad with terror."

"Poor Aesilesius," said Atalana.

"Let another attend upon him," said the slave.

"Surely you would not wish your trials to be visited upon another," said Atalana.

"One stronger, one wiser, than I," said the slave.

"He will have no other," said Atalana. "He cries, he screams, he rolls on the floor."

"He thinks I am a toy," said the slave, "only a toy, only another toy."

"Sweet, troubled Aesilesius is fond of toys," said Atalana, "especially pretty toys."

"I am no more to him than his blocks, his beaded strings, and colored globes, his small, stuffed, yellow *torodont*."

"Beloved, unfortunate Aesilesius is so fond of his toys," said Atalana, the empress mother, "particularly the pretty ones."

"Mercy, great Mistress," begged the slave.

"The one act of that barbarous lout, the arrant usurper, the so-called Ottonius, the First, who dares to sit upon my son's throne,"

said the empress mother, "his one act of which I can bring myself
to approve, is his giving you to dear Aesilesius."

"No!" cried the slave.

"I have not seen dear Aesilesius so tractable, so sweetly tem-
pered, so pleased, in years."

"Mercy!" said the slave.

"I am well pleased with the arrangement," said the empress
mother.

"I lift my hands to you," said the slave. There was a tiny sound
of metal from the linkage closely joining the two metal cuffs, these
attractively, snugly, upon her slender wrists. "I plead, piteously,
with all the helpless fervor of the slave."

"And with the meaninglessness, as well as the helplessness, of
the slave, my dear," said the empress mother.

"Please!" cried the slave.

"I wonder that you have not, in your desperation, appealed to
the boor who sits upon the throne," said Atalana.

"I have," said the slave.

"And?"

"He has refused to grant my plea," said the slave. "He is adamant."

"So, too, am I," said the empress mother.

"Surely not, kind Mistress," said the slave.

"I have granted this audience against my better judgment,"
said the empress mother. "I think it should now be concluded."

"No," begged the slave.

"I do not see," said the empress mother, "that you have so
much to complain of. Outside the chamber of my grandson,
outside of which you often are, you come and go much as you
please, save for your braceleting, your hands commonly braceleted before you, as they are now, in the palace, and commonly
braceleted behind you outside the palace. Many slaves would
envy you so generous a liberty of movement, even given the
braceleting."

The slave lifted her hands, parting them, with a small sound
of metal, to the tiny extent possible. "The noble Aesilesius," she
said, "will have me so."

"Surely not in his chamber," said the empress mother.

"Not so much then," said the slave.

"Men are beasts, brutes, and monsters," said the empress
mother. "They enjoy having absolute power over us. If they had

their way we would all be naked, squirming in chains at their feet, fearing to be whipped."

"Am I not to be granted mercy, any mercy, great Mistress?" asked the slave.

"No," said Atalana. "You are good for my son. He likes to have you kneeling behind him, to his left, in our audiences, your hands braceleted before you. He is more patient then, more willing to endure the tedious traffic of state, to the extent I am permitted, for the sake of appearances, to participate in it. Sometimes he even looks as though he might understand what was transpiring."

"There is no mercy for me then?" asked the slave.

"No," said Atalana, the empress mother.

"Please, please, noble Mistress," begged Nika.

"No," said the empress mother, "and do not bother me again about this matter."

"Forgive me, great mistress," said Nika, and stood, and backed away, and then, when it seemed appropriate, turned and left the room.

She was smiling.

CHAPTER FORTY

"So," said Abrogastes, clutching the bars of his cell, glaring across the wide corridor, into the cell into which Ortog had just been thrust, "I have sired a fool."

These cells were on the fourth basement level beneath the warehouse of Dardanis, of the Telnar Dardanii, importer of the wares of a dozen worlds.

Ortog turned about, to face his jailers and, across the corridor, his incarcerated father.

The cell door rang shut.

"I do not run from you now, monster," said blond Corelius, archly, facing Ortog. "And I never feared you, an ignorant, untutored bumpkin, before, not in the least. I feigned flight from you, and fear, merely to lead you into the patent ambuscade in which you found yourself trapped. A young boar, his tusks scarce erupted, could not have been snared as easily. Were it not for the plan I devised, which I wished to see implemented, I would have subdued you on the street."

"Why did you not do so?" inquired Ortog.

"My reasons were twice mighty," said Corelius. "First, a pedestrian grappling in public would too obviously link me with you, possibly compromising my future role in certain delicate matters. Second, I feared, in such a grappling, I might inadvertently slay you, a broken back or neck, a head dashed on the pavement, such things, in which case your value to my principal would be lost, and unrecoverable."

"I tremble," said Ortog.

"Do not do so," said Corelius. "It is not necessary. You are safe from me, here, where you are, and as you are, a prisoner."

"You are clever," said Ortog.

"I am Telnarian," said Corelius.

"Enter the cell," said Ortog, "that we may discuss these matters."

"I do not have time," said Corelius. "I give you leave to ponder such matters at your convenience."

"Come closer to the bars," said Ortog.

Corelius backed away.

Besides Corelius, there were five men in the corridor between the cells. Three had masked themselves before Ortog's blindfold had been removed. First amongst these three was Timon Safarius Rhodius, of the Telnar Rhodii, *primarius* of the senate of Telnaria. The other two were large, dangerous men, bodyguards of Safarius, each a former gladiator who had won his freedom following ten kills. The other two, who were not masked, were jailers. It had taken four of these men, the two former gladiators and the two jailers, once Ortog's blindfold and bonds had been removed, to get him into the cell.

"You do well to back away, dear Corelius," said Safarius. "You thoughtfully seek to protect the barbarian. He might injure himself by dashing himself against the bars to reach you."

"My thought exactly," said Corelius.

"You!" cried Ortog, suddenly pointing through the bars at Safarius. "You spoke above. You are first here! I would know you! Remove your mask!"

"Do you expect him to do so?" asked Abrogastes, scornfully, from across the corridor. "You have always been an unthinking, impatient fool."

"Perhaps," said Ortog, "I am more patient than you know. Perhaps I have learned to think."

"You might have petitioned, or negotiated, severance from the Drisriaks, to found a tribe, but your temper was short and your blood hot."

"I do as I wish," said Ortog. "I am of the Alemanni. I am of steel and blood. I am the son of Abrogastes, the Far-Grasper."

"And so," said Safarius, "father and son are blood enemies."

"The Far-Grasper tried to kill his traitorous, renegade son on Tenguthaxichai," said Corelius, amused, "but his stroke was faulty."

"It seems," said Safarius, "it would not be good to put these two in the same cell."

The jailers laughed, but the bodyguards were silent, observing, standing, with arms folded. They did not dismiss or underestimate men such as Abrogastes and Ortog. They had met such men on the sand. In the arena one learns quickly, or one does not learn at all.

"We shall leave you now," said Safarius. "I am sure you have much to talk about, stories to tell, memories to share, and such."

"Put us together," said Abrogastes, in a terrible voice.

"Perhaps later," said Safarius. "We wish to keep both of you alive, at least for a time."

Safarius made a sign to the others, and then he and they left the corridor, closed the corridor gate, and began to climb the steps.

"They could kill us," said Ortog, "what have they to gain otherwise."

"A great deal," said Abrogastes. "Through me they hope not only to hold the Drisriaks, and perhaps the Alemanni as a whole, at bay, but to enlist them for their own purposes."

"And if they kill you, the Drisriaks, and doubtless the other tribes of the Alemanni, and their allies, would seek blood vengeance."

"Hardly," said Abrogastes. "The killing would be secret. They would not know who to blame, who to hunt."

"Telnarians, Otungs," said Ortog. "An Otung sits upon the throne."

"It would be a pointless, mindless rampage," said Abrogastes.

"Such things are often satisfying," said Ortog.

"Unfortunately," said Abrogastes.

"I see little need for them to preserve my life," said Ortog. "The Ortungs are muchly decimated, scattered, their ships few."

"The schismatic Ortungs are of the Alemanni," said Abrogastes. "Even a few are dangerous."

"Perhaps I am wiser than you in some things," said Ortog.

"Enlighten me," said Abrogastes.

"They think a threat to the father might make the son more pliable," said Ortog, "and a threat to the son might induce the father to be more accommodating."

"How little they know of the Alemanni," said Abrogastes.

"Perhaps they know more of the Alemanni than the Alemanni," said Ortog.

"Do not forget," said Abrogastes, "I sought to slay you on Tenguthaxichai."

"I remember you failed to do so," said Ortog.

"The stroke missed its mark," said Abrogastes, angrily.

"Imprecision seldom characterizes the blade of the Far-Grasper," said Ortog. "His steel is commonly inerrant."

"Would that I had a blade now, and you were within its compass," said Abrogastes.

"Surely the galaxy is wide enough for both Drisriaks and Ortungs," said Ortog.

"No galaxy is so large," said Abrogastes.

"Let your pride not be stunned that a son should so resemble his father," said Ortog. "Be shamed rather that he should
not do so."

"Renegade, traitor!" cried Abrogastes.

"It was not my intention to steal a throne," said Ortog. "It was
my intention to create another."

Ortog went to the bars, and set his considerable strength
against them, trying to spread them, to bend them, to pull them
from the concrete.

"This cage could hold a *torodont*," said Abrogastes.

"But perhaps not a Drisriak," said Ortog, "—nor an Ortung."

"You are not only a renegade and traitor," said Abrogastes,
"but a fool."

"I may not be as much a fool as you think," said Ortog.

"You were unwary," said Abrogastes. "You did not think. You
permitted yourself to be led into a trap."

"And how are you here?" asked Ortog.

"I was betrayed by trusted allies, whom I had no reason to
suspect, proven allies who had served me well."

"Telnarians," said Ortog. "Men who are unfamiliar with winter trails, who do not know the smoke of the halls, who have not
shared horns of *bror*. Telnarians who betrayed Telnaria. He who
betrays his own hall will not hesitate to betray the hall of another."

"One casts the stones," said Abrogastes. "One abides the outcome."

"I, too, once cast stones," said Ortog.

"And lost," said Abrogastes.

"Stones once cast may be cast again," said Ortog.

"How is it that you are in Telnar?" asked Abrogastes.

"I sought you," said Ortog.

"To slay me, that you might revenge the decimation of the Ortungs," said Abrogastes.

"Perhaps," said Ortog.

"And now you are cooped like a wing-clipped *varda*," said Abrogastes.

"Where are we?" asked Ortog.

"I do not know," said Abrogastes.

"Others will know," said Ortog.

"Surely," said Abrogastes, "our captors."

"And others, now, as well," said Ortog.

At that moment, from the stairs, outside the corridor gate, there was a hideous sound of panting, of clawed feet, of growling, and snarling.

"Keep your hands inside the bars," said Abrogastes. "They will tear off a hand, or arm."

"War dogs," said Ortog.

The corridor gate was opened by a jailer and two large beasts, each the size of a small horse, thrust themselves into the corridor.

The two dogs turned instantly to Ortog and, hissing and squealing, eyes bright with hate, fangs wet with saliva, snapped at the bars. Then, frustrated, each, with a long, massive, clawed forelimb, reached through the bars and wildly raked the air between themselves and Ortog. Ortog retreated farther within the cell, and both beasts turned away, snarling, and lay down in the corridor.

"They are starved. They are trained. They are mistreated. They are taught hate. They can tear a man to pieces," said Abrogastes.

"Pleasant fellows," said Ortog.

"Here they are used as guards," said Abrogastes.

"They failed to threaten you," said Ortog.

The two beasts sprang up, snarling.

There was the crack of a whip.

"Back, back, down, down!" said a jailer, in the portal, whip in hand.

The two beasts backed away and crouched down, snarling.

Behind the jailer came two more jailers, each bearing a wooden platter of food and a shallow bowl of wine. These platters were put on the floor and thrust by a foot through the rectangular aperture at the bottom of the cell door.

"Feast well," said the jailer with a whip, and then the three jailers withdrew, closing and locking the corridor gate.

"Do not eat," said Abrogastes.

"Poison?" asked Ortog. "Drugs?"

"No," said Abrogastes.

"I do not understand," said Ortog.

"Wait," said Abrogastes.

The sound of the footsteps on the stairs faded.

One of the beasts rose up and rubbed itself against the bars of the cage of Abrogastes. The other rose up to a sitting position, regarding him.

"It would be wise to do as I do," said Abrogastes. He then cast most of the contents of his platter to the floor of the corridor where they were snatched up by the dogs. Ortog watched, wonderingly, and then imitated his father's action. Abrogastes then, through the bars, held out a piece of meat to each of the beasts, which took it gently. "Do not attempt this yet," he said, across the corridor. "They do not yet know you. They might tear your hand off."

"You enlist unusual allies," said Ortog.

"Into whose heart treason is unlikely to enter," said Abrogastes.

"I would I had a weapon," said Ortog.

"In your cell, as in mine," said Abrogastes, "there is a simple iron cot, on which reposes a thin mattress. This mattress is supported on springs, narrow strips of metal. Over time you can work one or more of these strips loose."

"Surely such a thing is no weapon," said Ortog.

"A pillow, a stylus, a splinter of wood, a rock can be a weapon," said Abrogastes. "A pillow can suffocate, a stylus can pierce, a splinter of wood can stab, a rock can crush."

"And your strip of metal?" asked Ortog.

"It can snap out an eye," said Abrogastes. "It can form a garrote, it can cut a throat."

"I shall arm myself," said Ortog.

"And seem unarmed," said Abrogastes.

CHAPTER FORTY-ONE

"Welcome back to Telnar, noble Ingeld, revered prince of the Drisriaks," said Sidonicus, the words like drops of oil, exarch of Telnar, from the draped throne in his private audience chamber.

Other than Ingeld, four individuals were present, Fulvius, high ministrant in Telnar, his purple only somewhat less so than that of his superior, Sidonicus; Timon Safarius Rhodius, of the Telnar Rhodii, *primarius* of the senate of Telnaria; and blond Corelius, once an officer of Phidias, captain of the *Narcona*, and later a member of the high command of the defensive batteries of Telnar, which were unaccountably silent during a surprise raid in which the two princesses, Viviana and Alacida, were abducted, to be later betrothed to Ingeld and Hrothgar, two sons of Abrogastes, king of the Drisriaks, called the Far-Grasper.

"You have met my esteemed colleague, Ministrant Fulvius, on Tenguthaxichai, I believe," said Sidonicus.

"In the matter of the Otung medallion and chain," said Ingeld.

"You may not know my dear friend, Timon Safarius Rhodius," said Sidonicus."

"We have not met," said Ingeld.

"He is *primarius* of the senate," said Sidonicus.

"A most exalted and noble post," said Ingeld.

Safarius bowed, appreciatively.

"I understand a coup failed," said Ingeld.

"I was not present at the time," said Safarius.

"Lastly," said Sidonicus, "may I introduce my young friend and colleague, of less than noble family, but of extraordinary merit, Corelius."

"I am honored," said Ingeld, scarcely glancing at Corelius.

"He collaborated in the plot wherewith your noble father became my guest," said Sidonicus, "and devised a further scheme by means of which your noble brother, Ortog, was induced to accept my hospitality."

"Ortog is detained?" said Ingeld.

"I understand he was your father's favorite," said Sidonicus.

"He is your guest?" asked Ingeld.

"With your father," said Sidonicus.

"I knew not the whereabouts of the traitorous Ortog," said Ingeld. "He has not yet been executed?"

"Not as yet," said Sidonicus. "For the moment we deem him, like your father, more valuable alive."

"I trust the moment, in neither case, will be overly prolonged," said Ingeld.

"As a result of my plan, noble prince," said Corelius, "in which I played a major role, the star of your future blazes more brightly in the sky of power."

"You were doubtless well paid," said Ingeld.

"He was given his life," said Fulvius.

"Why do you sit upon a throne while a prince stands?" asked Ingeld.

"I am a prince of the temple," said Sidonicus, startled.

"I do not think the humble Floon, on whose teachings you grow fat, sat upon a throne," said Ingeld.

"He was not the exarch of Telnar," said Sidonicus.

"How can one be a prince," asked Ingeld, "when he has no swords?"

"One need only make use of others, who carry swords," said Sidonicus.

"I thought that Floon rejected the sword," said Ingeld.

"Not at all," said Sidonicus.

"You have a text for that?" asked Ingeld.

"New texts are discovered, from time to time," said Sidonicus.

"When necessary?" asked Ingeld.

"If you like," said Sidonicus.

"The matter is obscure," said Fulvius. "Texts seem to conflict."

"Merely *seem* to conflict," said Sidonicus.

"Of course," said Fulvius.

"Get out of the throne," said Ingeld.

"Blasphemy!" said Fulvius.

"Now," said Ingeld.

"You would dare sit upon the throne of the exarch?" asked Fulvius.

"Off the throne, now," said Ingeld.

"Surely, if it would please the prince," said Sidonicus, softly.

"No!" cried Fulvius.

"Be easy, sweet brother, close friend, beloved ministrant," said Sidonicus. "As true Floonians, we are self-effacing and self-sacrificing. Remember, we reject prestige, power, wealth, and influence. We seek littleness and rejoice in our lack of importance. We imitate the sand in its docility and patience. Like the tree we yield ourselves to the ax. Like the fallen leaf we gladly accept the wind which carries where it wishes."

"Humility?" said Fulvius.

"Most precisely," said Sidonicus.

"How I have fallen!" said Fulvius. "My heart cries out with shame!"

"Petition *Karch* for forgiveness," counseled Sidonicus.

"Forgive me, *Karch*!" wept Fulvius, looking upward toward the ceiling of the chamber.

"Stop your blabbering and acting," said Ingeld. "I have no intention of sitting on, or otherwise desecrating, that pretentious, absurd object. It would sicken me to do so. A throne, indeed! Who deems it that, and with what justification? If it were not of value in my plans, as it impresses the ignorant and foolish, the mindless and gullible, I would topple it. I am proclaimed shrewd, ruthless, and cruel, but I am a child, an amateur, compared to the shrewdness, ruthlessness, and cruelty of frauds and hypocrites, who would rule through artifice and subterfuge, duplicity and deceit."

"I think we understand one another well enough," said Sidonicus.

"Then we shall sit with one another as equals," said Ingeld, "and conspire honestly, and plot our crimes and villainies openly, without cant and pretense."

"If you wish," said Sidonicus.

"Let our ambitions be unsheathed here, though concealed elsewhere," said Ingeld.

"It will be as the prince wishes," said Sidonicus.

"I have swords at my disposal," said Ingeld.

"I need only speak from the pulpit of the temple," said Sidonicus, "and I can have them at my disposal, as well."

"You are naive," said Ingeld, "to suppose that you can deal with Abrogastes, or Ortog, except on their terms. Honor intervenes. Have you heard of it? It seems you may be ignorant of that trammel. Do not judge them by yourselves. Too, you have not seized them in innocent childhood and contaminated them with contrived gibberish, tying strings of terror on their minds by means of which to manipulate them later as you wish, making them fear not to obey you, not to feed and clothe you, and not to enrich you, lest they be denied a place at the table of *Karch*, as if there was such a table and as if, if there was, you would know anything about it. If there is a *Karch*, or Orak, or such, let them appear and handle such matters themselves, or not, if they wish. If they truly wish a hundred pigs sacrificed on the summer solstice, though I assume they do not eat the pigs, they should be fully capable of making that wish known. Surely they do not need sweet, humble ministrants to assist them in the matter, or obese, pompous ministrants either. In short, given honor and a mind free of imposed weights, contrived burdens, and instilled illness, you cannot deal with an Abrogastes or an Ortog as you think; sooner you could deal with the hawk or *vi-cat*."

"How then shall we proceed?" asked Sidonicus.

"We shall kill both Abrogastes and Ortog," said Ingeld, "and manage the matter, where the bodies are found, amidst supposedly incriminating evidence, and such, to make it appear that they were murdered by Otungs. This will enflame the Drisriaks, the other tribes of the Alemanni, whom you call the Aatii, and their allied tribes. Meanwhile the temple pretends outrage and publicly deplores this perceived crime. This leads the Aatii, led by me, and the confederated tribes to regard the temple as an ally, one who will endorse the justice of their cause. You will also preach against the Otungs and your spies and provocateurs will ready your faithful in their mad throngs to take to the streets when the signal is given. We and the temple, together, will crush the Otungs. The usurper will be swept from the throne and the Otungs, and the other tribes of the Vandalii, will be crushed, their remnants, if any, scattered, driven as exiles and fugitives to remote worlds."

"And for our part in this?" asked Sidonicus.

"The new emperor, Ingeld, the First," said Ingeld, "will decree that your particular version of Floonianism, and none other, is the official religion of the empire."

"And all other faiths will be outlawed and their adherents will, by means of the secular authority, to which alone violence is permitted, be forcibly converted or slain?"

"Let us not do too much too soon," said Ingeld.

"Surely, later," said Sidonicus. "To save the *koos* of thousands, of millions, perhaps billions, false faiths, misleading and pernicious faiths, must be rooted out and their recalcitrant adherents exterminated."

"We shall see," said Ingeld. "I would be reluctant to pass a law under which I myself, as things are twisted about, might somehow be prosecuted."

"It is easy enough to be smudged with sacred oil from the pools of Zirus," said Sidonicus. "Beyond that you may do as you please."

"One must be careful," said Ingeld. "One step into quicksand might prove to be one's last."

"Things should work out nicely," said Sidonicus. "You will rule by the sword. We will rule by the *koos*."

"Two coffers," said Ingeld.

"One for the state, one for the temple," said Fulvius.

"I leave the details to you, my dear exarch," said Ingeld.

"We shall begin to arrange matters," said Sidonicus. He glanced to Safarius and Corelius. Both had paled.

"Do not delay," said Ingeld. "The sooner Abrogastes and Ortog are dead, the safer we shall be."

"We shall not delay, noble prince," said Sidonicus.

"I take my leave," said Ingeld, rising.

"Matters shall proceed apace," said Sidonicus.

Ingeld then threw his cloak about his shoulders and left the room.

"Gross boor," said Fulvius.

"Let us be mild and courteous," said Sidonicus.

"Insufferable barbarian," said Fulvius.

"He will prove of use," said Sidonicus. "We can dispose of him later."

CHAPTER FORTY-TWO

Abrogastes strode the confines of his cell like a nervous *vi-cat*. "As we are alive," he said to Ortog in the cell across the corridor, the words like blasts, "I do not understand why our captors have not interrogated us, have not challenged us, attempted to frighten, cajole, and influence us, given us terms and demands, striven to negotiate with us. Surely that would have been expected."

"Yes," said Ortog, standing at the bars, "if they wished to keep us alive."

"What?" said Abrogastes, stopping his tour, and facing Ortog.

"I think something has changed," said Ortog.

The two war dogs, serving as corridor guards, lay quietly in the corridor, sleeping. They had earlier been fed by portions of the meals given to Abrogastes and Ortog.

"What?" asked Abrogastes.

"I am not sure," said Ortog.

"Otungs must have contrived with Telnarians to have us imprisoned here," said Abrogastes.

"Otungs do the work of Otungs," said Ortog, "not hirelings."

"Otungs, somehow," said Abrogastes.

"Secret cells far below the street are not the way of Otungs," said Ortog. "We would be chained to a stake in some public place."

"Who then?" asked Abrogastes.

"Another, or others," said Ortog.

"We must soon be located, must soon be found," said Abrogastes.

"How so?" asked Ortog.

"Ingeld, even now, he, my loyal son, must be assiduously seeking me. In my absence he has the resources of the Drisriaks behind him. A thousand spies must be seeking this place."

"Ingeld may know more of this than you know," said Ortog.

"What do you mean?" demanded Abrogastes.

"I suspect treachery in high places," said Ortog. "I do not think your detention could have been accomplished without collusion."

"Such would violate the spear oaths," said Abrogastes.

"True," said Ortog.

"You speak without thinking," said Abrogastes, menacingly.

"I thought, I spoke," said Ortog.

"Renegade," said Abrogastes.

"One has long looked, this not known to you, with envy on the high seat of the Drisriaks," said Ortog.

"Who?" asked Abrogastes.

"Ingeld," said Ortog.

"I did not know you so hated your brother," said Abrogastes.

"I do not hate him," said Ortog. "I have never hated him. But long I have understood him, and feared him."

"Dare not, foul traitor," snarled Abrogastes, "to slander blood nobler than your own."

"He looks with desire upon the high seat of the Drisriaks," said Ortog.

"It is you who betrayed the Drisriaks," said Abrogastes.

"I did not betray the Drisriaks," said Ortog. "I left the Drisriaks. I did not want your high seat. I wanted my own."

"Treason!" roared Abrogastes.

"Departure," said Ortog.

"Would that I had you within my reach," said Abrogates.

"Or within the span of that slender, flexible, coiled band of metal you wrestled from your cot, now concealed in your tunic," said Ortog.

"Why have we not been approached, not dealt with?" muttered Abrogastes, turning angrily away.

"Plans have been changed," said Ortog. "If you were dealt with, on whatever terms, whatever bargains might be struck, whatever conditions might have been negotiated, you would still be king of the Drisriaks. That this has not taken place, no negotiation, or such, tells me that someone wishes the high seat of the Drisriaks to be vacant."

"Ingeld?" said Abrogates.

"I fear so, father," said Ortog.

"You called me 'father'," said Abrogastes.

"I came to Telnar to find you, and free you," said Ortog.

"Why?" said Abrogastes.

"I have challenged you, I have stood against you, I have defied you," said Ortog, "possibly because I am so much like you, for my blood, like yours, is hot, fierce, and deep, but, too, and I beg forgiveness for my weakness, I have always loved you, and do love you now."

"Liar!" said Abrogastes.

"And on Tenguthaxichai, I learned you loved me, too."

"I tried to slay you," said Abrogastes.

"You spared my life," said Ortog.

"What a fool you are," said Abrogastes.

"And I am an even greater fool than you think," said Ortog. "I have been betrayed by Otungs. A plot was formed. I was to permit myself to be apprehended, to seem to be trapped, even stupidly, but my apprehension, my feigned trapping, was to take place under the cognizance of Otungs who would thus, following my captors, be led to my place of incarceration, which, presumably, to abet their intrigues and policies, would be yours, as well. Thus, you would be found and freed."

"A most intelligent plan," said Abrogastes, "save for a grievous misplacement of trust."

"I think they will soon come to kill us," said Ortog. "Three were masked, to conceal their identity, he who was first amongst our captors, their leader, and two who were armed servitors, presumably ones commonly, publicly, associated with him. If they arrive unmasked, they deem their disguise no longer necessary. If they deem their disguise no longer necessary, they have come to kill us."

The two war dogs stirred, growling softly, almost inaudibly, lifting their heads.

"I hear footsteps outside, on the stairs," said Abrogastes.

A key was inserted in the lock of the corridor gate, and the gate was opened. Several men, each armed, entered.

Timon Safarius Rhodius, of the Telnar Rhodii, *primarius* of the senate of Telnaria, glanced at Ortog, and then stopped before the cell of Abrogastes, and faced its occupant.

"Greetings," said Abrogastes. "I see that you are not masked."

CHAPTER FORTY-THREE

"Greetings," had said Abrogastes. "I see that you are not masked."

"It is not now necessary," said Timon Safarius Rhodius, of the Telnar Rhodii, *primarius* of the senate of Telnaria.

About him were several men, who had served as jailers. Back in the corridor, just outside the gate, waited two large men, standing, their arms folded, bodyguards of Safarius, once feared by competitors on the sands of imperial arenas, once favorites of parties and factions amongst excited, roaring crowds.

"That you are not masked," said Abrogastes, "informs us that you are now ready to deal openly with us."

"Precisely," said Safarius.

Several of the men about him smiled.

The two war dogs, with a soft scratching of claws on the corridor tiles, rose up, manes stiffening, to a crouching position.

One of the jailers regarded them, apprehensively.

"I now know your face," said Abrogastes. "I would know your name, as well."

"I am Timon Safarius Rhodius, of the Telnar Rhodii," said Safarius, "*primarius* of the senate of Telnaria.

"I shall strive to remember that," said Abrogastes.

"I do not think you will remember it long," said Safarius.

"Are you so forgettable?" asked Abrogastes.

"Rather," said Safarius, "I think your memory will prove short."

There was a soft growl from one of the war dogs, which was seconded by his fellow.

"The dogs are uneasy," said the jailer who had earlier suspected a subtle disquietude in the beasts.

Safarius paid him no attention.

"I take it," said Abrogastes, "that we are now to be freed."

"Yes," said Safarius, "in a manner of speaking."

Two of the attendant jailers laughed.

At this point a bowman, equipped with a long bow, a heavy, strong-drawing bow, of the sort that might be used for hunting lion and *vi-cat*, even the massive *arn* bear, on worlds such as Tangara or Varna, entered through the opened gate. At his hip was a sheaf of arrows.

Safarius motioned the newcomer forward.

"Behold, dear king and dear prince," said Safarius to the two separately incarcerated prisoners, "your liberator."

"King and king," said Abrogastes, "king of the Drisriaks, and king of the Ortungen."

"Father!" said Ortog.

"I recognize the Ortungen as a tribe of the Alemanni," said Abrogastes.

"We accept the recognition of the Drisriaks, high tribe, hegemonic tribe, of the Alemanni nation," said Ortog, his voice breaking.

"It is done," said Abrogastes.

"This is all very touching," said Safarius, "a glad day for the Aatii, but I fear, too, a dark day for the Aatii, as on this day two kings of the Aatii perish."

"Speak," said Abrogastes.

"Behold," said Safarius, "the bowman's quiver."

Both war dogs growled, their bodies tensed, their eyes bright, their heads raised.

"What is wrong with the dogs?" asked Safarius.

"They are agitated," said the jailer.

"I have seen quivers before," said Abrogastes.

"But arrows such as these you have seldom seen, save in war," said Safarius. "Please," said Safarius to the bowman, "draw forth an arrow."

The bowman drew forth an arrow, and fitted it to the string.

The dogs growled, again.

"Behold the coloring of the arrow, the nature of the fletching," said Safarius.

"I see," said Abrogastes.

"It is an Otung arrow," said Ortog.

"So you are in the pay of Otungs," said Abrogastes.

"Scarcely," said Safarius.

"That is an Otung arrow," said Abrogastes.

"It seems so," said Safarius. "And we have no doubt but what it will be taken for an Otung arrow."

"These arrows, I take it," said Abrogastes, "are meant for us."

"Although you are a barbarian," said Safarius, "you are perceptive."

"Before you have your minion demonstrate his prowess and courage by shooting a caged *vi-cat*, I would that you might unfold your design to two barbarians who, otherwise, in their simplicity, might fail to understand it."

"Willingly," said Safarius. "Your lives were preserved until we could consult with an interested party. We had hitherto intended to work out a beneficial alliance, exchanging favors, your life, and then your lives, for political concessions. But we have recently been informed that you both might prove, or would prove, uncooperative, and even recalcitrant. It is apparently easier to deal with civilized parties than with those afflicted with primitive mentalities. Honor, for example, might prove a troubling obstacle, impeding mutually satisfactory arrangements. We became recently convinced that our goals might be more easily reached with a different monarch on the high seat of the Drisriaks. The problem remained of accounting for your prolonged absence, and now that of your son, in a way that would prove useful to our ends. It would also be helpful to shake, or remove, the Otung usurper, bringing a new barbarian to the throne, say, a Drisriak, or restoring the drooling, mindless dolt, Aesilesius, to the throne and ruling through him, until a royal birth occurs, the son of a princess, following which a regency would be emplaced, the regent being, naturally, the father of the royal heir. It will be arranged to appear that you and your son were held by Otungs, who then disposed of your bodies, clumsily, of course, which will be found in a field, or near the *carnariums*, heavy with Otung arrows. This would precipitate open warfare, a war of vengeance, between the Drisriaks and the Otungs, a war in which the mobs of Telnar, suitably aroused, would participate, on behalf of the Drisriaks. We would seize Telnar, and, as Telnar goes, so will the empire. Many gambling stones, handfuls, will be shaken and cast, but the odds are much in our favor."

"You have planned well," said Abrogastes.

"We have considered, I think, all plausible contingencies."

"Sometimes,'" said Abrogastes, "a contingency arises which was not plausible."

"I trust that your questions have been answered, and your curiosity satisfied," said Safarius.

"Quite," said Abrogastes.

"We may then proceed," said Safarius. "What is wrong with the dogs?"

"Nothing," said the jailer, uneasily.

"Why this business of arrows?" asked Abrogastes. "Simply enter the cells, and kill us. You can then fill our bodies with arrows later, at your leisure."

"Who, who was sane," asked Safarius, "would enter the cage of living *vi-cat*?"

"Yes," said Abrogastes, "it is easier to kill it in its cage."

"I do not like it," said the jailer. "The dogs are uneasy."

"And much safer, as well," said Safarius.

"Kings," said Abrogastes, "may not be as easy to kill as you think."

"We shall see," said Safarius. He then turned to the bowman. "Kill them," he said.

When he turned back to face Abrogastes, there was a sudden flash of metal, almost invisible, like a striking snake of steel, and Safarius screamed, his face cut open, streaming with blood, and he stumbled back, striking into the bars of Ortog's cell, and a loop of metal flashed forth about his throat and pulled him back, tight against the bars, and he could not move lest his throat be crushed, or, should the span be turned, he cut his own throat, and, at the same time, Abrogastes, screaming, and pointing wildly at the bowman and the men in the corridor, cried out to the trembling, excited, tensed war dogs, "Kill, kill, kill!"

CHAPTER FORTY-FOUR

The first dog lunged toward the bowman, seized an arm, and, shaking its head viciously, tore it from the bowman's body. There were shouts of consternation and alarm. The second dog, frenzied and violent, beside itself with hate for those who, to hone its murderous instincts, had starved and abused it, the door of its fury now flung open, its pent-up hatred unleashed, thrust itself into the midst of the small crowd of confused, twisting, screaming, stumbling, falling jailers, biting, tearing, and clawing. The jailers' motions were impeded by one another's bodies. Blades remained sheathed. Men thought only of escape. Flesh was torn, and a hand lost. Blood from the howling bowman rushed out, in arcs, as he spun about, it spurting, spattering men and bars. And this blood was joined by new blood, from a myriad cuts and bites. The robes of Safarius, his face streaming blood from his own wound, he pinned by the throat, back to the bars of Ortog's cell, were drenched. He could not speak. He closed his eyes, tightly, in horror, half-blinded, his eyes dashed with scarlet fluid. Men slipped on wet tiles. More than one fell, and was trampled by others, hurrying toward the corridor gate. A leg and neck were broken. The gate, which had been opened, was flung back, and men crowded through, struggling, some preventing others from entering. One fellow was pulled back by a foot into the corridor by the first dog. Another, pounced upon, had his neck bitten through, from behind, by the second dog, its long, curved claws, a half foot long, anchored in the body. Then a handful of men had passed through the gate, and joined the two gladiators in the hall behind the gate. One jailer still in the corridor, seized the bars of the shut gate, screaming to be admitted, and he was then pulled back into the corridor by the first dog. The bowman lay dead in the corridor, from loss of blood. Inert bodies were about him. Two jailers, sat, backed against bars, bleeding, fearfully eying the dogs, as they lapped blood, and fed.

One of the former gladiators, bodyguards of Safarius, stepped close to the bars.

"Release the noble Timon Safarius Rhodius," he called.

Neither Ortog nor Abrogastes responded. Safarius himself could not speak for the pressure on his throat. He opened his eyes, frantically, looking toward those on the far side of the gate.

"You are trapped," called the bodyguard to Abrogastes and Ortog. "You cannot escape. The keys to the cells are here, behind the gate. You are four floors down. The dogs can be killed with arrows. We can then enter the corridor and do with you as we wish. Release the noble Timon Safarius Rhodius."

This demand was met with silence.

Safarius lifted his hands, futilely, toward the band on his throat but quickly lowered them, for Ortog drew the band back, more tightly.

"You are to be slain," called the bodyguard, the former gladiator. "Your choice is simple. If you release the noble Timon Safarius Rhodius, your death will be quick and easy, attendant on a swift, merciful stroke. We are skilled in such matters. If you do not, your death will be slow, and, I assure you, one not to be envied."

Neither Abrogastes nor Ortog saw fit to respond to this offer, as generous as it might have been.

The dogs continued to feed.

The living jailers within the corridor shrank back more closely against the bars.

There was some consultation behind the gate, murmurs, and earnest whispers.

Then the former gladiator, who seemed spokesman for those in the hall, spoke once more.

"Very well, noble foes," he called. "We have lost. You have won. Release the noble Timon Safarius Rhodius and we will grant you not only your lives, but your freedom, as well. You will be released and escorted in safety to a destination of your choice."

"And given a hundred *darins* of gold, each, for our inconvenience?" asked Abrogates.

"Two hundred," said the former gladiator.

"Each?" asked Abrogastes.

"Of course!" said the former gladiator.

Abrogastes laughed, and such a laugh, emanating from the throat of the Far-Grasper, might have chilled the blood of a Tangaran wolf.

"We have weapons," the bodyguard reminded Abrogastes, "and the dogs can be killed."

"In whose name do you act, in whose name do you offer terms?" called Abrogastes.

"In the name of the noble Timon Safarius Rhodius, *primarius* of the senate of Telnaria," called the former gladiator.

"The senate is an instrument, a tool," said Abrogastes. "Who is behind the senate? Who wields the senate? Who stands in the shadows, unseen?"

Consultation took place once more behind the closed gate.

Then the former gladiator called out, "Otungs! The usurper, the false emperor, he who dares call himself Ottonius, the First!"

"Your response was less than prompt," said Abrogastes.

"Ottonius, Ottonius, the First!" said the former gladiator.

"It must be," said Abrogastes to Ortog. "It is as I thought. It can be no other."

"It was he," said Ortog, "by whom I was misled, and betrayed."

"Bring arrows, and bowmen, Otung arrows," said the former gladiator.

"It seems your prisoner can be spared," said Abrogastes to Ortog.

Safarius squirmed, unable to speak. He moved his left hand pathetically, pleadingly, at the closed gate.

"Kill the dogs first," said the former gladiator, "then the barbarians."

"Are you prepared to die well, my son," asked Abrogastes.

"How else should a Drisriak die?" said Ortog.

"Or an Ortung," said Abrogastes.

"I would have preferred an open field," said Ortog.

"Where one dies is one's field," said Abrogastes.

The jailers and the two former gladiators drew back a yard or so from the closed gate. Footsteps were heard, ascending the stairs behind them.

"As soon as you see the bow," said Abrogastes to Ortog, "act."

"I need only turn the span and jerk back," said Ortog, "and the head is gone."

The dogs, surfeited, lay down amongst the bodies in the corridor. The two living jailers in the corridor, their eyes wide with fear, dared move no more than to stanch their wounds with bloody hands. Blood spread between their fingers.

"I hear sounds on the stairs," said Ortog.

"Be ready," said Abrogastes.

"What is going on?" called the former gladiator, turning about, and looking upward, into the darkness, up the steep well of stairs. "Hurry! Hurry!"

There was then another sound on the stairs, much like a scuffle, and a short cry, and then there was the sound of a brief clatter of metal, and of something scraping, and then of an object, or weight, something, something rolling, or tumbling, down the stairs, and, twice, a snapping, as of a slender stick of wood.

"What madness is this?" cried the former gladiator, upward, into the darkness.

Suddenly, from behind the closed gate, there were cries of consternation and alarm. There was the heavy, sudden, quick sound of long shafts striking into bodies.

Borne lanterns, lifted, descending, illuminated the stairwell.

Twice more there was the sound, sudden, decisive, unmistakable, of long shafts striking targets.

"Otung arrows!" cried a man. "As you called for!"

"Stop, stop, fools!" cried the former gladiator. "You are confused! We are not the enemy! Hold your fire!"

Two more men fell.

The gate was then unlocked and opened, and the living jailers from outside, some seven or eight, pressed through the gate, swarming, crowding through it, and ran, now oblivious of the somnolent dogs and strewn bodies, to the blind end of the corridor. These were followed by the two gladiators, backing slowly, swords drawn, picking their way carefully, to the far end of the corridor.

Three bowmen appeared then in the portal, at the gate, with arrows set to the string.

"Ulrich, Citherix, Vandar," said a mighty voice from behind, "hold your fire."

The bows were lowered, but the arrows did not leave the string.

"Good," said the voice, as the speaker, a great sword hung behind his left shoulder, appeared behind the bowmen. He looked down, at various bodies, and turned one or more over with a foot. "One arrow per kill. Excellent. I had feared the softness, gentilities, and luxuries of civilization might have diminished your skill," he said. He then brushed past the bowmen, and entered the corridor, looking about.

Behind this figure then appeared two more, fierce, bearded Rurik, the Tenth Consul of Larial VII, of the Larial Farnichi, sword in hand, and Julian, he of the Aureliani, one of the foremost of the imperial families, cousin even to Aesilesius, occupant of the imperial throne prior to the accession of Ottonius, the First, he of the Aureliani, with a pistol in hand, containing four cartridges, any one of which could blast through a wall.

"*Filchen*," cried Rurik, "do you dare stand in the presence of your emperor?"

The jailers then knelt on one knee, their heads down. Even the two suffering jailers, grievously bitten and clawed, who had been unable to leave the corridor, lowered their heads. The two dogs looked up, curiously. The two gladiators remained on their feet, swords drawn.

"Greetings, noble Abrogastes, king of the Drisriaks," said Otto, "and greetings, too, to the noble Ortog, king of the Ortungen."

"Greetings to the emperor," said Abrogastes, "and to the king of the Otungs and chieftain of the Wolfungs."

"Dear Ortog," said Otto, "our friend, Timon Safarius Rhodius, appears uncomfortable."

Ortog released one end of the band about Safarius' throat and it snapped back, springing, striking against the bars, and Ortog withdrew it into the cell.

Safarius collapsed, shuddering, to the bloody tiles at the foot of the bars.

"Are we now to be killed, Otung?" asked Abrogastes.

"No," said Otto. "But perhaps in another time and another place."

"I have not been betrayed," said Ortog, wonderingly.

"No," said Otto. "I am Otung."

"Your arrival was tardy," said Ortog.

"We waited, hoping for the appearance of higher foes, who declined to reveal themselves, and wished, too, to allow time for the plans and proposals of your captors to be made clear."

"We, too, anticipated a period of bargaining, of flatterings and promises, of threats, of menaces, and such, but, it seems, matters had changed," said Ortog.

"I had not expected that," said Otto.

"Nor we," said Ortog.

"How is it to be accounted for?" asked Otto.

"A new order was given, a new proposal made," said Ortog. He did not elaborate on this remark.

"You are alive," said Otto.

"This does not diminish the enmity between the Alemanni and the Vandalii," said Abrogastes.

"Even foes can share a horn of *bror* upon occasion," said Otto. He then looked toward the far end of the corridor, where, on one knee, knelt the jailers, and where stood the two former gladiators.

"Bring keys," said Otto, "release the prisoners."

One of the jailers leapt up, and, taking keys from his belt, opened the two cells, after which he returned to his place with the others.

The two dogs, filled and content, lay quietly in place.

Safarius rose to a sitting position. He wiped the wound on his face with the sleeve of his robes. His eyes were glazed, vacant.

"You who manned this place, hirelings," said Otto, "may withdraw. Take with you your still-living, bloodied fellows."

Men looked at him, wildly.

"And tonight drink the health of Aesilesius of Telnaria," said Otto.

Uncertain, trembling, wondering, they rose to their feet.

"Noble ruler, Great Emperor!" cried a man, looking back, as they began, with their two bloodied fellows, to ascend the stairs.

"Hail Ottonius," cried others. "Hail Ottonius, the First, noble and merciful monarch!"

"Barbarians," said one of the former gladiators, "are not noted for mercy."

"Beware how you speak to the emperor!" said Rurik.

Julian leveled his pistol at the two gladiators. One cartridge could blow both to pieces and shatter the wall behind them.

"What are your names?" asked Otto.

"Boris," said one.

"Andak," said the other.

"I have heard of you," said Otto. "There are no cheering crowds in this corridor, in this basement."

"One would prefer," said Boris, "the canopied arena, the raked sand."

"We three," said Otto, "are long from the sand."

"It is true, the rumors?" asked Andak.

"Some, perhaps," said Otto.

"Otto, of the school of Pulendius?" said Boris.

"Otto, of the Dozen Worlds?" said Andak.

"You do not choose to sheath your weapons?" asked Otto.

"No," said the two facing the emperor.

"It is a long time since I have laughed with steel," said Otto.

"No!" said Rurik.

"Refrain!" said Julian.

"You have the long blade," said Boris. "You have much the reach on us."

"Do not engage," said Julian.

Otto removed the long blade from its shoulder sling and handed it to Rurik. "Your sword," he said.

"Surely not!" said Rurik.

Then he placed the shorter blade in the hand of Otto.

Otto then faced the two gladiators.

"Let the bowmen kill them now," said Rurik.

"No," said Otto.

"After we kill you," said Boris, "I take it we will be slain."

"Not at all," said Otto. "If you are successful, you may leave, unmolested and without fear of recriminations."

"No!" said Julian.

"You need not even wait for ten kills," said Otto.

"No, no!" said Julian, he of the Aureliani.

"I have spoken," said Otto.

"What of the throne, the empire, the future?" demanded Rurik.

"The usual things," said Otto, "politics, lies, favors, corruption, influence, betrayals, assassinations, uprisings, civil wars, such things, will determine matters."

"Surely the throne matters," said Julian.

"I prefer the saddle, the wind bending tall grass, boots treading fallen leaves, a forest trail," said Otto. He then regarded the two gladiators. "Will you come one at a time, or together?" he asked.

The two former gladiators looked at one another.

"It does not matter to you?" asked Boris.

"Not greatly," said Otto. "It does affect certain subtleties of engagement, the manner of defense, the timing of certain strokes."

"Together!" begged Safarius, rising to an elbow, the mark of the steel band still on his throat. "If he is so mad, such a fool, as to permit it, seize the opportunity. Together! Kill him! Kill him!"

Boris did not move.

"I have fought three several times," said Otto, "and twice I fought four, and once, on Inez IV, five."

"One at a time," said Boris.

"As you wish," said Otto.

"No!" cried Safarius.

The interaction was fierce, and brief. One could scarcely see the blades move, and then Boris reeled back, his blade struck away. He fell to his side. Andak rushed forward, and found a sword at his throat. He flung down his weapon and went to kneel beside Boris.

"You are the Otto of the school of Pulendius, the Otto of the Dozen Worlds," said Boris.

"Our lives are yours," said Andak. "We are at your mercy."

"Kill them and be done with it," said Rurik.

Otto returned the sword to Rurik, and received back the long blade.

"I can align them, all three, they and the *primarius*, kneeling, heads down, the backs of the neck exposed," said Rurik. "With your blade, the long blade, you could take three heads with one stroke."

"No, no!" cried Safarius. "Kill them! Kill them! Not me! They lifted weapons against you! Not I! They are nothings, hirelings, killers, dispensable minions. I am too important to be killed. I am of the Telnar Rhodii, the *primarius* of the senate! I have power, influence."

"In a day or two," said Abrogastes, "the dogs will be hungry again."

"No!" cried Safarius.

Otto stepped forward, regarding the fallen Boris, and the kneeling Andak. "Have you taken fee," he asked, "from Timon Safarius Rhodius?"

"We have," said Boris.

"Repudiate him," said Otto.

"We have taken fee," said Boris.

"Repudiate him, or die," said Otto.

"We have taken fee," said Boris.

"You would rather die than renounce your fee giver?" asked Otto.

"We have taken fee," said Boris.

"I thought it would be so," said Otto. "You are free to go."

"My emperor!" said Boris.

"You are not Otung," said Otto, "but I would have such men about me."

"We are your men!" cried Boris.

Otto then turned to face Safarius.

"They are yours," said Safarius.

Rurik then confronted Safarius, his sword drawn. "You are less than some," he said. "Who is greater than you?"

Safarius put his head down.

"Who is your leader, or leaders," demanded Julian, "your principal, or principals?"

"I dare not speak," said Safarius.

"Burning irons will encourage you," snarled Rurik.

"Mercy!" begged Safarius.

"The irons, the fire, the pincers, the nails," said Rurik, "then speech, then death."

"No, no!" whispered Safarius.

"You are free to go," said Otto.

"I am released?" asked Safarius, looking up.

"Yes," said Otto.

"They will think I have spoken," said Safarius.

"Only if you give them that impression," said Otto.

"I do not understand," said Safarius.

"Do you think the released jailers will make public their discomfiting and the loss of their prisoners?"

"I think not," said Safarius. "It could mean their lives."

"And yours, as well?" asked Otto.

"I fear so," said Safarius.

"Your principal, or principals," said Otto, "at least for a time, unless informed otherwise, will presume their plans have proceeded apace, will they not?"

"But what of the discovered bodies, riddled with arrows?" asked Safarius.

"That matter," said Otto, "is met without difficulty. Two of the slain jailers will do nicely, found in the garments of barbarians, their bodies abounding with arrows, bodies publicly proclaimed to be those of Abrogastes and Ortog."

"But surely some could recognize Abrogastes and Ortog," said Safarius.

"Few," said Otto, "other than Drisriaks and Ortungen."

"But Drisriaks and Ortungen," said Safarius.

"The faces will be torn away," said Otto, "and the bodies muchly mutilated, such depredations, given where the bodies are placed, to be attributed to the wild dogs of Telnar."

"I am to be released?" asked Safarius, again, uncertainly.

"If matters proceed awry," said Otto, "you would be well advised to claim you were not present at the actual killing of Abrogastes and Ortog, preferring to have left the matter in the hands of jailers."

"I might be faint of heart, or unwilling to have witnessed so distasteful or unaesthetic an event?" said Safarius.

"It is easy to see how you became the *primarius* of the senate," said Otto.

"Will anyone believe that?" asked Safarius.

"We shall hope, for your sake, they do," said Otto.

"I am truly free to go?" asked Safarius.

"It is part of my plan," said Otto.

"But I will be in danger," said Safarius.

"We are all in danger," said Otto.

"I am afraid," said Safarius.

"You will be protected," said Otto.

"I do not understand," said Safarius.

"Boris, Andak," said Otto. "You will go with the *primarius*. Guard him well. Too, in this way things must seem much as before."

"Yes, my emperor," said Boris.

"And if there is the least evidence of treachery, kill him, immediately."

"Our pleasure, my emperor," said Andak.

Safarius, then, slowly, and unsteadily, touching his throat gently, accompanied by Boris and Andak, left the corridor, and began to ascend the stairs. In a moment or two their footsteps could no longer be heard.

"You are clever, for an Otung," said Abrogastes to Otto.

"That is high praise, from a Drisriak," said Otto.

"You have *bror*, here in Telnar?" asked Abrogastes.

"Imported, from Tangara," said Otto.

"It is horrid stuff," said Rurik.

"Let us adjourn to the palace," said Julian.

The dogs lay amongst the bodies, sleepily.

Abrogastes crouched down, between them.

"Good dogs, good dogs," he said, affectionately shaking those massive heads. "I do not think you need more feeding tonight, but tomorrow you will be fed again, and well, though, I trust, differently."

CHAPTER FORTY-FIVE

"Splendid! Splendid!" cried Ingeld, rising from the chair and clapping his hands.

"We thought you would be pleased," said Sidonicus, on another chair, in his private audience chamber, forsaking the exarchical throne which dominated the room.

"How could it be better?" said Ingeld.

"Would you care for a sweet," asked Sidonicus, reaching into a box.

"No," said Ingeld, resuming his seat.

"Are you sure, dear Safarius," asked Sidonicus, placing a sweet in his mouth, "that we may speak openly before these other two?"

Toward the back of the room, standing, arms folded, were two figures, those of two large, strong men, who had accompanied Safarius to the meeting.

"Yes," said Safarius. "They may be trusted implicitly. Both are privy to these affairs. Both were present in the fourth basement of the house of Dardanis, on the day in question."

"They participated in the business?" asked Fulvius, deputy to the exarch.

"Very much so, as is my understanding," said Safarius.

"As is your understanding?" inquired Fulvius.

"I withdrew, once all was readied," said Safarius. "I feared blood, the dogs. I did not wish to risk the soiling of my robes."

"That is understandable," said Sidonicus. "It does you credit. I myself would have been reluctant to attend, personally, to such unpleasant details."

"You two," said Fulvius, addressing the two men in the rear of the room, "were present? You saw what occurred?"

"Yes, your excellency," said Boris.

"Good," said Fulvius, satisfied.

"It was clever," said Sidonicus to Safarius, "to have the bodies abandoned outside the walls, where they could be prey to the dogs."

"We thought," said Safarius, "that indignity would further enflame the Drisriaks, and the other tribes of the Alemanni."

"And it will," said Ingeld. "I promise you that."

"Sometimes," said Fulvius, "such beasts even find their way into the city. They are dangerous."

"Only in the streets and alleys of the poorer districts," said Safarius. "They live on garbage. One tries to exterminate them."

"Unsuccessfully," said Fulvius. "They can run in packs; they are dangerous to approach."

"Sometimes," said Safarius, "we are successful."

"But others find their way in," said Fulvius.

"Unfortunately," said Safarius.

"Amongst the keenest of motivations," said Sidonicus, helping himself to another sweet, "is hunger."

"Even now," said Fulvius, "reports of the Otung atrocity streak amongst worlds."

"I fear they will be largely ignored," said Sidonicus. "Events in Telnar seldom stir the worlds unless they are personally touched, even the comings and goings of emperors."

"I assure you," said Ingeld, "the Drisriaks will stir, and the other tribes of the Alemanni, too, and the allied tribes, as well. Blood is involved, and honor. I will bear a torch that will set fire to the tinder of outrage and vengeance. Our worlds, our thousand holdings and camps, will rise, and flame. I shall shortly take ship to the Meeting World, Tenguthaxichai, and send forth a summons to council."

"Be not too precipitate, dear prince, or now, I should say, king, for the Otungs control the batteries of Telnar. Such defenses could melt fleets."

"They may be overwhelmed, if not suborned," said Ingeld. "Hundreds of Drisriaks, and Dangars, and Borkons, and others, can find their way into Telnar in the guise of merchants, tradesmen, and laborers, waiting for the signal. Too, it will be simple to rally the remnants of the Ortungen from the towns they control in the delta of the Turning Serpent. They too will demand satisfaction. And, I trust, noble Sidonicus, that you can, upon short notice, bring your faithful into the streets with clubs, fire, and stones."

"If it is the will of Floon," said Sidonicus.

"I trust it will be," said Ingeld.

"It is highly probable," said Sidonicus. "It is I who pronounce the will of Floon."

"When the city swarms, and the batteries are seized," said Ingeld, "the fleet, unimpeded, will land and seal the doom of the Otung regime."

"I trust," said Sidonicus, "that the fair Viviana, your lovely spouse of royal blood, is now with child."

"Soon, I am sure," said Ingeld.

"Not yet?" said Sidonicus.

"It is curious," said Ingeld. "Not yet."

"It must be a male," said Sidonicus.

"I have no control over that," said Ingeld.

"What of gentle Alacida, she, too, of royal blood, espoused to your noble brother, Hrothgar?"

"Hrothgar has no more interest in thrones than a hunting dog or war horse," said Ingeld.

"Still," said Sidonicus. "Should Alacida bear a male, it would be in line for the throne, and Hrothgar could rule as regent."

"That will not occur," said Ingeld.

"Some misfortune might befall the infant?" suggested Fulvius.

"It is possible," said Ingeld.

"What if Viviana does not produce a male heir?" said Sidonicus.

"Should an accident befall my dear brother," said Ingeld, "I might wed his widow, and sire a son, or sons."

"And rule as regent," said Sidonicus.

"Of course," said Ingeld.

"Given the removal of Aesilesius," said Fulvius.

"A tasteless chemical mixed with a draught of wine?" said Sidonicus.

"Perhaps better a writ of removal on the basis of infirmity, unfitness, or incompetence, reluctantly promulgated by the senate," said Fulvius.

"That could be arranged," said Safarius.

"We should keep Aesilesius about," said Fulvius. "Should our first plans fail, we might need him, as a puppet, to rule through him, much as the empress mother and the Arbiter of Protocol, Iaachus, have done in the past."

"Our plans will not fail," said Ingeld.

"The writ of infirmity, unfitness, or incompetence," said Fulvius, "constitutes no obstacle. On the advice of carefully selected physicians, given new evidence, the senate might nullify the writ."

"That is easily done," said Safarius.

"But others, not we, might rule through him, as well," said Sidonicus. "Better the tasteless chemical."

"He would be the third of his line to so perish," said Safarius.

"I shall take ship tonight for Tenguthaxichai," said Ingeld. "It is fitting that the council summons be issued from that world. It is the Alemanni Meeting World."

"Soon, I trust, the usurper will be usurped," said Sidonicus.

"Let there be pretense of legitimacy," said Fulvius. "Rule for a time, dear Ingeld, in the name of the pathetic dolt, Aesilesius. Within a year or two, given a son by Viviana, or Alacida, he may be replaced. You will then rule as regent, in full legitimacy."

"The senate may be depended upon," said Safarius.

"As usual," said Sidonicus, drily.

"A ship is fueled," said Ingeld, rising. "I leave at dusk."

"Remember, dear Ingeld," said Sidonicus, "the cooperation of the temple is not without its condition."

"That condition is easily met," said Ingeld. "It costs not a *darin*. It is accomplished with an utterance, with the stroke of a pen. Floonianism becomes the official religion of the empire."

"There are dozens of versions of Floonianism," said Fulvius. "One must be specific. It must be our particular version of Floonianism."

"Religion is lucrative," said Ingeld. "It accumulates wealth. It is a facile source of income. It costs little; it gathers in much. It sells empty promises for gold. Naturally you wish the gold to stream in one direction, yours."

"How little you understand," moaned Sidonicus, dismayed.

"Right belief," said Fulvius, "is essential if one would sit at the table of *Karch*."

"Your beliefs," said Ingeld.

"As it happens," said Sidonicus.

"How do you know?" asked Ingeld.

"*Karch* has spoken," said Sidonicus.

"When and where, and before which witnesses?" asked Ingeld.

"At hundreds of times in hundreds of places, before thousands of witnesses," said Sidonicus.

"*Karch*, as I understand it," said Ingeld, "has no body, no eyes, no ears, no voice, and so on, so how does he speak?"

"Through his holy sayers," said Sidonicus.

"And how does one know that *Karch*, who has no body, no eyes, no ears, and no voice, speaks through them?" asked Ingeld.

"It is a matter of faith," said Sidonicus.

"And *Karch* reportedly says different things to different sayers," said Ingeld.

"There are false sayers, of course," said Sidonicus.

"Whose sayers are the true sayers?" asked Ingeld.

"Ours," said Sidonicus.

"How do you know?" asked Ingeld.

"It is a matter of faith," said Sidonicus.

"Next I will hear of miracles," said Ingeld.

"Possibly," said Sidonicus.

"What is the logical relationship between an interesting or surprising event and a claim?" asked Ingeld.

"The matter is admittedly obscure," said Sidonicus.

"Do not many faiths have their miracles?" asked Ingeld.

"There are evil miracles and false miracles," said Fulvius. "Only our faith has good miracles and true miracles. Indeed, most of the alleged miracles in other faiths are mere misunderstandings of natural events, or coincidences, anomalies, surprising occurrences, lies, tricks, frauds, or such."

"But yours are not?"

"No," said Sidonicus.

"How do you know?" asked Ingeld.

"It is a matter of faith," said Sidonicus.

"Putting aside subtle matters on which you are unqualified to form an opinion," said Fulvius, "just make certain that our version of Floonianism is decreed to be the official religion of the empire."

"And you will bring your faithful into the streets, to abet the coup?" said Ingeld.

"Surely," said Fulvius.

"It would help," said Sidonicus, "if you would be publicly smudged with oil from one of the sacred pools of Zirus."

"It is enough that I make your faith the official religion of the empire," said Ingeld. "You cannot expect me to believe it, too."

"It could help," said Sidonicus.

"Your views are confusing, contradictory, and often unintelligible," said Ingeld. "I would not know how to believe in them even if I wanted to, which I do not."

"I see," said Sidonicus, not happily.

"Besides," said Ingeld, "Kragon, the Alemanni god of war, would disapprove."

"That is a false god," said Sidonicus.

"His priests claim that *Karch* is a false god," said Ingeld.

"Absurd!" exclaimed Sidonicus.

"Perhaps all gods are false," said Ingeld.

"After you make the correct version of Floonianism the official religion of the empire," said Sidonicus, "you must then, shortly thereafter, outlaw other religions, suppress them, and see to the conversion or extermination of their unfortunately misguided adherents."

"That is not easily done, and would be costly, and not well accepted in certain quarters, particularly in those quarters occupied by other religions," said Ingeld. "That is an independent question."

"Very well," said Sidonicus. "One thing at a time."

"I would not approve of making myself a heretic," said Ingeld.

"As I understand it," said Fulvius, "you leave this evening for Tenguthaxichai."

"Yes," said Ingeld, "and shortly after arriving on Tenguthaxichai, I shall issue the summons to council."

"I trust," said Fulvius, "that all will proceed smoothly."

"It will," said Ingeld, "now that Abrogastes and Ortog are out of the way."

Safarius looked down. The two large, strong men in the background, arms folded, revealed no emotion or reaction.

"I fear only," said Sidonicus, "that nature will not see fit to abet our plans."

"How so?" asked Ingeld.

"That neither Viviana nor Alacida may bear sons in a timely fashion."

"Do not concern yourself," said Ingeld. "I have prepared for that contingency."

"How is that?" said Sidonicus.

"It is obvious," said Fulvius.

"Beware how you speak to the exarch of Telnar," said Sidonicus.

"Forgive me, your excellency," said Fulvius.

"Of course, it is obvious," said Sidonicus. "I merely wished to hear it spoken by our guest."

"Forgive me, your excellency," said Fulvius. "I failed to understand, to grasp your subtlety."

Sidonicus turned to Ingeld. "Please, speak," he said.

"One need only announce that Viviana, on Tenguthaxichai, has born a son," said Ingeld, "and then produce a male infant as the child. Male and female infants abound. Neither is in short supply."

"You see," said Sidonicus to Fulvius, "it is obvious."

"Yes, your excellency," said Fulvius.

"There will be much rejoicing in the empire," said Safarius.

"Of course," said Sidonicus.

"But what of Viviana?" asked Safarius.

"Yes," said Sidonicus, "what of Viviana?"

"I fear," said Ingeld, "she died in childbirth."

Ingeld then turned, and left the room.

"It is unfortunate that we had no opportunity to shape the mind of Ingeld from childhood," said Sidonicus. "We would then own him."

"In time, that problem will be ameliorated," said Fulvius. "Many schools will be closed, and others will be seized, or founded. We will control the mind. One takes the child; one molds the man."

"It is easily done," said Sidonicus. "It is a simple business."

"Yet some, somehow, a few, will think for themselves," said Fulvius.

"That is troublesome," said Sidonicus.

"Assuredly," said Fulvius.

"If they are wise, they will be silent," said Sidonicus. "Otherwise they may be dealt with."

"Easily," said Fulvius.

Sidonicus then helped himself to another sweet. He did not offer one to his deputy.

CHAPTER FORTY-SIX

"Much has occurred, Master," said Nika, going to her knees beside the couch on which young Aesilesius sat, in the quarters to which he was confined.

"Sit beside me, on the couch," said Aesilesius.

"I am a slave," said Nika, "I belong on my knees."

"As you wish," said Aesilesius. "I missed you."

"I am frightened," said Nika, adjusting the thin string at the left shoulder of her tunic. "I think the world is shaking beneath our feet. I know not what it might portend for my Master."

"Your hair is lovely," said Aesilesius. "I will comb it for you later. You must permit me to do so."

"Master may do with me as he wishes," said Nika. "He need not ask me such things. I must submit."

"I enjoy combing your hair, touching it," said Aesilesius.

"A Master may enjoy grooming his animal," said Nika, "combing the mane of his horse, smoothing the fur of his dog."

"I shall fetch the comb, and kneel behind you," said Aesilesius.

"Please wait, Master," said Nika, in agitation.

"Later, then," said Aesilesius. "You are very beautiful, you know."

"May I speak?" asked Nika.

"Of course," said Aesilesius.

"The city roils," said Nika. "The bodies of two barbarian kings, Abrogastes, the Far-Grasper, he of the Drisriaks, of the Aatii, and Ortog, he of the Ortungen, a dissident tribe of the Aatii, have been found outside the walls, near the *carnariums*. The bodies are half eaten by dogs, and pierced with many arrows, of the fashion of the Otungs."

"A most grisly discovery," said Aesilesius, shuddering, "regardless of the nature of the victims."

"Surely Master understands the import of such a thing," said Nika.

"Abrogastes was the father of the two barbarians to whom, by implicit force, my sisters were espoused," said Aesilesius.

"Yes, Master," said Nika, "but consider what this means."

"That Otungs are barbarians, violent and cruel, capable of heinous acts," said Aesilesius. "Doubtless this horror was perpetrated on the command of the beast now occupying the throne, to rid himself of rivals."

"I do not think so," said Nika. "It ill comports with Otungs I have known."

"What else then?" asked Aesilesius.

"I do not know," said Nika. "The city trembles."

"Over the demise of two barbarians?" asked Aesilesius.

"Two kings," said Nika. "Surely Master apprehends the danger."

"I know little of what occurs outside the palace, save what you tell me," said Aesilesius. "And within the palace they seldom speak before me, thinking I will not understand, fearing I will be disturbed."

"Abrogastes was a mighty king," said Nika. "And Ortog, his son, has pledged followers. One does not lightly kill a king."

"They were barbarians," said Aesilesius.

"Abrogastes was king of the Drisriaks, high tribe of the Aatii," said Nika. "He disappeared some weeks ago, mysteriously. Speculation abounded. Naturally suspicion fell upon Otungs. The Otungs, or Otungen, is the largest of the five tribes of the Vandalii, blood enemies for generations of the Aatii."

"I know something of this," said Aesilesius.

"The Aatii have threatened the empire, on a hundred worlds," said Nika. "Otungs were recruited to supplement the imperial forces, to resist the Aatii. Thus, Otungs were armed and trained."

"With the result," said Aesilesius, bitterly, "that there is now an Otung on the throne."

"But," said Nika, earnestly, "the empire has been stable, the Aatii, uncertain, held back, have been quiescent."

"That is known to me," said Aesilesius.

"There has been truce, if not peace," said Nika. "Fields are plowed, trade takes place, men no longer fear to regard the sky."

"A quietude purchased illegitimately, at the cost of a usurpation," said Aesilesius.

"A quietude now in jeopardy," said Nika. "It is believed that Otungs murdered the two kings of the Aatii, and cast their bodies away, in grievous insult, to be the feasting of dogs and birds."

"You fear war," said Aesilesius.

"It is rumored," said Nika, "that Ingeld, prince of the Dris-riaks, even now, filled with sorrow, and outrage, speeds to Teng-uthaxichai, to foment war, a war to the death with Otungs. This war will be fought in the skies, and on the lands, of Telnaria. Telnar itself could be burned to the ground. Thousands could die."

"This could end the time of the Otungs in Telnaria," said Aesilesius.

"Quite possibly, Master," said Nika, "but do not look to your restoration. Rather, when the fires die and the ashes cool, fear a Drisriak on the throne, one covered with blood and filled with anger, one who may well be far less tolerant and merciful than the supplanted Otung, one who may well wish, as a matter of political expediency, to exterminate all potential aspirants or claimants to the throne."

"Then it will be the end," said Aesilesius, "Telnar destroyed, the empire riven, a collapse into barbarism, the loss of law, the rise of brute savagery, the rise of bandits, carving out kingdoms for themselves, claiming crowns."

"I fear for Master," said Nika.

"You must be protected," said Aesilesius. "When they come for me with the bowstring or knife, you must be gone. I will have you sent away."

"Do not do so, Master," wept Nika. "I would die with you, at your feet, where I belong."

"Surely not," said Aesilesius.

"I would," she wept.

"Why?" he asked.

She put down her head, sobbing. "Do not make me speak," she begged, "lest you, in fury, outraged and scornful, slay me with your own hands."

"I could not do that," he said.

She looked up at him, wonderingly.

"You may ask me why," he said.

"I dare not do so," she said. "I am a slave."

"You fear for me?" he asked.

"Very much so, Master," she said.

"Few would," he said.

"Perhaps more than you know," she said.

"I am an embarrassment to many," he said.

"Not to me," she said.

"I am a pathetic monstrosity," he said, "a freak, a stain on a royal line, a reproach to the dignity and majesty of the empire."

"You are none of these things, truly," she said.

He then reached down, and drew her up, beside him. She shook in his arms, sobbing. He held her tenderly, comforting her.

"No, no," she whispered suddenly, frightened, and then squirmed from his arms to kneel beside the couch. There she put her head down, gently, against his left knee.

"As you will," he said, "sweet Nika."

They remained so, for some time.

Then Aesilesius began to speak, slowly, thoughtfully, choosing his words carefully. "Much must be sacrificed if the empire is to be saved. If two kings have been killed, viciously, wantonly, and without provocation, at the instigation of the Otung usurper, he arrogantly deeming himself Ottonius, the First, war may ensue. Indeed, it is likely. Even now, it seems a prince of the Drisriaks prepares to rouse his tribe and the Aatii nation, and doubtless their allied tribes, as well, to a war of vengeance upon the Otungs and the Otung regime, a war which may destroy Telnar and shake the empire. Could this catastrophe be averted? Is there some small act which, like crushing a dragon in its tiny shell before it hatches, feeds and grows, and spreads its wings and its sheet of fire over lands, like snuffing out a flicker of flame before it consumes forests and harvests, like devising a cure for a rushing, foreseen plague, a small act, perhaps easily performed, which might alter a looming path of history, which might turn aside floods of destruction, which might save the lives and properties, and futures, of populations? If so, were there such an act, small and easily performed, who could refrain from it? Who, in conscience, able, rightly placed and equipped, could refuse to perform that act, even at the cost of his own life, and particularly if that life were not worth living, if it were a life of futility and shame, a life which might possibly be redeemed and justified by such an act?"

"Master?" asked Nika, looking up.

"It is unlikely that war, if desired, can be prevented," said Aesilesius. "If men want their war they will have it. Have they not always behaved so? But a war often has a pretext. What if one were to remove that pretext? Might one then prevent the war? It is unlikely, but it is possible. Should one not then attempt such a thing? At the least, in such a case, motivations might be honestly unmasked, and faced."

"I grow uneasy, Master," said Nika.

"The Aatii want vengeance," said Aesilesius. "They want the blood of the Otung."

"Do not speak so, Master," said Nika. "I am frightened."

"I can give them their vengeance," said Aesilesius. "I can give them the blood of the Otung."

"No, no, Master!" said Nika.

Aesilesius stood up and went to the side of the room, and opened a chest. From beneath folded cloths he drew forth a knife."

"I stole this from the kitchen," he said.

"Do not, Master!" cried Nika.

He placed the knife in his belt.

Nika leapt up, and sped toward the door of the chamber, to pull at it, but Aesilesius, with the agility of a forest panther, interposed himself between her and the door.

"So you are a spy for the Otung," said Aesilesius.

"No, Master!" she cried. "It is you, you I fear for."

"You would save the Otung?" he said.

"Yes, yes," she said, "and in saving him, I would save you."

Aesilesius took her by the arm and drew her to the side of the couch. There he snapped a manacle about her ankle.

"You will not interfere," he said.

She went to the floor, sitting, sobbing, trying to thrust the manacle from her ankle. "Do not injure yourself," said Aesilesius. "Your ankle is pretty."

"Release me," she begged.

"The manacle is secure," he said, "the chain is heavy, the ring to which the chain is attached is sturdy."

"Please!" she wept.

"You will remain where you are," he said, "—slave."

"I shall scream!" she said.

"You will not be heard," he said. "This room is designed to contain sound, such as the screams of fear, the tantrums and cries, of a distressed, retarded child."

"Do not attempt what you contemplate!" begged Nika.

"We shall wait, some hours," said Aesilesius. "I wish to be sure the Otung is asleep."

"No, Master, please, no, Master!" wept Nika.

CHAPTER FORTY-SEVEN

"The emperor does not join us," said Rurik, Tenth Consul of Larial VII, of the Larial Farnichi.

"Again," observed Tuvo Ausonius, once a civil servant on Miton.

It was late evening in one of the private dining chambers in the palace. About the table were three men other than Rurik and Tuvo Ausonius; Iaachus, Arbiter of Protocol in the palace at Telnar, adviser to the emperor; Julian, he of the noble Aureliani, a naval officer; and Titus Gelinus, rhetor and attorney, envoy of the palace to the senate, and of the senate to the palace.

"He keeps much to his quarters of late," said Julian.

"How then is this night different?" asked Rurik.

"It is not," said Iaachus.

The dinner, well prepared and well served, was sedate. The men commonly spoke quietly.

Each was attended, as was often the case, by a personal slave. Though no free women were present, the slaves, though bare-armed and barefoot, were discreetly gowned, in palace slave livery. The neck of each was encircled by her collar.

"Wine," said Julian, and a lovely blonde, her hair dangling behind her, in two long braids, in the Alemanni fashion, rose to her feet, to fetch the decanter of *kana* on the nearby serving table. She was Gerune, a daughter of Abrogastes, who had joined her brother, Ortog, in his secession from the Drisriaks, to form his own tribe. After the decimation of the Ortungen, she had been given to Julian, then a tender of pigs, on Tenguthaxichai.

She served her master silently, and then withdrew, to kneel with the other slaves. The slave of Iaachus was brown-haired Elena, once a lady-in-waiting to the empress mother. Rurik's slave was Cornhair, once the Lady Publennia, of the Larial Calasalii, a family competitive with, and opposed to, in armed conflict, the Larial Farnichi. The slave of Tuvo Ausonius was dark-haired Sesella, once a stewardess on the line, *Wings Between Worlds*. She had been purchased for him on the "Summer World," that named for an imperial palace occasionally visited by the imperial family during Telnar's winter. The last of the five slaves was Pig. She belonged to Titus Gelinus, and had once been Lady Gia Alexia, of the Telnar Darsai.

The slaves were not, on these thoughtful, sober occasions, the men meeting to discuss serious matters, put to the pleasure of their masters. They would not be, following, or preceding, dessert, cast over the cushions of upholstered chairs, dragged beneath the table, or placed upon it, nor commanded to the carpets, to serve as the slaves they were. They looked at one another. They were not free women. Their eyes were moist with tears. In their bodies restlessness arose, refusing to be put aside or ignored. Slaves have needs, insistent, pressing, demanding, sometimes piteous, merciless needs. It is the way they are. Men had seen fit to make them so.

"Perhaps," said Iaachus, "the slaves might now be dismissed."

A soft moan escaped Sesella.

"Later," said Tuvo Ausonius.

Rurik slapped his hands together, sharply. "Leave us," he said.

The five slaves quickly rose to their feet and, heads down, withdrew.

"Ingeld is on his way to Tenguthaxichai," said Julian.

"Where is Abrogastes?" asked Titus Gelinus.

"I do not know," said Julian.

"Surely the emperor has not done away with him," said Tuvo Ausonius.

"He should have," said Rurik. "Abrogastes is a fearful enemy, to the empire, to the Larial Farnichi, to the Otungs, to the Vandalii, as a whole."

"If the emperor wished to do away with Abrogastes," said Julian, "he might easily have done so by letting him perish in the fourth basement of the house of Dardanis."

"How fares the house of Dardanis?" asked Tuvo Ausonius.

"It has not been razed," said Titus Gelinus.

"Nor should it be," said Julian.

"Things must seem normal," said Rurik.

"Where is Ortog?" asked Titus Gelinus.

"He barges on the Turning Serpent," said Rurik, "downstream, to rally the remnants of the Ortungs in the delta towns."

"Lawless, bandit towns," said Tuvo Ausonius.

"And thus appropriate to the remnants of the Ortungen," said Iaachus.

"At least," said Titus Gelinus, "the identity of the enemy is now clearly established, unmistakably, proven beyond any doubt."

"There was little doubt before," said Rurik. "Who had most to gain from the detention or destruction of Abrogastes?"

"Clearly Ingeld," said Julian, "heir to the high seat of the Drisriaks, the loving and loyal son."

"Yes, Ingeld," said Rurik, "abetted by some wealthy, ambitious, well-placed, powerful, favor-seeking ally, with its own interests and objectives."

"It could only be Sidonicus, the ministrant and exarch," said Iaachus.

"But now," said Titus Gelinus, "overwhelming suspicions, broadly entertained, are replaced with indisputable evidence. The two former bodyguards, once arena killers, Boris and Andak, now men of the emperor, were literally present at a meeting of Timon Safarius Rhodius with Ingeld, the exarch, Sidonicus, and his deputy, Fulvius."

"Why then does the emperor not arrest the exarch and his deputy?" asked Tuvo Ausonius.

"The earth would open," said Rurik. "Stones would be shaken from buildings. Telnar would burn."

"We have our proof now," said Titus Gelinus. "But it is only our proof. It is private proof, not public proof. Allegations need only be denied, doubtless with dismay, tears, astonishment, and outrage. Who would take the word of monsters, of arena killers, over that of the irreproachable, sacrosanct exarch of Telnar? Indeed, who would dare touch even the hem of that purple robe?"

"I do not understand one thing," said Tuvo Ausonius.

"Then you understand nothing," said Titus Gelinus.

"Please do not jest," said Tuvo Ausonius.

"If there is only one thing you do not understand," said Titus Gelinus, "you are very fortunate."

"I dare not match wits with a rhetor," said Tuvo Ausonius.

"Dear Gelinus," said Julian, "you are not now in a court, examining a confused, bewildered witness, winning plaudits from an amused crowd."

"Forgive me," said Titus Gelinus. "I fear it is a matter of habit. I meant no harm."

"Nor any good either," said Tuvo Ausonius.

"Very good," Titus Gelinus. "Two targets struck, mine and yours, in but a single moment."

"May Orak, father of the gods, preserve us from two rhetors at the same table," said Rurik.

"Dear Tuvo," said Julian, "please proceed."

"I may do so?" asked Tuvo Ausonius.

"Please do so," said Titus Gelinus.

"As I understand these things," said Tuvo Ausonius, "Corelius, a former officer on the freighter, *Narcona*, participated traitorously in the silencing of the batteries of Telnar, allowing the success of the raid by Abrogastes which resulted in the abduction of the princesses, Viviana and Alacida. He was then given refuge and shelter by Abrogastes, but later betrayed Abrogastes into the keeping of Sidonicus. He later let himself be seen by a seeking, vengeful Ortog, the son of Abrogastes, in order to lead him into a trap, which, in the view of the conspirators, who wished to make a captive of Ortog, as well as his father, was a trap well sprung. However, Ortog had intentionally let himself be apprehended in order that imperial forces might track his movements and thus be led to the location of Abrogastes. This utilization of one trap to spring a greater trap, an enclosing trap, was successful. This led to the events in the fourth basement of the house of the merchant, Dardanis."

"What is it you do not understand?" asked Rurik.

"The man, Corelius," said Tuvo Ausonius, "seems to have been importantly involved in these matters, indeed, as a primary participant. Yet, as I understand it, he disappeared shortly after the entrapment of Ortog. He was not, I gather, in the fourth basement of the house of Dardanis at the time of the freeing of Abrogastes and Ortog."

"That is true," said Julian.

"Where was he?" asked Tuvo Ausonius.

"We do not know," said Julian.

"Perhaps most importantly," said Tuvo Ausonius, "he was not, following the testimony of Boris and Andak, present at the meeting of Ingeld with Timon Safarius Rhodius, the exarch, Sidonicus, and the exarch's deputy, Fulvius."

"That is true," said Julian.

"I think," said Rurik, "Corelius is dead."

"How so?" asked Julian.

"Corelius was involved, and importantly, in various affairs, as you noted," said Rurik, "indeed, I think in too many."

"Speak further," said Julian.

"He was importantly involved," said Rurik, "but always as a minion, a minor figure, a figure with no standing, no power, no wealth, no men of his own."

"I see," said Julian.

"Therefore," said Rurik, "he, with a track of betrayals behind him, he, with little power, and expendable, knows too much of too many dark secrets."

"Such men are unnecessary and dangerous," said Iaachus.

"Of course," said Rurik, "so I expect our conspirators, long ago, must have noted his dispensability."

"He is dead," said Tuvo Ausonius.

"I would think so," said Rurik.

"Surely his dispensability and peril must have occurred to him," said Tuvo Ausonius.

"One would suppose so," said Rurik. "One does not know."

"Some men," said Julian, "ignore the most obvious signs of a prowling *vi-cat*, not wishing to understand them, even refusing to understand them, and some cling to a sack of gold even when it impedes their flight from a lion."

"Much proceeds, unseen," said Rurik.

"It is quiet now," said Julian.

"When the dam breaks," said Rurik, "a torrent of events will occur."

"In any event," said Iaachus, "we now have a signal advantage. By means of Timon Safarius Rhodius, *primarius* of the senate, we have access to the inner circle of our enemies, to their most secret plans."

"Unless the *primarius* is suspected," said Julian.

"Of course," said Iaachus.

"Ingeld will rouse the Aatii," said Tuvo Ausonius.

"But they will not attack until the batteries are silenced, either overwhelmed, suborned, or destroyed," said Iaachus.

"The defenses of the batteries are being strengthened," said Julian. "The emperor has placed Otungs in command."

"It is late, gentlemen," said Rurik.

"I would," said Julian, "that the emperor spoke more frequently with us."

"He keeps his own council," said Iaachus.

"He is deep," said Julian.

"Surely he has plans," said Rurik. "A thousand things could occur."

"For which," said Julian, "he may have a thousand plans."

"Let us adjourn our meeting," said Rurik. "By now the slaves, following our instructions, will be waiting, having chained themselves naked, to the foot of our couches."

"I noted earlier the preferred slaves of the emperor," said Iaachus, "Janina, Flora, and Renata. They were still in their cages. Usually the emperor has one or more sent to his chamber."

"I think not for three or four days," said Julian.

"I do not understand," said Iaachus.

"Nor do I," said Julian.

CHAPTER FORTY-EIGHT

"Greetings," said Otto, rising, sitting up on his side couch, turning, facing the panel which had just slid open, the darkness behind it. "I have been waiting for you."

A figure appeared from the darkness, bent over, clutching a small, stuffed animal, a yellow *torodont*.

"Did you hear the small coin that dropped, dislodged from its place, when you opened the panel?" asked Otto. "You must have heard it, and yet you did not immediately withdraw. Why is that? Or perhaps you thought that I, so asleep, would not hear it fall? Should you have risked that? Or should you have rushed forward, to strike instantly, hopefully before any possible response? In the darkness, or poor light, for the lamp is very dim, you would presumably attack the seeming figure on the great couch, but you would find it naught but curled cushions, wrapped in blankets."

The bent-over figure now appeared fully in the portal, clutching the stuffed animal to its chest.

"Surely you heard the dropping of the coin, as tiny a sound as it might have produced," said Otto. "Would not your every sense be keenly alert, at such a time? Might your hand not tremble in anticipation? Might you not wonder if the beating of your heart, like throbbing thunder in your breast, might be heard afar, from wall to wall? This would not be old business for you, as it might be for a controlled, cold, practiced assassin."

A small, childlike noise emanated from the figure.

"The falling of that coin," said Otto, "in such a place, at such a time, should have rivaled the clash of cymbals, the beating of drums, the blare of trumpets. Did you not hear it? Death seldom announces itself, approaching loudly. Commonly it comes on soft feet, like night, unseen like air. Were you camped on the Plains of Barrionuevo, on the Flats of Tung, with Heruls about, or resting in the forests of Varna or Tangara, roamed by the *vi-cat*, the forest panther, the *hroth*, the *arn* bear, the lion, you would become aware, if you were to survive, of small noises, the stirring of a pebble, the snapping of a stick, and aware, too, of the lack of noise, the sudden silence of night creatures."

A pathetic, snuffling, mewling sound escaped the figure.

"Ah," said Otto, "I see that it is the noble, tragic Aesilesius, puzzled and confused, who has somehow stumbled on clandestine avenues within the palace and has, wandering about, fortuitously, unwittingly, stumbled into my chamber."

An unintelligible mumble, a soft, soblike gurgle, came from the creature.

"I see you have your stuffed *torodont*," said Otto. "I hear you are fond of it. I hope you liked the other toy I gave you, as well, the small, red-headed, pretty toy."

The figure looked up, angrily.

"I assume the *torodont*, held as it is, serves to conceal a weapon," said Otto, "presumably the knife reported missing from the kitchen."

Aesilesius released the *torodont*, letting it slip to the floor.

"I thought so," said Otto.

Aesilesius faced Otto, the knife in view.

"That is not a toy, to be played with," said Otto.

Wavering, gurgling like demented child, Aesilesius, raised the knife over his head, awkwardly.

"I see you are innocent, and have no idea of what you are doing," said Otto. "Surely, if you did, you would not attempt an over-the-head downward stroke, as it is easy to block. You would do better to hold the knife down, edge up, and rip to the belly, following which you may go for the heart or throat."

Aesilesius, crouching, held the knife lower, edge up.

"Better," said Otto. "But it is safest, if less honorable, to attack, unnoted, from the rear, across the throat or into the back. To be sure, that option is no longer available to you, at least at present."

Aesilesius did not respond.

"You realize, of course," said Otto, "that you can be summarily killed, or killed unpleasantly, for entering this chamber, unannounced, without permission, let alone while bearing a weapon."

Aesilesius regarded Otto balefully.

"Discard your mask of imbecility," said Otto.

The creature raised its head.

"It is not necessary here," said Otto.

"You know?" said Aesilesius.

"Of course," said Otto.

"Your spy, Nika, has reported to you," said Aesilesius. "She has informed on me. She has betrayed me."

"No," said Otto, "she would die before she would betray you. I suspected the matter long ago, from missing volumes in the library, having to do with the plans of the palace, with politics, economics, statecraft, and war. And clearly your love of your mother and her weaknesses gave you away. Who else would be so concerned for her but a loving son, she to many a vain, tiresome old woman, and how could she be secretly provided with gifts in the absence of unrecognized corridors and passageways, doubtless recorded in one of the missing volumes from the library?"

"You put the slave into my chambers to spy on me," said Aesilesius.

"I put her there for two reasons," said Otto, "first, to spy not on you, but for you, that you might be better informed, and, second, a subsidiary reason, to teach you the delights and joys of the most beautiful, exciting, and precious possession a man can own, wholly, absolutely, and perfectly, a woman."

"She attempted to dissuade me from coming here," said Aesilesius.

"She is terrified for your safety," said Otto.

"Why should that be?" asked Aesilesius.

"Who knows?" said Otto.

"Call your guards," said Aesilesius.

"I would rather not," said Otto.

"They may arrive in time," said Aesilesius.

"Perhaps to remove your body," said Otto.

"I have a knife," said Aesilesius.

"If you will not return it to the kitchen," said Otto, "at least return it to your chamber and hide it, as before."

"Surely you understand why I have come here, in stealth, and armed," said Aesilesius.

"It is easy to have one's suspicions," said Otto.

"I must kill you," said Aesilesius.

"You are mistaken," said Otto.

"At least," said Aesilesius, "I must try to do so."

"Not at all," said Otto.

"You had two barbarian kings killed, needlessly and cruelly, even shaming their bodies," said Aesilesius. "A war of vengeance is now imminent. In this war Telnaria, and neighboring worlds, will be the battleground. Telnar itself, seat of the empire, may be destroyed. The empire will totter, and may fall. It is your dark, tyrannical blood which will be sought. If I can rid the empire of so heinous a perpetrator, war may be averted. If vengeance is obtained, it should no longer be sought."

"I suspect you have learned much from books and little from life," said Otto. "One lesson is that many things are not what they seem, and that much which is said is not what is meant. One who seems your friend may not be your friend, and one who seems your enemy may not be your enemy, and your friend may become your enemy and your enemy may become your friend. One who speaks much of honor may not be honorable, and one who speaks little of honor may die for it. Men are commonly aware of their own interest; it is then up to you to understand their interest, for that, far better than what they speak, is a guide to how they will act."

"I understand little or nothing of this," said Aesilesius.

"Words can illuminate reality," said Otto, "but too, they can darken and conceal reality. Try to look behind them."

"How can one look behind a word?" asked Aesilesius.

"Like an animal, like the lion and *vi-cat*," said Otto.

"I do not understand," said Aesilesius.

"See, smell, listen, taste, touch," said Otto. "Be alive, be aware, and when you think, think reality, what is, and what is not, and what may be, and how it may be, not words."

"This is hard to understand," said Aesilesius.

"Learn your books," said Otto, "but learn things, and men, and animals, and seasons and weathers, as well."

"If vengeance is obtained, it should no longer be sought," said Aesilesius. "If I slay you, I may avert a war. Thus, I must slay you, or, at least, try to do so."

"Some men who desire cities, lands, gold, and women," said Otto, "march out and seize them. Others invent reasons for doing so. Which are the more honest?"

"My knife is sharp," said Aesilesius.

"I could seize your wrist," said Otto, "and break it. I could crush your throat with either hand. I could break your neck beneath my foot."

"I fear it is so," said Aesilesius.

"I assure you it is so," said Otto.

Aesilesius sobbed, and handed Otto the knife, which Otto returned to him.

"I am a coward, a fraud, and failure," said Aesilesius, putting the knife in his belt.

"You are no coward," said Otto. "If you were a coward, you would never have come here. Too, I do not see you as a fraud. Rather I salute your brilliance, even from childhood. Deception and deceit, masking movements, misleading the enemy, are part of war, and the palace is at war. Such things are virtues of war, but there comes a time when one must, the place and time being propitious, put aside deception and deceit, and reveal oneself."

"I am a failure," said Aesilesius.

"You have succeeded, in your way, admirably until now," said Otto.

"I am a failure," insisted Aesilesius.

"Perhaps later," said Otto. "But not now, not yet."

"I do not understand," said Aesilesius.

"Now," said Otto, "if I were you I would return to your chamber."

"What shall I tell lovely Nika?" asked Aesilesius.

"You need tell her nothing," said Otto. "She is a slave."

Aesilesius regarded Otto.

"You may tell her that we met, amiably, and exchanged pleasantries," said Otto.

"She will not believe that," said Aesilesius.

"No," said Otto, "but she will understand."

"What of my secret?" asked Aesilesius.

"You may retain the clever, if dreadful, *persona* you have cultivated so carefully over the years," said Otto. "The future is uncertain. You may have need of it."

"My secret is safe with you?" asked Aesilesius.

"For now," said Otto.

"I may leave?" asked Aesilesius.

"Wait," said Otto, who then removed a bottle of *kana* from a cabinet to the side, which he placed in the hands of Aesilesius. "See the purple seal," he said. "This is the emperor's private stock. This will prove to your slave, should you wish to do so, that you were in my chamber."

"I hope this is not poison," said Aesilesius.

"I hope so, as well," said Otto, "for I might have drunk it. If you are concerned, have your slave drink first."

"No," said Aesilesius. "I would not do that."

"Interesting," said Otto.

"Should I permit her to have some?" asked Aesilesius.

"It is up to you," said Otto. "She is a slave."

"I think she would like some," said Aesilesius.

"The decision is yours," said Otto. "She is a slave."

"I take my leave," said Aesilesius.

"Take with you the stuffed toy, the *torodont*," said Otto. "It would not do for it to be found here."

Aesilesius picked up the toy, and turned to leave.

"I need not tell you this," said Otto, "but I choose to do so. It may lend solace to your concerns. I did not command, nor am I responsible for, in any way, the death of the two kings, Abrogastes and Ortog."

"Who then?" asked Aesilesius, turning back.

"Neither is dead," said Otto. "Both live."

"But," said Aesilesius, "the bodies?"

"Those of others," said Otto, "selected to perpetrate an illusion."

"I do not understand," said Aesilesius.

"Deceit and deception are part of war," said Otto.

"The kings live?" said Aesilesius.

"Remember," said Otto, "you do not know this."

"I understand," said Aesilesius.

"Nothing is to be said to Nika, nor to any other," said Otto.

"Accepted," said Aesilesius.

"My spies inform me," said Otto. "That some men in taverns drink the health of Aesilesius."

"Have you something to do with this?" asked Aesilesius.

"Who knows?" said Otto.

"Sometimes, I have heard," said Aesilesius, "an enemy is not an enemy."

"I have heard that, as well," said Otto.

CHAPTER FORTY-NINE

"Are the rumors true?" asked Lars Red Sleeves, of the Borkons, the third largest tribe of the Alemanni nation. He was of the Lidanian Borkons, the Coastal Borkons.

"We shall soon know," said Farrix, of the Teragars, or Long-River Borkons.

"Representatives of the Eleven Tribes are here," said Herman Two Ax. "I have counted the shields on the gate. Herman Two Ax was a Dangar, one of four on the Spear Council. The Dangars were the second largest tribe of the Alemanni nation, the Drisriaks being the largest.

"It is time," said Granath, "that the lion ships clawed at Telnar itself." He was of the Long-Toothed People, an allied tribe of the Alemanni. Representatives of several of the allied tribes were present.

"No wise lion charges into the muzzle of a gun," said Farrix.

"Better to nibble at the outer worlds," said an Aratar, "until Telnaria, harassed and bled, starved, succumbs, opening her gates to our grain ships."

"What if the guns are jammed, unloaded, or destroyed?" asked Granath.

"Excellent," said Farrix. "Accomplish it."

On the rude dais in the stoutly-timbered, high-roofed hall on the Alemanni Meeting World, Tenguthaxichai, loomed the high seat of the Drisriaks, unoccupied. Tables and benches lined the walls. There were more than four hundred men and nonmen present, delegates of more than a dozen species. In the long fire pit, the roasting racks and poles were cold, and in the pit lay inert, sullen ashes.

"I can remember," said Lars Red Sleeves, "when this hall was bright with laughter, with song, with shouting, with slaves, with fire and feasting."

"Meat roasted and *bror* flowed," said Herman Two Ax.

"In the time of Abrogastes," said Granath.

There was then a hush in the hall. "The prince," whispered a man.

All eyes turned to the side of hall, where, through a side portal, solemnly entered two individuals, one with her hand on the arm of the other.

"Who is the woman, escorted by the prince, she gowned, and so richly, in the fashion of Telnaria?" asked a man.

"That is the consort of the prince," said a man, "Viviana, of royal blood, sister of Aesilesius, former emperor, he deposed by a usurping Otung."

"I can remember," said a man, "when it was rare to see a Telnarian woman here who was not stripped and in a collar."

"She is lovely," said a man.

"Where is her collar?" asked another.

"Perhaps on a peg, waiting to be put on her," said another.

Ingeld, approaching, his face disconsolate, conducted Viviana to the dais. He then stood to the right of the high seat, Viviana to his right, and faced the assembly in the dirt-floored, rush-strewn hall, for the Alemanni, as many other peoples, are fond of old ways, and traditions.

"Brothers," declaimed Ingeld, "warriors in arms, fellows, comrades, sharers of blood, attend me. This is a dark day for the Drisriaks, for the Alemanni, for the allies, and a dark day, as well, for Telnaria, land and former abode of my dear spouse, Viviana. Many of you know what has occurred. Tidings abound. Horrors will out. How can one conceal darkness, the fall of night? My revered and beloved father, and my misled brother, whom I loved despite his treason, are no more."

A reaction shook the crowd, cries of disbelief, sorrow, and protest, though many, doubtless, were well apprised of the occasion of this meeting.

"They were foully and gratuitously slaughtered by malevolent Otungs, our hated and hereditary enemies, who cast the bodies forth, outside the walls of Telnar, abandoning them to the feasting of dogs and birds."

There were cries of rage, and fists were raised and shaken.

"Are we men?" asked Ingeld.

"We are men!" shouted men

"If so, shall we ignore this crime and insult?" asked Ingeld.

"No!" cried men.

"If so, must this insult be avenged?" inquired Ingeld.

"Yes, yes!" cried men.

"Death to Otungs!" cried more than a hundred voices.

"An Otung sits upon the imperial throne," said Ingeld.

"War upon Otungs, war on the Vandalii!" cried men.

"But hold!" called Ingeld, extending his hand. "Be not precipitate! Rush not headlong into the night of doom. An Otung sits upon the imperial throne. At his gesture armies march and navies, on towers of flame, climb the skies. The schemes of Otungs are interwoven in Telnaria's tapestries of war. We will strike but only when the target is vulnerable and the moment is opportune. I have a plan afoot, to be abetted by Telnarians, my spouse's people. When the Otungs are expunged in our cleansing war, there will be a melding of peoples, Alemanni and Telnarian. A son of mingled bloods, Drisriak and Telnarian, will grace the throne, and a hardier, stouter empire will rise and thrive."

"No," cried a man. "Do not wait! Do not dally! Act, act!"

"Vengeance now!" cried another man.

"While the blood is hot!" cried another.

"Now, now!" cried others.

"Patience, noble warriors," responded Ingeld. "Do you think I have forgotten my beloved father and dear brother? No. I pause only to brew a better vengeance. The excitement of vengeance stirs the blood; its torch cries out to be enflamed and lifted; and who does not desire to see it burn now, and fiercely; but there are other vengeances, too, planned vengeances, vengeances more sober and terrible, better vengeances, vengeances as implacable and unforgiving as ice. Are they less to be desired? Be patient. The spring and summer of vengeance is less to be dreaded than its winter. Be patient. The season of our vengeance approaches."

"Be it so, great prince!" cried a man.

"Accepted!" cried another.

"Yes, accepted!" cried yet another.

"Accepted, accepted," cried the assembled delegates and warriors.

Ingeld moved, and now stood not to the right of the high seat, the place of a prince, first in blood, but before it, and smiled, satisfied.

Viviana trembled, looking out upon that excited, rough-clothed, feral throng, fear in her eyes.

There were then gasps, and cries of astonishment, from the crowd, followed by a hushed silence.

"He has dared to sit upon the high seat," whispered a man.

Ingeld now reposed on the high seat in the hall of the Drisriaks, on Tenguthaxichai.

Men looked at one another uncertainly, apprehensively.

Then one cried, "Hail, Ingeld."

And then the cry went up, from all, over and over, ringing to the timbers of the roof, "Hail, Ingeld!"

It seems this acclaim might have rendered inaudible lesser sounds, the whine of a descending hoverer from outside the gate, the creaking of wagons entering the palisaded walls, cries of surprise and wonder in the yard, the celebratory striking of the flat of spear blades on shields.

When Ingeld lifted his hand to pause the tumult within the hall, some of these lesser noises became audible, the cries of men, the sound of metal on metal.

Men in the hall looked about, one to another, questioningly, and then turned to face the hall's mighty entryway. Some moved their hands to the hilts of blades. Herman Two Ax loosened the straps that held the crossed axes at his back, one to be wielded with each hand.

On those massive timbers, from outside, a spear butt struck three times, at measured intervals.

Hands moved from the hilts of weapons. Herman Two Ax tightened the buckle at his chest.

"A person of rank is without," said a man. This could be told, as all knew, from the three measured strokes on the timbers of the portal.

"Surely the kings of the tribes are here," said a man, "of the Alemanni, and those of many of the allies."

"Who would dare be so late, even a king, in responding to the great summons?" asked a man.

"Prince?" asked a shieldsman.

Ingeld nodded and the shieldsman signaled the two keepers of the portal to swing back the mighty leaves of the entryway.

In the portal stood a large figure.

"Greetings," said Abrogastes.

CHAPTER FIFTY

There was a half moment of stunned silence greeting the announcement of Abrogastes, and then the hall rang with cheers, and the keepers of the portal intervened, feet braced, with crossed spears, to protect Abrogastes from being swept from his feet and trampled by the glad throng that rushed toward him, hoping to touch him, or embrace him. With a great laugh, Abrogastes thrust up the crossed spears and, grinning, struggling, fought his way through the jubilant throng, toward the dais at the front of the hall.

Ingeld clutched the arms of the high seat, unwilling to release them. He could not move, so in shock he was. His vision swam; the room spun before him. He tried not to see what was before his eyes, tried to force away what he saw, not letting it enter his understanding. But it was there, a glad, grinning Abrogastes forcing his way through the crowd of well-wishers, as might a ship breast and cleave high waves, as might a *torodont* plow through thick brush.

"Greetings, beloved son!" called Abrogastes, reaching the dais.

Ingeld, suddenly aware of where he was, and the impropriety of his now being so ensconced, pressed down suddenly, forcibly, on the curved arms of the high seat, and thrust his body up, out of, and away from, that object.

"Beloved father!" he exclaimed.

Abrogastes leaped to the surface of the dais.

He embraced Ingeld, warmly.

"Does my daughter-in-law not greet me?" asked Abrogastes, looking down.

"She has fainted," said Ingeld, looking down to his left, at the soft, curved, crumpled figure in its Telnarian finery.

"Lovely," said Abrogastes, looking down at Viviana. "Had we no better use for her she might sell well as a slave."

"We thought you dead, slain by Otungs," said Ingeld.

"I trust she is now with child," said Abrogastes.

"No," said Ingeld.

"No matter," said Abrogastes. "We can always make do with one from Hrothgar's Alacida. One will do as well as another. Where is Hrothgar?"

"He is away, hunting," said Ingeld.

"What is going on here?" asked Abrogastes.

"We thought you dead, and Ortog, as well," said Ingeld, "killed by Otungs, and your bodies dishonored. I summoned a Vengeance Council."

"Then Hrothgar should be here," said Abrogastes. Hrothgar was the third son of Abrogastes. We recall that he was a large, jovial fellow fond of horses, dogs, falcons, *bror*, and slaves, such things. He had been named for the *hroth*, a large mammal similar to, and possibly related to, the *arn* bear.

"We could not reach him," said Ingeld. In actual fact, Ingeld had not tried to reach him; he had not included him in the Vengeance Summons. The reason for this is unclear. Perhaps Ingeld, who was not generally popular amongst the Alemanni, did not wish, at such a time, for his better-liked sibling to be seen in proximity to the high seat. At such a time Ingeld may have felt it judicious to maintain his paramountcy.

"Why should you think me dead?" asked Abrogastes.

"Bodies were found, abandoned, half-eaten, outside the walls of Telnar, filled with Otung arrows," said Ingeld, "bodies taken to be those of yourself and Ortog."

"The matter is obviously a mistake," said Abrogastes.

"You were missing, for weeks," said Ingeld.

"I was buying slaves," said Abrogastes, "mostly women of the high *honestori*, and several once of the Telnarian nobility. They are intelligent, can read, and look well, curled naked at the foot of a fellow's couch. I have several outside, in the wagons."

Viviana stirred.

"Up, girl," said Abrogastes.

Viviana rose to her knees, and, bending forward, kissed the hem of the long jacket of Abrogastes. "Greetings, beloved father of my husband and lord," she said.

"Greetings," said Abrogastes. "You seem warmer, less arrogant and haughty, softer, and more beautiful than I remember."

"Chains and a taste of the lash much improve a woman," said Ingeld. "They then learn that they are women, and not men."

"Have you now learned," asked Abrogastes, looking down, "that you are not a man but a woman?"

"Yes, beloved father of my husband and lord," said Viviana.

"Perhaps you should make her a slave," said Abrogastes. "Slaves are frequently seeded and are helplessly, vulnerably receptive. They may become pregnant far more readily and helplessly than a free woman."

"If they are permitted," said Ingeld.

"Of course," said Abrogastes.

"I fear," said Viviana, "that I would be of little political value if I were a slave."

"Where is my preferred slave, Huta?" asked Abrogastes.

"No slaves are present," said Ingeld. "This is a Vengeance Council."

"I do not understand the bodies outside the walls, their meaning and identity," said Ingeld. "What of the Otung arrows?"

"I see that as a simple matter to understand," said Abrogastes. "They are obviously the bodies of two Otungs, executed Otungs, Otungs executed by Otungs, that explaining the arrows, doubtless the bodies of two Otungs who were found disloyal, perhaps even treasonous. That is not surprising. Otungs no more than the Drisriaks, or the Alemanni, as a whole, and their allies, look lightly on disloyalty or treason. Traitors are to be dealt with according to custom and tradition."

Ingeld turned away, to the throng about the dais. "My beloved father lives," he called. "He is safe. He has returned to us. Rejoice! Hail, Abrogastes, all hail Abrogastes, king of the Drisriaks!"

Once again the hall rang with cheers, with shouts of relief and joy, with thunderous cries of acclaim from the assembly. In this raucous tumult, towering to the high, arched roof, resounding betwixt walls of stout timbers, men brandished weapons, and laced boots stomped in the rush-strewn dirt, in improvised martial dances. Kings and simple, hardy shieldsmen embraced, weeping.

Ingeld stepped to the side, unnoticed, his fists clenched.

Viviana, now risen, pale, unsteady, alarmed in the presence of such fierce jubilation, clung desperately to the back of the high seat, that she might not once more swoon.

"You arrived but recently," said she to Ingeld, "from far Telnar. What were you doing there?"

"Be silent," said Ingeld.

Viviana subsided into silence, for she feared to press unwelcome queries upon her unwilling spouse. If he did not discipline her personally, she dreaded, even more, being given again into the keeping of slender, dark-haired Huta who, of late, seemed to regard her with even greater hostility than hitherto.

"What a dismal gathering I find here," shouted Abrogastes from the dais. "The spits and cooking racks are cold. Is there frost upon them? The hinges of the portal creak. Have they not been rubbed with grease of late? Heaped ashes from long-extinguished fires, from happier times, not removed, make mounds in the fire pit. Rushes on the floor are dry, brittle, and broken. They have not been carried out, burned, and replaced. Do not tell me there has been mourning here, surely not here, not in this place, not in a house of the Drisriaks."

Men regarded him, suddenly silent, milling about, watchful, puzzled.

"What a sorry host I am," said Abrogastes. "Forgive me, shield brothers, that I should prove so lacking in hospitality!"

"Great king?" asked Farrix, of the Teragars, the Long-River Borkons.

Many of those present exchanged bewildered glances.

"Ho!" shouted Abrogastes, clapping his hands twice.

At this signal, dozens of servitors, earnestly hastening, variously burdened, pressed into the hall. Some carried wiping cloths, oils, and rakes. Others brought scoops and refuse buckets. Some had their arms filled with fresh rushes. Others were laden with tinder and fire logs, vessels, plates, drinking horns, salt, and rude utensils, cases of *kana*, kegs of *bror* to be heated in hanging metal vessels, sides of beef to be roasted, crates of cheeses and breads, and diverse boxes of viands from various worlds."

"Take your places, according to established rank and merit," said Abrogastes, gesturing sweepingly to the tables and benches that lined the sides of the hall.

Men crowded to take their places while the hall was readied and the feast prepared. Several men began to sing a rousing Alemanni warrior song.

Soon the smells of roasting meat on a dozen spits filled the hall.

"Tell stories," said Abrogastes, "share news!"

Abrogastes now resided upon the high seat of the Drisriaks. Short tables were brought to the dais, and two short benches. One of the short tables was placed before the high seat, and one, for Ingeld, with its short bench, was placed to the right hand of Abrogastes, and the other, for Viviana, with its short bench, was placed at the left hand of Abrogastes. In this way, Abrogastes sat between Ingeld and his forced bride, the Telnarian beauty, Viviana, sister to Aesilesius, dividing them.

If Ingeld noted this with uneasiness, he revealed no sign of agitation.

Viviana, on the other hand, was uneasy. She knew that amongst the Alemanni, as opposed to the Telnarians, a man might have more than one wife. If she failed to bear Ingeld a child, it was not certain she would be simply put away. She might, instead, be given to Hrothgar.

"The meat is near roasted," said Abrogastes to Ingeld. "Who will claim the hero's portion?"

This would be the first cut of the roasted meat; to have this cut, which is commonly sizable and choice, is an honor, or, upon occasion, to claim a priority and an honor. In some halls, rival claimants to the hero's portion fight to the death.

"Surely you, beloved father," said Ingeld.

"We shall see," said Abrogastes.

Often, in a feast, one of fellowship and conviviality, there is no hero's portion, though it is common for the first cut of the meat to be delivered to the hall lord, usually a chieftain or king, or to a ranking guest.

But here, Abrogastes had stated that there was to be a hero's portion.

Why was that?

Ingeld's mind raced. He had no intention of claiming the hero's portion. If he did so, in virtue of his blood and paramountcy amongst the Drisriaks, he being the likely heir to the high seat, Abrogastes, in his wily cunning, might have arranged for another, a mighty warrior, perhaps the redoubtable Lars Red Sleeves or Herman Two Ax, or perhaps even Farrix, the Long-River Borkon, to lodge an alternative claim. In such a way might not Abrogastes dispose of a treasonous son, seemingly innocently, utilizing the convenience of custom and tradition? Too, if, in such a case, Ingeld should refuse the contest, his standing and prestige would be much diminished amongst the Alemanni, and his presumptive right to succeed Abrogastes would be tarnished, if not lost altogether. The Alemanni, like the Vandalii, and such peoples, and unlike more civilized nations, which give little thought to the matter, are reluctant to follow cowards.

"Is the meat done?" called Abrogastes.

"It is, mighty king," called a servitor, following a cutting into, and inspection, of the meat.

"Let who will claim the hero's portion!" called Abrogastes.

Men looked at one another, uncertainly.

"Who but Abrogastes, our king and beloved lord," said Ingeld, "might more worthily claim the hero's portion?"

"Claim it," said Abrogastes, heartily.

"I am unworthy, father," said Ingeld, shaken. "I have stood first here, in right of blood, only in your absence. In this hall there are mighty warriors, chieftains and kings."

"Claim it," said Abrogastes, sternly, his tone brooking no allowance for demurring or hesitation.

Ingeld rose to his feet behind the short table, to which he clung briefly, perhaps to steady himself, and assure himself that his legs would not buckle beneath him.

"And unsheathe your sword," said Abrogastes.

Ingeld unsheathed the sword. He considered turning and lunging at Abrogastes, dealing him a sudden death blow, and then claiming the high seat of the Drisriaks, but he realized the likely result of such an action would not be the high seat but being, after perhaps a moment of shock and bewilderment, cut to pieces by hundreds of swords and knives, each eager to avenge the murder of the beloved king of the Drisriaks.

All eyes were upon Ingeld.

"Go," said Abrogastes.

Ingeld, his sword unsheathed, looked about, at the tables, on both sides of the long, narrow fire pit. Assembled were chieftains, kings, princes, captains, shieldsmen, and representatives of the eleven tribes of the Alemanni, and of many of the allied tribes. Present were even Aratars, Red Vessites, and, from Safa Major, Burons.

Ingeld tried to read faces.

He studied the countenances of many, including those of Lars Red Sleeves and Herman Two Ax, both formidable warriors much esteemed by Abrogastes, Red Sleeves, a master of the broad sword, and Two Ax, a master of the paired axes. He even scrutinized that of Farrix, of the Long-River Borkons, with whom he had had repeated dealings, who knew perhaps too much of his plans and intrigues.

Which, of all those present, might rise to his feet and issue a challenge, claiming for himself, doubtless at Abrogastes' instruction or command, the hero's portion?

Ingeld descended from the dais and walked slowly toward the far spit, the first spit, that closest to the entryway to the hall.

At any moment he expected to hear a voice behind him, or to the side, call out, in tones of force and might, "I claim the meat! It is mine!"

The heavy, hot, glistening burden of meat was impaled with four spears, and then, still on its spit, was lifted by four struggling servitors from the fire and laid on one of the two cutting racks closest to the main portal of the hall. There were ten such cutting racks, each with its corresponding spit, turned from either side, five on one side of the fire pit and five on the other.

Ingeld lifted his sword over his head, holding the hilt with two hands.

He paused for a moment, waiting for the cry of challenge, every sense alert.

He slashed down at the meat, again and again, and then lifted up, high, impaled on his sword, a large, cut slab of meat, hot and running with juice.

"Ingeld! Ingeld!" cried voices. Goblets clashed. Fists pounded on the tables. "Ingeld, Ingeld!" he heard.

He made his way back to the dais, amidst cheers and the cries of his name, ascended the dais, and took his place at the right hand of Abrogastes.

Abrogastes rose to his feet, brandishing a horn of *bror*. "To the hero!" he cried, lifting the horn, toasting Ingeld.

"The hero, the hero!" cried men.

Ingeld looked down. This was his father's doing, he knew. Who, uninvited, would gainsay the will of the king, who had, in effect, publicly ordered his son to claim the hero's portion? Who would dispute this with a king? Hrothgar, if he were not Hrothgar, might have, but to Hrothgar such things meant little compared to the pleasures of food and drink, the shaking of dice, the racing of horses, the chase, and slaves.

"Fellows, comrades, friends, brothers, and kinsmen," cried Abrogastes, "let there be rejoicing! Let meat be cut, let *bror* flow!"

There were glad cries from all the tables. Servitors addressed themselves to the replenishing of goblets and horns, and the cutting of meat.

"Let this night be sung on other nights!" called Abrogastes. Then he called out, "Enter! Enter!"

Into the hall, the signal given, through the opened portal, in motley-colored garbs, rushed mountebanks, jugglers, fire eaters, minstrels, and acrobats, these immediately, in their diverse ways, entertaining the guests.

An hour sped past and still the heated *bror* made its rounds from table to table, to curved horn after curved horn.

Abrogastes then dismissed these entertainers, and an awe came over the guests, as a white-haired scald, frail and bent with age, was led forward by a child to the dais, and then turned about, that he might face the hall. His hands clutched a seven-stringed lyre. He had been blinded in youth by rune priests on Kolchis IV, that he might thereby, wholly, without temptation or distraction, better serve his art.

A single note, like a ringing arrow, left a string of the lyre.

No other sound was heard in the great hall.

Then the old man, who lived alone in darkness, with his music and chanting, lifted a thin, quavering voice, and warriors listened.

He chanted of many things, of ships streaming fire, undertaking long voyages, of swift rivers with falls and churning waters, of lonely trails in dark forests, of deserts and mountains, of valleys and prairies, of animals and birds, of the wars of gods, and the battles of men, of loyalty and betrayal, of surfeit and hunger, of victory and defeat, of the sorrows of heroes and the deaths of kings.

Men were silent, and wept.

"Done!" cried Abrogastes. "Give him meat, and *bror*!"

Then Abrogastes again rose to his feet, and signaled once more to the portal, which was again opened.

The pounding of a drum was heard, and a medley of instruments, and six musicians came forward and took their place before the dais, sitting cross-legged.

Ten dancers, to the music, hurried into the hall with a clash of bangles, a ringing of ankle bells, a flash of veils and silks. Five of the dancers were to one side of the fire pit and five to the other.

The guests on the benches, behind the crowded, laden tables, cried out with pleasure, some leaping to their feet, others pounding fists and goblets on the tables.

"These," said Abrogastes to Ingeld, "are brought from Beyira II."

"From the central wastes, the sand belts," said Ingeld.

"Yes," said Abrogastes.

"Are the dancers slaves?" asked Viviana.

"Of course," said Abrogastes. "What free woman would dare to dance so?"

"Necklaces conceal collars," said Ingeld.

"Oh," said Viviana, and watched, awed, learning how beautiful women could be.

"Bring me my devoted slave, Huta," said Abrogastes to a servitor.

"Yes, lord," said the man, and hurried away.

"Forgive me, father," said Ingeld. "I did not expect you here. Had I realized you would be here, and were this not originally conceived as a Vengeance Council, I would have supplied slaves, to serve."

"No matter," said Abrogastes.

Huta was soon ushered forward. She wore a long, brown garment, of a sort common to Alemanni women. The collar, of course, close-fitting, and metal, was obvious on her neck. She seemed muchly agitated, and frightened. Ingeld, too, was muchly uneasy.

She stood before the dais.

Music swirled about her. The dancers were behind her.

Viviana knew that Huta belonged to Abrogastes. Why then, she wondered, if Huta were before her master, from whom she had been long separated, was she seemingly so troubled. Too, Viviana noted the tenseness of Ingeld. Viviana felt a surge of power.

"That is a pretty slave," said Viviana to Abrogastes.

"She is Huta," said Abrogastes, "once a high priestess of the Timbri."

"But now, it seems," said Viviana, "only an object, a property, a rightless chattel."

"Of course," said Abrogastes.

"It seems she is standing," observed Viviana, smiling.

"On your knees!" snapped Ingeld to the slave.

Huta, startled, knelt.

She cast a look of hatred at Viviana.

"Huta," said Abrogastes, "have you missed me?"

"Very much, Master," she said. "My heart and my body have ached for your return."

"Loyal and devoted slave," said Abrogastes.

"Yes, Master," said Huta.

"I trust you have been faithful to me in my absence," said Abrogastes.

"Surely, Master," she said.

Ingeld turned white.

"Dear father of my husband and lord," said Viviana to Abrogastes, "I know little of such things, but is she not dressed in the fashion of a Drisriak free woman?"

"How is it," asked Abrogastes, regarding Huta, "that you have dared to assume the garb of a free woman?"

Huta began to tremble.

"On Telnaria," said Viviana, "a slave might be slain for doing such."

"A slave," said Abrogastes, "should be clad, if clad, as a slave, preferably in rags, or revealingly. Her beauty is not her own, but belongs to the Master. Hence, in its way, it is as public as that of horse or dog."

"Forgive me, Master," said Huta.

"Some slaves," said Viviana, "abuse the indulgence of a master."

"That is not acceptable," said Abrogastes.

"Perhaps," said Viviana, "she has been too little whipped."

"It is good for a slave to be occasionally whipped," said Abrogastes, "if only to remind her that she is a slave."

"True," said Viviana.

"Remove the garment," said Abrogastes to Huta, "and ascend the dais, to be chained by the neck, naked, to the high seat, on my left, kneeling at the feet of the lovely and gracious consort of my son."

"Yes, Master," said Huta, frightened.

"And we will ponder the value of the lash on your softness," said Abrogastes.

"Yes, Master," said Huta.

"I suspect you need improvement as a slave," said Abrogastes.

"I shall try to be pleasing to my Master," said Huta.

"Pleasing as a slave is to be pleasing," said Abrogastes, "in all ways."

"Yes, Master," said Huta.

Shortly thereafter the proud Huta, slave-bare and neck-chained, fastened to the left side of the high seat, knelt at the feet of Viviana, consort of Ingeld, prince of the Drisriaks.

"You are the slave of Abrogastes," whispered Viviana, bending down to Huta. "Beware that you do not please Ingeld too much."

Huta was silent, self-stripped, her fists clenched.

"Yes?" said Viviana.

"Yes," said Huta, venomously.

"Yes?" inquired Viviana.

"Yes," said Huta, "—*Mistress*."

Abrogastes, with a clapping of hands, dismissed the musicians and dancers. "Bring dice," he called, "fifty cups of dice!"

"For what should we gamble?" called a man from one of the tables, to the left.

"For what, great king?" called another, from the right.

Once again Abrogastes clapped his hands, and from without the portal there was a snapping of switches and cries of fear, misery, lamentation, and pain.

"Ho!" cried more than one man, intrigued, looking toward the portal.

"Move, meaningless slave beasts, pathetic, worthless animals," called a young male voice, that of a boy, and the first slave in the long coffle appeared in the portal, naked, and exquisitely formed, a fifteen-*darin* girl in almost any market, blond and blue-eyed, her hands bound behind her, the coffle chain looped about her neck, the loop closed with a padlock, and the chain then extending back, behind her, to the next slave, similarly bared, bound, and secured.

"Hold!" called Abrogastes, gesturing, and the boy held his switch against the breasts of the first slave, halting her.

More boys, with switches, could be seen behind her.

Boys were often put in charge of fully grown female slaves. This is thought good for boys, accustoming them to see females as no more than females, as objects suitable for controlling, herding, and mastering, and good for the slaves, as well, that they be humiliated by being held in such custody, by mere boys, this also reminding them that they are no more than females.

"I have gathered together here," said Abrogastes, "for your interest, delectation, perusal, and sport, two hundred choice females, captured or stolen from the empire. Few are of the *humiliori*. Almost all are from the *honestori*, and the high *honestori*, and some from the imperial nobility, itself. All are your inferiors, totally so, as they are of the empire, whose pampered, spoiled, decadent women are wholly without worth save as they may be spared to be the abject slaves of younger, fresher, hardier, stronger peoples."

"Yes, yes!" cried men.

"Women are property and loot," said Abrogastes. "They belong to those who are strong enough to take them and own them!"

Approving shouts coursed about the hall.

"Beloved father of my husband and lord," said Viviana, "may I be excused?"

"Surely," said Abrogastes.

Viviana rose to her feet.

"Get with child, my dear," said Abrogastes. "You would yourself look well on a sales block."

Viviana hurried from the hall.

"It is the right of property and war, attested throughout history," said Abrogastes, "that the women of a conquered enemy become the slaves of the victorious, that they are spoils of war, goods like other goods, loot, as other forms of loot. This vital, undeniable truth is acknowledged, despite lamentations and unavailing protests, by the women themselves. Women, in their hearts, know they are the property of men. The laws of nature have decreed it. They are the fitting property of men. This truth they accept and acknowledge, even as they are put to all fours and the collars are locked on their necks! They long for masters. Only in chains do they learn their womanhood. Dominate them. It is what they want. It is the key that unlocks their sex."

The entire coffle then, to the pleased shouts of warriors, coupled with a pounding on the tables of fists and goblets, to the striking of switches, wielded by impatient boys, was herded, whimpering and weeping, to the sound of clinking chains, to cries of pain responding to stings of supple leather, into the hall, to be bunched and knelt down before the dais.

"Crowd, beasts," said one of the boy herders. "Make a nice round flock. Closer together, soft, curved beasts, get your heads down, dare not, without permission, look into the eyes of a free person!"

"Learn that you are nothing," said another boy, striking a sobbing slave between the neck and shoulder with his switch. "You now exist only for the service of masters."

"Yes, Master," she wept.

"You will grow familiar with cages and ropes," said another lad. "You will learn to beg and grovel for a handful of food and a caress. You are slaves."

"Yes, Master," said more than one of the kneeling, bound, neck-chained, frightened slaves.

"Send forth a delegate from each table," called Abrogastes. "Let each delegate select three or four of these slaves and then return with them to the table and rattle the dice."

"May we sell one we win?" called a man.

"Of course," said Abrogastes, "and if you see one you like and did not win her, negotiate with her owner."

"Shall they serve us?" called a fellow.

"You own them," said Abrogastes. "Let them all be set to serving, but, too, let them not be confused as to the identity of their actual master."

"Marking sticks, ribbons, a knot tied in the hair, a bit of cloth will do, tied about an ankle," said a man.

"Let some be blindfolded," said a man, "that they may be gambled for, not seeing the dice, knowing not the players."

"They are slaves," said Abrogastes, "do with them as you will."

A man from each table rushed to the bunched slaves, and servitors hastened to undo the padlocks which had closed the loops of chain that had held the slaves in the coffle. The selected slaves were then conducted to the tables, some thrust ahead of impatient warriors, some carried over shoulders, and, often enough, some, bent over, hurrying, endeavoring to keep up with the striding fellow whose fist was fastened in her hair.

Soon the sounds of dice were heard on tables to the left and right.

"It seems, dear father," said Ingeld, "that there will be serving slaves, after all."

"What is a feast without slaves," said Abrogastes.

"What, indeed?" said Ingeld.

Abrogastes then removed the chain from the neck of Huta. "You may now," he said, "crawl on all fours from the hall, and to my chamber, where you will lie beside my couch on your belly, with your legs widely spread, and your wrists crossed behind your back, that they may be conveniently thronged."

"Yes, Master," said Huta.

Abrogastes and Ingeld watched her take her leave.

"She will juice readily," said Ingeld. "She has missed you desperately."

"I am sure of that," said Abrogastes.

As the feast continued, Ingeld grew more calm. "It seems," he thought to himself, "that Abrogastes knows nothing, and suspects nothing."

Dice rattled on, sometimes spilling to the floor, and there were shouts of pleasure, and of frustration and disappointment, and screams and weepings, as slaves were seized by their new masters.

Most slaves soon had their wrists freed from behind their backs that they might participate in the serving, hurrying to the fire pit for meat, and to the serving tables for *kana* and *bror*, and assorted comestibles, staples and delicacies, some from far worlds. Some masters, perhaps jealous of their new acquisitions, or fearing their loss or misappropriation by others, fastened them, kneeling, beneath their table, to the legs of their table, at their feet, by their hair or a cord about their neck. Some masters, relieving the slaves of their back-binding, tied their wrists before their bodies, and fastened them, thusly, kneeling, to a table leg, by their front-bound wrists.

There was the blow of a boy's switch and a cry of pain from a slave. "Do not touch the food," he said.

"I am hungry, Master!" she wept.

"You are a beast," he said, striking her twice more, sharply. "You will be fed, if fed, only as a beast is fed, only as its owner sees fit."

"Yes, Master," she said. "Forgive me, Master."

Food was given, by hand, to some of the slaves kneeling beneath the tables, which provender they took eagerly.

One slave was cast on her back across one of the tables. Others found themselves put to the pleasure of their owners beneath the tables or on the rush-strewn floor.

The serving slaves, tears in their eyes, picked their way carefully amongst churning, roiling bodies, and then one, her vessel of *kana* spilling, was seized by an ankle, and drawn herself to the floor.

"The guests," said Ingeld, "grow somewhat unruly."

"One rewards, one punishes, one governs," said Abrogastes. Then he cried, "*bror!*"

A lovely brunette hastened to the dais and, ascending the dais, and careful not to meet the eyes of a free person, poured hot *bror* into the drinking horn of Abrogastes.

"See her left breast," said Abrogastes, "inscribed there, by a marking stick, the sign of Lars Red Sleeves."

The slave hurried away.

"The dice were kind to the Borkon," said Ingeld.

"Herman Two Ax," said Abrogastes, "won three. I watched."

"His boots will be well polished," said Ingeld.

"Three beauties will soon compete for the privilege," said Abrogastes.

"The luck of the Dangars is celebrated in more than one song,"
said Ingeld.

"So are the habits of Dangar dice," said Abrogastes.

"It grows late," said Ingeld.

"Men will sleep in the hall," said Abrogastes, "many with a
slave tied by her neck to his ankle."

"Doubtless you will soon retire to your chamber," said Ingeld.

"Huta awaits," said Abrogastes.

"You are fond of her, are you not?" said Ingeld.

"Not particularly," said Abrogastes. "But it pleases me to own
her. It was she, when a priestess of the Timbri, who, with her false
magic and honeyed words, led Ortog astray."

"Ortog was a storm, and clouds were gathering," said Ingeld.
"If it had not been Huta, it would have been another. The sky
menaced. Ambition flourished. Lightning would flash."

"Another, such as you?" asked Abrogastes.

"Surely not," said Ingeld.

"It is rumored," said Abrogastes, "that Ortog lives."

"That cannot be," said Ingeld. "You slew him, in this very hall,
here, on Tenguthaxichai."

"I think that I shall retire to my chamber," said Abrogastes.
"Huta languishes, unfulfilled, unroped, unbraceleted, lonely, un-
caressed, absent from love shackles."

"What misery for a slave," said Ingeld.

"She will soon be helpless, in the embrace of her Master," said
Abrogastes, regarding Ingeld closely.

"Of course," said Ingeld.

Abrogastes rose to his feet. "Perhaps it is time," he said, "that
you, too, retire to your chamber."

"I am eager to do so," said Ingeld.

"Seed the fair Viviana abundantly," said Abrogastes. "We are
looking to reap a harvest from that belly."

"Of late," said Ingeld, "she grows warmer, and more helpless."

"We can always put her in a collar," said Abrogastes. "After a
month in a collar, the most frigid of women will thrash, moan, and
beg, and, if permitted, conceive at as little as a snapping of fingers.
The breeding sheds are filled with such once tepid, haughty stock."

The breeding stock, at the time of its breeding, is hooded, and
also at the time of its delivery of young. In this way entangle-
ments or attachments are eliminated. Needless to say, verbal com-
munication is forbidden to the stock at the time of breeding, and

the matches or pairings, the crossings, are arranged by the stock owners involved.

"The collar has an interesting effect on a woman," said Ingeld.

"And the whip," said Abrogastes.

"Of course," said Ingeld.

"And, if things proceed slowly, or poorly, we can always sell her," said Abrogastes.

"'Sell her'?" asked Ingeld.

"Certainly," said Abrogastes. "Hrothgar's Alacida will do just as nicely for our purposes."

"Surely I have priority," said Ingeld. "I am the second son."

"You may have priority amongst the Drisriaks, dear Ingeld," said Abrogastes, "but if Hrothgar has a son, it is he who will sit as regent, the Otung deposed, on the throne of Telnaria."

"I see," said Ingeld, darkly.

At this point, Abrogastes turned away, preparing to leave the dais, but then turned back, and faced Ingeld.

"Tonight you received the hero's portion," said Abrogastes.

"Thanks to my beloved father," said Ingeld.

"See that you prove worthy of it," said Abrogastes.

CHAPTER FIFTY-ONE

"What is this you tell me!" cried Sidonicus, his great bulk leaning forward from the chair in his private audience chamber.

"Put aside your sweets," said Ingeld. "It is bitter news I bring."

"Impossible!" said Fulvius.

"I cannot believe it," screamed Sidonicus. "Abrogastes! On Tenguthaxichai!"

"Yes," said Ingeld. "I have seen him, I have touched him, I have embraced him, on Tenguthaxichai."

"He lives?" said Sidonicus.

"Yes," said Ingeld.

"Surely he was slain with his rebel son, Ortog, days ago, in Telnar, in the deepest basement of the house of Dardanis," said Safarius.

"You should have remained there, to witness the executions," said Sidonicus, "rather than squeamishly withdrawing, with your guards."

"You said yourself," protested Safarius, "you would have behaved similarly."

"It would not have been seemly for a ministrant of Floon, let alone the exarch of Telnar, to witness so bloody a spectacle," said Sidonicus.

"Nor for the *primarius* of the senate," insisted Safarius.

"Nonsense," said Sidonicus. "The two cases are in no way comparable. A ministrant is concerned with holy matters, matters pertaining to the *koos*. Being *primarius* of the senate is a secular post. It has nothing to do with the *koos*. It is concerned with mundane matters, matters political, profane, and such. You should have witnessed the executions, even seen to the matter."

"I withdrew, with my guards," said Safarius.

"You are sure of the matter?" Fulvius asked Ingeld. "That you encountered Abrogastes on Tenguthaxichai?"

"It is indisputable," said Ingeld.

"You are fortunate you were not torn to pieces on Tenguthaxichai," said Fulvius.

"Abrogastes does not associate me with what occurred in the house of Dardanis," said Ingeld.

"Nor the exarch, I trust," said Fulvius.

"No," said Ingeld.

"Good," breathed Sidonicus, leaning back in his chair, and reaching for a sweet.

"Who then would he see as having been involved in his detention and incarceration?" asked Fulvius.

"Otungs, of course," said Sidonicus.

"And who then to his rescue?" asked Fulvius.

"It is obvious," said Sidonicus.

"Who, your blessedness?" asked Fulvius.

"His own people," said Sidonicus, "obviously Drisriaks."

"Do we know that?" asked Fulvius.

"Who else could it be?" asked Sidonicus.

"I see," said Fulvius.

"This can work out well for us," said Sidonicus. "It can further enflame the ancient enmities, and hereditary hatreds, betwixt Drisriaks and Otungs."

"That is not clear," said Ingeld. "Abrogastes, on Tenguthaxichai, alleged he was absent, buying slaves."

"I trust," said Fulvius, "that you betrayed no skepticism or astonishment."

"I am not a fool," said Ingeld.

"I do not understand the silence of Abrogastes," said Fulvius. "Obviously he escaped or was rescued."

"The Far-Grasper is subtle," said Safarius.

"It seems he does not act," said Sidonicus.

"I trust he is not drawing together the cords of a net," said Safarius.

"In any event," said Ingeld, "our plans are much awry. I cannot now control the tribes. I cannot now launch them against Otungs. No invasion is imminent. My father's plan is to seize the throne by guile, and not by expensive, perilous force. Viviana or Alacida is to produce a son of mixed blood, Drisriak and Telnarian, who, once the Otung is deposed, will be seen as emperor, in whose name a regent, myself or Hrothgar, will rule."

"All this," said Safarius, "will be sanctioned by the senate."

"Of course," said Ingeld.

"As long as Abrogastes lives," said Sidonicus, "I fear he will oppose the imposition of a state religion, and the elimination of heretics."

"True," said Ingeld. "You cannot expect him to deny the gods of his house and tribe. Too, it is not the empire's way. The empire has always been tolerant of any religious faith which is not seen as subversive of, or dangerous to, the empire itself."

"I might point out," said Safarius, "as only a secular observation, of course, and thus of little interest, that the faith of his blessedness, the holy exarch, might easily be seen as subversive of, or dangerous to, the empire."

"Nonsense," said Sidonicus. "The faith celebrates the empire. What else will see to the extirpation of dissident beliefs and the eradication of heresy, to the suppression of dissidents and the extermination of heretics. One faith, one empire. The *koos* must direct the sword, and the sword must defend the *koos*. The *koos* guides the sword and the sword serves the *koos*."

"I do not understand," said Ingeld, "what occurred in the fourth basement of the house of Dardanis. There must have been several present, jailers, and such."

"I have inquired," said Fulvius. "They cannot be found."

"I understand," said Safarius, "that Abrogastes was on Tenguthaxichai."

"Yes," said Ingeld.

"What of the other," asked Safarius, "the rebel son, Ortog?"

"He was not on Tenguthaxichai, nor would he have dared to show himself there," said Ingeld. "He would have been slain instantly, the treasonous pig, cut down on the spot, or, as soon as the beasts were readied, put to the horse death, torn to pieces."

"There is a great enmity between father and son," said Fulvius.

"They would kill one another on sight," said Ingeld. "It was doubtless to slay Abrogastes that Ortog came to Telnar."

"Ortog is of no great interest," said Sidonicus. "He may be dead, and, if not, he is, in any event, estranged from his father and he has few men."

"Our plans must be revised," said Ingeld.

"How is it," asked Sidonicus, regarding the Drisriak, "that Viviana is not yet with child?"

"I do not know," said Ingeld.

"I suspect," said Sidonicus, "that chemicals have intervened."

"Let us proceed, rather as Abrogastes planned," said Ingeld. "I can proclaim that Viviana is with child and near to delivery. Soon there will be time enough for that to be believed. I need then only obtain a male child, on Tenguthaxichai, or elsewhere, and present it as the child, mourning, of course, the tragic death of Viviana in childbirth."

"That still leaves two obstacles," said Fulvius, "Abrogastes, and the usurping Otung."

"There are many routes to a throne," said Sidonicus. "Amongst them, commonly, is assassination. Indeed, both the father and grandfather of Aesilesius were assassinated."

"Yet, not effectively," said Fulvius. "There was no change of dynasty."

"But," said Sidonicus, "in our case, when Abrogastes is removed, Ingeld will rule the Drisriaks, and he is well prepared to abet our plans, and when the Otung is removed, an heir, the putative son of Ingeld, is emperor."

"The senate may be depended upon, if necessary," said Safarius, "to clarify and ratify matters."

"What if Julian, he of the Aureliani, of the current party, is proposed?" asked Sidonicus. "He is cousin to Aesilesius."

"He would not be first in blood," said Fulvius. "The child would be the putative offspring of a royal princess, the princess, Viviana."

"Further," said Safarius, "as I see Julian, he would honor the child's claim. Certainly he would not be likely to plunge the empire into civil war."

"I suppose the matter cannot be helped," said Sidonicus. "We must wait. We must be patient. At least we would not need to silence the batteries of Telnar."

"Palace revolutions are to be preferred," said Fulvius. "They are less time-consuming and expensive."

"We need to find eager daggers, wielders of strangling wires, servitors to administer poison," said Sidonicus.

"That may not be easy," said Safarius. "Abrogastes is surrounded by Drisriaks, the Otung with Otungs."

"There are always others," said Sidonicus, "servitors, envoys, guards, attendants, petitioners, physicians, guests."

"Obviously terrible risks are involved," said Safarius.

"I do not anticipate difficulties in the matter," said Fulvius. "Pave a path with gold, and few will refuse to follow it."

"Do not dismiss the possibility of slaves," said Ingeld.

"Perhaps you have one in mind," said Sidonicus.

"A preferred slave," said Ingeld, "one with easy access to Abrogastes, Huta, a former priestess of the Timbri."

"Excellent," said Sidonicus.

"The Otung," said Fulvius, "is popular with the people. If he is slain, there will be unrest in the streets, the threat of local insurrections."

"This should all be managed within Telnar," said Ingeld. "There is no need for worlds to perish."

"There have been many transitions in government," said Sidonicus, "scarcely noticed within the empire. To many worlds, what is an emperor but a name and a mystery? Most worlds, cities, and villages are more concerned with satraps and deputies, with administrators, and headmen, even chieftains, with those who can tax and steal, imprison and execute, those authorized by custom or law to apply force and coercion, those possessing the legal monopoly on violence."

"Still," said Safarius, "the streets in Telnar could rage and flame. Those who wish to loot and burn will not be lacking in pretexts."

"Yet," said Sidonicus, "I think we can take advantage of these propensities, turning them to our purposes, inventing, say, a "will of the people.""

"The will to profit without effort," said Fulvius.

"The people have no will," said Sidonicus, "until they are given one."

"And you will give them one," said Fulvius.

"The pretext they wish," said Sidonicus. "Its nature will depend on the political needs of the moment. We will give them appropriate banners and standards. That is all they want, something to march behind."

"To loot and burn behind," said Fulvius.

"I shall return to Tenguthaxichai," said Ingeld.

"The proper place for a loyal and devoted son," said Sidonicus. Ingeld then withdrew from the chamber.

"You can trust your two guards?" asked Fulvius of Safarius.

"Yes," said Safarius.

"Good," said Fulvius. "Nothing of what transpired here is to go beyond the walls of this chamber."

"Of course," said Safarius.

Safarius then took his leave, departing from the chamber, followed by his two guards.

"Your beloved blessedness," said Fulvius to Sidonicus, "I note that your valuable minion, Corelius, who assisted in silencing the batteries during the raid of Abrogastes on Telnar and who participated in the ensnaring of Abrogastes and Ortog has not been much present of late."

"He was not invited," said Sidonicus.

"I see," said Fulvius.

"The fewer who know of certain matters the better," said Sidonicus.

"Of course," said Fulvius. "The fewer who know of a secret the more likely it will be kept."

"Precisely," said Sidonicus.

"Corelius has already been privy to much that is sensitive," said Fulvius. "He knows much of many secrets."

"I agree," said Sidonicus.

"Too much," said Fulvius.

"I agree," said Sidonicus.

"I do not see that his services are required any longer," said Fulvius.

"Nor do I," said Sidonicus.

"Perhaps he should be invited into your chambers, the lower chambers, for a private audience," said Fulvius.

"My men cannot find him," said Sidonicus. "He has disappeared."

CHAPTER FIFTY-TWO

"I have received," said Iaachus, "an unusual message, one conveyed by a guard who received it from an asserted purveyor of food, claimedly an employee of some food shop."

The Arbiter of Protocol stood at the opened portal of the private chamber of the emperor, Ottonius, the First, in the royal palace in Telnar.

Four guards, Otungs, were farther down the corridor, at a convenient but discreet distance.

"So?" said Otto.

"It is encrypted in a naive manner," said Iaachus. "It purports to be from the elusive Corelius."

"Enter," said Otto, putting aside the soft, oiled, linen rag with which he was treating the re-edged blade of the long sword which he had carried since the Plains of Barrionuevo, or the Flats of Tung, as the Heruls would have it. It was the same blade he had carried when he had entered the Hall of the King Naming on Tangara, during the Killing Time, bearing the pelt of a white *vi-cat*. The light coat of oil protects against rust. Otungs, like Drisriaks, are reluctant to carry sullied or tarnished blades. Otto slid the long weapon to the side on the table. In the hands of one such as Otto that blade could fell a small tree or cut the head from a horse.

"I thought," said the Arbiter of Protocol, "you attended to that *torodont* of a weapon yesterday."

"Be seated," invited Otto.

Iaachus took his place across the table from the emperor.

"Some men," said Otto, "tap their fingers or feet, some rattle beads on a string, some whittle, some practice calligraphy, some draft poems, some touch the lyre."

"You are thinking," said Iaachus.

"You have news of our dear friend, Corelius?" asked Otto.

"Possibly," said Iaachus, thrusting a sheet of paper toward Otto.

"You know I cannot read," said Otto. "I am of the peasants, raised in the *festung* village of Sim Giadini. Learning is seldom wasted on peasants. They are good for other things."

One recalls that the *festung* of Sim Giadini, stronghold of an Emanationist Brotherhood, a sect of Floonianism, was destroyed in an air strike. Shortly before that, the medallion and chain, an artifact signifying leadership amongst the Vandalii, had been stolen by a renegade Otung, Urta, from the cell of one of the brothers, a salamanderine, as had been Floon, a Brother Benjamin.

"Look at it," said Iaachus. "You know the look of letters."

"Yes," said Otto, "I see letters."

"Even if you were an accomplished, skillful reader, as adept as Titus Gelinus, or your Flora, a former officer of a court on Terennia, or your Renata, you could not immediately read this."

"It is a secret writing?" said Otto.

"A cypher, I think," said Iaachus, "where a sign or mark may stand for a letter, or one letter stand for another letter, and such."

"I have heard of such things," said Otto, "a secret writing."

"A kind of secret writing," said Iaachus. "There are many kinds."

"Obviously such writings must be intelligible to the person or persons who use them," said Otto.

"Surely," said Iaachus.

"Thus, there is a method involved," said Otto.

"A key," said Iaachus.

"Once the method or key is discovered, the message becomes intelligible," said Otto.

"Precisely," said Iaachus.

"It must be difficult to discover the method, or key," said Otto.

"In some cases more so than in others," said Iaachus.

"How does one proceed?" asked Otto.

"Some letters occur more frequently in a language than others," said Iaachus. "This may provide a clue. If a given letter occurs, say, with such-and-such a frequency in Telnarian, then a sign or mark, or another letter, which occurs with the same or a similar frequency may stand for that letter."

"Then," said Otto, "it would be well to have more than one sign or mark to stand for that letter, and perhaps to have signs or marks which refer to no letter."

"That is frequently done," said Iaachus, "and, more interestingly, there are sophisticated cyphers in which a large number of keys may be used in a single message."

"How then can such messages be read by those not privy to the method or key?" asked Otto.

"It can be difficult, or impossible," said Iaachus, "particularly if the message is short, for then one has less to work with."

"Doubtless," said Otto.

"There are also cyphers," said Iaachus, "in which one has the actual letters of the message, but the letters are mixed in such a way as to obscure the meaning of the message."

"Once again," said Otto, "one must discover the method or key."

"By means of which to rearrange the letters in such a way as to reveal the message," said Iaachus.

"You spoke," said Otto, "of a message encrypted in a naive manner, one purporting to be from the elusive Corelius."

"The cypher is amateurish, embarrassingly simple," said Iaachus. "Each letter of the actual message is replaced by the third letter following it, and the last letters of the alphabet, as needed, by moving three letters, as before, returning, if necessary, to the beginning of the alphabet."

"That does not seem so simple, or amateurish, to me," said Otto, "certainly no more so than any other simple cypher, except that it has the advantage of being easy for those with the key to both write and read."

"Perhaps," said Iaachus.

"Too," said Otto, "there must be levels of such things and a cypher of the sort mentioned might be appropriate for certain situations and occasions, particularly where quick writing and reading are needed."

"Perhaps," said Iaachus.

"Also," said Otto, "the message was sent to you without the method or key. If it was sent to you, the sender would wish you to be able to read it. Thus, it would be judicious to put it in a form in which it would be mysterious and unintelligible to most, but still in a form in which you, with some effort, perhaps modest effort, could read."

"True," said Iaachus. "It was intended to be read by us. It is not as if we intercepted the message, or came upon it by accident."

"And so," said Otto, "let us not disparage the cypher but rather be grateful to the sender for providing us with a message we can read. Indeed, the simplicity, if anything, might be taken as something of a concession to our perhaps limited ability to unravel such a message. One could see the matter, if one wished, from the sender's point of view, as somewhat condescending, if not actually insulting."

"I see," said Iaachus, less than pleased.

"Convey to me the gist of the message," said Otto.

"It purports to be from Corelius," said Iaachus. "He claims to have information of momentous significance, which he would sell to us. He requests an emissary from the palace to bring a thousand gold *darins* to a specified address in the Varl district, tonight at midnight."

"Not an auspicious location for a rendezvous," said Otto, "and the hour seems a desperate one."

"Consider, as well, the dispatch with which he wishes the business to be concluded," said Iaachus.

"Speculate," said Otto.

"I conjecture," said Iaachus, "he is in hiding, in fear for his life. Consider the Varl district, and the hour. He wishes to obtain the means to flee the city."

"And wishes to betray his principal or principals, whom he justifiably fears," said Otto.

"He is no stranger to betrayal," said Iaachus.

"Long ago," said Otto, "he, with a Phidias, captain of a freighter, the *Narcona*, and a fellow officer, Lysis, delivered a poisoned dagger to the Lady Publennia, of the Larial Calasalii, then masquerading as a slave on Tangara, with the intention that she use it to assassinate me. The attempt failed. Interestingly, Phidias, Corelius, and Lysis fled, abandoning the Lady Publennia to her fate, even before the outcome of the attempt was known."

"They reported the attempt was successful," said Iaachus.

"You were instrumental in organizing the plot," said Otto.

"Yes," said Iaachus, "I thought it in the best interests of the empire."

"You do not now," said Otto.

"No," said Iaachus.

"The winds of politics are variable," said Otto.

"Let them blow and roar as they will," said Iaachus. "I no longer give them heed. I have been taught honor, and friendship."

"Oh?" said Otto.

"By a barbarian," said Iaachus, "an Otung."

"You deem the missive from Corelius?" asked Otto.

"I think it likely," said Iaachus. "I see no obvious trap in this, as one might if he requested a clandestine audience with the emperor."

"I assume the information he wishes to sell is that our enemies are Ingeld and the exarch of Telnar," said Otto.

"Yes," said Iaachus. "He would know nothing of what we know, from Safarius and the guards, Boris and Andak."

"What do you advise, dear arbiter?" asked Otto.

"We dare not arrest Corelius," said Iaachus. "If we do, Ingeld and the exarch will assume we are aware of their complicity, their plottings and treasons, this information having been extracted, by torture or other means, from Corelius. Better let them continue to think we are ignorant of such matters."

"Good," said Otto. "How then would you respond, or would you respond, to the missive of Corelius?"

"We must respond," said Iaachus. "If we do not respond, Corelius, and others, if they are involved, will suspect that we already have such information, and perhaps more."

"You would then pay him a thousand gold *darins* for information we already have?" said Otto.

"That it remain unknown that we have it," said Iaachus. "To purchase such an advantage I think a thousand gold *darins* is not unreasonable."

"I agree," said Otto. "Indeed, two thousand gold *darins* would not be unreasonable."

"We need not bring that to the attention of Corelius," said Iaachus.

"No," said Otto.

CHAPTER FIFTY-THREE

"You cannot do this to me," said Cornhair. "I am not a draft beast. I was of the high *honestori*! I was the Lady Publennia, of the Larial Calasalii!"

"And I am of the Larial Farnichi," said Rurik. "Surely you know that the women of the enemy are loot, and the suitable properties of the victors. And surely you know now that you are naught but a meaningless slave, and my slave. Harness her."

Lovely blond-haired, blue-eyed Cornhair, her hands braceleted behind her, standing in place, felt the straps cinched on her body.

"You are slight," said Rurik. "Otherwise I might enter you in the slave races. Do you think you might learn to prance?"

Cornhair moaned.

Such races are characterized by different gaits, and styles.

"To be sure," said Rurik, "such races are largely favored by free women, who are the most common attendees, and most often the drivers. Little love, it seems, is lost between free women and female slaves."

Cornhair was well aware of that.

The small, light wagon had two large wheels and a seat for one.

Rurik placed a small, iron-bound, locked, heavy box under the seat. It weighed a hundred weights. The Telnarian "weight" has ten divisions. The Telnarian gold *darin* is minted to a division of a weight.

"Bridle her," said Rurik, taking his seat in the buggy.

Cornhair was then bridled, the bit fastened in her mouth, and the reins passed back to Rurik.

"A snapping of the reins," said Rurik, "means move. If I draw back on the reins you are to stop. By means of the reins you will be informed to turn to the left or right. I have, incidentally, a whip at hand by means of which you might be urged to a greater speed, or encouraged not to dawdle."

It was late in Telnar, but not yet midnight.

Cornhair and Rurik were not alone. Flanking the wagon, ten on each side, were soldiers, drawn from Rurik's small, private army.

"Prepare to move, shapely draft beast, meaningless slave," said Rurik. "Dally, and you will feel the whip."

Rurik snapped the reins.

Cornhair, tears running down her cheeks, stripped save for her collar, leaned forward, pressing against the straps, and the wagon trundled forward.

She was far now from her former luxuries and riches, her silks and jewels, the palaces, resorts, and gaming tables of a dozen worlds.

"You should not be here," said Julian, of the Aureliani. "The district is dangerous, particularly at night."

"I often leave the palace at night," said Otto. "One is one's own spy. One learns much."

Both men were cloaked and hooded. Otto carried not the great long sword, but a shorter blade, one easily concealed within his cloak.

"The message," said Julian, "merely alluded to an emissary, certainly not to a person of rank, let alone an emperor."

"I am my own emissary," said Otto.

"What if Iaachus has been suborned, what if he has arranged for us to be set upon? Even our destination is known."

"That is interesting," said Otto. "Iaachus warned me, before departure, to beware of you, that you might strike at me in the darkness, and then blame the business on thieves, or assassins?"

"What a monster, and scoundrel!" said Julian.

"You might then have a claim to the throne," said Otto.

"As might a hundred others," said Julian.

"Iaachus does not trust you," said Otto.

"Nor I him," said Julian.

"I must be a fool," said Otto.

"Why?" asked Julian.

"Because I trust both," said Otto.

"You are emperor," said Julian. "Trust no one."

"I shall consider that," said Otto.

"Good," said Julian.

"You sound like Iaachus," said Otto.

"The palace is a jungle," said Julian. "It behooves one to be armed and tread warily."

"One wants friends," said Otto.

"Tread warily," said Julian.

"The throne is a lonely seat," said Otto.

"And a dangerous one," said Julian.

"By now," said Otto, "Rurik and his men must be at the dock district."

"I trust that those who might be watching the palace have him under surveillance," said Julian.

"The guards with him will surely suggest the transportation of a cargo of considerable value," said Julian.

"The small, weighty box, publicly placed in the wagon, should also be noted with interest," said Otto.

"Let us hope so," said Julian.

"It would be noted with less interest, or enthusiasm, though perhaps with greater surprise," said Otto, "were its contents revealed."

"A hundred weights of lead pellets," said Julian, "each pellet one division of a weight."

"We are now well within the Varl district," said Otto.

"It is muchly deserted," said Julian.

"The more deserted the better," said Otto.

"The dock lamps are extinguished," said one of the soldiers.

"Defense!" cried Rurik, drawing his weapon, leaping from his seat on the wagon, as shrouded figures approached, hurrying, in the darkness.

Cornhair twisted in the straps, and lost her footing, falling, tipping the wagon. The iron-bound box fell to the boards.

The soldiers wielded weapons, as they could, against crowding, dark figures. There was a sudden spray of sparks in the darkness as, by hazard, blades met blades. Thrusts were made. Some wove a compass of steel about themselves, a fence within which it might be death to enter. There was the sound of clubs, some striking bodies, some striking the seat or shafts of the wagon. Some of the assailants, in the confusion, doubtless struck their fellows. Cornhair, helpless, on her side, on the boards of the pier, the bit in her mouth, the reins about her, her hands braceleted behind her, tried to make herself small. "I have it!" cried a voice. "It is heavy! Help me! Help me!" "Hold, hold!" cried Rurik. The intruding, marauding figures hastened away, in the darkness. "A lamp, a torch, light, light!" called Rurik, a blade in hand, the steel running with blood. "Light, light!" A lamp approached, lifted, from the side, borne in the hand of a fellow emerging from the shack of a dock watchman.

"The dock lamps were out," said Rurik to the watchman.

"Surely recently," said the man. "All was in order when I made my rounds."

"Report," said Rurik, to a subordinate.

"Two wounded, one more seriously," said the subordinate.

In the pool of light from the lifted lamp, three bodies, clad in nondescript garb, of no known uniform or livery, lay on the boards.

"It is hard to kill in the darkness," said the subordinate. "It neutralizes skill."

"Tend to the wounded," said Rurik. "We return shortly to the palace."

"Woe," said a man, "I do not see the box."

There were sounds of consternation, and rage, from several of the soldiers.

"It is missing," said a man.

"We have lost it," said another. "The treasure is gone!"

"Let us pursue the thieves," said another.

"Do not rush on knives and clubs in the darkness," said Rurik.

"But the treasure," said a soldier.

"They are welcome to it," said Rurik. "May it do them much good."

"Our mission is a failure," said another soldier.

"Not at all," said Rurik. "It came out precisely as planned."

Men regarded him, wonderingly.

One man's wounds were being bound. Another, slumped, was supported by two comrades.

Rurik went to where Cornhair lay trembling.

He crouched down, beside her. "Are you all right?" he asked. Had there been concern, even tenderness, in his voice, Cornhair wondered. Could he care for her, she only a slave, once a woman of the hated Larial Calasalii, he of the Larial Farnichi? She made a tiny sound, against the bit.

"On your feet," he said, brusquely. "You tipped the wagon. You should be beaten for that."

Cornhair struggled to her feet.

She stood submissively, head down, in the traces. But she did not feel the whip. It did not strike her.

Then her heart flooded with slave emotion. She was owned, a collared slave. And she was suffused with the overwhelming feelings of an owned, collared slave. She wanted, with all her heart, to be at Rurik's feet, the feet of her Master. With every bit of her soft, owned body, she wanted to love, please, and serve him, wholly, helplessly, vulnerably, in all ways, as the slave she was.

Rurik and another placed the more sorely wounded man in the seat of the wagon. Two soldiers held him in place, one on each side. Two of the other soldiers attended their less injured fellow.

Rurik then picked up the reins and, walking ahead, led Cornhair, drawing the wagon, from the dock district.

"A gloomy area," said Otto.

"Tenements, and cheap shops," said Julian.

"Wooden buildings, easily gutted by fire," said Otto.

"The streets are deserted," said Julian. "It is hard to realize that thousands are crowded into such tiers of hovels."

"It must be near midnight," said Otto.

"There," said Julian, "the sign, the wine shop of Peleus, closed now, with the screens chained in place."

"The stairwell, that to the right, as one faces the shop," said Otto, "then the first door to the right, on the seventh floor."

"The stairwell is not lighted," said Julian.

"Few stairwells are lighted in this area," said Otto. "Lamps require oil."

"Who would live here?" asked Julian.

"Anonymous throngs," said Otto, "the ill-clothed, the hungry, the crowded, the ill, and wretched, and, too, men without names, without identities, men forgotten and men desiring to be forgotten, criminals, thieves, beggars, fugitives, dealers in smuggled goods and noxious substances, those desiring to reside under a mantle of invisibility, those wishing to live unseen and unrecognized, those who hope to disappear in crowds."

"Let us return to the palace," said Julian.

"Ah," said Otto. "This street is not as deserted as heretofore."

"Stand back," said Julian, unsheathing his weapon, drawing it from beneath his cloak.

The bent-over figure, head down, hobbling, muchly cloaked, and hooded, stopped, some feet from Julian and Otto. "Please, noble sir," said a quavering voice, "do not strike me. I am only a poor beggar, innocent and defenseless, lame, alone in these dark streets." At this point, the figure held out a shallow metal pan, and shook it, gently, pleadingly. Some coins rattled about in the pan. "A coin, a coin, a penny, a penny, please, noble sirs."

"Do not approach," said Julian.

"Wait," said Otto, "I have a coin."

"Do not approach him," said Julian. "Consider the district, the time of night."

Otto dropped a coin in the pan.

"Thank you, noble sir," said the quavering voice, its owner not looking up from within the darkness of the hood. He then turned about and hobbled away.

Julian and Otto looked after him. Then he turned a corner and was gone. Then Otto said, "To the stairwell, and hence to the seventh floor."

"It is dark, and forbidding," said Julian, looking up the stairwell.

"Do not bother sheathing your blade," said Otto, as he drew his own weapon.

"I will not," said Julian.

Julian and Otto then, Otto in advance, began to feel their way up the stairs.

"I smell urine, and excrement," said Julian.

"Do not be critical," said Otto. "It is late, the floor buckets, on the landings, by the stairs, may be full. The nearest public latrine may be hundreds of yards away."

"Perhaps some tenants are impatient, even lacking in civility," said Julian.

"It is not impossible," said Otto.

They had ascended some four flights when Otto stopped.

"What is wrong?" whispered Julian.

There are two or more on the stairs, above us, ahead of us," said Otto.

"I hear nothing," whispered Julian.

"You are not a hunter in the forests of Tangara or Varna," said Otto.

"What shall we do?" asked Julian.

"Do not conceal our presence," said Otto. "We live here. We are returning home. Climb normally, possibly stumble, it being dark, mutter, curse, hum a tavern tune, such things. If they take us for residents and they are departing, or are eager to depart, they will pass us on the stairs. If they wait on a higher landing, in silence, prepare to use your weapon."

Accordingly, Otto, followed by Julian, blades poised, began to ascend the stairs, rather as might rightful residents, incautiously, unsuspectingly, returning to their rooms.

They had ascended but one more flight, when they heard clearly, above them, descending, the sounds of feet.

"There are at least three," said Otto. "Stand to the side."

"Out of the way," said a rough, gruff voice, and a dark bundled figure brushed past Otto and, on a lower step, past Julian.

Three more such figures followed, hurrying, as they could, in the darkness.

"It seems they are in haste," said Julian.

"The next landing is the sixth," said Otto.

Otto and Julian then ascended to the sixth level, and then to the seventh level, and felt their way to the first door on the right.

The levels in such a structure are close to one another, and the ceilings are low. In this way lumber is conserved, and more levels can be crowded into a given space. In a typical room, a grown man cannot stand upright. Given the stresses on wood, particularly on cheaper wood, such buildings are seldom more than seven or eight stories in height. In such buildings, the wooden construction, coupled with in-room cooking and the use of braziers in colder weather, tends to increase the hazard of fire. Indeed, not too long ago, a terrible fire had ravaged the city, the worst in some four hundred years, destroying, it is estimated, between a tenth and a fifteenth of the city. Reportedly, it began in a Floonian temple, one practicing the rites of, and subscribing to the beliefs of, the Illusionists, a Floonian sect teaching that *Karch*, in his compassion and mercy, would never have permitted a sentient, living organism to suffer and die on his behalf. Accordingly, what was taken as the salamanderine, Floon, must have been an image, a projection, an illusion, or such. The Illusionist sect, it might be noted, had been denounced as heretical by Sidonicus, the exarch of Telnar, ministrant of another Floonian sect, claiming itself to be Floonian orthodoxy, namely, that Floon and *Karch* were the same, though different.

"The door is open," said Otto, feeling his way.

"I feared it would be so," said Julian. "The spies of Sidonicus are everywhere. The lair of Corelius was found. Surely those who passed us on the stairs, given the hour, were dispatched to deal with him. I shall strike a light. We will examine the body."

"There will be no body," said Otto.

In a moment Julian had switched on, and lifted, a lighting cartridge.

"There is no body," said Julian.

"No," said Otto.

Julian moved the ignited cartridge about. "This is a hole, a hovel," said Julian. "A *filch* would keep its nest cleaner and in better order."

"I knew Corelius from the *Narcona*, and from Tangara," said Otto. "He was very particular about his appearance, and such. Hiding here must have been very stressful for him."

"He is not here," said Julian. "He did not keep his appointment."

"But he did," said Otto.

"I do not understand," said Julian.

"Would you wait here? With no exit?" asked Otto. "Would you not, rather, wish to wait outside, to see who might approach, and if they came alone? Or if they might be followed?"

"Doubtless some reconnaissance would be desirable," said Julian.

"That would be wise," said Otto, "particularly if one suspected there might be killing squads about, searching for one."

"The lame beggar!" said Julian.

"Yes," said Otto.

"Corelius!" said Julian.

"Yes," said Otto.

"You put a coin in his pan," said Julian.

"A gold *darin*," said Otto.

"That sealing a bargain, pledging agreement to his terms," said Julian.

"Yes," said Otto. "Arrangements, of course, are pending. One would not be well advised to carry a thousand gold *darins* about. To transport such easily would require a large, powerful man, a cart, or small wagon. And how could Corelius manage such a weight, subtly, judiciously, concealing it or transporting it?"

"But why, then, the matter done, did you enter the building and ascend the stairs?" said Julian.

"To conceal the identity of the beggar," said Otto. "Corelius was in quite enough danger as it was, to pretend begging, in this district, at this hour. I suspect few genuine beggars would court such peril."

"What of the men who passed us on the stairs?" asked Julian.

"I suspect," said Otto, "as I gather you did, assailants, presumably a killing squad."

"Corelius was fortunate he left his room before their arrival," said Julian.

"Very much so," said Otto.

"Do you think he noted their entry into the building?" asked Julian.

"It is very likely," said Otto.

"He must be terrified," said Julian.

"Quite possibly," said Otto.

"He will contact the palace later," said Julian.

"If possible," said Otto, "if still alive."

CHAPTER FIFTY-FOUR

"We are sure," said Sidonicus, "that Corelius has taken refuge in the dock district. It was there that this treasure, well seized, was to be delivered to him."

"Better," said Fulvius, "that the treasure was followed, it leading us to Corelius."

"Not at all," said Sidonicus. "The treasure was stoutly guarded. It could be acquired only in an arranged darkness. It served its purpose, informing us that Corelius is somewhere in the dock district. Even now I have men combing the area, every inn, tavern, warehouse, alley, byway, shelter, camp, and shop, every ship and barge, every pier and wharf."

"Still," said Fulvius.

"In a lighted area, our men, following and discovered, would have been slaughtered under the blades of professional soldiers," said Sidonicus.

"How wise you are, great blessedness," said Fulvius.

This conversation took place in the basement of the exarchical palace. Four men were present, ponderous Sidonicus, exarch of Telnar, his high deputy, smooth-cheeked Fulvius, and two others, large, plain-tunicked men, bearded, of somber visage, one grossly scarred. Light in the chamber was supplied by a single lamp, resting on a stout table, that about which the four men were gathered.

"Lift the box, Buthar," said Sidonicus. "Place it on the table."

The more scarred of the two plain-tunicked men lifted the box, and carefully placed it on the table.

The box was small, but, judging from the apparent stress involved in its relocation, weighty. It was of thick, dark, lacquered wood, bound with two bands of iron, and secured in two places, with heavy padlocks.

"Note," said Sidonicus to Fulvius, "the seals."

"Those of the palace," said Fulvius.

"Unbroken," said Sidonicus.

"I trust, my dear Buthar, your esteemed, reticent colleague, Grissus, has brought tools."

The second of the two plain-tunicked men placed a hammer and a tapered wedge, a narrow, rather cylindrical cone of iron, flat on one end and pointed on the other, on the table.

"We were quite right to be concerned with the fidelity of our friend, Corelius," said Sidonicus to Fulvius. "Not only did he vanish from our purview, his absence unauthorized, but he wished, as well, the ungrateful, treasonous *filch*, to enter into dealings with the usurper. What sort of dealings? Those of profit to himself and of value to the usurper. Something to sell, doubtless. And what would he have to sell but information, and what information would fetch a better price than the revelation of our identities and the nature of our plans to seize and manage the empire, for the most blessed and appropriate of purposes, ours?"

"As the box has not been opened and the seals are in place," said Fulvius, "it seems clearly that any projected transaction on the part of the loathed Corelius had not yet been consummated."

"Even if it had been, we need but deny it with astonishment, tears, and outrage," said Sidonicus. "Who would take the word of a usurper, and barbarian, over that of the exarch of Telnar, a native Telnarian, who speaks in the name of Floon and *Karch*?"

"A barbarian arrow does not review or question its target," said Fulvius.

"The barbarian is not a fool," said Sidonicus. "He does not want the empire to be riven, broken into flaming halves."

"It is unfortunate that Corelius eluded us," said Fulvius.

"He, too, is not a fool," said Sidonicus. "He must have sensed that he was no longer of value to us and that his prolonged existence, given what he knows, might imperil our projects and programs."

"I was sure we had located him in the Varl district," said Fulvius. "Descriptions were recognized, streets were guarded, exits were watched. But then it seemed he vanished once more. He had withdrawn from sight, avoiding the streets. But he must eat and drink. So food shops and markets were put under surveillance. Inquiries established that meals were being delivered to a particular address, a certain room in a certain dismal tenement."

"And who, living in such a place, in such poverty and squalor, could afford to pay for the regular ordering and delivery of food?" said Sidonicus.

"It seemed certain he had betrayed himself," said Fulvius.

"The room was found unoccupied," said Sidonicus.

"Clearly another fugitive had been making use of the premises," said Fulvius. "We did not know at that time that Corelius was in the dock district."

"Our spies will locate him," said Sidonicus. "Our men will see to the rest."

"We may not have apprehended the treasonous Corelius as yet," said Fulvius, "but the day was not lost."

"Indeed, not," said Sidonicus. "How much wealth is in the box, would you suppose?"

"Its weight suggests a goodly sum," said Fulvius.

"Surely more than a hundred *darins*," said Sidonicus.

"Much more," said Fulvius.

"My dear Buthar," said Fulvius, "what would you conjecture?"

"There might be a case within the box, and a case within that," said Buthar, "it is hard to say."

"Conjecture," suggested Sidonicus.

"Five, perhaps six, hundred *darins*," said Buthar, "—of gold."

"Ah," breathed Fulvius.

"It cost me three men," said Buthar.

"No matter," said Sidonicus, "they now revel at the table of *Karch*."

"Three men," said Buthar, evenly.

"Do not menace me," said Sidonicus.

"Three," said Buthar.

"Very well," said Sidonicus. "I will give you a silver *darin* for each."

"If the chest contains gold," said Buthar, "give me three *darins*—of gold."

"Do not seek to feed a hungry purse to the point of gluttony," said Sidonicus.

"Three," said Buthar.

"We accept the contents of this stout coffer on behalf of the temple," intoned Sidonicus. "There, it is said; it is done."

"Three," said Buthar, "—of gold."

"Do not risk sacrilege," said Sidonicus. "With a word I could deny you a place at the table of *Karch*."

"Friend Grissus," said Buthar, "remove your hand from the hilt of your knife."

"We are all friends," said Fulvius.

Grissus perhaps failed to understand Buthar's suggestion, for he not only failed to remove his hand from the hilt of the knife, but, rather, drew the weapon.

This was noted by Fulvius, if not by Sidonicus.

"In your days in the bloody square," said Sidonicus to Buthar, "in a hundred bouts you would not make three *darins* of gold."

As one may recall, the visage of Buthar was muchly scarred, and, indeed, if it must be known, much of his body was scarred, as well. Until recruited by Sidonicus he had survived four years in the bloody square. While not a record, this was unusual. In the bloody square one dons the leather belt and has one's fists wrapped with bands of leather, often studded with hooks and bits of metal.

"Three—*of gold*," said Buthar.

"He must pay his men, excellency," said Fulvius, with a glance drawing attention to the unsheathed knife of Grissus, "and good men, applied to dark projects, possibly involving risks, deserve to be well paid."

"Of course," said Sidonicus, now observing the drawn knife. "Who could gainsay so fair an observation? Let us open the chest, and observe the treasure. If necessary, scales may be brought."

"Perhaps our colleague, Grissus," said Fulvius, "might be pre-vailed upon to open the chest."

Grissus resheathed the knife, and picked up the hammer and the tapered wedge.

Soon, by means of the wedge and hammer, the two padlocks were sprung, and jerked free from their staples. The hasps were then flung back, freeing the lid.

"Open it," said Sidonicus.

Scarred Buthar lifted the lid, revealing a dark, wide leather sack, filling the box. This sack was knotted shut, the two ends of the knotted cord attached to one another by a wrapped paper, closed by a wax seal.

"Bring the lamp closer," said Sidonicus.

"The palace seal, again," said Fulvius.

"Break the seal, read the paper," said Sidonicus, eagerly.

"It is a certification and confirmation," said Fulvius, "of the contents, of the weighing and counting out of one thousand *da-rins* of gold."

"One thousand!" said Sidonicus.

"One thousand!" said Buthar.

Grissus was silent. His hand went, again, to the hilt of his knife.

"Our friend, Corelius," said Sidonicus, "cannot be faulted for his lack of arrogance and ambition."

"Nor greed," said Fulvius.

"He puts a high price on the goods he sells," said Sidonicus.

"But, interestingly," said Fulvius, "one the palace is willing to meet."

"With such gold," said Buthar, "one could buy an army, one could master a world."

"I am certain the temple can find worthy causes to which it might be applied," said Sidonicus.

"Surely," said Fulvius.

"Dear Buthar and Grissus," said Sidonicus, "you have done well, and you will be neither forgotten nor neglected. You may now withdraw."

"Grissus," said Buthar, "free the cords."

Grissus whipped out his knife, put his hand on the sack, holding it still, and, with one quick motion of his knife, slashed open the cords.

"Do not think we are not grateful for your service," said Sidonicus. "It is much appreciated. You may now leave."

"I am in no hurry," said Buthar.

"Your presence here is no longer necessary," said Sidonicus.

"I would see the gold," said Buthar. He then looked to silent Grissus. "Empty the sack," he said.

"Please," protested Sidonicus.

"Spill the gold, heap it on the table, here," said Buthar to Grissus.

Grissus did not sheath his knife, but held it between his teeth.

"Wait," said Sidonicus, reaching into the open sack. "I will give you your three *darins* of gold."

"I think, your excellency, your blessedness," said Fulvius, quickly, "reliable men devoted to dark designs, involving possible risks, like to be well paid."

"Oh?" said Sidonicus.

"Very much so," said Fulvius.

"Of course," said Sidonicus, "six *darins* of gold!" He then reached into the sack, with two hands, seized a portion of its contents, and offered them to Buthar.

"What is this?" cried Buthar in rage. He then, himself, with effort, drew up the sack, half way, and then wholly, and turned it over, showering the table with its contents.

"Lead! Lead pellets!" cried Buthar.

Grissus pulled the knife from between his teeth, and, in rage, struck the table a dozen or more times, slashing amongst pellets, scattering them about, often to the floor, gouging and splintering wood.

Sidonicus and Fulvius fled from the basement.

They halted their flight only behind the bolted door of the exarch's private audience chamber.

"Lead," said Sidonicus, "only lead!"

"Be pleased, your excellency," said Fulvius. "Had it been gold, we might now be dead."

"We were tricked," said Sidonicus.

"And are alive," said Fulvius. "It is not well to display honey to the *arn* bear nor sheep to the *vi-cat*."

"Lead, tricked!" said Sidonicus.

"I am sure that Buthar and Grissus, under more modest and guarded circumstances, will once more prove to be valued minions," said Fulvius. "Buthar is not likely to desire to return to the bloody square, nor Grissus to the petty work of the cheap assassin, hiding in doorways, lurking in alleys."

"Lead pellets!" said Sidonicus.

"More valuable to us than gold, as it turned out," said Fulvius.

"Perhaps," said Sidonicus, grudgingly.

"In any event," said Fulvius, "we have learned one thing. It is no longer obvious that Corelius conceals himself in the dock district."

CHAPTER FIFTY-FIVE

"Your name is Urta?" said Viviana.

"Yes, great lady," said Urta.

"An Otung?" she asked.

"Summoned from Tangara to Telnaria," said Urta, "and from thence here, to lovely Tenguthaxichai."

"I have heard of you," said Viviana, "from the time of the King Naming on Tangara, and in connection with savage, scaled Heruls."

"The great lady," said Urta, "must not believe everything she has heard."

"If you are Otung," said Viviana, "how is it that you dare to appear here, amongst Drisriaks?"

"I come in peace, permitted and credentialed, as the loyal servitor of two glories of the empire," said Urta, "Sidonicus, exarch of Telnar, and your beloved husband and lord, Ingeld, prince of the Drisriaks."

"Your appearance is not prepossessing," said Viviana. "You seem an unlikely agent of so exalted a principal as the exarch of Telnar, or of so worthy and handsome a prince as Ingeld, son of mighty Abrogastes."

"A jewel may reside in a plain container, great lady," said Urta, "and the ugliest of dogs is often the most loyal."

"And a *vi-cat* may turn on its master without warning," said Viviana.

"Only if the *vi-cat* finds it to his advantage," said Urta.

Viviana, gowned and jeweled, clad in Telnarian finery, had received Urta in her quarters, at the request of Ingeld. Her chair, the arms of which were carved in the likeness of the mane and head of a forest lion, was mounted on a small dais. In this fashion her station was attested. In the dais, at each side of the chair, was a slave ring. To such a ring, she would occasionally chain Huta, clad in scraps of rags, as a low slave, a laundering and cleaning slave, whose services Abrogastes had placed at her disposal, save in the evenings, when he housed her, in her rags or less, at the foot of his couch. Given the return of Abrogastes, the relationship of Huta and Ingeld had undergone, at least publicly, a radical transformation. They had scarcely dared to glance at one another in public. Ingeld, in public, had treated her with indifference, even coldness, and she, at least in public, had avoided him as if she were a terrified slave, fearing his whip. Certainly he had forbidden her to enter his quarters. Needless to say, this was found acceptable by Viviana. Huta was, after all, owned by Abrogastes, and, as she had no wish to be boiled alive, and Ingeld had no wish to face the wrath of his father, that perhaps extending even to a public expression of disapproval, both sought to avoid any hint of interest or attraction between them. Huta's fear and wariness was increased when Viviana informed her that her behavior would be scrutinized, and the least suspicion of any interest in Ingeld, or lack of faithfulness to her master, on any count, would be summarily brought to the attention of Abrogastes. In this fashion Viviana had much reduced Huta's activities, and her potentiality as a rival. Similarly, Huta sensed that she was now much less in the favor of Abrogastes than hitherto. And might she be in actual disfavor? Surely that was a terrifying thought to be entertained by a female slave. As Ingeld feared his father might know more than he cared to reveal, of plots and behaviors, so, too, Huta feared he might suspect, or know of, her infidelity.

Urta smiled, and looked up at Viviana.

"I enter your presence at the invitation and urging of your husband and lord, Prince Ingeld," said Urta.

"I am aware of that," said Viviana. "You are admitted."

"Thank you, beautiful and gracious lady," said Urta.

"Are you not he who stole an Otung artifact, a medallion and chain, from the *festung* of Sim Giadini, shortly before its destruction?" asked Viviana.

"Surely it must be another," said Urta, as though dismayed. "I know nothing of such things."

"My husband and lord wishes you to speak to me," said Viviana. "You may speak."

"Surely you are aware of the nature of the matter," said Urta.

"I am not," said Viviana.

"Your husband and lord did not inform you?"

"No."

"The matter is sensitive, even delicate," said Urta. "I trust that what transpires here is to be kept in the utmost confidence."

"Speak," said Viviana.

"The empire totters," said Urta. "Barbarians, of a thousand tribes, prowl the perimeters of the empire. Weapons are sharpened. Raids occur. Storms of war gather."

"It is my understanding," said Viviana, "that Otungs ally themselves with the empire, and perhaps others of the Vandal tribes, as well. Indeed, an Otung currently occupies the imperial throne. On the other hand, the Aatii, or the Alemanni, as you may know them, amongst them the Drisriaks, sheath their weapons and rest their ships. They tend their fields and graze their cattle. Abrogastes, my esteemed father-in-law, will have it so. Small wars occur, many of them amongst the barbarians themselves. But the empire holds. The standards and banners of Telnaria have not been so secure in years. Do you seek to change that? Do you seek to threaten Telnaria?"

"Certainly not, great lady," said Urta.

"There are many ways to conquer an empire, or seize an empire, or come to power in an empire," said Viviana. "As the saying has it, common amongst barbarians, as you are doubtless aware, there are many paths to one hall. A sword carves one path, law, a child, and a regency another."

"But," said Urta, "there is no child, and thus no regency."

"Why do you not speak openly?" asked Viviana.

"As there is one empire," said Urta, "there should be one mind, one belief, one creed, one faith, to unify the empire."

"Faiths divide men," said Viviana.

"Not if there is a single faith," said Urta.

"And thus a single pan for offerings?" said Viviana.

"An inevitable consequence," conceded Urta.

"As my husband and lord has insisted upon this interview, which I find neither comprehensible nor tasteful," said Viviana, "I request that you speak clearly and quickly, and then, with dispatch, take your leave."

"Do not be too curt or lofty with me, great lady," said Urta. "Despite your dais and heavy, carved chair, and your gowns and jewels, you have little power on Tenguthaxichai. At a word from Ingeld or Abrogastes you could be stripped, branded, and collared, and sent to the pens to tend pigs, or transported to a mud world, naked and in chains, to be auctioned off to the highest bidder, perhaps a four-armed simian or insectoid."

"*Filch!*" seethed Viviana.

"Surely you know," said Urta, "that beneath your jewels and silks, you are as naked as the least of slaves."

"Leave my presence," said Viviana.

"You might even find yourself my property," said Urta. "I might buy you."

"Go!" said Viviana.

"I think not, lovely, haughty Telnarian," said Urta. "You will hear me out."

"No!" said Viviana.

"Shall I then inform your husband and lord that you are reluctant to listen, which is contrary to his expectation and desire, and which intelligence he might find disappointing?"

"You may speak," said Viviana, "but do so quickly, and then, with haste, depart."

"As you know," said Urta, "plans obtain, devised by Abrogastes, the Far-Grasper, whereby the throne of Telnaria may, following some discord, come into the keeping of either Ingeld or Hrothgar."

"Following Drisriak infiltration and a popular uprising in the streets of Telnar," said Viviana.

"Precisely," said Urta, "coupled, of course, with the availability of a royal child, one of shared Telnarian and Drisriak blood, such events leading happily to a joining of peoples and a benign regency."

"I am aware of all this," said Viviana.

"But there is unlikely to be a useful insurrection, a popular uprising in the streets, something important to our plans," said Urta, "unless it is arranged by, and summoned forth by, the exarch of Telnar."

"Surely he would be guilty of no such crime," said Viviana. "He is a pious, holy man, one who humbly wears the sign of the Burning Rack, one who speaks in the name of gentle Floon."

"One envisions a world as one wishes the world to be," said Urta. "One then acts to bring that world about. Reasons, justifications, and such are afterthoughts. Such things are always at hand. They are common, like weeds and dirt. They are easy to find. One can find one to justify anything."

"The exarch would never be party to death, ruin, and destruction," said Viviana.

"Say, rather, to life, growth, and progress," said Urta, smiling.

"I see," said Viviana.

"For such collaboration, for such cooperation and complicity, there is, of course, a price," said Urta.

"Doubtless," said Viviana.

"As I said," said Urta, "as there is one empire, there should be one mind, one belief, one creed, one faith, to unify the empire."

"Floonianism," said Viviana.

"One particular version of Floonianism," said Urta.

"It is not difficult to speculate on which version the exarch has in mind," said Viviana.

"It is to be made the official religion of the empire," said Urta, "and then, later, though Prince Ingeld need not be informed of this at present, the only religion of the empire, its teachings and observances to be imposed by the sword of the state."

"Murder," said Viviana.

"Salubrious purification," said Urta. "One must prevent the spread of pernicious lies and false faiths, faiths inimical to the welfare of the *koos*. Men are to be saved, if necessary, even from themselves, not misled. They are to be guided into the paths of righteousness, by those who know such paths, for the sake of their *koos*. It is a holy duty."

"That is a bloody monstrosity," said Viviana.

"Beware how you speak and how you think," said Urta.

"I thought gold paved the path to power," said Viviana.

"The instillation of fear and guilt, the control of words and thought, careful teaching, frowns, sneers, denunciations, and such, may do so as well," said Urta. "And gold will later follow, of its own accord."

"I know the father of my husband and lord," said Viviana. "He will not agree to such a price. He would never stand for such things. He may or may not believe in the gods of his people, I do not know, but he will not forsake them. He wants land, gold, power, and, I fear, women, but he would not seek his ends by poison, either of the body or mind. He is Drisriak, of the Aatii, or Alemanni. Such doings would not be honorable. The empire means much to him, but less than his honor. Perhaps you cannot understand that."

"I understand that very well," said Urta. "So, too, does the exarch of Telnar and your beloved husband and lord, Prince Ingeld. That is what brings me to the foot of your dais."

"I do not understand," said Viviana.

"Obviously," said Urta, "Abrogastes must go."

"He is the father of my husband and lord," said Viviana.

"He must be removed," said Urta.

"What has this to do with me?" asked Viviana.

"I have here, within my tunic," said Urta, "a small package, obtained in Telnar, through the auspices of his blessedness and excellency, the exarch of Telnar. It contains a tasteless powder which, in a moment, placed surreptitiously in a drink, say, *kana* or *bror*, will dissolve, leaving no trace. Its effect takes place in a few minutes. It produces no great pain, no agony. You need not be concerned on that score. One subsides, gradually, gently, almost unnoticeably. With Abrogastes gone, Ingeld will be king of the Drisriaks, hegemonic tribe of the Alemanni, and the path to the throne of Telnaria will be open."

"Take it away," said Viviana. "I do not want even to look upon it."

Urta placed the small packet on the dais, at the slippered feet of Viviana.

"Does my husband and lord know of this?" asked Viviana. "Why is he not here? What is his part in this? Does he have a part in this? Speak!"

"The noble Prince Ingeld did not choose to be present," said Urta. "I prefer not to speak further of the matter."

"So he is not involved?" said Viviana. "So he seems to know nothing of this business?"

"I prefer not to speak further of the matter," said Urta.

"It is all on me?" said Viviana. "I am to be the culprit, I, to bear alone the wrath and vengeance of a bereaved nation?"

"You are in no danger," said Urta. "The death will seem one of natural causes. The powder has been selected with great care."

"I am not a murderer," said Viviana. "I will not administer this powder to the father of my husband and lord. I refuse to do so."

"Then, dear lady," said Urta, "I fear you are in great danger."

"I do not understand," said Viviana.

"For one thing," said Urta, "you now know of the matter, which places you in great jeopardy. For a second thing, you will have proved displeasing to your husband and lord which, I fear, places you in even greater jeopardy. This plot discovered, for example, you would be fortunate to avoid more than the horse death, in which, ropes attached to your fair limbs, you will be torn to pieces by horses."

"I have few opportunities to discharge this grievous business, even did I wish to do so," said Viviana.

"You will be in no danger," said Urta. "The slave, Huta, is privy to our design. She is each night in the chamber of Abrogastes. She would have no difficulty, in her serving her master, to see that the contents of this small packet find their way into, say, a goblet of *kana*."

"I see," said Viviana.

"She is informed," said Urta. "She expects to receive the packet from you. She will be waiting."

"I see," said Viviana.

"Were I to be seen consorting with the slave, Huta," said Urta, "questions, even suspicions, might be aroused."

"Of course," said Viviana.

"Now," said Urta, "having supposedly conveyed to you the good wishes of the exarch of Telnar, who presided at your nuptials, as I pretended to do with your sister, Alacida, I think I may take my leave."

"I take it that Alacida knows nothing of this," said Viviana.

"Nothing," said Urta.

"She has no dealings with Huta," said Viviana.

"No," said Urta.

He then smiled, bowed, turned about, and withdrew from the chamber.

Viviana sat for a long time in the heavy chair, the arms of which were carved in the likeness of the mane and head of a forest lion.

Then she bent down, and picked up the small packet.

CHAPTER FIFTY-SIX

"I thank Master for his kindness," said Huta, kneeling humbly at the feet of Abrogastes, who sat upon his massive couch, "for permitting me to wear so lovely a tunic, white and silken, in the hall, about the compound, and here, in your chambers."

"The rags in which you were kept by the Princess Viviana," said Abrogastes, "ill-befitted your standing as a high slave, a preferred slave."

"I thought such garmenture, so brief, soiled, and demeaning, was put upon me by your will," said Huta.

"How could you think that?" asked Abrogastes.

"In it I was forced to perform the most servile tasks," said Huta, "tasks more appropriate for a Drisriak's Telnarian slave girl."

"How could that be?" inquired Abrogastes.

"I fear I am not in favor with the Princess Viviana," said Huta.

"I thought to please the princess and honor you, by permitting you to serve her," said Abrogastes.

"I do not think the princess Viviana likes me," said Huta.

"Why not?" asked Abrogastes.

"I have no idea, Master," said Huta.

"Well," said Abrogastes, "you need no longer report to her, unless summoned."

"A slave is grateful to her Master," said Huta. "And I thank you again for my tunic, its opacity and length, short perhaps, but modest for a slave."

"You look well in it," said Abrogastes.

"A slave is pleased if Master is pleased," said Huta.

"It is a slave tunic," Abrogastes reminded her.

"Yes, Master," said Huta.

"My bath is drawn?" asked Abrogastes.

"All is attended to," said Huta.

"I shall refresh myself," said Abrogastes.

"I am happy to see you in so pleasant a mood," said Huta.

"How so?" inquired Abrogastes.

"I confess I had feared of late that you might have begun to view me with less favor than hitherto," said Huta.

"How could you believe that?" asked Abrogastes.

"A slave muchly fears that her Master might frown upon her, or tire of her," said Huta.

"Put such thoughts from your mind," said Abrogastes.

"My heart leaps with joy," said Huta.

"Perhaps, then, we shall celebrate," said Abrogastes.

"I shall pour your wine," said Huta.

"From the locked, sealed stock, as usual," said Abrogastes.

"Surely, Master," said Huta. "You will, of course, as always, supply the keys."

"Do you wonder," he asked, "why that stock is locked and sealed?"

"To prevent theft, and unauthorized usage," said Huta.

"To prevent tampering," said Abrogastes.

"'Tampering'?" asked Huta.

"Many are those who, in their hatred, smallness, envy, malice, and jealousy, would bring down those who stand above them," said Abrogastes. "The small, compared with the large, cannot deny their smallness. If all are small they can pretend no one is small. Too, other dangers lurk. Rank, distance, and hierarchy rule the worlds, and many hope to replace one such arrangement with another, in which they expect to be better placed. They are not opposed to rank, distance, and hierarchy, only to the current occupants of a particular hierarchy. Does not the denunciation of hierarchy invariably lead to hierarchy anew? How could it be otherwise? They do not renounce gold, only that which is not within their own purse. And so many would praise, and hope for, the unsheathed dagger, the uncoiled strangling wire, the vial of poison, the swift, silent arrow sped from a rooftop."

"How dreadful, Master," said Huta.

"And that, slender, dark-haired, charming Huta," said Abrogastes, "explains the locked, sealed stock."

"That it cannot be tampered with, that it cannot be poisoned," said Huta.

"To be sure," said Abrogastes, "it could be poisoned before being sealed, or after having been opened. Tasters militate against the first possibility, and devoted, trusted servitors against the second."

"Tasters are employed by some of power, might, and rank," said Huta, uneasily.

"In decadent, suspicious, wary Telnarian courts perhaps, those fraught with ambition and intrigue, where who knows who can be trusted," said Abrogastes, "but amongst the Alemanni such things are not necessary and would be deemed insulting to servitors, shieldsmen, and allies, men bound together by blood, spear oaths, and sword oaths."

Abrogastes then delivered the keys to the wine chest to Huta, turned about, and left the room, to take his bath.

"I will pour your wine, Master," called Huta.

"A red *kana*," he called, "from Larial IV."

Larial IV was noted for the quality of its wines.

"Yes, Master," said Huta.

CHAPTER FIFTY-SEVEN

"I trust you poured the wine carefully," said Abrogastes, standing barefoot in his lounging robe, toweling his shaggy head of hair, looking down on the metal goblet on the small stand near the Master's chair.

"I did not spill a drop," said Huta.

"It came by way of Safa Major," said Abrogastes, "received in a trade mission from Burons."

He then slipped into sandals and reclined in the Master's chair, putting the towel over its arm. Huta knelt at his side.

"Will Master drink before or after putting me to his pleasure?" asked Huta.

"Perhaps both," said Abrogastes.

Huta put her head down. "Let me serve you now," she whispered.

"If you wish," he said.

Huta then looked up, and took the goblet with two hands.

"You are unsteady," observed Abrogastes.

"The wine is expensive," said Huta. "I fear to spill it."

"Put it on the table," said Abrogastes. "Fetch another, one less daunting."

"No, no, Master," said Huta. "This wine is fine. On this day I received a fine tunic, on this day I am reassured of the favor of my Master. This night is special. Drink, dear Master, this wine, drink it tonight, a special wine on this, so special a night."

"You are in a celebratory mood," said Abrogastes.

"Very much so, Master," said Huta.

"I, too, then," said Abrogastes. "It pleases me that you, who are so beautiful, so lovely in your collar, perhaps worth twenty *darins*, are pleased."

"Thank you, Master," said Huta.

"Therefore," said Abrogastes, lifting the goblet, "we shall share the *kana*."

"Surely not, Master," said Huta. "Such a wine is far too precious for a mere slave."

"Nonsense," said Abrogastes. "You are a high slave, a favored slave, a preferred slave."

"No, no!" said Huta.

"Drink first," said Abrogastes. "Here."

"Please, no, Master!" said Huta.

"It is my will," said Abrogastes.

"I dare not," said Huta, drawing back. "Drink before my Master! I might die of fear!"

"Very well," said Abrogastes, "as you will."

Abrogastes then took a deep draft of the wine.

Huta drew back, even further.

"Drink more, drink more, Master," she said.

Abrogastes once more drank, and deeply.

"It is your turn now, lovely slave," he said.

"The unworthy lips of a slave should not be permitted to soil the rim of a cup from which the Master drinks," said Huta, carefully.

"Nonsense," said Abrogastes, holding out the cup. "Drink."

"I beg not to do so," said Huta.

"As you wish," said Abrogastes, once more drinking deeply.

Huta then rose to her feet, and backed away.

"How is it that you stand, how is it that you back away?" asked Abrogastes, the sentence slurred, though he seemed not to notice that.

"Because I wish to," said Huta, taking another step back.

"I do not understand," said Abrogastes, slowly.

"So you are the mighty Abrogastes, the Far-Grasper," said Huta, "the king of the Drisriaks, the terror of a hundred worlds?"

Abrogastes regarded her, his eyes half closed.

"You are nothing," she said, "only a drunken sot, a fool, inert, a fallen tree, a bag of sand, a dull, sickened *arn* bear, scarcely able to move, half paralyzed, slumped in a chair."

Abrogastes did not respond.

"I trust you are conscious for a few moments more," said Huta. "Know that I am Huta, a former high priestess of the Timbri. You have dared to put me in a collar and have my thigh marked with the slave rose, as though I was a common woman! You have put me, who was a high priestess of the Timbri, in the garment of a slave! Even now I wear so degrading and humiliating a garment! How ugly it is! How demeaning it is! How I hate it! I shall have robes and veils, and cinctures, and stoles, and cloaks, and footwear, covered with jewels. I shall be rich, and have slaves and servants, and houses, and horses and carriages, of my own. I shall share the throne of Telnaria!"

Abrogastes closed his eyes, and then, after a moment, opened them again.

"I hope that you can hear me," said Huta. "You have only moments, if that, to live. Know that your dread enemy is Ingeld, your son. Learn that, understand that, in your last, declining, darkening, helpless moments. Yes, he has coveted your throne for years, and now, thanks to me, will become king of the Drisriaks, hegemonic tribe of the Aatii. He will bend tribes and worlds to his will. I am his lover, and will later be his consort in Telnar, his empress. Urta, the Otung, brought poison to Tenguthaxichai, delivered it to Viviana of Telnar, who vouchsafed it to me, to administer it to you, as I have done. The poison which I have tricked you into imbibing is particular. Its effects are undetectable. It will be assumed you died of natural causes. I shall be distraught and horrified at the demise of my beloved Master. Then I will, in the cleansing games, be freed by Ingeld, and will become his queen, the queen of the Drisriaks, and, later, will sit beside him in the imperial palace at Telnar. I hope that you can hear me!"

"I can hear you, quite well," said Abrogastes, rising from the chair.

"Master?" whispered Huta, startled, puzzled, eyes wide, stepping back, further.

"The princess, Viviana," said Abrogastes, "unwilling to be party to your plot, brought me the powder, the poison, and explained its purpose. Accordingly a harmless powder, from the ground, sweet cane of Inez II, was substituted. It was this harmless substance which reposed in the envelop she delivered to you, that you emptied into my *kana*. Urta, the Otung, who delivered the poison to Princess Viviana, is in custody."

Huta screamed in terror, turned about, and fled from the chamber.

"Your majesty," said a guard, appearing at the portal, presumably startled by Huta's wild departure from the chamber.

"The slave will flee from the compound," said Abrogastes. "She will seek refuge in the forest. There she would die, being torn to pieces by wild animals, probably by tomorrow morning. Hunt her down with dogs, and bring her back."

CHAPTER FIFTY-EIGHT

"How shall we judge these two, beloved son?" asked Abrogastes.

"Harshly, as they deserve," said Ingeld.

Before the high seat of the Drisriaks on Tenguthaxichai, in the king's hall, knelt Urta, the Otung, and Huta, the slave, once a high priestess of the Timbri, both swathed in chains. Ingeld sat at the right hand of Abrogastes, and at Ingeld's right hand sat the princess Viviana.

"Perhaps, dear son," said Abrogastes, "you have heard that the slave, Huta, in her failed attempt to assassinate me, sought, while the supposed poison was doing its work, to implicate you in in the nefarious plot."

"I have heard so," said Ingeld. "Am I expected to deny so absurd an allegation?"

"Certainly not," said Abrogastes. "The origin of the plot lies in Telnar, deriving either from the imperial palace, governed by an Otung, a hereditary enemy of the Drisriaks, or from the exarchical palace, the residence of the exarch of Telnar, Sidonicus, who desperately sought political concessions I would not grant, or both. The Otung pig, Urta, was the tool of one or the other, and perhaps of both."

"It is true that I requested an audience with the princess Viviana for Urta, the Otung," said Ingeld, "but it was merely that he might convey the good wishes of the exarch of Telnar to the princess. I made a similar request to Princess Alacida, spouse of my beloved brother, Hrothgar, which, as I understand it, was also acted upon."

"The Princess Viviana has cleared you of all guilt, or even suspicion, in this matter," said Abrogastes. "She has testified that you were not present at her interview with Urta, and that, to the best of her knowledge, his intent was unknown to you."

"It is so," said Ingeld.

"But the slave, Huta," said Abrogastes, "while believing in the effectiveness of the supposed fatal toxin, and awaiting the culmination of its lethal effect, spoke of you in terms of vile treachery."

"Perhaps the ravings of a mad slave," said Ingeld. "I assume so palpable a canard needs no response."

"But I am curious," said Abrogastes.

"Pray, speak," said Ingeld.

"What, at such a time, could be the motivation for allegations so obviously false?"

"Who knows the mind of a woman?" said Ingeld.

"May I speak, beloved father of my husband and lord," said Viviana, "and may I speak, my beloved husband and lord?"

"By all means," said Abrogastes.

"Surely," said Ingeld.

"An obvious motivation suggests itself," said Viviana, "a motivation obvious to a woman, but perhaps less so to a man. A hateful woman, desiring to darken the dying moments of a hated man, wishing to fill them with torture and misery, with doubt, suspicion, and agony, might say anything that would be germane to her malicious purpose."

"Of course," said Abrogastes.

"That explains the matter," said Ingeld.

"And very well," said Abrogastes.

"What I said was true!" cried Huta, kneeling in her chains. "Speak for me, dear Ingeld! Protect me, dear Ingeld! Act on my behalf! Do you not love me? Save me!"

"Ingeld is guilty!" cried Urta. "He was privy to the plot! Spare me, great king. I am but a minion, a negligible tool."

"Bring the two goblets," said Abrogastes to a servitor.

Two identical goblets were brought and placed before the kneeling Urta.

"The deadly powder you brought from Telnar will not be wasted," said Abrogastes. "Examine the goblets. Which contains poison? Choose one."

"Mercy, great king," said Urta.

"Choose," said Abrogastes.

With trembling hands, his wrists chained, Urta lifted one of the goblets to his lips and drank.

"More," said Abrogastes, sternly.

Urta had taken little but a swallow more when he turned white. His chains shook, as he trembled. "The poison, the poison!" he rasped.

"Take him away, to his quarters," said Abrogastes. "There, remove his chains and wash them, lest they carry any trace of poison."

"It will be done," said a servitor.

"Handle them carefully," said Abrogastes. "We know little of the nature of the toxin, other than its lethality. It may infuse sweat, oils, and flakes of skin."

"Yes, your majesty," said another servitor.

"The poison, the poison," said Urta, as he was carried from the hall.

"He chose unwisely," said Ingeld.

"Take those goblets away," said Abrogastes. "Empty them, carefully. Do not let the liquid touch your skin. Rinse them, wash them, scour them, cut them in pieces, and cast away the pieces."

The two goblets were removed by another servitor.

"Bring now," said Abrogastes, "the other two goblets."

Two more goblets were brought and these were placed before Huta.

"Mercy, Master," begged Huta.

"Examine the goblets," said Abrogastes. "Which contains poison? Choose one."

"Beloved Ingeld, Master Ingeld," wept Huta. "I have served you well and faithfully. Do you not love me? Am I not to be your queen? Am I not to be empress of Telnaria? Intervene on my behalf! Save me!"

"Drink," said Abrogastes.

"Dear Ingeld!" cried Huta.

"Drink," said Ingeld.

"She is slender and lovely," said Abrogastes. "Her hair is as glossy and black as the wing of the night gull of Safa Major."

"There is now some gray in it," said Ingeld.

"From last night, and the forest, and the dogs," said Abrogastes.

"She would bring less in the markets now," said Ingeld.

"I see it as a charming touch," said Abrogastes. "How could she be more beautiful?"

"Mercy, Masters!" begged Huta.

"Which one?" asked Abrogastes.

She placed her small hands on one of the goblets, looking desperately at Abrogastes, and then Ingeld, and then back to Abrogastes. Then she moved her hands to the other goblet, and, in turn, tried to read the faces of the two men.

"Please," said the Princess Viviana, suddenly, "show her mercy. She is but a slave."

Huta regarded Viviana, startled.

"Spare her," said Viviana.

"Be silent," said Ingeld.

"I beg it," said Viviana.

"Be silent," said Ingeld. "Only a slave would plead for a slave."

"Please," said Viviana.

"Be silent," said Ingeld.

"Yes, my husband and lord," said Viviana.

"Choose," said Abrogastes.

"Pick a goblet, and drink," said Ingeld.

"Now," said Abrogastes.

Huta picked one of the goblets.

"Drink," said Abrogastes.

"Drink," said Ingeld.

"Drain it," said Abrogastes.

Huta closed her eyes, lifted the goblet, put it to her lips, and then, head back, eyes closed, drained the goblet. She remained so for a few moments, and then opened her eyes, and looked to the high seat.

She smiled, tentatively, wonderingly, questioningly.

"She is fortunate," said Ingeld, uneasily.

"It is a red *kana*," said Abrogastes. "It derives from the vineyards of Larial IV. We received it in trade from Burons."

"Our allies," said Ingeld.

"It is much too good to be wasted on Otungs and slaves," said Abrogastes, "but the bottle was opened."

Huta put the goblet down before her.

She was trembling. The chains, locked on her small, fair limbs, made small, soft noises.

"It seems," said Ingeld, "one chose well, and one not. It is interesting is it not, that Urta chose the poison and the slave the harmless beverage."

"It does seem interesting," said Abrogastes.

"To be sure," said Ingeld, "it is not altogether improbable. Each had one chance in two. Thus, there was one chance in four that this particular outcome would obtain."

"Not quite," said Abrogastes. "Both of the goblets placed before Urta contained poison. Neither of those placed before the slave contained poison."

"Master?" said Huta, looking up to the high seat.

"No," said Ingeld. "She is guilty. Let justice be done. Kill her, immediately."

"You wish her dead?" said Abrogastes.

"Certainly," said Ingeld.

"Dear Ingeld!" wept Huta, looking up, lifting her chained wrists.

"Why are you so earnest in this matter?" asked Abrogastes.

"To be earnest in the pursuit of justice becomes a prince," said Ingeld.

"Quite true," said Abrogastes, "particularly when one defines justice as one pleases."

"Father?" asked Ingeld.

"But it is I, the king, who defines justice as he pleases."

"How is that?" asked Ingeld.

"I have the power," said Abrogastes.

"Be it as you say, dear father," said Ingeld.

"It will be as I say," said Abrogastes. "I am king."

Abrogastes then regarded Huta, who, kneeling in her chains, bent over at the waist, put her head to the floor. "Thank you, Master," she said.

"Surely, fair slave," said Abrogastes, "you do not think I would let you off so easily as all this, that I would allow you to slip away gently, painlessly, drifting into the mercy of a quiescent oblivion?"

"Master?" asked Huta, looking up, fearfully.

"That would be far too easy," said Abrogastes. "How dubious and unsatisfactory a vengeance that would be. Not only did you wish to kill me, and would have done so if your plot had not been betrayed, but you gloated over the success you thought you had achieved, and endeavored to torment me most cruelly. As I listened to you, pretending to suffer the effects of poison, I was considering what might constitute a meet punishment for your crimes."

"Please no, Master!" cried Huta.

"I see I am now once more "Master,"" said Abrogastes.

"Yes, Master!" said Huta.

"Kill her," said Ingeld.

"No!" begged Viviana.

"So," said Abrogastes, "I decided that I would keep you as my slave, and I encourage you to conjecture what will be the nature of your slavery."

"Sell me, give me away, anything," begged Huta, "but do not keep me, not after last night, as your slave!"

"It will be so," said Abrogastes.

"What is wrong with her?" asked Abrogastes, regarding the small, crumpled, chained figure on the rush-strewn, dirt floor before the dais.

"I think," said Ingeld, "she has fainted."

CHAPTER FIFTY-NINE

"Excellent," said Ingeld.

"The infant is freshly born, sturdy, male, and healthy," said Farrix, he of the Teragars, the Long-River Borkons. The Borkons were one of the eleven traditional tribes of the Alemanni.

"It has been examined by physicians, ones trustworthy?" asked Ingeld.

"Yes," said Farrix.

"I trust that its origins are obscure," said Ingeld.

"It is a foundling, from Inez IV," said Farrix. "It cannot be identified or traced."

"Of what blood is it?" asked Ingeld.

"From Inez IV, presumably Telnarian," said Farrix. "Does it matter?"

"Not really," said Ingeld. "It can be done away with when we wish."

"Beware," said Farrix. "Should it die there will be scions of a dozen factions and families who will claim the throne. Any of these will have a stronger claim to the throne than a Drisriak regent."

"Factions and families can be set at one another's throats," said Ingeld.

"The senate can nominate a pretender," said Farrix.

"Let them nominate whom they wish," said Ingeld. "Who will take seriously the word of a purchasable gaggle of sycophants?"

"Still," cautioned Farrix.

"Do not concern yourself," said Ingeld. "In five to ten years our power will be so consolidated, by force, habit, and custom, that we can deal easily with dissension."

"What of law?" said Farrix.

"When has law not yielded to the spear?" said Ingeld.

"Prince Ingeld plans well," said Farrix.

"Amongst the Teragars you will advance," said Ingeld, "and the Teragars amongst the Borkons, and the Borkons amongst the Alemanni."

"It is time Viviana bore her child," said Farrix.

"Rumors, like seeds, have been cast widely," said Ingeld. "Delivery is expected momentarily. Even now the princess is sequestered, for her health, safety, and privacy, in a secret hall of the prince."

"Worlds await the announcement of the birth," said Farrix.

"It must be soon," said Ingeld, "or we shall have to dispose of this child and find another, one more recently born."

"Once the announcement is made," said Farrix, "the empire will rejoice, and you and the exarch of Telnar will be free to act."

"Sweeping the Otung usurper from the throne," said Ingeld.

"Unfortunately the joyful tidings will be marred by a tragic fact," said Farrix.

"Yes," said Ingeld. "Viviana, to the sorrow of worlds, will have died in childbirth."

CHAPTER SIXTY

"Worlds reel," said Rurik, Tenth Consul of Larial VII, he of the Larial Farnichi.

"Dismay darkens the empire," said Julian, of the Aureliani.

"Clouds gather," said Iaachus. "I fear the storm is nigh."

Several had gathered in the small, private audience chamber of Ottonius, the First. It was late afternoon. No slaves were present.

"It is tragic that the Princess Viviana perished in childbirth," said Otto.

"Aesilesius must be terribly grieved," said Titus Gelinus.

"No," said Rurik, "he is reported to have sung a little song, and returned to playing with his blocks."

"Horrid," said Titus Gelinus.

"Not at all," said Rurik. "It is not clear he even understood what he was told. He is a retardate, an idiot child wandering aimlessly about, lost in the body of a young man."

"The scheme of Abrogastes proceeds," said Tuvo Ausonius, "a child having been born to Viviana, a royal princess, spouse of Prince Ingeld, the Drisriak, a child on behalf of which, it being male and of royal blood through his mother, a claim may be made to the throne."

"Which will doubtless be made," said Titus Gelinus.

"The throne is occupied," said Rurik.

"By a usurper, unrelated to the royal family, unrelated even to a noble house or family," said Julian.

"Such as yours," said Iaachus.

"I stand for the empire," said Julian. "I stand with our emperor, Ottonius, the First."

"Sovereignty is fragile," said Iaachus, "a riot, an uprising, a minor insurrection, a revolution, even a dagger in the dark or a fatal draft of poison, and the winds of power, wayward and capricious, ignorant and uncaring, blow afresh and differently, toppling regimes and ruining families."

"Now that the child is born," said Titus Gelinus, "the schemes of Ingeld and Sidonicus may unfold."

"Hopefully we will have time to prepare and guard against them," said Rurik.

"Timon Safarius Rhodius, and Boris and Andak, are well emplaced to keep us informed," said Julian.

"I much regret that Princess Viviana is dead," said Otto. "I remember her, haughty, vain, and petty, but beautiful."

"I doubt that she died in childbirth," said Iaachus.

"I do not understand," said Otto.

"I think she was killed," said Iaachus.

"Speak," said Otto.

"Consider," said Iaachus. "The marriages of Viviana and Alacida were both contrived artifacts of statecraft; love was not involved, and scarcely was consent. Both were essentially forced marriages, marriages essentially performed, despite the sacerdotal trappings of the exarch, under duress. Consider further, that for so a long a time there was no sign of pregnancy, let alone a birth. Now we are given to understand that Viviana was actually with child, and recently gave birth. I suspect that Viviana's long time of seeming barrenness, of fruitlessness, was consequent on chemical deterrents militating against conception."

"You do not believe that she gave birth?" said Otto.

"I do not," said Iaachus.

"Then the child is not hers," said Otto.

"No," said Iaachus.

"And she was done away with?" said Otto.

"Rather of necessity," said Iaachus.

"I do not think Abrogastes would be party to such a thing," said Otto.

"But might not be Ingeld, a cunning, impatient, ruthless prince?" asked Iaachus.

"That is possible," said Otto.

"I have received communications from Abrogastes, from Tenguthaxichai, only this morning," said Iaachus, "communications not to be delivered directly from a Drisriak to an Otung."

"But through a Telnarian?" said Julian.

"I do not choose to gainsay the will of a Drisriak king," said Iaachus. "I do choose to deliver his message to the emperor."

"I understand," said Otto. "He is Drisriak, I am Otung. Drisriaks and Otungs, the Alemanni and the Vandalii, have often met in war, on the fields and in the forests, even in the corridors of space. We would seldom address one another openly, save in the matter of threats and challenges. So, wily diplomat, dear friend Iaachus, speak."

"In this message," said Iaachus, "it is accepted, rejoicingly, that a child is born and it is accepted, with lamentation, that the mother perished. There is no hint that Abrogastes doubts that the child is genuine or suspects that the Princess Viviana was killed."

"Perhaps," said Julian, "the child is genuine and the mother did perish in childbirth."

"Perhaps," said Iaachus. "But the content of the message is devoted to other matters. Abrogastes reports that an attempt was made on his life, in which an Otung, a man named Urta, was involved."

"I know of him, a renegade and spy," said Otto, fingering the hilt of his dagger.

"Abrogastes," continued Iaachus, "takes it as incontrovertible that his son, Ingeld, was involved in the assassination attempt, but lacks proof on which to move, largely because of protestations and testimony which had been rendered by the Princess Viviana, who apparently, for some reason, sought to defend and exonerate Ingeld. Her views were taken with great seriousness, for she had been instrumental in foiling the assassination plot. Abrogastes, however, is adamant. He takes it as assured that Ingeld is in league with the exarch of Telnar. He also supposes that these conspirators, Sidonicus and Ingeld, wish him gone, Ingeld to ascend to the high seat of the Drisriaks, and Sidonicus to secure an eventual ally on the throne of Telnaria, one who will agree to his political and economic demands, as Abrogastes would not. As the plot failed, and Ingeld must suppose himself suspected, Abrogastes warns that matters are now likely to move differently and quickly. He thinks it likely that a projected coup will be imminent. Indeed, Ingeld has already departed Tenguthaxichai, and is *en route* to Telnar. He may be in Telnar now."

"Ingeld will have men in Telnar, waiting," said Rurik.

"He will have anticipated action, though doubtless not so soon," said Tuvo Ausonius.

"How disappointing for Ingeld," said Julian, "that he does not hold the high seat of the Drisriaks, that the full might of the Drisriaks is not at his disposal."

"He does not need it, if Telnar rises at the word of Sidonicus," said Rurik.

"What of the city guard," said Tuvo Ausonius.

"It is likely to side with Sidonicus and the senate," said Titus Gelinus.

"Consul Rurik has men," said Tuvo Ausonius.

"Not enough," said Rurik.

"Friend Julian," said Tuvo Ausonius, "has partisans in the navy."

"Not enough to brook a flood, not enough to thwart a tide," said Julian.

"What of Ortog, son of Abrogastes, rescued from the house of Dardanis?" asked Tuvo Ausonius. "He has men in the delta of the Turning Serpent."

"Again," said Julian, "not enough, too few."

"But he will be contacted?" said Tuvo Ausonius.

"Surely," said Julian.

"We need more men," said Rurik.

"Send out word," said Titus Gelinus. "Contact provincial worlds. Summon *comitates*, spear guards, auxiliaries, and others."

"And surrender borders?" asked Tuvo Ausonius.

"There may not be time," said Rurik.

"I shall contact Tangara," said Otto.

"It was there you were named king," said Julian.

"You will draw troops from Tangara?" asked Rurik.

"Perhaps," said Otto.

"The medallion and chain, symbol of the Vandalii, once worn by the great Genserix himself, honored even by Heruls, is on Tangara," said Julian.

"I trust so," said Otto.

"I fear there is too little time to summon troops from Tangara," said Rurik.

"I, too, fear that," said Otto. "But we do not know how much time we have. There may be enough time. We do not know."

"Summon them," said Rurik.

"You cannot, you dare not, dear Otto, dear friend," said Julian.

"Why can he not?" asked Tuvo Ausonius.

"Heruls," said Julian. "They would pour forth unchecked, unresisted, from their camps, in their hordes, from the Plains of Barrionuevo, from the Flats of Tung, as they will have it, looting and killing, burning crops and seizing cattle. It would be the end of Tangara, as we know it."

"Perhaps not," said Otto.

"There is one other thing, though it is doubtless of little importance," said Iaachus.

"Beware of things which seem of little importance," said Otto. "What is it?"

"It involves a subtle calculation by Abrogastes," said Iaachus. "The conspirator, Urta, captured and chained, was made to drink a poison, the very poison intended to be used in the assassination of Abrogastes."

"Rightfully poetic," said Julian, "a most suitable and appropriate form of execution."

"But one surprising, is it not?" asked Otto.

"How so?" asked Julian.

"You know much of *civilitas*, but, I fear, little of *barbaritas*, my friend," said Otto.

"I do not understand," said Julian.

"Would such a death not seem a most mild and merciful punishment for so great a crime, as attempting to kill a king?"

"Perhaps," said Julian.

"In any event," said Iaachus, "Abrogastes had the wretch, Urta, carried to his quarters where his chains were removed, and he was supposedly left to die. The calculation of Abrogastes was twofold, first, that Urta would still be alive when he reached his quarters and his chains were removed, and, second, that the bearer of such a poison, presumably a dangerous, extremely lethal poison, would have an antidote on hand, to be used if needed. It was then arranged that a servitor, one supposedly of the party of Ingeld, would see to his escape from Tenguthaxichai."

"It seems the calculation was subtle, indeed," said Rurik.

"We note that Abrogastes was willing to take the risk," said Julian, drily.

"With the life of another," said Tuvo Ausonius.

"Brave Abrogastes," said Titus Gelinus.

"Had he miscalculated, nothing of importance would be lost," said Rurik, "only the life of a loathsome *filch*. It is easy to be brave in risking the loss of a penny, not so easy in risking the loss of a *darin*."

"But what," said Otto, "was the point of the calculation in the first place. What had Abrogastes in mind?"

"I do not know," said Iaachus. "He did not say."

"I suspect," said Otto, "he had more data on hand than we, in his calculation of the odds, say, the likely interval between inges-

tion and death, and the availability and effectiveness of the antidote. I suspect that the poison was identified and its properties
were investigated. Thus, we may suppose that he was very sure
that Urta would survive. The question then is why? Why did he
wish for Urta to survive and escape?"

"We do not know," said Iaachus.

"But it is easy to speculate," said Otto. "Had the assassination
of Abrogastes taken place, conspirators might have proceeded in
patient leisure. There would be time for Ingeld to assume the high
seat of the Drisriaks, consolidate his power, and, his rule established, align the tribes of the Alemanni, and their allies, for, if
needed, a many-pointed and massive attack on Telnaria. In the
meantime, Sidonicus, and his minor ministrants, from the pulpits
of a hundred temples, do their work, priming a gullible faithful
for rising in the streets. They denounce an Otung on the imperial throne. They note with joy the supposed offspring of Princess
Viviana, and thus the availability of a plausible heir to the throne.
They note, as well, Ingeld, supposed father of the child, Ingeld,
mighty amongst the feared Aatii, yet ready to save the empire,
the throne, and senate, who will, when in power, decree their
faith as the official faith of the empire. All that is necessary then
is to remove the hated Otung from the throne. Then there will be
love, peace, and harmony; then will wine flow, flowers bloom, ribbons and banners flutter, maidens dance and sing, and perfume
be poured in the streets."

"But Ingeld is not on the high seat of the Drisriaks," said Rurik.

"Precisely," said Otto. "And Abrogastes is inimical to the policies of the exarch."

"An uprising then must be local to Telnar," said Tuvo Ausonius.

"But nonetheless formidable," said Otto. "Consider thousands,
wild in the streets, enflamed, armed with torches, clubs, knives,
tools, and stones, burning and looting, calling for blood, in the
name of Floon and *Karch*, abetted by dissident guards, malcon-
tented troops, and foreign infiltrators, Drisriaks sworn to Ingeld."

"I fear we are lost," said Iaachus.

"We will attempt to draw aid from Tangara," said Otto.

"Surely not," said Julian. "Recall the Heruls."

"I have a plan," said Otto.

"I doubt there is time for any such intervention," said Rurik,
"even discounting its attendant hazards, the swarmings of Heruls."

"I fear you are right," said Otto. "We shall see."

"But why should Abrogastes have spared the spy and would-be assassin, Urta?" asked Tuvo Ausonius. "Why should he permit him to escape?"

"I think," said Otto, "to bring matters to a head, to alarm the exarch, and thus prematurely hasten his plans. Urta will inform the exarch that Abrogastes lives, and may well suspect his collusion with Ingeld. The wrath of a king is not a light thing. Presumably then, to avoid his own jeopardy, Sidonicus must act expeditiously, to seize power in Telnar, and thus in the empire. As a private person, even as an exarch, he is in mortal peril, by assassins or otherwise; I am sure he does not covet the role of a martyr; he would be more than content to leave that for others; if, on the other hand, he has the protection of Ingeld, as regent in Telnar, the regent backed by the resources and might of the empire, Abrogastes would be wise to stay his hand, to sheath his sword and wait."

"It seems then that Abrogastes, in releasing the Otung, Urta, is impatient, that he chooses to force matters, that he is eager for matters to be resolved," said Titus Gelinus.

"I think so," said Otto.

"And we are warned, that we be prepared," said Iaachus.

"There may be little time," said Rurik.

"Ingeld may even now be in Telnar," said Iaachus.

"It is quite possible," said Rurik.

"Abrogastes plans well," said Otto. "If the coup is resisted, the exarch is foiled. If it succeeds, we are done, and the throne is clear for the regency of his son, Ingeld, however unreliable and treacherous."

"But," said Iaachus, "we were warned."

"Which suggests to me," said Otto, "that Abrogastes has not forgotten the events which took place in the fourth basement of the house of Dardanis."

"In either case, it seems Abrogastes wins," said Julian.

"One enemy is pitted against another," said Rurik.

"He is clever," said Iaachus.

"He is called the Far-Grasper," said Otto.

CHAPTER SIXTY-ONE

The blond-haired, blue-eyed slave touched, softly, gently, the collar locked on her neck. Then, delicately, she touched the Slave Rose, burned into her left thigh. Most masters are right-handed.

She sat, her back against the wall, in a small, barred room, on a scarlet carpet. She was naked, as slaves are often kept.

She heard someone at the door.

Two men entered. She did not know them. She had never seen them before. She knelt, for she knew that slaves commonly knelt in the presence of free persons.

"Palms of hands on floor, head down, to the floor," said one of the men.

She immediately assumed that position. She knew that slaves obeyed, and might be punished, terribly, if they did not do so. She knew that slaves might be so punished, even if they were slow to obey, or showed the slightest indication of, or suggestion of, unwillingness.

The men walked about her, looking at her. Then they returned, to stand before her.

"Kneel up, palms on thighs, back straight," said one of the men.

She complied.

"Again, more gracefully," said one of the men.

She assumed her former position, head to the floor, and then knelt up, again.

"Good," said the man.

She knew that slaves were to be graceful.

"How do you feel?" asked one of the men.

"There is a collar on my neck," she said.

"You are a slave," said the man.

"I am branded," she said.

"You are a slave," he said.

"I am naked," she said.

"You are a slave," he said.

"Am I a slave?" she asked.

"Yes, you are a slave," said the man. "How do you feel?"

"Well," she said, "—Master." She knew that slaves called free men 'Master' and free women 'Mistress'.

"Do you know where you are?" asked one of the men.

"No, Master," she responded.

"But you do know you are a slave," he said.

"Yes, Master," she said.

"You may speak," he said. "And be grateful that you are permitted to speak," he said.

"A slave is grateful, to be permitted to speak," she said.

Then she looked, wonderingly, at the two men.

"I do not know you," she said. "And I am confused. Things circle about, and are unclear. I know nothing of my origins, or owners. I do not recall my embonding or my sales. I do not recall my marking, nor my collaring. How strange that a girl would not recall her branding, when the iron first seared her skin, marking her as a slave, or when the collar was first snapped about her neck, so momentous a moment. I remember little, or nothing. It is as though much of my memory was wiped away."

"The drug is effective," said one of the men to the other.

"I have seen it so, in hundreds of cases," said the other.

"I do not even know my name," she said.

"You have no name," said one of the men, "save as it pleases Masters to put a name on you."

"You have been called 'Yana'," said the other man. "That will do."

"What is your name?" asked the first man.

"'Yana'," she said.

"We will tell you a little about yourself, Yana," said the second man. "Keep it in mind. Remember it. You were taken in a town war on Safa Major, and sold to an itinerant slaver, from a town victory camp. You need not know the towns. Slaves need know little, other than that they are slaves. You were taken to Carleton, on Inez II, where you were exhibited, where the first sales plaque was hung about your neck. Following that you had five Masters, on three worlds."

"I remember nothing of this," she said.

"Nor need you," he said.

"Your body is shapely," said the other man. "It is a good body for a slave."

"I am pleased, if Masters are pleased," she said.

"It looks well in a collar," he said.

"A slave is pleased, if Masters are pleased," she said.

"You know the duties of a slave, do you not?" asked one of the men.

"A slave is to be pleasing to her Master," she said, "—in all ways."

"You understand that—"in all ways"?" asked the second man.

"Yes, Master," she said.

"Do you know what this is?" asked one of the men, holding forth a coiled, dread implement.

"A slave whip," she said.

"And you are a slave, are you not?" he asked.

"Yes, Master," she said.

"Do you wish to feel it?" he asked.

"No, Master," she said.

"Be pleasing," he said.

"Yes, Master," she said.

"In all ways," he said.

"Yes, Master," she said.

"Instantly, and unquestioningly," he said.

"Yes, Master," she said.

"You are Yana, only Yana," he said.

"Yes, Master," she said.

"Do not forget it," he said.

"Yes, Master," she said.

"What do you think we can get for her?" asked the first man.

"Fifteen, perhaps seventeen, or eighteen, *darins*," said the second man.

"Chain her, and put her with the others," said the first man.

"On all fours, and follow me, Yana," said the second man.

"Yes, Master," she said.

CHAPTER SIXTY-TWO

The longboat grated gently on the sand.

Rowers leapt over the side and, wading, drew the boat on the beach.

"This is a desolate place," said Corelius.

Rurik took his hand from the tiller and climbed overboard, wading ashore. "It is a secret, barren place," he said, "little more than a skerry, some rocks and sand, a small island, a day from the delta, north, apart from familiar sea lanes, a good place to transact private business."

"The thousand *darins* of gold are here?" asked Corelius, uneasily. He was in the bow of the longboat.

"There, waiting," said Rurik, pointing.

"I see," said Corelius. "The tiny shack."

"The gold is inside," said Rurik.

"I should have asked for more," said Corelius. "The information I sold may save the empire, save it to be as it has been; it may keep the Otung on the throne; it may prevent the throne from falling into the hands of the Aatii; it may defeat various heinous plots of unsuspected conspirators."

"Who," asked Rurik, "could possibly have guessed that the secret enemies of the state would be the great and blessed exarch himself, humble ministrant of the rites of Floon; or Ingeld, the very son of Abrogastes, betraying his father's wishes; or Timon Safarius Rhodius, the seemingly loyal and patriotic *primarius* of the senate?"

"I should have asked for more," said Corelius, climbing over the side of the long boat, stepping onto the sand. The sand was soft and his sandals sunk into the sand, and a bit of water, washing ashore, beside the boat, entered the footprints, and then sunk away, disappearing in the sand.

"Accept the thanks of a grateful empire," said Rurik.

Corelius advanced, climbing the beach, reaching the dry, hot sand. "I but did my duty," he said. "The gold is in the shack?"

"Yes," said Rurik.

"This is a strange place to store waiting gold," said Corelius.

"Not at all," said Rurik. "It is a safe place, a secure place. Would you rather have had the gold delivered to you in the plaza before the imperial palace or on the steps of the senate, or in an alley in the Varl district?"

"You must understand," said Corelius, "that I must count the gold."

"It is there," said Rurik, "certified, under the imperial seal, but do as you wish."

"Accompany me," said Corelius.

"Very well," said Rurik.

Corelius, followed by Rurik, climbed toward the shack.

"You already received a gold *darin*, did you not, some days ago?" asked Rurik.

"That was a mere token of good faith, to seal a bargain," said Corelius. "It is not to be counted as part of the agreed-upon sum."

"I see," said Rurik.

"In devising these arrangements, so decreed the Otung," said Corelius.

"The emperor," said Rurik.

"If you wish," said Corelius, trudging ahead, hastening his steps.

"The emperor is generous," said Rurik.

"It should be a thousand *darins*," said Corelius, suddenly stopping, not looking back.

"It is," said Rurik.

Corelius then resumed his climb to the shack.

In a few moments, a little short of breath, he thrust open the door of the small shack. It was loose on its hinges. There was some light in the shack, from a small window. Motes of dust were discernible in the shaft of light, falling through the window. In the shack, on the wooden floor, were a chair and table, and on the table was a simple, sturdy box. It was of dark wood; it was closed; it was secured with a padlock; and a key lay on the table, beside the box, to its right. Corelius, sweating, thrust the key into the padlock, and, fumbling, turned the key, sprung the bolt, put aside the padlock, and opened the box. In it were four sacks, each tied with cords, their junctures bearing the imperial seal, impressed on a scrap of parchment.

Rurik stood in the doorway of the shack. "Each sack contains two hundred and fifty *darins* of gold," he said.

Corelius pulled at the opened box, which scraped on the table, bringing it closer to him. "It is heavy," he said.

"A thousand *darins* of gold is heavy," said Rurik, behind him.

Feverishly, trembling, Corelius broke the seals, and tore open the sacks. "Gold!" he cried. Grunting, he lifted one sack, it was not easy, and poured its contents on the plain table, in a lengthy shower of bright metal.

"I must count it," he said, and he began to separate the coins, sorting them into piles of ten coins each.

It took several minutes for Corelius to assure himself that the sack contained two hundred and fifty *darins* of gold. Indeed, he inspected each coin. Then, when he had twenty-five piles of ten coins each, he replaced them in the sack and knotted its cord. He then proceeded to the second sack, and determined its contents similarly, counting the coins carefully, and then returning them to their sack, which he then tied shut. This procedure was repeated with the third and fourth sack. He then lifted the four sacks, one by one, with some difficulty, as they were heavy, as had been noted, put them in the box, closed the box, secured the box with the padlock, and placed the key in his wallet.

He then turned about and noted that Rurik was no longer standing behind him, waiting in the doorway.

He shrieked with terror, and fled from the shack, running to the beach, which was empty. He screamed, and waded out, into the water, to his waist. The horizon was clear. There was no sign of the longboat.

CHAPTER SIXTY-THREE

"You have a suitable child?" asked Sidonicus.

"Yes," said Ingeld. "It is on Tenguthaxichai at present, but it, or another, can be produced when needed."

"Excellent," said Sidonicus. "And the Princess Viviana?"

"Died in childbirth," said Ingeld.

"Of course," said Sidonicus.

"The empire mourns," said Fulvius.

"He is here?" asked Ingeld, looking toward the back of the private audience chamber, where, standing in the shadows, rather behind Timon Safarius Rhodius, and two guards, there was a small figure.

Sidonicus motioned that the small figure might approach.

"I believe you know our friend, Urta," said Sidonicus.

"We have met," said Ingeld.

"I feared you were serious, great prince," said Urta, "when, on Tenguthaxichai, you feigned to favor my execution."

"Oh?" said Ingeld.

"You were a superb actor," said Urta.

"I was not acting," said Ingeld. "I feigned nothing. The work was bungled, and you knew too much. Your continued existence did much imperil a momentous clandestine enterprise."

"I bungled nothing," said Urta. "I delivered the poison to the Princess Viviana and explained its purpose. She betrayed the plot."

"We miscalculated," said smooth-cheeked Fulvius, high ministrant in Telnar, second only to the exarch himself. "We anticipated she would work on our behalf, to bring Ingeld, her husband and lord, to the high seat of the Drisriaks."

"She did not do so," said Urta.

"Why?" asked Sidonicus.

"Who knows?" said Urta.

"Perhaps she resented her forced marriage to Ingeld, and wished to foil his plot," said Fulvius. "Perhaps she cares for, or fears, Abrogastes. Perhaps she even cares for Ingeld, and hoped to protect him, keeping him from participation in such a matter. Perhaps she simply did not wish to be a party to murder."

"Please," said Sidonicus, "righteous political expediency."

"Of course," said Fulvius. "Forgive me, your excellency."

"I trust," said Urta to Ingeld, "we are still friends."

"You are Otung, I am Drisriak," said Ingeld. "How could we be friends? Sooner might a lion befriend a *filch*."

"Associates then, great prince," said Urta.

"Regrettably," said Ingeld.

"Let there be gentle amity amongst us," said Timon Safarius Rhodius, *primarius* of the senate. Behind him stood his two guards, Boris and Andak.

"Be not in doubt, noble Safarius," said Fulvius. "There exists such amity."

"You are fortunate, dear, brave Urta," said Sidonicus, "to have escaped from Tenguthaxichai with your life."

"I outwitted Abrogastes," said Urta, "availing myself of a ready antidote."

"Abrogastes," said Ingeld, "is not easily outwitted."

"We did not expect you so soon in Telnar," said Fulvius.

"I fear we must advance our plans," said Ingeld.

"How so?" asked Sidonicus.

"My father suspects," said Ingeld.

"I did not speak," said Urta to Sidonicus. "Abrogastes suspects nothing of Prince Ingeld."

"He suspects, I am sure," said Ingeld.

"Surely not," said Urta.

"I know my father better than you," said Ingeld. "That is why I have come so soon to Telnar."

"Interestingly, independently," said Sidonicus, "we were thinking of summoning you to Telnar, with the very object of just such an advancement in our plans."

"On what grounds?" asked Ingeld.

"Corelius, of whom you have doubtless heard, who was involved in the silencing of the defensive batteries of Telnar at the time of the raid of Abrogastes that seized the two princesses, Viviana and Alacida, who was instrumental in the capture of Abrogastes and, later, that of Ortog, and such, has taken leave of our company. Further, we have evidence he has betrayed us to the imperial palace, and, quite possibly, given further evidence, on which we need not elaborate, for a thousand *darins* of gold."

"Deny accusations," said Ingeld. "Who would believe charges leveled by a deserter, an ambitious, disgruntled minion?"

"The palace," said Sidonicus.

"Where is he now?" asked Ingeld.

"We do not know," said Sidonicus.

"How is it he was not traced and slain?" asked Ingeld.

"We made every effort to do so," said Sidonicus. "We failed."

"Wherever he is," said Fulvius, "he is carrying his death in his own hands. In a given day in Telnar scarcely a dozen gold *darins* enter the banks or markets. As soon as he spends one *darin* he will signal his position. He will place himself in mortal jeopardy, not only from our kill squads, alerted by our spies, but from common thieves and murderers, as well."

"In any event," said Ingeld, "as I do not have the high seat of the Drisriaks, and I believe that Abrogastes suspects us, it behooves us to come to power as soon as possible, that we may have the resources of the empire at our disposal, these to give caution to Abrogastes, should he be tempted to move against us."

"Agreed," said Sidonicus.

"How soon can we act?" asked Ingeld.

"Soon," said Sidonicus. "I shall send out a confidential exarchical letter to all our temples, instructing our ministrants how to proceed. It is a foul crime that the throne should have been seized by a hateful barbarian. He is a wicked tyrant. His rule is unlawful. His officers steal from the people. He despises and hates you. He holds you in contempt. He exploits you. When will the sufferings of Telnaria be relieved? And now, in these times of trouble and tribulations, of sorrow and misery, a child of royal blood is born, one who by birth belongs upon the throne. Let us rejoice and set things aright. All that is needed is for the people to speak, and speak forcibly, in the language of righteous iron, blood, and fire. Prepare to perform a blessed and holy act. It is the will of Floon and *Karch*! Await the signal!"

"Do you truly think your people will believe your lies, despite the evidence of their own senses?" asked Ingeld.

"Certainly," said Sidonicus. "They will believe whatever they are told to believe. We teach them so. We train them so. People do not look for themselves and think for themselves. That is difficult. Who wants to do that? They believe words about things. That is easier. Who looks at the things themselves to see if the words are true? Only eccentrics who dare not tell the truth, aware of the dangers and penalties attending honesty."

"How soon," asked Ingeld, "can your deluded puppets be brought into the streets?"

"Our courageous and righteous faithful," said Sidonicus.

"How soon?" asked Ingeld.

"A few days," said Sidonicus. "It takes time for a pot to boil. It must be heated; it must simmer; then it boils; then, at the signal, it pours forth, rushing and scalding, into the streets."

"The palace is not naive," said Ingeld. "It will prepare countermeasures. It will summon aid."

"Countermeasures will be ineffective," said Fulvius. "And we can seize Telnar, and the throne, finishing matters, before aid can arrive."

"Good," said Ingeld.

CHAPTER SIXTY-FOUR

"He has by now discovered he cannot eat gold," said Rurik.

"Nor drink it, should it be melted," said an oarsman.

The longboat was eased to the beach, and oarsmen went over the side and, wading, thrust it up, on the sand.

Rurik left the tiller, and waded ashore.

He put his hands to the sides of his mouth, to amplify his voice, and cried, "Ho, wealthy *filch*, ho!"

"There is no answer," said an oarsman.

"Can he be dead already?" asked another.

"He should have been left here to die," said another. "It is what he deserved."

"The emperor would not have it so," said Rurik. "It is a matter of an understanding, of an implicit word given, some article of honor."

"Look," said another, pointing toward the shack. In the portal, clinging to the doorjamb, was a haggard figure. It stepped forth, and fell, and then rose again, took a few steps, and then fell, again. On its hands and knees, it lifted its head, and seemed to cry out, but there was no sound. It lifted one hand, plaintively, toward the group on the beach. Then it began to crawl toward them, slowly. It collapsed a few feet from the longboat. Rurik, and two oarsmen, went to the collapsed figure, and Rurik lifted it to a sitting position. It opened its mouth. Its tongue was dark and swollen. The eyes did not seem to focus. "Water," it rasped, the noise a hoarse whisper. Then the body stiffened, as if contorted by cramps. Then, again, it lay back, propped in Rurik's arms. Its skin was dry and papery.

"Bring water," said Rurik, and one of the oarsmen went to the longboat and returned with a flask. Most of the oarsmen remained near the boat.

"Water," said Corelius, reaching toward the flask.

"Water in this place," said Rurik, "is expensive."

"—*Water*," said Corelius, reaching again toward the flask.

"It costs one thousand *darins* of gold," said Rurik.

"Leave him here," said an oarsman.

"I pay, I pay!" rasped Corelius.

Rurik held the flask of water to the parched lips of Corelius, and, looking up, said to the two oarsmen with him, "Fetch the gold."

A bit later the two oarsmen had returned to the beach, and placed the small, weighty box on the sand, near the longboat.

Rurik then rose to his feet.

"You may keep your gold," he said.

Corelius looked up, startled.

"You are not dead yet," said an oarsman. "We are not thieves."

Then Rurik said, "Oars."

"Wait!" said Corelius.

Rurik climbed into the longboat and grasped the tiller.

"Wait, wait!" said Corelius.

The oarsmen thrust the boat back into the water, turned it about, clambered aboard, and set the oars in the oarlocks.

"Wait!" cried Corelius, rising unsteadily to his feet, clutching the now-drained flask. "Do not leave me here!"

Rurik turned about, looking back.

"Take me with you!" begged Corelius.

"The fare," said Rurik, "is one thousand *darins* of gold."

"Leave him," said an oarsman. "Retrieve the gold later."

"I pay it," cried Corelius. "Take the gold. Save me! Rescue me! Do not leave me here! Take me back with you! Surely you are noble and honorable men! You cannot leave me here! Take the gold! The gold is yours! It is yours!"

"Stow the box, there," said Rurik, pointing to a space between two thwarts.

The two oarsmen who had brought the box down to the beach climbed from the longboat, waded to the beach, gathered up the box, and returned to the side of the longboat. They then lifted the box into the hands of two others who placed it in the area Rurik had designated. These four then reassumed their places on their respective thwarts.

Corelius staggered into the water, and seized the side of the longboat.

"Take me with you!" he begged.

"Bring him aboard," said Rurik.

An oarsman pulled Corelius over the side of the longboat, and Corelius crawled to the small, weighty box, clasped it, and lay with it, held in his arms.

"My gold, my gold," he said.

It was night when the longboat reached the delta of the Turning Serpent.

The shore was little more than a darkness to starboard. One could hear the surf.

Corelius lay between two thwarts, clutching the box.

"Are you awake?" asked Rurik.

"Yes," said Corelius.

"You may keep the gold, as before," said Rurik.

"I do not understand," said Corelius.

"Had you a sense of honor," said Rurik, "you would understand. You would know we would return for you and that the gold would not be taken from you. You have tormented yourself. The emperor thought it would be so. You lack trust. His experiment is now complete. It is common for one who is dishonest, who lies, who betrays, to fear being treated dishonestly, to fear being lied to, to fear being betrayed. You had the word of a chieftain, of a king, of an emperor, and yet you doubted."

"This is some mad game?" asked Corelius.

"Neither mad nor a game," said Rurik. "It is a lesson, which an emperor has devised, but does not expect to be learned, a lesson in values, that many things, even a flask of water or a place between the thwarts of a simple longboat, may outweigh the value of gold, and that one may rely on the pledged word of an honorable man."

"Who is honorable?" asked Corelius. "To pretend honor is wise, to be honorable is to be foolish. Honor is a deceit. It is a facade, a curtain, behind which to conceal intrigue and the secret stratagems of power. Who does not know this? Let the emperor, if he is truly so naive and foolish, learn lessons, let him learn the ways of the world."

"The emperor," said Rurik, "is prepared to provide you with protection, and an escort, to a destination of your choice."

"He is gracious, indeed," said Corelius. "Put me ashore."

"Beware of how you handle gold," said Rurik. "It can be more dangerous than a handful of vipers."

"It will provide me with all I need," said Corelius. "I need only spend it."

"What is the color of gold?" asked Rurik.

"Gold is the color of gold," said Corelius, puzzled.

"Sometimes it is the color of death," said Rurik.

"Absurd," said Corelius. "It is the color of power."

"Often," said Rurik. "Not always."

"Always," said Corelius.

"Avail yourself of the aid of the emperor," said Rurik. "Beware of spending even a single *darin*."

"Put me ashore," said Corelius. "Or am I to be slain now, and the gold taken?"

"I see the lesson has not been learned," said Rurik. "The emperor thought it would be so."

Rurik then directed his oarsmen to beach the longboat.

Corelius managed to get the small, sturdy, heavy box in his arms, and climb over the side of the longboat. He then stood on the beach, holding the box.

"Go," he said, in the darkness.

"You have a thousand *darins* of gold," said Rurik, "but I would not be you."

CHAPTER SIXTY-FIVE

A mighty fist pounded on the door to the chamber of Aesilesius. It pounded three times. Had young Aesilesius known more of the customs of Drisriaks and Otungs, he might have recognized that such a knock commonly signals the presence of a person of importance or rank. It is common in the halls of various peoples, peoples who may even be enemies to one another, that, interestingly, one may find similar, even identical, customs, practices, sayings, and ways. That this phenomenon occurs suggests a harkening back to common origins and a past no longer recalled. As it was, Aesilesius was merely startled, shocked at the intrusiveness of such a sudden, bold announcement of presence. Nika cried out in fear, sitting up the couch.

Aesilesius quickly rose from the couch, and drew his robe about himself.

The door then, from the outside, was unlocked.

Aesilesius bent over, making himself appear small, frail, and weak, and seized up a toy, the small, stuffed, yellow *torodont*, which he clutched to his bosom.

The door opened.

Aesilesius straightened up, putting aside the toy.

"Cover yourself," said Otto to Nika, "and leave."

Nika leaped from the couch, and seized up a tunic, which she held before her. She cast a wild look at Aesilesius.

"Away, slave," said Otto.

"Speak gently to her," said Aesilesius.

"Get out, slave," said Otto.

Nika sped from the room.

"Be kind," said Aesilesius.

"Slaves are slaves," said Otto, "and they are to be spoken to as slaves, and treated as slaves. When a woman is a slave and knows she is a slave, she expects to be treated as a slave, and wants to be treated as a slave, for she is a slave. It is what she needs and wants. If you want her at your feet, juicing and begging, treat her as what she is, and wants to be, a slave."

"Have you come to kill me?" asked Aesilesius. "Have you finally decided on that? Have you come at last to understand the danger I might pose to you? But if you wished to kill me, presumably you would dispatch underlings to my chamber, to finish the business. Why should an emperor stoop to such chores? Such things are better delegated to menials."

"You let her on the surface of the couch?" asked Otto.

"Yes," said Aesilesius.

"Interesting," said Otto. "Is she "slave satisfactory"?"

"Very much so," said Aesilesius.

"Good," said Otto.

"Surely you have not honored my chamber to ascertain the satisfactoriness of a slave," said Aesilesius.

"A free woman need not be satisfactory," said Otto, "but a slave, a collar slut, a chain bitch, must be."

"I understand," said Aesilesius.

"And extremely so," said Otto.

"I understand," said Aesilesius.

"Has your slave, based on her inquiries in the palace and her peregrinations in the city, informed you of untoward circumstances and looming events?"

"All seems level, and serene," said Aesilesius.

"It is not," said Otto. "Much brews beneath the surface. Has the slave informed you of what occurs in many temples, in Telnar, and its vicinity?"

"Slaves are not allowed in temples," said Aesilesius, "even at the feet of their masters, nor are dogs."

"Sedition emanates from pulpits," said Otto. "In this we see the hand of the exarch of Telnar, his glorious blessedness, Sidonicus."

"My mother," said Aesilesius, "repudiated his smudging, annoyed to learn that women, even those of noble blood, are denied a *koos*."

"That is doubtless temporary," said Otto. "She need not fear. Revelation will be trimmed to meet the needs of the day."

"Unfolding revelation?" asked Aesilesius.

"Whatever is required," said Otto. "Documents can be read in any way the reader wishes."

"You are troubled," said Aesilesius.

"Graffiti attacking the throne are scrawled on walls and pavements," said Otto. "Men shun guardsmen and are evasive and

surly when approached. There are whisperings and sudden si-
lences in the taverns. Men gather in dark places."

"Such things connote restlessness," said Aesilesius. "But I
think such things would not justify your appearance here, this
night, at this hour, unless danger was imminent. I suspect you are
more deeply apprised than such trivia would suggest."

"Perhaps," said Otto.

"I take it you have not come to kill me," said Aesilesius.

"No," said Otto.

"What is it you fear?" asked Aesilesius. "Of what would you
warn me?"

"Shortly, perhaps as early as tomorrow, and certainly within
the next few days," said Otto, "there will be a revolt. Thousands
will swarm into the streets, muddled, exploited fanatics, and hundreds of others, as well, eager to take advantage of any disruption
or breach of order, looters, killers, thieves, rapists, and arsonists,
the unruly, cruel, vicious, destructive, greedy, and violent, those
seeking anonymity and license."

"To be resisted and quelled by guardsmen, by soldiers?" said
Aesilesius.

"We do not know how guardsmen and soldiers will stand,
what they will do," said Otto. "They might join the mobs, shouting slogans of rightfulness. How do they think the wind is blow-
ing? Is it not better to have it at one's back? How seriously are
civil oaths and pledges to be taken? In the ranks there may well
be confusion, and mixed loyalties. One does not know. In a raging
river most will follow the current. In any event, they are too few
to stand against swarms of heedless, rushing *filchen*."

"Surely help might be sought," said Aesilesius.

"I have summoned auxiliaries, *comitates*, from Tangara," said
Otto.

"Not from Tangara," said Aesilesius, with dismay.

"I have done so," said Otto. "I can count on their loyalty. It is a matter of Spear Oaths, which you might find it difficult to understand."

"You would surrender Tangara to Heruls?" asked Aesilesius.

"It is my hope not to do so," said Otto.

"Events transpire," said Aesilesius.

"Rapidly," said Otto.

"There is hope?" asked Aesilesius.

"Very little," said Otto. "Time is short. Abrogastes, the Far-
Grasper, if no other, has precipitated events. The dogs of war are

loose, and hasten to their feeding. We need time, and there is no time."

"All is lost?" said Aesilesius.

"I fear so," said Otto.

"Why have you come to tell me this?" asked Aesilesius.

"Because your life is in great danger," said Otto.

"I do not understand," said Aesilesius. "I need but return to my calculated façade of idiocy, and survive, as the means whereby others rule, my mother, a new Arbiter of Protocol, some scion of a noble Telnarian family."

"It would not be so," said Otto. "It is claimed that a child is born to the union of Ingeld, the Drisriak, and your sister, Viviana, who, if she did not die in childbirth, as is alleged, was doubtless done away with. That child would have royal blood. The coup effected, the child would be pronounced emperor, this predictably ratified by the senate, and Ingeld would rule as regent. In such an arrangement there would be no place for the embarrassment of an Aesilesius. He would not long survive. There are many ways to die, many seemingly natural. Doubtless his death would be publicly mourned."

"Poor Viviana," said Aesilesius.

"Think of yourself," said Otto.

"I have thought of myself too much, for too long," said Aesilesius.

"You could take a painless, quick-acting poison," said Otto.

"Would you do so?" asked Aesilesius.

"No," said Otto. "I would die fighting."

"I would do so, as well," said Aesilesius.

"You are not Otung," said Otto.

"I am Telnarian," said Aesilesius.

"Do not tell me that I look upon a man," said Otto.

"Whatever I may be," said Aesilesius, "boy or not, man or not, I am he upon whom you look."

"I think now," said Otto, "for the first time, I am proud to do so."

"One thing must be done, however," said Aesilesius.

"What is that?" asked Otto.

"Nika must be provided for," said Aesilesius. "She must be freed, given wealth, and placed safely somewhere, secretly."

"Do not be absurd," said Otto. "She is a slave."

"Even so," said Aesilesius.

"It is not practical," said Otto. "She is now part of your *per-*

sona, your nurse, governess, confidante, informant, toy, and play-mate. Were something to change, notice would be taken. Thoughts would soon spring from the soil of curiosity. Things must seem the same. Appearances must be maintained."

"I am to maintain the farce of imbecility?" asked Aesilesius.

"In public, of course," said Otto. "Do not let enemies suspect the truth. You are in quite enough danger, as it is."

"From you?" asked Aesilesius.

"If you like," said Otto.

"From Ingeld, the Drisriak?" asked Aesilesius.

"Certainly," said Otto. "You would constitute a most grievous impediment to his plans. I can think of nothing which might more thoroughly put them into disarray."

"Thank you," said Aesilesius, "for speaking to me of these things."

"I gave you words," said Otto. "I hoped that you would be capable of hearing them."

"I have heard them," said Aesilesius.

"Let your meaningless collar slut know nothing of these things," said Otto.

"Why?" asked Aesilesius.

"She is a slave," said Otto.

"Perhaps she may now return," said Aesilesius.

"Of course," said Otto. "In the meantime, I suspect that the guards in the hall were not displeased to look upon her. She is an attractive slave. I trust you have found her so."

"Yes," said Aesilesius. "I have found her so."

CHAPTER SIXTY-SIX

"How is it, if you have been sold before, more than once, three or four times, you know so little?" asked Teela. "If you are at a post, back to the post, facing forward, your hands braceleted behind you, about the post, as now, or examined in a cell, chained on a shelf, or such, in good daylight, or in adequate torchlight, there is much you can do, or try to do. To be sure, if the slaver catches you at it, and disapproves, you will much regret your indiscretion. If the buyer interests you, if you want him to buy you, show him that, in a thousand ways, with smiles, with tiny movements, with parted lips, with sighs, with pleading looks. But you must be subtle. If he thinks you are being forward, you may be called to the attention of the slaver, which will probably result in a whipping, or, if you are fortunate, simply being cuffed. He wants you to be appealing, to be beautiful, and desirable, but he wants there to be no doubt that the decision is his, and his alone. Read the buyer. Sometimes it is good to pretend indifference, even disdain, that he will be tempted to have you at his feet, broken, subdued, conquered, and tamed, mastered, pleading for his caresses. If the buyer offends, or repulses, you, you might feign inertness, aimlessness, distraction, or stupidity. Who would want a stupid slave? A plain woman who is intelligent is far more interesting, exciting, and desirable a slave than a more beautiful woman who is dull."

"I think I am intelligent," said Yana.

"What is most fearful," said Teela, "is the night auction, where you cannot well make out the buyers. It is much like voices shouting from a darkness. You are in the light; they are not. There you will perform, for most practical purposes, blindly. But be as desirable as you can, or you will feel the whip. Obviously the seller wants to make money on you. You might not even know who bought you until you are collected or delivered."

"I am afraid," said Yana.

"Here, at the post," said Teela, pulling a bit at the bracelets which confined her hands together, behind the post, "it is easier. Needless to say, other things being equal, one would like to have a Master who is well fixed. In such a house, the chores are likely to be lighter and the whip more likely to remain on its peg. So consider the apparent weight of his wallet, and hope he has not stuffed it with rocks or iron. Consider his carriage, his attitude, how he holds himself, his robes, his diction, and hope that such things are reliable indications of his background, station, and resources. Some men feign standing and background, assuming manners and robes misleading as to their station. Others may assume manners and garments beneath their station, to influence bargainings, to avoid envy and attention, or reduce the likelihood of finding themselves the target of cutpurses and thieves. Read the buyer, as best you can. And when in doubt, be beautiful, and hope for the best, hope for chains in which you will rejoice and thrive, and may even find love, for many men come to love, often despite themselves, the woman at their feet, a property which belongs to them, and them alone. They wish to own, and we wish to belong. They are master; we are slave."

"I understand," said Yana.

"Remember," said Teela, "we are not free women. We are slaves. We are nothing. We are to serve and obey, unquestioningly and instantly, and with perfection, and, as we are not free, we must be prepared to give our masters, at any moment, in any manner they wish, inordinate pleasure."

"I want to do that," said Yana. "I want to be a slave."

"It is what we want," said Teela. "We are women."

"But I am afraid," said Yana, pulling at her braceleted wrists, fastened together behind the post, "terribly afraid."

"Of course," said Teela. "We are collared. We are marked. We are slaves. We are vulnerable, and absolutely helpless."

Yana moaned.

"Be silent!" whispered Teela. "A man approaches!"

When lovely Yana, sitting on a red carpet in a strange room, first discovered herself, as though awakening from a dream, and found herself a stranger to herself, she had no idea where she was or how she had come there. She did not know who she was, or had been, but, from her lack of clothing, the brand on her thigh, and the collar on her neck, there was no doubt as to what she now was; she was a slave.

There was a jumble of discordant memories following the strange room, being chained with others, by an ankle or the neck, being herded about with switches, and occasionally feeling the sting of the same devices, the pans on the floor, learning to eat on all fours, the closed wagons, the ascending and descending, barefoot, of warmed, corrugated metal ramps, the unmarked ships roaring into the sky, being pressed against the metal flooring of the slave bin during their accelerations, the hosing down of the bins, the different slave camps, different spaceports, different ships, the holding stations, the being sorted into one lot or another, being vended in batches, learning to walk with shackled ankles, hoping not to be beaten, envying girls permitted tunics, and finally, outside some unknown town or city, on some world, being tied to a sales post.

To introduce some order and coherence into the narrative, the strange room with the red carpet was at Tinos Station, on Tinos, a world which now lay within the sphere of influence of the Aatii. Tinos was a rather obscure world, which lay outside major space lanes. Whereas the empire might regard Tinos as peripheral, at best, to its interests, she was, given her location, important commercially to six essentially independent worlds, namely, worlds unaligned with the Aatii and associated only nominally, if that, with the empire. On Tinos, at Tinos Station, Yana had been sold for two *darins* to agents of the slaving company, *Flowers of the Six Yellow Stars*. The word "Flowers" often, but not always, occurs in the names of companies dealing with slaves. There are hundreds of such companies in the empire. Two of the largest are *Bondage Flowers* and *The House of Worlds*. There was surely something unusual in the case of Yana. Her origins and background were obscure and her asking price, for some reason, was far beneath her obvious market value. She was clearly priced for a quick sale. It is little wonder then that the agents of the company in question purchased her promptly and asked few, if any, questions. Beyond that, Yana seems to have been involved in group, or batch, sales, rather than individual sales. Lots, so to speak, were conveyed amongst worlds, where they, or portions of their contents, were sold or exchanged. These lots were sometimes added to, and sometimes diminished. All this was largely, if not entirely, managed on a wholesale basis. Many buyers and investors did not concern themselves with the lots themselves, not even inspecting them, but rather with numbers, seasons, trends, and potential markets.

Speculation in slaves was rampant. Later, trades were also effected between various houses, large and small. Some houses would be likely to favor, and feel that they had a need for, at least at a given time, one sort of goods, or stock, over another. For example, although most slaves were female, it must be understood that not all females were human. Female slaves of many species would be marketed on one world or another. The males of most species tended to prefer, naturally, at least on the whole, female slaves of their own species. As nearly as this can be traced, Yana was, at one time or another, the property of several camps and, at least, four houses. Indeed, for a time, she may have been owned by *Bondage Flowers* and possibly even *The House of Worlds*. It was on Inez II, closer to the core of the empire, that it was decided that a lot of fifty slaves, amongst whom we find Yana, in response to a requisition, would be shipped to Inez IV, to be broken up and distributed amongst a variety of markets for individual sales. It was shortly thereafter that an untoward and unexpected event occurred. The transport *en route* to Inez IV, the *Turona*, on whose manifest appeared the lot in question, that including Yana, was overtaken by, and engaged by, a corsair. Although certain matters are not clear, it seems the *Turona* carried, as well as slaves, a quantity of copper and silver, and five cartridges, two for a Telnarian pistol and three for a Telnarian rifle. Given the general depletion of resources in the empire, and the desire on many worlds to disarm populations, so that they could be ruled, bled, and exploited with impunity, these cartridges were of great value, possibly bringing four or five *darins* of gold apiece in the black-market. That this information came into the cognizance of the corsair, this constituting an egregious breach of security, suggests the likely collusion of an informant. In any event, the corsair disabled the *Turona*, and, by means of magnetic, drilling lock ports, boarded her. Probably the slaves, in the hold, in slave bins, were not even aware of the pursuit, and had very little understanding, even later, of the crippling, the boarding, and such. Members of the crew of the *Turona*, commanded by masked corsairs, blindfolded or hooded the slaves, and tied their hands behind their backs. A string was then tied about the upper left arms of the slaves, constituting a light coffle tether, a "string coffle," following which the slaves were taken from their bins, conducted through corridors to a freight elevator, raised to the deck where the drill locks had forced their entry, and taken from the *Turona* into and through the corsair to improvised pens where they were decoffled, untied, and their blindfolds or hoods removed, by masked corsairs. These precautions were presumably instituted so that the slaves might not recognize unmasked corsairs in their march to the pens, or recognize the interior, the appointments, or any identifying details of the corsair itself. The men of the *Turona* then sealed off the penetrated deck of their ship, and the corsair disengaged. The *Turona* would limp back to Inez II. Given the scarcity of ships and the preciousness of fuel the corsairs may have wished to preserve the ship and its resources, if only to have it eventually available for carrying new, vulnerable loads. Too, the informant, if there was one, might have been on the *Turona*. In this way his cover would be preserved, and he might be once more of value to them. Some days later the corsair made landfall on some world, presumably at a prearranged point, and the slaves, once more bound, their hands again fastened behind their backs, once more string-coffled, the string again about the upper left arms, and either blindfolded or hooded, were led down a metal ramp to what they could tell, being barefoot, was a grassy field. There they were knelt. Shortly thereafter there was a great roar, and a blast of heat which made some of the slaves cry out with fear, and the ship departed. The slaves were then put in new collars, and the old collars, their shipping collars, were removed. In this way there was no moment in which they were not in at least one collar. The new collars were plain. They marked the girls well as slaves, but, unlike most collars, gave no indication of their masters. There was a smell of expended fuel in the air. They were then, as they knelt, fastened together by neck rings and chain. The coffle string was removed. Then the blindfolds and hoods were removed. "On your feet," they were told. They rose to their feet. It seemed to be early afternoon. There was a slight breeze. To one side they could see a circle of smoking, scorched grass. There were some tunicked men about, two of whom carried whips. Two slave girls then approached. Both were tunicked. How the stripped slaves envied them, for clothing, however demeaning, brief, shaming, and revealing, as is suitable for slaves, is desperately desired by slaves, save when they are alone with their masters, who commonly enjoy seeing them "slave naked" in their collars. One of the slaves, a sturdy slave, carried water, in a bucket, which she served to each slave with a dipper. The other slave, also sturdy, for large, strong, female slaves are often put in charge of smaller, lovelier, more feminine slaves, carried a basket of rolls. She thrust a roll into the mouth of each slave in the coffle. A bit later one of the men cracked his whip. The leather struck no one, but the coffle recoiled. Yana, bound and coffled, was dismayed. She had the sense that she once, somewhere, somehow, had been lashed with such a tool. She had no desire to feel it again. She would endeavor to obey impeccably, and be pleasing, in all ways, as a slave is to be pleasing. "Ho," called the man with the whip, "you curvaceous stock, you pretty, two-legged, meaningless cattle, you are on the way to market!" He then cracked the whip again. "Move," he said, "move!" He then cracked the whip once more, and the coffle stepped out, through the grass, the first step being taken, as is prescribed, with the left foot.

It is not known what became of the *Turona*'s silver and copper, or, at least for a time, the five cartridges, but it is reasonably clear what became of the slaves. As they were technically stolen goods, or contraband, and the statute of limitations on their recovery had not yet expired, they were disposed of discreetly, in small groups, in fairs, festivals, camps, and minor markets. Certainly major houses would be unlikely to risk dealing with them, at least while the statute of limitations was still in effect. Some were sold from itinerant, wheeled platforms and some, as you have doubtless surmised, informally, from slave posts at one crossroads or another. In a sense, they were disposed of in one black-market or another. Some worlds, and some areas, of course, are more tolerant of such dealings than others. It was even rumored that some magistrates, possibly for a consideration, welcomed such dealings in their districts.

Yana, frightened, turned her head away, and her body tightened and stiffened. How aware she was of the sun, the post, her nudity, her braceleted wrists, her helplessness. In the moment, Teela's counsel was lost, forgotten, flown away like a startled bird. She was aware that the small, rectangular placard which hung about her neck, on its thin leather cord, was lifted in the hand of a man, who was doubtless perusing it. She did not meet the man's eyes. A bold look, or even a direct look, into a man's eyes can be interpreted as a confrontation, a challenge, a defiance or insolence. Such an indiscretion usually occurs only in the case of a new slave, who may not yet understand fully that she is a slave, and only a slave. Such mistakes are seldom repeated. To be sure there are situations and relationships in which a direct eye contact between the master and slave is not only permitted, but welcomed and encouraged. Much depends, obviously, on the individual master and slave, and the nature of the eye contact.

"There is not much information here," said the man, releasing the placard. Yana felt it fall back, against her bosom.

"Forgive me, Master," she said.

"There is little here but a name and a caveat," he said, "warning a buyer of an absence of certain forms of memory."

"I have little recollection of my past," said Yana, "except for the last few days."

"I have heard of such cases," said the man. "One loses one's identity, who one is, where one lives, and such. It is commonly consequent on a blow, a fall, some emotional trauma, or such."

"Yes, Master," said Yana.

"Perhaps you will recover your memory," said the man.

"As I am a slave," said Yana, "it matters little."

"True," said the man. "Indeed, it is perhaps just as well, or better, that you do not regain your memory."

"Yes, Master," said Yana.

"It might make you easier to train," he said.

"Yes, Master," said Yana.

"It is not like a scar, a limp, a lost ear," said the man.

"No, Master," said Yana.

At that point the man turned away, to examine the girl at the next post.

When he had moved further down the line, Teela turned to her left, to regard Yana, somewhat reproachfully.

"I am sorry," said Yana. "I did not know what to do, how to act."

Then Teela turned away, and smiled.

"Here is a pretty one," said a fellow.

A little later, Teela gasped, and said, "Oh!"

"She is responsive," said the fellow.

Teela was shortly thereafter sold.

Another girl was brought out of the holding tent and braceleted at the post. In such situations, as a girl may be for hours at a post, she is braceleted, rather than thonged. Thonging is usually reserved for shorter confinements. Husbandmen, so to speak, tend to be watchful and careful of their stock. Bracelets are more secure than thongs, which anyone might untie or cut away. Also, bracelets, while confining the slave with perfection, are usually looser, and more comfortable, thus minimizing any risk of impairing circulation.

Yana backed against her post, feeling its roughness. The linkage of the bracelets made a tiny noise. Wagons and carts passed, moving down the larger, more trafficked, of two roads. It was parallel to this larger road that, back some feet, was the line of selling posts, twenty-two posts. Other traffic, including a number of pack merchants, single file, afoot, was traversing the smaller, intersecting road. She also noted a hoverer, some yards overhead, following the larger road. As it was permitted, she knelt at her post, her hands fastened behind it. She closed her eyes, and put her head down.

The sun passed meridian.

"Slave," said a male voice.

She struggled to her feet, that her placard be easily read.

When she felt the placard drop back against her breast, she looked to the side, to avoid possible eye contact.

"Can you read?" she was asked.

"I do not know," she said, frightened.

She was cuffed twice, sharply, and she felt blood at her lip.

"Anyone knows whether they can read or not," said the voice.

"I do not remember," she said. "I think I can read. I feel I can read."

She was then struck again, twice.

Many slaves, of course, cannot read. Presumably it would have been safer for Yana had she denied being able to read. That might easily have been believed. With most forms of memory loss, of course, basic skills, such as knowing a language, being able to read, and so on, are not affected. I think there is little doubt that Yana could read. She had not read, of course, since awakening in the room with the red carpet at Tinos Station. Her response was presumably motivated by the fear that if she were challenged to read, she might find the marks unintelligible. We do note that she thought she would be able to read, that she felt that she would be able to read. Much in her mind was confusion, still, and, to some extent, terror. Presumably it would be a frightening experience to awaken, a stranger to oneself, and learn that one is a slave.

The man turned away, annoyed, exasperated. "What an incredibly stupid slave," he muttered. There were tears in Yana's eyes. She did not think she was stupid. How can one help what one can remember, and not remember? She then ran her tongue over her cut lip, and tasted a bit of blood. She then knelt again, and closed her eyes, listening to the cries of passing birds, and the trundling of wagons and carts on the intersecting roads. She also heard the hum of another passing hoverer.

She did not even know, given the confusions, variations, and changes of the past few days, the different confinements, camps, ships, and routes, on which world she was.

She and the other slaves, toward the late afternoon, were watered and grueled. The watering slave took some strands of Yana's hair, moistened them, and wiped away the dried blood on her lips and chin. For that Yana was grateful. Slaves, as other women, tend to be sensitive with respect to their appearance.

Two hoverers passed by overhead, each following the larger road, but traveling in different directions.

Occasionally a hoverer, one which did not contain free women, would reduce its altitude and slow or poise its flight to examine the girls at the stakes, to inspect and review, so to speak, the proffered "stake meat." When this took place the slaver's men would often hail the hoverer and invite it to land. Three times hoverers did land, and Yana had seen two girls purchased, one from the tent and one from the stakes.

More wagons on the main road now were traveling in one direction, away to Yana's right. This suggested to her, given the time of day, that they might be in the vicinity of a town or, more likely, a city, as some municipalities restrict wagon traffic, particularly that of heavy wagons, to night hours. This reduces congestion. On the other hand, even in municipalities without such ordnances, many deliveries are at night, in order that the markets may be supplied before dawn.

Yana now sat at the stake, her hands braceleted behind it.

"Does a slave not kneel in the presence of a free man?" she was asked.

Yana, startled, struggled to a kneeling position, and put head down. She had not noted the man's approach.

"Up, girl," she was told.

Yana stood. Her placard, then, might be the more easily accessed. She kept her head down.

"Raise your head," she was told.

She raised her head, but avoided eye contact.

Her placard was read, and then, again, it dangled on its leather cord.

"You remember little?" she was asked.

"Very little," she said. "I am told I was embonded on Safa Major, and first sold, formally, placarded, in Carleton, on Inez II. I have also been told that I have had five Masters on three worlds."

"You were told?" he said.

"Yes, Master," she said. "I remember nothing of it."

"You had a fall?" he asked.

"Perhaps," she said. "I do not know."

"If you have had five Masters, on one world or three," he said, "it seems you were not satisfactory."

"I fear it must have been so," she said.

"Yet you are comely," he said, "and are nicely curved."

Yana put her head down.

Suddenly she cried out, and, as she twisted, frightened, helpless, trying to withdraw, felt the post roughly abrade her back.

Her body, stimulated, was suffused scarlet. Her body then, suddenly, reflexively, thrust itself forward, pleadingly. Her arms were straight behind her, held in place by the braceleting. Then, recovering herself, she pushed back, head down, against the post. "Forgive me, Master," she said.

"Do not be absurd," he said. "You are not a free woman. You are a slave. You are free to be the sexual creature you are. Indeed, you must be the sexual creature you are, and wholly, for you are a slave. Rejoice in your vitality. Understand your collar and love it. Revel in your sexuality. You are free to do so. You are not a free woman. You are a slave."

"Yes, Master," she whispered, head down.

"It seems to me," he said, "that you would be quite satisfactory."

She kept her head down.

When she looked up, he had gone.

Yana tried to understand her feelings. How was it that her body, seemingly of its own accord, had behaved as it had? She was confused and bewildered. Had it betrayed her, or revealed her? She had a profound sense then of what it might be to be a slave, to be submitted, owned, and mastered. "I am a slave," she thought. "It is my nature, and being. I do not want to be free. Let others be free, if they wish. I want to be a slave. It is what is right for me. I know that now. I want to serve, yield, and love. I am a slave. Why should I not live so, and be so? I want to live so, and be so. Why should I not be a slave? I want to be a slave. But, I am

vulnerable, and helpless. I cannot choose my master. I have nothing to say about who owns me!"

Then, again, braceleted to the post, she was frightened.

The evening was warm, a summer night on this world, and it
took some time for night to fall. Once again, Yana sat at the post.
Some four torches were set amongst the stakes. Traffic continued
to move on the large road, mostly moving to Yana's right. There
was little traffic on the intersecting road, save that which turned
at the larger, and that moved to Yana's right. Some of the wagons
bore lamps. To the side, two slaver's men conversed. As midnight
approached, the girls would be freed of the posts and chained in
the large tent. Yana had drifted off to sleep, when she woke, still
half asleep, hearing the hum of a hoverer in the night. She looked
up. She, rising and turning, detected it, after a bit, in the darkness, the poised, disklike shape, some forty feet in the air, behind
the line of stakes. Oddly, given the hour, it bore no lights. It descended, and landed behind the stakes, several yards away from
the road. She heard men talking, and then saw one of the slaver's
men lift a torch, and approach. He was followed by three men, two
large, and one small, the small one closely behind him.

Yana worked her way back about the post, so that she faced the
road. She then knelt, head down.

So, too, did the other girls, those near to her, to her left and
right.

But it was before Yana that the men stopped. She felt herself
illuminated in the torchlight.

"Raise your head, slave," said the slaver's man.

"She is still here," said one of the newcomers, one of the larger
men.

"Good," said the smaller man, rubbing his hands together in
satisfaction.

Yana dared to glance at the smaller man, and quickly moved
her head to the side, recoiling, shuddering. She had never seen a
man whose face wreaked so of deceit and corruption. Many are
the ugliest of men whose interior man is straight, fine, and strong,
and many are the handsome fellows whose smooth and clever
looks fail to reveal a dishonest or trustless heart, but Yana sensed
that the interior man of the smaller figure was well manifested in
the hideous configuration she feared to behold.

"It is she?" said the second of the two larger men.

"Indeed," said the smaller man.

"I thought it might be so, from the ship, this afternoon," said the second of the two larger men. "I thought you would wish to inquire into the matter."

"You did well," said the smaller man. Then he said to Yana, "Look at me."

Yana, shuddering, obeyed, then looked away, quickly.

"Do you know me?" he asked.

"No, Master," said Yana.

"You are sure?" he asked.

"Yes, Master," said Yana.

"Perhaps it is not she," said one of the two larger men.

"She is not bad looking," said one of the slaver's men. "Are you interested in her?"

"Possibly," said the smaller man.

"Stand, slave," said the slaver's man, "that your placard may be examined."

Yana rose to her feet, and backed against the post.

"We need not examine the placard," said the smaller man.

"No," said one of the two larger men, he who had just spoken. "Something is strange here. Read the placard."

The smaller man looked at him, angrily.

"He is a barbarian," Yana thought. "He cannot read."

"I will read it," said the larger man.

The slaver's man with the torch approached and lifted the placard, turning it a bit to the side, to make it easier for the larger man to read it, from where he stood. Yana looked to the side, to the right, away from the glare of the crackling torch. She could not look directly at it. She felt its heat on her bared skin. She then, naked, braceleted at the post, under the torchlight, listened while the contents of her placard were read aloud. This was the first time she had been apprised, with any specificity, of her placard's contents. Horses, pigs, slaves, and other goods, as is obvious, need not be informed as to how they are described or advertised. Such matters are the proper concern of sellers and buyers, of merchants and customers, not of goods.

"Ah, memory," said the smaller man.

"Perhaps it is not she," said the second of the two larger men.

"It is she," said the smaller man, rubbing his hands together.

"Slaves may resemble one another," said the second of the two larger men.

"It is she," repeated the smaller man, continuing to rub his hands together.

At this point, having emerged from the tent, and seeing the position of a torch at a post and the five men gathered there, the slaver himself approached.

"Have we interest in a slave here?" he asked.

"Possibly," said the smaller man.

"This one," said the slaver, "is one of my best."

"Doubtless," said the smaller man.

"As the hour is late, and we may seek a new location tomorrow," said the slaver, "I am willing to let you have her at a bargain price."

"That is generous," said the smaller man.

"Sixty *darins*," said the slaver.

Yana was startled, for she knew her market value, in a minor market, in a roadside market, indeed, one dealing with suspect slaves, possibly stolen slaves, who had doubtless been acquired at very low prices, would be expected to be closer to eight to ten *darins*. In such matters, buyers, as well as sellers, were shrewd. Indeed, Teela, whom she thought was quite beautiful, had sold for only fifteen *darins*. Too, she was not trained, could not play a musical instrument, and knew only one language. She had little to commend her, save what could be seen at the post. Too, there was the problem of the loss of so much personal memory. She was not even sure she could read.

"Too high?" asked the slaver.

"Perhaps, a bit," said the smaller man.

"I could not let her go for less than fifty-five *darins*," said the slaver, regretfully.

"This is a roadside market," said the smaller man. "I doubt that you are renting space. I suspect that you have little, or no, overhead. I doubt that you have much more than a tent, a wagon, and some posts. In such a market, one expects bargains."

"You are obviously a master bargainer," said the slaver. "I fear I am outdone. How can a poor, struggling merchant cope with one who negotiates so fiercely? Fifty-four *darins*."

"May I make a counter-proposal?" asked the smaller man.

"Of course," said the slaver.

"I suggest you give her to us, for nothing," said the smaller man.

"You are mad," said the slaver.

"Not at all," said the smaller man.

"I do not understand," said the slaver.

"This is a stolen slave," said the smaller man.

"I do not deal in stolen slaves," said the slaver.

"Where are her papers?" asked the smaller man.

"Many slaves have no papers," said the slaver, angrily.

"Perhaps she is not a stolen slave," said the smaller man, "but she may be a stolen slave."

"So might be any slave without papers, and many with papers, forged papers," said the slaver.

"Your innocence will doubtless be established following the hearing," said the smaller man.

"What hearing?" asked the slaver, warily.

"That to be called for by an appropriate administrator," said the smaller man. "I am sure you have nothing to fear. I am sure that many of these slaves, if not this one, are fully aware of whether or not they have been stolen. And we shall suppose, in your favor, that none have been stolen. But, still, their testimony would be routinely required. Too, as you doubtless know, the testimony of slaves is taken under torture. This procedure guarantees that the slave will speak the truth, or, at least, agree quickly with whatever is suggested to them as the truth."

"What do you want?" asked the slaver.

"Not your stock," said the smaller man, "only this slave."

"She is yours," said the slaver.

Yana cried out, in misery, then put her head down, shuddering.

"Bring chains, from the hoverer," said the smaller man to one of his two companions. He then turned to the slaver. "When her ankles are shackled, free her of the bracelets. We will then complete her chaining."

In a short time, Yana's ankles were shackled while she stood at the post. The shackling was adjusted so that her ankles were confined within six inches of one another. A new collar was then placed on her neck and the simple, plain collar removed. Her bracelets were then removed and one of the two larger men, he who seemed the lesser in status, looped the belly chain about her waist, with its two attached wrist rings. She then stood by the post, illuminated in the torchlight, her ankles shackled, her waist snugly encircled by the belly chain, her hands confined before her body, closely.

"Excellent," said the smaller man.

"We shall withdraw," said the slaver, now flanked by his two men, one bearing the torch.

"You acknowledge, do you not," asked the smaller man, "that I have had the best of this business?"

"Quite so," said the slaver.

"Then," said the smaller man, "I choose to buy this slave at my own price, five *darins*."

"I thought you wanted her for nothing," said the slaver.

"How could you think that of me?" asked the smaller man. "Do I seem one who would take advantage of an honest man? No. Certainly not. I want this to be wholly legal. There must be no question about it. I wish to own her, with a perfectly clear title."

"Five *darins* is not much," said the slaver.

"I think it is an exquisite, delicious price for her," said the smaller man. "Let her remember she was sold for only five *darins*."

"Accepted," said the slaver.

"Pay him," said the smaller man, handing his purse to the first of the two larger men, he who seemed higher in status.

"Kneel, head to the grass," said the smaller man to the slave.

Yana remained in this position while the coins were counted out and the purse returned to the smaller man.

To the other of the two larger men, the smaller man said, "Go to the hoverer, turn on the beam light, and bring a slave whip."

Yana trembled.

In a few moments the beam light shone forth from the hoverer, across the grass, to the stakes.

"Let me assist you to your feet," said the smaller man to Yana, and lifted her, politely, to her feet, so that she faced the hoverer. She was unsteady for the close chaining of her ankles. The smaller man then stood near her, to the side, and held out his hand, into which one of the two larger men, he of seemingly lesser status, placed the slave whip.

Yana then stood in the grass, facing the hoverer, shackled, wrists held close to her body, fastened to the belly chain, illuminated in the beam light.

The smaller man then walked a few feet ahead of Yana, and stood before her. She could not then see his features, for the light was behind him. It was a darkness, an ominous darkness, silhouetted by the light. She, however, was well illuminated.

"Stand well," said one of the two larger men, he who seemed of the higher status.

Yana recalled that slaves, as they were not free women, were to be lovely and graceful. How had she forgotten that? Soon such

things would be part of her being, without thought, uncon-
sciously and naturally.

"Excellent," said the smaller man.

Yana knew herself savored, as a slave is savored.

The smaller man then returned to stand near her, the whip in
his hand.

"Regard me," he said.

"Yes, Master," whispered Yana.

"You do not know me, do you?" he asked.

"No, Master," said Yana.

"Have you never seen me before, in your life?" he asked.

"I do not think so, Master," said Yana.

"I have heard of such things," said one of the larger men, he
who seemed of highest status. "It is done by a drug. I think I
know the drug."

"And there is an antidote, I trust," said the smaller man.

"Yes," said the larger man.

"Excellent," said the smaller man. He then, having changed
his position, spoke from behind Yana. "Slave," he said.

"Yes, Master," she said.

She dared not turn, unpermitted, to face him.

"It is late and we must be on our way," he said. "We have dallied long enough. You see the hoverer before you, some twenty
yards away. Hurry to it. Run!"

"I am shackled, Master!" wept Yana.

"Run!" said the smaller man. "Run!"

The lash then struck her, and Yana cried out in misery, and
tried to move toward the hoverer, but almost instantly, thrown
by the shackling, her ankles fastened so closely together, tumbled
to the grass. The whip then struck her again, and she struggled
to rise, but fell, again. "Disobedient slave," snarled the smaller
man. "Mercy Master!" she wept. She tried to rise yet again, but
fell again. She was again struck. Then, unable to regain her feet,
she was struck, again and again. She twisted in the grass under
the rain of blows showered on her body, and she then, sobbing,
helpless, stopped struggling, drew up her legs, and made herself
as small as possible. She then lay there, under the blows, until
they suddenly stopped.

One of the two larger men, he of possibly greater status, had
stayed the hand of the smaller man. "It is enough," he said. "Are
you mad? She strove to be pleasing. Do you wish to destroy her

market value? Would you maim or blind her? Do you wish to kill her?"

"No," said the smaller man, breathing heavily, gasping for breath. "Of what use is a dead dog, or a dead slave?"

He then crouched down by the huddled, beaten figure. "Do you begin to sense now, my dear," he asked, "what it will be, to be my slave."

The slave nodded, weakly, miserably, her shuddering body afire, unable to speak.

"And remember, my dear," he said, "that you were purchased for only five *darins*."

"Have you a reason for treating her so, for hating her so?" asked one of the two larger men, he of seemingly higher status.

"Perhaps," said the smaller man. Then he turned to the second of the two larger men, he of possibly lower status. "My dear Grissus," he said, "may I trouble you to stir and warm the engine of our humble craft?"

The man turned about and strode toward the hoverer.

"And you, my dear Buthar," said the smaller man, "may I prevail upon you to carry this worthless cargo of collar meat to the ship?"

The fellow addressed then lifted up the slave, went to the hoverer, which was now humming, and put her on the metal grating.

Shortly thereafter the smaller man joined the other two aboard the small craft. While the engine was warming, he rearranged the belly chain and wrist rings on the slave in such a way that her hands were confined behind her back. He then took a small thong and, by means of it, tying it about both the linkage of her shackling and the chaining at her wrist rings, drew her ankles up behind her, fastening them, in effect, to her wrists.

He then picked up a tarpaulin, and bent down to the slave, his lips close to her ear. "Would you like to know where you are?" he asked.

"Yes, Master," she said.

"You are on Telnaria," he said, "near Telnar."

"I have heard of these places," she said.

"Would you like to know the name of your Master?" he asked.

"If it pleases Master to tell me," she said, in pain.

"You are fortunate to belong to so important a man," he said.

"Yes, Master," she whispered.

"I am an Otung," he said. "My name is Urta."

"Yes, Master," she said.

"Does that name mean anything to you?" he asked.

"No, Master," she said.

"It will," he said, and covered her, completely, with the tarpaulin, which he buckled down at the edges, to recessed deck rings.

Shortly thereafter the hoverer, as the men held to the railings, rose into the air, leaving the stakes and torches behind.

CHAPTER SIXTY-SEVEN

"Hold," said Otto, noting Nika scurrying down the corridor, toward the chamber of Aesilesius, her wrists braceleted before her. Her white tunic came to slightly above her knees. Perhaps her Master did not wish too great an extent of her to be exposed to the casual view of others. Was he so jealous of her? Did he not relish a Master's pleasure in displaying one's slave, so that others can realize how fortunate he is to own so lovely an animal?

Nika immediately knelt, having been addressed by a free person.

"You seem eager to return to your Master," said Otto.

"Yes, Master," she said.

A contented, loving slave commonly longs for the attention, presence, and touch of her Master. She is his slave.

"You have been in the city," said Otto.

"Yes, Master," she said.

"I gather that your haste betokens more than a slave's simple desire to return to her Master's feet," said Otto.

"I fear so," she said.

"How go things in the city," he asked.

"Surely you have informants, and spies, and doubtless many," she said. "My Master has only me. I hurry to report to him."

"Report to me first," said Otto.

"I am afraid," she said. "Things stir, the day seethes, unrest is rampant, furtive looks abound. Sticks are being sharpened, axes are being brought in from fields, who knows what is concealed beneath cloaks? Some shops are shuttered, wagons leave the city. Peasants bring less produce to the markets. Special services are being held in the temples. Ministrants march in processions, chanting and ringing bells, bearing images of burning racks and carrying pots of smoking incense. There is much talk of the infamy and tyranny of the usurper, Ottonius, the First, and of the infant emperor, born on Tenguthaxichai, and of the noble and heroic Ingeld, the benevolent Drisriak, friend to the empire, father of the child."

"You may return to your Master," said Otto.

"Thank you, Master," she said, leaping up and speeding down the corridor.

CHAPTER SIXTY-EIGHT

Yana looked up, frightened, from her knees, at her Master, an Otung named Urta.

"You are going to drink this," he said, holding a goblet before her, half filled with a warm, foaming liquid, the chemical result of pouring a cheap wine over a mysterious white powder.

Yana regarded the goblet, with the foaming contents.

"I am generous," he said. "I permit you wine."

Yana knelt on the tiles. She was naked. Her Master saw no reason to grant her clothing. Her ankles were shackled, allowing her some eighteen inches of play. In this way, she could walk but not run. Her wrists were chained together with a separation of a foot. About her neck was a "number collar." Such a collar does not directly reveal, as would most collars, the slave's owner. The number correlates with a matching number, given the collar, in one of the city's slave registries. An anonymous collar, so to speak, is often favored by a master who, for one reason or another, does not wish to be publicly identified, at least not without research. To further conceal his identity, the collar was registered under an assumed name.

"You are pretty for a five-*darin* girl," said Urta.

Yana wondered if this were still true.

She was exhausted, and her body ached. She had sweated much, and had not been washed. Her hair was straggly and unkempt. She had worked hard during the day, briefly tunicked and unchained, carrying water, the paired buckets suspended from a yoke, filling street troughs at which dogs, horses, and slaves might drink, and cisterns and reservoirs on various levels of nearby tenements. She was also familiar with char work in public buildings, and, in various private domiciles, with that task and others, such as laundering and polishing. Urta rented her out, for a penny here and a penny there, as he pleased. He rented her out cheaply, so he had many offers for her services. It seemed he was less interested in making money on her than in seeing to it that she was put to tasks which, if she were a free woman, would have been regarded as arduous, lengthy, humiliating, shameful, and degrading. He himself seemed to have some source of income which far transcended the collection of pennies reaped from a slave's labor. The source of this income was not evident.

Urta slowly swirled the contents of the goblet before the kneeling, chained slave. The surface of the liquid still roiled.

Yana, worn and weary, unwashed, her hair neither brushed nor combed, her body in pain, regarded the goblet, apprehensively.

"Tomorrow," said Urta, "is a special day, a day of which a grateful history will gladly take note. Things will change. A throne will change hands. An empire will be born anew. An official faith, to be promulgated by love, and fire and sword, as absurd as it is, will be imposed upon a thousand worlds. I will have access to the coffers of a palace. I will be recognized and promoted to high office. This is a day for celebration, and I want you, poor, simple Yana, with your truncated memory, to appreciate it fully."

"I am a simple slave, Master," she said. "I know nothing of politics and worlds. What do I know other than work, the chain, and the whip?"

"Your anguish, my dear," he said, "has been largely physical, the miseries of an ill-treated, despised, abused work slave."

"Master has made me suffer much," she said.

"Not enough," he said, "for you do not truly understand who you were, what you have lost, what has been done to you, and who has done it to you."

"How strangely Master speaks," she said. "I was a simple town or village girl, taken in a town or village war, on Safa Major. I changed hands several times. I was first officially placarded in Carleton on Inez II. I have had three masters on two worlds."

"Lies," said Urta, "told to you to obscure your origins, to give you a sense of self."

"I am a simple slave," she said, "only that, no more. Please do not torture me further. If you would make me grievously suffer, use, as is your wont, the whip of leather, terrible as it is, not one of uncertainty, confusion, anxiety, and fear. That is too cruel."

"You do not yet know what cruelty is," he said.

She looked at him, comprehending nothing.

He held the goblet toward her. "Drink this," he said.

"Yes, Master," she said, taking the goblet in two hands.

She looked into the liquid, which still seemed alive, coldly boiling in the cup.

"Do not be afraid," he said, "—not now."

She lifted the goblet to her lips, put back her head, and, slowly, drained the goblet. She then looked at Urta, puzzled.

"Master?" she said.

"Did you enjoy the beverage?" he asked.

"I tasted the wine," she said, "little else."

"My vengeance," he said, "will shortly be complete."

"I do not understand," she said.

He then took the goblet back, and placed it on the floor beside his chair, a simple curule chair.

He watched the slave intently for a time.

The body of the slave then wavered. She shut her eyes, tightly. There was a sound of chain. She put her hands, palms down, on the floor, that she not fall. Then she lowered herself to the tiles, slowly. It seemed then she lost consciousness, lying at the feet of her Master.

Urta was patient. He waited; he rubbed his hands together; he listened to the sounds outside the tenement apartment, carts passing, the click of shod hooves on the pavement, voices, the cries of children, unaware of the morrow, the sounds of birds; he sung Otung songs to himself, and one he remembered from secret meetings in a Herul camp, that of the Herd of Chuluun, east of the Lothar, on Tangara.

Yana made a small noise, and sought to stretch her limbs, but she could move her wrists and ankles only to the extent permitted by her chains. Her eyes opened, suddenly, startled, widely. "I am chained!" she said. "Where am I? Why am I chained? What has happened? How can this be done to me on Tenguthaxichai? Where are my slaves? I find myself unclothed, as though I might be a slave myself! Is this a dream, some madness! It seems so real!"

"It is real, slave slut," said Urta.

"You!" she cried. "You, in my madness, my dream?"

"You are not mad, nor are you dreaming, shapely pig," said Urta.

She sprang to her feet, naked, in her chains, furious, enraged.

"Remove these chains," she cried. "Take them off!"

"Chains become beautiful slaves," he said.

"Cover me!" she cried. "Bring me clothing!"

"Slaves are beasts, and they, as you know, need not be clothed, unless the Master pleases," said Urta.

"I am not a slave!" she cried.

"Who do you think you are?" asked Urta.

"Viviana," she cried, looking down upon him, where he sat in the simple curule chair, "sister of the emperor, Aesilesius, daughter of Atalana, the empress mother, spouse of Ingeld, prince of the Drisriaks!"

"Viviana," said Urta, looking up, "died in childbirth, and her offspring, tomorrow or the next day, will be recognized as the heir to the throne of Telnaria."

"I have borne no child!" said Viviana.

"Records and testimony," said Urta, "will say otherwise."

"*Filch*! *Filch*!" she cried.

"Beware," he said.

"I know you!" she cried.

"I hoped you would," he said.

"You are Urta, the Otung, who brought poison to Tenguthaxichai!"

"And one whom you did not treat well," he said.

"I demand to see Abrogastes!" said Yana.

"You are no longer on Tenguthaxichai," said Urta, "and Abrogastes believes the reports."

"Where am I?" asked Yana.

"In Telnar," said Urta.

"Take me to the palace!" demanded Yana.

"On what grounds would one take a low slave to such a place?" asked Urta.

"Where is Ingeld, prince of the Drisriaks, my husband and lord?" asked Yana.

"You do not have a husband and lord," said Urta. "You are a slave, and have only a Master, and I am he."

"No, no!" she cried, recoiling in horror. "I must not belong to you! I cannot belong to you!"

"But you do," he said, pleasantly.

"Where is Ingeld?" she said.

"In Telnar," said Urta.

"Contact him," she said.

"What interest might a prince of the Drisriaks have in a lowly slave?" he asked.

"Contact him," she said.

"I think that would be unwise," said Urta. "Viviana of Telnaria supposedly died in childbirth. Indeed, I am surprised that you were not succinctly done away with. Would that not have been politically judicious? Would it not be embarrassing if you were now to appear? Your life would not be worth the penny I have been renting you out for. I suspect that Ingeld did not wish to waste a slave, and, in consequence, disposed of you, presumably in a far location, and did not expect to see you again."

"Surely not!" she said.

"Surely so," said he.

"I am free," she said.

"You are mistaken," he said. "Feel your neck."

She lifted her chained hands. "I am collared!" she said.

"Appropriately so," he said.

"I, collared?" she said, disbelievingly.

"You did not even notice, did you?" he said. "But have no fear. It is locked on your neck."

"Remove it, immediately!" she said.

"I am sorry," he said. "Law prescribes collars for slaves."

"I am not a slave!" she said.

"Consider your left thigh," he said.

"No, no!" she cried, in disbelief and dismay.

"The Slave Rose," he said, "nicely incised in your lovely thigh."

"I cannot be a slave!" she cried.

"You are suitably branded and collared," he said. "All is fully legal, pretty slave."

"No, no, no," she wept.

"I note you are standing," he said.

She sank to her knees.

He then rose from the simple curule chair, and went to a sideboard, from which he removed an implement, a slave whip.

"I have many scores to settle with you, slut," he said.

"Please do not whip me," she said.

"Have you not forgotten something?" he asked.

"Please do not whip me—*Master*," she said.

He resumed his seat, the whip in hand.

"As you learn your collar," he said, "which you must do quickly, thoroughly, and perfectly, that word, 'Master', so difficult to you now, will come more easily to you, and, soon, even in your own mind, it will be addressed appropriately, rightly, and naturally, to all free men."

"Yes Master," she whispered, her eyes wide, and frightened.

"As Viviana of Telnaria reputedly died in childbirth," said Urta, "should you be so unwise as to proclaim yourself Viviana of Telnaria, you would be dismissed as an insane slave. Too, should you come to the attention of certain parties, you would be done away with quickly, and quietly. Do you understand?"

"Yes, Master," she said.

"Have you the memories of Yana, the slave?" he asked.

"No," she said. "I remember Tenguthaxichai, and awakening here."

"The name 'Yana' will do for now," he said. "We can always change it later."

"Yes, Master," she said.

It might be observed, in passing, that many slaves, from time to time, may have different names. As is the case with other pets and beasts, their names are at the discretion of their Masters.

"Whereas," he said, "you do not now have the memories of the interlude between Tenguthaxichai and your coming to consciousness here, after imbibing the drink I proffered to you, that will change."

"I do not understand," she said.

"Let me explain the whole," he said. "There is a drug which produces a loss of many personal memories. It produces effects which sometimes occur following an injury or a psychological trauma. You can well imagine the value of such a drug in certain hands, for certain purposes, for example, expunging the recollections of a crucial witness, wiping away the memory of a crime or transaction, benignly incapacitating a rival or foe, and so on. I was recently apprised of the likelihood that you had been subjected to this drug, and that an antidote existed. Accordingly, supposing you had indeed been administered the drug, I obtained the antidote and administered it to you. It was in the wine you drank. My supposition turned out to be correct, and, by means of the antidote, I counteracted the effects of the original drug, restoring your memory."

"Yes, Master," she whispered.

"Then," said he, "your memories of the interlude between Tenguthaxichai and few minutes ago were lost."

"Yes, Master," she whispered.

"But that, as I mentioned," he said, "will change."

"I remember nothing of that time," she said.

"I inquired into the matter," he said. "It takes time, usually a few hours after the antidote is administered, for the mind to readjust. Then the interlude memories, so to speak, will come back. You will then remember both your former memories, which were blocked from consciousness by the drug, and your inter- lude memories, as well, which were temporarily rejected, as they seemed incompatible with your former memories."

"A part of my life was lost," she said.

"Not irrevocably," he said.

"There was a red carpet, in a strange room, two men," she said.

"Anything else?" he asked.

"No, Master," she said.

"It is a beginning," he said.

"Yes, Master," she said.

"Do you remember being brought to the stakes, the road, the hoverer, such things?"

"No, Master," she said.

"Still," said he, "you have made a beginning."

"I am afraid," she said, "to recognize what was done to me, what I did, how I was."

"The memories will come back to you," he said, "whether you wish them to or not. Perhaps now you will be horrified and of- fended, but you should not be. As a slave you were a slave, and behaved as a slave. What choice had you? In bondage a woman learns what she is, and wants to be. She is forced to face needs in herself which she may have fought for years to deny and suppress. Collared, she is liberated; collared, she is free to be the truest, deepest, and most female of women, the slave. In the collar she learns herself, finds herself, and becomes herself."

"I dare not think such thoughts," she said.

"I do not now wish you to do so," he said. "I prefer that you think back now on what you were."

"Master?" she said.

"Think back," he said. "Remember yourself as you were. Re- member how you were so fine, so superior, so lofty, in your rich, costly gowns and jewels, so far above others, not merely the *hu- miliori*, but even the high *honestori*, you, of noble blood, indeed, the sister of an emperor, how you were so imperious, so proud, so vain, so petty, so shallow, so spoiled, so securely ensconced in your status and station."

"Please be kind," she said.

"Now look at you," he said. "She who was Viviana of Telnaria is now a common slave, filthy and unkempt, collared, branded, naked and chained, the helpless property of a man she dared once look down upon and despise."

"Please do not whip me, Master," she said.

"On your belly, slut," he said.

She who had once been Viviana of Telnar went to her belly on the tiles before her Master.

"Now you are where you belong," he said.

"Yes, Master," she said.

"Behold," he said, "how merciful I am. I cast aside the slave whip."

"Thank you, Master," she breathed.

"Now," he said, "get up, on all fours, and, head down, fetch it. Pick it up in your teeth and bring it back to me."

"Please, no," she said.

"Now," he said.

In a bit, Yana, on all fours, lifted the whip, held between her teeth, to Urta.

He took the whip, and stood up. She remained on all fours, as she had not been permitted to break position.

She looked up at him, miserable.

"Now," he said, "kneel before me, with your head to the floor."

She assumed this position, with the palms of her hands on the floor.

"You may now," he said, "beg to be whipped."

"Surely not!" she said.

"Beg," he said.

"Do not whip me," she begged.

"Beg to be whipped," he said.

"I beg to be whipped," she whispered.

"If you wish it," he said.

"I do not wish it, Master," she said.

"But you begged," he said.

"What if I had not begged?" she asked.

"Then," said he, "you would have disobeyed a command, for which I, being a kindly Master, would let you off, this time, with no more than a sound whipping."

"But," she said, "I must beg or not beg!"

"And thus," he said, "you have made your choice, to be whipped or whipped."

The slave trembled, moaned, and kept her head to the floor.

"Before I generously accede to your request to be whipped," he said. "I shall explain something to you. As Yana was used as the lowest and most negligible of work slaves, despised, frequently beaten, and rented for pennies, so, too, will be you, only now, Yana anew, you will have the memories of your former existence, as Viviana of Telnaria. I think you can guess at the pleasure that this will give me. Your misery, physical and psychological, realizing what has been done to you and who has done it to you, all this contrasting your former state with your present state, should be consistently and keenly felt, particularly when you appreciate the deliciousness of my vengeance, given your former pride, disdain, and effrontery."

"Please do not whip me, Master," she said.

"You will be pleased to learn that you will have tomorrow to rest, for I think tomorrow would be a good day to remain indoors. The streets may be dangerous. After you have had your well-deserved session with the whistling leather, to be shortly delivered, you will be chained by the neck to a floor ring. The reason for this is that when your memories as the slave, Yana, return, as they should by morning, you will recall certain things I said to you, pertaining to thrones and empires, these things said before you drank the antidote. Recalling such things, with your present consciousness of the former Viviana of Telnaria, might tempt you to do foolish things, like rushing into the streets and, at all hazards, attempting to reach the palace before dawn."

"I do not understand," she said.

"Of course not," he said, "not now."

He then rose to his feet, the whip in hand.

"Please do not whip me, Master," she said.

"Remember how you treated me badly," he said.

"Forgive me, Master," she begged.

"The former Viviana of Telnaria," he said, "now at my mercy, my slave. Excellent."

The slave trembled, and wept.

She was then beaten.

CHAPTER SIXTY-NINE

"It has begun!" cried Fulvius.

"It should not begin before noon," said Sidonicus, blinking, and sitting up amongst the heaped cushions on the broad couch in the private chambers of the exarchical palace.

Bells could be heard throughout the city and distant shouts.

"The signal is premature," said Fulvius.

"Impatient fools," said Sidonicus. "They cannot wait, so eager they are for blood and treasure."

"Garb yourself, your blessedness!" said Fulvius. "Hurry into the streets. Lead the resisters of tyranny! Inspirit them!"

"Do not be foolish, beloved deputy exarch," said Sidonicus. "It will be dangerous in the streets. After attiring myself, and enjoying breakfast, breaking my fast with the exarchical chocolate, I will march solemnly to the temple and do my part for the revolution, praying for its success. That is the appropriate role for a holy man."

"Indeed," said Fulvius. "Why court martyrdom?"

"Martyrdom is for others," said Sidonicus, "for the simple and the blind, for the zealous and deluded, for our implements and tools, those we have taught to believe our contrived nonsense."

"Many thousands take the faith, honestly and deeply, profoundly, with great seriousness," said Fulvius.

"Of course," said Sidonicus. "Fortunately for us, simple souls are abundant."

"They are prepared to die for it," said Fulvius.

"Excellent," said Sidonicus.

"Expecting their *koos* to flutter off, up to the table of *Karch*," said Fulvius.

"Happily, as they will be dead," said Sidonicus, "they will never experience the least disappointment in the matter."

"Could you not at least make a public appearance," said Fulvius, "locate the fore, rush to it, cry "Follow me!" and then step discreetly aside?"

"My place is in the temple," said Sidonicus. "I authorize you, if you wish, to carry a golden image of the burning rack bravely into the streets."

"I do not understand how the bells have rung early," said Fulvius.

"Perhaps the signal was betrayed," said Sidonicus.

"Some knew the signal and the day," said Fulvius. "But few knew the hour."

"Eagerness," said Sidonicus. "A premature act, a hungering to begin the festival of destruction."

"We are not utilizing soldiers, equipped and trained, with an accepted chain of command," said Fulvius. "It is not certain how things will turn out, what will occur. There is always danger implicit in the unleashing of crowds."

"Who can stop the wind?" said Sidonicus. "It blows as it will. It is not easy to divert the flood, quench the raging conflagration, convince trembling, opening, breaking, heaving ground to lie still."

"And what if the storm destroys those who have called it into being?" asked Fulvius.

"Do not fear," said Sidonicus. "Those who have called the storm into being are wise enough to shelter themselves from it. After the storm is done, they will emerge, interpret the ruins, pronounce on their meaning, and arrange a new reality."

"Where is Ingeld?" asked Fulvius.

"In a place of safety, I trust," said Sidonicus.

"He is to be part of the new reality?" asked Fulvius.

"Of course," said Sidonicus, "he and the putative child of poor Viviana, who, supposedly, perished in his delivery."

"I trust she was done away with," said Fulvius.

"Ingeld will have seen to it," said Sidonicus.

"Good," said Fulvius.

CHAPTER SEVENTY

"It has begun," said Urta, stepping back from the narrow window in his tenement domicile, looking down into the street. Men were rushing about, below. "Hear the bells. But it seems early."

"Please release me, Master!" begged Yana, lying on her side, her neck fastened closely to a floor ring."

"Be silent," said Urta, turning about. "I have heard enough of your inane whining and begging, after midnight and early this morning. If I must tie your hands behind you and gag you, I will do so."

After her beating the preceding evening, Urta had fastened her to the floor ring, and then removed her wrist and ankle chains. It was his practice keep her so at night, on the floor, on her thin scrap of a blanket, though commonly he had permitted her somewhat more slack in her neck chain. He had shortened the chain, so that it now held her head closer to the floor, that after she had learned that she was the former Viviana of Telnaria. In this way she was further instructed in her slavery. She had pulled the small scrap of a blanket about her. It was somewhat about midnight when Yana had awakened with a scream of misery, as a thousand memories had suddenly flooded back to her, irresistibly, harrowingly, washing about her, of the time between the room with the red carpet and the drinking of the wine-diluted, foaming contents of a goblet proffered to her by her Master, Urta, the Otung. Among these memories were those in which Urta had alluded to thrones and empires. She had jerked futilely at the chain which held her to the floor ring. Allusions which last night had been meaningless or incomprehensible to Yana, the slave, had been alarmingly, excruciatingly meaningful to the former Viviana of Telnaria. "Please, Master," she had begged. "Release me! Let me run naked through the streets, if you wish to deny me the kindness of a tunic, or rag. Let me attempt to reach the palace! Let me attempt to warn the palace of the impending rising! Perhaps my brother, poor, helpless Aesilesius, and my dear mother could be sped to safety! Let me warn the palace, lest all perish in some wild, mad, misbegotten insurgency. Please, please, Master!"

"Be silent, and sleep," had snarled Urta, "lest I treat you to an entertaining lullaby of leather."

Later that night in the very early hours, she had pleaded once more with him, but this time she had received two peremptory strokes of the whip, after which she had remained silent, red-eyed, clutching the chain which held her head down, to the floor ring.

Urta mixed some water with meal in a pan and put it on the floor next to Yana. "As before?" she asked her Master. "Of course," he said. As she now had the memories extending from the room with the red carpet to those of imbibing from the goblet of yesterday's evening with its foaming contents, she went to her knees, her head down, close to the floor ring, and, the palms of her hands down on the floor, fed from the pan.

Urta then went back to the window, to look down into the street.

It did not take Yana long to finish the gruel as there was little of it. Urta was sparing of the gruel. Such parsimony was common in the feeding of female slaves. Whereas most female slaves are well-nourished, for one wishes one's animals to be well fed and healthy, they are seldom overfed. In this way the Master assures himself of an attractive, well-figured beast. An obvious concomitant virtue of this practice is that less money needs be spent on slave feed.

"May I be told what is occurring?" asked Yana.

"No," he said.

Suddenly Urta jerked back from the window, and, almost at the same time, a rock struck the side of the window, gouging the wood. Yana screamed.

A bit later Urta returned, warily, to the window.

Lying on the floor, Yana had drawn the small blanket about her.

The bells were still ringing.

"Master," said Yana. "I smell smoke!"

"It is elsewhere in the city," said Urta. "It is carried by the wind."

"Fires can spread," said Yana.

Her apprehension was not ill-founded. Within the last year a terrible fire had ravaged several sections of Telnar. Estimates var-

ied, but it seemed clear that at least a fifteenth of the city might
have been destroyed. The fire had supposedly begun in an Illusionist Temple, one of the several sects or versions, or views,
within Floonianism, one not to be confused with that of Sidonicus, the exarch of Telnar, which maintained the identical-but-
different view of the nature of Floon.

"The city is not to be destroyed," said Urta. "Certainly not the
entire city. That is no part of the plan. The city, seat of the empire,
is the prize. Of what value are ashes, cinders, and charred wood?"

"Fire, Master," said Yana, "seldom acknowledges the plans of
others, seldom responds to instructions."

"It must not get out of hand," said Urta.

"It is heedless and voracious," said Yana. "If it had its way it
would burn forever."

Urta turned about, angrily, went to the prone Yana, and jerked
away her small blanket. He then, with a long thong, looping it
several times about her ankles, tied them together, tightly. He
then relieved her of the neck chain, so that she would no longer
be chained in place. He turned her and drew her up to a sitting
position. "Sit there," he said, "and do not touch the thonging on
your ankles. If the fire approaches I will free your ankles and you
will accompany me to safety."

"A slave is grateful to her Master," she said.

"You might prove of value," he said.

This form of tying is not that unusual. As long as her ankles
are tied, she is, in effect, kept in place. This also frees her hands,
so that she may do handwork, groom herself, feed herself, and so
on. Needless to say, this arrangement is normally in place only
when a master or mistress is about and the slave, thus, is under
supervision.

Urta went again to the window.

"There is unrest in the streets?" she asked.

"There is little action here," he said.

"Elsewhere?" she asked.

"Doubtless," he said.

"I still smell smoke," she said.

"The signal should not have been given early," he said. "It
disrupts plans and phases. Leaders do not know whether to act
upon the signal or wait until the proper time. Confusion obtains."

"Things, I gather, are awry," she said.

"Possibly," said Urta.

"Crowds are dangerous," said Yana. "Like fire, they can go where they wish and do what they want."

"Leaders were to be put in place, shortly before noon," said Urta. "The crowds, like stampeding cattle, were to be guided, directed to planned streets. Now the leaders will not have been at their posts. And now the crowds are loose."

"All is in jeopardy?" asked Yana.

"Not at all," said Urta. "Do not hope so. The coup may be delayed, but it is not foiled."

"Unwanted fires must be fought," said Yana.

"True," said Urta. "And that will divert resources, which should be directed on the palace."

"And valuable time is lost," said Yana.

"It will make no difference in the long run," said Urta, "for the palace has been taken unawares by this movement and will have had no time to call for assistance. Success will be secured before help can arrive, even if help should be offered, which I doubt. What help would be offered to a usurper, a barbarian, when victory already blazes upon, and crowns, the silver standards of legitimacy?"

"I understand little of this," said Yana.

"All was in place," said Urta. "Rioting and arson were to be strictly controlled, limited to poorer districts, performed under the guise of justice, objecting to privilege and power, to wealth and success."

"Wickedness thrives best under a moral cloak," said Yana.

"Of course," said Urta.

"But now?" she asked.

"Now wolves are loose," he said. "The privileged and powerful, the wealthy and successful, those of your former sort, those who were to profit by the coup, may themselves be at risk. That will not do at all."

"But you are not afraid?" said Yana.

"No," said Urta. "Fire burns out when there is a lack of fuel, crowds grow weary, and bored, when there is nothing left to burn, break, and steal. Then legitimacy will be welcomed, and will mercifully prevail, and Prince Ingeld, who was your husband and lord, will reside in the palace and sit upon the throne as regent."

"If there remains a palace and a throne," said Yana.

"The smell of smoke grows stronger," said Urta. "I fear the wind has changed."

"You are a bold Master," said Yana.

"Of course," said Urta, "but how so?"

"Suppose we must flee the domicile," she said.

"So?" he said.

"In a time of unrest, possibly lawlessness," said Yana, "it is a bold Master who will take a naked slave into the streets. Might he not be slain, and robbed, and the slave be raped and stolen?"

Angrily Urta turned from the window, and went to the side, seized up a bit of cloth, and hurled it at Yana.

She gratefully, quickly, slipped the loose, brief tunic over her head, drew it down about her thighs, and tied the knot at her left shoulder. The knot in such garments is almost always at the left shoulder as most masters are right-handed. The knot is also such that it may be easily undone, with so little as a light tug. In this way the girl is reminded that she is not a free woman, but a property, a slave.

"The signal sounded too soon," said Urta, returning to the window, "too soon."

The cacophony of the bells, which apparently had constituted a signal of sorts, continued unabated. Had it not been clear that a signal was involved, one might have taken the sounding of the bells as, given its nature, an alarm, signifying, for example, an invasion or fire.

CHAPTER SEVENTY-ONE

"It has begun," said Iaachus.

Even in the throne room of the imperial palace, one could hear the bells, as though from far off, across the great plaza, through the mighty walls.

On his knees, at the foot of the throne, Timon Safarius Rhodius, of the Telnar Rhodii, *primarius* of the senate of Telnaria, struggled against the ropes that swathed his upper body. Behind him, on either side, stood two dark, strong figures, the guards, Boris and Andak.

"Shall we kill him now?" inquired Boris.

"Hold," said Otto.

He sat upon the throne, the great sword across his knees.

"He attempted to escape," said Boris.

"But failed to do so," said Otto

"I beg you to stay your hand, great majesty," said Safarius. "I have served you well, however unwillingly."

"It must be admitted," said Otto, looking down on the bound Safarius, "that your presence, accompanied by guards loyal to me, at the secret councils of our enemies, your standing in high regard with them, they taking you into their confidence as a fellow conspirator, has been a boon to our party. The conspirators might as well have reported to the throne in person."

"Be merciful," said Safarius. "I even gave you the signal and time."

"We received the signal and time," said Otto, "from our informants, Boris and Andak. You were merely present."

"I have been their prisoner," said Safarius, "day in and day out, in constant danger of having my throat cut, if I gave the least sign of waywardness."

"And it would have been, had you done so," said Otto.

"What is to be done with me?" asked Safarius.

"I am thinking," said Otto, "of having you chained and returned to Ingeld and Sidonicus with a placard wired about your neck, detailing your services to the throne."

"Mercy!" begged Safarius.

"It is true," said Otto, "that we should be grateful to you for having ordered the signal for the insurrection to be sounded unseasonably, indeed, several hours before expected."

"You forced me to do so," he said. "Otherwise I would have been killed."

"A consideration, to be sure," said Otto.

"Disruption has doubtless occurred," said Safarius.

"I trust so," said Otto.

"Last minute preparations and orders would not be issued," said Safarius. "Leaders would not be in place. Explanations would be sought. Hundreds of men would not know whether to spring into action, or wait upon clarification and new orders."

"We shall hope so," said Otto.

"All this will do you no good," said Safarius. "At best it will buy you time, but far from enough, and for what? You are without recourse and assistance. What does it matter whether you are destroyed today, or tomorrow, or the next day? It is uncertain that forces will be loyal to you. Many will quail and desert. You are a barbarian, a killer, a usurper. There is now a legitimate heir to the throne. Tremble! Even if handfuls of guards or soldiers remain loyal to you, they will be outnumbered, by hundreds to one. Resistance could be no better than token resistance, and it will be crushed like a *varda* egg under the nailed foot of a *torodont*, swept away like dried leaves before the wind of Umba, shattered like the *vance* tree by the bolt of Orak. Free me, and I will plead with Ingeld and Sidonicus to permit you and selected followers, a limited number of your choice, passage to some remote world, to enjoy the lenience of honorable banishment."

"You are most generous," said Otto.

"Free me," said Safarius.

"Take him away," said Otto, "and chain him in some remote cell."

"Do not keep me here, not in the palace, helpless!" cried Safarius as Boris and Andak pulled him to his feet. "The mobs will be mad for blood. Sidonicus has made them so. The palace will be stormed. You do not understand their hatred. They will kill, destroy, or burn everything in sight, even dogs and *filchen*."

Otto made a small gesture, dismissing Safarius.

"No, no!" screamed Safarius, as he was dragged from the room.

Iaachus approached the throne. "The city is in danger," he said. "Looting and rioting already takes place. Night will be terrible. It will be red with blood. Ravaging will be unabating. Districts will blaze."

"Many citizens," said Tuvo Ausonius, "board their domiciles and conceal themselves within."

"One cannot expect them to challenge unbridled, hostile mobs, to risk criticizing their carnival of destruction, robbery, and arson," said Julian. "It would be worth their lives. The reed of reason fares ill in the gale of passion."

"Against passion," said Iaachus, "naught can prevail but passion. It is a war of lions."

"Surely," said Tuvo Ausonius, "some attempt to restore order must be offered."

"The emperor is unwilling to sacrifice men in futile gestures," said Titus Gelinus.

"There are, proportionally, few on whom we can depend," said Julian. "Rurik has secured the dock district, which accounts for his men. Ortog is in the delta of the Turning Serpent, and has, surely, no more than a hundred or a hundred and fifty men, the remnants of the Ortungen. I have some twenty officers from the imperial navy. Guardsmen and soldiers of the city garrison barricade themselves in their guard stations and barracks. We do not know where their loyalties lie, if anywhere. The emperor has ordered most Otungs away, putatively on missions of reconnaissance, of patrolling, and the pacification of supposed unrest in the countryside, that they not be overwhelmed in the deluge of rising, enflamed mobs."

"Tens and hundreds cannot stand against thousands," said Titus Gelinus.

"Mobs rule," said Iaachus. "Who can challenge their sovereignty?"

"And so," said Tuvo Ausonius, "we wait here to die?"

"I granted freedom to depart, to all who desired it, days ago," said Otto.

"I would not leave my emperor," said Tuvo Ausonius.

"Nor would those here," said Julian.

"I think," said Titus Gelinus, "we should have spirited away the boy, Aesilesius, and the empress mother. They are not involved in these dark and terrible matters."

"The young, noble Aesilesius," said Otto, "chose to stay and his mother would not leave without him."

"Young Aesilesius," said Titus Gelinus, "is a pathetic retardate, a tragic, idiotic simpleton. He is incapable of even understanding what is going on, let alone making a judgment on the matter."

"He chose to stay," said Otto.

"I discovered that several of the servitors," said Iaachus, "perhaps Floonians, of one sort or another, before departing, fouled water and contaminated food."

"*Filchen*," said Julian.

"Some private stores are untouched," said Iaachus.

"Used sparingly," said Otto, "how long will they last?"

"Some days," said Iaachus, "presumably longer than it will take murderous swarms to force their way into the palace, looting and killing."

"Word has been sent to Tangara," said Otto.

"You should not abandon Tangara to savage Heruls," said Julian.

"Perhaps I have not done so," said Otto.

"I do not understand," said Julian.

"In any event," said Iaachus, "there is insufficient time for aid to reach us from Tangara."

"All is lost," said Tuvo Ausonius.

"How many cartridges have you?" asked Otto of Julian.

"Four," said Julian, "for the pistol."

"Iaachus?" asked Otto.

"Two," said Iaachus, "too, for the pistol."

"Six cartridges are of great value," said Otto. "And the enemy may fear we have more. Judiciously fired, they may give pause to even a mob."

"True," said Julian.

"And we may rest assured," said Otto, "given the rarity of cartridges, that our foes lack even one."

"The mobs are busy in the city," said Iaachus. "I doubt that they will turn their attention to the palace until tomorrow or the next day."

"There are fires, too," said Tuvo Ausonius. "They may hold back mobs."

"Hopefully," said Iaachus, "even insurgents, determined as they are, will have the common sense to address themselves to fire, their enemy as much as ours. What has one won if one's prize is consumed in flame?"

"We may survive for a time," said Julian. "This is not fifty thousand, or a hundred thousand, years ago, a time of greater resources. Few weapons of power now exist, and some that do might tilt the axes of worlds, affect orbits, even shatter planets. Both we and our enemies are largely confined to weapons of steel and wood, arrows, spears, the knife and sword. Indeed, the depletion of resources lending themselves to destruction may account for the survival of civilization."

"Our walls are high and thick," said Otto. "Even unguarded they will mock for a time the pounding of rams, the blows of hammers."

"And," said Julian, "the throne room, from centuries ago, was shielded with steel. The walls of the throne room can withstand the impact of a cartridge, they were designed to do so, perhaps even two cartridges."

"Perhaps then," said Tuvo Ausonius, eagerly, "we may be able to hold the palace until help arrives."

"If it arrives," said Julian. "I find it unlikely that Otungs on Tangara will surrender their lands, their women and children, their world, to Heruls."

"Perhaps they will not do so," said Otto.

"Then indeed," said Tuvo Ausonius, "all is lost. It is only a matter of time."

"What of the slaves?" asked Titus Gelinus.

"They will be safe," said Otto, "even if our friends from the streets would kill even dogs and *filchen* in the palace. Slaves are valuable loot, precious possessions. Even the most ill-disposed of enemies is unlikely to neglect available loot."

"I trust so," said Iaachus.

"So, Arbiter," said Otto, "you think it will be tomorrow, or the next day, that our fellow citizens, with their knives and sticks, their axes and flaming brands, their cries, screams, and enthusiasms, will turn to the palace?"

"That is my estimate," said Iaachus. "Tonight I expect them to be engaged in their festival of fire, so stimulating to the looting soul."

"How long," asked Otto, "would you expect the palace to resist incursion?"

"Not long," said Iaachus. "But the throne room, from long ago, was built to be a keep. It is our hope."

"For how long?" asked Otto.

"Attacked by picks and axes, by hammers, by chisels and wedges, day and night, gouged and scratched away bit by bit, say, four days."

"Help could never arrive within that time," said Tuvo Ausonius.

"Let us add a day or two, in which we expend our cartridges, say, from the roof or a balcony," said Julian.

"Still not enough," said Tuvo Ausonius.

"Far from enough," said Iaachus.

"Would you care to be provided with lethal tablets?" asked Otto.

"Not really," said Iaachus.

"The likely alternative," said Otto, "is to die fighting."

"I am not an enthusiast for dooms," said Iaachus, "but amongst them, I suspect that is one of the least despicable."

"I no longer hear the bells," said Tuvo Ausonius, lifting his head.

"They have stopped ringing," said Julian, he of the Aureliani.

"Then things have indeed begun," said Iaachus.

CHAPTER SEVENTY-TWO

"Smoke rises from the city," said Julian.

"From the Varl district," said Titus Gelinus.

"Little compared to two nights ago," said Iaachus.

"Should the palace not be stormed by now?" asked Titus Gelinus, a crossbow cradled in his arms.

"Our fellow citizens are engaged elsewhere," said Julian.

"I am pleased I am not elsewhere," said Iaachus. He carried a Telnarian pistol, secured from the Arbiter's office. Julian wore such a pistol holstered at his right hip. Between them they possessed six cartridges. One such cartridge could shatter a wall; two, judiciously placed, could bring down a floor.

Above the great gate of the palace, before high-windowed rooms of state, there was a balcony from which, commonly on state occasions, civil holidays, and such, appearances might be made and announcements transmitted to the public. From this balcony there had been announced victories and the acquirings of worlds. From it had been announced royal births and the recoveries from illnesses of members of the royal family. On it had appeared generals and emperors. Four times, though years ago, on his birthday, a child emperor, Aesilesius, bundled and propped up, had been exhibited to an awed public. Of late, for years, he had been concealed from the public. Most Telnarians were unaware of the seeming nature of Aesilesius. Many regarded him as merely reclusive, or disdainfully solitary, given to books and music. To many he was little more than a name. Rumors, of course, abounded. Still, on the whole, his seeming frailties and weaknesses, his hideous debilities and shocking infirmities, were unknown to the public. Certainly such things had been concealed as much as possible. Many Telnarians suspected he had died or had been quietly done away with in the palace, on the accession of Ottonius, the First, the Otung emperor. It was on this balcony that, on the morning of the third day, beginning from the ringing

of the bells, that four men had gathered, Iaachus, the Arbiter of
Protocol, of the imperial palace; Titus Gelinus, a rhetor and attorney, double liaison between the senate and the throne; Tuvo
Ausonius, a former high-ranking civil servant posted on Miton, a
"same world," like Terennia; and a cousin of Aesilesius, a lieutenant in the imperial navy, Julian, of the Aureliani.

"It is too quiet," said Julian.

"Do not be impatient," said Iaachus. "Rejoice, we may have a
day more to live."

"The plaza is empty," said Tuvo Ausonius, looking over the
wall of the balcony, at the broad expanse of the tiles and fountains
stretching out from below, the stately building of the senate, and
other public buildings, to the left.

"We hear nothing from Rurik," said Titus Gelinus.

"We hear nothing from anywhere," said Tuvo Ausonius, bitterly.

"He holds the dock district," said Julian. "He holds the ware-
houses, the shipping. He controls the great artery of the Turning
Serpent."

"He may have fled," said Titus Gelinus.

"Would you have fled?" asked Julian.

"No," said Titus Gelinus.

"Nor would any man of honor," said Julian, "and Rurik, Tenth
Consul of Larial VII, scion of the Larial Farnichi, is a man of honor."

"Still we have heard nothing," said Titus Gelinus.

"Perhaps there is nothing to hear," said Tuvo Ausonius.

"If there were, the bell would have sounded," said Julian.

Lest this allusion be obscure, it might be mentioned that Iaachus, at the behest of Otto, anticipating a possible need for commu-
nication, had arranged a code with Rurik. There are many ways of
arranging signals, of course, hoisted flags, blasts on horns, flashes
of light on mirrors, fires covered and uncovered, and so on. The
arrangement in place, alluded to above, had to do with a bell, the
sound of which was controlled. The bell in question lacks a clap-
per, and is sounded, as many bells in Telnarian history, by being
struck from the outside by a large, wielded hammer. This arrangement both allows for different tones and lengths of tones, depend-
ing on where and how the bell is struck. Otto was familiar with
this sort of thing from his childhood in a village located at the foot
of the pass leading up to the *festung* of Sim Giadini, a *festung* of
Emanationist Brothers, which *festung* had later been destroyed in

a Telnarian air strike. A double arrangement of signals had been put in place; the first arrangement dealt with very simple signals, connected with such things as fires, attacks, stresses, arrivals, and such; the second arrangement, devised by Iaachus, was correlated with the Telnarian alphabet, in which particular tones and lengths of tones were correlated with individual letters. In this fashion, particular words and sentences could be transmitted.

"What of the servitors?" asked Tuvo Ausonius.

"The last have fled," said Iaachus, "released by the emperor."

"Have the great doors been sealed?" asked Tuvo Ausonius.

"Yes," said Iaachus.

"I do not understand why the palace has not yet been stormed," said Titus Gelinus.

"Nor do I," said Iaachus.

"How fare the slaves?" asked Titus Gelinus.

"You fear for Pig?" asked Julian.

"For others, as well," said Titus Gelinus, defensively. Who would be so embarrassed as to manifest concern for a slave? Still, as has often been noted, many men would risk fortunes and their very lives to possess them, and many would die for them.

"They are well enough," said Julian, "one supposes."

"Are they informed?" asked Titus Gelinus.

"Certainly not," said Julian. "They are slaves."

"But surely they suspect the desperateness of the situation," said Titus Gelinus.

"Doubtless," said Julian. "Consider the alterations of routine, the rationing of food and water, the smell of smoke, the disappearance of servitors, the absence of familiar guards, such things."

"I have not seen the emperor today," said Tuvo Ausonius.

"Nor I," said Titus Gelinus.

"Where is he?" asked Tuvo Ausonius, uneasily.

"I do not know," said Iaachus.

"I am afraid," said Tuvo Ausonius.

"Do not speak your fear," said Julian.

"It need not be spoken," said Tuvo Ausonius.

"One understands the concern of our friend, Ausonius," said Iaachus. "At one time, I, too, might have shared such concerns, but I now do not do so."

"Nor I," said Julian, "but it is easy to understand how many might. He is emperor. He might easily have arranged a convenient egress from predicaments even more dire than ours, if such could exist. Orders are issued, a path is smoothed, a ship awaits, and the departure is effected, discreetly, gracefully."

"Where is he?" asked Tuvo Ausonius.

"I am sure I do not know," said Julian.

"Perhaps he is dead," said Tuvo Ausonius. "Perhaps he has taken a lethal tablet."

"It is not the Otung way," said Julian.

"Perhaps he has fled," said Tuvo Ausonius, in a whisper.

"It is not the Otung way," said Julian.

"Surely not all Otungs follow the way of the Otungs," said Tuvo Ausonius.

"True," said Julian.

"You are sure of him?" asked Tuvo Ausonius.

"Yes," said Julian, "even from the forests of Varna."

"Where is he?" asked Tuvo Ausonius.

"I do not know," said Julian.

"Friend Ausonius' fears may be warranted," said Iaachus. "The emperor may be dead. He would not desert us, but why is he not here? Several times in the past I attempted to contact him late at night or early in the morning, on matters of palace business, sometimes urgent business, and his chamber was empty. He was abroad, incognito, in the city. It is easy to suppose he left the palace in such a way last night and fell afoul of rioters, assassins, arsonists, or looters."

"Well supposed," said a great voice, "and several such, much to their regret, fell afoul of me."

"Otto!" cried Julian, joyfully, and rushed to embrace the massive figure of the somber-clad Otung. Soot besmirched the Otung's features, and his cloak reeked of smoke. "Ottonius!" wept Iaachus, pressing forward. "The emperor!" cried Titus Gelinus and Tuvo Ausonius, both hurrying to greet their friend and sovereign.

In the joy of this impromptu reunion the group which had been on the balcony failed to note a bedraggled figure, in torn garments, its upper body bound with ropes, and its wrists crossed and bound before its body, which was cast to the floor of the balcony.

Once the Otung had managed to break free of the embraces of his friends, he reached down and, seizing the figure by its hair, as though it might have been no more than a female slave, pulled it up to its knees.

"Corelius!" cried Iaachus.

"The traitor and informer," said Julian.

"He to whom Rurik delivered a mighty treasure," said Titus Gelinus.

"I do not understand this," said Tuvo Ausonius.

"I found him in the city," said Otto. "A crowd was preparing to tear him to pieces, alive. I intervened, with a sword, and the war cry of the Otungs, "Blood Upon Steel," cut several fellows away from him, and gestured wildly, meaningfully, behind me, shouting, "Forward, men!" and the crowd panicked and broke apart, its tatters fleeing from the street. I then gathered in this piece of meat, dragged it into the darkness, bound it, and brought it back with me."

"Better you had left it to the crowd," said Julian.

"Perhaps an emperor has erred," said Iaachus.

"Few are without flaws," said Otto.

"You should not have risked your life for a worthless *filch*," said Iaachus.

"Why did you save him?" asked Julian.

"His end would have been unjust," said Otto. "And it is the duty of an emperor to uphold justice."

"I do not understand," said Tuvo Ausonius.

"Many are the crimes for which this handsome, cowardly, traitorous *filch* might be well punished," said Otto, "but not that with which he was charged."

"The crowd would kill him?" asked Tuvo Ausonius.

"Yes," said Otto.

"What was his crime?" asked Titus Gelinus.

"Wealth had been found in his possession," said Otto.

"I do not understand," said Titus Gelinus.

"His crime was to be rich," said Otto.

"Is that a crime?" asked Titus Gelinus, rhetor and attorney.

"To some," said Otto.

"But surely he had caused the crowd no harm," said Titus Gelinus.

"That seems to be irrelevant in such matters," said Otto.

"Where is the treasure," asked Titus Gelinus, "the small, weighty chest of gold?"

"It purchased us some time," said Otto. "Had our friend, Corelius, availed himself of the proffered safe-conduct to a destination of his choice, he would now be elsewhere and rich instead of a prisoner and a pauper, in great peril of his life. And we might well be dead. But, as I expected he would, trusting no one, doubting good faith and honor, seeing others in terms of himself, he refused that offer."

"There is much here I do not understand," said Iaachus.

"What of the treasure, what of the treasure?" said Titus Gelinus.

"Speak," said Otto to Corelius.

But Corelius seemed too terrified to speak.

Otto then, his hand fastened in the blond hair of the kneeling figure, shook its head, and it cried out in misery, and Otto then, by the hair, flung it to the floor of the balcony. "Speak," said Otto.

"I had the gold," said Corelius, gasping and cringing, half prone. "But how could I spend it? I was starving. I had gold, and was one of the wealthiest men in the empire, but I had not a crust of bread. I tried to convert one of the coins into silver at a bank, and did so, but I was somehow marked, and followed. Men set upon me and stole the chest. Its contents were soon discovered. There was rejoicing and drunkenness, followed by murder. I fled, as they began to fall out, even more, amongst themselves. Others, suspecting loot, like sharks smelling blood, as though from nowhere, appeared. Then, as I understand it, several of the strongest barricaded themselves in a sturdy house, which was soon assailed by others. Some were taken into the house, to assist in its defense, whilst many others laid siege to the dwelling. I myself was recognized by one or more of the original group, who had been refused entrance to the house. I was seized, and held prisoner for days, and abused and tortured, that I might reveal the whereabouts of even more gold, about which I could know nothing. I was not believed. Where there was so much gold, there should be more gold, and more, and more, and so on. Then bells began to ring, and the streets to fill with looting crowds. Then my captors, finally convinced I knew no more, and could be of no value to them, put me out before looters, proclaiming me a scion of the wealthy in the city, one of the hated rich. When the mob was to set upon me, eager and jubilant, with their bare hands, their knives, their sharpened sticks, their hammers and tongs, their fish hooks, needles, and awls, a mighty figure thrust itself amongst them, howling of war, thrusting and slashing with a blade the motion of which one could scarcely follow. It was the emperor, as I learned. And thus it was that you find me now at your feet, a prisoner."

"Give him to Ortog or Abrogastes," said Julian.

"No, no!" begged Corelius.

"I shall complete the story," said Otto. "I and my prisoner must negotiate dangerous streets, sometimes lonely and deserted, sometimes raucous and crowded, sometimes bright with flame and sometimes dark with smoke, to return to the palace. Too, we must elude scattered remnants of the crowd, remnants pursuing us, now aware of my ruse, that of calling out as though upon imminent and ready aid. Sometimes we made our way through the ashes and broken, charred wood of ravaged districts, sometimes between burning buildings. Twice we encountered impediments, once three men, once four. These regretted the success of their pursuit. Sometimes we passed amongst riotous crowds, achieving anonymity by mingling with these. Once we took refuge in a crowded tavern, for who would look for fugitives in such a public place? It was in the tavern that we learned news which bodes ill for us."

"What news?" asked Iaachus.

"The siege of the sturdy house was done," said Otto.

"Speak," said Iaachus.

"Stout poles and metal railings, wrested free, had been used as prods and battering rams. Hammers struck at walls. Men leaped to the roof from adjoining buildings, tore shingles away, pried up boards, and cast stones on defenders. Bundles of flaming straw were thrust through windows. Oil was cast on walls and ignited. Assailants, by means of ropes, tied to rafters, lowered themselves within the dwelling, few reaching the floor alive, succumbing to the blows of axes, the thrust of knives. Soon, in smoke and flames, the portal splintered and ajar, men rushing inward to be the first to obtain gold, attackers and defenders were mixed, attackers falling upon attackers, and defenders upon defenders. Men waded in blood and fire. Those who could seized a coin, or a handful of coins, and rushed, seared, coughing, and choking into the street, where they were seized, thrown to the pavement, and robbed, by men who, as often or not, were themselves soon robbed. The building was afire and the timbers of the roof collapsed. Screams rent the neighborhood. Vessels of water were sought, to be put upon the flames. Some, impatient, mad with greed, trod into the fire, daring its menace, and several perished thereby, some so wild that they did not realize they were afire. Some fled like torches into the street."

"Men will do much for gold," said Tuvo Ausonius.

"Conflicting leaders, self-proclaimed and assertive," said Otto, "in the midst of men fetching water, forbade entry upon the premises. The stink of burned, and burning, flesh was about. Finally, the unreluctant, tenacious flames, protesting amidst hissing steam and billowing smoke, must subside, that to the point where men might, to the consternation of erstwhile leaders who counseled patience and division, invade debris and ashes. They did so, from all sides, unheeding, like swarms of eager *filchen*. Coins abounded, strewn about, some dark, defaced with ash and soot, others scattered here and there like bright, hot pebbles. Men scrambled to seize them. Bodies were rifled. And woe to those who seized a prize and foolishly sought to escape. Many were hunted down in the streets and alleys. Some flung gold about, that others, retrieving it, would be delayed in their pursuit. The wisest, finding a coin, would endeavor to conceal it. Many fortunes were won and lost that day."

"And so," said Titus Gelinus, "a thousand or so pieces of gold were distributed in the streets of Telnar."

"And doubtless now still, under the behest of knives and clubs, continue to change hands," said Julian.

"Without law," said Tuvo Ausonius, "even crime becomes impractical."

Solemnly was the emperor regarded.

"So," said Otto, "it was in the tavern I learned that it was done, the siege of the sturdy house, a war, small but terrible."

"Ill news, indeed, for us," said Iaachus, "the fall of the sturdy house, it no longer concealing the trove of Corelius."

"Wolves could then seek new prey," said Tuvo Ausonius.

"Rejoice," said Otto, "some time was purchased."

"At least," said Julian, "our puzzle has been solved, the respite, the silence, the vacant square, the mystery of delay."

"Let me go!" cried Corelius, bound, lying on the floor of the balcony. "I have no wish to die with you!"

"Time was earlier purchased, as well," said Otto, "when we encouraged Safarius to issue the signal prematurely, this disrupting the plans of Sidonicus, and loosening unguided, uncontrolled crowds into the streets, crowds soon, following the lure of license, turning to arson, destruction, and looting."

"Predictably," said Tuvo Ausonius, "fires were ignited, intentionally or inadvertently, and must be dealt with, not only to save the city, but the very lives of the rioters, the arsonists, and looters as well."

"But flames much subsided and circumspect calm soon prevailed," said Julian.

"Then," said Iaachus, "the agents of Sidonicus doubtless began to harangue and regather the crowds, to direct an attack upon the palace itself."

"As the palace goes, so goes Telnaria," said Tuvo Ausonius.

"But," said Iaachus, "the beasts of the street, goaded and guided, did not yet pounce."

"It was then we were indebted to dear Corelius," said Otto, "who had tried to change a gold piece into silver."

"Better I had drunk from puddles and stolen bread," muttered Corelius.

"Following the seizure of the trove of Corelius," said Otto, "rumors of obtainable wealth abounded, initiating a new cycle of savage inquiry and methodological looting, this further disrupting the plans of Sidonicus."

"Giving us more time," said Julian.

"But," said Otto, "it soon became clear that much wealth had left the city, or was concealed, perhaps secured in walls or buried in cellars, or that it existed, but was distributed in tens of thousands of households, a handful of coins here, a handful of coins there, any coin of which might be stoutly defended. A man whose life depends on pennies will defend those pennies as gold. One calculates; one balances risk and gain. Few will choose to risk death for copper. So it soon became clear that the trove of Corelius might well be unique. Then, as might be expected, those who had seized the trove, and those whom they had recruited as allies, and guards, were sought. Did they not have graspable riches? Surely. Then, as they were closely pursued and found themselves unable to flee, they seized, and retired to, a stout house, a sturdy house, the house in question, to fortify and defend it, and set themselves to withstand the inevitable assault and siege."

"Which house has now fallen," said Julian.

"Yes," said Otto.

"Which indeed bodes ill for us," said Iaachus.

"The agents of Sidonicus," said Julian, "doubtless hint that a hundred troves, such as that of Corelius, lie within the palace."

"Of course," said Iaachus.

"I see nothing," said Julian, peering outward. "The great square, the plaza, is clear."

"The palace is silent," said Tuvo Ausonius.

"It is muchly deserted, largely empty," said Iaachus.

"We are few," said Julian, he of the Aureliani, "some officers, a handful of Otungs."

"There is no signal from the dock district," said Iaachus.

"The Otungs on Tangara will not intervene," said Tuvo Ausonius. "They would not surrender their lands, their women and children, to the Heruls."

"In any event," said Julian, "there is no time. Tangara is far."

"I see no hope, friends," said Iaachus.

"'Friends'?" asked Julian.

"Even you," said Iaachus.

The two men clasped hands.

Otto lifted his head, and raised his hand. "Do you hear it?" he asked.

"Yes," said Julian, after a time.

The sound was far off and faint.

"It is a hymn of Floon," said Iaachus.

"There must be a great number of voices," whispered Tuvo Ausonius, listening, awed.

"It is easy to see why religion is so popular," said Julian. "It appeals to what is darkest and most terrible in human beings. It may be used to justify any crime or horror. One wishes to be special and superior, so one is. One wishes to burn, loot, and kill, so, properly guided, one may. Hatred and intolerance, suitably directed, become virtues. How many, I wonder, have died in the names of a thousand gods? Those who yesterday were arsonists, looters, rioters, killers, and thieves, the hating, rabid, destructive mobs, are now the devout and faithful, the redeemed and exonerated, ready now, eager now, singing, to burn and kill, as permitted, as directed, in the name of sweet, gentle Floon, loving prophet of the god, *Karch*."

"Floon is betrayed," said Tuvo Ausonius.

"Perhaps he should not have preached to beasts," said Julian. "He should have left them in the jungle."

"How hungry they are in their holiness," said Iaachus.

"Flee," begged Corelius. "Take me with you!"

The sound of the hymn was now much clearer, and much louder.

"I see them," said Tuvo Ausonius.

It seemed dark swarms, or herds, were at the far edge of the square. The street behind them was filled, like a river between buildings.

"They advance," said Julian.

"Is Sidonicus with them?" asked Tuvo Ausonius.

"It is unlikely," said Otto. "The crowd is his weapon. Weapons are dangerous. They are most safely wielded from afar."

"Crowds may be manipulated with impunity," said Tuvo Ausonius.

"Not always," said Iaachus.

CHAPTER SEVENTY-THREE

Urta, the Otung, looked down at the bellied slave at his feet.

"Off your belly and on your feet, meaningless slave," said Urta. "From here we can see."

The slave struggled to her feet.

Wind, swift, chilly, fierce, and relentless, sped across the roof of the building, on the east side of Palace Street. Yana, barefoot in her thin, brief, ragged tunic, shivered, her eyes half closed, her uncombed, tangled blond hair swept to her left. About her throat, locked, was a number collar. She felt a tug on the leash, and hurried to respond. She then stood beside him, looking over the balustrade. Her hands were braceleted behind her back. She was gasping, breathing heavily, for she had been hurried through the streets, into the building, and up the long flights of stairs. The sweat on her body, from her climb, was cold on her body. Her leash looped up to his hand. It was a long leash; coiled and shortened, it afforded, like the common leash, perfect slave control; uncoiled, it afforded the master enough material to bind a slave, hand and foot, with enough material left over, folded on itself two or three times, to administer discipline.

"We can see the plaza, and the palace," he said.

"Yes, Master," she whispered.

She saw the great plaza, or square, and the fountains, now dry, and, beyond, in the distance, stately and imposing, the palace.

"See the palace?" he asked.

"Yes, Master," she said.

"It is faraway, is it not?" he asked.

"Yes, Master," she said.

"Worlds away from you," he said.

"Yes, Master," she said.

"Once, you lived there," he said, "in indolence and pampered luxury. Perhaps you remember your former life, your riches and grandeur."

Tears formed in her eyes.

"You were a worthless free woman," he said. "Now for the first time in your life, you have some value, slave value, if only in pennies."

"Please be kind," she said.

"That is enough," he said. "Belly, slave."

She lowered herself to her belly. "How helpless are slaves," she thought. "How men keep us!"

Yana was familiar with Telnarian custom, and Telnarian law. She had no hope of regaining her freedom, not merely because of the onrushing course of contemporary events, so inimical to the fortunes of her family, but even in more stable, placid, or typical times. Abundant was the folk wisdom on such matters. "An enslaved woman is besmirched and stained, to the last cell of her body. She can never again be free. She is spoiled for freedom. It is dishonorable and offensive, unthinkable, for a woman who has once worn the collar to be freed. How insulting to free women! Would you permit a woman who has once been a slave to walk again amongst free women, as though an equal? How demeaning and insulting that would be to free women! She has been irretrievably changed and degraded. Let her then be despised, scorned, and beaten. She is a slave." "If a woman is in a collar she belongs in a collar. If she is in a collar, she should be in a collar." "For a man the whip is right, for a woman, the collar." "All women wish to be in collars, and thus, knowing in their hearts that they are worthless and despicable, put them in collars." "The woman who wants a master knows she is a slave, and should be a slave." "By nature, man is master and woman slave." "Women belong on their knees, at the feet of men." "Women wish to be subject to the whip. In that, they know they are women." Much was the tumult of thought in the mind of Yana. She knew that she had never felt so feminine, so sexual, so helplessly and fully female, as in her collar. Families who recovered an enslaved daughter or sister, she knew, were commonly so scandalized and dishonored, that they did not free her, but disposed of her in some market, commonly faraway. If she was freed and kept, she was commonly kept sequestered, hidden away from public view, that her shame be concealed from society. Yana feared and hated Urta, and the miseries he inflicted on her, but she did not fear and hate being a slave. Never before had she felt so alive and vital. Being owned, being possessed as an object, she felt radiant and fulfilled. She wished to submit, will-lessly and joyfully. She remembered the arms of Ingeld. She felt ready, even eager, to be chained naked to the foot of his couch. Why not? Had she not learned she was a slave?

"The attack, temporarily disrupted and delayed, given an inadvertence in signals, is now readied," said Urta.

"I beg, again," she wept, her cheek to the surface of the roof, "to be permitted to warn those in the palace."

"There is no time, even were I to permit it, which I would not," said Urta.

He then looked, again, over the balustrade. The wind tore at his hood.

Yana felt warmer, now, prone, lying on the roof, sheltered from the wind by the balustrade.

Urta looked out toward the square and palace. Yana pulled a little at the bracelets which confined her hands behind her back. Thoughts raced in her mind. "He is distracted," she thought. "If only he would drop the leash, I might rise up, and slip away, descend to the street, and hurry across the square. I could be gone before he noticed!"

"By nightfall," said Urta, "the palace will be in the hands of the people, the glorious, sovereign people, herded forward to do the will of their masters. All slaves do not know they are slaves. All puppets do not know they are puppets. The terror of the usurper will be ended. Your supposed son, the infant, will be acclaimed emperor. Ingeld, his putative father, will be proclaimed regent. All will be ratified by the senate and blessed by the exarch of Telnar."

"What of my brother, Aesilesius, and the empress mother?" asked Yana.

"Gone, dead," said Urta.

"No!" protested Yana.

"Aesilesius, deposed and superseded, would have been put away by the usurper, long ago. Why should Aesilesius, an embarrassment, a useless presence, a possible center about which resistance might coalesce, be permitted to live?"

"Do not speak so, I beg you," said Yana.

"How ignorant you are of statecraft," said Urta.

"The usurper, though a barbarian, is a man of honor," said Yana.

"On his part, an expedient hypocrisy," said Urta.

"Surely not," said Yana.

"Meanwhile a pillow, a blanket, a cushion, not the honor of
a knife, or bow string, has sufficed to silence the vain, half-mad
hag, the empress mother," said Urta. "No longer does she rule by
means of an idiot child. I surmise two dark sacks, months ago,
one moonless night, were discreetly lowered into one *carnarium*
or another."

"No," said Yana. "No!"

"Listen!" said Urta. "Hear it?"

"What?" said Yana.

"The hymn," said Urta. "Thousands march, singing."

"Yes," said Yana, suddenly. "Far off."

"It grows louder," said Urta.

"Let me hurry to the palace!" begged Yana.

"I do not understand why there are no Otungs, no auxiliaries,
no soldiers, no police, no guards, before the palace," said Urta.

"Let me go!" begged Yana. "Perhaps warned, some could escape."

"Strange that you should be solicitous of those who ruined
your family, seized its throne, and slew your brother and mother."

"Please!" begged Yana.

"Quiet," said Urta, looking over the balustrade, and then
back, to his right, up Palace Street. "I see them!" he said. He then
shielded his eyes and looked, again, toward the palace. "I see no
signs of defense, or flight," he said. "Perhaps the palace is empty,
abandoned. I trust it will not be pulled down, brick by brick,
stone by stone, or burned."

The singing was now easily audible.

Yana looked about as she could, back, toward the door through
which they had reached the roof.

As Urta looked toward the palace, intently, Yana rose to her
feet in such a way as to stress the leash as little as possible. It was
held, with its coils, in Urta's right hand, loosely. She suddenly
lunged away, the leash strap at the side of her neck, jerking the
leash from Urta's hand, and sped toward the door.

"Stop!" cried Urta, spinning about.

In a moment Yana had reached the door.

She jerked wildly, desperately, at the cuffs that confined her
hands behind her back, and turned her back to the door, reaching back for the handle to lift it, to then turn, slip through the
opening, and rush down the stairs. But her confined hands were
no sooner clutching at the handle than she, back to the door, of

necessity facing back toward the balustrade, saw, to her misery,
the rushing form bearing down upon her, saw that she could not
escape, that Urta was upon her. Urta seized her by the hair and,
with the palm and back of his hand cuffed her several times, striking her head back and forth. The world seemed to jerk about her,
and her face burned and raged with the sting of her master's attentions. Urta then recovered the leash and, turning about, angrily,
dragged her rapidly, stumbling, back to the balustrade. There,
with his foot, he swept her feet from beneath her and she fell to
the floor of the roof. She felt Urta's bootlike sandal on her back,
holding her in place.

"You are a stupid slave," he said.

Yana suddenly felt a slave's terror, that of having been found
displeasing by her master.

Urta stepped to the side, loosening, and then folding together
the strands of the leash.

"Forgive me, Master!" she begged.

A rain of blows then fell upon her, angrily, fiercely, from the
triple-folded leash, and she wept in misery, punished.

"Please, stop, please stop, Master!" she cried.

How natural, and appropriate, she felt her cry. Shaken, she
realized its authenticity. It was an indisputable slave's plea to her
master for mercy!

Urta took the leash down and back, beneath her trembling,
prone, stinging form, pulled her ankles up, high, behind her,
crossed them, and tied them together.

"You have not behaved well," said Urta, standing up, looking
down at his lovely, well-tethered property, surely a not unattract-
ive girl beast.

"Let me proceed to the palace," she wept. "There may yet be
time to urge flight!"

"You are a slave," he said. "I may dispose of you in a *carnarium*."

"Please, no, Master!" she begged. She was a slave. It could be
done with her, as with any animal.

She, a slave, was overcome with terror, and horror.

Urta thrust his bootlike sandal toward her, where her head was
tied down by the leash strap, inserting the heavy sandal between
the surface of the roof and her mouth.

She put her head down, as she could, and pressed her lips to
the heavy sandal, and, terrified, kissed it, fervently, and hopefully, desperately, again and again.

"I see," said Urta, sneeringly, "that you might be trained to kiss well."

"Masters train their slaves as they wish," whispered Yana. "And it is the hope of a slave to be trained in such a way that she may be found pleasing by her master." Had she actually said that, and to such a man? Yes, she had said it, and, as she realized, a moment later, it had been uttered instantly, sincerely, naturally, and without thought. "Who could say such a thing?" she asked herself. "And what could that tell her about herself," she wondered.

"Do you beg to be trained by me, or any man?" asked Urta.

"Yes, Master," she said.

"Why?" he asked.

"Because I am a slave," she said. How could she say such things?

"There is no way back to freedom for you," he said.

"I desire none," she said. How could she have said that?

"Why?" he demanded.

"Because I am a slave, Master," she said. And she knew, suddenly, that what she said was true.

Urta withdrew the sandal.

"You were displeasing," he said.

"Forgive me, Master," she said. "I beg forgiveness, Master." She heard her voice as though it was the voice of another, and then she realized that it was truly her voice, a voice soft, humble, submissive, and deferent, a voice which she well recognized, from thousands of experiences as a free woman, as the voice of a slave. A free woman may speak as she pleases, abruptly or harshly, imperiously or arrogantly, slurringly or indistinctly, clumsily or inarticulately, but a slave is to speak with excellent diction, softly, clearly, and deferently. She may be punished if she does not. "Yes," she thought, "I am now a slave. It is what I am." And then she added, half marveling, "and it is what I want to be." To be sure, she now had no choice in the matter. On her neck was a collar; and on her thigh, seared into her flesh, was a mark, the lovely and delicate "slave rose."

Urta turned away from her, contemptuously, and once more peered over the balustrade.

"Yes, I am a slave," she thought. "I belong in a collar. I hope he will sell me. I need a master. If only I had a master, a strong master, who would own me and treat me as the needful slave I am, a master who might be kind to me, his meaningless animal, a master whom I might joyfully love and serve."

The singing of the many throats in the street below was roaring upward between the buildings.

"They are at the edge of the square," said Urta. "They are variously armed. They are determined. They march on the palace! Surely they will destroy all free persons they find within, and seize slaves and other loot. I trust that, in their ransacking and despoiling, they will not fire the palace. Prince Ingeld, to whom you were wedded, your former husband and lord, wishes to rule from it, in the name of whatever brat it may be who will be passed off as your offspring. Behold, they do not hesitate!"

Yana wept, and groaned with misery.

"They are well upon the square now," said Ingeld. "They are eager. They hasten!"

Suddenly there was a flash of light, brighter than daylight itself, and Urta recoiled, crying out, darting down, behind the balustrade, and, a moment later there was a sound as of erupting rocks and descending tiles and stonework, and then, one after the other, there were three more such flashes, and then, after each, a moment later, a sound as of gouged, upheaved, falling rubble. Even from where she lay, Yana, looking up, as she could, saw spumes of dust rising in the air and then being swept away by the wind.

"Master!" she cried, frightened.

Urta, shaken, rose up a bit, looking over the balustrade, and then, satisfied, straightened up, shielding his eyes from the sun.

No longer was there singing below, but rather sporadic, disjointed cries of frightened men.

"The palace was not abandoned," said Urta. "It is being defended. They must have thousands of cartridges at their disposal. See how freely they expend them! Free women, even cities, have been given for one. It is supposed they scarcely exist. Often there is no more than one or two on a world, if that. Such things go back to a time of plenty, of fabulous resources which could be devoted to widescale destruction, a time when a moment could suffice for the slaughter of a population, the leveling of a city."

"What was done?" pleaded Yana.

"I do not understand," said Urta. "They did not fire on the crowd. How foolish! They might have burned hundreds, thousands alive. But they killed no one. They merely blasted out great craters, four great craters, in the path of their advance."

"That a warning be issued," said Yana.

"The crowd has scattered," said Urta. "It flees back, up Palace Street."

"The palace is safe!" said Yana.

"What fools they were," said Urta. "They could have killed hundreds, even thousands, of their enemies, and they refrained from doing so."

"Some are less hungry for blood than others," said Yana.

"It will do them no good," said Urta. "The palace is isolated. It will be surrounded. We know that the food and water at its disposal is in short supply. Our operatives within the palace saw to that before their withdrawal from the grounds. I doubt that more than three or four days will take place before the usurper sues for terms. Generous terms will be granted to lure the defenders out, and then, when they are at our mercy, they will be seized, tried, and executed."

"You would betray honor?" asked Yana.

"Not at all," said Urta. "That might displease worlds. It will be discovered, rather, that the treaty was illegal, that it was without standing, having not been ratified by the senate."

"Perhaps the palace will be able to hold out indefinitely," said Yana.

"No," said Urta. "If it is not soon surrendered, it will be breached."

"You would risk damage to the palace, even its destruction?" asked Yana.

"Unfortunately," said Urta.

"I do not understand," said Yana.

"It has to do with the *Turona*," said Urta.

"The *Turona* was intercepted, and looted, by a corsair," said Yana. "I, and others, were seized on the *Turona*."

"And had you not been," said Urta, "you would not now be at my feet."

"It was robbed of copper and silver, as well as slaves," said Yana.

"It was robbed, as well," said Urta, "of something far more valuable than slaves, silver, and copper."

"I do not understand," said Yana.

Urta bent down, over her prone form, pushed her ankles forward to reduce the tension on the confining leash, and undid the taut straps which had bound her crossed ankles together, so uncomfortably, so high, behind her back, and then drew the freed leash forward, from under her body, and stood up, the leash in his hand.

"On your feet," he said.

Yana, her hands fastened behind her, struggled to her feet. As she had been tied, her balance, for moment, was uncertain.

Yana noted that her Master's grip on the leash was now firm.

His eyes appraised her, as a slave may be appraised.

"Master looks upon his slave boldly," she said.

"Do you object?" he asked.

"I may not," she said.

"You are not a free woman," he said.

"No, Master," she said.

"The name 'Viviana' is a familiar Telnarian name," he said. "There are few who would recognize the former Viviana, the sister of a deposed emperor, she of royal blood, in the unkempt, bedraggled slave before me."

"I am no longer, legally, the sister of Aesilesius," she said. "I am now a property, an object, an animal. Too, I am no longer, legally, of royal blood. I am now of slave blood."

"I see that you know the law," he said.

"Yes, Master," she said.

"I think," he said, "I will name you 'Viviana'. It pleases me to own you under that name."

"Master may do with me as he wishes," she said.

"You are 'Viviana'," he said. "What is your name?"

"'Viviana', Master," she said.

"You understand," he said, "that that is a mere slave name, put on you as one might put a name on a dog or pig?"

"Yes, Master," she said.

He lifted the leash before her.

"You attempted to escape," he said.

"Only to warn those in the palace," she said.

"You failed," he said.

"Yes, Master," she said.

"Do you think escape is possible?" he asked.

"No, Master," she said.

"Ever?" he asked.

"No, Master," she said.

"Why not?" he asked.

"I am a slave," she said. "I am in a collar."

"We shall now leave the roof," he said. "I must take counsel with highly placed ones."

Viviana regarded her master.

"I will chain you somewhere," he said. "The doings of moment in which I am embroiled, doings of great importance, are not the concern of pigs, dogs, and slaves."

Viviana, barefoot, tunicked, and helpless, felt the cool wind coursing across the roof.

"I trust you understand," he said.

Viviana recalled the many audiences and assemblies of state which she had been required to attend, at which policy had been discussed and decisions made, decisions sometimes dealing with worlds, meetings she had found tiresome, meetings at which she had been perforce present, distracted, inattentive, disinterested, and bored.

"Yes, Master," she said.

She then, on her leash, her hands braceleted behind her, followed her Master from the roof.

CHAPTER SEVENTY-FOUR

"Drink, Master?" asked Flora, once an officer of the court, on Terennia.

Otto held forth his goblet, and a bit of water was poured into it, carefully, from a pitcher.

"Bread, Master?" inquired Renata.

"Yes," said Otto, and Renata put a crust of bread on the golden plate.

All the slaves in the room were clothed in brief tunics. Men often prefer to have slaves so, as the sight of the female figure, scarcely clad, pleases them, indeed, often arouses and excites them. One speaks, of course, of true men. It is well known, as well, that the sight of a scarcely clad slave improves the appetite. Such garmenture, too, serves to remind the slave that she is a slave and, if it must be known, given her display and bareness, arouses and excites her, as well. Had the occasion been less somber, the slaves might have served even more simply, clad only in their collars.

Several men were gathered about the makeshift table set in the throne room. There was Iaachus, the Arbiter of Protocol, his slave, Elena, in attendance; and then there were Tuvo Ausonius, once a finance officer on Miton; Julian, he of the Aureliani, an officer in the navy; and Titus Gelinus, a rhetor and attorney, who was the envoy of the palace to the senate, and the envoy, as well, of the senate to the palace. Rurik, the Tenth Consul of Larial VII, of the Larial Farnichi was not present. He, as it may be recalled, was stationed in the dock district. Some slaves knelt nearby, unobtrusively, but at hand, should they be summoned. These were Sesella, owned by Tuvo Ausonius; Gerune, a former barbarian princess, who had sided with her brother, Ortog, in his secession from the Drisriaks, now in the collar of Julian; and Pig, a former ambitious, avaricious Telnarian beauty, the Lady Gia Alexia, now the property of Titus Gelinus. Lovely Filene, or Cornhair, the former Lady Publennia, of the Larial Calasalii, Rurik's slave, was not amongst the other slaves. She was presumed to be with her master, somewhere in the dock district. It was not unusual for a man to wish his slave at hand, for his convenience. Amongst other slaves present were two slaves of Ortog, of the Ortungen, the first son of Abrogastes, king of the Drisriaks, commonly referred to as the Far Grasper. These were Delia and Virginia, both once of Telnar, the first the former Lady Delia Cotina, of the Telnar Farnacii, and the second, the former Lady Virginia Serena, of the lesser Serenii. Ortog was rumored to be in the delta of the Turning Serpent.

Aesilesius, the young, deposed emperor, was not present. His absence provoked neither surprise nor curiosity, but was, rather, taken for granted. Of what value or interest might be the presence of a feeble, uncontrollably salivating, retarded stripling? His familiar plaything, nurse, companion, and mentor, a delicate, red-headed slave named 'Nika', was also not in evidence. Aesilesius would often scream, cry, and tear at his hair and clothing that she be brought to him. The most piteous pleas of Nika to be relieved of her onerous charge, that of attendant upon the former, deposed emperor, had been scorned by the empress mother, and, it seems, had gone unheeded by the emperor himself, Ottonius, the First, sometimes, in whispers, spoken of as the Usurper.

A captive, blond Corelius, was also not present. He was chained in the kitchen, unshod, clad in the tunic of a slave.

Iaachus had suggested that he might be turned over to the restless mob hovering about the far edge of the square, several of whom might well remember him, or be surrendered to the mercies of Sidonicus and Fulvius, the exarch and deputy exarch of Telnar, but the emperor had demurred.

"It was wise to expend four of our six cartridges at once, rapidly, altogether, four days ago," said Iaachus to Otto. "As you surmised would be the case, the enemy withdrew precipitously, and, suspecting that we must be stocked with ammunition, having been so free in its expenditure, were reluctant to renew their advance."

"It won us a reprieve of four days," said Tuvo Ausonius.

"Indeed," said Julian, wryly, "a day per cartridge."

"I anticipated a week," said Otto, "but already probes and provocations multiply."

"Perhaps Ingeld has penetrated our ruse," said Tuvo Ausonius.

"Sidonicus, impatient to proceed, may have assured useful, gullible fanatics that being torn to pieces by blasts and consumed by fire is a quick, sure route to the table of *Karch*," said Julian.

"That we have not fired again has doubtless heartened the foe," said Iaachus.

"There is another possibility, as well," said Otto, "one I view with dread."

"Speak, dear friend," said Julian, concerned.

"Through purchases or bargainings, through pledges or promises," said Otto, "the foe may be accruing resources. Indeed, he may already have them at his disposal, but has been reluctant to apply them."

"Resources?" said Julian.

"Cartridges," said Otto, "five cartridges, two, as I understand it, for a pistol, and three for a rifle."

"I do not understand," said Julian.

"There was a ship," said Iaachus, "the *Turona*, which carried such treasures, which was intercepted by a corsair."

"You think such devices have found their way to Telnar?" asked Julian.

"It is possible," said Iaachus.

"Why then have they not been used?" asked Tuvo Ausonius.

"They are incredibly precious," said Iaachus. "One waits. One ponders. One does not spend gold recklessly."

"But one may spend it freely," said Otto, "for what is worth more than gold."

"Such as an empire," said Titus Gelinus.

"Precisely," said Otto.

"I think," said Julian, "Ingeld is unwilling to destroy the palace."

"I think that is it," said Titus Gelinus. "I think that is true."

"A palace can be rebuilt," said Otto.

At that moment a great explosion rocked the palace, and, a moment later, another. Slaves screamed, men leaped to their feet, the table shook and dishes rattled, and outside the throne room could be heard, as though in the distance, a tumbling of masonry.

"The great doors are sealed, are they not?" inquired Julian.

"Surely," said Otto.

"Our question is answered," said Iaachus. "Ingeld and Sidonicus have cartridges."

"From the *Turona*?" said Titus Gelinus.

"Presumably," said Iaachus.

"They would then have three left," said Julian. "We have two."

"Pistol cartridges," said Otto.

"The great doors," said Tuvo Ausonius, "were designed, were they not, to withstand the force of such weaponry?"

"Yes," said Julian.

"To resist one strike," said Iaachus, "perhaps two."

"So few?" said Tuvo Ausonius.

"Two cartridges were expended," said Otto. "They would presumably be those for the pistol. The three not yet fired would presumably be stronger charges, those for the rifle."

"One must not expect too much of a foot of steel," said Iaachus. "It is only a foot of steel."

"We may all die," said Julian, "choked with dust, crushed in debris."

"Or wading, drowning, in molten metal," said Iaachus, pleasantly.

There were cries of consternation from the slaves, who were now again, as was appropriate, on their knees.

"Be silent," snapped Iaachus.

The slaves then lowered their heads, trembled, and were silent. They must await their disposition. It would be done with them as with other animals, as their masters pleased.

How exalted are free women!

How lowly are slaves!

CHAPTER SEVENTY-FIVE

"What is the damage?" inquired Otto.

"The great guard doors, gouged, and shaken, are awry on their hinges, but muchly hold," said Julian. "As they hang, there is a narrow crevice at their height. One would need ladders, from the outside, to reach it."

"I hear no swarmings, nor cries of battle," said Otto.

"They have demonstrated their power," said Iaachus, "and are uncertain of our resources. Their next step will be one of cunning, a recourse to deception, doubtless a pretense to parley."

"Dear Tuvo," said Otto. "Use the side passage, and the interior ascents, if they are practical. Some walls must stand. See if the observation ports are unblocked."

Tuvo Ausonius withdrew from the throne room.

"I smell smoke," said Titus Gelinus.

"The approach corridor will have been demolished," said Iaachus. "The anterior façade will be gone, the balcony of address will be collapsed. Much will be rubble. The architraves, pylons, gates, and vaults of a thousand years will be a shambles."

"Such things may be rebuilt, to last a new thousand years," said Otto.

"Iaachus weeps," marveled Julian.

"No," said Iaachus, angrily. "It is penetrant dust, the stinging of particles of smoke."

At that point a long, thin, piercing note was heard, which carried even to the throne room.

"They lose little time," said Iaachus.

"What is the sound?" said Otto. "I think it speaks not of the charge."

"It is the herald's trumpet," said Iaachus.

"A parley then," said Titus Gelinus.

"Let them wait," said Iaachus. "This may lure them into expending another cartridge, perhaps two."

"Rather," said Otto, "let us appear eager for some truce, over which we might haggle and dally, thus purchasing time."

"Time for what?" asked Iaachus.

"Only fools rush to death," said Julian.

"Fanatics hurry to the table of *Karch*," said Iaachus.

"And they will know no disappointment," said Julian.

"For they will be at the table of *Karch*?" asked Iaachus.

"For they will be dead," said Julian.

"Idiots are useful," said Iaachus. "What tyrant would choose to dispense with them?"

"The curtain of the future is not yet drawn," said Otto.

"It never is," said Iaachus.

"Yet tomorrow becomes today," said Otto.

"If they have the purloined *Turona* cartridges, three more firings would put us at their mercy," said Julian.

"I think so," said Otto.

At this point once more blared the herald's trumpet.

Tuvo Ausonius reappeared in the throne room. "Walls are muchly intact," he said. "Most ports, those examined, are clear. Ruination is muchly confined to the great portal and the façade giving on to the square. The balcony of address is crumbled. Tumbled masonry rears, heaped upon the broad stairs and the vantage porch. In the square a small party of civilians, attended by Floonian clergy, holds aloft the life flag, with its shimmering green, the color of mercy, and peace."

"So truce is offered," said Titus Gelinus.

"Or seems to be offered," said Iaachus.

"In this I see the hand of Sidonicus," said Julian, "the pretense of conciliation and compassion, staged for the consumption of the Floonian faithful."

"Much more," said Iaachus, "who would not prefer deception to danger, toil, and blood? Falsity is useless if it does not masquerade as truth. Generous terms will be offered, only to be soon rescinded and betrayed. Diplomacy is often the prelude to murder. A lie is a most significant weapon."

"Only if the lie is believed," said Otto.

"True," said Julian.

"But let the lie seem to be believed," said Otto, "that we may turn it to our advantage."

"Thus let lies clash," said Iaachus.

"Are Sidonicus, exarch of Telnar, or Ingeld, prince of the Drisriaks, visible?" asked Otto.

"No," said Tuvo Ausonius. "I do not think so. I see no exarchical purple, I do not see one who is clearly in the trappings of the Drisriaks."

"They are wise to remain out of range," said Julian.

"One in the lesser purple, one of the high clergy, is in evidence," said Tuvo.

"That would be Fulvius, the deputy exarch," said Iaachus.

"Sidonicus is willing to risk him," said Otto.

"The exarch is content to risk others," said Iaachus.

"It is a skill of his," said Julian, "one improved by much practice."

"Is Fulvius, if it be he," asked Otto, "first before the flag?"

"No," said Tuvo Ausonius. "He is not paramount. Prominent rather is a seeming barbarian, one of small stature and crooked frame."

"I think I know him," said Otto.

Again the trumpet blared.

"It is the third note," said Iaachus.

"That is of purport?" asked Otto.

"I fear so," said Iaachus. "If it be ignored, onslaught will ensue."

"Then," said Otto, "we shall respond without delay. Open the subgate in the guard door."

"Remain here," said Julian. "I will go."

"I will go," said Titus Gelinus. "I am envoy to the senate."

"I am known, and will be recognized," said Iaachus.

"Who would trust you?" asked Julian.

"Send me," said Tuvo Ausonius. "I am least here. My loss would be politically negligible."

To the side, kneeling, Sesella, his slave, cried out in protest, and then, frowned upon, trembling and weeping, put her head to the tiles.

"Not negligible to all," said Otto.

"Do not go!" said Julian.

"I have seized the throne, I am chieftain of the Wolfungs, I am king of the Otungs, I am first in the Vandal nation," said Otto.

The men stepped aside, and Otto, unattended, made his way through the narrow subgate.

CHAPTER SEVENTY-SIX

"It is impossible!" screamed Sidonicus.

"It is true," said Fulvius. "The premises have been examined, in detail. The palace is deserted."

"It cannot be," said Sidonicus.

"After the third blast the guard doors were melted from their hinges. The palace keep, the throne room, was ours," said Fulvius.

"And empty," said Buthar.

"The rooms and adjacent corridors were searched," said Fulvius, "all rooms, store rooms, the great library, reception chambers, banquet halls, closets, the royal quarters, accommodations for guests and dignitaries, guards' quarters, servants' housings, slave pens and cages, everything, all empty."

"What of blackened skeletons, charred bodies, scattered limbs, surfaces disfigured with dried, brittle cakes of shed blood?" asked Sidonicus.

"Nothing," said Grissus.

"I will not have it so," said Sidonicus. "What is destruction without carnage? Surely this mockery is not the visage of victory. Where is the foe, butchered, or chained, at our feet? Why is he not in custody, marked for execution? Why is he not shackled in the quarries or laboring in the damp and cold of the mines? Is conquest hollow?"

"Please, blessed Holiness," said Fulvius, "let the storms of your discontent subside. Let the contentment of *Karch* and the sweet peace of Floon attend you."

"Fool," hissed Sidonicus.

"Your Holiness?" inquired Fulvius.

"Save such mindless, pattering drivel for the simple," said Sidonicus.

"Forgive me, your Holiness," said Fulvius. "I meant no harm, or disrespect. I accept, as I must, and as is fitting, your well-deserved rebuke, but I assure you nonetheless that there is little to justify your agitation or disappointment. The victory is ours. Success is clear, and complete. The prize is won. The guerdon is seized. Resistance is absent. Even now Prince Ingeld moves to occupy the palace."

"Bring me a sweet," said Sidonicus.

"It has been four days," had said Sidonicus, earlier.

"I have done as you asked," had said Urta. "Four times in four days I have addressed the foe, following the trumpet of parley, he, the usurper himself, standing atop the rubble of masonry strewn upon the vantage porch and steps leading to the palace, and, as you directed, three times in three days, sweetened the terms of the truce, and he has withdrawn again and again, supposedly to consult with his colleagues, only to return with more cavils or amendments."

"My patience is not infinite," said Sidonicus. "The cable of my renowned forbearance is strained. It grows taut."

"The vile Otung has no intention of accepting any terms, even amnesty, riches, and the empire itself, were it offered," snarled Ingeld.

"That is hard to believe," said Fulvius.

"You are not Otung, or Drisriak," said Ingeld.

"You deem him insane?" asked Fulvius.

"I deem him perceptive," said Ingeld.

"Surely he will, sooner or later, rely on the pledge of the exarch, the sworn oath of his Holiness, according him protection and safe-conduct," said Fulvius.

"Would you?" asked Ingeld.

"Who could anticipate," said Fulvius, "that the pledge of the exarch, uttered in all integrity, proffered in all openness and honesty, would be abrogated by a senatorial dictate?"

"I find it hard to believe that the people will accept such blatant treachery," said Ingeld.

"They will accept it," said Urta. "It will be a ruling of the senate. It will be legal. Who will go against the law? Law makes all things possible."

"But Safarius is missing," said Buthar, he, as Grissus, in fee to Sidonicus. "Was it not he who was to arrange for the senate to reject the truce, deeming it unauthorized?"

"Once the Otung had accepted terms, and surrendered, thus clearing the way for his detention and destruction," said Grissus.

"Of course," said Buthar.

"Where is the *primarius* of the senate, worthy Timon Safarius Rhodius?" asked Fulvius.

"Disappeared," said Sidonicus.

"We must then choose another," said Fulvius. "Second in the senate is Clearchus Pyrides, of Inez IV."

"I do not trust him," said Sidonicus.

"He is said to be honest," said Urta.

"And is thus not to be trusted," said Sidonicus.

"How then shall we proceed?" asked Fulvius.

"The senate is a tool," said Sidonicus. "We can choose another to wield that tool. Ambitious hypocrites and groveling sycophants abound."

"I think," said Ingeld, "we have overestimated the power of the Otung. Were his resources as rich as we initially feared, he would not have pretended to participate in negotiations, but might have destroyed half of Telnar. I doubt that he has more than a dozen charges left."

"Then he is finished," said Buthar.

"Why then does he prolong the farce of negotiation?" asked Fulvius.

"Surely to postpone the inevitable," said Ingeld.

"How many charges have we, from the *Turona*," asked Sidonicus.

"Three are left," said Buthar.

"Maximum charges, rifle charges," said Grissus.

"Buthar," said Sidonicus, "how many charges will it require to open the palace?"

"One, perhaps two," had said Buthar.

"Use three," had said Sidonicus.

"Here, your Holiness," said Fulvius, "is your sweet."

"Prince Ingeld," said Sidonicus, "moves to occupy the palace?"

"As we speak," said Fulvius.

"I trust that the plans for the coronation of the royal child, the supposed son of Ingeld and the Princess Viviana, are in readiness," said Sidonicus.

"Yes, and have been for days," said Fulvius. "On the day of the coronation Prince Ingeld will accede to the regency."

"The Princess died in childbirth," said Sidonicus.

"The public lamentations have it so," said Fulvius.

"Expediency is the coin of public truth," said Sidonicus.

"Indeed," said Fulvius.

CHAPTER SEVENTY-SEVEN

"I have used the tunnel often, to depart the palace and traverse the city," said Otto.

"Emerging in the dark of night," said Julian.

"We shared such adventures," said Otto.

"Fortunate that the house of the senate is empty," said Tuvo Ausonius.

"It is not in session," said Iaachus.

"Who would think of looking for us here?" said Julian.

"It was not practical to move fugitives, slaves, and prisoners far," said Otto. "So large a group, several in number, would surely be quickly noted. And fortunately our fellow, Gelinus, as envoy to the senate, possessed the access combinations to enter the house surreptitiously by means of one of the secret entrances, a discreet convenience, designed for private comings and goings."

"Ingeld will move quickly, to have the mysterious child, he alleged to be the son of the Princess Viviana, proclaimed emperor, and will then assume the regency," said Titus Gelinus.

"There will be a coronation," said Iaachus. "Sidonicus will insist upon it. It will be a part of his scheme of things."

"From here, across the square, to the side, we can see the palace," said Tuvo Ausonius.

"Perhaps we can then see the processions of the intended coronation," said Otto. "Surely they will assemble at the palace, to proceed to the great temple."

"Sidonicus, in his scheme of things, will preach that the sanction of the temple, his temple, and no other, is required for the crowning of the emperor, thus subordinating the crown to the temple," said Iaachus.

"Many are the paths to power," said Titus Gelinus.

"And some are subtler and more sinister than others," said Julian.

"The most dangerous foe to society and the state, to justice and freedom," said Titus Gelinus, "is a foe not noted, a foe not recognized, an invisible foe."

"It will not end there," said Iaachus. "The temple will drain and expropriate populations; it will close schools; it will train and narrow minds; it will, with righteous, unquestioned zeal, force a single faith on diverse communities and utilize the state to exterminate or exile dissidents; it will rule through terror, guilt, and the obedient, secular sword; it will even threaten and intimidate rulers; it will claim the right to absolve citizens of their obligations and duties to them; it will erode loyalties and sever ties essential to civil order; it will unleash anarchy and use confusion and chaos as a weapon; it will generate civil strife; it will depose kings and subvert thrones."

Those gathered in the deliberation chamber, in the semicircular well at the foot of the tiers, were then silent.

The sound of a wagon passing by could be heard.

"It is morning," said Julian.

"We cannot stay here indefinitely," said Titus Gelinus. "Workers will come."

"Water and supplies brought from the palace will be soon exhausted," said Iaachus.

"Is the empress mother suitably situated?" asked Otto.

"In one of the robing rooms," said Tuvo Ausonius. "She insisted on being returned immediately to the palace."

"You explained to her the inadvisability of that, I trust," said Otto.

"Yes," said Tuvo Ausonius, "torture, dismemberment, being cast as garbage into a *carnarium*, and such."

"Did such considerations alter her view?" inquired Otto.

"She agreed to give the matter further thought," said Tuvo Ausonius.

"And what of young Aesilesius?" asked Otto.

"He crouches in the senate library, against a wall, whining, confused, shuddering, sputum dribbling from his mouth, being cared for by the small, red-haired beauty, Nika, his slave."

"I see," said Otto.

"Many of us are sorry for her, though she is a slave," said Tuvo Ausonius. "How miserable for her, a vital, lovely slave, well-curved and doubtless worth many *darins*, to be assigned so onerous a duty, essentially to be caged with a monstrosity, a man's body inhabited by the mind of a feckless, short-tempered, irresponsible, unpredictable child. Relieve her of her duties, before she is driven mad, or at least assign others to lighten her labors and share her miseries."

"Sesella, for example?" asked Otto.

"Be it, I beg you, as though I had said nothing," said Tuvo Ausonius.

"You have said nothing," said Otto.

"Thank you, your highness," said Tuvo Ausonius.

"I deem the present arrangement satisfactory," said Otto.

"It is eminently so," said Tuvo Ausonius.

"I fear you have shown solicitude for a slave," said Otto, "first for the slave, Nika, and then for the slave, Sesella."

"A lapse, two lapses, your highness," said Tuvo Ausonius.

"What of the prisoners, Safarius, *primarius* of the senate, and faithless, handsome Corelius?" asked Otto.

"Both chained in a storeroom, apart from one another," said Ausonius, "under the guard of Boris and Andak."

"Excellent," said Otto.

"I fear Safarius is losing his mind," said Ausonius. "He fears he is to be done away with. He is going mad. He claims he is to be poisoned. He lives in terror of being poisoned. It is a madness with him. He refuses to eat until his guards prove to him that his simple provender, each meal, is free of toxins."

"I thought him of sterner stuff," said Otto.

"He evinced signs of this dementia even in the palace," said Ausonius.

"What of the slaves?" asked Otto.

"Confined in a cloak room, and ordered to silence," said Ausonius.

"Good," said Otto. "Few things better impress on a woman that she is a slave than not permitting her to speak when she pleases."

"Having her on her knees, naked, and her neck in a collar, as well," said Ausonius.

"It is pleasant to own a woman," said Otto.

"I have found it so," said Ausonius.

"It solves many problems," said Otto.

"And for the woman, as well," said Ausonius.

"The "same world" seems far behind you," said Otto.

"It is," said Ausonius. "It is incomprehensible how that unnatural insanity could infect a world."

"And yet, at one time, you accepted its aberrations unquestioningly," said Otto.

"I knew no better," said Ausonius. "Much depends on how one is raised, how one is taught, what one is permitted to know, and so on."

"You were unacquainted with nature, and biology," said Otto.

"Clearly," said Ausonius.

"Master! Master!" cried Nika, frenzied and distraught, suddenly emerging from a ground-level side passage, rushing forward into the lofty, tiered, deliberation chamber. "My Master, Aesilesius, is gone!"

CHAPTER SEVENTY-EIGHT

"Speak!" demanded Otto.

"I was sent for bread," cried Nika. "When I returned, my Master was gone."

"A ruse," Julian.

"Do not be absurd," said Iaachus. "Aesilesius is incapable of such things. He has wandered off, like a lost dog."

"He did not come this way," said Tuvo Ausonius.

"We will search the building," said Titus Gelinus. "We will find him, we will bring him back."

"Do not," said Otto, sharply. "He will not be in the building."

"How do you know?" asked Iaachus.

"He will have availed himself of the secret entrance, the same as that through which we entered."

"If he is not in the building, he must have done so," said Titus Gelinus. "The private entrances, with their panels, are concealed, both inside and outside. He would be familiar only with that through which we entered."

"And he would be familiar only with that combination," said Otto.

"Do not jest," said Iaachus. "A mind like that of Aesilesius could not even keep in mind the simplest of combinations, or even understand the nature of such things."

"Let me go," begged Nika. "Let me go, and search for him!"

"She has a palace collar," said Iaachus.

"Few are likely to inspect it," said Julian.

"Please, Master," begged Nika. "Let me go, Master."

"Remain where you are," said Otto. "Perhaps later."

"One of us should go," said Julian.

"Wait," said Otto.

"He cannot have gone far," said Julian.

"He may have gone farther than you think," said Otto.

"He can hardly walk," said Julian. "He will attract attention, lurching about the streets."

"Perhaps not," said Otto.

"I can find him," said Julian.

"Perhaps not," said Otto, "if he does not wish to be found."

"I do not understand," said Julian.

"It is nothing," said Otto.

"He will not know his way, the districts, or the streets," said Julian.

"He may be more familiar with such things than we know," said Otto.

"How?" said Julian.

"Do not concern yourself," said Otto.

"Few know of his affliction," said Iaachus. "His relationship to the royal family will not be understood. He can hardly speak. He may not even know his name. He will be regarded as no more than crippled, misshapen simpleton. Guardsmen will pick him up and have him examined by authorities, following which he will be remanded to one of the charity pits reserved for the insane, to be thrown bread from time to time from the spanning bridge."

"Perhaps it is all for the best," said Julian. "When the forces of Sidonicus and Ingeld locate us, as they must, we will all be slain, sooner or later, slowly or more quickly."

"Perhaps you are right," said Otto. "Perhaps Aesilesius is the wisest of us all."

"You seem disappointed," said Julian.

"Aesilesius, with his childlike mind, does have a large body," said Iaachus. "In the charity pit, when sufficiently hungry, he is likely to prove a formidable foe. I myself would not choose to challenge him."

"You speak of him as though he were a wolf or *vi-cat*!" cried Nika.

"Be silent, slave," said Iaachus, "lest your tongue be cut out."

"Forgive me, Master," said Nika, frightened, kneeling, putting her head down.

"What are we to do?" asked Titus Gelinus.

"For now, as we have done for days, wait," said Otto. "There is little else to do."

"And for what are we waiting?" asked Julian.

"The curtain of the future is not yet drawn," said Otto.

"It never is," said Iaachus.

"Yet tomorrow becomes today," said Otto.

At that moment Andak who, with his cohort Boris, supervised the prisoners Safarius and Corelius, reeled into the deliberation chamber, stumbling toward those gathered in the semicircular well at the foot of the tiers.

"He is ill," said Julian.

Andak, white-faced, stumbled forward and was caught and held, by Titus Gelinus. Andak's eyes did not focus. His lips moved but no sound escaped them.

"What is wrong?" demanded Iaachus.

"Violently, desperately ill," said Julian.

Titus Gelinus lowered Andak to the floor, and supported him there, in a sitting position.

"I think he has gone blind," said Ausonius.

The body of Andak begin to tremble and then, slowly, the muscles contracting, stiffen.

"I have seen this, I am sure," said Julian, suddenly, "long ago, on Naxos." He knelt beside the sitting Andak, and, with two hands, spread his jaws.

A sound of dismay, of revulsion escaped Ausonius.

"Yes," said Julian.

The tongue was black and swollen.

"What is it?" asked Iaachus.

"A toxin, eloidial mercury," said Julian. "It proceeds rapidly, but is not a merciful poison. It paralyzes the lungs and induces suffocation. One suffers terribly. It is like acid in the blood stream. I do not see how he reached the chamber. On Naxos it is used for executions, of those guilty of the most heinous crimes."

"I have been a fool, a mindless fool," said Otto.

"I think he is dead," said Titus Gelinus.

"Quite dead," said Julian, rising.

"How could he have obtained the poison?" asked Ausonius. "How could it have been administered?"

"Where is Boris?" asked Iaachus.

"He will be dead, in the storeroom," said Julian. "He may have imbibed more of the compound."

"The appearance of madness is not always madness," said Otto. "Timon Safarius Rhodius planned well. This was prepared for, for days, perhaps weeks. He waited until the opportune time and then struck."

"I do not understand," said Iaachus.

"The pretense of madness," said Otto. "The feigning of the terror of poisoning. The refusal to eat until assured the food was free of poisons."

"The guards proving the harmlessness of the food by themselves tasting it, one or both, to assure Safarius of his safety," said Ausonius.

"And this time, one of the times for which Safarius was waiting, it being tasted by both," said Otto.

"Safarius was chained," said Iaachus.

"But not encelled," said Ausonius.

"And locks respond to keys," said Otto, "keys easily available from the wallet or pouch of a dead or dying guard, otherwise the deed would not be practical."

"Let us seek Safarius," said Iaachus.

"It would be useless," said Titus Gelinus. "He is *primarius* of the senate; he would know every foot of this building and its devices. He would have taken his departure within moments of his deed."

"How could he have obtained poison, or dispensed it?" asked Ausonius.

"From a ring, worn," said Iaachus, "from a sachet concealed about his person, from a raveling on a sleeve, a raveling imbued with the substance, in many ways."

"One thing is clear," said Otto. "Our location is now known, and will be instantly communicated to Sidonicus and Ingeld."

"We have run out of time," said Iaachus.

"Perhaps not," said Otto.

CHAPTER SEVENTY-NINE

"We owe you much, noble Safarius," said Sidonicus.

"I did no more than my duty to the state, the throne, and the temple," said Timon Safarius Rhodius, modestly, he of the Telnar Rhodii, *primarius* of the senate of Telnaria.

"Were it not for you we might not now have in custody the usurper and his treasonous associates."

"I expected them to die fighting," said Ingeld.

"They were cowards," said Fulvius. "They made not the least show of resistance."

"One might have thought them ministrants," said Ingeld.

"Ministrants, dear prince," said Sidonicus, "remember, are forbidden the shedding of blood."

Buthar and Grissus, both in fee to the exarch, stood to the side, their arms folded.

"Why are we in this basement room, below the exarchical residence?" asked Safarius.

"The throne room," said Sidonicus, "is being dealt with, freshened, cleaned, recarpeted, refurbished, and such. The stately pomp of office is being restored. Surely you can understand this. Smokened walls, burnt hangings, ruined carpeting, cold droplets of melted metal, rubble, and such, ill befit the majesty of empire."

"Of course," said Safarius.

"You were very clever in managing your escape," said Sidonicus.

"It was well thought out," said Fulvius.

Safarius nodded gracefully.

"And you wisely left the fugitive, your fellow prisoner, Corelius, at the mercy of his captors."

"I thought it best, excellency," said Safarius. "His companionship might have delayed or jeopardized my escape. Too, as I knew he was one whom you had long sought to apprehend, I left him in place, helpless, yours to do with as you pleased, once you had invaded and recaptured the house of the senate."

"Excellent," said Sidonicus.

"Doubtless, fearing for his life at the hands of the usurper and his villains, he pleaded with you to be released, either to accompany you or to be freed to seek his fortune elsewhere," remarked Fulvius.

"Quite so, sweet, holy ministrant," said Safarius. "And he pleaded most piteously, most desperately."

"We had long sought him," said Sidonicus. "He betrayed us grievously."

"He will be dealt with accordingly," said Fulvius.

"We do not deal lightly with traitors," said Sidonicus.

"Nor should you," said Safarius.

"As I understand it," said Sidonicus, "you feigned an irrational fear of being poisoned, this pretense being credited by your guards, and generating their pity, indeed, to the extent that, as you refused, in seeming terror, to eat, they grew accustomed to assuring you of the provender's innocence, this done by sampling it themselves."

"I had poison, concealed in my tunic, in a clasp at the left shoulder," said Safarius. "When the usurper left the palace and took refuge in the senate house, an edifice without cells, an edifice muchly deserted, an edifice with which I was intimately familiar, I awaited my opportunity. When it presented itself, I proceeded as I had planned."

"You are extremely clever," said Sidonicus.

"Thank you, your excellency," said Safarius.

"But I wonder if you were clever enough," said Sidonicus.

"Your excellency?" asked Safarius.

"We trusted you," said Sidonicus.

"Appropriately," said Safarius, uneasily.

"Boris and Andak, whom you poisoned, were your guards, your captors, in the senate house?" asked Sidonicus.

"He made that clear," said Fulvius.

"Is that not interesting?" asked Sidonicus.

"How so, your excellency?" asked Safarius.

"We took them to be your bodyguards, attending you at various secret councils," said Sidonicus.

"Now, it seems," said Fulvius, "you were their prisoner, that you were in their custody."

"The signal for the planned coup was prematurely issued," said Sidonicus, "confusing matters, disrupting plans, introducing bewilderment and chaos into what should have been a rapid, smooth, effective seizure of power. Rioting and looting ensued. The city was in turmoil, for days. Only now is the city in our power. The scales could have tipped either way. Who knew how the reed might lean, how the dice might fall? Anarchy is a thoughtless beast. Who knows on what it might turn or whom it might attack? From it a dozen competitive factions might emerge."

"It was not I who betrayed the signal!" cried Safarius. "It was Boris or Andak, or both! Unknown to me they were suborned by the foe!"

"You and they survived the killings beneath the warehouse of Dardanis, in which Abrogastes and Ortog were freed," said Sidonicus. "Then somehow Boris and Andak became your custodians. It is not hard to guess on what terms your life was spared."

"If I had not done the will of the foe, his minions, either one of them, Boris or Andak, would have killed me!" said Safarius.

"You spied, you revealed secrets," said Fulvius.

"I had no choice," said Safarius.

"You could have resisted, you could have refused, you could have defied them, you could have denounced them," said Fulvius.

"And died?" asked Safarius.

"Certainly," said Sidonicus, "and then rushed jubilantly to the table of *Karch*."

"I am not one of your dupes," said Safarius.

"But you are ready to obey now, are you not?" asked Sidonicus.

"Certainly," said Safarius, sweating, relieved.

"Excellent," said Sidonicus. "Buthar, fetch the plate."

"I do not care to see this," said Ingeld. "I take my leave." He then withdrew, not speaking, from the room.

"What is going on?" asked Safarius.

"The food, I fear, is now cold, and dry, and stale," said Sidonicus.

"But it will do," said Fulvius.

"I do not understand," said Safarius.

"You did not finish your supper," said Sidonicus. "You may do so now."

"What supper?" said Safarius.

"That which Boris and Andak sampled for you, in the senate house," said Sidonicus. "We had it picked up, and saved for you."

"No!" cried Safarius.

"We do not think lightly of traitors," said Sidonicus.

"Eat," said Fulvius.

"Ministrants do not shed blood!" said Safarius.

"This does not shed blood," said Fulvius.

"Eat," said Sidonicus.

In the dimly lit basement room beneath the temple, Safarius looked about, first at Sidonicus and Fulvius, and then at Buthar and Grissus, and then partook of what lay, hitherto little touched, on the plate.

CHAPTER EIGHTY

Julian struck the metal door, again and again, angrily, in frustration.

"Desist," said Otto. "You will bloody your fists, you could break your hands."

Julian spun about, enraged. "We could have sold our lives dearly," he said. "That would have been an honorable death, heated, noble, and swift. Now, at the mercy of Sidonicus we can be disposed of as he wishes, shamefully, in prolonged agony."

"We will be thought cowards," said Tuvo Ausonius.

"Certainly," said Otto.

"Why did you not permit us the satisfaction of a worthy death?" asked Julian. "Why did you order us to lay down our arms, and submit, like sheep, offering not the least resistance? I had two cartridges in my pistol. They might have slain dozens."

"And they will think us cowards," said Ausonius.

"Does that concern you?" asked Otto.

"Yes," said Ausonius.

"It should not," said Otto.

"Why not?" asked Ausonius.

"Because you are not a coward," said Otto. "To be thought a coward should be of concern only to cowards."

A narrow, descending, placid shaft of light entered the chamber by means of a small barred window set high in the wall, some fourteen feet above the straw-strewn floor. In this shaft of light floated tiny, sparkling particles of dust.

"I am an attorney," said Titus Gelinus. "I know the law. They cannot just dispose of us. I can argue from a hundred precedents. There must be a trial."

"There will be no trial if it is not in the interests of Sidonicus," said Otto.

"The law!" protested Gelinus.

"It can be invoked or ignored," said Otto. "It exists or does not exist at the will of those in power; it means one thing or another, as those in power choose what they wish it to mean."

"I do not think you a coward, my friend," said Iaachus. "I know better. Yet I acknowledge I am surprised that you did not have us die at the entrance to the senate."

"You had us surrender," said Julian, reproachfully.

"True," said Otto.

"And placed us in gross jeopardy," said Ausonius, "subject to an ignoble, shameful fate."

"That is true," said Otto.

"And what has this gained for us?" asked Iaachus.

"A day, perhaps two," said Otto.

"Ah," said Iaachus, "I see."

"I thought you would," said Otto.

"The curtain of the future is not yet drawn," said Iaachus.

"It never is," said Otto.

"Yet," said Iaachus, "tomorrow becomes today."

"Precisely," said Otto.

At that moment there was a stirring and a shuffling on the other side of the stout metal door. With a creak it was swung open and a figure, half stumbling and then catching its balance, had been thrust through the opening.

"We are joined," said Julian.

"But by whom?" asked Iaachus.

The figure, that of young man, was hard to discern in the half-light.

"Who are you?" asked Julian.

"We know him not," said Tuvo Ausonius. "He is a spy, thrust amongst us to descry plans or acquire information on allies, their dispositions, locations, and numbers."

"You do not know me?" asked the young man.

"I do," said Otto.

"He wears not the garb of the Otungen," said Titus Gelinus.

"Who are you?" asked Iaachus.

"Show them," suggested Otto.

The figure of the young man, tall, straight, and large, strong and proud, stepped forward.

"Now you know him," said Otto.

"I do not," said Julian.

"Nor I," said Iaachus.

"From Vellmer, from Tangara?" said Titus Gelinus.

"I think not," said Julian.

"I cannot place him," said Iaachus. "But I am sure I have seen him. There is an uncanny resemblance to another, some other whom I cannot place."

"Show them," said Otto.

Then, in the half-darkness a remarkable transformation took place in the figure before them. It seemed to shrink visibly, in and on itself, and to grow twisted and crooked. Its head wagged back and forth, and intermittent puling noises escaped its lips.

The group in the chamber regarded the newcomer.

"Foul actor," cried Julian, suddenly, "mocking us, insulting us, disguising himself as Aesilesius."

"What is the point of it?" asked Titus Gelinus.

"The Aesilesius you knew," said Otto, "was the disguise, now once more feigned. This is no actor, no counterfeit. This is the true Aesilesius before you."

"Do not be absurd," said Julian.

"Do you think I do not recognize you, my allegedly ambitious cousin?" asked the contorted figure, looking up, speaking with clear, aristocratic diction.

It then straightened up, and stretched its limbs. "That is better," it said. "Muscles held rigid soon grow stiff and cramped. I have known much such pain, and, I assure you, it is far less than pleasant. Indeed, not all my weeping and whimpering was mere pretense. Being oneself entails great risk, but there is at least this to be said for it. It is more comfortable."

"My emperor," said Iaachus, going to one knee.

Tuvo Ausonius then knelt, as did Titus Gelinus. Then Julian, too, knelt.

"Rise," said Aesilesius. "This is no place for the pomp of court."

"Indeed," said Iaachus getting to his feet. "We are all fellow prisoners, subject to a common doom."

"He is truly Aesilesius?" said Julian, rising, wonderingly.

"Yes," said Otto.

"How long have you known of this?" asked Julian.

"I suspected it for a long time," said Otto. "I have known it for some time."

"And you did not kill him?" said Iaachus.

"It slipped my mind," said Otto.

"Politics prescribes certain actions," said Julian.

"So, too, does honor," said Otto, "and they are not always the same actions."

"I accord greetings," said Aesilesius. "I hope they will be accepted. I apologize for appearing as I did, perpetuating a hoax of several years' duration. In cowardice I maintained a façade, one unworthy and deceitful. It was a choice motivated by a fear of dying. I have now chosen manhood, motivated by a willingness to live, or die, as a man should. It is a lesson taught to me by two who did not fear to give lessons to an emperor, a man and a woman, a barbarian and a slave."

"Your greetings are accepted," said Iaachus.

"They are accepted," said Tuvo Ausonius and Titus Gelinus.

"They are accepted," said Julian, he of the Aureliani.

"And you, Otung, come from arenas and wars, chieftain, captain, and king, defender of an empire not always kind to your people, preserver of an empire once an enemy, an empire alien to your origins, background, and blood, do you accept my greetings?" asked Aesilesius.

"I wonder," said Otto, "if you well learned the lessons of manhood."

"I have done my best, little and inadequate as it may be," said Aesilesius.

"You deserted us," said Otto. "You fled the senate house. You would not, your guise of imbecility discarded, be recognized as Aesilesius. Few, in any event, would know you. You were much hidden from the public. There are those here, even in this dismal chamber, ones well familiar with the court and palace, who did not recognize you. You would mingle with crowds. You would escape. You would live."

"I knew you would not permit me to leave the senate house," said Aesilesius. "For some reason I seemed important, or precious, to you. I sensed you might have in mind a role for me to play. I sensed you might even care for me, as one might a son, a troubled, wayward son. You would not risk me. You would not let me leave. Accordingly, I availed myself of the opportunity to leave when, and as, I pleased."

"You were not authorized to do so," said Otto.

"On the contrary," said Aesilesius, "I authorized it."

"I feared you were confused, distracted, infantile, and irresponsible," said Iaachus, "that you had merely wandered away, and that you would be apprehended as one helpless and incompetent, as one ill, or lacking, in mind, and would be consigned to a charity pit, to be maintained at public expense."

"Dear, kind Iaachus," said Aesilesius.

"But your scheme failed," said Otto. "In vain you abandoned your friends, deserted your post, and left others to die, while you sought to save your own life."

"Indeed," said Aesilesius, "my scheme failed, but I do not think you know the scheme."

"The matter is clear enough," said Otto.

"Perhaps not, hasty Otung," said Aesilesius. "How is it that I am here now with you?"

"You were recognized," said Otto.

"No," said Aesilesius. "They do not know who I am."

"Then why have you been put in with us?" asked Otto.

"After you abandoned the palace," said Aesilesius, "you had no way to communicate with Rurik, the consul of Larial VII, your ally in the dock district. Accordingly, he might well be ignorant of how matters stood in the heart of Telnar. I hoped to reach him, to apprise him of the situation, and have him organize a sortie into the city to attempt to extract you from danger, hopefully before your hiding place in the senate house was discovered. Unfortunately, in trying to reach the dock district, I was apprehended by Drisriak guards loyal to Ingeld, troops stationed to seal off the dock district, prior to a planned move by Ingeld to deal with Rurik and his men."

"How is one to believe this?" asked Otto.

"I was not recognized," said Aesilesius. "The city is large, and filled with strangers, men unknown to one another. Who would notice me? It would have been easy to avoid the militarized dock district, to pretend sympathy with the uprising, even leave the city, by a hundred routes. I did not do so."

"You were not recognized as Aesilesius?" said Otto.

"No," said Aesilesius, "and I am not recognized as Aesilesius even now. I have called myself Vorn, a name common in the countryside, to the west of Telnar. I am here with you because I am thought a spy, a confederate of the usurper."

"And now must share our fate," said Iaachus.

"I fear for the empress mother," said Aesilesius.

"We all do," said Iaachus.

"Where are Boris and Andak?" asked Aesilesius.

"Dead," said Iaachus. "They were poisoned by Safarius, who escaped, and revealed our ensconcement in the senate house. That is how you find us here."

"And Corelius?" asked Aesilesius.

"Incarcerated, separately, for his own safety," said Iaachus. "They were afraid we would kill him."

"Doubtless Safarius now stands high in the ranks of our foes," said Aesilesius.

"Doubtless," said Iaachus.

"His place is secure, his fortune is made," said Julian.

"You risked your life for us," said Otto.

"And for Nika," said Aesilesius.

"She is a slave," said Otto.

"No matter," said Aesilesius.

"May I now accept your greetings?" asked Otto.

"I would be pleased if you would do so," said Aesilesius.

"I accept them," said Otto.

CHAPTER EIGHTY-ONE

The throne room had been freshened, recarpeted, and refurbished. New hangings were in place. The guard doors, blown from their hinges, half melted, lay to the sides of the passage leading inward.

Ingeld, dangling a golden cloak in his right hand, moved to place himself on the throne.

"Do not yet assume the throne, noble prince!" said Sidonicus. "You are not yet regent. The royal infant has not yet been smudged, anointed, and jeweled, nor crowned and invested with the dignities of office."

Ingeld seated himself upon the throne, adjusting the golden cloak.

"You look an emperor, prince," said Fulvius.

"I am an emperor," said Ingeld.

"Soon," said Sidonicus, "but not in name."

Ingeld let his glance rove to the entrance to the throne room, the fallen guard doors lying to each side of the passage.

"I do not recognize the livery of the two guards, one on each side of the portal," he said.

"The guards are Captain Buthar and Captain Grissus," said Sidonicus. "The livery is that of the newly instituted temple guard."

"The temple needs no guard," said Ingeld.

"We must protect ourselves against thieves, dissenters, intruders, vandalism, and such," said Sidonicus.

"They are armed," said Ingeld.

"True," said Sidonicus.

"I thought that ministrants do not shed blood," said Ingeld.

"They are not ministrants," said Sidonicus.

"Noble prince," said Fulvius, "as is our agreement, there must be no impediments placed in the path of the true faith. The true faith is to be the official faith of the empire. All other faiths are not only to be discouraged, but to be denied, denounced, forbidden, and suppressed. They are to be uprooted and exterminated. This is vital. We cannot risk the loss of a single *koos* to ignorance, neglect, or heresy."

"I gather so," said Ingeld.

"A substantial temple tax, a tax distinct from secular revenues, is to be imposed on the populations. This tax is to be instituted by, collected by, and guaranteed by, the state. This will enable the construction of new temples, new schools, and new missions, facilitating the further propagation of the true faith."

"There are thousands of faiths," said Ingeld, "and, as I understand it, several Floonian faiths."

"Yes, but there can be but one true faith," said Fulvius.

"That there can be but one true faith," said Ingeld, "does not imply that there is one true faith."

"Considering the thousands of faiths," said Fulvius, "surely one must be true."

"They could all be false," said Ingeld.

"Without the backing of the temple," said Fulvius, "your position on the throne is precarious."

"How do you recognize the one true faith?" asked Ingeld.

"It is the one which rises victorious from the killing and torturing, from the blood and fire," said Fulvius.

"An unusual test for truth," said Ingeld.

"*Karch* would have it so."

"What of the peace and gentleness, the love, tenderness, compassion, and sympathy of Floon?" asked Ingeld.

"Floon has nothing to do with this," said Fulvius.

"I see," said Ingeld.

"Floon is naive, no more than an embarrassment to the true faith," said Fulvius.

"What of the writings pertaining to Floon and his early followers?" asked Ingeld.

"Reinterpreted, and superseded, by oral tradition," said Fulvius.

"Who nurses and keeps, and discovers, or invents, this oral tradition?" asked Ingeld.

"Holy ministrants," said Fulvius.

"I am not a theologian," said Ingeld.

"Much is likely to be obscure to the profane," said Fulvius.

"Sidonicus," said Ingeld. "You are certain you can hold the city?"

"Certainly," said the exarch. "I can bring thousands into the street at any moment. We can go from house to house, hunting down any who might be partisans of the usurper, who might be loyal to the old regime. Viable opposition does not exist. Those who are uncertain will be moved by the cards of the future. Who does not wish to survive? Who does not wish to nestle in the cradle of safety? Who does not wish to be sheltered in the arms of victory? Who does not wish its wind at his back? We can thrust villainous, cowardly Rurik, the Tenth Consul of Larial VII, aside in an afternoon. The city guard is ours, the temple guard is ours. Battalions of zealous insurgents are armed. We have imported troops. As Telnar goes, so goes the empire."

"I trust the city is being readied for the coronation," said Ingeld.

"The festivities will take ten days," said Sidonicus. "The preliminary ceremonies take place two days from now."

"Why not tomorrow?" asked Ingeld.

"Tomorrow," said Sidonicus, "is reserved for executions."

CHAPTER EIGHTY-TWO

"I am afraid the handsome features of Corelius are somewhat marred," said Iaachus.

"He would now be less in demand in a male brothel," said Julian.

"Back, back," said a fellow in the livery of the city guard, trying, from the side, to thrust the pressing, screaming, hissing crowd back.

"Way, way!" said another, "give way," pushing men to the side with the butt of his spear.

Two other guards, with leveled spears held diagonally before them, like wedges or plow shares, cursing, thrusting, were forcing their way forward.

"Let us through," demanded another. "Let the prisoners pass. You can all see when they reach the platform. Back, back!"

It is not easy to take a line of bound prisoners, derided and abused, through an incensed and demonstrative throng.

Certainly one must pity the guards, of which there were several; one must sympathize with their endeavors.

Crowds are difficult to deal with.

That is well understood.

What is a crowd?

Is it not a beast with many heads and no mind?

Is it not a cloak which conceals assailants, a locale within which all is permitted?

Is a crowd a number of individuals, or a crowd; is a wave drops of water, or a wave; is an avalanche grains of earth, or an avalanche; is a beast cells, or a beast?

Is nature one or many? She eludes names. She disregards grammar.

Otto, castigated as The Usurper; Iaachus, Arbiter of Protocol; Julian, he of the Aureliani; Tuvo Ausonius, a former civil servant from Miton; Titus Gelinus, a rhetor and attorney; and a young man, Aesilesius, taken by authorities to be a peasant named Vorn, allied with Otto, had their hands tied behind their backs, and were roped together by the neck. Corelius, too, as indicated, was a member of this coffle. This had been seen to by Sidonicus. "I do not belong with these miscreants," he had cried, "free me, free me," his voice lost in the raucous cacophony.

Tuvo Ausonius turned his head away, struck by a handful of gravel.

A switch lashed Titus Gelinus across the cheek.

Hands reached out from the crowd to claw or strike at the prisoners. Pebbles had been cast at them, and garbage, and excrement.

Often enough these missiles had struck, spattered, or soiled unintended targets.

"Forgive me, friends," said Otto. "It seems we should have ended matters at the door of the senate."

"One casts the dice," said Iaachus. "They fall as they will."

"Ai!" said Julian, angrily, his face scratched by a woman.

"How brave they are when supported by a hundred men," said Iaachus.

"I would not give a *darin* for her," said Julian.

"What of the empress mother?" said Aesilesius, agonized, turning, his neck in the loop of rope.

"We do not know," said Otto.

"It would not be popular to execute an old woman publicly," said Iaachus. "Presumably she will just disappear."

"She might be spared," said Otto, "to give additional credence to the schemes of Sidonicus. The child to be recognized as emperor by the senate is allegedly that of her daughter, Viviana. Thus her public acknowledgement of, and acceptance of, the child would be of political value to Sidonicus and Ingeld."

"After we have been slain?" said Aesilesius.

"Yes," said Otto.

"They do not know my mother," said Aesilesius.

"After that," said Iaachus, "she could be done away with quietly."

Aesilesius struggled in his bonds.

Tuvo Ausonius felt the butt of a spear prod him forward.

"Move, move," said a guard.

"We have been given no trial!" Titus Gelinus cried to the crowd.

He was answered by a chorus of jeers.

"Do not concern yourself, dear Gelinus," said Iaachus. "The records of a trial can be written up any time, if one so wishes, and inserted in the public records. All will be in perfect order. It would satisfy even you."

The group was now near the foot of the stairs leading up to the surface of the newly constructed, large wooden platform, it located in the great square, several yards before the steps leading up to the palace.

"At least," said Julian, "we need not fear execution by the burning rack."

"I do not understand," said Otto.

"In the past," said Julian, "execution by burning rack was common. Sometimes hundreds, even thousands, surrendered armies and helpless populations, were so executed, publicly, in arenas, along highways and thoroughfares, near markets, and such. Exasperated generals commonly dealt in this fashion with besieged city populations which had refused to surrender and had put up a lengthy and costly resistance."

"I hope," said Otto, "an exception was made in the case of attractive young women."

"Certainly, commonly," said Julian. "Who would wish to waste such loot? They would be stripped, collared, branded, chained, and sold."

"Drisriaks favor the horse death," said Otto, "in which a bound prisoner is dismembered by driven horses. Heruls often run prisoners naked for the dogs."

"The burning rack," said Julian, "was an ignoble death, a thing of shame, suitable for murderers and thieves. Floon, as you know, was executed by the burning rack. After that, as the faiths of Floon, incompatible as they are, began to spread, the burning rack took on a new significance. Eventually execution by burning rack became less common and more rare. Today the burning rack is often an object not of shame, but of reverence. Accordingly, the last thing one would wish to do today, at least in areas where Floonianism is recognized and respected, is execute a common criminal in such a manner."

"Up the steps!" said a guard.

Otto, who was first in the coffle, began to ascend the stairs.

When the prisoners were aligned on the platform, a great cry arose from the crowd.

"Now they can see," said Iaachus.

Corelius tried to pull away, but was detained by the coffle rope, burning his neck. "I do not belong here!" he cried. "Stay in line!" said a guard, striking him on the side with the shaft of a spear.

Such a blow could break ribs.

"I see no block, no axes," said Julian.

"Nor will you," said Iaachus. "An ancient death, it seems, from a thousand years past, has been restored for us."

"What death?" asked Julian.

"We were not informed of the nature of the execution," said Tuvo Ausonius.

"The crowd will have been informed," said Iaachus.

"Perhaps that is why there are so many," said Tuvo Ausonius.

"What death?" said Julian.

"The beast death," said Iaachus, "one antedating even the burning rack, one reserved for criminals denied the dignity of our species, criminals regarded as less than men."

"I have heard of it," said Tuvo Ausonius shuddering.

"Sidonicus is a clever fellow," said Titus Gelinus. "He is erudite. He is to be congratulated. He has consulted old records. He has a sense of political theater. The symbolism is clear. We are to be exterminated as *filchen*, as vermin. The crowd will applaud."

"How a beast death?" asked Otto. "I see no beasts. This is not an arena. I would that my hands were not bound."

"Do not think it will be a beast fight," said Iaachus, "one in which you might attempt, however futilely, to protect yourself, even to prolong your life for a bit, by flight or resistance."

"Ho, prisoners!" called a voice, from below the platform.

The crowd was then silent.

"It is the wretch, Fulvius," said Iaachus.

"Where is Sidonicus?" asked Otto.

"Doubtless in the temple," said Iaachus, "immersed in prayer."

"Your actions," called Fulvius, "have proclaimed you beasts. Accordingly you are to die as beasts."

"Smudge me!" begged Corelius. "I beg it!"

"Corelius seeks to save himself," said Iaachus.

"How so?" asked Otto.

"When one is smudged," said Iaachus, "as the Floonians have it, all evil, all crimes, all wickedness, of which one might be guilty, however dark and heinous these things might be, is instantly gone, wiped away, done away with."

"Interesting," said Otto.

"The person then is innocent, and the innocent, of course, are not to be punished, and so on."

"So he should be freed?" said Otto.

"I am not sure how *Karch* would view these matters," said Titus Gelinus, "but the state takes a dim view of the business."

"So, too, would headsmen, hangmen, and such," said Iaachus.

"The *koos*, I gather," said Titus Gelinus, "whatever that is, following the killing of the mere body, flies off to the table of *Karch*."

"The body to the state, the *koos* to the temple?" said Otto.

"Something like that," said Titus Gelinus. "It is hard to understand."

"Corelius is no fool," said Iaachus. "The temple is much involved in this, and might profit from some gesture of lenience or mercy."

"Smudge me! Smudge me!" cried Corelius.

"One does not smudge beasts," said Fulvius.

Corelius cried out in misery.

"However," called Fulvius, "a public expression of sorrow, a crying out for forgiveness, a profound manifestation of repentance, might not be inappropriate, even for beasts."

Fulvius waited a moment, and then, satisfying himself that a response was not in the offing, lifted his hand, signaling the guards on the platform. "Proceed," he said.

The tunics of the prisoners were torn down to their waists.

Guards, in city livery, with whips, climbed the stairs, to the surface of the platform.

"We are to be softened, prior to the beast death," said Iaachus.

"Stand, as long as you can," said Otto.

"I survey the crowd," said Julian. "I do not see Timon Safarius Rhodius, *primarius* of the senate. I was sure he would wish to be present."

"He stands high amidst our foes," said Otto. "His absence is puzzling."

"He who is second in the senate, Clearchus Pyrides, senator from Inez IV, is present," said Titus Gelinus.

"He does not seem pleased to be here," said Tuvo Ausonius.

"He seems in the custody of two guards, in a livery I do not recognize," said Iaachus.

This livery was that of the newly formed temple guard.

"I see vendors in the crowd," said Aesilesius, "selling drinks and sweets."

Behind the line of prisoners whips were uncoiled.

"While the attention of the crowd is occupied," said Iaachus, "pickpockets and cutpurses will be active."

"I decline to sympathize with the victims," said Titus Gelinus.

"Let the festivities begin!" called Fulvius.

A roar of pleasure arose from the crowd.

There was the sharp blow of a whip, and Otto stiffened.

Then, methodically, a guard behind each prisoner, blows were delivered, in serial order, one after the other, moving down the line, and then beginning again, once more, with Otto. The first to lose his footing was Corelius at the end of the line, after only the ninth blow. His subsequent blows were administered to his kneeling, and then, later, to his collapsed, sobbing, twisting, writhing form.

After a time only the tall, mighty form of Otto, once of the *festung* village of Sim Giadini, at the foot of the heights of Barrionuevo, on the provincial world of Tangara, remained on its feet.

"He does not fall!" complained the captain of the city guards on the platform.

The crowd was growing restless, dissatisfied.

"Enough, enough!" called Fulvius. "We cannot have the others die under the whip. We must not cheat the beast death. Freshen the prisoners, revive them, and then proceed with the beast death."

"Yes!" called several from the crowd.

Leather buckets filled with water were carried to the platform and dashed on the collapsed, insensate prisoners. Then, as they recovered consciousness, and could again feel the fire of their pain, they were lifted to a sitting position and administered draughts of water. They were then knelt, their knees on the bloody boards of the platform. Only Otto remained standing. He was given no water.

Julian was the first to rise from his knees, to stand beside Otto.

"I welcome you," said Otto.

"At this time," said Julian, "where better to be?"

The others then, with the exception of Corelius, struggled to their feet.

"I think I hear a strange sound, faraway," said Iaachus.

"The crowd," said Titus Gelinus.

A small, crooked figure, in the livery of the temple guard, climbed the steps of the platform, carrying a broad tray, on which reposed an ugly burden.

"Greetings, vile Otung," said the small figure.

"We are honored," said Otto, "to be visited by noble Urta, the King Namer, high on Tangara, betrayer of his people, agent of Heruls, thief of the medallion and chain, tool of the temple, and would-be assassin."

"Jest while it pleases you," said Urta. "On this tray I bear your death."

"I know not your livery," said Otto.

"It is that of the temple guard," said Urta.

"Liveries are sewn for larger men," said Otto.

"A *filch* may prosper where a lion perishes," said Urta.

"In any event," said Otto, "I gather you are now a servitor of *Karch*."

"Gods are conveniences," said Urta. "One believes in them selectively."

"It seems we are to be doubly honored," said Iaachus. "Holy Fulvius, deputy exarch of Telnar, intends to grace us with his presence."

"He would be exarch, I am sure," said Titus Gelinus.

Fulvius had ascended to the platform, and, turning to face the crowd, congratulated it on its piety, assured it that it basked in the sunshine of Floon, and that the doings of the day were prescribed by *Karch*. He concluded by blessing the crowd with the rectangular sign of the burning rack. He then turned to the prisoners. "Behold the grim contents which lie upon the tray borne by my loyal minion, the noble Urta," he said.

"You contemplate murder," said Titus Gelinus.

"As a man of law," said Fulvius, "you know it is impossible to murder a beast. One can kill a beast, but one cannot murder it."

"We are not beasts," said Titus Gelinus.

"Law is subject to interpretation," said Fulvius. "It means what those in power will have it mean."

"Caviling monster," said Titus Gelinus.

"Behold the tray," said Fulvius. "On it lie two objects, each the severed paw of a black *vi-cat*. A hand can be thrust, glovelike, into each of the paws. The five claws, long and curved, on each paw have been hollowed out, and opened at the tip. They are thus rather like the fangs of a venomous serpent, say, the asp of Naxos. Each claw, as you now suspect, is laden with poison. Raked across a living body, breaking the skin, even slightly, the poison is introduced into the blood stream."

"An eloidial mercury," said Julian.

"Nothing so merciful or benign," said Fulvius. "It is a rare poison unknown even to most professional suppliers of poison. It is seldom duplicated, apparently because it is extremely hazardous to handle and analyze. We think it is a medley of horrors designed to produce a variety of symptoms. From that property it derives its entertainment value. Needless to say it is expensive. It has many names on many worlds, 'Torment', 'Rainbow', and such. We purchased it under the local name 'The World Convulses'. There is much speculation as to its ingredients but it is commonly thought it has, at least in part, some relation to the venom glands of the tiny golden toad of Inez VI."

"Doubtless you have tested it," said Otto.

"Secretly, in the prisons, four times," said Fulvius.

"I take it that the results were impressive," said Iaachus.

"Quite," said Fulvius.

"It is called the beast death, I gather," said Aesilesius, "because it is introduced into the body by means of the claws of a beast, rather as though it might feign the attack of an animal."

"Think of it as a beast killing a beast, so to speak," said Fulvius.

"I see," said Aesilesius.

"Free me!" begged Corelius, still on his knees. "I will serve you faithfully and well!"

"We have had our fill of your faithfulness and service," said Fulvius.

"Please!" wept Corelius.

"If death is inevitable," said Titus Gelinus, "it may as easily be faced bravely as fearfully."

"Please, please, sweet, kind, holy Fulvius, ministrant of merciful all-forgiving Floon!" wept Corelius.

"Following the envenomed lacerations," said Fulvius, "the bursting of blood from pores, the shrieking for unobtainable breath, the blotching of skin, the bleeding of eyes, the convulsions, the nausea, vomiting, and diarrhea, your intestines will be drawn out and your bodies will be dismembered, the parts then, tied together with gut, to be hung outside the gates of Telnar."

"Mercy!" begged Corelius.

Fulvius turned to Urta.

"The prisoners are helpless, weakened, well bound, bloodied from the whip," he said. "There is no danger. You may now thrust your hands into the claw gloves and tear their flesh, thus administering the liquids of justice and rightfulness."

Urta looked down, trembling, at the two heavy, inert, severed paws. "I fear to touch these things," he said. "I have borne the tray. It is enough. Let another go further."

"Do you hear it?" asked Iaachus.

"Yes," said Otto.

"What?" asked Julian.

"Bells," said Otto, "from the dock district."

"I hear nothing," said Titus Gelinus.

"Captain," said Fulvius.

One of the guards on the platform responded, stepping forward, he who had been first amongst the attending city guardsmen. He had supervised the ascent to the surface of the platform and the beating of the prisoners.

"This is Captain Harst, of the City Guard," said Fulvius. "He will administer the poison."

"I would not do so, if I were you," said Otto.

Captain Harst, carefully, thrust his hands into the gloves.

"Given my office," said Fulvius, "I abhor the shedding of blood."

He then withdrew from the platform.

Some in the crowd moved, uneasily, looking about.

"Throughout the crowd," said Otto, "there are troops, city guardsmen, and, I gather, temple guardsmen. Too, there are numerous armed retainers, many in inconspicuous garb, presumably to conceal their numbers. I suggest you remove them from the field."

"From the field?" asked the captain.

"They cannot meet the enemy as they are," said Otto. "Withdraw them, assemble them, take up positions, form your lines of battle."

"Are you mad?" said the captain.

The poison gloves were now fully on the captain's hands.

"Surely you hear the bells," said Otto.

The captain lifted his head, warily, straining.

Urta cast down the now-bare tray and hastily descended from the platform.

"What is going on?" said the captain.

"Can you read the sounds, the letters?" Otto asked Iaachus.

"Yes!" said Iaachus.

At that point four ships streamed over the square.

"The four lion ships of Ortog!" said Julian.

"They will land near the *carnariums*, as did the vessels of Abrogastes," said Iaachus.

"The gates will be shut against them," said Titus Gelinus.

"That the ships have passed overhead," said Otto, "means that the gates have already been secured."

"I see other ships!" said Tuvo Ausonius. "From the opposite direction! What ships are they?"

"I know not," said Otto.

"I advise you, Captain," said Iaachus, "to withdraw while you still have time."

"The defensive batteries did not fire," said Aesilesius.

"Men have infiltrated from the fields, from the countryside," said Otto. "The batteries have been seized."

"The crowd senses something is amiss," said Titus Gelinus.

"It wavers, stirs, and mills," said Tuvo Ausonius.

There was a long sound, the prolonged note of some device, wild and menacing, coming from the direction of the dock district.

"You hear that?" asked Otto.

"What is it?" asked Iaachus.

"It is the war horn of the Otungen," said Otto.

"Prepare to die," said Captain Harst.

"I recommend that you withdraw while you can," said Otto.

"We are helpless!" said Iaachus.

"So much the better," said the captain.

"Save yourself," said Otto.

"Die!" cried Captain Harst, raising his gloved hands, both of them, high, with the ten long, curved, venom-laden claws, poised to rake and tear flesh.

Otto, though bound, and coffled, drove his booted foot into the officer's belly once, and then again, fiercely, forcing him from the platform, over the edge, he then, his footing lost, tumbling back down, rolling, stair by stair, to the level of the square below.

Sounds came from behind the prisoners.

The guards on the platform, those who could, leapt from the platform, fleeing into the panicked crowd. Three lay bloody on the platform.

Otto sensed a figure near him, one clambered up from behind to the height of the platform, and then felt a knife move against the ropes which bound his wrists. Another stroke freed him of the coffle loop.

"Vandar!" said Otto.

"My king!" said Vandar.

Vandar was he who had first, long ago, on Tangara, pledged himself to Otto, first to accept liege meat from the Hero's Portion claimed by Otto, that in the Hall of the King Naming.

Ulrich, a second liegeman from Tangara, pressed a sword into Otto's hand.

"Good," said Otto. "Now we may laugh with steel!"

The Otungs from the nearby countryside, who had slipped into the city and infiltrated the crowd, began to free the other prisoners.

"Not that one, not the one in the tunic of a slave," said Otto, indicating Corelius, who had risen to his feet.

"Your majesty!" protested Corelius.

"Back on your knees," said Otto.

Otto then strode to the front of the platform, sword in hand.

Those in the crowd near the platform began to turn, and pull away, in consternation.

Then came another blast on the Otung war horn, much closer.

"There!" said Vandar, pointing to his right.

Waves of horsemen stormed into the square, seemingly small and far off.

The crowd ceased to be one and, at its edge, broke into its thousands of scattered, running, buffeting, screaming, stumbling, falling, terrified bits. The larger portion of the crowd, inert and puzzled, had not yet realized what was occurring.

"They will be trampled like *filchen*!" said Vandar.

One could see the horses slowed, half arrested in the throng, their riders forcing them forward, as though pressing through flood waters or breasting drifts of snow.

"Unfortunate," said Ulrich. "It is too dense for lance work."

Lances were grasped in the left hand, the butts of the lances in the stirrup sheathes.

"No matter," said Vandar. "See the riders, leaning down in their saddles, wielding the threshing sabers!"

"It is the scarlet harvesting," said Ulrich.

"The crowd will soon break," said Vandar. "It will then be easy to pick and spit targets."

"Hunting the wild boar is better sport," said Ulrich. "It is swift, it changes speeds and directions, its dartings are hard to anticipate, its tusks are like knives, it can turn, abruptly, and charge the hunter. Horses can be disemboweled, dismounted hunters torn to pieces."

"Now," said Vandar, "I think the crowd has some sense of its danger."

"Yes," said Ulrich.

This was doubtless true, for what had been packed and massive, excited, gleeful, and righteous in its hate, hungering for blood, greedy for death, competing for positions to witness murder, became fugitives, prey, flight, and quarry.

"Now," said Ulrich, "the square begins to clear."

"Riders couch lances," said Vandar.

"There are many fallen bodies," said Ulrich.

"Many, in their attempt to escape, were trodden to death by their fellows," said Vandar.

Portions of the crowd had retreated up Palace Street; most it had fled before the charge of the horsemen, running to the left, seeking refuge in the side streets and houses near the square. Some had died at portals on which they had hammered, begging admittance; some had sped to take refuge on the steps of the palace, or those at the house of the senate, but horsemen had urged their mounts up the steps and, as they could, left bodies on the porches and steps.

"Citherix commands, does he not?" asked Otto.

"No other," said Vandar.

"He must regroup," said Otto. "There will be resistance. He must not divide his forces in the streets. One cannot fight from house to house on horseback."

There were four notes winded on the battle horn.

"He regroups," said Vandar.

"I have seen carnage, slaughter," said Iaachus.

"It is the way of war," said Otto.

"Were the enemy in position to do so," said Julian, "we would have been treated as roundly or worse."

"Worse," said Titus Gelinus.

While the events just recounted were ensuing, Captain Harst had lain half-conscious at the foot of the steps to the platform, shaken by his injuries and fall. Now he grasped much of what must have occurred. He moved his body, bit by bit, imperceptibly, to the lowest step.

"I fear," said Otto, "the enemy is in a position to do so." He pointed to the left.

Otto, the blood on his back now cold, from the beating he had withstood, thrust his sword into the belt of his tunic, its tatters loose about his waist, and raised his hand, hailing a rider.

Captain Harst remained completely still, at the foot of the stairs, seemingly no more than another lifeless body.

"My king," said Citherix, riding to the platform. His lance and saber were stained. The legs and chest of his horse were bloody.

"Leave the square," said Otto. "There is little time."

Citherix wheeled his mount about.

"Why do you think there is little time?" said Julian.

"Because," said Otto, "I do not wish to lose a hundred or more men and horses."

"I do not understand," said Julian.

"Your pistol, confiscated at the senate house when we surrendered," said Otto, "contained two cartridges."

"Look, toward the senate house," said Iaachus, shading his eyes.

"I see," said Otto.

"Hundreds, armed, with bows, spears, swords, knives, pikes, axes," said Titus Gelinus.

"City guardsmen," said Iaachus, "troops, regular and raised, adventurers, mercenaries, belligerents, without uniforms, zealots."

"Doubtless temple guards, as well," said Julian.

"The city is far from ours," said Tuvo Ausonius.

"They approach, they spread out, they cast a wide net," said Julian.

"We had best withdraw," said Otto, "or we are lost."

At the foot of the stairs, Captain Harst stiffened. Within the death gloves, formed from the severed paws of a black *vi-cat*, with the poison-filled claws, his hands tensed.

"I do not think so, my mighty and beloved king," said Vandar, smiling.

"How so?" said Otto.

To the left the extended ranks of advancing men were suddenly halted, and men turned about, startled, and crying out, for, sweeping down upon them from a side street, now spilling into the square, were ranks of riders, staggered, so spaced, that lines of bow fire, one rank behind another, were open, and following these came a column, in rows of ten abreast, with slender lances couched.

"What cavalry is this?" said Iaachus.

"Come from the dock district, circled about the square, through the city, to take the enemy by surprise, unexpectedly, suddenly, without warning, from behind," said Vandar.

"They are dark riders, in their clouds," said Titus Gelinus, shading his eyes.

"Who are they? What are they?" said Iaachus.

"They are no strangers to Otungs," said Ulrich.

Iaachus viewed the bloody square, and the dark, surgent riders. Then he turned to Otto. "These riders," he said, "was this part of your plan?"

"Yes," said Otto.

"How so?" asked Iaachus.

"Many have speculated, from my mien and such," said Otto, "that I am the son of a former leader of the Otungen, a great champion, a warrior king, Genserix."

"Is it true?" asked Iaachus.

"I would suppose not," said Otto.

"But you do not know?" said Iaachus.

"No," said Otto.

"But this figured in your plan?"

"Yes," said Otto, "given how Heruls think."

"I understand little of this," said Iaachus.

"The lancers draw back," said Ulrich. "New bows leave the bow cases. The riders no longer close. The enemy, in its terror, gathers together, naturally, but unwisely. The riders continue to urge their mounts, never still. How fix on such a target? They now turn, approach, and withdraw. They now hang at the edges of the square."

"The horn bow has great striking power," said Vandar.

"Its range exceeds that of the smaller, wooden bows of the enemy," said Vandar.

"It is butchery," said Iaachus.

"See," said Julian, "the enemy casts down its weapons, it disarms itself, it begs to surrender!"

"One does not turn one's throat to the wolf," said Vandar.

"An enemy dead needs not be fought again," said Ulrich.

"Behold," said Tuvo Ausonius, dismayed, "the victors give no quarter."

"It is not their way," said Vandar.

"The enemy is male," said Ulrich. "There are no females to be caught and sold."

"Remnants scatter," said Julian. "Some will escape, into the streets."

"I fear, few," said Tuvo Ausonius.

"What riders, what demons, are these?" asked Titus Gelinus.

"Riders approach," said Aesilesius, "one in the forefront."

A rider, his tentacled appendage grasping a lance, from which standard streamed tatters of fur, brought his mount, snorting and squealing, to the platform, and jerked it up short, its clawed fore-legs pawing at the sky.

Captain Harst, at the lowest step, did not move.

The rider's mount was hard to control. Its lathered body trembled, its nostrils flared. Such beasts are stimulated by exertion, by the chase, the hunt, the smell of blood. At the sides of the saddle tied in place by the hair, there were four heads, two on each side.

"You know me?" inquired the rider.

"I do know you," said Otto.

"Your father, Genserix," said the rider, "was our greatest foe. How wonderful it was to do battle with him. It was long ago. How is it then that we would not honor his son?"

"I am a peasant, from the *festung* village of Sim Giadini, at the foot of the heights of Barrionuevo, on the provincial world of Tangara," said Otto. "I knew neither my mother nor my father. I was called 'Dog', having purportedly been suckled by a dog. I chose the name 'Otto' later, for my body and features resembled those of the Otungen."

"You are the son of Genserix," said the rider. "I found you in the snow, newly born, freezing, soiled with blood and the fluids of a drained womb. I cut away your cord and bound it. With you was the medallion and chain of the Vandalii. I knew you by this artifact to be the son of Genserix. I delivered you to the salamanderine brother, Brother Benjamin, of the *festung* of Sim Giadini."

"He was as a father to me," said Otto.

"I suspect there are more to hunt and kill," said the rider, turning his mount abruptly about. "Come, Mujinn. Our lances are still thirsty." The rider then, followed by several others, departed, in the direction of the house of the senate.

"Who is that?" asked Iaachus.

"His name," said Otto, "is Hunlaki."

"He seems quite old," said Iaachus.

"He is quite old," said Otto, "for a Herul."

"You have known him from before?" asked Julian.

"At least from the time I was run naked in the snow, on Tangara, for the dogs," said Otto.

"I gather that few survive such an experience," said Iaachus.

"I think he suspected I would," said Otto.

"Look," said Aesilesius, pointing across the square, now empty of riders, desolate and bare, but littered with bodies, "three men, one a herald, approach, two bearing green flags, the flags of peace and truce!"

"Beware," said Tuvo Ausonius.

"It is too early for Sidonicus to sue for peace, and Ingeld would not do so," said Julian.

"Stop!" called Otto. "Stay where you are! Approach no more closely!"

"*Civilitas!*" called the herald.

"He says *civilitas*," said Aesilesius.

"Stay where you are," called Otto.

"Do you know the herald?" asked Iaachus of Titus Gelinus.

"I do not recognize him," said Gelinus. "I do not think he is of the senate."

"He is not in the garb of the temple," said Julian.

"He may be a zealot, an expendable dupe," said Gelinus.

"*Civilitas!*" called the herald, once more.

"You cannot refuse an authentic petition to parley," said Aesilesius. "It would be an unconscionable act of barbarity. On all worlds of the empire the significance of the green flag is respected."

"Why do you move to the side of the platform?" asked Tuvo Ausonius of Otto.

"Do not stand near to me," said Otto. "Be ready to depart the platform."

"We are prepared to yield the city," called the herald, taking a step forward. "Let the ravages of war be done. You will find us practical men, not bereft of reason. The day is yours. Let us speak. Let us recover our dead. Let us negotiate a fair and civilized capitulation. Let us speak of forgiveness, amnesty, tolerance, and reconciliation. Do not hold the city responsible for the unauthorized acts of lawless, unbridled, repellant mobs. We stand as aghast as you at their actions. Let deeds of mercy be done."

"Stay where you are!" said Otto.

As the herald spoke, he and his fellows, little by little, almost imperceptibly, had been advancing toward the platform.

"The location of the two missing cartridges," said Otto, "is now clear."

"Soon they will be unable to miss," said Julian.

"I do not understand," said young Aesilesius. "Can you not see? They lift the flag of life and peace."

"Had I a bow!" growled Otto. "Do not stand close to me!"

"Let us shield you," whispered Tuvo Ausonius.

"There is no shield," said Otto. "A cartridge could take out a wall."

"In the name of *civilitas*, beloved to us all," said the herald, "let concord flourish."

Otto waited only an instant, that instant which was required by the herald to remove the weapon from beneath his cloak, lift, level, and train it. Then in the moment between settling the aim and pulling the trigger, Otto hurled his body down and to the side. A torrent of fire burned away the side of the platform where Otto had stood but a moment before. Burning boards reeled behind the platform, some bending end over end. One could hear running feet approaching the platform. "They will have another cartridge," said Otto. "They will fire at point-blank range." "We are lost," said Julian.

But there was then a flash of fire and a scattering of dust and debris from yards before the platform, and, almost simultaneously, another roar of fire, one which burned an erratic, meaningless path to the right of the platform, blackening stones, expending itself at last in a swirling torch of smoke and light before the steps of the palace. Following this, almost immediately, there were three more bursts of fire, these placed muchly where the first had struck.

Otto rose to his feet, standing on the uneven, half collapsed surface of the platform. Boards were charred to his right, and, in places, there was a running trickle of fire. The others, with the exception of Corelius, who had not been given permission to rise, rose to their feet.

"The herald and his fellows are no more," said Iaachus.

Three bodies or the remains of bodies, burned flesh, blackened, scorched bones, a skull, darkened, free of flesh, lay some fifteen to twenty yards, before the platform. Two of the bodies, or parts, a torso and shoulder, had been melded together.

"You need not look," said Otto to Aesilesius.

"*Barbaritas*," said Iaachus.

"Suitably so," said Otto.

"I do not understand this," said Aesilesius. "They bore the sign of truce, the green flag."

"You have read books," said Otto. "You have not yet learned to read men."

"One who would hold the throne," said Iaachus, "must learn that skill."

"One discharge," said Tuvo Ausonius, "was erratic, wild, that wide of the platform, that exhausted near the palace steps."

"It was not aimed," said Otto. "The herald, running toward us, had his finger on the trigger when engulfed with flame."

"That would be the second, and last, of the two cartridges," said Julian.

The pistol of the herald lay to one side, an almost unrecognizable lump of metal. There was no sign of the green flags. A portion of a staff on which one might have been mounted, lay among the bodies.

"There were four independent explosions, destroying the herald and his fellows," said Iaachus. "Who possesses such might, such riches?"

These four explosions had been recorded on the pavement of the square by four elongated, seared ellipses.

"Look," said Otto, pointing.

"There is no mistaking that size, that frame and form," said Julian.

Some fifty yards away, gazing toward the platform, in garb which was not that of Telnar, were two large men.

"Who is that with him?" asked Aesilesius.

"His eldest son, Ortog," said Otto, "prince of the Drisriaks, king of the secessionist tribe, the Ortungen."

"He is reloading his pistol," said Tuvo Ausonius.

"We may be his next target," said Julian.

"That is possible," said Otto.

"No," said Tuvo Ausonius, relieved, "he replaces it in its sheath."

"Look," said Vandar, "Citherix returns."

The riders of the Otung cavalry were to the right, emerging onto the square.

"Behold," said Ulrich, "to the left, Heruls!"

"These are fierce, terrible enemies," said Julian.

"Separated by the Lothar," said Otto, "the plains of Barrionuevo, the flats of Tung, ranged by the Heruls, the forests by the Otungen."

"When have they not met without feasts of blood?" asked Julian.

"We brought horses from Tangara," said Vandar, "but Rurik, and his men of the Larial Farnichi, his private soldiers, obtained hundreds more from the countryside, and the lands drained by the Turning Serpent, even to the delta. Rurik, too, cleared the path to Telnar from the dock district, dismantling barricades and uprooting hundreds of horse traps and sharpened stakes, and forcing Drisriaks loyal to Ingeld from their posts, at the last minute, of course, in bloody fighting, to conceal our assembling forces. Without his help we would have lost the element of surprise, and might have been detained, and perhaps stopped, at the piers."

"I see the banner of the consul now," said Julian pointing to the right.

"His men are afoot," said Julian.

"Infantry," said Otto, "can hold trenches, clear streets, scale walls, investigate narrow places, climb to roofs, can fight from house to house, from room to room. There is no victory without infantry."

"The cavalry of Citherix and the Heruls approach one another," said Julian apprehensively.

"Slowly," said Otto. "And note, lances are not couched, bows remain encased, quivers are tied shut."

"They mingle," said Julian, wonderingly.

"This afternoon," said Otto, "they are fellow warriors."

"And tomorrow?" said Julian.

"I do not know," said Otto. "Species can grow bored, and the waters of the Lothar are easily forded."

"Abrogastes and Ortog now approach," said Julian.

"Let us greet them," said Otto.

Otto moved to the front edge and center of the damaged platform, where the steps which led up to its surface were intact.

He lifted his hand, to hail those who approached.

At the same moment Captain Harst, at the foot of the steps, gathering his legs beneath him, rose up and sped upward, climbing to the height of the platform, the death gloves, with the venom-laden claws, reaching out to tear at the face and half-bared body of Otto.

"Beware!" cried Vandar.

But already, Otto, responding with the suddenness of a startled *vi-cat*, was struggling with his assailant, his hands on the wrists of

Captain Harst. The two men, locked together, turned and swayed, leaning to one side and the other. The claws were but inches from Otto's face, straining to reach his face, when, bit by bit, they were separated, wavering, and the strength of the blond giant began to assert itself against the fury and driven madness of the captain of the city guard. Captain Harst's face was wet with perspiration and, as he began, in slow moment by slow moment, to understand the inevitable denouement of his desperate action, his eyes grew wide with comprehension, and terror. Then the clawed gloves, on his own hands, were turned against him, and then, as his strength failed, each of his cheeks suddenly bore the furrows of five claws, each furrow brimming with blood.

"You did not withdraw," said Otto.

He then thrust the body of the captain of the city guard reeling down the steps. At the foot of the steps, the captain rose to his feet, looked upward and back, once, and then turned, took two steps, and fell to the pavement.

"He was a good officer," said Julian.

"No," said Otto, "his position was with his men."

"The poison begins to take effect," said Iaachus, in horror, looking down from the platform.

"You need not look," said Otto to Aesilesius.

"Do you so despise me, think so little of me, that you would guard me from the world?" said Aesilesius.

"Forgive me," said Otto.

There was wild, piteous screaming from the foot of the stairs, below the platform.

"Is this how men kill in cities?" asked Vandar, looking down.

"Sometimes," said Otto.

"The difference between *civilitas* and *barbaritas*," said Julian, "is sophistication and technology."

"And lying," said Otto.

"How so?" said Julian.

"Civilization is only barbarism denied," said Otto, "civilization proclaiming innocence."

By this time Abrogastes and Ortog, followed by shieldsmen, had neared the platform, and now both, with their followers, stood back, observing the writhing thing at the foot of the stairs.

"Is that human?" inquired Abrogastes.

"It was," said Otto.

"You can tell from the clothing," said Julian.

"We owe you and others our lives," said Otto.

"All who live owe their lives to others," said Abrogastes. "Consider yourselves now repaid for the succor you once rendered in the basement of the house of Dardanis."

"Then we are sword level once more, friend foe," said Otto.

"I drew profit from that day," said Abrogastes. "I recovered a son, and gained two pets."

"Two pets?" said Julian.

"Two," said Abrogastes.

"It no longer moves," said one of the shieldsmen at the foot of the stairs.

"Draw the gloves from it carefully, avoiding the claws," said Otto, "then have them burned, but stand not close to the flames. Afterwards scrape together the ashes or what might remain and dispose of it in some *carnarium*."

The shieldsman looked at Abrogastes.

"Have it done so," said Abrogastes.

"You and your fellows appear to have been beaten," said Ortog.

"It is hard to stand," said Iaachus.

"Healing balm is in the ships," said Ortog.

"The field is clear," said Abrogastes, gesturing behind, "save for the gathering of the dead."

"Heruls are ghastly," said Julian. "I fear they will feast tonight."

"I see a slave, he kneeling on the platform," said Abrogastes.

Corelius, kneeling, his hands still tied behind him, part of the coffle rope still on his neck, put down his head, trembling.

"Not a slave," said Otto, "but a free man, denied footwear and clad in the tunic of a slave. Perhaps you know him."

"I know him well," said Abrogastes. "How much do you want for him?"

"He is not a slave," said Otto.

"A collar and brand will remedy that," said Abrogastes.

"Resistance may linger," said Ortog, looking uneasily to the side, past the senate house.

"Little now," said Otto. "We will cleanse or redeem the city guard. The temple guard will be disbanded. Levied troops will be returned to their posts. Order will be restored. Abject defeat should assure dupes, and even zealots, that gods did not favor their cause."

"Beware, dear Otung," said Iaachus, "the temple is unscrupulous and patient, it seeks power like the snake, silently and with subtle venoms."

"It is little to be feared if it is denied the sword of the state," said Otto.

"Crush it," said Julian.

"No," said Otto, "persecution provokes attention, curiosity, inquiry, and sympathy. What might the state fear? Could it be the truth? Too, if the state should crush difference how is the state different from the temple?"

"Let schools be free," said Aesilesius, "let a thousand faiths flourish."

"And lacks of faith," said Iaachus.

"Vandar," said Otto. "Let the bells of the city ring. Let it be proclaimed that war is done. Let it be proclaimed that the good citizens of Telnar, bystanders of strife, may exit their dwellings and resume their lives."

"Peace will be in the streets," said Iaachus.

"In three days," said Otto, "I invite you to the palace, with high officers of our allies."

"Until then," said Abrogastes.

CHAPTER EIGHTY-THREE

Sidonicus, head down, was kneeling on the upholstered kneeler before the small, linen-draped altar in his private chapel, in the exarchical palace. The only light in the chapel was furnished by two candles on the altar. Above the altar, illuminated in the flickering light, golden against a dark, brocaded background, was a stylized image of a burning rack.

"Your holiness," said Fulvius, breathing heavily, in robes clutched about him, hastening into the chamber, "plans have gone amiss, unexpectedly and tragically so, much blood has been shed, crowds have scattered, ridden down in the square, the usurper and his villainous cohorts live, our forces are muchly perished in red slaughter, remnants flee, our foes, unimpeded, seize strategic positions, bells ring in jubilation!"

"I am aware of this," said Sidonicus, not lifting his head. "Buthar and Grissus have told me."

"I passed them on the way in," said Fulvius. "This is a dark day for the temple."

"No," said Sidonicus. "In all this we are innocent. We know nothing of crowds and secular designs. What has transpired has taken place without the collusion of, or even the knowledge of, the temple. Who shall prove otherwise?"

"What of Ingeld?" asked Fulvius.

"Who is Ingeld?" said Sidonicus. "We know of no such person."

"Hundreds know of our role in this," said Fulvius.

"And thousands do not," said Sidonicus.

"The temple may be closed, outlawed," said Fulvius.

"Can one outlaw air, or the sky?" said Sidonicus. "The faith of Floon has been outlawed before."

"Only sporadically, here and there, from time to time," said Fulvius. "The policy of the empire, with the faith of Floon as well as with thousands of other faiths, foolishly, has almost always been tolerance. It never did as we would have it do, force a particular faith on cultures and populations with the sword, extirpating other faiths, dictating beliefs, and murdering dissenters."

"Do not despair, friend Fulvius," said Sidonicus, "we will control the mind of the child and thus the mind of the adult."

"You must give the female a *koos*," said Fulvius. "In that way the child will be shaped almost in the womb."

"There is little in the teachings of Floon to authorize that," said Sidonicus, lifting his head, and turning a bit toward Fulvius.

"Floon," said Fulvius, "was a salamanderine from Zirus. He may have been a neuter. I do not think he gave the matter much thought. He was filled with love, and blessed, and preached to, all things, rational and nonrational, living and nonliving, to insects, flowers, toads, snakes, trees, even rocks, roads, and mountains."

"He was insane, of course," said Sidonicus.

"We must give a *koos* to women," said Fulvius.

"Nothing in the teachings of Floon authorizes that," said Sidonicus.

"Nor forbids it," said Fulvius.

"I see," said Sidonicus.

"I have many ideas for the increase and exaltation of the exarchate," said Fulvius.

"I am sure you do," said Sidonicus, lifting his ponderous form, rising and facing Fulvius.

"All now understand Floon to be a salamanderine from Zirus," said Fulvius.

"Of course," said Sidonicus, "and appropriately. He was a salamanderine from Zirus."

"This has made it difficult on certain worlds," said Fulvius, "to proselytize amongst certain species, who do not care that the offspring of *Karch* should not be of their own species. Indeed, some find that idea repellant. Accordingly, let us identify the offspring of *Karch* not with a particular form but with a *koos*. In this way we can present Floon as being of a multitude of different species on a multitude of different worlds, one *koos*, but different forms, worlds rich enough to justify missionary efforts."

"That would necessitate certain adjustments in doctrine," said Sidonicus.

"The exarchate would ascend to new heights," said Fulvius, "heights from which it might then view new worlds, many worlds, rich worlds."

"Doctrine must be responsive to truth," said Sidonicus.

"Rather, your holiness," said Fulvius, "truth must be responsive to doctrine."

"You are ambitious," said Sidonicus. "A ministrant is to be humble."

"I assure you, your holiness," said Fulvius, "no one is more humble than I."

"I hear the bells," said Sidonicus, lifting his head, "even here in the chapel."

"Celebrating the victory of the usurper," said Fulvius. "These times may prove dangerous times for the temple. Despite our denials there is a broadcast public perception that the temple is implicated in the insurrection, the rioting, the burning and looting, the tumult and turmoil of the past several days."

"A mistaken perception," said Sidonicus.

"But one which might redound to the detriment of the temple, and the encouragement of skepticism, even heresies."

"We will plan anew," said Sidonicus. "In the top drawer of the chest to the right, containing vestments and ceremonial paraphernalia, you will find a flat case of sweets. Fetch it."

Fulvius then went to the mentioned drawer, and, in a moment, returned to Sidonicus, who took the case of sweets from him.

"I have a plan," said Fulvius.

"You seem fertile with plans," said Sidonicus.

"I think you will approve," said Fulvius.

"I attend," said Sidonicus, placing a sweet in his mouth. "Speak."

"The prestige of the temple is in jeopardy," said Fulvius. "Men suspect that the temple has ends in view, economic ends, social ends, political ends, which are incompatible with the sweet, loving, tolerant, anarchistic teachings of Floon. They dare to think, if only privately, that we seek wealth, prestige, and power. Indeed, many think the temple has betrayed Floon. Once again we must see to it that the temple is regarded with reverence, that it is respected as a selfless vessel, divinely instituted, by means of which *Karch* hopes to improve and exalt the weak and small, the miserable and unhappy, the neglected and despised, that they, or a select few amongst them, for one must keep them apprehensive, may find places at his table."

"And how, dear Fulvius, is this to be brought about?" asked Sidonicus, placing another sweet in his mouth.

"Suspicion must be diverted from the temple," said Fulvius. "The temple must no longer seem the perpetrator but the victim. The temple itself must seem attacked by the very forces which brought about so much disorder, suffering, and destruction. Thus the temple cannot be guilty, and, indeed, might it not even seem that the disorder and chaos might have been raised by enemies of the temple itself, perhaps heretics, say, illusionists or emanationists, to cast suspicion on the temple, to discredit it in the eyes of the faithful."

"And how, sweet Fulvius," asked Sidonicus, "is this fruitful and valuable illusion to be brought about?"

"Simply, your excellency," said Fulvius. "We need an innocent victim, one who is irreproachable, beloved, holy, and saintly, one whose death will seem shocking and piteous, one whose end will provoke outrage and generate sympathy, a martyr."

"Excellent," said Sidonicus. "It should be an individual reasonably well known, one of some position and station, one revered for his selflessness, his devotion, orthodoxy, piety, sanctity, and such, preferably a ministrant."

"That is my view, exactly," said Fulvius.

"Have you someone in mind?" asked Sidonicus, reaching into the box of sweets. "What are you drawing forth from beneath your robes?" asked Sidonicus.

"Surely you recognize an altar knife," said Fulvius. "Have you not, often enough, in the ceremonies of Floon, used such a knife to cut apart the loaf of blessed bread symbolizing the riches of the table of *Karch*, the bread you then distribute to the faithful?"

"Do not!" cried Sidonicus, as the knife was plunged into his breast.

The case of sweets fell to the floor.

"Now I am exarch of Telnar," said Fulvius.

He replaced the knife in his robes, and looked about. He regarded the altar with the white, linen coverlet, the two candles, and the representation of the burning rack on the wall, gold against the brocade. He then looked down at the crumpled body of Sidonicus. "I am not a manipulable fool," he said, "nor do I fetch for fools." He then bent down and, from the fallen case of sweets, picked out a sweet, and placed it in his mouth. He then turned about and left the chapel.

Outside the chapel, in the dark corridor, Fulvius paused briefly, listening to the bells outside. Then he continued on, moving through the corridor to the exit through which he had entered. This exit, where it entered the building, was several blocks from the great square. He accounted himself fortunate, in such times, to have made it safely through the streets. Once he had even seen a Herul rider, small and fur-clad, far off, a lance in his grasp. When Fulvius reached the exit he found, waiting for him, Buthar and Grissus. They plunged their knives, several times, into his body.

"That is done," said Buthar, at last.

"Let us go now," said Grissus, "and collect our pay from the exarch."

CHAPTER EIGHTY-FOUR

"We must leave the city," said Urta, tearing away the livery of the temple guard.

"What has happened?" said Viviana, rising, frightened, to a crouching position, for the ring and chain which confined her permitted her no more.

"Back on your knees, homely, despicable slave," said Urta.

"Yes, Master," said Viviana, again kneeling, but with agitation.

'Yes, Master' is the common response of a slave to an instruction or command, unless the slave is owned by a woman, in which case the common response is 'Yes, Mistress'. Consider the female slave. She speaks the word 'Master' frequently, and understands that it is appropriately spoken. Such small things enhance and deepen her awareness of her bondage. The common verbal formula, for example, reminds her that she is a slave, a property, and the awareness that she is owned and at the complete mercy of her master stimulates her sexually. She knows she has no choice, and she does not desire a choice. Most female slaves are easily aroused. They cannot help it; they are slaves. Many, in the vicinity of their masters, are in an almost constant state of readiness. To the slave even small things, such as cooking, dusting, laundering, sewing, ironing and folding clothes, serving at the table, pouring wine, and such, can be a sexual experience, it being done as a slave.

Viviana did not regard herself as homely, though, indeed, she was now unkempt, unwashed, and clad in no more than a brief filthy rag. As a free woman she had regarded herself as quite beautiful, and she well knew how a woman's beauty was enhanced manyfold by bondage. Is that not why free women so envied and hated slaves? A free woman may be beautiful; a slave is beautiful.

"Master has been gone for hours," said Viviana.

"Do not concern yourself," said Urta.

"Something has happened, clearly, Master," said Viviana, her small hands clutching her neck chain. "Please tell me! I am a slave! I am helpless! I know nothing!"

"You need know nothing," said Urta, drawing a street tunic over his head, the removed livery of the temple guard at his feet.

"I heard bells," she said. "What is their meaning? But yet the streets seem quiet. Perhaps they are empty. What has occurred?"

"Nothing," said Urta. "But I choose to leave the city."

"I heard a horse race by," said Viviana.

"Some rider," said Urta.

"Master hastens," said Viviana. "Has he resources?"

"Enough," said Urta.

"I, too, heard, far off, dogs, the baying of hounds."

"Doubtless wild dogs," said Urta, "slipped in through an unguarded gate."

"Why should a gate be unguarded?" she asked.

Urta looked down at the discarded livery of the temple guard. "I will burn this garmenture outside, somewhere outside," he said. "There are fires enough, here and there. It would not do for it to be found here."

"I do not know the livery," she said.

"You need not know it," said Urta.

"It is satin, and fine," she said. "Why should it be put aside, why should it be done away with?"

"It is dark now," said Urta. "It could not have come soon enough for me. I must be on my way."

"I hear the dogs," said Viviana. "They are closer."

Urta paused for a moment, listening. "This far within the city," he said, "they must be domestic dogs. There is nothing to fear from domestic dogs. One waves them away. One speaks, sharply. They withdraw, snarling, or flee."

"Am I to be left behind?" asked Viviana.

Urta removed a knife from his belt.

"I am worthless, dead," said Viviana.

Urta replaced the knife in his belt.

"I will take you with me," he said. "I can sell you. I should be able to get a *darin* or two for your sleek hide, even as it is."

"Had I been better rested and better fed, and beaten less often," she said, "your profit might be greater."

Her face was lashed to the side as Urta slapped her, sharply, on the left cheek.

"Forgive me for having been displeasing, Master," she said, tears in her eyes, her cheek burning. "How stupid you are, slave," she thought to herself. "Do you still think you are a free woman? Do you not yet know you are a slave?"

"Do not be afraid," said Urta. "The marks, the residue, of the whippings will soon disappear. Combed, brushed, washed, and suitably tunicked, you might not be a displeasing item, exhibited with other items, on a chain. Put your hands behind you, with your wrists crossed."

"Yes, Master," whispered Viviana.

Her wrists were then tied behind her back. Following this, Urta put a leash on her neck. He then freed her of the chain and ring, dropping the ring collar and chain to the floor. "On your feet, beast," he said.

"Yes, Master," said Viviana, rising.

"Stand straight," he said. "You are a slave."

"Yes, Master," said Viviana. "Are we returning later to the city?" she asked.

"I do not know, I do not think so," said Urta.

Urta then gathered up the discarded livery, and wound it, turned so that its colors could not be seen, about his waist. He then slung a small bag of his belongings, gathered from the side, apparently earlier prepared, over his shoulder, which action surprised Viviana, for slaves are commonly used to port a master's belongings, if within their strength. Many Masters would be embarrassed to personally transport such an object, if a slave, a lovely beast of burden, so to speak, were at hand. "For some reason," she thought, "he wishes to retain that bag himself. Perhaps it contains *darins*. It seems to have been prepared earlier. Why would that have been? Did my Master anticipate the possibility, however remote or unlikely, of this departure from the city? Is he afraid I might be taken from him, and the bag, as well, were it tied about me? My Master is clever. What is going on in the city? Little it seems, but I suspect much."

Urta then, the livery about his waist and the small bag over his shoulder, the leash of his slave in his left hand, exited the apartment, descended the stairs, opened the portal at the foot of the stairs, surveyed the street in both directions, and then left the building.

They had moved only some blocks, keeping to the side of the street, when her Master, Urta, stopped.

"The streets are deserted," said Viviana.

"Not entirely," said Urta, looking about. To be sure, a furtive figure, little more than a shadow, was occasionally sensed, usually on the other side of the street.

"There is a refuse fire," said Urta. "I dared not leave the livery in the apartment, lest it be traced to me."

"I do not understand," said Viviana.

"To wear it could be death," said Urta.

There were two men standing near the fire, who drew back as Urta neared.

"That is a good-looking slave," said one of the men, from the darkness.

Viviana, briefly tunicked, bound and on her leash, had been illuminated in the shifting light of the fire.

She realized, suddenly, vividly, as another fact of her bondage, that she, as a property, could be stolen, as any other property.

"Stand back," said Urta. "I have a knife."

Urta dropped the leash.

Viviana felt it dangle against her body.

She remained in place.

With his left hand Urta loosened the livery from about his waist and cast it into the fire.

"The livery of the temple guard," said one of the men.

"So that is the nature of the livery," thought Viviana. "I did not even know there was a temple guard. Why should he discard it?" Viviana, however, said nothing, nor asked a question. Other men were present, and she knew she had not asked permission to speak.

"Burn it," said the other man.

Viviana, puzzled, watched the livery burning in the flames. "Why," she wondered, "would anyone burn so seemingly new, and fine, a livery, and one apparently pertaining to the temple itself?"

"What have you in the small bag about your shoulder?" asked the first of the two men in the shadows.

"And why is it not borne by the slave?" asked the other.

Urta drew his knife and backed away from the fire.

Viviana kept behind him.

The two men remained standing, back in the shadows.

Urta replaced the knife in his belt, retrieved Viviana's leash, and, leading her, continued on his way.

"I think we are in the Varl district, indeed, on Varl Street itself," thought Viviana. "Surely this seems an unlikely, an inauspicious, route to choose, to leave the city. It gives access only to lesser gates, obscure gates, minor gates."

"I hear the dogs, Master," said Viviana.

The baying did seem closer.

"They are going down Varl," said Urta. "We shall turn aside and let them pass us, continuing on their way."

Viviana stumbled, jerked on the leash to the side, as Urta turned into a side street. After a few blocks Urta stopped.

"I hear the dogs," said Viviana, "I think they are still behind us."

"It is a coincidence," said Urta. Then he turned left. "This is Circumspection Street," he said. "It runs parallel to Varl."

Viviana knew of Varl Street, for who did not know of Varl Street? It is a well-known thoroughfare in Telnar. She, however, raised in the palace and concerned with little for years but her appearance, jewelry, clothing, and amusements had little concerned herself with the streets and districts of Telnar. She had never heard of Circumspection Street.

"Hurry," said Urta, hastening forward.

Viviana, leashed, had no option but to comply.

"Can Master but untie my hands," she begged.

It is not easy to hurry when one's hands are tied behind one.

In a bit Urta stopped.

"I no longer hear the dogs," he said.

"Nor I," said Viviana.

"They have continued past," said Urta.

"I do hear footsteps, Master," said Viviana.

"There is light ahead," said Urta, "a hanging lantern."

Such lanterns are not that uncommon. Some shopkeepers and householders illuminate their gates and portals. This is particularly the case in poorer districts where public light tends to be meager or nonexistent.

"Something moves, Master," whispered Viviana.

"To the light," said Urta, drawing his knife.

Darkness is the friend of villainy, Viviana had heard, as light is its foe.

"Hold, small friend," said a voice.

"We would renew our acquaintance," said another voice, soothingly.

Viviana could not see the faces, but she recognized the voices, those of the two men earlier encountered near the refuse fire.

"The streets are dangerous," said the first voice. "After you left, we shared our concern. We feared for your safety."

"We will afford you protection," said the second voice. "We will escort you."

"Stay back," said Urta. "Keep your distance. I may be small, but I am armed, and I am Otung."

"Do not be afraid," said the first voice.

"We are your friends," said the second. "Let us be of assistance."

Urta, knife now drawn, backed across the street, to stand beneath the light. He looked about, wildly, at closed portals, at that behind him, and those to his left, and right.

"What do you carry in the small bag at your shoulder?" asked the first voice. "Why is it not borne by the slave?"

"In the filthy thing beside you, in tattered rags," said the second voice, "I think I see the promise of a comely slave, one a man might enjoy having at his feet. Perhaps you do not know how to keep a slave and get the most, and best, from her."

The two men then separated, by some seven or eight feet.

Viviana saw that each carried a stout club.

Urta dropped Viviana's leash.

She remained much where she had been, backing against the wall behind her.

"Give us the bag about your shoulder and the slave," said the first man.

"We will keep them safe for you," said the second.

"Stand back," said Urta.

"We mean you no harm," said the first man.

"Put down the knife," said the second man.

"Perhaps you would spare me?" said Urta.

"Surely," said the first man, who seemed to be first amongst the two.

"Indeed," said the second.

"Do you think I am a fool?" said Urta. "If I disarm myself I die. If I am spared, I might live to recognize you and bring you to the river galleys. If I am spared, I might have you traced through the slave or the contents of my small satchel, in which you seem so interested. I do not think you would risk such things."

The two men looked at one another.

"I see you are not a fool," said the first, "save in going out in the night with valuables, say, jewels or *darins*, and a bound slave."

"I am Otung," said Urta. "At least one of you will die!"

"I think not," said the first man.

Viviana pressed back, harder, against the wall behind her.

The two men then were tensed, and bent over. Each now held his club in two hands. So held, a fierce and mighty blow could be struck. Viviana realized, clearly, as must Urta, as well, that the clubs could reach him before his knife could reach either of them.

"Hold!" said the first man, suddenly, and he and his fellow, startled, stepped back, paces, turning uneasily toward the darkness, trying to see into it.

"There is something there, I hear it," said the first man.

"Yes," said the second.

There was a snuffling noise, and a sound of scratching on pavement, and then a growl, darkly menacing, and then a second growl, even more menacing than the first.

"See the size of them," said the second man, backing away to the side.

Two immense forms emerged from the darkness.

"You see," cried Urta, suddenly. "I am not such a fool! These are my dogs, my guardians. See the collars, domestic beasts, fierce and terrible, mine! Examine the collars, if you dare, and find my name! These are mine. They are trained to kill, at a word. Flee, lest I set them upon you!"

Both of the brigands began to back away, further, and to the side. Then they withdrew, to a post yards away, where they could scarcely be seen.

"Run, run, save yourselves!" cried Urta.

At this point, from behind the heavy, closed portal, over which the lantern hung, a voice was heard. "What is going on there?" it said. "Who are you? Go away!"

"Open, open!" cried Urta, backing against the door.

The two dogs were crouched down, their eyes fixed on Urta. Their nostrils were flared. One could sense the beating of massive hearts within the barrels of their furred chests, trembling with excitement.

"Open, open!" cried Urta, turning and pounding on the door, and then, an instant later, turned to face again the two dogs, which had inched closer.

"They are not wild dogs, Master!" said Viviana. "See the collars. They are domestic dogs, trained to obey and fear men! Order them away! Frighten them! Frown upon them! Gesture them gone! Speak sharply to them! Send them crawling, or running, frightened, back to their kennels."

Urta's knife seemed small in the face of the two fanged, gigantic brutes tensed before him.

Without turning about, Urta hissed back, desperately, over his shoulder, "Open, open, now, now, riches, riches for you, gems, rings, *darins*, gold *darins*, if you let me in! Let me in. Let me in!"

The door opened a crack and Urta tried to force his way through, backing against it, but it was held firm.

"The slave first," said the voice. "I saw her through the window. Did you not hear the shutters? She will have value. I do not know what else you have. You must buy your entrance here."

"I have a hundred times, or more, her value with me," whispered Urta, urgently.

"I do not know that," said the voice. "I have seen the slave. She has value. So, she first. Thus I guarantee myself something of value."

"Into the domicile," hissed Urta.

"Yes, Master," said Viviana, moving behind Urta, her back to the building, slipping through the narrow aperture. In an instant Urta, thrusting the knife in his belt, had followed her inside. No sooner had he done so than the householder slammed the door shut, and the two dogs leapt against the stout wood, snarling, and scratching.

The householder thrust two bolts in place.

Viviana shrank back in the room and Urta stood near the door, breathing heavily.

The light in the room was furnished by a single candle on a nearby table, to the right as one would enter.

"I heard the dogs, from afar," said the householder. "The crying out came closer and closer, and then was silent."

"It has to do," said Urta, "with the ancestry of the wolf. They bay and howl on the scent. It is a token of pack excitement. The calling summons other members of the pack, ever more members, ever more excited, ever more fleet. It keeps the pack together. When several follow a scent, the chance of losing it are very small. If the quarry is large and dangerous, a pack is more likely to bring it down. The baying may also flush new prey out, frightened, laying down new roads of scent."

"But then there was silence," said the householder.

"Prior to closing and attack," said Urta. "What point noise then?"

"Perhaps you are wanted by the city guard?" said the householder.

"Yes," said Urta, "that is it!"

"And the two fellows outside are city guards?" said the householder, ironically.

"No," said Urta, "rogues, brigands."

"Those beasts," said the householder, "are not the hunting dogs of the city guard. They are massive, things of a different breed, much larger and fiercer. The guard, bold as they be, would fear them. They would be reluctant to handle them, even to be near them."

"I understand nothing of what transpires here," said Urta.

"You do not know why you are sought, how it is that you are sought, or could be sought, or who seeks you?" asked the householder.

"No," said Urta. "I understand nothing. I fear it is some terrible mistake."

"Scents can be crossed, or similar," said the householder.

"It must be so," said Urta. "I have no enemies, I have offended no one, I have left behind nothing, have given away nothing, that might be used to set these beasts on my trail. It is all some terrible mistake."

"You are safe here, small fellow," said the householder.

"My thanks, noble sir," said Urta.

"But the rent on my walls is high," said the householder.

"I will give you a *darin*," said Urta.

"Too little," said the householder.

"The *darin*," said Urta, "and the slave."

"The *darin* is of gold, of course," said the householder.

"It can be, if necessary," said Urta.

The householder turned to look at Viviana, in the candlelight. Observed, she knelt instantly.

She realized, with a sinking feeling, that she, a slave, could be beaten for such a lapse.

"She was standing," said the householder.

"She has the body, blood, needs, and instincts of a slave," said Urta. "It is only that she is not yet that far from her freedom. Thus she is not yet fully conversant with the vulnerable softness and grace of the slave, the behaviors of the slave, even the diction of the slave."

"Observe her," said the householder. "She is far more of a slave now than you know."

Viviana trembled, for she knew the householder spoke the truth. In her collar she knew herself fulfilled as only a woman can be fulfilled, having a Master, being a property, a possession, owned by a man.

To her relief, the householder looked away from her.

She breathed more easily.

A whip would not be sought, at least not now.

One of the dogs could be heard outside the door, restless, stirring.

"What is in your small sack?" the householder asked Urta.

"Very little," said Urta, quickly.

"Objects of sentimental value?" asked the householder.

"Yes," said Urta.

"Of negligible value?" said the householder.

"Yes," said Urta.

"You did not speak so before," he said, "when you hoped for entrance."

"I was lying," said Urta. "I was in fear for my life."

"I am very much like you," said the householder. "I, too, am a fellow of sentiment. I am particularly sentimental when it comes to gems, gold, and such."

"What is your price?" asked Urta.

"My price," said he, "is half of what you have in that small sack."

"Never!" said Urta.

There was a fierce scratching at the door.

"I think the dogs grow restless," said the householder. "Shall I open the door?"

"They would tear you to pieces," said Urta.

"I do not think I have the least to fear from them," said the householder.

"It is too much," said Urta.

"What do you think your life is worth?" asked the householder.

There was more scratching at the door.

"I could take it all," said the householder.

"Very well," said Urta, "half!"

Urta unslung the sack from his shoulder and carried it to the table, opened it, and spread its contents on the wood. He then stepped back. Gems, knots and tangles of jewelry, gold and silver coins, distributed, shone and sparkled in the candlelight.

"Divide it fairly," said Urta.

The householder rushed past Urta and eagerly addressed himself to sorting through the small trove glistening on the wood.

Viviana screamed and threw herself to the side, on her shoulder, as Urta's knife was thrust deeply into the back of the householder.

Urta wiped the knife on the shirt of the householder, and then lifted the body from the table and let it slide to the floor.

"He would have been wiser," said Urta, "to have taken my knife."

Viviana, aghast, her shoulder aching and bruised, rose to her feet and backed away.

"Do not fret or be naive," said Urta. "It was my plan to kill him, from the start. He might have identified us."

Viviana stepped back, her eyes wide, even further into the shadows.

"Now," said Urta, "you know better the nature of your Master."

At this point there was the sound of a great body throwing itself against the outside wall, scratching at it, trying to climb it.

"The upstairs window!" cried Viviana.

"The beast cannot reach it," said Urta. "Too, it will be shuttered, the shutters secured."

"There will be a ledge!" said Viviana.

"It is a dog, not a *vi-cat*," said Urta. "And the shutters will be secured."

At that moment there was the sound of a wild scratching, or scrambling, on the wall outside, at the upper level, and a ripping and splintering of wood. Viviana screamed again. From where she stood, near the foot of the stairs, she saw the snout of the animal thrusting itself through the wood. A scrap of wood bounded down the stairs. Then she saw the shoulders of the beast, and then part of the torso, and then it was half through the aperture.

"They are coming through the window!" screamed Urta.

Scarcely had he said this, when the beast scrambled through the window and was crouching, eyes bright in the darkness, blazing like copper, at the head of the stairs. Urta seized Viviana by the arm and drew her forcibly across the room, toward the door, putting her between the beast and himself. The beast descended three stairs, and then four stairs. Urta threw back the two bolts on the door. "I will close the door behind me," he said. "I will trap them in the house!" He then thrust Viviana deeper into the house, flung open the door, hurried through, and slammed the door shut behind him. The beast in the house, seeing its prey escaping, scurried down the stairs. Viviana, within the house, put herself to the side of the closed door. She pulled futilely against the thongs which confined her hands behind her back. The leash dangled from her neck. At that moment there was a cry of horror from outside the door, and a great weight must have hurled itself against the door, because it burst inward, torn from its latch and hinges, and, lying across the fallen door, on the floor of the house, was the body of Urta, one of the two dogs, its muzzle, thrusting and active, half buried in the body, feeding. It was joined momentarily by its fellow, and they began to contest the prey, dragging it about, tearing at it, gorging themselves in their common feast. Outside the doorway a club smote the lantern hanging over the threshold, so that it no longer shed light on the street and portal. A moment later the two men who had accosted and threatened Urta and his slave, Viviana, crowded into the room. Clearly they had not departed the vicinity but had been waiting outside, back in the darkness. The two beasts took no notice of them, and may not have realized they were in the room. "The table!" cried one of the men. "I see it!" said the other. Despite the tumult in the room the candle, flickering now that the door was gone, was still alit, and the sack, and its spilled, sparkling contents, lay manifest on the wood. The first of the two men rushed to the table, thrust aside the body of the householder with his boot, and regarded the lovely miscellany before him. The two animals, the fangs of each tearing at their common quarry, contesting their prize, moved back and forth in the room, their claws scratching on the wooden floor. The second man joined the first at the table. "We did well to wait," said the second man. "The dogs pose us no danger," said the first man. "They want meat, not gold." "They are otherwise occupied," said the second man. "Who would have thought the little pig had such treasure," said the first man. "Scrape it together, get it in the sack," said the second man. "Let us be on our way." But then, the two beasts, twisting about, lost their footing, possibly in the blood, and rolled together toward the table, not releasing their prey. The first man cried out, angrily, cursing. The two beasts then regained their footing but under the table, and, as they reared up, the table was flung to the side, and the candle flew away and went out. "Find the candle, light it!" screamed the first man, then on his hands and knees, trying to feel about for jewelry, coins, and whatever else might have been spilled to the floor. The two dogs had now separated, each with a portion of their spoil. "Curse the darkness, the blood!" said one of the men. "Get the candle! Light it!" Viviana, who had been standing to the left of the door as one would enter, her back pressed against the wall, then slipped through the opened portal and fled away, hurrying into the night.

CHAPTER EIGHTY-FIVE

Viviana lay on her right side, in an alley in the Varl district, in the early morning, her back to one of the high, windowless walls. She had fled from the house on Circumspection Street. She did not know how long she had run, or how far. Her hands were still tied behind her. As in many high cultures in which the institution of slavery exists even children learn how to secure a slave, rendering her helpless. The leash was still on her neck. After her long flight though the darkness, street after street, alley after alley, she had stopped, exhausted, and had lain down, and then, though she did not remember it, she had fallen asleep.

She opened her eyes slightly, a tiny crack, her cheek on the paving stones of the alley, and was aware of the heavy, furred, clawed feet of a mount before her.

Then she cried out softly, in protest, as she was jabbed by the point of a lance. Awakened, she was aware of the soreness and weariness of her body, the dampness and coldness of the pavement, and her hunger. She struggled to her knees, a miserable slave. She looked up and shuddered. The rider seemed high above her. He was clad in fur, even to a fur cap. Over the fur jacket was a breast plate. A conical helmet was slung behind him, and, at his side, he wore a short, flat bow case and quiver. "How," she wondered, "could so small a case carry a serious weapon?" The lance was grasped in a tentacled appendage. The eyes of the rider were narrow, the face was scaled, and, oddly, reptilian, or snakelike. She saw no visible ears. The mouth seemed wide for the width of the face. The saddle was small, but ringed, such that objects might be suspended from it, and the stirrups were high, this compensating for impact, should a lance meet resistance. Viviana, in her days in court, in various entertainments, banquets, receptions, audiences, and state functions, had seen many alien forms of life, alien to Telnarians, as Telnarians would be to those other forms of life, but she had never seen an alien such as this. Viviana had never before seen a Herul.

The rider gestured with the lance that she should rise, and she did so, standing in the alley, the leash on her neck and her hands bound behind her.

"What was such a creature doing in Telnar," she wondered, "mounted, and clad in the gear of war?"

The lance dipped toward her and she closed her eyes. She tensed, waiting for the quick, light thrust which would penetrate to her heart, or the saberlike slash which would cut through the tunic and open her belly. She felt the leash strap move and opened her eyes. The rider, with a quick, delicate motion, had looped the strap about the lance point and lifted it up. He now had it wound it about the pommel of his saddle.

She looked up at the rider, but she saw no keen interest in his eyes. Although there are certainly exceptions, Heruls, statistically, found human females of little but economic interest. Viviana knew that in time of war the slave was in far less jeopardy than the free female, who might, like a free male, particularly in hours of fire and blood, be summarily slain. The slave, like other domestic animals, had value. Free women were worthless, save for what they might bring, once stripped, marked, and collared.

The rider turned his mount, and began to ride, slowly, toward the opening at the end of the alley. Viviana walked beside the mount, on its left side, tethered to the pommel.

Viviana, brushed, combed, and scrubbed, in a short white tunic, her hands chained before her, and her ankles shackled, knelt before an officer in the guard station on Palace Street. How natural, and comfortable, it was for her, a slave, to kneel before a man. How happy she had been yesterday morning, to have been turned in by the Herul to authorities. Gratefully she had crawled to the bowl of gruel placed for her on the floor of the guard station and had fed appropriately. Often she had fed so, head down, not permitted to use her hands. This modality of feeding reminds the slave that she is an animal. With this clearly in mind, she well understands how it is that she is fittingly bought and sold. Kneeling before the master and being hand fed, being on all fours under the table and being hand fed, or retrieving scraps thrown to the floor, and such, is similarly instructive. The slave is never to be allowed to forget that she is a slave.

"You claimed," said the officer, "that you were owned by a man known to you as Urta, an Otung?"

"Yes, Master," said Viviana.

"Our records do not suggest that any such man exists," said the officer. "You were wearing a number collar. The number has been traced to a Regius of Telnar, a dealer in copper, residing in the house of Menippus, on Market street."

"I have only now heard the name of Regius of Telnar," said Viviana. "But my master did reside in the house of Menippus on Market Street."

"The second floor of that house is now empty," said the officer.

"My Master wished to flee the city," said Viviana.

"Why?" asked the officer.

"I was not informed, Master," said Viviana.

"He was accosted by brigands, and threatened by dogs, on Circumspection Street," said the officer. "Doubtless wild dogs."

Viviana was silent.

"After that, it is reasonably clear what ensued," said the officer. "He gained admittance to the dwelling, but one or more of the dogs forced their way into the building and attacked him. Following this, brigands entered the domicile and, it seems, killed the owner of the dwelling and robbed the premises."

Viviana did not speak.

"You were frightened and fled," said the officer.

"Yes, Master," said Viviana.

"Did you attempt to escape?"

"Master?" said Viviana.

"Did you attempt to escape?"

"Not in the sense that I fear you mean, Master," said Viviana.

"And what sense is that?" he asked.

"That of a fugitive slave, a runaway slave," said Viviana.

The officer smiled.

"We are marked, we are in collars," said Viviana, "we know there is no escape for us."

"There is no record of a Regius of Telnar, nor of an Urta, an Otung," said the officer.

Viviana was silent.

"You are an attractive slave," said the officer.

Viviana was silent.

"You have blonde hair and blue eyes," said the officer. "Some men like that. And you are nicely curved."

The slave did not speak.

"You have the sort of body that excites men," said the officer. "Do you have slave reflexes?"

Viviana was silent.

"Speak," said the officer.

"I am helpless in my collar," said Viviana.

"Good," said the officer.

"Yes!" said Viviana. "I will tell you what you wish to know. I will admit it, freely, gladly. I am no longer a free woman. I need lie no longer. I need sex! I want sex. I crave sex! I cannot help myself, nor do I wish to do so! It is what I am! I do not apologize! I have learned myself! I wish to be owned by a man! I want a Master, I need a Master! I am a slave!"

"Good," said the officer.

"What is to be done with me?" asked Viviana.

"You will be remanded to a market, where you will be sold," said the officer.

"Yes, Master," said Viviana.

CHAPTER EIGHTY-SIX

"What is going on?" whispered Viviana, to the girl next to her. "It is early. The sales do not begin until noon."

"I do not know," said the brunette.

The room was a basement room, long, low-ceilinged, ill-lit, and narrow, below Varick's Market, on Hestle Street in Telnar. There were forty girls in the room, mostly sitting or lying, aligned against one wall, that facing the heavy metal door at the foot of the stairs. Each wore Varick's "emporium collar" and over that collar there was another collar, an independent collar, with its yard of chain, by means of which each was fastened to the wall behind her. Interestingly, each, though a slave, and chained, was clothed, at least in the sense that a slave may be regarded as being clothed. Each wore a brief tunic, of plain gray. Permitting a chained slave a garment, as opposed to, say, a short, light blanket, was a consequence of Varick's views on the value of clothing in controlling a woman. Whereas the body of a slave is public, as is the body of any other animal, it is well known that slaves treasure even the mockery of a garment, even a rag, to shield their soft, precious, vulnerable, owned beauty from the idle, appraising, contemptuous scrutiny of the free, at least in public. Few slaves, for example, care to be exposed, wholly and helplessly, in the streets and markets. Accordingly, clothing, like rations and the whip, may serve for purposes of discipline. When a woman's clothing, its nature, and if she is clothed, depends on another, she well knows she is owned. Thus, even a tunic can be of great importance to a slave. To be sure, Varick was often scorned by other dealers for his indulgence in this respect. Who expects, for example, a slave in a holding area to be clothed? Varick's Market, incidentally, was one of the most prestigious in the city, and was noted for the quality of its merchandise. It could boast a rich and discerning clientele. Amongst its patrons might be numbered even members of the aristocracy and senators. Many slaves hoped

to be sold in Varick's Market. They often brought high prices and
were vended to affluent masters. To be sure, when a woman was
sold in Varick's Market she was exhibited raw as one would expect. Masters wish to see what they are buying. This was not the
only such holding room associated with Varick's Market, incidentally, and each, in its way, was special. The differences amongst
them depended on such things as languages, accomplishments,
origin, background, and so on. The girls in this room, as you may
recall, wore gray tunics. In the color coding of Varick's Market,
this commonly identified slaves received from the state, usually
abandoned slaves, unclaimed slaves, and such, whose purchase
price would be returned to the state, minus a vender's commission. To be sure, only the best of these would be accepted by Varick's Market. Viviana, inspected, had been accepted by an agent
from that market. She had pleaded to be retained for a lesser,
more obscure market but her pleas had been unheeded, as often
are those of a female slave. She, in her degradation and shame,
well aware of what she had learned about herself, the rightfulness of a collar on her neck, and knowing a slave's standing in
Telnarian law, feared being exposed in Varick's Market, for in
such a market, given its fame, quality, and prestige, she might be
recognized. How could that be endured? A proud princess, now
collared and marked, now naught but a humbled, abject, needful slave! What scandal and disgrace might ensue! What infamy,
ignominy, mortification, and humiliation might shock the city!
Might not the throne itself totter? Perhaps the senate might attempt to seize it? Might she be discreetly slain and disposed of in
some *carnarium*, hurried away to some market on a Mud World,
kept sequestered for life in the palace, a prisoner, alone with the
secret knowledge of her deepest self, her slave needs starved?
What if a disgruntled aristocrat, hostile to the royal family, might
buy her and keep her secretly, using her for a proxy on which to
vent his spleen? Too, surely there were several young men, high-
born and rich, of noble blood, whom she had treated curtly and
with contempt. What if she found herself naked, and at the feet
of one of them?

A moment ago the door had been opened, and two men had
entered the chamber, one richly dressed, one bearing a lantern.

"What is going on?" had whispered Viviana, to the girl next to
her. "It is early. The sales do not begin until noon."

"I do not know," had said the brunette.

The slaves stirred in the straw.

"One is one of Varick's men," said a girl near them. "I do not know the other."

"He is surely well-placed," said another.

"Do these sluts not know enough to kneel in the presence of a free man?" asked the richly dressed visitor.

"Kneel," barked Varick's man, lifting the lantern.

There was a movement of straw, and the line at the wall was kneeling.

"They are clothed," observed the richly dressed man.

The fellow with the lantern did not respond.

"Varick spoils his girls," said the richly dressed man.

"That they may better learn, by contrast, once sold, what it is to be a slave," said Varick's man.

"In so sharp a change," said the richly dressed man, "shocked and terrified, they sooner learn their collars?"

"Precisely," said Varick's man.

"Let us look at them," said the richly dressed man.

The two entrants into the chamber, one of them with the lantern lifted, Varick's man, then began to peruse the line of kneeling slaves.

"Get your head up, slut," said the richly dressed man.

"Yes Master," said Viviana, lifting her head, looking away from the lantern.

The line was perused twice, carefully, and, at the indication of the richly dressed man, sixteen girls, including Viviana, with a rattling of chains, were removed from the line.

"I would see these in the light," said the richly dressed man. "Take them upstairs, and put them with the others, in the rear court. We will make our selections there."

The sand of the rear court, behind the house of Varick, within its rear wall, closing the grounds, was warm to Viviana's bared feet.

She was one of some fifty girls standing, waiting.

"Days ago, bells rang," said Viviana.

"It was holiday," said one of the other girls.

"I know little of what has occurred," said Viviana.

"The matter is muchly done," said the girl.

"My Master was unable to flee the city," said Viviana. "Affairs, I gather, went awry. He was killed before he could reach an outer gate."

"I heard guards speaking," said the girl. "A revolt was afoot, thousands roving and ransacking in the city, for days, looting, and burning. How hard to accrue, how easy to seize, how hard to build, how easy to destroy, particularly under the cover of crowds and fire. The palace was attacked, the emperor, Ottonius the First—"

"The Usurper," said Viviana, quickly. "Aesilesius is the emperor."

"You are quite wrong, slave," said the other. "The sword determines such matters, and, even if it did not, the accession was approved by the senate. It was accepted and ratified, all in a perfectly legal manner."

"Law itself rests upon the sword," said another girl.

"Ottonius, the First, is emperor," said the first girl. "Do you dispute it?"

"No," whispered Viviana. She knew it was so.

"Do not concern yourselves," said the second girl. "What are matters of state to horses, pigs, and slaves?"

"Pray, rather to Dira, the goddess who became the slave girl of the gods," said another girl, "for a master who will not beat you as often as you deserve."

"To continue," said the first girl, "the palace was attacked, and the emperor, Ottonius, the First, and others, escaped, but, days later, were apprehended. Eventually, fires diminished and a semblance of order was restored. The regime was to be swept away. An infant prince was to be crowned, the son of Viviana, of the house of Aesilesius, who died in childbirth, and the child's father, a Drisriak, a tribe of the Aatii, was to be appointed regent by the senate."

"Viviana," said Viviana, "did not die in childbirth, nor has she ever borne a child."

"How do you know?" asked a slave.

"I have heard so," said Viviana.

"The revolt became understood as a revolution," said the first girl. "It is well known that things are named for purposes, and that fools seldom look behind names. They see realities as they are named and fail to see realities as they are. A day of festival and regeneration was proclaimed, and the captured emperor, Ottonius, and selected cohorts, were to be put to death on a platform set up in the square before the palace, almost at the steps of the palace. The square swarmed with celebrants. One could scarcely move.

The mood was joyful. Guards, soldiers, ministrants, servants of the temple, the rich and the poor, the high and the low, were in evidence. Citizens vied for points of vantage. Abroad was eagerness to see death. But the revolt or revolution was short lived. The time of vandalism and murder, blessed and sanctioned, was at an end. The legislation of the streets was over, the decree of mobs was no more. Authority abolished hoped to be replaced with authority renamed. But it was not to be. At the last moment barbarians, horsemen and others, Otungs and Heruls, intervened. The great square ran with blood, it is said to the knees of horses. Thousands perished. Men who came to see death themselves died. The revolt or revolution was done; ambitions were thwarted, fortunes were reversed; the barbarian, the Otung, Ottonius, the First, was again on the throne."

"It was on that day, I do not doubt," said Viviana, "that my Master chose to flee the city."

"He was doubtless of the failed party," said the first girl.

"I fear so," said Viviana

"A man!" said a frightened voice.

"Masters!" said another.

The fifty slaves then knelt in the sand.

"A line," said one of Varick's men, indicating a place.

The girls then formed the line, as had been indicated, and then again knelt, facing the masters.

Some six men were with the richly dressed person whom Viviana had seen in the subterranean chamber.

"The tallest, that is Varick himself," whispered the first girl.

That was the first time Viviana had ever seen Varick, the man whose collar she wore. To be sure, the collar was a sales convenience, as she knew she was, strictly, a property of the state, whom Varick was expected to market, obtaining thereby his commission.

Yet this gathering in the court did not seem a sale, at least not in any usual sense of a sale.

"Stand," said one of Varick's men, he whom Viviana recognized as the same who had held the lantern earlier.

The line rose obediently to its feet.

Viviana stood well. She did not wish to be cuffed or switched. Slaves are not free women, who may behave and act as they wish. The slave, who is goods, and an animal, is to present herself well, as the beautiful, desirable, purchasable object she is.

"Remove your tunics," said the man. "Drop them to your feet, on the right side."

Viviana felt the slave girl's thrill, obeying a dominant male. Even new captures, not yet marked and collared, sense such feelings. How keenly are they then aware of their womanhood, of the radical dimorphism of the sexes, of their slightness and softness, their marvelous difference from men, and what it might be to belong, as a woman, to a man.

Viviana felt the sand beneath her feet and the warm sun on her back.

The richly dressed man, accompanied by the fellow who had earlier carried the lantern and at whose command the girls had unhesitantly bared their bodies, then began to make his way about the line, sometimes pausing, and then, sometimes, going back a bit, and then again proceeding. He then returned to the line, coursing it a final time.

"I will take this one, and this one, and this one," he said. In the end, twelve girls, one of them Viviana, were pointed out.

"Reclothe yourselves," said the fellow who had carried the lantern, and the slaves slipped back into their tunics.

The twelve girls designated, now again tunicked, were arranged, standing, in a vertical line, one behind the other, in order of height, the tallest girl first, which is common in such arrangements. This line was oriented facing the interior gate of the court. Viviana was seventh in the line.

"Return the others to their holding areas," said Varick to one of his men.

"You others, form a line, follow me," said the fellow.

Shortly, the only slaves left in the court were the twelve who had been selected out from the others.

"An excellent choice," said Varick to the richly dressed man.

"Not an easy choice," said the richly dressed fellow. "They are all superb."

"We endeavor to have them so," said Varick.

"I do not know what is going on," thought Viviana to herself. And she was reasonably sure that the other girls were as ignorant of matters as herself. One seldom explains matters to slaves. Why should one? They are slaves. Who would stop and explain matters to domestic animals, to *vardas*, pigs, horses, or slaves?

One of the men with Varick had withdrawn from the court, and had now returned with a length of chain, with collars.

"How is it," asked Varick, of the richly dressed man, "that you are not in the livery of the palace?"

"Few are now to know of this," said the richly dressed man. "It is to be a surprise."

"He spoke of the livery of the palace," said Viviana to herself. "Can he be of the palace? I am afraid."

"Have you heard aught of the Drisriak prince, the conspirator, Ingeld?" asked Varick.

"No," said the richly dressed man, "but he must be in the city. They search for him, door to door, domicile to domicile. He cannot escape."

"It is said," said Varick, "that the exarch, Sidonicus, and the deputy exarch, Fulvius, have disappeared."

"I know nothing of that," said the richly dressed man.

"It is rumored that they were slain by order of the crown," said Varick.

"I do not think it likely," said the richly dressed man. "It is unpopular, even hazardous, to kill a common ministrant, and surely it would be politically injudicious, extremely so, to kill an exarch or a deputy exarch. Instantly they would be transformed into martyrs, even saints."

"But secretly?" asked Varick.

"Unlikely," said the richly dressed man. "Secrets are dangerous. They are seldom kept."

"Perhaps they are in hiding," said Varick.

"I see no point in that," said the richly dressed man. "They are ministrants. If accused or charged, they need only appear dismayed and scandalized, and deny complicity in any crime, of whatever magnitude. Blood seldom sticks to such hands."

"Perhaps they were done away with by their own followers, outraged and resentful, after the fiasco of the revolution, and the massacre in the palace square," said Varick.

"Perhaps," said the richly dressed man, "but I think it unlikely. It seems to me that ignorant dupes would not associate them with the disaster, and that dissident elements would wish to retain the cunning and prestige of their leadership."

"To try again," said Varick.

"Of course," said the richly dressed man.

"But where then are they?" asked Varick.

"I do not know," said the richly dressed man.

"I suspect they were slain, somehow, by someone, their bodies then disposed of in some *carnarium*," said Varick.

"Perhaps," said the richly dressed man. "I do not know."

"There are many mysteries in the world," said Varick.

"True," said the richly dressed man.

Varick then turned to the line of standing, waiting girls, that selected twelve, amongst whom, in seventh place, was Viviana. All stood well, as was fitting, soft, slender, and tunicked; none dared meet his eyes. Such boldness might be deemed effrontery. He regarded the line for a moment. "I trust they will prove satisfactory," he said.

"I have no doubt of it," said the richly dressed man.

Varick then nodded to the fellow who had withdrawn from the court, and then returned with the chain and collars.

That fellow then moved to the back of the line.

The line was then knelt.

At this point the richly dressed man withdrew.

Kneeling is common with slaves, as it betokens their radical difference from the free, their inferiority, their meaninglessness, and submission. The slave, aware of what she is, accepts and welcomes this position. She feels its rightfulness for her. She wants to be on her knees, and is thrilled to be so. Often even the body of a free woman flames with femininity when she finds herself on her knees before a man. How perfect and right, despite her chagrin, her possible protests and tears, it suddenly seems to her. How she then understands what she is, a female. Another advantage of kneeling the woman is that she is then better held in place. Viviana heard the sound of chains behind her. A kneeling woman is less likely to bolt. One commonly begins a coffling with the last girl in the line, and then moves forward. This practice, like kneeling, particularly in the case of new slaves, tends to reduce the possibility of bolting. The girl may not even see the collar until she is its prisoner. There is a click, and she knows she has been added to the chain. Women, incidentally, understand chains and ropes. Few have not, if only in their imagination, felt them on their bodies. Many women have brought their fingers to their throats, softly, delicately, carefully, apprehensively, wondering what it would be to feel that wonderful, marvelous part of their bodies closely encircled with the locked collar of a master. Sometimes a woman, a free woman, of course, as a joke, is chained in her sleep, and placed gently on the floor, her neck fastened to the foot of the bed, thus to awaken, in consternation, and realize her womanhood and what might be done with it, should men choose. Sometimes an interested party contacts a dealer and requisitions a particular woman. The woman, usually wholly unsuspecting, is then, commonly, when convenient, rendered unconscious, usually as a result of the administration of a drug. She is then, while unconscious, after being stripped and chained, delivered to the appointed venue. There she awakens, to begin her new life. Perhaps she is aware of the collar on her neck. Surely she is aware of the chains on her fair limbs. Perhaps, in one corner of the room, she sees a glowing brazier from which protrudes the handle of an iron.

Viviana, as she knelt in the sand, in line, heard the snap of a collar behind her, and knew that the girl behind her was now on the chain. She, Viviana, knew that she would be next. She knelt straight, preparing her body.

"May I speak, Master?" asked the girl behind her.

"How bold," thought Viviana, "that she would dare speak. She must be a very brave girl. Perhaps she is unusually beautiful, and thus hopes to trade on her attractions. Still, even though she is beautiful, even very beautiful, she is only a slave. Might she not be beaten for her presumption?" Viviana was sure that she herself would have been cuffed or switched, perhaps even lashed, had she dared be so bold.

"What do you want?" asked the master. There was a tiny sound of links. Viviana could sense the chain and collar dangling from his hand.

"Handsome Master," said the girl behind her, "though I am only a worthless slave, yet I am a woman and as such am subject to the pangs and torments of an unsatisfied curiosity. I am helpless and in agony. I suffer. Please have mercy on a meaningless beast and assuage its curiosity. Please consider my agony, and do as much for me, unworthy though I am, as you might for a nobler animal, could they but speak and understand, a pig or dog. I beg it, kind, handsome Master! What is to be our lot, what is to be done with us?"

Viviana winced expecting to hear the striking of flesh and a cry of pain, as though she herself might have been so bold, so forward, so unwise, but the denouement of this tiny interaction was both prompt and unexpected.

"Rejoice, lovely collar slut," said the master. "Be glad. You and your sisters are incredibly fortunate. First, you have been accepted as goods worthy of Varick's Market; on that you may congratulate yourselves; from what block might you be better vended; second, the regime has survived and holidays are proclaimed. It is a time of celebration and victory. There will be fetes and banquets throughout the city. Gold, silver, jewels, and hundreds of girls will be distributed, lavishly bestowed, and, where you are concerned, the palace itself, recognizing the quality of our house, has patronized us, in search of a small number of girls who, in addition to other gifts, special prizes, awards, and such, are deemed worthy of being distributed amongst the high victors, the heroes and favorites of the throne."

Sounds mingled. There were cries of joy from most who heard the master's words but this unrestrained irruption of gladness and relief was penetrated by a cry of anguish from Viviana.

"Thank you, Master! Thank you, Master!" cried the girl behind Viviana. "No, no, no!" wept Viviana. "Not the palace! Not the palace!"

Viviana tried to leap to her feet but she had scarcely half risen when the fellow, dropping the chain and collars, seized her by the hair, and forced her down, again, on her knees.

The master's hand was cruelly tight in her hair and he shook her head angrily. Her head seemed to burst with blinding fire.

"No!" she wept. "Please, no! Not the palace! Not the palace!"

"Are you mad, slave?" asked the girl behind her. "What could be better than the palace?"

"Yes, yes!" said other girls, who had heard.

Viviana tried to struggle to her feet once more, to run, though there was nowhere to run, but she was thrown by the hair to the sand on her right side. Indeed, her shoulder was thrust deep in the sand, and she was aware, on her side, of the master's hands somewhere near her throat, and, an instant later, she heard the heavy, definitive snap of the collar, and she knew herself added to the chain. "No, no!" she wept. The master pulled her rudely up to her knees again. She became aware of a robed figure near her, and, looking up, saw that it was Varick himself. Instantly she threw herself to her belly in the sand, seized an ankle, and, sobbing, began to cover his sandaled foot with kisses, again and again, frantically, desperately. "Please, Master," she begged. "Free me from the chain. Do not let me be taken to the palace! I will do anything, not to go to the palace."

"You are a slave," said Varick. "You will do anything, and everything, immediately and unquestioningly, which a Master might wish."

"Master!" wept Viviana.

"Do you seek to bargain?" inquired Varick.

"No, Master. No, Master," wept Viviana. "I am a slave."

"She is in terror of the palace," said one of Varick's men.

"Good," said another. "Let us hope her terror is well justified."

"She must know something of the palace, or its occupants," said another.

"And they of her," laughed another, he who had collared her.

"Excellent," said another. "That might make her somewhat special as a gift, to someone or other."

"True, it might well add flavor and spice to her bestowal," said he who had collared her.

"Mercy, Master," begged Viviana. "I am a poor slave who begs mercy! I beg mercy! Mercy! Do not let me be taken to the palace! Please, Master, do not let me be taken to the palace, not the palace!"

"Proceed," said Varick to the fellow who had been forming the coffle. The girl before Viviana was then collared, and the fellow moved forward, to the next in line. Shortly thereafter the last collar was snapped shut, and the coffle was formed.

It remained on its knees while Varick spoke with his men.

Viviana, on her knees, in the sand, in the coffle, shuddered, miserable with shame. Tears streamed down her cheeks.

When Varick turned again to the line, Viviana again appealed to him. "Please, Master," she wept, "do not have me taken to the palace!"

"You have been selected," said Varick.

"Please, Master," begged Viviana. "Free me of the chain."

"You have been selected," said Varick. "You are on the chain."

"Up, curvaceous beasts," said he who had formed the coffle.

The coffle then rose to its feet.

"Stand well, be proud," said Varick.

"The slave girl is surely the most desirable form of livestock," said one of Varick's men, admiringly.

"Yes," said another.

"Remove the coffle," said Varick.

He who had formed the coffle then conducted it from the court.

"When is delivery to be made?" asked he who had borne the lantern earlier.

"We will be notified," said Varick.

"But soon?" asked he who had borne the lantern earlier.

"I think quite soon," said Varick.

"How are they to be presented?" asked his fellow.

"That has been specified," said Varick. "Things are to be simple, plain, even demure. There must be nothing to distract from the slave herself. She is to be presented clothed, but in such a way that it is clear that she is a slave. She is to be almost nude. There is to be little doubt as to the nature of her lineaments."

"May I then suggest," said his fellow, "brief tunics of white silk?"

"I think that will do very nicely," said Varick.

"Quite brief?" asked his fellow.

"Of course," said Varick.

Varick and his men then prepared to leave the court.

At the interior gate, that leading into the house, Varick hesitated. "Oh," he said, "do you recall the blonde, the one who made such a nuisance of herself?"

"Surely," said he who had earlier borne the lantern.

"See that she is given ten lashes," said Varick.

"It will be done," said he who had earlier borne the lantern.

CHAPTER EIGHTY-SEVEN

Corelius, in the garb of a slave, on his hands and knees, his ankles shackled, was scrubbing tiles in one of the corridors of the palace, a task typical of those to which he was commonly put. The bucket of water was at his side. His head was down. He became suddenly aware that a mighty figure stood over him. He did not dare raise his head.

"Such work is commonly done by slave girls," said Abrogastes, called the Far-Grasper, king of the Drisriaks. "On the worlds of the Alemanni, it is done, ideally, by female slaves who were formerly of high birth in the empire, scions of families wealthy in the empire, and such. How interestingly the emperor deals with you, keeping you a free man, but putting you to the shameful tasks of the slave."

Corelius kept his head down.

Then Corelius cried out as Abrogastes seized his hair and pulled his head up, and turned it from side to side. Then Abrogastes thrust his head down, again, rudely, and released it. "You are not so handsome now as before," said Abrogastes. "Few women would now be interested in buying you for a male couch slave."

The left side of Corelius' face was deeply scarred. It had been furrowed by the claws of a gardening implement wielded by an angry woman. This had taken place several days ago when he was being conducted through the gantlet of an angry, abusive crowd to the steps of a punishment platform, that on which the emperor and certain others, he amongst them, were to be put to death.

"It was you who betrayed me, and others," said Abrogastes. "You betrayed Telnar to its enemies, and its enemies to Telnar. Your treasons, ignoble *filch*, draw no distinctions; they do not discriminate; they are manifest, frequent, and opportunistic. What will be done with you? The horse death on Tenguthaxichai would be too good for you. It is too quick. Better to tie you in a cage with starving *filchen*. It might take them days to eat you."

Corelius, trembling, did not speak.

"I will petition the emperor, to acquire you," said Abrogastes. "I will buy you from him."

"Mercy, great lord," whispered Corelius.

But Abrogastes had strode away.

Corelius then, trembling, returned to his work.

CHAPTER EIGHTY-EIGHT

"Your majesty," said Mujinn, respectfully.

"Noble rider, noble Herul," said Otto, rising from the throne on its dais, and descending to sit behind a black-lacquered, marble-topped table set near the throne. He knew that Heruls did not care to raise their head to a human. Heruls commonly addressed humans from horseback, lance in hand. Mujinn remained standing.

"Arrangements have been made," said Otto, "to return your people, and beasts, to the Plains of Barrionuevo, given the conclusion of the days of holiday."

"We look forward to having the turf of the Flats of Tung once more beneath the paws of our horses," said Mujinn.

"How is noble Hunlaki, skilled commander of the Herul cavalry, to whom we owe so much?" asked Otto.

"Old, but otherwise quite well," said Mujinn.

"I am pleased to hear it," said Otto.

"He thinks to conclude his life suitably," said Mujinn.

"He did not fall in the action in the great square," said Otto.

"No," said Mujinn.

"You understand," said Otto, "that we cannot permit a large force of armed Heruls to remain in Telnar."

"Nor would we wish to do so," said Mujinn, "there is no grazing for our herds in the streets of Telnar."

"Your people, and mounts, and many Otungs, and their mounts, will be returned to Tangara at the same time."

"On the same ships, differently housed," said Mujinn.

"Yes," said Otto. "In that way Heruls need not fear that Otungs will arrive first to harvest meat from poorly defended herds and Otungs need not fear that Heruls will arrive first to raid and burn poorly defended Otung villages, halls, and encampments. Too, Heruls need not fear that ships will be deliberately crashed or destroyed, for in such an act prize Otung forces would find themselves likewise destroyed."

"Some Otungs will remain in Telnar," said Mujinn.

"Yes," said Otto, "some, to keep order in the city."

"We shall look forward to further days of celebration and then to our triumphal return to Tangara," said Mujinn.

"I shall hope that you, and other high officers of the Heruls, will honor us with your presence at the culminating victory celebration, the great banquet in the palace."

"That is our intention," said Mujinn.

"I suspect," said Otto, "that this visit to the palace is little motivated by a wish to confirm details as to your return to Tangara."

"True, your majesty," said Mujinn. "I come on behalf of my mentor and tutor, my friend and fellow, one with whom I have ridden for many years, in hunting, in herding, and in battle, Hunlaki."

"That was my conjecture," said Otto.

"Perhaps you suspect the nature of the commission with which I have been entrusted," said Mujinn.

"I fear so," said Otto.

"At the great feast, Hunlaki will make a request of you. He will ask of you a boon, a favor."

"I do not think," said Otto, "I will grant Hunlaki his favor."

"You realize," said Mujinn, "things are not so simple."

"I know," said Otto.

Mujinn then bowed and withdrew.

Otto remained seated at the table for a long time. Eventually, Iaachus, Arbiter of Protocol, entered the throne room.

"What is wrong, your majesty?" asked Iaachus.

"Hunlaki," said Otto, "wants a favor."

CHAPTER EIGHTY-NINE

"What word," inquired Otto, "of Ingeld, prince of the Drisriaks?"

"The search continues," said Rurik, Tenth Consul of Larial VII, of the Larial Farnichi.

"Perhaps he has escaped the city," said Otto.

"Unlikely," said Rurik. "In any event, his power is broken. Drisriaks allied with him have been pardoned and recalled to the banner of Abrogastes."

"How goes the temple?" asked Otto.

"The temple guard has been disbanded," said Titus Gelinus, attorney and rhetor. "The temple has been denied its exemptions and subsidies. It is thought appropriate that it support itself, on its own resources, such as they may be. No longer is there danger that the might of the state will be enlisted to coerce and murder citizens who do not subscribe to its witless verbalisms."

"And what of the many other faiths of Floon?"

"They are now safe, to prosper or falter, as the case may be," said Titus Gelinus.

"And the faiths in the thousands of other gods, on the hundreds of other worlds?" asked Otto.

"They, too, are now safe, to prosper or falter, as the case may be," said Titus Gelinus.

"Has aught been heard of the exarch and deputy exarch, ponderous Sidonicus and smooth-cheeked Fulvius?" asked Otto.

"In a way, "No," and, in a way, "Yes,"" said Titus Gelinus.

"I do not understand," said Otto.

"In a way, we have heard nothing," said Titus Gelinus. "We have had no word from them, have had no verifiable appearances of them, have had no traces of them, have had no discoveries of bodies, or such. On the other hand, in another way, we have heard much. Thousands of men claim to have seen them flying through the air to the table of *Karch*."

542 John Norman

"How is it determined that they were flying to the table of *Karch* and not somewhere else?" asked Otto.

"I do not know," said Titus Gelinus.

"Where is the table of *Karch*?" asked Otto.

"The table of *Karch* is perhaps up, and to the east," said Titus Gelinus. "Yet some say they were flying in another direction, and, indeed, in several other directions. It is very confusing."

"This was witnessed by thousands of men?" asked Otto.

"And more, later on, at least until recently, came forward, attesting to the same phenomenon," said Tuvo Ausonius.

"Interesting," said Otto.

"Who were the first to note this remarkable phenomenon?" asked Iaachus.

"Two fellows, of little fame and obscure antecedents," said Titus Gelinus, "a Buthar and a Grissus, both of Telnar."

"I do not know them," said Iaachus.

"Nor I," said Otto.

"I regret to inform you," said Rurik, "we have been unable to determine the whereabouts of Timon Safarius Rhodius, of the Telnar Rhodii, *primarius* of the senate."

"I think we shall have to appoint, or see to it that the senate nominates and elects, a new *primarius*," said Iaachus, "one acceptable to us."

"Clearchus Pyrides, senator from Inez IV, current moderator of the senate," said Otto.

"Very good," said Iaachus.

"He is invited to the great banquet," said Otto. "That will be time enough for him to learn that he is to be freely elected the new *primarius*."

"Very good," said Titus Gelinus, envoy to the senate, and envoy from the senate to the throne.

"Will Atalana, the empress mother, and Aesilesius, now deposed as emperor, be invited to the victory banquet?" asked Iaachus.

"Of course," said Otto.

"Is that wise?" asked Iaachus.

"Of that the future will decide," said Otto.

"The infant which was to be proposed as the offspring of Viviana," said Julian, "has been located, as you requested. It is a foundling. It has been traced to somewhere in the Inez system."

"Settle it on some civilized world," said Otto, "and let no records be kept of its disposition."

"What is this strange business on Tangara?" asked Iaachus.

"That dealing with the Heights of Barrionuevo?" asked Otto.

"Yes," said Iaachus.

"I am having the *festung* of Sim Giadini rebuilt," said Otto.

"How is that compatible with the proclaimed policy of the throne?" asked Iaachus. "The *festung* was a citadel of Emanationist brothers, and Emanationism is one of the many Floonian faiths."

"The emperor," said Julian, "was raised in the *festung* village."

"That is immaterial," said Iaachus.

"The *festung* was destroyed by imperial cruisers," said Julian. "Doubtless then, the emperor feels it is appropriate, in this case, that restitution be made."

"Is that it, your majesty?" inquired Iaachus.

"I have my reasons," said Otto.

"Rumors have reached us," said Rurik, "that Alacida, spouse of Hrothgar, third son of Abrogastes, on Tenguthaxichai, is pregnant."

"May things proceed apace and well," said Otto.

"What if the child is a male?" said Iaachus. "It would be of royal blood and a grandson of Abrogastes."

"So it would be," said Otto.

"It would have a claim on the throne," said Iaachus.

"Only in its turn," said Otto.

"I do not understand," said Iaachus.

"How, dear Rurik," asked Otto, "is your slave, Cornhair?"

"She licks, kisses, moans, and squirms well," said Rurik. "I am not yet tired of her. I think I shall keep her, at least for the present."

"You are familiar, perhaps," said Otto, "with my slave, Flora?"

"The one who was an officer of the court, on Terennia?"

"Yes," said Otto.

"Of course," said Rurik.

"I am having her trained in dance," said Otto. "I am going to include her in the entertainment. I think it will be amusing to see her dance, to entertain us, as a slave."

"Preparations for the great feast are well underway," said Iaachus.

"Musicians, dancers, singers, jugglers, acrobats, rope walkers, eaters of fire?" said Otto.

"And magicians, and knife dancers, and others," said Iaachus.

"Good," said Otto.

"Markets on a dozen worlds will be ransacked for delicacies," said Iaachus. "The palace chefs will be joined by others, from amongst the finest in the city."

"There should be a thousand guests at the tables," said Julian.

"Even the great hall will be crowded," said Titus Gelinus.

"Gifts and prizes are to be abundant and lavish," said Otto, "worthy the bestowing hands of an emperor."

"Gold, silver, rings, jewelries, slaves, villas, estates, and such," said Iaachus.

"To the noblest the richest of prizes, the greatest of gifts," said Rurik, "the most esteemed and best remembered, will be the gratitude of an emperor."

"They shall have that, and more," said Otto.

"It will be strange to have an imperial feast attended by Abrogastes, king of the Drisriaks, and Ortog, prince of the Drisriaks, and king of the Ortungen," said Julian.

"They have graciously delayed their departure from the city, to join us in the fete," said Otto.

"They are currently housed in the palace," said Tuvo Ausonius.

"Stranger yet," said Rurik, "to have Heruls indoors, and in a palace."

Men laughed, save Otto.

"I gather that certain high men from the city will be in attendance," said Julian.

"Yes," said Iaachus. "That seems in the best interests of the throne."

"And some common folk, as well?" said Julian.

"A selected handful, a token," said Iaachus.

"Well publicized?" said Julian.

"Of course," said Iaachus.

"That, too, in the best interests of the throne?" said Julian.

"Of course," said Iaachus.

"What of free women?" asked Julian.

"Some," said Iaachus, "spouses of high men, ambassadors, dignitaries, wealthy merchants, and such."

"They can avert their eyes, whenever they wish," said Titus Gelinus.

"There will be many tables," said Otto, "and not everything need be the same at every table."

"In a way," said Iaachus, "there will be many feasts."

"But only one emperor's table," said Julian.

"Of course," said Iaachus.

"Presumably it will be large and well attended," said Julian.

"Naturally," said Iaachus, "but with its places reserved for particular guests."

"There will be too many in attendance," said Rurik. "I fear for the safety of the emperor."

"Precautions have been taken," said Iaachus. "There will be a public feast, to be sure, but a private one, as well. The emperor will be seen, appear amongst the tables, accept salutations, welcome guests, and such, but will then retire to a more secluded venue, a reserved dining area, one ample, but better secured."

"One in which the business of the banquet, its purposes and paramount considerations, may be better pursued?" said Julian.

"Precisely," said Iaachus.

"That seems wise," said Julian.

"It was deemed so," said Iaachus.

CHAPTER NINETY

Viviana, seventh in the coffle, her hands braceleted, fastened behind her, made her way, in her place, weeping, miserable with shame and fear, in her tiny, degrading tunic of clinging silk, through the jubilant throngs in the great square, toward the steps of the palace. Men greeted the coffle's passage with cries of interest, laughter, hootings, unsolicited appraisals, and lewd noises. Even if it had consisted of the captured women of a hated enemy little would have been different. The coffle was flanked by guards, that its contents not be accosted, seized, and fondled in its course.

Viviana lifted her head and saw before her the broad steps of the palace.

Beneath her feet she felt crushed flowers.

She, no more than the others, now wore the emporium collar of Varick's Market. Her neck, and those of the others, was now encircled with a palace collar. How the others had been delighted at this change; how she had been filled with a sense of distress and dread as this change had been effected!

The palace, blazing with light, furnished by dozens of lamps and mounted torches, was strung with ribbons, banners, and streamers.

She then, in her place, obedient to the chain, began to climb the broad steps leading to the now-rebuilt, great portal, the central entryway into the palace.

Many times before she had ascended these same steps but never as she did now, scarcely clad, helpless, and on a chain. She, with the others, had originally expected to be entered into the palace by an obscure side entrance, as would be common with slaves, denied, as other animals, the prestige of a portal better reserved for the free, but she had learned while in the House of Varick, the Market of Varick, that many valuables, weighty chests, bound with gold bands, silver standards hung with jewelry, elaborate candelabra, large precious vessels, rugs from Beyira II, and such, were to be ostentatiously introduced into the palace, evidencing the wealth of the city, the regime, and the empire.

"Oh!" she cried, for a hand had dragged at her arm.

"Back," said a guard, brandishing his spear.

The coffle hurried on.

A free woman hissed and spat, and sputum struck the cheek of Viviana, mingling there with the tears streaming from her eyes.

Viviana recalled the contempt in which she herself had once held female slaves, worthless beasts so fascinating to, and desired by, strong men.

Shortly thereafter Viviana had entered the palace.

"I must try to be unnoticed," thought Viviana to herself. "I must be unobtrusive, be so much a slave that none will note me."

In her days of freedom Viviana had frequently been served by slaves whom, an hour later, she would have been at a loss to recall.

A servitor, in a vestibule to the side, had received the coffle. The captain of the coffle guard had turned the key pouch over to the servitor, and then he, with his men, had withdrawn.

The servitor inspected the coffle.

He wiped Viviana's face with a soft cloth, removing the stains of tears and the traces of the free woman's displeasure. "Why do you weep?" he asked. "Forgive me Master," said Viviana. "Weep no more," he said. "Yes, Master," she said. He then, as he did with the others, straightened and adjusted her tunic, pulling it downward, a bit, and then more back, more tightly against her body.

The coffle then, the guards having retired, followed the servitor.

In the great hall, Viviana's head began to swim, dazzled by color and movement, by crowding and merriment, by dozens of tables filled with laughing, jesting, conversing guests, by scurrying slaves and servitors, with the swirl of music, with the movements of mountebanks and acrobats performing amongst the tables. The odors of succulent viands, many of them unfamiliar to Viviana, permeated the hall. Never in her days in the palace had she experienced anything like this, so seemingly momentous an affair, so busy with noise, crowding, light, and commotion. She looked up and saw a rope walker cavorting yards above the tables. She cried out in fear, while men laughed, as a torrent of fire burst forth beside her, emitted from the mouth of a turbaned fire eater.

The coffle continued to follow the servitor in whose charge it was.

Threading through the tables Viviana was heartened. She

began to grow cautiously optimistic, and then, as they continued on their way, even more so, and ever more so.

"There are many here," thought Viviana to herself. "I do not know them, and they do not know me. In such a gathering who pays attention to a slave? In such crowds who truly sees a slave? I have little, if anything, to fear."

She wondered how long the feast, or banquet, had been in progress. It was clearly much underway. Surely it had not just begun.

Then, to her surprise, the coffle was turned to the right, and then, a bit later, to the left, where there was a carpeted aisle amongst the tables. The coffle, following the servitor, was conducted up this aisle, tables on both sides. Viviana felt the deep nap of the rug beneath her bared feet. At the termination of this aisle there was a closed portal, flanked by guards. Viviana, though raised in the palace, was not familiar with many of its precincts. She had, for, example, never been in the kitchen, the servitors' quarters, the guard rooms, various store rooms, or even the great library. She was familiar, of course, with the great hall, but she had never seen it so busy, so strewn with tables and crowds. She recalled it largely as an imposing, spacious, empty area, presumably designed to impress visitors with the vastness of the palace, a place where general audiences might be held. She had seen the portal at its termination, but had never been behind it. She did not know if a large or small chamber, perhaps a robing room, lay behind it, or, possibly, merely a corridor, by means of which the great hall might be discreetly reached from inner recesses of the palace.

It was before this portal that the coffle was halted, tables on each side.

Suddenly Viviana was very frightened.

She saw the chain on her neck looping up to the back of the collar of the girl before her, and sensed its weight, as well, going to the girl behind her.

She jerked at the close-linked metal circlets which confined her wrists behind her.

"You slaves are special," said the servitor to the coffle.

Viviana, in the passage amongst the tables, in the tumult of the feast, seeing hundreds of strangers, and busy servitors and slaves, had cautiously discounted the apprehensions which had so disturbed her in the rear court of Varick's Market and outside the palace, and on the steps. She would be unremarked, one slave amongst many, even were she to be given to, or won by, a guest. Who knew what guests were high victors or heroes? Were not all the guests favorites of a generous emperor?

"You slaves," said the servitor, "with others, private slaves, will serve at the emperor's table, after which you will be gambled for, or distributed, to the guests."

"The emperor's table!" cried a girl, delightedly.

There were cries of joy from the coffle, save from its seventh occupant, a blue-eyed blonde who shook with fear and misery.

"Oh, let the room be large," thought Viviana to herself, "and let the guests be many. Let there be light, noise, and good cheer. Let entertainers charm the guests, engaging their attention. Let inebriating beverages flow, heating the blood, instilling contentment, dulling perception and clouding the mind. Let me be unnoted!"

Keys were inserted into the bracelets confining the girls' hands behind their backs, and their hands were freed. One of the portal guards took the impediments from the servitor and dropped them into a basket situated to the left of the portal, as one would enter. Viviana rubbed her wrists. The bracelets had not been cruelly tight, as might have been those inflicted on women of the enemy shortly after capture, but they had been snug, and, as one would expect, unslippable. Next the coffle was crowded before the closed portal, with its two stout panels, and the coffle chain was removed. Viviana began to tremble, and feared her legs would give way beneath her. The coffle chain was deposited in the same basket as contained the now-removed bracelets. Viviana might have turned to run, back, amidst the tables, but she feared she would, in her weakness, fall. "What is wrong?" asked the girl beside her. "Nothing, nothing," Viviana whispered.

"'Nothing'!" she wept to herself. "In the affairs of Telnaria, were my abasement known, the house of Aesilesius would be wrought with scandal. It would be dishonored, shamed, and perhaps ruined. A hundred noble families, such as the Orsini, the Aureliani, the Veii, the Farnichi might spring forth and eye the throne. Order might totter and civil war rage. The empire itself, a thousand worlds, might tremble. How could I bring that about, such disruption, scandal, shame, and peril? And what fate would be mine? Might I not, to prevent such misery and chaos, be hastily done away with in one fashion or another, slain and disposed

of, perhaps in some *carnarium*, or sold on some remote world, perhaps to an alien form of life? But who would risk selling me? Or
might I be simply hidden away, say, in one palace or stronghold,
or another, on one world or another? And how could I be restored
to liberty, if that was to be my fate, without affronting public
opinion and custom, and even the law? There has been a collar
on my neck. How could I take my place amongst free women?
What an insult to them! How could they endure my presence, as
though I might be an equal? I would be shunned, avoided, despised, and scorned. But, too, how I could I endure to be amongst
them, trapped in their robes, prejudices, and conventions, knowing what I now know of myself, that I desire to be on my knees
before a master, that I rightfully belong to men, that I wish to be
owned, possessed, and dominated, that I am a needful slave!"

Viviana could hear music from within. At the moment, though
the instruments were doubtless similar, it was quite different from
the music of the main concourse, that in the great hall itself. In the
great hall, the music was designed to enhance the pleasures of dining and provide an unobtrusive background for conversation. Here,
from behind the door, could be heard music intended not only to
delight the ear but stir the blood. Odd, thought Viviana, how similar instruments in the same hands can effect such incredible varieties, subtleties, and nuances of sound, sinking to the depths of night
and pain, soaring to the heights of cloud and sky. How is it, she
wondered, that men can draw from simple, silent, mechanical objects, bowls, boxes, strings, bits of metal, tubes of wood, placidity,
despair, hope, resolution, fury, ecstasy, and passion, the gamut of
sensibilities without which a species could not be itself?

As the slaves were grouped before the panels of the portal, it
seemed they would be introduced into the area behind the portal
as a whole.

"Forgive me, Master," whispered Viviana to the conducting
servitor, "but I trust that we will not be introduced individually
before the guests within."

She received the response for which she had hoped.

"Certainly not," he said. "Do you think you are important?"

"No, Master," said Viviana. "Thank you, Master."

"There is hope," thought Viviana. "Let there be many guests,
let there be many distractions. Who notices a slave as other than
a slave? Are we not all the same, identical in our collars, meaningless, purchasable work and pleasure beasts?"

"Too," she thought, "what have I to fear, truly? All, or most, believe that Viviana died in childbirth, or, I suppose, was somehow done away with. I know this sort of thing from my former Master, Urta, the Otung. Who then would recognize the royal princess, Viviana, in a common slave, tunicked, marked, and collared? To be sure, there might be a resemblance. But how could I help that? Thus, if questioned, I need only deny being Viviana. It would be simple to feign ignorance of the royal princess, her background, and such, to whom I might accidentally bear some resemblance."

The music within the room surged to a climax and suddenly ceased, and, a moment later, there could be heard an odd mixture of sounds, ranging from the raucous, ardent cries of men, accompanied by the rude pounding of fists on wood, to the light, restrained, perhaps reluctant, tapping of metal on metal or glass.

The guards then pressed open the two panels of the portal, revealing what lay within.

Gasps of delight, soft cries, scarcely suppressed exclamations of pleasure coursed amongst the slaves, save for one of their number, but even she, too, to whom the room was as new as to the others, was startled and impressed. Within that portal, beyond the opened doors, lay a large, rectangular room bright with color and light. Lamps were many, both mounted and suspended. The room was dominated by a long table, white with linen, laden with festive provender, resplendent in a service of crystal and gold. This table was set parallel to the long sides of the rectangular room. About the table were at least a hundred guests, women and men, most robed in finery appropriate for the occasion. There were many slaves in the room, some attending on the guests, others kneeling to the sides, unobtrusive, but ready, in a moment, summoned, to serve. Wary guards were in evidence, as well. The walls of the room and its high, domed ceiling were covered with murals depicting scenes from dozens of worlds, forests and jungles, rivers and lakes, deserts and mountains, varieties of plants and animals, scenes pastoral and urban, scenes of clearing land and building homes, scenes of ships under sail and scenes of soldiers on the march. The character and condition of the murals, and their nature, bespoke a room's long history, the waxing and wanings of fortunes, the shifts and interests, the victories and defeats, of a thousand years. The music had surged to a climax and suddenly ceased, following which the dancer, a slender dark-haired slave of medium height, in her bit of flaming silk, had sunk to the floor and knelt, her head down. As the new slaves, amongst whom was Viviana, were ushered into the room, the dancer, breathing heavily and sheened with sweat, leapt up and fled to the head of the table where she inserted herself beneath the table, at the robed knee of the individual who occupied that place of distinction.

"Noble guests," called the servitor, "amongst the many gifts, grants, emoluments, and tokens of the emperor's generosity, previously or later to be distributed, behold twelve exquisite properties, obtained from Varick's Market, well-known in Telnar for the quality of its merchandise."

Again there were cries of approval, and some appreciative strikings of fists on the table. Some goblets were lifted, saluting the figure at the head of the table. "Long live Ottonius, the First," called more than one fellow. In this case there was little, if any, lifting of utensils and tappings of metal on metal or metal on glass.

Viviana, shrinking down, concealing herself amongst the other slaves, was aware of the frowning scrutiny of the free women, some several, at the table.

"Are they rented?" asked a fellow. "Need they be returned?"

"He is drunk," laughed a fellow.

Many of the guests, Viviana knew not. But there was no mistaking the mighty figure at the head of the table, the Usurper, an Otung, Otto, from Tangara. She glimpsed, too, several she well knew, amongst them Iaachus, the Arbiter of Protocol and Julian, an officer, a scion of the proud Aureliani. She did recognize Clearchus Pyrides, senator from Inez IV. She did not see Timon Safarius Rhodius, of the Telnar Rhodii, *primarius* of the senate of Telnaria. She was startled to see Abrogastes, king of the Drisriaks, at the table. Too, he was seated at the emperor's side, to the emperor's left. What business had he here in Telnar? She knew him well from Tenguthaxichai. Behind his chair, lying down, were two large, terrible creatures, seen once as fierce and implacable, now as passive and docile, blinking, even somnolent, well recalled from Circumspection Street. She feared to be in the same room with them. Beside Abrogastes was another barbarian, one she did not know, presumably also a Drisriak. Some slaves she was familiar with but did not recall their names. All the slaves in the chamber, save Viviana and those with her, and the dancer, were modestly garmented, clad in light robes falling to their ankles, a concession, doubtless, to the free women present. To her surprise two Heruls sat high at the table, one, an older one, at the emperor's right hand. Two places near the head of the table were empty.

"The collars on their necks are palace collars," called Otto, the emperor, at the head of the table.

This clarification, needless as it was, was greeted with acclaim by several of the men at the table.

"For now," called the servitor, "we will put them to work. Consider them later, as they serve, regard them with care. Which might well please you, or which the most? Make choices. If more than one guest is interested in a given slave, you may later amuse yourselves by playing for her." The servitor then turned to the slaves. "Hasten now, be quick," he said, indicating a door to the side, to the right, "to the kitchen and pantries."

Viviana, her head down, amidst the others, hurried through the door indicated.

"Oh!" she breathed, startled, turning her head away. A slave had passed her, not even noticing her, carrying a tray, moving toward the dining area. She was older than the others, or, rather, seemed older, as there was white hair about her temples, and lovely white streaks in her sheen of otherwise black hair. Viviana recognized her as the slave who had been enamored of Ingeld, she who had so resented her on Tenguthaxichai, the slave who was owned by Abrogastes, she who had conspired with Urta to poison him and might have succeeded had it not been for Viviana's intervention, Huta, the once-priestess of the Timbri. Viviana's heart leaped. "She did not recognize me!" she said to herself. "Who, then, might do so?" In the kitchen, while she was standing in line, waiting to be commanded, Viviana noted, sitting with his back against the wall, his knees drawn up, a male figure, bound and gagged. As there was no collar on his neck, Viviana supposed him a prisoner of some sort, perhaps an apprehended thief. He was blond-haired, and blue-eyed, and might once have been quite handsome, though the left side of his face was now muchly scarred. His head was down. He was clad in the garment of a slave.

Shortly thereafter Viviana had been given a pitcher of *kana* and returned to the dining area. She waited, hovering about the table, happily not the only tender of *kana*. Commonly a guest would merely, wishing more, lift his cup, and it would be filled, to the extent desired, commonly from behind. In this way, the slave might be scarcely noticed. Viviana's fellow slaves, on the other hand, would have little of that. "Good," thought Viviana to herself, "let them smile, let them turn and twist, let the plates and vessels they bear melt in their hands, let them be slaves such as they might seduce the very figures painted on the wall, that they would tear themselves free from the wall and rush forth to embrace them. The better for me, as I shall not attract the attention of Masters. Let me be overlooked. I will be not as a slave, but as a free woman wrongly garbed, stiff, awkward, unfeminine, unneedful, proud, cool, superior, disinterested!" But then, with a sinking feeling, she realized that such a feigning, now so distasteful and false to herself, herself as she now knew herself to be, as nothing else, might draw attention to her, and even suggest a reminiscence of the vain, haughty, royally clad, bejeweled Viviana of her days of freedom. In this torment, she saw, to her terror, the eyes of the Otung, Otto, the Usurper, upon her. She stood still, absolutely. She thought of turning, and running to the portal, but it was closed, and flanked by guards. Without taking his eyes from her, the emperor motioned, with a lifted goblet, that she should approach him. "Has he recognized me?" she asked herself, trembling. She began to pour *kana* into the emperor's cup, and had hardly poured a drop when he said, "Enough." She made to turn away, but he said, "Stay. I may wish more."

Viviana remained where she was, trembling.

The two beasts behind the chair of Abrogastes began to stir. The nearest lifted its head, and its ears, and, almost inaudible, a low growl rumbled in its furred throat. The other animal then aroused itself, as well. Its tail lashed twice.

"My dear friend," said Otto, goblet in hand, leaning toward Abrogastes, "Otungs, and guards and police, have long sought in vain for a renegade Otung, once a King Namer on Tangara, one I would take into custody. He was recently a member of the now-disbanded temple guard. His name is Urta. He was in Telnar, but I fear he has now escaped the city."

Abrogastes looked carefully at Viviana, and she feared she might fall.

"Remain where you are, slave," said Otto.

"Yes, Master," said Viviana.

"What is your name?" asked Otto.

"Whatever Masters may please," said Viviana.

"What have you been called?" asked Otto.

"I have been called 'Yana'," said Viviana.

"You are pretty, Yana," said Otto.

"Thank you, Master," said Viviana. "May I leave now?"

"Tarry a moment," said Otto.

"Yes, Master," whispered Viviana.

Abrogastes turned from Viviana, musingly, as though puzzled, and then back to Otto.

"I know the Otung, Urta, of whom you speak," said Abrogastes. "He was involved in a plot to kill me, a plot in which he was joined by a slave. He did not escape the city."

"Your dogs seem to be interested in this slave," said Otto.

"I obtained these pets," said Abrogastes, "as you recall, in the fourth basement beneath the warehouse of Dardanis, a Telnarian merchant."

"I recall," said Otto. "You do not think Urta escaped the city?"

"I thought he might be in Telnar," said Abrogastes. "I had brought bedding on which he had slept in Tenguthaxichai to Telnar. From this I gave his scent to my pets. The rest was easy."

Both dogs were now crouching, eying Viviana. They growled softly, tails lashing.

"No," said Abrogastes. "No, no. Down."

The two beasts then subsided.

"A slave was with Urta when he was discovered, attacked, torn, and eaten," said Abrogastes.

"I was she," whispered Viviana.

"That explains the interest of the dogs," said Otto. "You were recognized."

"This slave reminds me," said Abrogastes, "of the Princess Viviana, who saved my life, of whom I was fond."

"Surely not," said Otto. "Look at her. This woman is every inch a slave. One might buy her sort in any market."

"True," said Abrogastes. "Yet there is a resemblance."

"You may withdraw," said Otto.

"Thank you, Master," said Viviana, and she withdrew, backing away from the emperor. "*Kana!*" called a fellow, and Viviana hurried to him. "I have been recognized," thought Viviana to herself, in misery. "The emperor, I am sure, knows me. I can tell. I saw it in his eyes. I do not think Abrogastes knows me. He may, but I do not know. They did not speak. Are they toying with me? Abrogastes was fond of a princess. Surely he sees in me only a lowly slave, one present when the Otung, Urta, fell to his dogs. How could she be Viviana, who supposedly perished on Tenguthaxichai? He believed that, that I died, but does he believe it now? I do not know. The emperor knows the child is not mine, I am sure. If it were truly mine would I not have been spared, to be its mother, to further Ingeld's ambitions? The emperor, I am sure, is aware of the child's origins, which would doubtless be far from Tenguthaxichai. He may even know some system, or city, or village, from whence it came. Now he knows I am not dead, as well. Am I now to be done away with? But perhaps he is not sure. Even so, would he risk my survival? But I am a slave! What more could he want! There is nothing to fear, in Telnarian law, from a slave. I might be simply marketed. Perhaps he knows me. Perhaps he does not know me. I am afraid."

Conversation continued about the table, amongst the guests. The music, now, as it had been since the finish of the dancer's performance, was subdued and unobtrusive, pleasant, refined, and scarcely noted.

"My dear Clearchus," said Iaachus, across the table, "we are delighted to find you present at our small collation. Your presence does us honor."

"It is I who am honored," said Clearchus Pyrides, senator from Inez IV. "Indeed, such an honor I did not think it wise to refuse."

"I wish to congratulate you," said Iaachus.

"On what?" asked Clearchus Pyrides.

"On your accession to the post of *primarius* of the senate of Telnaria," said Iaachus.

"Timon Safarius Rhodius, of the Telnar Rhodii, is *primarius* of the senate of Telnaria," said Clearchus.

"The noble Safarius," said Iaachus, "seems to have disappeared. It seems possible that his absence may prove permanent. Too, should he appear, he will be arrested for perpetrating a double murder in the house of the senate. As you can see, both considerations suggest the advisability of a replacement."

"A *primarius* can be elected only by a majority vote of the senate," said Clearchus Pyrides.

"Up to now," smiled Iaachus.

"I see," said Clearchus Pyrides.

"But the throne is sensitive to such matters," said Iaachus. "It would prefer to respect tradition, honor proprieties, and such. Thus, you will be elected by a majority vote, indeed, considering your worthiness and qualifications, by acclamation."

"Such would be unusual," said Clearchus Pyrides.

"So, too," said Iaachus, "would be the slaughter of senators,

the confiscations of their properties, and the abolition of the institution of the senate itself."

"I shall do my best," said Clearchus Pyrides.

"Enjoy your *kana*," said Iaachus.

"Two places at the table remain empty," said Tuvo Ausonius to
Titus Gelinus, attorney and rhetor.

"Those reserved for Aesilesius and Atalana, the empress
mother," said Titus Gelinus.

"It grows late," said Tuvo Ausonius.

"Presumably the empress mother does not wish to sit the table
of an Otung," said Titus Gelinus, "and, I suppose, she has pre-
vailed upon Aesilesius, for reasons of state, to remain apart, as
well."

"I do not think the emperor bears ill will to Aesilesius," said
Tuvo Ausonius.

"Nor Aesilesius to the emperor," said Titus Gelinus. "Indeed,
at the side of the emperor, Aesilesius has become a man."

"Or nearly," said Tuvo Ausonius.

"He is the son of Atalana," said Titus Gelinus.

"He is a son," said Tuvo Ausonius. "He is not yet a man."

"Slave," snapped a free woman, glaring at Viviana.

Viviana, with her vessel of *kana*, which had now been twice
refilled in the kitchen, hurried to the free woman.

She prepared to pour, but the free woman placed her hand
over the goblet.

"Mistress?" said Viviana, uneasily.

"Look about you," said the free woman. "See the other slaves.
Most are modestly tunicked."

"The emperor defers to your sensibilities, beautiful, noble
lady," said Viviana.

"But the tunics of twelve, as I count, including yours," said the
free woman, "are quite short."

"We are clothed, if clothed," said Viviana, "as Masters please."

"I think you rejoice, are pleased, and thrilled, to be so treated,
to have no choice in such matters," said the free woman.

Viviana was silent.

"Slave are brazen, appetitious, and meaningless," said the free
woman. "They are despicable, worthless beasts."

"Yes, Mistress," said Viviana.

"Have you "learned your collar"?" asked the free woman.

"It has been taught to me," said Viviana.

558 John Norman

"You are a Varick's-Market girl, are you not?" asked the free woman.

"I was purchased from Varick's Market," said Viviana.

"Purchased, like a clasp or sandal, a pig or dog," said the free woman.

"Yes, Mistress," said Viviana.

The free woman then stood up in her place, and faced the head of the table. Viviana, sensing she was dismissed, backed away and knelt, in the background.

"Your majesty," called the free woman.

The conversation grew silent about the table.

The musicians ceased playing.

"Lady," said Otto, respectfully, attending to her.

"Great lord," she said, "difficult times have been in the city, and the empire has been troubled. Following perils and tribulations, despair and doubt have at last been routed. Order is restored. Commerce recurs. *Civilitas* soars. We salute your success, we wish prosperity, security, glory, and duration to your regime. May it last a thousand years. Tonight we celebrate peace, contentment, and victory."

Otto inclined his head, and there was polite applause, the tapping of utensils on the table and dinnerware, and, here and there, vocal affirmations of support and agreement.

"We are all grateful for, and welcome, your hospitality and generosity," continued the free woman.

This addition to the free woman's discourse was received even more readily and appreciatively than its precursor.

"But, your majesty," said she, "it must be recognized that, however welcome and great your contributions to our welfare and safety may be, your antecedents and background are not identical to ours, and, in the light of this, I might wish to call to your attention certain traditions, understandings, customs, proprieties, and conventions of which you might be unaware and on which you might welcome enlightenment."

Men and women looked at one another, apprehensively.

"Please proceed," said Otto.

"Whereas slaves are useful and necessary," said the free woman, "and a desirable component of any civilized society, and particularly of any high civilization, such as Telnaria, like horses and dogs, yet slaves are slaves, and not free women."

"True," said Otto.

"Accordingly," said the free woman, "I protest, on my behalf, and on that of the free women present, the public display of several, I believe a dozen, half-naked collar girls. I, and doubtless others, find their presence offensive."

"Not me," said a male voice, from somewhere.

"Perhaps," said Julian, "because they suggest what you, or some of you, might be like beneath your robes."

"Look upon a slave, and see what a true woman is," said Vandar, an Otung.

"Do you wish you were so clothed?" asked a man, safely across the table from where the free woman stood.

"That you might be more attractive to men?" inquired another.

"There is more to being a slave than a garment, a mark, and a collar," said another.

"Why do you hate slaves, who are helpless and owned?" asked another.

"Because men find them more attractive," said another.

This remark, uncalled for as it was, brought forth cries of rage from several of the free women.

"Your majesty!" protested the free woman.

"Let us select a slave," said Otto, rising.

He looked about and, as he stood, could easily see the slaves in the room, both those standing, with their diverse paraphernalia of service, and, too, those kneeling, at the sides of the room, with their trays, vessels, plates, large and small, bowls, shallow and deep, decanters, pitchers, and such. His eyes rested on Viviana, and he smiled. "He knows me," she thought to herself, but could not move. "I am lost," she thought. But then the Otung's gaze roved elsewhere, and he regarded a brunette, she who had been fourth in the coffle, and she considered, at least by the men of Varick's Market, as the fairest on the chain. "Go to the dancing place," he said. She put down her tray, on the floor, and hastened to kneel in the square where the dark-haired dancer, in her bit of scarlet silk, had reminded men of how maddeningly desirable a human female could be, especially in a collar.

Viviana, now unnoticed, now relieved, now kneeling gratefully in place, felt a breath of air on her right shoulder. She looked to her right and noticed that the portal to the chamber had been opened. The guards were in place. She saw no reason for the portal to be opened. No one was entering, no one was leaving.

She then returned her attention to the brunette slave who was kneeling in the dancing square.

All eyes were upon her.

"Shall we garb her as a free woman?" asked Otto.

The brunette trembled, for she well knew the dire penalties which could be inflicted on a slave found in the garments of the free.

"Certainly not, your majesty," said the free woman. "Such would be unthinkable. She is a slave."

"To do so," said Otto, "would be an insult to free women?"

"A most grievous insult," said the free woman.

"Shall we free her?" asked Otto.

"Is that lawful?" asked the free woman.

"The matter has been disputed," said Titus Gelinus, attorney and rhetor, rising. "Worlds differ. There is no imperial judgment imposing a uniform view on the empire. Let us restrict ourselves then to Telnaria. On this world, Telnaria, the common judgment, upheld by several precedents, and disputed by some, is that a slave can be freed. Some people, to be sure, even judges, do not accept that. The matter seldom comes up as slaves are seldom freed. What is to be done with a freed slave, or, say, a freed horse or dog? To continue, obviously she cannot free herself, but not to allow her master to free her would seem to constitute a limitation or infringement on the power of the master, he who owns her. Such a limitation or infringement is commonly regarded as legally insupportable. Accordingly, a slave can be freed. Indeed, a master can, legally, as suggested earlier, free any animal, a horse, a pig, a dog, or any other animal, and the slave, of course, is an animal, and thus, by deduction, may be freed as well. To be sure, there seems little justification, or point, in freeing a dog, or horse, or such, and so, too, there seems little justification, or point, in freeing a slave. And, of course, it is often regarded as foolish, even reprehensible to do so."

"What, then, is the legal certitude?" asked Julian.

"That there is no legal certitude," said Titus Gelinus, "only a presumption and practice, namely, that a slave may be freed."

"As that is the preponderant opinion," said Otto, "we shall accept that, at least provisionally."

"The high court of Telnaria has never ruled decisively on the matter," said Titus Gelinus.

"So, then," said Otto, turning to the free woman, "shall we free the slave?"

"Certainly not," said the free woman. "She is in a collar. Look at her. She is obviously a slave."

"Noble lady," said Julian, "many free women have fallen to barbarians, even free women of Telnaria, sometimes of high place and lofty station, even of noble blood. Should they not, if recovered, be freed?"

"No," said the free woman. "They have been with masters, sported with, clasped in the arms of beasts. They are no longer fit to take their place amongst free women. Their presence in the garb of the free would be an insult to free women. We would not accept them. We would have nothing to do with them. We would despise them and hate them. They have been forever spoiled for freedom. Once a slave, always a slave. If recovered, let them have new masters, be given away, sold, or such. Let the empire not be shamed. Let them remain in their chains and collars, to be used, handled, caressed, and worked as the free may please."

"To clothe a slave as a free woman would be an insult to free women?" said Otto.

"Certainly," said the free woman. "Even one who was ever a slave. Once a slave, always a slave."

"One supposes then," said Otto, "that some difference in garmenture would be appropriate, to enable the free to be clearly and easily distinguished from the slave."

"Yes," said the free woman.

"And slaves are worthless and degraded animals," said Otto.

"Yes," said the free woman.

"Then," said Otto, "it seems that those slaves in the room who are more amply tunicked, those of whom you seemed to have more approved, are wrongly garbed, indeed, shamefully overdressed."

"Your majesty?" said the free woman, warily.

"As the slave is a meaningless and worthless animal, to be despised and degraded," said Otto, "it seems the difference in garmenture between the exalted free woman and the lowly slave should be as clear as possible. Accordingly, if the slave is granted clothing, which she need not be, as she is an animal, it seems her clothing should be as plain, simple, and scanty as possible, be the mere mockery of a garment, a rag or a brief, revealing tunic. Thus, of all the slaves in the room the twelve whom you called to our attention are those most appropriately garbed. Thus, you should most approve of those purchased from Varick's Market. Their garmenture should thus please you most."

"Yes, yes!" said several of the men.

"Your majesty!" protested the free woman.

"You think little of slaves," said Otto.

"Of course," said the free woman.

"Has it ever occurred to you that slaves, in their chains and collars, helpless, rightless, and vulnerable as they may be, so much at your mercy, might think little of you?"

"I do not understand," said the free woman.

"Although a slave has no say in such matters," said Otto, "yet we might, as a matter of interest, invite her opinion. Do you, slave, desire to be free?"

"No, Master," she said. "I have been at the feet of men. I love my collar, and would remain in it."

"Disgusting!" screamed the free woman. "Disgusting! Disgusting! Slave, slave!"

She then turned about with a swirl of robes, and withdrew from the chamber, followed by the other free women in the chamber.

At a gesture from Otto the brunette who had been kneeling in the dancing square and had so outraged the free woman leaped up, retrieved her tray, and sped about the table, to resume her serving. Several of the guests had already determined to play for her.

Otto looked to the portal.

"Welcome," he said.

In the portal stood Aesilesius, in a sparkling dinner robe, heeled by his property, small, exquisite, red-headed Nika, modestly tunicked.

"Did you hear?" asked Otto.

"Yes," said Aesilesius. "I delayed entry. I stood by the door."

"Aesilesius," whispered a man, awed.

"Is it Aesilesius?" asked another, quietly.

"It cannot be Aesilesius," said another.

"Dear friends," said Otto. "It is indeed Aesilesius, of Telnar. Those of you who did not recognize him in the great square, it was he. And those of you who were acquainted with him in the palace in the past, in audiences or presentations, rejoice to learn that he is recovered."

"I knew Aesilesius," said a man softly. "This tall, strong, clear-eyed young man cannot be he. This is an impostor. The true Aesilesius must have been done away with."

"Greetings, dear Ramos," said Aesilesius, "I also have keen hearing. Are you still as fond of olives and the game of five cups as always?"

"Forgive me," whispered the man.

"Where is the beloved empress mother?" asked Otto.

"She preferred to remain in her quarters," said Aesilesius.

"But it seems she did not persuade you to do so as well," said Otto.

"No," said Aesilesius.

"You are here despite her wishes?" asked Otto.

"Yes," said Aesilesius.

"Welcome," said Otto, indicating the two empty places at the table.

Aesilesius then took one of the two seats, that closest to the head of the table. Nika knelt beside his chair, a bit behind and to the left.

Food and drink was promptly brought to him. He fed Nika from his own plate. Viviana remained on her knees, back and to the side, remaining as inconspicuous as possible, until one of the governing servitors gestured impatiently that she should rise and continue serving. As she could, she remained away from Aesilesius. They had never been close and they scarcely knew one another. In the palace, given the hoax of Aesilesius and his general seclusion, they had scarcely seen one another. Normally she had seen him only at state functions, and had seen him then in his twisted pretense of imbecility, had contemptuously viewed him as an embarrassment to the throne. She suspected he would not recognize her, as she now was. Too, he would doubtless have been informed, as had been worlds, that she had perished in childbirth on Tenguthaxichai. At most, he might, as had Abrogastes, note some resemblance.

"Great lord," said Mujinn, rising, "Hunlaki has a request."

CHAPTER NINETY-ONE

"I, Mujinn," said Mujinn, "rider of the Heruls, of the camp of the Herd of Chuluun, of the Flats of Tung, herewith, formally, publicly, great lord, chieftain of the Wolfungs, king of the Otungen, Emperor of Telnaria, submit a request on behalf of Hunlaki, rider of the Heruls, of the camp of the Herd of Chuluun, of the Flats of Tung. His request may be easily satisfied. It costs the empire nothing. It means much to him."

"I know his request," said Otto. "I do not choose to satisfy it."

"Your majesty," said Iaachus, "we owe the Heruls much. Satisfy his request, if at all possible, whatever it may be."

"No," said Otto.

"Do so, if possible," said Julian, he of the Aureliani.

"You know nothing of Otungs and Heruls," said Otto.

"What is the request?" asked Titus Gelinus.

"Yes," said Rurik, Tenth Consul of Larial VII, of the Larial Farnichi, "what is the request?"

"It is to die in combat, at the hands of a worthy foe," said Mujinn.

"I am not his foe," said Otto.

"Otungs and Heruls are hereditary enemies," said Mujinn.

"Once, no more," said Otto.

Hunlaki then stood, and all eyes in that large, bright chamber, those of the free and those of the slave, regarded him.

"Great lord," said Hunlaki, "I once dipped the blade of my lance in the blood of your father, Genserix."

"So, doubtless, did many," said Otto.

"Thereby honoring our weapons," said Hunlaki.

"It was you, as I learned," said Otto, "who, long ago, lifted a newborn infant from the snow."

"The son of Genserix," said Hunlaki, "as known by the medallion and chain, cold, stained with the frost of afterbirth."

"A child delivered into the keeping of an Emanationist Brother,

Brother Benjamin, of the *festung* of Sim Giadini, in the heights of the Barrionuevo Range."

"Who became a great warrior and statesman, ascending to the throne of Telnaria."

"Surely, great lord," said Mujinn, "you cannot fear Hunlaki. He is old. His eye is no longer sharp. His muscles are no longer quick and supple, responding instantly to the subtlest glimpse of opportunity."

"I do not fear Hunlaki," said Otto. "I fear his request."

"The emperor," said Julian, "is swift, strong, and powerful, skilled with weapons, practiced in their employment. He has survived in the arena, in the forests, on the plains. It would be no duel, no small war. It would be a slaughter, a butchery."

"It is a slaughter, a butchery Hunlaki craves," said Mujinn.

"I do not choose to accede to his request," said Otto.

"Consider the matter more carefully," said Mujinn.

"I decline to do so," said Otto.

"Very well," said Mujinn. He then darted forth his hand, reaching under the table to where the lightly-clad dancer was kneeling and dragged her forth by the hair. She screamed and, in a moment, Mujinn was behind her, holding her, with a knife at her throat. Her eyes were wide with terror as she felt the thin blade, like a line of steel, at her throat. Guards stirred, springing forth, drawing weapons, but Otto motioned them back.

"Now," said Mujinn, "call for weapons!"

"Release her," said Hunlaki. "Sheath your blade. You are a guest. Do not behave in an unbecoming manner."

Angrily Mujinn thrust the dancer, Flora, from him, and sheathed the knife. She fled to the other side of the emperor's chair, and knelt there, wide-eyed, trembling.

"You are serious in this matter," said Otto to Hunlaki.

"I am Herul," said Hunlaki.

"Very well, then," said Otto. "Let weapons be brought. And let none interfere."

Two swords were brought, furnished by guards, one delivered to Otto, the other to Hunlaki.

"Weapons more familiar to Heruls," said Mujinn, "would be the lance and bow."

"These will do as well," said Otto, "for our purposes."

Otto then drew his chair away from the head of the table, and placed it on one side of the dancing square. He then sat upon the chair, the sword, ungrasped, across his knees. "I am ready," he said.

"No!" cried Julian.

"No!" cried Aesilesius, and others.

Guards would surge forward, but Otto warned them back. Flora ran to him and knelt beside him, but he pushed her to the side.

"I am ready," said Otto.

"Be on your feet," said Mujinn. "Hunlaki is old. He is not decrepit. You cannot defend yourself as you are. Grasp the sword. Hunlaki is old, but he is not slow. He is still a warrior and could slay many, a great many. Be ready! Lift the sword!"

"I am ready," said Otto.

Hunlaki came about the table and raised the sword, holding it over his head, grasping the handle in two hands.

"If you will have a death," said Otto, "let it be mine."

Hunlaki wavered, and then lowered the sword. He turned away, his body shaking. Keen sorrow, seldom affecting a Herul, manifests itself so.

"Do not turn the blade against yourself," said Otto, rising, and laying the sword across the table.

"It was a small enough thing to ask," said Hunlaki.

"Much greater than you understand," said Otto.

Hunlaki turned to face Otto.

"What shall I do now?" he asked. "How can I be? I could have died. Now I am dead without dying."

"You are not," said Otto. "You live."

"How can that be?" asked Hunlaki.

"You have much to do," said Otto. "I have need of you, old warrior, old friend. Even now Brother Benjamin, dear to me, friend to you, is on Tangara, assisting in the rebuilding of the *festung* of Sim Giadini. He puts his tiny body and his small strength to what stones he can, lifting them and placing them as he can, that the *festung* may rise once more. I fear he may die in this endeavor. Do not let him be unwise in his labors, and in his devotions and exercises. He has in his enthusiasms little sense in such things. He must be watched and cared for. Too, I want you to protect the *festung* and those brothers who come to join it. Protect them from predatory Heruls, of the camps of other herds, and renegade Otungs. It is to be a place of harmony, peace, and sanctuary."

"I have no understanding of, or affection for, the competitive, bickering faiths of Floon," said Hunlaki. "What have they to do with the sky, from which the rain falls, watering the grass, which grows and feeds the herds?"

"Do what you can," said Otto.

"Very well," said Hunlaki. "The small salamanderine is my friend."

"It is my intention," said Otto, "to see to it that he is first in the *festung*. I want him to be foremost amongst the brothers."

"That will not be," said Hunlaki.

"Who will thwart that aim, who will dare contest my will?" asked Otto.

"Brother Benjamin," said Hunlaki. "He is humble. He would be, had he his way, the least amongst the brothers."

"Return to your place, with Mujinn," said Otto. "If you must seek death, do so in another place, in another manner, at another time."

"I will seek life," said Hunlaki. "I have learned that from an Otung, though none need know that."

Otto returned his chair to its place, at the head of the table. He then said. "Converse, feast!" and took his seat. He signaled to the musicians and they began, once more, to play.

"I am glad to see you live," said Iaachus.

"I, too," said Otto.

CHAPTER NINETY-TWO

"Put her on the table!" cried men.

The comely brunette who had been knelt in the dancing square during the conversation of Otto and the free woman was hoisted bodily and cast on the table, where she stood, laughing, regaining her balance, steadying herself.

She had been fourth in the coffle, and so would be fourth in the playing.

Ramos of Telnar, sportsman and breeder of horses and slaves, had, a short time ago, at the invitation of Otto, an invitation doubtless prearranged, drawn from his pouch the five small silver cups which he commonly carried with him, much as one so inclined would not be likely to be without a favorite paraphernalia of gambling, tops and mats, figured placards, dice, marked stones, and such. He had cleared a place on the table before him, arranged the tiny cups, inverted them, and moved them about with practiced skill. "Behold," he had said, "I now place one small object, say, an olive, like this, or a pea, or a grape, or such, beneath one cup. You need then only identify the cup covering the object, to win."

"That is easy," had said Vandar. "One need only watch carefully."

"Beware, Vandar," called Otto.

Six times Vandar failed to detect the proper cup, it lost in the dazzling movements of Ramos' hands.

"You have removed the olive," said Vandar at last. "For such cheating many would use your head as a ball in the horse game."

"It is here," said Ramos, lifting a cup, revealing the olive.

This feat was applauded by the men who had risen from their places and crowded about the cups.

Vandar threw back his head and laughed.

"One is not well advised to do lance sport or cross swords with one whose skills far exceed one's own," said Otto.

"Let others now move the cups," had said Ramos.

"No, no, Ramos, Ramos," said the others.

"Very well," had said Ramos. "But if I choose to gamble, say, for a certain brunette, another must move the cups."

"Yes," said the others.

"Give her to him now," had said a guest.

It was late in the evening now. The feast was largely done. Only liqueurs, nuts, dried fruit, and sweets, remained on the table.

Many gifts had been distributed by servitors earlier. It had then been the time for the gamblings.

The musicians had withdrawn, each with a gold *darin*.

The modestly tunicked slaves stood largely aside, watching while the Varick's-Market girls were played for. Amongst these was Huta, once a priestess of the Timbri, slave of Abrogastes, and Delia and Virginia, both once of Telnar, one the former Lady Delia Cotina, of the Telnar Farnacii, and the other, the former Lady Virginia Serena, of the lesser Serenii, both now slaves of Ortog, son of Abrogastes. Pig was present, once the Lady Gia Alexia of Telnar, now the property of Titus Gelinus. Rurik's slave, Cornhair, the former Lady Publennia, of the Larial Calasalii, clung close to her Master. Iaachus' slave, lovely gray-eyed, brown-haired Elena, once a lady in waiting to Atalana, the empress mother, stood beside the chair of her Master, who was now attending the gambling. She hoped he would not acquire another slave, unless it were to market her. The emperor's three favorite slaves knelt about his chair, while he, sitting, watched the men at the silver cups. One was Flora, still in a bit of dancing silk, who had once been an officer of a court on Terennia, a "same world." She had once, in her days of freedom, been named 'Tribonius Auresius', a not uncommon sort of name for a woman on a "same world," it being masculine or gender-neutral. In a collar she had learned her womanhood. Another, Renata, had been met on the street of a Summer World, near a Summer Palace, one in which the royal family was then in residence. Otto, a barbarian chieftain, conducted by Julian, of the Aureliani, who recognized the need for new and strong blood in the empire, was to be introduced to the royal family, that a captaincy might be granted him. She, weakened, overcome, and stunned, helpless before a masculinity and power she had not realized could exist, after a night of hope and torment, had presented herself to the mighty barbarian whose glance had, in effect, collared her, and begged to be kept as a slave. Her request had been granted. The third slave was lithe Janina, a prize girl who had been acquired long ago, on the *Alaria*, a cruise ship.

Attention might be called, as well, to three other slaves, amongst
those modestly tunicked. We have already met Nika, a small,
exquisite red-head, who had been given to Aesilesius by Otto.
Another was Sesella, once Sesella Gardener, a stewardess in the
employ of a commercial spaceline, *Wings Between Worlds*. Tuvo
Ausonius, a former civil servant, once of the "same world" Miton,
was her Master. The last slave to whom we might draw attention
was owned by Julian, he of the Aureliani. She had been a Drisriak,
the daughter of Abrogastes, the Far Grasper, king of the Drisriaks.
She had joined her brother, Ortog, in his attempted secession from
the Drisriaks, to form his own tribe, to be called the Ortungen.
Captured, in lieu of execution, she had been given as a slave to
Julian who, at that time, clad in rags, was a lowly, muchly worked
prisoner of Otto, chieftain of the Wolfungs on Varna.

Ramos himself, as agreed, moved the cups, unless he himself
gambled, and they were then shifted about by a servitor, one who
only too obviously had been prepared for the task. The order in
which participants gambled was determined by numbered slips
drawn from a bowl, this in the keeping of another servitor. If
seven were to gamble for a given slave, and she was not won in
the first specific round, then a second specific round took place,
in the same order, and a third, and so on, until the girl was won.
Given the skill with which the cups were moved, victory was essentially a matter of fortune, each player having, given a specific
round, one chance in five of success.

Ramos himself failed to win the brunette, doubtless to his
chagrin, but the approval of the other players. She was won by
a high merchant, a slaver, who subsequently, naturally enough,
promptly put her up for bidding, a bidding in which Ramos, to
his satisfaction, proved successful. The merchant received twenty
gold *darins* for his property, which had cost him nothing. This
muchly pleased the slave who, by her glances and smiles, had left
little doubt but what she would not be loath to decorate the chains
of Ramos, the master of the silver cups. Ramos himself gambled
no more that night, nor did he continue to move the cups, but
respectfully took his leave of the emperor, and left the chamber,
leading his new slave on a leash. His duties were then assumed by
the servitor who had been his alternate in moving the cups. Most
of the slaves from Varick's Market were more than pleased to figure as prizes in such a gambling. Few slaves would be so fortunate
as to have a master of so high a station, and probably wealth, as to

have feasted at an emperor's table. The exception amongst them, expectedly, was Viviana.

Amidst the shouts of men, gamblers and onlookers, the slave who had been fifth in the coffle was lifted to the table.

She smiled, and posed, her hands behind the back of her head.

"How insolent, how brazen!" thought Viviana.

"At least the prizes were not put nude upon the table," thought Viviana. "This is a gambling, not a selling."

Viviana noted the movements of the girl on the table.

"There is something stressful about her, beneath those smiles," thought Viviana. "I think she is desperate for the touch of a Master."

Girls are often starved for caresses prior to a sale. Viviana's own belly was restless. By such things and a thousand others one is reminded that one is a slave.

Additional men who had not intended to gamble now hastened to the servitor with the bowl, to draw numbers.

The cups, now in the hands of the servitor, began again to spin and twirl, their motion a blur of silver on the table.

Viviana clutched the vessel of *kana* to her body, tightly.

How could she bear to be so displayed?

Why could the gambling not be discreet, or aside, only one of various entertainments?

The fifth girl was shortly won, as the second contestant guessed the cup which contained the olive.

The sixth girl was seized and lifted to the table.

Viviana, clutching the vessel of *kana*, moved as subtly and unobtrusively as possible toward the corridor that led to the kitchen and pantries. If questioned, could she not pretend the vessel needed refilling? She would linger in the corridor. In the kitchen or one of the pantries a servitor would be sure to note her. Surely she would not be missed, not for a time, hopefully a time long enough. Who was counting girls? Might they not move to the eighth girl, and so on, and eventually to the twelfth, and the gambling would be finished. Might she, overlooked and forgotten, not even be sold back to the Market of Varick?

Viviana, with her vessel of *kana*, now cowered in the short hallway leading to the kitchen and pantries. From where she was, she could see the gagged, bound figure of the male seen earlier, he sitting on the floor, his back against the wall, his knees drawn up, clad in the tunic of a slave. He, now that the evening was drawing to a close, seemed more apprehensive than before. In his eyes, there was dread and fear. He struggled in his bonds, futilely. He looked at Viviana, pleadingly, as though he would enlist her aid, if not to free him, at least to understand his plight.

Viviana turned away, in the short corridor, at the edge of the portal leading to the floor. Occasionally a slave passed her, coming from the floor to the kitchen or a pantry, or proceeding from one or the other back to the floor.

As the gambling proceeded, one after the other of the girls from Varick's Market were placed, standing, on the table. After the sixth girl, Viviana, in her weakness, clutching the *kana* vessel, struggled to stay on her feet, and not slip, terrified, to her knees. Then, to her relief, the eighth girl was put in place, standing on the table. Viviana, who had been seventh in the coffle, had not been seized, or conducted, to the platform of display. The eighth, ninth, tenth, eleventh, and twelfth girl were won, no one calling for, or seeking, Viviana, and then, as men called for more sport, the emperor, lavish in his role as host, contributed to the evening's entertainment by designating several of the modestly tunicked palace slaves to be played for. Two of those slaves had been displayed and played for, and won, when Viviana, to her uneasiness, sensed a figure near her, behind her.

"What are you doing here?" said a masculine voice, presumably that of a servitor.

"I hurry to the kitchen, to refill the vessel," said Viviana, turning about to move toward the kitchen.

But her way was blocked. It was indeed a servitor, but, happily, not he who had supervised the coffle after its delivery to the palace.

"It is a third full," said the servitor.

"I thought to freshen its contents," said Viviana.

If the servitor had just made his appearance, as was apparently the case, Viviana was sure he would not realize how long she had lingered in the corridor.

"See her!" said a feminine voice, from the floor. There was a group of palace slaves there, waiting to be taken to the table.

"See her tunic!" said another.

"One of the pigs from Varick's Market," said another.

"Five Masters were counting," said another. "There was dispute on the matter. Some thought twelve were won, some only eleven."

"Two were heard inquiring about a blonde, a Varick's girl seen serving," said another. "It was thought she had been won earlier and taken from the palace."

"That is she!" said another.

"She dallied, she hid, she will be well whipped," said another.

"Let her nose and ears be cut off," said another.

"What is going on here?" said another servitor, coming to the portal of the corridor.

"It is nothing," said the first servitor. "One of the kitchen masters kept this slave occupied in the kitchen, not realizing she was due on the floor."

"Then no harm is done," said the servitor near the waiting slaves.

The first servitor then took the vessel of *kana*. "Join the others," he said.

"Thank you, Master," said Viviana. "Thank you, Master."

Viviana then went to the modestly tunicked, waiting slaves, and would have concealed herself behind them, but they seized her and thrust her, struggling, resisting, to the head of the group. She was held there by the arms, tightly, each arm in the grasp of one of the modestly tunicked slaves. "Is your tunic not a bit short, slave?" asked the girl holding her right arm. "I think I will bite off your ear, dallying slave," said the girl holding her left arm. "Your hair will cover the place, and the blood."

"Mercy, Mistress!" begged Viviana.

Viviana, surrendered, helpless, looked about. This tiny fracas had attracted the attention of several of the men. This dismayed her. She saw Otto and Abrogastes, still at the table, observing her. Did they recognize her? Did they know who she was? She feared so, but was sure it could not be. How could they? Across the table, near Iaachus, not far from Julian, within feet of two Heruls, she saw herself also regarded by a large, good-looking, young fellow in a sparkling dinner robe, an officer perhaps, poised, at ease, and confident, until, suddenly, again, she realized that this stalwart stranger was her brother, Aesilesius, the deposed emperor, so different from the Aesilesius with whom she was familiar, a timid, misshapen, puling retardate. She shook her head, this rushing her hair down about her face, and lowered her head.

"Ho!" cried a man, triumphantly, for the manipulator of the cups, lifting a cup, had revealed an olive.

The modestly tunicked slave who had been won was drawn from the table and turned over to her new master, who pressed upon her parted lips a kiss such that a woman is left in no doubt but what she is a possession. Within moments he had bound her wrists behind her and fastened her neck in his leash, and then, shortly thereafter, after taking his leave of the emperor, he hurried her from the chamber.

"Next!" called the mover of the cups.

Viviana was thrust forward and a guard lifted her bodily from her feet, carrying her to the table.

"Please, no!" wept Viviana.

She was lowered to the table.

"Get on your feet," said the guard.

Viviana, terrified, stood on the table, unsteadily. She put her hands out, to stabilize her balance. Then she lowered them to her sides, and put her head down, turning away from Aesilesius.

"What is wrong with her?" asked a man.

"This, if I am not mistaken," said the manipulator of the cups, "is the last of the Varick's-Market girls. Who will draw from the bowl, for the order of playing?"

"Hold!" cried Aesilesius, rising.

Men regarded him.

"What is wrong?" asked Otto.

"I know this woman!" cried Aesilesius.

"How can that be?" asked a man.

Viviana swiftly knelt on the white table cloth, terrified, head down.

"Get on your feet!" cried Aesilesius to the slave. "How dare you kneel, as a slave?"

"I am a slave, Master," said Viviana, remaining, trembling, on her knees.

"Do you think I do not know my own sister?" cried Aesilesius, whipping off the shawl of his dinner robe. "Cover your body!" he said, spreading the shawl. "There are men here. Do you wish to be looked upon as though you might be no more than a simple, half-naked, neck-ringed beast?"

"Master is mistaken," said Viviana. "I am a slave."

"You are Viviana," he said, "my sister, daughter of Atalana, the empress mother of Telnaria, sister to Alacida, espoused to the Drisriak, Hrothgar, son of Abrogastes."

"Forgive me, Master," said Viviana. "Master is mistaken."

"Do not think to sport with me," said Aesilesius. "Do not confuse me with the pathetic thing you despised in the palace. Even in the midst of my protracted imposture, I was aware, keen-eyed, and perceptive. "You are Viviana of Telnar, my sister."

"No, Master," said Viviana.

"Do you think I was unaware of your airs, your vaunted superiority, your vanity, your contempt for me?"

"I do not know what Master is talking about," said Viviana.

"This cannot be she," said a man.

"Viviana died in childbirth on Tenguthaxichai," said another.

"Describe for me," said Aesilesius to Viviana, "the location and appointments of the chamber of the Princess Viviana in the palace."

"I cannot do so, Master," said Viviana. "This is the first time that I have been in the palace."

"You lie!" said Aesilesius.

"Your claim is scarcely to be believed," said Iaachus. "Are you sure?"

"It is she," said Aesilesius.

"Perhaps you are mistaken," said Julian.

"How could that be?" asked Aesilesius. He turned to Nika. "Is she not Viviana, Princess of Telnaria?" he asked.

"I do not know, Master," said Nika, plaintively. "I did not know your sister well."

"Perhaps you are misled by a resemblance," said Titus Gelinus.

"The resemblance is indeed remarkable," said Iaachus.

"You once, craven courtier, pretentious knave, despite your lowly origins, presuming on your influence in the palace, dared to aspire to her hand," said Aesilesius. "It nearly cost you your position, and your head."

"Fortunately I retain both," said Iaachus. "In sober moments I share your outrage at so preposterous an ambition."

"What do they call you, slave?" asked Julian.

"Whatever Masters please," said Viviana. "I am commonly called 'Yana'."

"'Yana' will do nicely," said Julian. "This young man in the dinner robe, holding the shawl, rather pointlessly in my view, is Aesilesius. He is a resident of the palace, a member, I trust, of the party of the emperor. He seems to think you are his sister."

Viviana remained silent.

"His sister died on Tenguthaxichai," said a man.

"Perhaps not," said Aesilesius.

"Speak, slave," said Julian.

"Master?" asked Viviana.

"Tell us of yourself."

"I am Yana," said Viviana. "I am of lowly origins, of the *humiliori*, the daughter of a bootmaker on Safa Major. There was a town war. I was captured and delivered to a victory camp. From this camp I was sold to an itinerant slaver. I was later taken to Inez II, where I was sold in the merchant city of Carleton. I have worn various collars on three, no, now four, worlds."

"Your majesty!" said Aesilesius.

"It seems she is not Viviana," said Otto.

"He knows me," thought Viviana to herself. "I am sure of it."

"Great Abrogastes, king of the Drisriaks," called Aesilesius, "you knew my sister, Viviana, on Tenguthaxichai. Is this woman not she?"

"It does not appear so," said Abrogastes. "I acknowledge a resemblance."

"He knows me, too," thought Viviana. "I am sure of it. How kind they are not to expose me, not to let me shame and endanger the house of Aesilesius and the empire, to allow me to be the slave I now know myself to be. But do they know me? Now, again, I am not sure."

"Can I be mistaken?" asked Aesilesius.

"Blue-eyed and blonde-haired slaves are less common than dark-haired, dark-eyed slaves," said Iaachus, "but they are all alike, blue-eyed and blonde-haired, and thus might be more likely to be confused with one another than slaves with more familiar eye and hair colors, where we are accustomed to the necessity of making subtler discriminations."

"She is Viviana," said Aesilesius.

"No, Master," said Viviana.

"I met Viviana," said Rurik, Tenth Consul of Larial VII, of the Larial Farnichi. "She was, in my assessment, forgive me, young friend, very different from this woman, who is obviously a slave, indeed, a natural slave. Viviana, as I recall her, was cold, stiff, awkward, selfish, short-tempered, vain, loftily spoken, contemptuous of inferiors, and concerned with little but her greed, pleasures, gowns, and jewels. This woman, on the other hand, is soft, feminine, graceful, and, doubtless, not only slave beautiful, but, I suspect, slave responsive."

"'Slave responsive'!" said Aesilesius. "She would not dare be so."

"She may, and must," said Rurik. "Do you not note the collar locked closely about her lovely neck."

"It is true," said Aesilesius. "This woman is very different."

"Let her be gambled for," said a man.

Aesilesius stepped back and looked about the table, and to Otto and Abrogastes, and then replaced the shawl about his shoulders, and resumed his seat. "Yes," he said. "She is very different. She cannot be Viviana. Let her be gambled for."

Several of the men expressed approval, uttering sounds of satisfaction. Two struck the table with their fists.

"Do you wish to draw a slip from the bowl, to join in the gambling?" asked the manipulator of the silver cups.

"No," said Aesilesius.

"On your feet, slave," said the manipulator of the silver cups. "Put your hands behind your head. Turn slowly."

"Ah," said more than one man.

Several of those present then hurried to join the line at the bowl, to draw forth, each in turn, slips, these marked with the numbers which would determine the order of the gambling.

Viviana, tears in her eyes, then stood still, lithe and slender, her head up, and her arms at her sides.

"It is they who are betting," thought Viviana to herself, "but it is I who have lost, and I who have won."

The manipulator of the silver cups reached to the cups.

At that moment there was clearly a disturbance of sorts in the great hall, cries of fear, anger, awe, and outrage, stirrings of guests coming to their feet, a cessation of music, a sudden absence of the sounds of dinnerware, an abeyance of the murmur of discourse and laughter, a woman's scream, all this detectible through the still-opened doors of the emperor's dining chamber, through which Aesilesius and Nika had entered, and through which the free women and other guests had taken their leave.

A tall figure stood framed in the portal.

Otto, Abrogastes, and Ortog rose to their feet.

Angrily, the tall figure in the portal shook himself loose from the two guards who held him.

"He is unarmed, your majesty!" called one of the guards.

"Let him approach," said Otto.

The tall figure strode forward and then stopped, and stood still, his large arms folded across his chest.

On the table a slave lay prone, unconscious.

"We are honored by the presence of a prince of the Drisriaks," said Otto.

"Ingeld," said Iaachus.

CHAPTER NINETY-THREE

"Torture!" cried a man.

"Ropes, irons!" cried others.

"Let the execution be public, and lengthy!" cried another.

Otto held up his arms for silence.

Ingeld regarded those who had cried out. In his eyes was contempt.

"We have sought you," said Otto.

"He came alone, unarmed, to the steps of the palace, ascended them slowly, came to the great portal and made himself known, and demanded to be brought into the presence of the emperor," said a guard.

"We determined he was unarmed, and then complied with his wish," said another guard.

"Even so," said another, "few would come near him, though he bore no arms. Conducted, he made his way through the tables. Men drew back. None approached him. We lay hands on him only at the entryway to the dining area, where he made it clear, disdaining our clasp, he did not care to be touched."

"You have surrendered," said Iaachus.

"I am your prisoner," said Ingeld. "I have not surrendered."

"He could not escape the city," said Iaachus.

"I could have slipped away, a hundred times," said Ingeld.

"How is it that you have come here?" asked Julian.

"My cause is lost, my war is done, my banner is furled, my sword is put aside," said Ingeld. "I will not hide, as might a *filch*."

"Bring chains," said Otto.

"We acknowledged the wisdom of your flight," said Ingeld. "We searched for days, only to discover you were at our elbow, so close as the house of the senate. It was clever of you to conceal yourselves almost within our grasp, where you would never be suspected. We did not understand, however, your surrender in the house of the senate. How odd that seemed for an Otung, not to die armed and fighting, but to surrender, to gain some days of shameful life, before the humiliation of a public execution. That seemed cowardice, a forfeiture of honor, a braving of the contempt of enemies. We did not realize until the day of the square the meaning of your ruse, the waiting, the winning of time. And who would have anticipated a conjoint action of Otungs and Heruls, blood enemies for centuries? We did not understand, until too late, the nature of the wager, even that there was a wager. You gambled; you won."

In the presence of the guests, and slaves, Ingeld was shackled, hand and foot.

"It is pleasant to have one's enemies thus," said Rurik, Tenth Consul of Larial VII, of the Larial Farnichi.

"Conduct him to the side," said Otto, "to the place where a slave danced, near where I put my chair, when considering the request of a Herul."

Ingeld then stood in the dancing square, the place specified.

"Let a military court be convened," said Iaachus.

Otto, Abrogastes, and Ortog resumed their seats.

"The supreme judge in the empire is the emperor," said Titus Gelinus.

"Let it be burning irons, the flaming slivers, the thin needles!" said a man.

"The flesh saws," said another. "The gouges, the thousand hooks, the scrapers!"

"Remove the skin, a ribbon at a time," said another.

"Dangle him in a vat of tiny fang fish," suggested another. These small fish were almost transparent until they fed.

"Stake him out, for *filchen*," suggested yet another.

"Run him for dogs," said another.

"No! No!" screamed a woman's voice.

"A slave!" said a fellow, startled.

A distraught figure, slender, collared, blue-eyed and blonde-haired, in the brief, white, silken, degrading tunic of one of the girls from Varick's Market, raced from the side of the table from which she had descended when she had recovered consciousness, and threw herself on her knees between Ingeld and the head of the table. "Be merciful, great Master, kind Master," she cried. "Spare him! Be merciful! I beg it! Mercy! Mercy!"

"Who dares to interfere?" said a man.

"A slave," said another.

"A beast, dabbling in the affairs of the free?" said a man.

"Strip her, rope her, and whip her," said a man.

"Please, Master, be merciful!" said the slave.

"Take her to the kitchen and beat her," said a man. "Let her remember that she is a slave."

Ingeld looked away from the slave, angrily.

"This prisoner," said Otto, rising, "betrayed, and would have had slain, his father, a king, and his brother, a prince. He is cunning and unscrupulous. He would have assumed the high seat of the Drisriaks, first tribe amongst the Alemanni, and by means of conspiracy, subversion, and revolution seized the throne of Telnaria. Whom would he spare, what could restrain his greed, what could excuse or mitigate his treachery, what could limit his ambition?"

"Show him mercy!" begged the slave.

"Who begs on his behalf?" asked Otto.

"A poor, miserable slave," wept Viviana, "but one who was once Viviana of Telnar, sister of Aesilesius, of royal blood!"

"Viviana!" cried Aesilesius, rising from his place at the table, tearing off his dinner shawl, and rushing to the side of the slave, over whom he cast the shawl.

"She is a slave," said Otto, sternly. "Do not cover her."

"Your majesty!" protested Aesilesius.

"Remove the shawl," said Otto.

Aesilesius drew away the shawl and looked away from the slave.

"The slave is not Viviana," said Ingeld. "I know the princess. This slave is not she. This is a lying slave. Take her away, and beat her."

"No, Ingeld!" she wept. "Do not deny me!"

Ingeld turned to her, fiercely, and looked down upon her.

"Forgive me, Master!" she cried, frightened.

"I am shackled," said Ingeld, angrily. "Punish this insolent, presumptuous slave, who dared address a free man by his name."

A guard, at a nod from Otto, seized Viviana by the hair, she on her knees, and turned her to face him.

"Six strokes," said Ingeld.

"No!" cried Aesilesius.

"Do not interfere," said Otto. "Surely you can see there is a collar on her neck, and a palace collar. She is thus not only a slave, but a property of the state."

"Six strokes," said Ingeld.

The guard then struck Viviana six time across the face and mouth, first with the palm of his hand, and then with the back of his hand. Her cheeks burned and there was blood at her lip.

"Thank him, and suitably, for instructing you," said Otto. "And be grateful you were not whipped, as you should have been."

Viviana put her lips to the guard's feet, kissing them.

"No!" cried Aesilesius.

"Thank you for instructing me, Master," said Viviana to the guard.

"No!" said Aesilesius.

"Do not interfere with the discipline of a slave," said Otto.

Viviana then crawled to Ingeld, licking and kissing his feet.

"Stop!" said Aesilesius.

"Do you truly not know me, Master?" she wept.

"Who is this importunate, meddlesome slave?" Ingeld snarled.

Viviana's blonde hair lay about Ingeld's boots.

"Take her away," said Ingeld.

The guard drew Viviana back from Ingeld. She lay on her belly, sobbing, a yard from where he stood, on the dancing floor.

"Get up, be on your feet!" said Aesilesius.

"I dare not," said Viviana. "I am in the presence of free men. Forgive me, Master."

"Do not call me 'Master'," said Aesilesius.

"I must, Master," she said, her face streaked with tears.

"She is not a slave!" said Aesilesius, turning to Otto.

"You are mistaken, my friend," said Otto. "She is a slave, clearly, a palace slave, a property of the state."

"No!" cried Aesilesius.

"You see the tunic, the collar," said Otto. "Do you wish me to command her to reveal her thigh to you, that you may see the mark, burned there, the slave rose?"

"No!" said Aesilesius.

Abrogastes then rose to his feet. "The prisoner," he said, "is a Drisriak. I am king of the Drisriaks."

Ingeld stiffened.

"The prisoner is a prisoner of the Telnarian state," said Otto.

"While we are dealing with recreants, culprits, and traitors," said Abrogastes, "I might request consideration, a favor."

"He, the other, will be shackled and brought forth," said Otto.

"Two defendants may figure in the same action," said Titus Gelinus, "though the charges differ. This is supported by ample precedent."

"Your majesty," said Aesilesius.

Otto turned toward Aesilesius.

"If she is truly a slave," said Aesilesius, indicating prone Viviana, "give her to me!"

"No," said Otto.

"Then let me buy her," said Aesilesius, "to free her, instantly, and restore her to her dignities, honors, and privileges."

"Despite her shame?" asked Otto.

"Even so," said Aesilesius.

"You would forge weapons for dissidents, waiting to seize them?" asked Iaachus. "You would risk outrage, retaliation, revolution, divisions of populations, the loss of the empire?"

"We could seclude her in the palace," said Aesilesius. "Let her not venture beyond its gates. Let her be confined to her quarters. None need know of her shame. She may live with it, alone. Nothing need proceed beyond troublesome, unverified rumors. Let this be kept a private affair."

A wordless utterance of distress and protest escaped Viviana, prone on the smoothed, polished boards of the dancing square.

"Sell her to me," demanded Aesilesius, "that I may free her, that her shame be wiped away."

"Such shame can never be wiped away," said Iaachus.

"That it be concealed then!" said Aesilesius.

"Such an approach might prove feasible," said Iaachus.

"Sell her to me," insisted Aesilesius.

"She is a slave," said Otto. "She remains in her collar."

"Am I not your ally, your friend?" asked Aesilesius.

"I trust so," said Otto.

"Then!" said Aesilesius.

"She remains in her collar," said Otto.

Shortly thereafter there was a cry of misery, presumably from the kitchen or one of the pantries off the corridor leading to the dining area.

"Corelius is being fitted with shackles," said Otto.

"I have come here voluntarily," said Ingeld. "I am owed something for that. Let me then die as I wish, armed, at the hands of a professional killer, at the hands of the scourge of a hundred arenas on a dozen worlds, at the hands of the Wolf of Tangara, at the

hands of the Lion of Varna, not at the hands of a Telnarian hang-
man or headsman, but at the hands of one like myself, of the forest, a hereditary enemy, a traditional foe, an Otung, even though,
hair short and clad in robes, he sits upon a throne."

"You have not earned a quick death," said a man.

"Let the emperor not stain a blade with dishonorable blood,"
said another.

"I am willing," said Ingeld, "to do battle with any champion,
or champions, of your choice, even though I be weighted and ill-
armed."

"He craves a merciful execution," said a man.

"Whatever else I might be," said Ingeld, "I am a prince, a
prince of the Drisriaks."

Corelius, pale, trembling, shackled, was conducted forth, to
stand beside Ingeld.

"Put that one, the lowly one, on his knees," said Otto.

Corelius was thrust down to his knees.

"We have two prisoners before us, one standing, one kneeling," said Otto. "Their crimes are well known, their guilt transparent."

"Mercy!" begged Corelius.

"I ask for no mercy," said Ingeld, "nor do I expect any."

"You will receive none!" cried a fellow at the table.

Viviana moaned.

"Great Abrogastes," said Otto, "had you been granted custody
of this prisoner, Ingeld, prince of the Drisriaks, this prisoner of
the Telnarian state, how might he be dealt with, given the justice
of the Drisriaks?"

"I have something in mind," said Abrogastes.

A burst of anguish escaped Viviana.

Ingeld had not flinched.

"To act against one's own father and brother," said Otto, "is to
betray one's own blood. That seems more heinous than those who
might, for gold, betray states or strangers."

"Yes, yes!" said Corelius. "My faults, if any, do not compare.
They are few, and surely less! I beg mercy!"

"Yet," said Abrogastes, "Ingeld was consistent, in seeking
his own advancement and power, brilliantly and with cunning,
no matter the cost. I see him as a son of mine, as I see Ortog, as
well, sons capable of mighty things and towering ambitions. This
kneeling wretch, Corelius, fittingly in the tunic of a slave, in his

diverse treacheries, sought not kingdoms and an empire but only gold, like a cheating peddler or dishonest merchant, his crimes not mitigated by the lure of vast temptation, not redeemed by breadth or vision."

"Thus his crimes are less excusable," said Otto.

"No!" cried Corelius.

"And his punishment should be more dire," said Otto.

"No, no!" cried Corelius.

"Give him to me," said Abrogastes.

"I may," said Otto.

Corelius shrieked with fear.

"It is interesting, Otung, how you speak of justice," said Ingeld, "you who deposed a child, subverted a senate, and seized a throne."

"A difference exists between us," said Otto. "I was successful."

"Yes," said Ingeld.

"No," said Iaachus. "There was no choice. It was necessary, to save the empire."

"There was an infant," said Ingeld, "proposed as the child of the Princess Viviana, the child to be emperor, I, its putative father, to rule as regent until his majority. What became of it? Was it cast into a *carnarium*?"

"We found it," said Otto. "It was healthy. It was sent away, to be safe and cared for, to be free of the tumults and dangers of politics. It need never fear the assassin's knife. It will never know what might have been. No records were kept."

"Proceed," said Ingeld. "We must, perforce, abide your decision."

"No!" cried Corelius. "Mercy!"

"Your majesty," wept Viviana, raising a hand to Otto, "your prisoner, Lord Ingeld, prince of the Drisriaks, might have killed me, to protect his designs, to eliminate the threat of exposure, which would have brought his plans to naught, but he let me live, though disposing of me to the markets. Was this not gentle of him, kind of him, merciful of him?"

"Surely it was a most grievous diplomatic indiscretion," said Iaachus.

"I beg mercy for him!" wept Viviana.

"Who is this slave?" said Ingeld.

"She was Viviana, sister of Aesilesius, of royal blood, of the house of Aesilesius," said Otto.

Viviana, prone, cast Otto a look of wild gratitude.

"She was your spouse, according to the vacant, false rites of the exarch of Telnar," said Abrogastes.

"Thank you, Master!" cried Viviana.

"Not truly espoused," said Ortog. "No horses were given."

"As a matter of law," said Titus Gelinus, "all is altered, superseded and abolished, with the affixing of the collar. The state of marriage obviously cannot exist between free and slave, no more than between a free person and a horse, pig, or dog."

"I know her not," said Ingeld.

"Master!" protested Viviana.

"Why do you deny, prince of the Drisriaks," asked Otto, "that this slave who lies before us was once Viviana of Telnar, sister of Aesilesius?"

"Do you deny it, that she be not shamed?" asked Aesilesius.

"Of what import would that be, for one such as Ingeld, the Drisriak?" asked Rurik. "Would he not rather gloat in her shame, his foot upon her belly?"

"He cares for me," said Viviana. "He did not have me killed."

"Who would care for a slave?" said Ingeld. "They are meaningless pleasure objects."

"I would be such to you, Master," wept Viviana.

"Be silent!" shouted Aesilesius.

"He pretends not to know me," said Viviana, "for my sake and safety, that our paths not cross, that our fates be independent, that we in the eyes of worlds be dissociated in all respects, that his faults and stains, as they may be, not mark me."

"Who will take this stupid slave away?" said Ingeld.

"He fears for me, that I would be endangered at his feet," wept Viviana.

Ingeld turned away from the slave.

Viviana rose to her knees, tears in her eyes. She reached toward Ingeld, but dared not touch him.

"Come away, Viviana," said Aesilesius. "Stand up, cover yourself with this shawl. There are men here. You are tunicked. They might look upon you."

"The free may look upon the slave," said Viviana. "Her beauty, if beauty it be, is to be patent, clear, and obvious to all."

"Like that of a dog?" asked Aesilesius.

"Yes, Master," said Viviana.

"Come away," said Aesilesius.

"Am I to be ashamed of my body?" she asked.

"I shall petition the emperor for your freedom," said Aesilesius.

"Your petition would be denied," said Otto.

"And rightly so," said Abrogastes.

"Your majesties?" said Aesilesius.

"The Princess Viviana," said Abrogastes, the Far-Grasper, king of the Drisriaks, "saved my life, at great risk to her own, on Tenguthaxichai, preventing me from imbibing poison, which would have been administered by the slave who now crouches behind my chair."

"I was coerced, Master!" cried Huta. "I am guiltless!"

"Tonight," said he, "lying slave who misled Ortog, my first son, encouraging him by signs and craft to secede from the Drisriaks—"

"The seed, if poisoned, fell on receptive, fertile ground, father," said Ortog.

"And would have slain me," said Abrogastes, "will be stripped and whipped this night, and serve me in a thousand ways!"

"Mercy, Master," wept Huta.

"What is there about having your sleek, well-curved hide about my ankles, your lying lips upon my feet, that so pleases me?" said Abrogastes.

"Master!" cried Huta.

"You will have no doubt, worthless, treacherous she-*filch*, who is your Master," said Abrogastes.

"I know who is my Master. I know who is my master, Master!" cried Huta, sinking to her belly on the floor behind her Master's chair, and touching its foot, carved in the semblance of the paw of a forest lion, with one trembling hand. "He is Abrogastes, king of the Drisriaks, whose frown I fear, for whose merest touch, enflaming me with a slave's need, I have learned to beg."

"If, great king of the Drisriaks," said Aesilesius, "she who was my sister saved your life, surely you must urge the emperor to grant her freedom."

"How naive you are, boy," said Abrogastes.

"I do not understand," said Aesilesius.

"She is a slave," said Otto.

"Free her!" cried Aesilesius to Otto.

"The collar remains on her neck," said Otto.

"No, no!" said Aesilesius.

"Guard," said Otto, indicating Viviana, "bring chains for this slave."

"Do not!" said Aesilesius.

"Let him look upon her, and see her as the slave she is," said Otto.

"Free her!" cried Aesilesius.

Chains were brought, suitable for a woman, light, attractive, supple, gleaming, and closely linked.

"Do not chain her!" said Aesilesius.

"These are display chains," said Otto. "But they are superbly effective as custodial devices. Slaves are quite helpless in them."

Viviana was snapped into the restraints.

"See how lovely she is," said Otto. "What do you think she should bring on the sales block?"

"Free her!" said Aesilesius.

And then Viviana knelt, head down, her wrists chained before her, separated by some six inches of chain, her ankles chained behind her, as she knelt, separated by some ten to twelve inches of chain.

"She is beautiful," said a man.

"What a beautiful slave," said another.

"You shame her!" said Aesilesius.

"She is not shamed," said Otto. "She is a slave. Nor are you shamed, though you may think yourself shamed."

"And needlessly, foolishly, and pointlessly so," said Iaachus.

"See her," said Otto. "Look upon her. Is she not an attractive slave?"

Aesilesius turned away, in rage and tears, and hurried toward the far portal, that leading to the great hall.

"Close the doors!" called Otto.

At the portal, Aesilesius found it closed, and blocked by guards. Angrily he returned to his place at the table.

Viviana, distraught, her cheeks stained with tears, lifted her chained wrists and pressed her lips to the metal, the bracelets and chain, and then knelt as she had, head down, in place.

"Your majesty," said Aesilesius.

"Noble Aesilesius," said Otto.

"The doors have been shut against me," said Aesilesius.

"They will be opened," said Otto.

"Let sentences be passed," called a man.

"Wine has flowed, lamps burn low," said Otto.

"Public deaths to the prisoners," said another at the table.

"Deaths of lengthy, excruciating pain," said another.

"The day is gone, the night is muchly passed," said Otto.

"We can set upon them with knives, now," said a man.

"No!" cried Corelius.

"Do as you please," said Ingeld.

Viviana looked up, wildly, tears in her eyes.

"A slave may speak," said Otto.

"A slave begs mercy for Master Ingeld!" wept Viviana.

"Take this slave away," said Ingeld, angrily.

Otto turned to the guests.

"Friends," said he, "pray attend me."

All attention turned to the head of the table.

"There is a time for victory, for feasting, for holiday, for festival," said Otto. "Let there be another time, a quiet time, a patient time, for deliberation and judgment."

"It seems," said Iaachus, "the horses of state are weary."

"It is hours since one once of the Larial Calasalii, nicely curved and now well collared, was enjoyed by one of the Larial Farnichi," said Rurik, glancing at his slave, Cornhair.

This remark was met with approval by several at the table whose slaves were in attendance.

"Noble Gelinus," said Otto. "I conjecture an adjournment would be acceptable, even welcome."

"At the will of the emperor," said Titus Gelinus.

"Be it so," said Otto.

"It is so," said Titus Gelinus.

"Three days from now," said Otto, "in the morning audience, in the throne room, before scribes, judges, and high men, we will meet again."

"Until then," said Iaachus.

"Until then," said Otto.

CHAPTER NINETY-FOUR

"Allies have departed," said Iaachus, "Otungs and Heruls, sharing ships but not quarters."

"The empire owes them much," said Otto.

"Sufficient Otungs remain," said Julian, "supplementing others, to police the streets and guard the palace."

"Private troops from Larial VII, sworn to me," said Rurik, "are enclaved less than a march away."

"The senate will convene within the month," said Clearchus Pyrides, senator from Inez IV, *primarius* of the senate, "given the pleasure of the emperor."

"It will conduct unexpected business," said Otto.

"Your majesty?" said Clearchus Pyrides.

"But first," said Otto, "it will be disbanded and abolished, following which it will be reinstituted, at the command of the emperor."

"Is that not pointless?" asked Clearchus Pyrides.

"Not at all," said Titus Gelinus. "That establishes, and clearly, the priority and preeminence of the throne, and the dependence of the senate on the palace."

"I see," said Clearchus Pyrides.

"Otto, emperor of Telnaria, king of the Otungs, chieftain of the Wolfungs," said Ortog, first son of Abrogastes, the Far-Grasper.

"Speak, prince of the Drisriaks, king of the Ortungen," said Otto.

"I speak on behalf of Hrothgar, my brother on Tenguthaxichai," said Ortog. "His mighty heart has been won by the Princess Alacida of Telnaria, who even now bears his child."

"I have heard so," said Otto.

"He wishes to wed her," said Ortog.

"It is my understanding," said Otto, "that he and the princess are already espoused, having been wed long ago in Telnar."

"Hrothgar is uneasy," said Ortog. "He cares much for the princess. It is important to him, therefore, that he be properly married to her."

"Continue," said Otto.

"Therefore," said Ortog, "Hrothgar offers to Aesilesius, her brother, one hundred horses for the hand of his sister, Alacida."

"One hundred horses," said Otto, "does not seem much for a princess."

"It must be remembered," said Ortog, "she is only a Telnarian."

"That is true," said Otto. He then turned to Aesilesius, who was within feet of the throne.

"Do you accept this offer?" he asked Aesilesius.

"What would I do with a hundred horses?" said Aesilesius.

"Give them to the imperial stables," said Otto.

"Is Alacida happy?" asked Aesilesius.

"Very much so," said Ortog.

"Is it her wish that I accept this offer?" asked Aesilesius.

"Most earnestly," said Abrogastes, stepping forward, "she entreats you to do so."

"Then," said Aesilesius, "though this business seems pointless to me, given the facts of the matter, I accept the offer, and I wish health, happiness, and prosperity to them and theirs."

"He adds ten horses, in gratitude, and for good will," said Ortog.

"Thank him," said Aesilesius.

"The matter is done?" said Otto.

"Done," said Ortog.

"How high would Hrothgar have bid?" asked Otto.

"As many as was necessary," said Ortog.

"A thousand horses?" said Otto.

"Easily," said Ortog.

"What if no offer was accepted?" said Otto.

"Then he would have kept the princess, under the aegis of different customs, as a prize of capture," said Ortog.

"Aesilesius is young," said Otto. "He is untutored in the games of negotiation."

"I am content," said Aesilesius.

"Men wait outside," said Iaachus. "The hour of the general audience is now upon us. Let us now open the doors to the throne room."

"Open them," said Otto.

∎ ∎ ∎

"Bring forth the prisoners," said Otto, from his seat upon the throne.

Those who had attended the victory feast were in attendance, but now standing, as the emperor was seated upon the throne, but there were several others, as well, dignitaries, envoys, ambassadors, department administrators, judges, high officers, and such. Other than the emperor, only four, to the side, were seated. These were four scribes, two imperial scribes, and two city scribes. Each had his own small table, and his own tablet, ink, and pens. Some slaves, at the edge of the throne room, knelt.

Ingeld and Corelius were brought forward, each still in the chains in which he had been placed at the victory feast.

Ingeld was permitted to stand, but Corelius, in his tunic of a slave, was forced to kneel. He viewed Abrogastes, with dread.

"The imperial court resumes its session," announced Titus Gelinus. "The charges against the prisoners, matters of public record, of which you have been informed, are numerous, clear, and not contested, and their guilt is established, recognized, and accepted. Nothing remains now but the disposition of the prisoners, the deciding of their fates."

Corelius moaned.

Ingeld stood proudly before the throne.

"The emperor's court is the highest court in Telnaria, and amongst the Telnarian worlds," said Titus Gelinus, "and the emperor himself is the supreme and only judge, beyond which there is no right of appeal."

"It is so, be it so," said several in the assembly.

"It is in session," said Titus Gelinus.

"It is so, be it so," was heard from several in the hall, again, a formulaic utterance taken to be indicative of assent.

"These prisoners," said Otto, "are prisoners of the Telnarian state, and are subject to the exclusive jurisdiction of the Telnarian state. Yet, the state, without relinquishing in the least or compromising in any way its jurisdiction, reserves the right to solicit views and opinions of diverse parties, and consult as it will with whomsoever it may please."

"This right is acknowledged and is absolute," said Titus Gelinus.

"Consider the prisoner, Ingeld," said Otto. "He is a prince of the Drisriaks. Therefore, it seems meet that he not be subjected to the fates which might be appropriately levied against a common miscreant."

Corelius began to shudder.

"Excoriation, the death by hooks and needles, being eaten alive by *filchen*, a bit at a time, over several days, and such," said Otto.

"The privileges and gentilities of *civilitas*," said a man, "need not cover barbarous royalty."

"I am king of the Otunjen," said Otto.

"But they may, of course, if the emperor wishes," said the man backing away, losing himself amongst his fellows.

"Ortog, prince of the Drisriaks, king of the Ortungen," said Otto.

"I am here," said Ortog.

"The prisoner, Ingeld, would have had you, and your father, slain," said Otto.

"That is true," said Ortog.

"Would you then, a prince, a fitting peer, be willing to serve as executioner, administering a swift and easy death to the prisoner, Ingeld, the Drisriak?"

"How merciful is the emperor," said a man in the witnessing throng.

"No," said Ortog. "I will not shed the blood of a brother."

"Why?" asked Otto.

"I am not Ingeld," said Ortog.

"Noble Abrogastes, king of the Drisriaks, hegemonic tribe amongst the Alemanni," said Otto, "you acknowledge, do you not, the gravity of the charges against, and the weight and force of the offenses of, the prisoner, Ingeld, a prince of the Drisriaks?"

"I do," said Abrogastes.

"And you petitioned custody of the prisoner some nights ago, that he be subject to the justice of the Drisriaks?"

"I did," said Abrogastes.

"When petitioning for custody of the prisoner," said Otto, "you said you had "something in mind.""

"I did," said Abrogastes.

"Might you inform the court, what fate, what penalty, you had in mind?"

"The court is curious?" said Abrogastes.

"Yes," said Otto.

"I lost one son," said Abrogastes, "to mutiny and secession, a fine, proud son whom I should have better understood, a son I have now pardoned and regained. I do not care to risk losing another."

"Yet the crimes of the prisoner, Ingeld, are unconscionable and fearful," said Otto.

"They are," said Abrogastes.

"What fate, what penalty, would satisfy the justice of the Drisriaks, the outrage of a betrayed king, and yet the mercy of a grieving father?" asked Otto.

"Exile to a remote world, one as yet uncharted, one rude and primitive, one far from the routes of commerce, without retainers," said Abrogastes.

"What greater cruelty could be concealed within so deceptive a wrapper of kindness?" said Ingeld. "Better the knives and needles, the feeding of *filchen*!"

"The court," said Otto, "accepts the view of the king of the Drisriaks."

"No!" cried Ingeld. "No!"

"It is so, be it so," said Titus Gelinus.

"It is so, be it so," said several in the chamber.

"Remove the prisoner," said Otto.

Ingeld, raging and struggling, in the grasp of guards, was dragged from the room.

"My thanks to the king of the Otungen, the chieftain of the Wolfungs, the emperor of Telnaria," said Abrogastes.

"Another prisoner is to be considered," said Otto, "he before us, kneeling, chained, clad in the garb of a slave, the conspirator and traitor, Corelius of Telnar."

"Mercy!" begged Corelius.

"He lacks noble blood and high station," said Otto. "Thus, he qualifies as a common miscreant. Thus, tradition, custom, and propriety, not to speak of law, place before us a plethora of penalties, these widely ranging in degrees of severity."

"My crimes were nothing compared to those of Ingeld, the Drisriak!" cried Corelius.

"What should be done with him?" inquired Otto.

A number of suggestions were then forthcoming from the throng in the throne room. These need not be listed nor elaborated upon but Corelius more than once shuddered with fear, a reaction for which few, under the circumstances, could blame him.

"His crimes were not only against Telnaria," said Otto, "but also against others, not of Telnaria. He was generous in his treacheries, bestowing them liberally."

"Give him to me," said Abrogastes. "Deliver him the justice of the Drisriaks."

"Do not!" wept Corelius.

"One might consider delivering him to a male brothel," said Otto, "but his left profile, which he might be expected to exhibit, would make him a bad investment."

There was laughter in the room.

No free women were present.

"Perhaps one could make him a slave in a woman's prison," said Otto.

"Hooks, knives, fang fish!" cried several in the room.

"Justice is often swayed by public preferences," said Titus Gelinus. "What judge does not consider the public consequences of his decisions, including those to his future, irrelevant to the law as they may be."

"Many judges," said Iaachus, "decide with an eye to their tenure and promotion, decide with an eye on the approval of their superiors, and, ultimately, of the emperor."

"I am the emperor," said Otto.

"The city wants the blood of Corelius," said Julian, "for his facilitating and abetting the raid of Abrogastes."

"And Abrogastes," said Rurik, "wants his blood for the treachery done to him, that leading to his capture and, subsequently, to the capture of his son, Ortog, prince of the Drisriaks, king of the Ortungen, putting both in mortal peril."

"Even an emperor," said Titus Gelinus, "is well advised to attend to murmurs in the taverns, markets, theaters, and streets."

"Power is never absolute," said Iaachus.

"It cannot be, as long as the leader needs the led," said Julian.

"Or as long," said Iaachus, "as a ring can contain poison or a folded handkerchief conceal a dagger."

"Abrogastes," said Otto, "dear friend, mighty enemy, I have spared one life; I would that you might spare another."

"I understand," said Abrogastes, "one life for another."

"I am Telnarian," cried Corelius, "do not give me to a barbarian!"

"I herewith deliver, as a gift, the wretch, Corelius of Telnar, to Abrogastes, king of the Drisriaks."

"No, no!" cried Corelius.

"He will tend pigs on Tenguthaxichai," said Abrogastes, "far from fine linen and gold, barefoot and in rags, wading amongst swill and mud."

"No!" cried Corelius, lifting his chained wrists to Otto.

"It is so, be it so," said Titus Gelinus.

"It is so, be it so," said others in the chamber.

"Remove the prisoner," said Otto.

Corelius was led from the chamber.

The seated scribes added a further notation to their records.

At a nod from Otto, Titus Gelinus announced that the session of the court was concluded, after which most of the throng in attendance, including the scribes, then excused, withdrew from the chamber. A small number, however, mostly intimates of the emperor, were asked to remain.

"A little business," said Otto, "remains to be done."

CHAPTER NINETY-FIVE

Viviana knelt before the throne, much as she had knelt earlier, some days ago, in the dining chamber, in the same brief, silken tunic, from Varick's Market, though it had been washed the day before. The slave, too, her chains removed and then replaced, had been washed, and brushed, and combed this morning. Slaves are expected to be cleanly, and meticulous in their appearance. As owned animals, as with dogs and horses, their grooming is important. She, too, had been well fed and watered. The slave is expected to be well cared for, including being well rested and well exercised, as any other valuable animal. Too, of course, these attentions lead to the health, vitality, and attractiveness of the animal, and it is generally accepted, at least amongst free men, that the most attractive and desirable of all animals is the female slave. Certainly, they seek them out, fiercely, buy and sell them, raid for them and fight for them. The women of the enemy are always prize loot. What woman, in her heart, does not understand that she is booty?

"We are going to call you 'Viviana', slave," said Otto.

"I am Viviana," said the girl.

"That is a slave name, of course," said Otto, "as slaves, as other animals, have no name in their own right, merely a name put on you by the will of the free, and changeable at will."

"Yes, Master," said Viviana.

"It must be an interesting feeling for you," said Otto, "to kneel before the throne, a slave, when you had often, on your own throne, near the emperor's throne, attended state functions, audiences, and such."

"Yes, Master," she said, "but I now belong where I am."

"And even before?" asked Otto.

"Yes, Master," said Viviana. "Even before."

"You are an attractive slave, Viviana," said Otto. "You might bring several *darins* in a market."

"Thank you, Master," said Viviana.

"Free her," said Aesilesius, angrily, standing near the arm of the throne.

"No," said Otto.

"May I withdraw?" asked Aesilesius.

"No," said Otto.

"I do not care to see my sister so," said Aesilesius.

"Legally," said Titus Gelinus, "she is no longer your sister, but an animal, a slave."

"By blood," said Aesilesius.

There were not many in the throne room, certainly not compared to the throng which had filled the chamber earlier, but there were several, other than some guards. As indicated, Aesilesius and Titus Gelinus were present. Also in attendance were Iaachus, the Arbiter of Protocol; Julian, of the Aureliani; Tuvo Ausonius, originally from Miton; and Rurik, the Tenth Consul of Larial VII, of the Larial Farnichi. Interestingly, two barbarians, other than the emperor himself, if we dare to count him as a barbarian, were present, Abrogastes, the Far-Grasper, king of the Drisriaks, and Ortog, prince of the Drisriaks, and king of the Ortungen. There were no women present, other than the slave, either free or slave.

"Look upon this slave, kneeling, in her tunic and chains," said Otto.

"I do not care to do so," said Aesilesius, looking away.

"Do so," said Otto.

Aesilesius, angrily, turned to view the slave.

"Does she look different, different from any other slave?" asked Otto.

"No," said Aesilesius.

"You were not close to one another," said Otto.

"No," said Aesilesius. "She despised me, as a cripple, a weakling, a timid, mindless fool."

"How you must have hated her," said Otto.

"As she did me," said Aesilesius.

"She is a slave," said Otto. "You could now put her under the lash."

"I do not care to do so," said Aesilesius.

"I do not think you know your sister," said Otto.

"I know all I care to know," said Aesilesius.

"You know much of what it is to be a man," said Otto, "but you may not know much of what it is to be a woman. Many men project what they know of men onto women. That is a mistake. Men and women are both precious and marvelous, but they are not the same. Women will strive to be like men if they fear and hate men, or will try to be like men to please men, thinking that is how men want them to be, more men, other men, but they are not truly more men, or other men. They are different, deeply and wonderfully so."

"I understand nothing of this," said Aesilesius.

"Regard that woman, kneeling in her chains," said Otto. "She is a slave."

"Legally," said Aesilesius.

"Legally, yes," said Otto, "but far more so in her heart and mind."

"Surely not," said Aesilesius.

"Look upon her," said Otto. "Women desire strong men and respond sexually to them. Why before strong men do they feel yielding and weak and their bodies burn with flaming need? They know in their heart they have been bred by nature to belong to masters. Why do they despise and strive to manipulate accommodating weaklings, and are all too often successful? They would punish them for not being the masters, dominant and confident, they crave."

"I understand nothing of this," said Aesilesius.

"Look upon her," said Otto. "She is now wholly, and only, a slave, in her heart, mind, and belly. No longer does she have a place amongst free women. Let them not be shamed, and scandalized, by her presence. She has been at a man's feet, and has discovered she belongs there."

"See her, dear Aesilesius," said Julian. "It has been done to her."

"Once a slave always a slave," said Iaachus.

"Let her remain in chains," said Julian. "It is where she belongs."

"Let the empire not be shamed," said Iaachus.

"If she is a slave, let her be a slave," said Otto. "If she belongs in a collar, let her be in a collar."

"I do not care to see her so," said Aesilesius. "She is shamed."

"Do you see all such women as shamed?" asked Otto.

"Certainly not," said Aesilesius, "not if they are slaves, and should be slaves, and it is right for them."

"I suspect," said Abrogastes, "that young Aesilesius is concerned more with himself than the slave."

"She is shamed," said Aesilesius.

"She is not shamed," said Otto. "She is fulfilled."

"Shamed!" said Aesilesius.

"If so," said Otto, "let her then rejoice in her shame, welcoming it, and loving it, for in it she finds her fulfillment."

"Do you not want she who was your sister to be happy?" asked Abrogastes.

"Only if properly so," said Aesilesius.

"Who decides what is proper?" asked Abrogastes.

"I do," said Aesilesius.

"You would impose your views, your values, upon her?" asked Abrogastes.

"Of course," said Aesilesius.

"Have you so little feeling for her, care for her so little, have so little respect for her, have so little understanding of her wants and needs?" asked Abrogastes.

"Free her," said Aesilesius to Otto.

"Freedom is precious," said Otto.

"So, too, is love, and being what one is in one's heart," said Viviana. "Let each woman be what she is and wants to be."

"No," said Aesilesius.

"I have never felt more real and more free than in my collar," said Viviana. "The collar has liberated me to be myself. I am thankful."

"No!" cried Aesilesius.

"Scorn me, if you wish!" said Viviana. "I am a slave! It is what I am, and want to be! How can one be more free than when one is oneself?"

"Do you wish to be whipped?" asked Aesilesius.

"No, Master," said Viviana, "but I wish to be subject to the whip, and I wish to know that I will be whipped if I am not pleasing."

"And so you strive to be pleasing?" said Aesilesius.

"A girl hopes to please her Master," said Viviana.

"I see," said Aesilesius.

"Yet," said Viviana, "an occasional stroke, hopefully rare, is sometimes useful. It helps to remind a girl that she is a slave. It reassures her. Even the kindest and most loving of Masters should never let a girl forget that she is a slave."

"I see," said Aesilesius.

"The slave wants to know she is a slave," said Viviana.

"And the lash," said Iaachus, "reminds her well."

"So you are a slave?" said Aesilesius.

"Yes, Master," said Viviana.

"We shall see," said Aesilesius. "Have her chains removed."

"Remove her chains," said Otto to a guard.

The slave's chains were removed. The slave remained kneeling, not having been given permission to rise.

"Now," said Aesilesius, "crawl to that other guard, he farther off, not he holding the chains, and beg to lick and kiss his feet."

Viviana went to all fours and crawled to the other guard. She put her head down, humbly.

"I beg to lick and kiss your feet," she said.

The guard looked to Otto. "Permit it," said Otto.

"You may do so," said the guard.

Viviana put her head down, her hair like a loose, blonde shower about the guard's feet. In a few moments Aesilesius cried out, angrily, "Enough! Return!" Then he said to the guard who was near, he who held the chains. "Put her in chains. She belongs in chains."

"Chain her," said Otto.

Shortly then, Viviana knelt again, as she had before, half naked, helpless, a slave, chained before the throne.

"How dared you obey such a command?" asked Aesilesius.

"How would I dare not obey?" asked Viviana.

"Were you not horrified to obey such a command?" asked Aesilesius.

"It does not horrify a slave to be a slave," said Viviana. "It fulfills and pleases her."

"It pleased you?" asked Aesilesius, angrily.

"It pleased me to obey the command of a free man," she said. "It pleases me to be the slave I am, and want to be. It pleases me to be humble and grateful, and please the free. It pleases me to be owned, to be willingly and joyfully choiceless, to be marked, collared, and mastered."

"No!" said Aesilesius.

"Do not torment her," said Otto.

"Take this slave away," said Aesilesius.

"A moment," said Otto. "Slave," he said.

"Master?" asked Viviana.

"As a slave," said Otto, "it would doubtless be wise to keep you in ignorance. There seems little need to inform animals of the doing of Masters. Who would explain things to a dog or horse? Yet, in this case, I am prepared to make an exception."

"Master in his kindness," said Viviana, "would explain to me the fate of Master Ingeld, prince of the Drisriaks."

"You know of it?" asked Otto.

"The news coursed through the corridors of the palace like the flash of light," said Viviana. "Lord Ingeld is to be sent to a far world, a rude, primitive world, one far from the lanes of commerce, one as of now uncharted. Too, he has been denied followers, men, cohorts."

"Does this sentence seem too cruel?" asked Otto.

"It is far less cruel than what I, in great fear, had anticipated," she said. "I feared not only execution, but an execution of prolonged horror. I thank Master for sparing his life."

"You are interested in the matter?" asked Otto.

"Desperately, profoundly," she said.

"I surmised so," said Otto.

"While I waited in the corridor, crouching in a slave cage, waiting to be brought before the imperial throne, an unbelievable thing for a slave, Lord Ingeld, wild in his chains, in fury, was hastened past me. I cried out to him, at the risk of a whipping, and extended my hand through the bars, but he paid me no attention."

"Perhaps he did not recognize you," said Otto.

"No," said Viviana, tears in her eyes, "he knew me. He merely scorned me as the worthless slave I am."

"It seems," said Iaachus, "that Prince Ingeld would have preferred an execution, even one lengthy and decidedly unpleasant, to years of isolation, futility, and loneliness on a remote world, one possibly uninhabited, even without life, or, it may be, one roamed by savage and dangerous life forms, rational or irrational, say, hostile, isolated tribes, far from civilization, or strange, predatory animals."

"I read Ingeld differently," said Otto. "Once his rage passes, I think he will cling to life with tenacity, vowing vengeance and return."

"I trust that no records are to be kept," said Iaachus, "indicating on which of the thousands of such remote and uncharted worlds Ingeld is to be marooned."

"Correct," said Otto.

"Then," said Iaachus, "let him storm, rage, and howl as he will. He could not be rescued, even if some mad faction should desire to do so."

"I think we have little to fear in that respect, such a desire on the part of dissident factions," said Otto.

"How is that?" asked Iaachus.

"There is never a lack of those who would strive for kingdoms," said Otto, "and those who would so strive would not be eager for competition. The lion who wishes to rule is not likely to call his jungle to the attention of a larger, stronger, fiercer lion."

Otto then returned his attention to the slave, who seemed small, kneeling on the tiles before the throne.

"You are pleased that Ingeld lives?" he asked.

"Deeply, relievedly, profoundly so," she said.

"You are grateful that Ingeld did not do away with you, in furtherance of his schemes, despite the diplomatic advisability of doing so?" said Iaachus.

"Yes, Master," said Viviana. "Certainly I would know that the child was not mine."

"As I understand it," said Iaachus, "you were administered a drug which impaired your memory, and were sold to slavers."

"Yes, Master," said Viviana.

"Interesting," said Julian. "That would have involved great risk for Ingeld. You might have been recognized, you might have recovered your memory."

"I fell into the hands of Urta, an Otung, whose scheme to kill Abrogastes, king of the Drisriaks, I had foiled. He recognized me though I did not know myself. To sweeten his vengeance I must realize who I was and what had been done to me. Accordingly, he obtained a drug, an antidote to that which had affected my memory, and, by means of this antidote, my memory was restored."

"Why did Ingeld not have you killed?" asked Iaachus.

"I do not know," said Viviana.

"You were espoused to Ingeld," said Rurik.

"As was my sister, Alacida, to Hrothgar, following the rites of the exarch of Telnar," said Viviana.

"The marriage ceased to exist, instantly, upon your embondment," said Titus Gelinus.

"Yes, Master," said Viviana.

"In your marriage," asked Otto, "did Ingeld touch you?"

"Do not ask such a question!" said Aesilesius.

"Did he?" asked Otto.

"Though free I was as a slave in his arms," said Viviana.

"No!" said Aesilesius.

"I did not know what it was to be in the arms of such a man," said Viviana. "I did not know such sensations could exist. I would have competed with slaves for his love."

"Shameful!" cried Aesilesius.

"At the feet of such a man there is no shame," said Viviana.

"You love Ingeld?" asked Otto.

"Yes, Master," said Viviana.

"Impossible!" said Aesilesius.

"With the deepest and most helpless of all loves," said Viviana, "the love of a slave for her Master."

Aesilesius turned angrily to Otto. "May I withdraw?" he asked.

"No," said Otto.

"Subside," said Abrogastes.

"Now," said Otto, regarding the slave, "what is to be done with you?"

"It will be done with me as Masters please," said Viviana. "I am a slave."

"Have you a preference," asked Otto, "a given market, a given world?"

"No, Master," said Viviana.

"In any event," said Titus Gelinus, "a slave's preference is unavailing. It is immaterial to her disposition."

"You know the sentence passed upon Prince Ingeld," said Otto.

"Yes, Master," said Viviana.

"Is it not a terrible sentence?" said Otto.

"Yes, Master," she said. "It is a fearful thing to contemplate."

"Consider the isolation, the distance, the loneliness," said Otto.

"Consider the enormity of his crimes," said Iaachus.

"The justice of Telnaria and that of the Drisriaks coincide," said Titus Gelinus.

"At least he lives," said Viviana.

"Perhaps the worst," said Julian, "is that he is to be alone, that he may not be accompanied by retainers."

"And what retainer, in any case, would choose to share such banishment, to endure such exile?" asked Iaachus.

"Must he be alone, so dreadfully alone?" asked Viviana.

"Yes," said Iaachus. "He is to be denied retainers."

"Even a slave?" asked Viviana.

"The sentence said nothing of slaves," said Titus Gelinus.

"I beg to be given to him, Masters!" cried Viviana.

"What you wish makes no difference," said Iaachus.

"The will of a slave is immaterial," said Titus Gelinus.

"The free will decide what is to be done with slaves," said Rurik, Tenth Consul of Larial VII, of the Larial Farnichi.

"I love him!" said Viviana. "I love him!"

"Do not speak so," said Aesilesius.

"I love him without qualification or reservation," wept Viviana, lifting her chained wrists piteously to the throne. "I love him without measurements and countings, without contracts and negotiations, without stipulations and calculations, without questions and assurances, without documents and bargainings! I love him with the profound and abject love of a slave for her Master!"

"I did not know such love could exist," said Aesilesius.

"Ask Nika," said Otto.

"Ingeld has rejected the slave," said Iaachus. "He refuses to recognize her as she who was once the Princess Viviana, sister of Aesilesius."

"Do you think he knows you?" asked Julian of the slave.

"I am sure of it, Master," said Viviana.

"Why then would he not recognize her?" asked Julian of Otto.

"Perhaps," said Otto, "that he not jeopardize her, that he not put her in the path of dangers which might attend him, perhaps that she not share his obloquy, and his fate."

"Ingeld is proud," said Abrogastes. "He may fear his feelings, he may fear love."

"Who would be so foolish as to love a slave?" said Rurik.

"I can think of one," said Otto, "of the Larial Farnichi."

Rurik growled in resentment.

"Am I to understand," asked Aesilesius of the slave, disbelievingly, "that you wish to not only remain in bondage but to be given as a slave to the cunning and unscrupulous prince of the Drisriaks, a condemned criminal and traitor, and would accompany him in profound and shameful exile?"

"Yes, Master," said Viviana. "She who was once your sister has learned herself, found herself, discovered herself, freed herself— in the collar of a slave."

"I fear Ingeld would never accept such sacrifice on the part of a slave," said Ortog. "How could he repay it? He would be furious, and shamed."

"He might kill her," said Julian.

"No," said Otto, "but he might, to salve his vanity, treat her, at least for a time, until his love was won, with great contempt and cruelty."

"There is an easy remedy for that," said Viviana. "Let it be understood that I am dismayed and reluctant to share his exile, that I am distraught and disconcerted to do so, but that I have no choice, that I must, that Aesilesius, he who was my brother, has had me banished, as the slave I am, to conceal the shame my bondage has brought on the line of Aesilesius. I would thus be an unwilling victim, a fellow exile."

"Ingeld, I fear," said Iaachus, "would be a hard master."

"What woman does not want a firm and uncompromising Master?" asked Viviana. "How could she love one who was not?"

"The guards who patrol the cells at night," said Otto, "have reported to me that sometimes Ingeld calls out a name in his sleep."

"A woman's name?" asked Viviana.

"Yes," said Otto.

"The name of a slave?" asked Viviana.

"It seems so," said Otto.

"'Huta'?" asked Viviana, frightened.

"No," said Otto, "'Viviana'."

"Ahh," breathed Viviana.

"Are such arrangements in accord with your wishes?" asked Aesilesius of the slave.

"Yes, Master," said Viviana.

"I fear you are lost for freedom," said Aesilesius.

"Freedom comes in many forms, Master," said Viviana.

"Take this slave away," said Aesilesius.

"Yes," said Otto, to the guards, "take the slave away."

"Thank you, Masters," said Viviana.

When the slave had been led away, Otto descended from the throne. "Aesilesius," he said, "I would speak to you in the presence of these others, advisors and confidants, friends, and brothers in battle."

"The matter is then serious?" inquired Aesilesius.

"Quite so," said Otto.

"I do not place you in peril," said Aesilesius. "Yet I have often wondered why, in the games of statecraft, you have permitted me to live. Is that lenience now to be revoked?"

"You have read books," said Otto. "You must learn to read men."

"I do not understand," said Aesilesius.

"Those here," said Otto, "will do all they can to help you. You must listen to them, but you must make your own decisions. A hundred factions lurk and yearn for power. Law without the sword is empty. He who sits upon the throne is alone; he is in a sense banished, though ensconced in a palace; surrounded by thousands, he is yet alone; to occupy the throne is to be in exile."

"I do not understand what you are talking about," said Aesilesius.

"I have discussed the matter with these and others," said Otto. "I have even discussed the matter with the empress mother."

"What matter?" asked Aesilesius.

"The future of Telnaria," said Otto.

"I do not understand," said Aesilesius.

"I am an Otung, a barbarian," said Otto. "I do not belong on the throne of Telnaria. I seized it in a time of troubles, abetted by barbarian forces, that the empire might be saved."

"That is true," said Iaachus.

"Shortly," said Otto, "we will disband and abolish the senate, a nest of conflict and ambition, and then reestablish it, its jurisdiction then clearly subordinate to the throne. One of the first acts of the newly formed senate will be to celebrate the peaceful accession to power of a new emperor."

"I?" said Aesilesius.

"Yes," said Otto.

"No!" cried Aesilesius.

"In your veins," said Otto, "flows the blood of the line deriving from the first usurper, another Aesilesius. Do not be concerned. It is common for time to legitimize piracy, theft, and crime. You must be true to your blood."

"I am afraid to be emperor," said Aesilesius.

"Many seek power," said Otto. "But only a fool does not fear it."

"It will make you a better emperor," said Iaachus.

"I am not ready to be emperor," said Aesilesius.

"By study in the secrecy of your chamber, you prepared yourself for this day," said Otto.

"How did you know?" asked Aesilesius.

"You are not the only one who can prowl about the corridors of a palace," said Otto. "Too, few retardates are likely to rifle libraries, stealing, hoarding, and hiding books, books which often dealt with things an emperor should know."

"You saw through my hoax," said Aesilesius.

"Long ago," said Otto.

"On a suitable day," said Iaachus, "Ottonius, the First, in a plenitude of power and custom, of his own free will, unforced and benignly motivated, will publicly and lawfully abdicate. In the same ceremony, Aesilesius, the Sixteenth, will assume the throne."

Aesilesius was silent.

"You will, of course," said Iaachus, "given the politics of the day, and the security of the line, require an empress."

"I do not want an empress," said Aesilesius.

"You must have one," said Iaachus.

"No," said Aesilesius. "You do not understand. I love Nika. I am unwilling to replace her. What would become of her?"

"You can keep a dozen slaves, a hundred slaves, on the side," said Iaachus.

"You do not understand," said Aesilesius. "I love her."

"I have spoken to the empress mother of these things," said Otto, "of the empire, of your restoration, of the need for an empress, and such."

"I was told nothing of this," said Aesilesius.

"The empress mother loves you," said Otto. "And she knows of your love for Nika and her love for you. She wants what is best for you, and for the slave, as well. Indeed, she herself cares deeply for Nika, whom she believes saved you, bringing you from mindless futility to health and manhood. She is grateful to Nika, and loves her. Many see the empress mother as a selfish, stubborn, wily hag, which she may be, but she is also a loving mother."

"I love her," said Aesilesius. "I much regret causing her dismay and pain for so many years."

"The empress mother and I have conceived a scheme," said Otto. "With your consent, we will send Nika to the summer world, to a residence near the summer palace, where the royal family occasionally vacationed, where, in a state audience, I first saw you, your sisters, and the empress mother. There, on the summer world, while she is being trained in arts suitable for a possible empress, a new identity will be devised for her, complete with a genealogy. You need then merely encounter her on the summer world, while you are supposedly seeking a brief respite from the burdens of office. Romance and marriage swiftly ensue, and, shortly, you return with your bride to Telnar, and, to the acclaim of a jubilant population, see to her institution as empress."

"This will never work," said Aesilesius.

"Such things often work," said Otto. "I have that on the authority of the empress mother. You merely hear of the ones which do not work."

"I suppose it depends on who writes the history," said Aesilesius.

"Most likely," said Otto.

"What if it does not work?" said Aesilesius.

"Let us hope it does not," said Otto. "That would be more honest. Who will gainsay an emperor's choice of spouse?"

"Any free woman may legally become an empress," said Titus Gelinus.

"Even a former slave?" asked Aesilesius.

"Certainly," said Titus Gelinus.

"Free women may not accept her," said Aesilesius.

"The greatest fear of all free women," said Iaachus, "is that they will not be accepted by an empress."

"I do not know if Nika wishes to be freed," said Aesilesius.

"She has nothing to say about it," said Titus Gelinus. "She is a slave."

"Do not be afraid," said Otto. "She loves you. She will do anything to please you."

"You have discussed this with Nika?" asked Aesilesius.

"Of course not," said Otto, "she is a slave."

"May I withdraw?" asked Aesilesius.

"Certainly," said Otto.

Aesilesius glanced at the throne, now unoccupied, and then hurried from the chamber.

"He speeds to Nika," said Iaachus.

"I suspect so," said Otto.

"Were you not unduly solicitous in the case of Ingeld?" asked Iaachus.

"He was a worthy foe," said Otto.

"Telnaria owes you much," said Julian, he of the Aureliani.

"Perhaps we can again, one day, ride together on Vellmer," said Otto.

"Had you remained longer on the throne," said Iaachus, "I might have made a diplomat of you."

"What better reason for leaving the throne?" said Otto.

"You have served Telnaria well," said Rurik.

"Long live the Larial Farnichi," said Otto.

"You will now let your hair grow, and put aside silken garments," said Iaachus.

"Otungs will remain allies," said Otto. "Bloods will mix, and one day there may be a stronger, finer Telnaria."

"I have long thought," said Julian, "that *civilitas* and *barbaritas* have much to learn from one another."

"I trust there is good hunting on Varna, and Tangara," said Rurik, of the Larial Farnichi.

"One misses the forests, the wind in the trees, the quiet, the moss, the rain," said Otto.

"You are welcome on Tenguthaxichai," said Abrogastes.

"Yes," said Ortog.

"An Otung, amongst Drisriaks?" said Otto.

"One Otung," said Ortog.

"Such an Otung," said Abrogastes.

"I am unclear on this," said Titus Gelinus. "Can one just leave a throne?"

"I am an Otung," said Otto. "I do not belong in a palace."

"Still," said Titus Gelinus, "can one just leave a throne?"

"Yes," said Otto, "when the throne no longer needs one."

"What is before you?" asked Iaachus.

"The same that is before everyone," said Otto, "universes."

"What will you do, where will you go?" asked Tuvo Ausonius.

"Away, to be forgotten," said Otto. "There was once a peasant, who became a chieftain, a king, and an emperor, and was then forgotten, his is a history to be judiciously overlooked, an embarrassment to proper chronicles, one not fit for remembering."

"You have put your hand upon an Empire," said Iaachus. "Your name may be excised from the histories but the grasp and force of that hand has left its mark on worlds."

"Serve Aesilesius loyally and well," said Otto.

"We will," said the others.

"In some days then," said Otto "farewell."

"In some days then," said the others, "farewell."

EPILOGUE

I find reality mysterious.

I wonder if others do, as well.

We have a small, comfortable world, situated happily, appropriately, in the center of all that can be, a plate beneath the inverted bowl of the sky, all details of which have been arranged by the gods.

How different is our little world from the vastnesses of space and time hinted at in the Telnarian chronicles! It is no wonder that the wise ones, in their holiness, have begun to search the libraries, to remove all allusions to, all traces of, the Telnarian world. To speak briefly, the Telnarian Histories were long undiscovered, or neglected; they were then, when discovered or noted, proscribed, and denounced as heretical; later, despite considerable evidence, archeological, linguistic, numismatic, and such, it was proclaimed that the Telnarian world had never existed. Alternative explanations were then provided to account for, or dismiss, the evidence, ruins and such, which suggested the actuality of the Telnarian world. Recently, manuscripts pertaining to the Telnarian world are being systematically sought, presumably to be consigned to private destruction. They are no longer burned because this called public attention to their existence. I have managed, in my role as a scholar, and librarian, a dabbler in antiquities, often alone in the library, to remove certain references to certain manuscripts from the catalogs, and obtain and conceal the associated manuscripts. Among these manuscripts, dealing with Telnaria, is that known as Valens 122b, on which these chronicles are largely based. More particular details pertaining to these matters I recounted earlier, elsewhere.

I myself, though ostensibly a trusted scholar loyal to the one true and holy regime, have little doubt, personally, that there is, or was, a Telnarian empire. To my mind, as simple and uninformed as it may be, the evidence for the Telnarian empire, or world, is indisputable, and overwhelming. Truth is often embarrassing to piety; and it is often, understandably, felt as threatening to establishments founded on its denial.

I mentioned that I find reality mysterious. Perhaps you do as well. Surely it is interesting that something exists. Does it not seem more probable that nothing should exist, even empty space? We have one reality. Why might there not be more than one? Perhaps there are. Might not our space and time, with their mysteries, be derived from, or founded in, other spaces and times, with their own mysteries?

I think I have mentioned, at one time or another, that I once had an unusual experience, in which I glimpsed, or seemed to glimpse, another reality, one in which my sleeve brushed, or seemed to brush, a golden pillar. I think, for a moment, I had touched Telnaria. But it was not a Telnaria of rain-worn statuary, of worn, cracked, furrowed pavements, of gray shards of once-bright pottery, of crumbled ruins, but a sturdy, vibrant, bright, beautiful, sunlit reality, momentarily glimpsed and then gone.

Can reality turn, and repeat itself?

Is Telnaria gone, or is it with us, at our elbow, a neighbor?

Is it ancient, or contemporary?

Are we in the vicinity of Telnaria, perhaps somehow on its porch or within a stone's throw of its wall? Are we perhaps a part of Telnaria, a fragment temporarily dissociated from a golden mainland?

I do not know.

Did the story in these chronicles take place long ago or is it continuing to take place, even now?

I do not know.

I will mention one last thing.

Perhaps it is not important, but it is interesting.

Yesterday afternoon I saw something I had never seen before, something the orthodoxy deems impossible, something it does not permit.

A ship crossed the sky.